READER'S DIGEST

CONDENSED BOOKS

FIRST EDITION

THE READER'S DIGEST ASSOCIATION LIMITED
25 Berkeley Square, London W1X 6AB

**THE READER'S DIGEST ASSOCIATION
SOUTH AFRICA (PTY) LTD**
Nedbank Centre, Strand Street, Cape Town

Printed in Great Britain by Petty & Sons Ltd, Leeds

Original cover design by Jeffery Matthews M.S.I.A.

For information as to ownership
of copyright in the material in this book see last page

ISBN 0 340 24759 2

Reader's Digest
CONDENSED BOOKS

THE PRIDE OF THE PEACOCK
Victoria Holt

THE DEVIL'S ALTERNATIVE
Frederick Forsyth

FRIENDS AND
FRIENDLY BEASTS
Gerald Durrell

EARTHSOUND
Arthur Herzog

COLLECTOR'S LIBRARY
EDITION

In this Volume:

The PRIDE of the PEACOCK

by Victoria Holt   p.9

Jessica Clavering was unhappy with her bitter, bickering family when, as an escape, she accepted a proposal to marry Joss Madden. With him she left England and went to live in Peacocks, his grand Australian mansion. Soon Jessica was in a turmoil. Strangely attracted to her new husband, she was also in fear of him and—most of all— curious about his connection with the fabulous opal, the Green Flash at Sunset. To what lengths would he go to possess that glorious jewel? A spellbinding novel in the finest Victoria Holt tradition.

Friends and Friendly Beasts

by Gerald Durrell   p.341

This is a unique selection from the works of Britain's most popular author/naturalist. The editors have chosen three of Durrell's very best stories to illustrate his wonderfully varied life—from his idyllic childhood in Greece, through his first job in an extraordinary pet shop in London, to a typically chaotic return visit to Greece with his irrepressible family many years later. It is, as with the best of Durrell's writing, charming, instructive, and hilariously entertaining— often all at once.

The Devil's Alternative

by Frederick Forsyth p.127

"Whichever option I choose, men are going to die." This is the Devil's Alternative—the appalling choice that faces the statesmen of the Western World. It lies at the heart of Forsyth's latest and most ambitious novel.

As the gripping story gathers momentum, the reader is transported from Moscow to London, from Rotterdam to Washington, from a country house in Ireland to the world's biggest oil tanker which threatens to pollute the whole of the North Sea. The climax is the most exciting that even this master storyteller has contrived.

EARTHSOUND

by Arthur Herzog p.401

Earthquakes? In the peaceful country haven of Rhode Island? Impossible. Still, Harry Vail had been hearing rumblings in the ground. And he'd noticed the crack in his cellar getting larger, and his books were toppling from their shelves.

His friends said it was his imagina-tion. His wife said the house was haunted. Old-time residents were evasive. Yet as the earthsounds grew louder, Harry knew disaster was certain. It was only a matter of time.

This is an extraordinary story—a chilling, thrilling novel, full of fascinating lore on one of the world's most unpredictable, terrifying, natural disasters.

The
PRIDE
of the
PEACOCK

A CONDENSATION OF THE BOOK BY

VICTORIA HOLT

ILLUSTRATED BY JEAN-LÉON HUENS

PUBLISHED BY COLLINS

Jessica Clavering's father has gambled
away Oakland Hall, and the family seems
doomed to a dreary, pinchpenny
existence. But Jessica refuses to accept
her lot. Her rough-hewn friend, Ben Henniker,
suggests marriage to his handsome
illegitimate son, and Jessica decides to take
the gamble of wedding a virtual stranger.
Having travelled to the wilds of Australia,
Jessica begins to fear Joss Madden, her proud
and wilful husband. What is his obsession
with the Green Flash at Sunset, a magnificent
opal men would stop at nothing to possess?
Soon Jessica finds that the adventure she craved
is turning into a terrifying nightmare.
With this superb tale of romantic suspense,
Victoria Holt surpasses even her popular
Lord of the Far Island.

Chapter 1

I was quite young when I realized that there was something mysterious about me, and a sense of not belonging came to me and stayed with me. I was different from everyone else at the Dower House.

It became a habit of mine to go down to the stream which ran between the Dower House and Oakland Hall, and gaze into its clear waters as though I hoped to find the answer there. That I chose that particular spot was somehow significant. Maddy, who was a general servant and a sort of nurse to me, found me there once, and I shall never forget the look of horror in her eyes.

"Now why do you want to come here, Miss Jessica?" she demanded. "If Miss Miriam knew, she'd forbid it."

I wanted to know why. This was characteristic of me and resulted in Maddy's calling me Miss Why, Where, and What.

"It's morbid, that's what it is," she declared. "I've heard Miss Miriam say so. Morbid!"

"Why? Is it haunted?" I asked.

"It might well be," said Maddy. "Now don't keep going there."

"I like it," I retorted stubbornly; and, as forbidden fruit could never have tasted sweeter to anyone than it did to me, I went to the stream all the more.

What was wrong with the pleasant stream and pretty bridge which crossed it? It was especially attractive to me because on the other side loomed the magnificent grey walls of Oakland Hall. The stream itself was shallow, and I could see pebbles on its brownish bed. A weeping willow drooped on the opposite bank.

9

In those early days I would sit by the stream and dream about myself, and always the theme of my wonderings was: You don't really belong to the Dower House.

Not that the thought disturbed me. I was different and wanted to be. My name for one thing was different. It was Opal Jessica Clavering. I was never called Opal and I often wondered how my mother had come to give me such a frivolous name, because she was a far from frivolous woman. She seemed very old; she must have been in her forties when I was born; and my sister, Miriam, was fifteen years older than I, and my brother, Xavier, nearly twenty. Miriam served as my governess, for we were too poor to engage one. In fact, our poverty was the remorseless theme of our household, for we had slid down in the world from the utmost luxury to what my mother called penury.

My poor sad father used to cringe when she talked of "better days", when they had been surrounded by a myriad of servants and there had been brilliant balls and elegant banquets. But there was always enough to eat at the Dower House, and we had poor Jarman to do the garden, and Mrs. Cobb to cook, and Maddy as maid of all work, so we weren't exactly penniless.

I was about ten years old when I made a portentous discovery. There was a weekend party at Oakland Hall, and the grounds on the other side of the stream were noisy with the hearty voices of the guests. I wished they would invite me to call, for I longed to see the inside of the big house. True, I could catch glimpses of the Hall in winter, when the denuded oaks no longer shielded it, but I could see no more than its distant grey stone walls.

On this day I was in the schoolroom with Miriam, who was not the most inspiring of teachers and was frequently impatient with me. She was a tall, pale woman, and as I was ten she must have been twenty-five.

When a hunting party from Oakland Hall came riding by, I ran to the window. "Jessica," cried Miriam, "what *are* you doing?"

"I only wanted to see the riders," I replied.

She gripped my arm, none too gently, and dragged me from the window. "They might see you," she hissed, as though that would be the depth of degradation.

"What if they did?" I demanded. "They did see me yesterday. Some of them waved and others said hello."

"Don't dare to speak to them again," she said fiercely.

"Why not?"

She hesitated for a moment, and then, as though she were considering that a little indiscretion was creditable if it saved me from the mortal sin of being friendly towards the guests from Oakland Hall, she said, "Once Oakland Hall was ours. Those barbarians took it from us."

"Took it from us? How?"

"They *bought* Oakland Hall." Her mouth hardened. "We could no longer afford to live there."

"Oh," I said, "*penury*. So it was there that we had our better days."

"*You* never had them. It all happened before you were born. *I* lived my childhood at Oakland Hall. I know what it means to come down in the world."

"But why did we become so poor?"

"You wouldn't understand," she said. "But now perhaps you see why we do not want you to stare like a peasant at the people coming from Oakland Hall. Now it's time for our algebra lessons."

But how could one be interested in x plus y squared after such a discovery? I was desperately anxious to know something of the barbarians who had taken our house, and in my energetic and, as I thought, subtle way, I began to probe.

It seemed to me that I might have more success with the servants than the family so I tried poor Jarman, who kept the Dower House garden in good order under Mama's supervision. Poor Jarman! He was kept poor, he told me, by Nature, who presented his wife with a new baby every year.

I followed him around for a week hoping to prize information from him. I collected flowerpots, stacked them in the greenhouse, watched him prune and weed. He said, "You're getting interested in ortyculture all of a sudden, Miss Jessica."

I smiled artfully. "You used to work at Oakland Hall."

"Aye, them was the days," he said ecstatically. "Best lawns in the country. Just look at this St. John's-wort. You only have to turn your back and it's all over the place."

"Nature's bounty," I said. "She's as generous with St. John's-wort as she is with you."

He looked at me suspiciously.

"Why did you leave Oakland Hall?" I wanted to know.

"It seemed the faithful sort of thing like. Mistress sent for me.

11

'Jarman,' she said, 'we've sold the Hall. We're going to the Dower House.' You could have knocked me down with a dove's feather, though there had been some talk. She said, 'If you come with us, you could have the cottage on the bit of land we're keeping. You could marry.' That was the beginning. Before the year was out I was a father."

"You said there was talk. . . ."

"Yes. Gambling was in the family. Mr. Clavering had been very fond of it, and he'd lost quite a tidy sum. There was mortgages—and that's not good for a house, and what's not good for a house ain't good for them that works there. Sometimes wages wasn't paid for two months. Then this man took the Hall. Miner, he'd been. Made a fortune."

"It all took place before I was born," I commented.

"Yes. 'Tis so. Must have been two years before that."

So it was twelve years ago—a lifetime—mine anyway.

All I had learned from Jarman was that my father's gambling had been responsible. No wonder Mama treated him with contempt. Poor Father stayed in his room, playing patience—a solitary game in which he could not lose to an opponent who would have to be paid, yet preserved contact with the cards he loved.

My father, with the heavy weight of guilt on his shoulders, was definitely not the one to approach for more information. To me he was a sort of nonperson, which was an odd way to feel about one's own father, but as he seemed scarcely aware of me, I found it hard to feel anything for him—except pity.

As for Mama, she was even more unapproachable. When I was very young and we sang in church:

> Can a mother's tender care
> Cease towards the child she bear?

I had thought of a little female bear cub beloved by its mother bear. I commented to Miriam that my mother's tender care could never cease, because it had never really existed. At this, Miriam had grown very pink and told me that I was a most ungrateful child and should be thankful for the good home I had.

My brother, Xavier, looked after the farm and pastures we had been able to salvage from the Oakland estate. He was kind to me in a vague sort of way, as though he recognized my right to be in the house but wasn't quite sure how I'd got there and was too polite to ask. I had heard that he was in love with Lady Clara Donningham, but because he couldn't offer her the luxury to which she was accustomed, he wouldn't ask her to marry him. This gave Xavier a very romantic aura in my eyes. He was a chivalrous knight who went through life nursing a secret passion because decorum forbade him to speak. *He* certainly would tell me nothing.

Miriam might be lured into betraying something, but she was not one for confidences. There was an understanding between her and the Reverend Jasper Crey's curate, but they couldn't marry until the curate became a vicar, and in view of his retiring nature that seemed unlikely for years to come.

Maddy told me that if we'd still been at Oakland Hall there would have been coming-out dances, and it wouldn't have been a curate for Miss Miriam. Oh dear, no. There would have been Squire This or Sir That—and maybe a lord.

As I might have known, Maddy was the only one who could really help. She had worked in the nursery at Oakland Hall and she loved to talk. As long as I could be sworn to secrecy, she would let out little scraps of information.

"It was all very grand. Lovely nurseries they was."

"Xavier must have been a good child," I commented.

"He was. *He* wasn't the one to get up to mischief."

"Who then? Miriam?"

"No, not her either."

"Well, why did you say one of them was?"

"I said no such thing. You're like one of them magistrates, you are. What's this? What's that?" The question had disturbed her. It was only later that I realized why.

Once I said to Miriam, "Fancy, you were born in Oakland Hall, and I was born in the Dower House."

Miriam hesitated and said, "No, you weren't born in the Dower House. Actually . . . Mama was in Rome when you were born."

My eyes widened with excitement. "But wasn't travelling costly?"

She looked pained. "Suffice it that she was there."

So there was more to brood on. Perhaps Mama had called me

Opal in a moment of frivolity inspired by the Italian skies. After looking it up in the dictionary, I had mixed feelings about my name. It was not very flattering to be named for "a mineral consisting chiefly of hydrous silica". That did not sound in the least romantic. I discovered, however, that opal had varying hues of red, green, and blue—in fact, all the colours of the spectrum—and was of a changing iridescence, and that sounded better.

Soon after I had seen the guests riding out from Oakland, I heard that the owner had gone away. Only the servants remained, and there were no longer sounds of revelry across the stream.

My life went on in the old way. As the years passed the mystery remained, and my curiosity did not diminish. I became more and more certain that there was a reason why the family gave me the impression that I was an intruder.

PRAYERS WERE said at the start of each day, and every member of the household had to be present. We met in the drawing room, "since," my mother often commented coldly, "we have no chapel now!" And she would throw a venomous glance towards my father.

My mother conducted this solemn ceremony, and I thought she was inclined to be a little hectoring towards God. It was: "Look down on this . . ." and "Don't do that . . ." as though she were talking to one of the superior servants she'd had at Oakland Hall.

I always found morning prayers irksome, but I did enjoy the church services, though perhaps for the wrong reasons. The church was a fine one, and the stained-glass windows, with their beautiful colours, a joy to see. Opal colours, I called them with satisfaction.

We still had the Clavering pew in the church. This consisted of the two front rows with a little door, which had a lock and key, and when we walked in, I believe my mother felt that the good old days were back. Perhaps that was the reason why *she* enjoyed going to church.

On one particular Easter Sunday when I was sixteen years old, the service had an interesting theme: "Be content and thankful with what the Lord has given you." A very good homily for the Claverings, I thought, and I wondered whether the Reverend Jasper Crey had had them in mind. Was he reminding them that the Dower House was quite grand by standards other than those of Oakland Hall? My father should be allowed to forget that he had brought us to our present state; and my mother should rejoice in what she had. As for myself, I was happy enough, except that somewhere inside me I yearned to be loved. I wanted someone's eyes to light up when I came by. I wanted someone to be a little anxious if I were late coming home.

O God, I prayed, let someone love me.

Then I laughed at myself, because I was telling Him what to do, just as my mother did.

After luncheon, we went to the churchyard to put flowers on the family graves. Here again, prestige was restored, for the Clavering headstones were the most elaborate of all. I liked to read the engraved words on them. There were memorials to John Clavering, who had died at the Battle of Preston in 1648, and James, who had died at Malplaquet. There was another for Harold, who had been killed at Trafalgar. We were a fighting family.

"Come away, Jessica," said Mama. "I do declare you have a morbid streak."

Called from the guns of Trafalgar, I walked solemnly back to the Dower House, and later that afternoon I wandered out to the stream. Beyond the Dower House gardens there was a stretch of meadow in which the grass grew long and unkempt. Very few people ever came here, and it was called the Waste Land.

As I walked across it, I noticed a bunch of violets tied with white ribbon. When I stooped to pick them up, I saw that they had been lying on a spot which was slightly raised. I knelt and pushed aside the grass. It was a mound, about six feet long.

Like a grave, I thought.

Who could possibly be buried on the Waste Land? I sat by the stream and asked myself what it meant.

Back at the house, I found Maddy at the linen cupboard, sorting out sheets. "Maddy," I said, "I saw a grave today."

"It's Easter Sunday so I reckon you did," she retorted.

"Oh, not in the graveyard. In the Waste Land."

She turned away, but not before I had seen her horrified expression. She *knew* about the grave in the Waste Land.

"Whose was it?" I insisted.

"Miss Jessica, it's time you stopped putting people in the witness box. You're too inquisitive by half."

"I don't see why I shouldn't know. I thought someone might have buried a pet dog there."

15

"That's as like as not," she said with some relief.

"But it was too big for a dog's grave. No, I think it was a person there . . . a person buried long ago but still remembered. Someone had laid a little bunch of violets there for Easter."

"Miss Jessica, will you get out from under my feet?"

She bustled away with a pile of sheets. She knew who was buried in the Waste Land, but, alas, she wasn't telling.

For several days I worried her but could get nothing out of her. "Oh, give over, do," she cried at length. "One of these days you might find out something you'd rather not know." That cryptic remark lingered in my mind and did nothing to curb my curiosity.

That spring there was great activity across the stream at Oakland Hall. Tradesmen called constantly, and the servants shouted to each other. There were regular thwacks as carpets were brought out of the house and beaten.

Then one day a carriage turned into Oakland's drive. I darted across the stream, crept close to the house, and hidden by bushes, I saw a man lifted from the carriage and placed in a wheelchair. He had a very red face and a very loud voice.

"Get me in, Wilmot!" he shouted. "Come out and help Banker."

I wished that I could see better, but I had to be careful. The red-faced man was clearly a forceful personality and it was, I felt, necessary indeed for me to remain hidden.

The little procession went into the house at last, and as I made my way back to the bridge I fancied that I was being followed. I ran as fast as I could, and it was only when I had crossed the bridge that I paused to look back. I saw a movement among the trees, but I was unsure whether it was a man or woman. I began to feel uneasy, wondering whether whoever had seen me would tell Mama. There would certainly be trouble if he—or she—did.

The next afternoon I decided to ask Maddy about the owner of Oakland Hall. She always gave me the impression that she could tell me a good deal if only I could make her talk.

I said, "Maddy, a man in a wheelchair was taken into Oakland Hall yesterday. I think he's had some sort of accident."

She nodded. "That's *him*," she said. "He's what you call one of them new rich."

"*Nouveau riche*," I informed her grandly.

"Have it your own way," she said, "but that's what he is."

"I'd like to get into the Hall. Will he be there for long?"

"You can't get about all that easy when you've had one of your legs off. Mrs. Bucket says she reckons he's home to stay."

"Who's Mrs. Bucket?"

"She's the cook at Oakland. I know her from when I was there."

"And you see her now and then?"

Maddy pursed her lips. "Well, it ain't for me to stick my nose up in the air when I pass someone I've known for twenty years. It wasn't as though there was a place for Mrs. Bucket or Mr. Wilmot, the butler, here."

"I understand perfectly. So he lost a leg, did he?"

"You're on your cross-questioning again, miss. You stay on the right side of the stream and don't keep asking about things that don't concern you."

IT WAS a sultry July day and I was sitting by the stream looking over Oakland territory when suddenly it happened. A wheelchair, with a man sitting in it, came towards me. There was a tartan rug over the man's knees, so I couldn't make out whether or not he had one leg. As I watched, the chair seemed to gather speed.

Then I realized it was out of control. It moved so fast down the incline that in a few moments it would reach the stream, where it would surely overturn.

I wasted no time. I ran down the slope, waded through the stream, and ran up the slope on the other side just in time to catch the chair before it went down into the water.

The man had been yelling, "Banker! Where in God's name are you, Banker?" until he caught sight of me. I was clinging to the chair, and it took all my strength to stop it.

The man was grinning at me, his face redder than ever. "Good-o!" he shouted. "You've done it."

He guided a steering bar in front of him, and the chair started to move along parallel with the stream.

"There," he said. "That's better. I'm not used to the perishing thing yet. Do you know, I'd have turned over but for you."

"Yes," I said. "You would."

"Where were you?"

"On the other side of the stream. Our side."

17

He nodded. "Lucky for me. Do you live over there?"

"Yes. In the Dower House."

"You're not a Clavering?"

"Yes, I am. What are you?"

"A Henniker."

"You must be the one who bought Oakland."

"The very same."

I started to laugh, and he started to laugh, too. I don't know why it should have seemed so funny to us both, but it did.

"Well, Miss Clavering, let's get acquainted. It's uncomfortable here. I'm going to drive my chair over to the trees."

I walked beside him, thinking this was a marvellous adventure. He brought the chair to rest in the shade, and I sat down on the grass. We studied each other.

"Are you a miner?" I asked.

He nodded. "Opals."

A shiver of excitement ran through me. "Opals!" I cried. "My name is Opal, but they never call me that. I'm always Jessica. That's rather ordinary after Opal, don't you think?"

"Opal Clavering. It sounds grand to me," he said. The reddish tinge in his cheeks deepened, and his eyes were a very bright blue. "There's nothing more beautiful than an opal to an old gouger."

"A what?"

"An opal miner."

"What do you do? Tell me about it."

"You smell out the land and you hope and you dream. Every miner dreams he'll find the most beautiful stones in the world."

"Where do you find them?"

"Well, opals have been mined in Hungary for centuries. That milky kind. Give me the black opals of Australia."

"You're from Australia?" I said.

"That's where I found opal, but I started out from the old country. Australia's rich in opal. We haven't scratched the surface of the land yet."

He paused and looked up at the sky. He was scarcely aware of me, I was sure. He was miles away on the other side of the world, gouging, as he called it, for his black opals.

"Australian opals are the best," he went on. "They're harder. They don't splinter as easily as some. They're lucky stones. Long ago, people used to believe opals brought good fortune and the

18

gift of prophecy. Emperors and nabobs used to wear opals to guard themselves against attack. It used to be said that an opal could protect you from poison and cure you of blindness. What more can you ask than that?"

"Nothing," I agreed heartily.

"They're called *oculus mundi*. Do you know what that means?"

I confessed that my education did not carry me so far.

"The eye of the world," he told me. "And you say Opal's your name? Jessica, too. Do you know, I like that. Jessie. It's friendly."

He took a ring from his little finger and showed it to me. I slipped it on my thumb, but even that was too small for it. I watched the light play on the opal. It was deep blue shot with red, yellow, and green lights.

"It's beautiful," I said as I gave it back to him.

"The stone comes from New South Wales. There are going to be some big finds there one day. I won't be in on it though." He tapped the tartan rug. "Hazards of the business. I'll never forget the day this happened. I was deep in a cave, collecting nobbies. Clinging to the roof, they were, like oysters. I couldn't believe my luck. Suddenly there was a rumble and down came the roof. It was three hours before they could get me out. I'd got my opals though, and one of them—well, it was a real beaut, worth losing a leg for, or so I told myself. When I came round in a hospital, the first thing I said was, 'Show me that green opal.'"

"It ought to have brought you protection against the falling rock," I commented.

"Well, you see, it wasn't mine until the rock started to crack. I look at it like this: it was the price I had to pay for my nobbies. I knew it was the end of my mining days, so I thought the best place to come to was Oakland. And here I am, relying on this old chair to carry me round, and you see what nearly happened to me but for a certain young lady . . ."

"I'm so glad I saw you."

"There's been a sort of feud. . . ." He laughed aloud, and I laughed with him. The laughter was a bond between us. I thought then—and I became sure of it later—that he liked the idea of snapping his fingers at my family.

He said, "The Claverings had lived at Oakland Hall since 1507, until this rough Henniker came along and took it from them!"

"They should never have let it go if they wanted to keep it so

19

much. As for you, Mr. Henniker, you worked to get it and you've got it . . . and I'm *glad*."

"Strange words from a Clavering," he said. "Ah, but this one's an Opal. I have to go now, but let's meet here tomorrow."

"I'd love it."

I watched him guide his chair towards the house, and then, in high spirits, I ran down to the bridge. I stood on it, looking back. The trees hid the house—his house now—but I was picturing him in it, laughing because a Clavering had become his friend.

He's an adventurer, I thought, and so am I.

I TRIED to hide my exuberance, but Maddy noticed it and commented that I resembled a cat who'd stolen the cream. "Very pleased with ourself," she added suspiciously.

"It's a lovely day," I answered blithely.

"Thunder in the air," she grumbled.

That made me laugh. Yes, indeed, the atmosphere would be decidedly stormy if it were discovered that I had spoken to the enemy. But I could scarcely wait to see him again.

Next day he was there when I arrived. He talked and talked, telling me about his early days in London.

"London!" he cried. "What a city! I never forgot it, no matter where I was. But there were some hard memories, too. I left school at the age of twelve, and by that time my father had died. He was a drinker so it wasn't much of a loss, and I started to keep my mother in a degree of comfort to which she had not been accustomed."

I wondered why he was telling me all this, but I was fascinated. I had never met anyone like him.

"I was born to make money," he said. "The Midas touch, that's what I've got. I found selling things was the answer. You find something people want, and you bring it out better and cheaper than the next man. I knew where to get the cheapest and give the best value—sheep's trotters, sherbet, ginger beer, and lemonade. When I got the idea of making gingerbread, it seemed I was set fair to make my fortune. I hit on the idea of making it in fancy shapes—horses, dogs, girls, boys, the queen herself. My mother made 'em and I sold 'em. We had a fine little shop. The business grew and we were comfortably off. Then my mother died."

"What did you do then?"

"I got me a lady friend. Pretty as paint but a fiery temper, and she couldn't make the cakes right. Business fell off and she left me. I took a job in a gentleman's home looking after the horses. I was eighteen then, and it was my job to ride at the back of the carriage, and I'd jump down and open the door for the ladies when we stopped. One day we went out visiting in the country, and where do you think we came to—Oakland Hall."

"You were calling on the Claverings!"

"Quite right, but calling in a humble capacity. I thought it was just about the most beautiful place I'd ever seen. I went round to the stables to look after the horses and talked to the stablemen of Oakland Hall. They were very superior, I can tell you."

"That must have been years ago," I cried.

"Long before you were born, Miss Jessie. It was more than forty years ago that I first set eyes on this place. I remember feeling the age of it. That's what I liked—all those stone walls and the feeling that people had been living there hundreds of years. I said to myself, One day I'm going to have a house like Oakland Hall. And in six months' time I was on my way to Australia."

"To look for opals?" I asked.

"No. I hadn't thought of opals then. I was after what everyone else was after—gold. But disappointments, frustrations . . . that was my lot. Shifting from place to place, living in the fields. I had my first big find at Castlemaine—not enough to make me rich, but an encouragement. I banked it in Melbourne right away. I wasn't spending it on women, like so many did."

"So you made your fortune," I said.

"It wasn't done in a night, but after I struck gold at Heathcote and Ballarat, I wasn't a poor man any more. I had time to look about and ask myself, Which way now? It's a funny thing about mining. It gets in your blood. But there's other things besides gold."

"Opals!" I said.

"Yes, opals. I went on a trek into New South Wales and fell in with a party which was looking for opal. Within a month I was a proper gouger. Then I started to get my first real finds. As soon as I held them in my hands and they twinkled at me, I knew that it was opals for me. You know, they say there's a story in each stone." He looked at me and laughed. "I'm going to show you my collection. Next time, you come to the house, eh?"

"I'd like to, but my family would forbid it."

He winked. "What do people like us care for a bit of forbidding, eh? Tomorrow I have visitors—and they'll be with me for a while. But you come next Wednesday. I'll entertain you in a fashion worthy of a Clavering."

I was so excited I could scarcely thank him.

Chapter II

That week seemed a long time in passing, for I was eager to see more of Ben Henniker, who had shown me a different kind of world and made my own life seem colourless in comparison. He made mining so vivid to me that I could picture myself holding a candle, peering into crevices, gouging out the opal—the beautiful iridescent stone which told a story, Nature's story.

I sat by the stream and hoped Mr. Henniker would come in his chair. "I know we were to meet next Wednesday," he would say, "but it was too long to wait."

But it was no use. He didn't come. Sadly I stood up and wandered along the stream until I found myself in the Waste Land kneeling by the grave.

Oh yes, it was a grave. There was no doubt of that. I pulled up the weeds, and then I made a startling discovery. A small plaque protruded slightly from the earth. I yanked it up and knocked off the earth. What was revealed made me feel as though icy water were trickling down my spine, for on that plaque was my own name—JESSICA CLAVERING.

I sat back on my heels studying the plaque. I could just make out some figures—1880—and, above them, JU––. The other two letters were obliterated. This was even more disturbing. I had been born on the third of June, 1880, and whoever lay in that grave not only bore my name but had died at the time of my birth.

Momentarily I had forgotten Ben Henniker. I could think of nothing but my discovery, and I was still thinking of it when I went in to dinner.

Meals were dreary occasions at the Dower House. Conversation usually centred on local affairs, what was happening at the church and to people of the village. We had very little social life,

for when invitations came they were declined. "How could we possibly return such hospitality?" Mama would cry.

On this occasion we were seated around the table in the really rather charming dining room. Xavier was saying that the summer's drought had not been good for the crops.

"I remember the disaster last year," my father said. "Most of Yarrowland crops were under water." This was a mistake, because Yarrowland was a farm on the Donningham estate, and it would remind Xavier of Lady Clara.

"The Donninghams can take disaster in their stride," said Mama. "*They* retained their fortune throughout the generations."

"That's true," my father agreed in his resigned way.

I was sorry for him, and to change the subject, I blurted out, "Who was Jessica Clavering?"

There was immediate silence. Everyone was looking at me, and I saw the faint colour begin to show under Mama's skin.

"Is it some joke?" said Miriam, her thin lips twitching slightly. "You know very well who you are."

"I'm *Opal* Jessica. And I often wonder why my first name is never used."

Mama looked relieved. "It's not very suitable," she said.

"Why did you give it to me then?" I demanded.

Xavier, who always came to the rescue when he could, said, "Most of us have names we'd rather not own to, but I suppose when we were born they seemed suitable enough."

"But who is this Jessica who is buried in the Waste Land?" I insisted. "I found a stake there with her name on it."

"And what were you doing in the Waste Land?" demanded Mama.

"I often go there," I told her.

"You should be better employed. There is a whole stock of dusters to be hemmed. Isn't that so, Miriam?"

"Indeed it is, Mama. There is much to be done."

This gave my mother an excuse to go off on one of her sermons on industry and giving to the needy, for the dusters— made from cast-off garments—were distributed to the poor.

Xavier listened gravely; so did Miriam, and my father, as usual, was silent while the cheese was brought in and eaten. Then my mother rose from the table before I had time to pursue the matter of the grave.

As I was mounting the stairs after the meal, I heard my parents talking in the hall. "She'll have to know," my father was saying. "She'll have to be told sooner or later."

"Nonsense!" retorted Mama. "If it hadn't been for you, it would never have happened."

They went into the drawing room, and I was as bewildered as ever. It seemed that everything came back to the fact that my father had gambled away the family fortune.

AS WEDNESDAY approached, I forgot my curiosity about the grave in my excitement at the prospect of visiting Ben Henniker. In the early afternoon I set out for the Hall. Oaks—solid, proud, and beautiful—grew on either side of the winding drive. They had caused me some irritation in the past because I had been unable to see the house from the road, but now I was glad. As soon as I had rounded the bend, I was out of sight to any passer-by.

When I saw the house I caught my breath in wonder. It was magnificent. It had always looked interesting seen through the trees from the stream, but to come face to face with it was thrilling. I could even forgive my mother's rancour, for having once lived in such a place it would be hard to lose it. It was Tudor in essence, and it could not have looked very different in the days when Henry VIII had visited, as I had heard my mother say he did. I stood awestruck looking up at the two towers. Over the gateway was a coat of arms. Ours, I supposed.

I went through the gateway into a courtyard, where I faced a massive oak door. I pulled the ancient bell and listened delightedly to the loud ringing.

A second or so later a dignified butler opened the door. I placed him at once as Wilmot. "You are Miss Clavering," he said before I could speak, and somehow he made the name sound very grand. "Mr. Henniker is expecting you."

As he led me across the hall, I was aware of a big refectory table with pewter dishes on it, and suits of armour at each end of the room. I heard whispering and the scuffle of feet. Wilmot looked up sharply and I guessed we were being observed.

A faint smile touched his lips. "You see, Miss Clavering, this is the first time we have received a member of the family, since . . ."

"Since we were obliged to sell," I said bluntly.

Wilmot winced a little and bowed his head. I realized later that

25

this coming to the point and calling a spade a spade would have been considered bad taste in anyone outside the family. I wondered then how Ben Henniker and Wilmot got on together.

"Mr. Henniker will receive you in the drawing room," Wilmot said as he opened a heavy oak door.

Ben Henniker wheeled his chair towards me. He was laughing. "Ha!" he cried. "Welcome to the old ancestral home."

I heard the door shut discreetly behind me as I went forward to greet him.

He continued to laugh and I joined in. "Well, it is funny, don't you think?" he said at length. "You, the visitor. Miss Clavering—Miss *Opal* Jessica Clavering."

"I shall begin to think you asked me just for the pleasure of showing a Clavering the family mansion."

"Not only that. I enjoyed our meetings. Did you tell your family you'd made my acquaintance?"

"No."

He nodded. "Wise girl. Better for 'em not to know, eh?"

"It saves a lot of forbidding and disobeying."

"I can see you're a rebel. Well, I like that. It's good for you to learn something of the ways of the world, and you'll never learn much if you cut out this one and that one because they're not nice to know. That's why it's good for you to know me. We're on different sides of the fence. But deep down you're not one of them, are you? You're not shut in with cramped ideas. You're free, Miss Jessie." He winked at me. "That's why we get along together. Now I'm going to take you into my own special hideaway."

He reached for a crutch and hoisted himself out of the wheel-chair. Then he opened a door. Two steps led down into a smaller room, which had panelled walls and leaded windows. He unlocked a cupboard and inside was a steel safe. Twirling knobs, he opened the safe and took out several flat boxes.

"Here are some of the finest opals that have ever been gouged out of rock," he said.

He sat down at a round table, and I drew up a chair to sit beside him. He opened a box and inside, lying in little velvet hollows, were the opals. I had never seen such beautiful gems. On the top row great pale stones flashed blue and green fire; those on the next row, also of remarkable size, were darker—blue, almost

26

purple; and in the last row the stones had an almost black background, which was the more startling because they flashed red and green lights.

"There," he said, "your namesakes. What do you think of them? Keep your diamonds. Keep your sapphires. There's nothing anywhere in the world to beat these gems."

"I have never seen a great many diamonds or sapphires," I said, "but I can't imagine anything more lovely than these."

"Look at this!" he commanded as, with a gnarled finger, he gently touched one of the stones. It was deep blue with a touch of gold. "They've got names, these opals. This one is the Star of the East. The wise men must have seen something like it on that Christmas night years ago. I tell you this . . . it's unique. Opals are like people, no two alike. Now the Star of the East tells its owner that the best is yet to come, for didn't the Star rise to announce the birth of the Christ child?"

"So *your* best is yet to come, Mr. Henniker?"

"You're to call me Ben. I'm Ben to you as I am to all my friends, and I trust you're one of them."

"I want to be . . . Ben." I put out a finger and touched the Star of the East.

"That's right," he said. "Touch it. Look at the light on the stone. And here's Pride of the Camp. Not quite up to the Star of the East, but a fine gem."

"Do you sell them?" I asked.

He was thoughtful for a moment. "Well, that would seem to be the object, but sometimes you just can't sell a stone, no matter what it can bring you. You get a sort of feeling for it. You'd rather have it than all the money in the world."

"So you feel like that about all these stones?"

"That's it. Some are there for their beauty and some for other reasons. Look at the Green Lady. See the green fire in it? That cost me my leg." He shook his fist at it. "You cost me dear, my beauty," he went on, "and for that reason I keep you."

He opened more boxes, and as he pointed out the qualities of various stones, I was caught up in his enthusiasm.

Then he took out a small box that was meant to cushion one single stone. In the centre of the black velvet was a hollow, almost accusing in its emptiness. He gazed at it in a melancholy way for some moments.

"What was there?" I asked.

He turned to me. His eyes had narrowed and he looked murderous. I stared at him, astonished by this change of mood.

"Once," he said, "the Green Flash at Sunset was there."

"It was a specially beautiful opal?" I ventured.

His eyes blazed. "She was the queen of the opals. Not another like her in the whole world. She was worth a fortune, but I would never have parted with her."

"You talk about the Green Flash as though she were a woman."

"That's how she was to me. I loved her. I used to take her out and look at her when I was downcast. I'd say, 'Times will change. You'll find happiness as well as stones, old Ben.'"

"What happened to her?"

"She was stolen," he said. "Before you were born."

He snapped the box shut and put it back in the safe with the others. "Now," he said, "we're going to have some tea. So let us go back to the drawing room."

The spirit lamp and silver teapot were already there, with plates of sandwiches, scones, and plum cake. Beside Wilmot stood a maid. "Miss Clavering will pour," said Ben.

"Very good, sir," replied Wilmot graciously; and I was glad when he and the maid had retired.

"All very ceremonious," said Ben. "I've never quite got used to it. You can imagine how a man feels when he's boiled his own billycan and cooked his own damper round a campfire. Today is special though. Today a Clavering is my guest."

"But not a very important one, I'm afraid," I said.

"*The* most important. Never underestimate yourself, Miss Jessie. People will think you're not much if you think that way yourself."

I asked how he liked his tea, poured it, and when I carried it to him, he smiled at me appreciatively. I felt very pleased with myself as I returned to my place behind the silver teapot.

"Miss Jessie," he said, "have you ever heard of the green flash?"

"Only this afternoon."

"I don't mean the opal . . . that other green flash. When the sun goes down—just before it disappears—there is a green flash on the sea. You can see it only in the tropics, and then conditions have to be exactly right. It's a rare phenomenon. If you as much as blink your eyes you could miss it. I saw it once on a voyage back to England from Australia. I was on deck at sunset watching that great ball of fire drop into the ocean. It's different in the tropics. There's little twilight like we have here. Suddenly the sun was gone and there was this green flash. 'I've seen the green flash,' I cried out loud. On that journey home I carried my opal with me. It was a deep, deep blue; and there was a red fire in it like the sun. If you were looking at the right moment, the red would disappear and you'd see the green flash. I couldn't call her anything else but the Green Flash at Sunset."

"And you loved it best of all your stones?"

"There is no other like it. I'd never seen that green flash in a stone before. It was the way the light caught it; you had to watch for it. It was something about you as well as the stone."

"Did you never find out who took it?"

"I had my suspicions. In fact, everything pointed to him, the young devil. By God, if I could lay my hands on him . . ." He seemed to be lost for words, which was rare with him.

I refilled his cup and said softly, "Where did it happen?"

"There," he said, pointing to the room we had just left. "I hadn't had the house long then. I was anxious to show it off. I used to have people stay here because I wanted to say, Look what I've got. This is what all these years of toil have got for me. It was pride, pride going before a fall. There were four of us on that occasion. I brought out my opals, and that was the last I saw of the Green Flash at Sunset. I put her back in the safe. The next time I looked, all the opals were there except that one."

"And you knew who stole it?"

"There was one young man. He disappeared and I never saw him again. He was clearly the one who had the Green Flash. Funny thing was I'd never have thought it of him. He had that determination which almost always ends in success. But when he set eyes on the Green Flash, that was his downfall."

"Do you think he sold it?"

"It wouldn't have been easy. Any dealer would have reported the sale. He may have taken her just to have her to himself. She had such a fascination for everyone who saw her. In spite of the tales of bad luck, everyone who saw that stone wanted it."

"What tales, Ben?"

"Well, one or two owners experienced misfortune. The Green Flash meant death, people used to say."

"So *you* didn't find it in the first place then?"

"Oh, dear me, no. You might say I won it."

"How did you do that?"

"Old Harry Wilkins had this stone, and from the moment he showed it to me I wanted it. Ill luck dogged Harry. People said it was the stone. His son went out one night and never came back. He was found with his neck broken. Old Harry went to pieces after that. He was a great gambler, and so was I. He staked the Green Flash for a fortune; I took the gamble and won. He shot himself a few weeks later."

"And what about you?"

"I wouldn't believe in the curse."

"You lost the stone, so perhaps you escaped it."

Suddenly it seemed as though he could no longer bear to talk of his loss. He said perhaps I'd like to look around the house. "Then you can think what it would have been like if you'd lived your life here, as you would have if a get-rich-quick johnny hadn't grabbed the ancestral home."

"I shall always be glad of that now," I assured him, and he looked very pleased. He pulled a bell rope and Wilmot appeared.

"Miss Clavering would like to see the house," said Ben. "Have Hannah show her round."

I went to Ben's chair and took his hand. "Thank you. I have enjoyed it so much."

His face looked strange. If he had been anyone else, I should have said he was about to cry. Then he said, "Off with you."

HANNAH was a tall, spare woman with gaunt features, and large dark eyes which seemed to bore right into me. "I came here when I was twelve years old," she told me. "I was with your family for five years. When they went, they couldn't afford to keep me."

"That happened with many, I'm afraid."

"Would you care to start at the top of the house, Miss Clavering, and work down?"

I said I thought that seemed an excellent idea, and together we climbed the newel staircase to the roof.

"You can see the turrets best from up here," she said. "And there's a good view of the Dower House."

It looked like a doll's house nestling among the trees, and the lawn looked like a square of green silk. I could see poor Jarman working on the flower beds.

"You have a better view of us than we have of you," I commented. "You must have seen us in the garden now and then."

"Oh, often."

I felt a little uneasy at having been watched by Hannah.

"Do you prefer it now to the days when my family were here?"

She hesitated, then said, "In some ways. Mr. Henniker goes away a lot, and we have the place to ourselves. He's easy to work for." I could see she was implying that my mother was not.

"Shall we go down now, Miss Clavering?" suggested Hannah.

I nodded and we descended the circular stairs and entered a room. I admired the moulded beams of the ceiling, the panelled walls, and the carved fireplace.

"There are so many rooms like this that you lose count," said Hannah. "But Mr. Henniker can afford to keep the place up."

"It must be a comfort to work for Mr. Henniker after my family."

"It's all so different. Mr. Wilmot says it's not what he's used to, and I reckon he hankers for a house with more dignity. But it's nice to have your wages come prompt, and not have to pinch and scrape." We had come to a gallery. "Once," Hannah went on, "there were pictures of the Claverings all along here. A gallery's not a gallery without pictures of the family, Mr. Wilmot says."

The gallery was beautiful, with carved pillars, and tall stained-glass windows which threw a lovely glow over the place. There were curtains of rich red velvet at intervals around the walls.

"They say this was haunted," Hannah told me. "But no one's seen or heard anything since Mr. Henniker's been here. They used to hear music coming from a spinet that was there. Mr. Henniker had it shipped out to Australia. It meant something special to him, I heard."

We went on with our tour and, as Hannah said, there were many rooms of the same kind. I hoped that if I visited Mr. Henniker frequently I could explore the house at my leisure. Hannah was not the most comfortable of guides, because whenever I looked at her I would find her eyes fixed on me.

Finally we came down to the hall. At one end there was a door which shut off the servants' quarters. Hannah opened it, and we entered a vast kitchen. An enormous fireplace took up almost the whole of one side. In this were bread ovens, roasting spits, and great cauldrons. A large woman came sailing in, followed by three maids. Hannah said, "This is Miss Clavering, Mrs. Bucket."

31

"How do you do, Mrs. Bucket," I replied. "Maddy often mentions you."

"Is that so?" she asked, pleased. "Well, Miss Clavering, this is a great day for us to have one of the family here."

I felt a little embarrassed because I could see they were all assessing me.

"Miss Clavering has become acquainted with Mr. Henniker," said Hannah, "so he asked her to tea."

Mrs. Bucket nodded. "And did you enjoy the scones, Miss Clavering? I always remember Miss Jessica . . ."

Hannah was staring at Mrs. Bucket as though she were Medusa. I could see she was imploring her to be discreet. But I was not going to allow that. I said, "Miss Jessica? Who was she?"

"Mrs. Bucket meant Miss Miriam," said Hannah. "This is Miss Jessica, Mrs. Bucket. It was Miss Miriam who used to love your scones. I reckon that Mrs. Cobb's are not a patch on yours."

"Nobody's are a patch on mine," said Mrs. Bucket emphatically.

"I thought they were delicious," I said, but I was wondering why she had said Miss Jessica.

Hannah asked quickly if I would like to see the stables. I said I thought I'd better not, for it had just occurred to me that though my visits were supposed to be secret, some of the servants would certainly talk, so the fewer I saw the better. I was seventeen years old, and I had to obey orders to a certain extent, rebel that I was. I told Mrs. Bucket that I was glad to have made her acquaintance, thanked Hannah for showing me the house, and left.

I went straight to the Waste Land and found the plaque, which I had stuck back into the ground: JESSICA CLAVERING, JU—— 1880. She must be the Jessica of whom Mrs. Bucket had spoken.

ALL THROUGH THE MONTH of August I went to Oakland Hall. Ben practised walking with a wooden leg and seemed to be showing progress. He called himself Ben Pegleg and said he reckoned he'd do as well with wood as most people did with flesh and blood. He'd hold my arm and we would walk along the gallery together.

Once he said to me, "There ought to be family pictures here. But my ugly face wouldn't add much to it."

"It's the most interesting face I have ever seen," I told him.

The face in question twitched at that. Underneath his tough exterior he was a very sentimental man. Once I said to him, "Ben, you should have had a wife. Then you'd have had some sons and daughters to fill the gallery."

"I've got the odd one or two," he said with a grin. "At least they claim me as father, or did when I began to grow rich."

"Perhaps they would have claimed you if you were poor."

"Who's to say?"

And so we talked.

I was friendly with the servants, too. Mrs. Bucket had taken me to her heart, and even Wilmot accepted my visits to the servants' hall. I was sure he worked it out that although I was a Clavering, I was not really an Oakland Hall Clavering. He treated me with respect, but it was tempered with condescension.

Ben and I used to laugh a great deal over it, and I would wonder how I had endured the monotony of my life in pre-Ben days.

Only one thing made me uneasy. Once Ben could walk more readily, he planned to return to Australia, where he had a place north of Sydney, in opal country.

"You mean you'd go mining again?" I asked.

"Oh, I wouldn't go off with my pick. But I have mines out there and men working for me."

"What's happening to all that now?"

"The Peacock's looking after it." Ben began to laugh. "You'll have to meet the Peacock. The name suits him."

"He must be vain."

"Oh, he's got a good conceit of himself. Mind you, I'm not saying it's not warranted. He's got blue eyes the colour of a peacock's feather, and my goodness, can he flash them when he's in a rage. There's not a man in the company who would dare cross the Peacock. That can be very useful. I know he'll take care of everything while I'm away."

"So you can trust this Peacock?"

"Seeing the closeness of our relationship, I reckon I can."

"Who is he then?"

"Josslyn Madden. Known as Joss the Peacock. His mother, Julia Madden, was a beautiful woman. Her husband, Jock, was a poor fish who couldn't manage a job or hold a woman. Julia and I were very fond of each other. And when young Joss came along there wasn't a shadow of doubt."

"You mean he is your son?"

"That's about it. I built my place—Peacocks—some time after

Joss was born. I put the peacocks on the lawn and gave the house its name. Julia used to come over to see me. She was thinking of leaving Jock. Then one day on the way over she was thrown from her horse and killed. Jock married again when Joss was seven. My young peacock didn't like the new household at all, so he packed a bag and marched over to my place. He told me, 'I am going to live here now.' Not 'May I?' but 'I am!' That was Joss Madden aged seven and that's Joss Madden today. He makes up his mind what he wants and that's how it's going to be."

"And is he one of those who claimed you as his father when you grew rich?"

"At seven I don't know how knowledgeable he was about wealth. I think he just hated his home and liked the peacocks. He paid more attention to them than he did to me. Then he became fascinated by opals—particularly those with peacock colourings. He took an interest right from the start, and when Joss takes an interest it's a big one. I know the place is safe with him. But the urge comes over me to be out there. Sometimes I dream I'm down in an underground chamber with my candle. The roof is a mass of gems, and right at the heart of them is another Green Flash."

"It's unlucky, Ben," I said. "You're rich; you've got Oakland. What does the Green Flash matter?"

"I'll tell you one of the nicest things I've found since I lost the Flash," he answered. "Well, that's you."

We didn't speak for some time. We just stumped along the gallery, but my misgivings had started. I knew the day would come when he would go away.

At Oakland Hall I always made a point of going down to the kitchen. Mrs. Bucket delighted in cooking little delicacies for me. She liked to talk about the past, and from her I learned much that I wanted to know about my family.

"Mr. Xavier used to call me Food Bucket." She purred and shook her head. "Nothing disrespectful, mind. 'Of course you're Food Bucket,' he used to say, 'because nobody can make food taste like you do.' He could eat, and so could Miss Miriam. I caught her more than once stealing the sugar. And Miss Jessica . . ."

There was a deep silence before Hannah said, "Have you made those currant buns for tea, Mrs. Bucket?"

Mrs. Bucket burst out, "What's the good of all this pretending? You can't keep that sort of thing in the dark for ever."

"Tell me," I demanded rather imperiously, as though I were an Oakland-bred Clavering, "who was Jessica?"

"There was another daughter," said Mrs. Bucket almost defiantly. "She came between Miriam and Xavier."

"And she was called Jessica?" I went on.

Hannah bowed her head. It was tantamount to agreement.

"What happened to her?" I looked at Mrs. Bucket appealingly.

"She died," said Mrs. Bucket.

"When she was very young?" I asked.

"It was after they left Oakland," Hannah told me. "She was about seventeen. But Mrs. Bucket shouldn't have . . ."

"I'll do what I like in my own kitchen," said Mrs. Bucket.

"This is no kitchen matter," protested Hannah.

I could see that they were making a quarrel to avoid telling me. But I was determined to find out. I left the Hall and went to the churchyard and looked at all the graves. There was only one Jessica Clavering, and she had died about a hundred years before at the ripe age of seventy.

Then I went to the Waste Land. There it was—the grave and the plaque. "So this is where they buried you, Jessica," I murmured.

THE NEXT DAY, when I was sitting by the stream, Hannah appeared with a large envelope, which she thrust into my hands.

"What is this?" I asked.

"It was given to me to give you when the time came, or on your twenty-first birthday—whichever came first. I reckon, after all that's been said, that the time is now."

"Who gave it to you?"

"It's all in there. I hope I've done what was right."

She hesitated for a moment, her brow puckered in consternation, then she turned and hurried away. I opened the envelope and pulled out several sheets of paper covered in neat writing.

I glanced at the first page. "My darling child, Opal," it began.

"It will be many years after I write this that you will read it, and I hope when you do you will not think too badly of me. Always remember that I loved you, and that what I am going to do, I do because it is the best way out for all of us. I want you to know that my last thoughts were of you. . . ."

I took the papers to the Waste Land to read them, close to the grave of Jessica.

"I shall start at the beginning. I want you to know me, so you will understand how everything happened. I think in every family there is one who is different, the one in the litter who doesn't bear much resemblance to the rest.

"Well, I was like that—always a bit of a rebel. I used to pretend I was a ghost. I'd play the spinet in the gallery and then go and hide when people came to look, so the rumour started that the gallery was haunted.

"I was Papa's favourite, and he taught me how to play poker. I shall never forget when Mama found us with cards in our hands. She said, 'Fiddling while Rome's burning!' I said, 'This isn't fiddling, Mama. It's poker.' And she picked up the cards and threw them into the fire. 'Now it's cards that are burning, not Rome,' I said, for I never guard my tongue. Mama slapped me across the face. I remember the shock it gave me. Papa was shocked too. He said sternly, 'Never lift your hand against the children again.' Then it came out: 'And who are you to tell me how to behave? You are teaching our daughter to be as dissolute as you are. Cards, gambling . . . and gambling means debts, which is why we are in the position we are in today.'

"There were scenes quite often. Money was wanted to pay for this and that, and it wasn't there. I knew Papa was doing wrong. It was some devil's streak in the family. Finally there was only one course open to us. We had to sell Oakland.

"Papa was so miserable that I feared he would take his life. Mama was bitter. She kept saying it need never have happened. We had to sell not only the house but so much that was precious in it. The lovely tapestries, some of the silver and furniture. Then we went to the Dower House. 'It's a beautiful house,' Xavier kept saying, but Mama wouldn't hear of it and grumbled continually. Nothing was ever right.

"Miriam caught my mother's bitterness. I never did. I understood the irresistible urge, the compulsion which had beset Papa. I had that myself—not for cards, but for life. I was of a nature to follow my impulses, to act first and consider the wisdom of that act afterwards. I hope you will not grow up to be of that nature, dear Opal, because it can bring you trouble.

"A Mr. Ben Henniker bought Oakland. He was a friendly man and one day called on us at the Dower House. Maddy brought him into the drawing room, where we were having tea.

"'Well, ma'am,' he said to Mama, 'I'm having a bit of a gathering next week, and it struck me you might like to join us.'

"Mama could freeze people with a look. 'A gathering, Mr. Henniker?' she said, as though he were suggesting a Roman orgy. 'I'm afraid that is quite out of the question. We shall most certainly be engaged during the week you mention.'

"Mr. Ben Henniker's face was quite purple with rage. He said, 'I understand, ma'am, you would be engaged any time I had the impertinence to invite you. Have no fear. You'll never again be asked to Oakland Hall while I'm there.' Then he walked out.

"I was so angry with Mama. It seemed absurd to resent him merely because he had bought Oakland. *We* had put it up for sale. I slipped out and ran after him. 'I'm so ashamed that my mother spoke to you like that,' I panted. 'I do hope you won't think badly of us all.'

"His blue eyes were blazing with fury, but as he looked at me he began to smile. 'Well, fancy that,' he said. 'And you're little Miss Clavering, I reckon.'

"'I'm Jessica,' I told him.

"'You don't take after your mother,' he said.

"'She has some good points,' I defended her, 'but they are a little hard to recognize.'

"He started to laugh, and it was impossible not to join in. Then he said, 'I like you for running after me like this. You must come and see me in your old home. What about that?' He almost choked with laughter. 'You come and meet some of my friends. It'll be an eye-opener for you, Miss Jessica. I reckon you've lived in a cage all your life. How old are you?' I told him I was seventeen. 'It's a beautiful age,' he said. 'It's an age when you ought to be setting out on your adventures.'

"What an escape those visits to Oakland Hall were. . . ."

I paused in my reading and stared at the grave before me. My life was repeating an old pattern; what had happened to Jessica was happening to me. I continued reading.

"I went frequently to Mr. Henniker's house, and it soon seemed more like home than the Dower House ever could be. Once when we were in the gallery I told Mr. Henniker how I used to play the spinet and frighten the servants. He was very amused and thereafter he often asked me to play for him. He loved to listen while I went through the Chopin waltzes. I used to think it would

37

go on like that always. I wish I could tell you how he interested me. I had never known anyone like him."

She didn't have to try to make me understand that. I had experienced the same thing myself.

"There had once been a lot of talk about my coming out. We had had some lovely dresses made. The most beautiful one was a cherry-coloured silk trimmed with Honiton lace; it fell off the shoulders, and I had a pretty neck and shoulders.

"I told Mr. Henniker about the dress. It was strange that he— a miner, really, and a rough one—could understand how I felt. He said, 'Why should the world be deprived of a glimpse of your shoulders just because your father was a gambler? We'll have a ball and you shall wear the cherry-red dress to it.'

"So on Ben's suggestion I smuggled the dress into Oakland, and on the night of the ball I slipped over there and changed into it.

"It was an enchanted evening. There had never been such an evening in the whole of my life and never will be again, for at the ball I met Desmond Dereham.

"I wish you could have seen the gallery as it was that night. There were musicians, and flowers from the greenhouses, and candles flickering in their sconces. It was not a crowded ballroom, because Mr. Henniker had asked none of the neighbours who would know me. Right at the first Desmond found me and asked me to dance. He was young . . . not much older than I, but twenty-one seemed a responsible age to me. He was tall and fair and his hair was bleached by the sun. He had what I call Australian eyes, which meant that they were half closed and had thick lashes. 'It's the sun,' he told me. 'It's brighter and hotter than here. You half shut your eyes against it. I expect Nature provides the lashes as a protection.' He talked like Ben Henniker about opals. He was fanatical about them.

"'There never has been anything so fine as the Green Flash at Sunset,' he told me. 'You ought to ask Ben to show it to you sometime.' I wasn't interested in the Green Flash at Sunset. I wasn't interested in anything that night but Desmond.

"He told me he intended to go back to Australia in about two or three weeks' time. He had discovered land which he was sure was opal country, and he was longing to prospect it. Ben and some others were interested in the project; it was going to need a good deal of money to develop it. Some of the old miners laughed at him. They called it Desmond's Fancy. But he believed in it.

"When the ball was over, Hannah helped me to change into my day dress. She was about my age, which I suppose made her understanding. Maddy helped too. She crept down the Dower House stairs and let me in. Without those two it would have been very difficult for me.

"When Hannah brought my dress back next day, there was a note from Desmond. He must see me that afternoon. Of course I met him. We walked through Oakland park and talked and talked, and that night I went once more to Oakland to dine. You guess, of course, that we were in love. We were absolutely sure before the first week was out that there couldn't be anyone else for either of us. Every night I would slip across the bridge into the park, where he would be waiting. I cannot describe the bliss of those September nights. Mama felt poorly that summer and spent a great deal of time in bed. That made it easier for me.

"Desmond and I planned it all carefully. We were going to be married in three weeks' time. He would get a special licence, and then we would go to Australia together. We told no one . . . not even Ben. Then we came to that terrible night.

"Some of Ben's associates were coming to Oakland to discuss Desmond's project. Desmond was very excited. Because of a conference with them, he wouldn't be able to see me that night. But he'd told me he would be waiting by the stream the following afternoon, as usual.

"But he never came. Desmond had gone. He had disappeared without saying goodbye to anyone, and the Green Flash at Sunset had disappeared at the same time.

"As the days passed, I felt that I was living through a nightmare. I felt sick with fear, but I kept telling myself that it was a silly mistake and that Ben would find he had put his opal in another place. I went to see Ben. He was like a raging bull. 'He's got it,' he shouted. 'I'll shoot him dead, the young devil.'

"'He didn't take it, Ben,' I cried. 'I know he didn't.'

"He stopped raging and stared at me. 'He's deceived you,' he said soberly. 'Such a good-looking boy . . . such a pleasant young man. But he wasn't all he appeared to be.'

"I couldn't bear to hear Ben talk like that, so I stopped going to Oakland. I shut myself in with my grief, and everyone thought I was ill, for I grew pale and listless. For a time I simply didn't care what happened to me. Then Hannah told me that Ben was going back to Australia.

"I saw him before he went, but our friendship had changed. Desmond was between us. Ben was so sure he was guilty; I was so certain that he was not.

"I cannot describe the desolation which had come into my life. Ben had gone and I had lost Desmond. I could not imagine greater tragedy. And when the fear first came to me, I tried to ignore it. It couldn't possibly be, I told myself. Yet there had been those meetings in the park when we had talked and dreamed and loved so passionately. Desmond had said, 'We are married, really.' And I had thought of myself as his wife. Before Christmas I knew I was going to have a child. I did not know what to do. I told Hannah because I could trust her. We talked and talked but could find no solution.

"On Christmas Day I told Miriam. She was horrified. She didn't understand much, but she did know that one of the servants had once 'got into trouble' and had been sent back to her family, disgraced for ever. 'Disgraced for ever,' she kept repeating, until I wanted to scream.

"I knew that the rest of the family would have to be told, so I told Xavier next. He looked at me as though he thought I had gone mad. There was nothing to do, he said, but tell my parents.

"When a woman is going to have a child, she seems to acquire some special strength. That was how it was with me. Even the scene with my parents did not distress me as much as might have been imagined. Xavier told Mama and Papa that there was something they must know, and the four of us went into the drawing room. Xavier shut the door and said very quietly, 'Jessica is going to have a baby.' There was a moment's silence. I thought that that was how it must have been before the walls of Jericho came tumbling down. My father looked blank; my mother just stared at us.

"Then she turned on me like an enraged tigress. She said the most bitter things to me. I don't remember them; I deliberately shut my ears to them. I kept thinking of the baby. I wanted that baby, and I thought then, even in the thick of my trouble, that having it would make up for a great deal.

"It was Xavier who decided what to do. My pregnancy could be disguised for a few more months. Skirts were voluminous, and

40

mine could be let out. The baby was due in June. In April my parents and I would go to Italy. My mother's health could be said to be giving us concern. We would sell the silver punch bowl and salver which George IV had given to one of our ancestors; they would provide the money for the trip and the expenses of the birth. My child would be born abroad; and when we returned we would say that my mother's ill health had been due to a pregnancy, which she had not suspected, and because of her time of life there had not been the usual symptoms. This would mean we could return with a child and give no cause for scandal.

"How unhappy those months were! We took a villa in Florence for a while—Florence with its golden light! How I should have loved it in other circumstances. I used to escape from my misery by imagining myself strolling along the Arno with Desmond.

"A few weeks before my confinement we went to Rome, and there my baby was born in June 1880. I called her Opal. Mama said it was a foolish name and that she should be given another. So the baby had my name too; she was Opal Jessica.

"We came home, and such was my mother's indefatigable energy that although some might have put a certain construction on our return with a newly-born baby, no one dared mention it. You, my dear Opal, as you have guessed, were that child. Never be ashamed of your birth. You were conceived in love. Always remember that, and no matter what people may tell you of your father, do not believe them. He was not capable of stealing that miserable opal. One day the truth will be known. I'm sure of it.

"Now, my dearest child, I come to the end of my story. After you were born, I was beset by such despair that I did not know where to turn. Mama made our lives a misery. I would look up suddenly and see her eyes fixed on me with utter distaste.

"I used to go down to the stream and stare at the cool shallow water. I thought a lot about my life then, and the belief came to me that I should never see Desmond again, for since he would never have deserted me, he must be dead. Someone had stolen the opal and killed him so that he might appear to be the thief. My conviction was so strong that the waters seemed to beckon to me. It was as though Desmond himself were asking me to come and join him.

"As I sat by the stream, I thought of all the trouble I had brought the family and how much better they would be without me. Even you would be better off not to know that I had brought disgrace on the family.

"I dreamed then of lying face downward in that cool water, and I experienced a perfect peace. I couldn't talk about it to anyone but Hannah. When I told her what I felt, she cried out, 'It's wrong. You mustn't think like that.' I said, 'It might be for the best. The baby would be all right. They'll care for her.' Hannah said, 'If you were to do away with yourself, they couldn't bury you in consecrated ground.'

"I thought about that quite a lot, but I continue to go down to the stream, and one day I shall go down there and not come back. I think of you, my daughter, growing up, and I wonder what they will tell you about me and your father, and I have written this so that you can know the truth as I saw it. I shall give this to Hannah, and she will give it to you when the time comes.

"Goodbye, little Opal. May God bless you. One day you will discover the truth about your father. I promise you there will be nothing to discredit him."

I stared ahead of me. I was seeing it all so clearly. Then I knelt by her grave, and when I touched my cheeks I found that they were wet, although I had not known that I was weeping.

I DID NOT appear at dinner that evening because I could not face the family. They drove her to it, I thought. If they had been kinder to her, she would have been alive today. I wanted to storm at them—my poor ineffectual grandfather, my proud unloving grandmother. How glad I was that she was not, after all, my mother!

I feigned a headache, and when Miriam came to see me I closed my eyes and turned away.

The next day I saw Hannah, who, I think, had been watching for me. "So you read the letter, Miss Jessica?" she said. "I never thought she'd do it or I'd have found some way to stop her."

I nodded. "Tell me what happened afterwards."

"They found her lying face downward in the stream."

"And they buried her in the Waste Land," I said.

"Reverend Crey was very strict about it. They don't bury suicides in consecrated ground. That's all. People didn't speak of it much. It was put about that she'd fallen in love and that he had gone away. I always put flowers on her grave at Easter time."

"Thank you, Hannah. Did anyone suspect I was her child?"

"If they did, it wasn't said. You were accepted as an after-thought. It can happen that way, and Miss Jessica drowned some time after your birth. It was the last day in July. And you were born on the first of June." She turned away, her lips quivering.

"How she must have suffered! I know my father never took that opal. My mother would never have fallen in love with a thief."

"That's how your mother used to talk, but he was gone and so was the opal."

"I wish I could find out what really happened to it."

"Bless you, miss. I reckon Mr. Henniker has never given up the search. And you think *you're* going to be the one to find it! You just don't know anything about these things."

"But he's my father. That makes all the difference."

Hannah shook her head sadly.

ALTHOUGH I could not talk to my family about the tragedy, I could do so to Ben, and at our next meeting I blurted out, "I know about my mother and father." I explained about the papers she had left for me.

We were sitting in the drawing room, he in his chair with his crutch propped up beside him. He did not speak for a few moments, and I saw that a great sadness had come to him.

"You knew?" I asked.

"I guessed. You're so like her, with your dark eyes and your turned-up nose and your mouth which somehow says you're going to laugh at life even at its worst. I could believe she was sitting there at this moment."

"You didn't mind when she fell in love with my father?"

He hesitated. "It wasn't for me to mind," he said at length. "I could see how it was with them from the moment they met. I thought he was a good, honest young fellow then."

"He didn't do it, you know, Ben."

"He broke her heart, didn't he! I'd kill him for that."

"You loved her, Ben," I said. "You would have liked to marry her yourself."

"That wouldn't have been right. She was a dainty creature. And look at me—a rough old gouger."

"If you had," I reminded him, "I'd be your daughter."

"That's not a bad idea." He was becoming his old self again, and I was finding comfort in talking to him. "Yes," he went on, "I loved her. I blame myself for not being here when she died. If I had been, it wouldn't have happened."

"What would you have done, Ben?"

"I would have married her. Perhaps she would have had me then."

I ran to him and hugged him. "Oh Ben, wouldn't that have been wonderful? We should all have lived here together."

He stroked my hair and said, "Well, it didn't work out that way. It's no use looking back and saying if. It's today that's important. We got acquainted and we're good friends."

I went back to my chair and said, "Tell me about my father."

"Desmond Dereham was a handsome boy, good family, too. He had a feeling he'd stumbled on one of the richest opal fields in New South Wales. We joked about it and called it Desmond's Fancy. Then we started to think there might be something in it, and gathered together at Oakland to discuss it."

"What actually happened on that night?"

Ben appeared to consider carefully. "There were Joss, Desmond, an opal merchant called David Croissant, and myself. Joss was fourteen then, going to school over here. My goodness, he was a sharp one. He already knew what he was going to do. He was going to be the biggest opal man in the whole world! That was his way of looking at everything. He was already telling me what to do. He towered above me, and he hadn't finished growing. Six feet five inches. That's Joss now in his stocking feet."

"Yes, yes," I said a little impatiently. I was tired of hearing about Joss Madden's perfections.

"Well, we studied Desmond's plans for the Fancy and worked out where to sink the shafts. We were going to keep it fairly small at first, and then if Desmond's hunch proved correct, we'd go all out. I remember Desmond's enthusiasm. There was something about him . . . a sort of sheen of confidence. Every one of us believed that Desmond's Fancy was going to yield big fine opals. But I said we'd never find anything as good as the Green Flash at Sunset. Then we got talking of the Flash and they wanted to look at it.

"I took them all into the study and opened the safe. There it lay in its velvet nest. Desmond Dereham stretched out his hands

44

to take the Flash. He let her lie in his palm for a moment, and then he called out, 'I saw it. I saw the green flash.' I snatched the opal from him, but I couldn't catch the flash. Joss swore he saw it too. He always had to be there right in the centre of everything. The next morning your father had gone. And the Green Flash had disappeared."

"I can't believe that my father stole it."

Ben leaned forward and took my hand. "I understand how you feel. But what happened to the Green Flash? David Croissant wouldn't have taken it. He was a salesman. He knew the quality of opals as few people did, but he didn't feel sentimental about any one stone. He'd see its market value, and what market value would the Green Flash have had? It would be recognized at once, and he'd be exposed as a thief. Joss?" Ben chuckled. "Granted Joss would be capable of anything. I knew how he felt about the Green Flash, but he could see it when he wanted to. Unless, of course, the urge came over him to own it. . . ."

"My father wouldn't have deserted my mother."

"He didn't know you were on the way then. Perhaps that would have made a difference or perhaps not. You've never seen the Green Flash. If you had, you might understand its effect on people."

"What happened to my father's Fancy?"

"It's now one of the finest opal fields in Australia."

"Do you believe he would have given up his Fancy and my mother for the sake of one opal which he would never be able—openly—to call his own?"

"I can only repeat, Miss Jessie, that you have never seen the Green Flash."

WHEN I left that day, my grandmother, as I must learn to call her, saw me in the Oakland drive. "Jessica," she cried incredulously, "where have you been?"

I answered almost flippantly, "Visiting Mr. Ben Henniker!" and waited for the storm to burst. It didn't immediately, of course. Her sense of decorum would always govern her anger, but back at the Dower House, she gathered the family together in the drawing room and shut the door.

"Now Jessica," she said, "you had better explain at once how you came to be at Oakland Hall."

45

"First, will you explain why you pretended to be my mother all these years and why you made her so miserable that she drowned herself . . ."

They were all staring at me. I was sure it was the first time in her life that my grandmother had felt at a disadvantage.

"Jessica!" cried Miriam, looking from her mother to Xavier, while my grandfather looked about him as though searching for *The Times* to cower behind.

"I suspect someone has told you the story of your birth," Xavier said. "It was a tragic time for us all."

"This," said my grandmother, "is what comes of friendship with miners."

"Mr. Henniker is a good man," I said. "If he had been here, he would have helped my mother, as none of you did."

"On the contrary," went on my grandmother, "we inconvenienced ourselves greatly to help her. We sold our silver to take her abroad. I accepted you as my daughter."

"You didn't give her kindness; you didn't love her and comfort her. You let her die. As for you"—I turned to my grandfather—"you haven't any guts." I saw him wince. "Not you nor Miriam nor Xavier. You're all despicable. Miriam can't face life with her curate because he's too poor. Xavier can't marry Lady Clara because she's too rich. What are you all made of? Straw!" And coming to the end of my tirade I ran out the door and up to my room.

I was shaking with emotion. I had told them what I thought of them, and for once they had no answer for me.

Miriam came up soon afterwards. She looked bewildered, and what she said was, "We shall no longer have to hide the family Bible." This struck me as so funny that I burst out laughing. Then she went on as though talking to herself. "I suppose it's better to be poor than let everything pass you by."

Later I saw the family Bible, which had hitherto been locked away in the drawing-room cabinet. There was my mother's name inscribed in beautiful copperplate, and mine too. When I went down to dinner that night, they said nothing about my outburst. The conversation was all about the weather and village affairs. In a way I had to admire them.

But of one thing I was certain. No one was going to stop my friendship with Ben Henniker, and after that I made no secret of my visits to Oakland Hall.

Chapter III

I was eighteen, and change was in the air. Miriam had grown a little bolder, and my grandfather was less subservient. The really alarming change, however, came from Oakland Hall.

Ben was gleefully hobbling around on his crutch. "This old wooden stump will soon be as good as a leg," he kept saying.

"Then you won't be content to stay here," I suggested fearfully. "Shall you go back to the opal fields?"

"I reckon so. The end of the summer would be the best time to sail. The seas would be kinder." Then he talked a great deal about the company and the town called the Fancy or Fancy Town. He often mentioned Joss, but the more I heard of that arrogant gentleman the less I was able to share Ben's enthusiasm for him.

I did enjoy our talks though. I loved hearing about his home out there, and I felt I already knew the ostentatious house called Peacocks. There was a housekeeper, a Mrs. Laud, a most efficient woman, for whom Ben felt some affection. She had a son and a daughter—Jimson, who worked in the company, and Lilias, who helped her mother in the house.

One day he said, "You'd miss me if I went away, Jessie."

"Please don't talk of it," I begged.

"But I've got something very important to say about it. If I went, I'd want you to come with me."

"Ben! They'd never let me go!"

He gave his sly laugh. "You leave that to me," he said.

THERE WAS a knock on the door of my room, and Miriam came in. She looked quite pretty. "I want to talk to you, Jessica," she said. "Ernest and I are going to get married."

I put my arms around her and kissed her. "I'm so glad, Miriam," I cried. "You should have done it years ago. Never mind. You have at last. I hope you'll be very happy."

"As you know," she went on, "we were waiting for Ernest to get St. Clissold's. But the vicar there could live for another ten years, and Ernest says there is no sense in waiting any longer. I still have to tell Mama."

"Don't let her stop you."

"Nothing could stop me now. We'll live in Ernest's little cottage on the vicarage grounds. It's rather a blessing that we have been so poor—though not as poor as Ernest and I shall be. It means that I have learned how to make things go a long way."

"I'm sure you're right. When is the wedding to be?"

Miriam looked really frightened. "At the end of August. Ernest says we'd better put up the banns right away."

My grandmother was naturally angry and sceptical. She spoke slightingly of old maids who made fools of themselves in the mad rush to marry anybody—just *anybody*—before it was too late.

Miriam was wounded, and she wavered, but only slightly. She was Ernest's future wife now, not merely my grandmother's daughter, and she quoted him whenever possible. I was delighted, and we grew more friendly than we ever had been.

AT THE end of August, Miriam was married, as she had said she would be. There was a permanent sneer about my grandmother's lips when she referred to the married pair. She called them the church mice, and gloated over their future poverty "in that miserable little hut."

One day my grandfather spoke up. "Sometimes there can be more joy in a humble cottage than in a mansion. Miriam can only congratulate herself that she has escaped from this place."

He picked up *The Times* and walked out of the room. It was indeed a change when my grandfather stood his ground.

A week after Miriam's wedding, Ben was walking in the grounds when his crutch slipped and he fell. It was an hour before he was discovered. He was carried in by Banker and Wilmot, who called the doctor. The wound on Ben's leg had burst open, and he would have to remain in bed until it was healed.

He was looking not only disgruntled but ill when I called.

"Look what the old fool's done, Jessie," he grumbled. "It means postponing our going to Australia. But that doesn't seem to upset you."

"I don't think I ever really believed I would go."

"That's not like you, Jess. You wanted to go, didn't you? The Dower House is no place for a bold spirit like yours. Look at it like this. It's a postponement. One day you'll go to Australia, I promise you."

"Well, Ben, all you have to do is get better."

But he didn't.

September passed and October was with us, and still the wound did not heal. Ben cursed the doctors and tried to get up, but the effort was too much for him and he had to admit defeat.

I saw him every afternoon. I knew that he watched the door at half past two, so I made a point of never being late, and it made me happy when I left him more cheerful than I found him.

One day towards the end of October the doctor arrived with a consultant, and there were grave faces at Oakland Hall. Ben insisted on knowing the truth, and when I called he told me what he had got out of the doctors.

"I've got some blood disease. That's why the leg won't heal. They give me a year at the most. You might think that there goes all Ben Henniker's fine plans, but if you think that, you don't know Ben Henniker. You follow me, Jess?"

"Of course," I said.

"All right then. Don't look so sad. I've had my day, and a pretty good day it's been. The point is I don't want to be snuffed out like a candle. It's always been a dream of mine to see my grandchildren peacocking on my lawn."

"You mean Joss's children."

"That's right. I used to picture them . . . sturdy little boys and girls . . . looking just like him. Joss is on the other side of thirty, and he's shown no signs of marrying yet. Oh, he's been involved here and there. He likes women, and they like him." Ben chuckled fondly. "He's got a roving eye, but he never seemed anxious to settle."

"He gets more attractive than ever," I said sarcastically. "He's now added promiscuity to his arrogance."

"Joss is a man, remember. He's strong, proud, sure of himself. I gave him the right education too, which is what I missed. I sent him to school in England when he was eleven years old. I was a bit worried about that. Afraid it might change him. Not at all. An English education just gave him something more. When he was sixteen, he refused to stay at school any longer. He was raring to get to work. He was mad about opals and mining and all that went with it. When I showed him the Flash that night, I remember the look in his eyes. . . . But that's past. What I want to talk about is now. I have a year at the most, they say. Well, before I go, everything will have to be in order. You can help me."

"I'll do everything I can. You know that, Ben."

"Well, first I want you to write to my solicitors, Vennor and Caves, in London. Tell Mr. Vennor to come here without delay."

I wrote the letter and said I'd post it. Then I sat by his bed, and he said, "I'm glad there's some time left to us, Jessie."

"The doctors could be wrong," I insisted.

He took my hand and held it. "Later on," he said, "I shall send for Joss." His shrewd eyes were on me. "I can feel your pulse quicken. The thought of seeing him excites you, doesn't it?"

"Why should it?" I asked. "I know you think a great deal of him, Ben, but what I have heard doesn't make me admire him very much. Are you really going to ask him to come here?"

"Not yet. He's got work to do out there. He can't dilly-dally, shilly-shally for a year. But when the end is near, I'll know it and I'll send for Joss. I'll have to tell him what to do before I go."

This time next year, I thought, and was filled with melancholy.

THE WEEKS passed, and I continued to visit Ben every day. He used to talk incessantly about the Green Flash, and once or twice he seemed to be wandering in his mind, because he talked as though he still had it.

"People get fancies about opals," he said. "In the past they were omens of good fortune. Now people say they bring bad luck. I've always thought the stories started because some opals chip easily, and so a stone a man has regarded as his fortune can lose much of its value. Of course, there would be legends about the Green Flash. It was one of the first black opals to be found."

"Who found it?"

"An old miner called Unlucky Jim. When he found her, the rock collapsed on him. It was rather like what happened to me with the Green Lady. He died clutching the Green Flash in his hand. Perhaps that's what started all the stories. His son discovered the body and the stone, and he knew right away that she was a winner. Then a bushranger shot him, and his younger brother inherited it. So that was two deaths already."

"What happened to the stone then?"

"It was cut and polished and, by heavens, what emerged dazzled everyone. But the tragedies continued. The younger brother fell downstairs, and spent two years in acute pain before he died. His daughter put the Green Flash in the hands of a dealer. From him it passed to an Eastern ruler, who was assassinated, and then to his eldest son, who was sold into slavery. One of his captors stole the Flash and ran off with it. When misfortune started to hit him, he blamed the stone. Before he died, he told his son to take it back where it belonged. That was how it was brought back to Australia. Old Harry won it in a gamble."

"And you weren't afraid when you had it?"

"No." He held my hand firmly and began, "Jessie . . ." I thought he was going to tell me something, but he changed his mind.

He looked very tired and I said, "Go to sleep now, Ben." I quietly left him and went back to the Dower House.

THE NEXT YEAR was with us. Every now and then Ben rallied so that I thought he was going to defy the doctors and get well, but at other times he would appear exhausted in spite of his efforts to hide it.

Then came a cold, snowy day in the middle of February. When I arrived at Oakland, Hannah looked sad.

She whispered, "He's failing, I think."

So I was prepared when I went into his room. His face had a bluish tinge, but he smiled when he saw me.

"What I call roast-chestnut and hot-spud weather," he said. "I once did very well selling them on a London street corner. Lovely to warm your hands on. It's cold today, Jessie."

I took his hands. They were indeed very cold. Then I made tea on the spirit lamp, which he liked to see me do.

"I picture you boiling the billycan out in the bush," he said. "That's what I used to think we'd be doing one day. They say man proposes and God disposes. He's disposing a bit today, I'm afraid, Jess." I must have looked very sad, because he went on. "Cheer up, my girl. Oh yes, you're going out there. I won't have it otherwise."

I didn't answer. I let him go on with his fancies.

"I've been thinking of something," he said. "I reckon the time has come for Joss to be told."

I took paper and pen and sat down by the bed. "What do you want to say?"

"I'd like you to write it in your own way. I want it to be a letter from you to him."

So I wrote:

Dear Mr. Madden,

Mr. Ben Henniker has asked me to tell you he is very ill. He wants you to come to England. It is very important that you should leave as soon as possible.

Yours truly,
Jessica Clavering

"Read it to me," said Ben, and I did.

"It sounds a bit unfriendly," he commented. "But when you meet him, you'll feel like all women do."

"I'm not a silly little peahen content to goggle at the magnificent peacock, you know, Ben."

That set him laughing so much that I was afraid it might be bad for him. When he was quiet, he lay back smiling happily as though, I thought, he had discovered a rich vein of opal.

"Anyone would think you'd found the Green Flash," I told him, and a strange expression crossed his face. I could not guess what he was thinking.

In due course I received a reply from Josslyn Madden addressed to me at Oakland Hall. I took it up and read it to Ben:

Dear Miss Clavering,

Thank you for your letter. By the time you receive this I shall be on my way. I shall come immediately to Oakland Hall when I arrive in England.

Yours truly,
J. Madden

APRIL HAD COME. I would be nineteen in June. I was feeling very sad. Ben's health had taken a turn for the worse, and I wondered what would happen when he died. The future stretched out drearily before me. I was still doing what my grandmother called those duties expected of people in our position. That meant taking dusters to the poor, managing a stall at the church fête, attending the sewing class at the vicarage, helping decorate the church, and such activities. I could see myself growing old and sour.

Our gardener's wife had recently been delivered of another child, and one day my grandmother packed a basket with a pot of raspberry jam, a small chicken, and a flask of broth. "You can take this over to Mrs. Jarman, Jessica," she said.

That was how on a breezy afternoon in late April I came to be walking over to the Jarman cottage with a basket on my arm.

Outside the house there was a muddy pond and a scrap of garden overgrown with weeds. In the midst of this neglect there were little Jarmans playing games which seemed to involve the maximum of noise, confusion, and litter.

One of the young ones had a small flowerpot into which he was shovelling dirt and turning it out into neat little mounds, which he patted with grimy hands. Two others were tugging at a rope, and another was bouncing a ball beside the pond.

There was a brief silence as I approached, all eyes on the basket, but as I went into the cottage the noise broke out again.

Mrs. Jarman was in bed, the new baby in a cradle beside her. She was very large—like a queen bee, I thought.

"Another little girl, Mrs. Jarman," I said.

"Yes, Miss Jessica," said Mrs. Jarman, rolling her eyes reproachfully up to the ceiling, as though Providence had whisked this one into the cradle when she wasn't looking.

I talked for a while and then came out of the house. The maker of dirt mounds was now kicking them over. The boy with the ball had thrown it into the pond and walked away.

I was about to cross the road when the mound maker decided to retrieve the ball from the pond. He walked in and fell flat on his face. The other children were watching with interest, but none of them thought of getting the child out. I waded into the pond, picked up the little boy, and angrily strode onto dry land.

As I stood there with the child in my arms, I was aware of a man on horseback watching the scene. He said imperiously, "Can you tell me the way to Oakland Hall?"

I said, "Go up the road, take the first turn to the right, and you will see the gates."

"Thank you." He brought some coins out of his pocket and threw them at us.

I was furious. I hastily put down the child and stooped to pick up the coins with the intention of throwing them back, but before I could reach them, two little Jarmans had swooped them up and had run off as fast as they could.

I strode off to the Dower House. As soon as I reached my room, I looked in the mirror. There was a smudge on my cheek, my blouse was muddy, and my skirt wet at the hem. No wonder the man on horseback had taken me for a cottage girl! I guessed who he was. Hadn't he asked for Oakland Hall? Hadn't he behaved in an arrogant manner? Hadn't he the conceited looks of a peacock!

"I knew I'd hate him," I said aloud.

I COULD NOT bring myself to go to Oakland Hall the following afternoon. Ben will be all right, I thought jealously. He's got his precious Peacock. He won't want me.

I was wrong.

Maddy knocked at my door. "Hannah gave me a message from Mr. Henniker. He wants to see you." I dressed with care in my blue alpaca, which gave me an air of dignity.

As soon as I arrived at Oakland, I was aware of tense excitement in the atmosphere. I went straight up to Ben's room and knocked on the door. I heard him say, "This will be Jessica." Then loudly, "Come in, my dear."

Ben was sitting in a chair with a rug about his knees. A tall figure came towards me. I was annoyed because I had to look up so far. He took my hand.

"So," he said, "we meet again."

"Hey? What's this?" cried Ben. "Come over here. I want to make a proper introduction. This is a very important occasion. When you get to know each other, you're going to like each other a good deal. You're two of a kind."

I couldn't help showing my resentment at being compared with this man. I noticed his eyes then—deep blue eyes the colour of a peacock's feather; I noticed the slightly aquiline nose, which suggested arrogance, and the rather thin lips, which could have been cynical or sensuous or both.

What I disliked most was the mocking expression which told me that he was remembering me emerging from a muddy pond with a grubby child in my arms.

"We have met before, Ben," he said.

I said quickly, "I'd been to see Mrs. Jarman. As I was leaving the house, one of the children fell into the pond. I got him out and Mr. . . . er . . ." I nodded towards him.

"You must call him Joss, my dear," said Ben. "We don't want any formality. We're all too friendly for that."

"But I don't know him," I protested. "Mr. Madden came by, asked the way—and paid for the information." I turned to him.

54

"I can assure you the fee would have been returned had not the children run off with it."

Ben laughed. "Fancy that. And you didn't know who he was."

"I guessed it was Mr. Madden. His actions fitted what I had heard of him."

"I trust that was meant as a compliment," Joss Madden said, "because I'm going to take it as such."

Ben was smiling. "It does me good to see you here getting along so well with Jessica," he said. "Come on. Bring the chairs up, one of you on either side of me. There. Now I'm going to be sentimental. There's two people who mean more to me than anything else in the world, and I've set my heart on one thing. I want them to be together . . . work together. . . ."

I could feel Joss Madden's eyes on me, assessing me. No man had ever looked at me like that before. I suddenly remembered that my alpaca was not very becoming. I heard myself say shrilly, "Work together! Whatever do you mean, Ben?"

"Well, I'm coming to that. I can see Joss thinks it's a bit soon. I reckon he's thinking you and he ought to get better acquainted first. Is that it, Joss?"

"It may be that Miss Clavering would find the shock too great. Give her a day or two to get used to me."

"This is all rather mysterious."

"It's really very straightforward and practical," said Joss Madden. "Are you practical, Miss Clavering?"

"Now what did I say," interrupted Ben. "No formality."

"Are you practical, Jessica?" asked Joss Madden.

"I think I am," I answered.

"Yes. You have that air. I would say you take pride in being a sensible young woman." He turned to Ben. "That will be very helpful, if she decides to accept your terms."

"Terms?" I demanded. "What terms?"

"I thought you said it was too soon to talk," said Ben.

"So it is," replied Joss Madden. "If we did, I reckon we'd get a blank refusal. You've got to give Miss Clavering time . . . er, I mean Jessica. You're not a puppet master, Ben, because neither Jessica nor I are of the stuff which puppets are made of. Don't you agree . . . Jessica?"

"I can assure you that I am not. But I think you ought to let me into the secret."

Ben looked at Joss, who shook his head. Then Ben said, "There's something I have to tell you first, Jessica. But I'll wait until we're alone."

"That's a hint," said Joss. "I'm going to have a look at your stables, Ben. We'll meet again soon . . . Jessica."

He left, and Ben asked eagerly, "What do you think of him?"

I said cautiously, "I don't feel I know him. But what were you going to tell me, Ben?"

He hesitated. "This is going to hurt a bit, Jessie. I know you have a beautiful picture of your father and his love for your mother, but it wasn't quite like that. Your mother was a sweet pretty creature, and I was more than a little bit in love with her."

"Yes," I said. "I know that."

"Desmond was a bit of a rogue, and he was always one for the ladies. When he came down here to persuade me to invest in the Fancy, he took up with your mother. In his way, he was in love with her. I reckon he would have married her, but he couldn't the way it turned out.

"That brings me to the night I showed them the Green Flash. Desmond couldn't take his eyes off it. I remember now how his fingers curled round it. Desire! There's no other word for it. I knew what the result would be, so I was ready. That night I left my bedroom door open and I sat fully dressed, listening. Then I heard footsteps creeping down to the study. I followed.

"He was there at the safe. He had the Flash in his hands. I said, 'What are you doing, Desmond Dereham?' He just stared at me. I said, 'You've seduced little Jessica Clavering and now you're trying to steal the Green Flash. And when you've got it, there's only one thing you could do—get out of here fast . . . and desert Jessica. Do you know, I reckon you're not fit to live.' "

"Oh, Ben," I cried, "you killed my father!"

He shook his head. "No . . . not that. I had a gun, but I didn't want his life on my hands. So I said, 'Put that opal back in the safe and get out of here. If you ever show your face here or at the Fancy, I'll expose you for a thief.' I marched him back to his room. Sure enough, his bags were already packed. He had planned to get the opal and clear out like a thief in the night."

"My poor mother!"

"I wanted him out of the way for her sake. I didn't know you were on the way then. That would have been different."

"You said he had stolen the Green Flash."

"That's what I want to tell you. It was a pretence on my part. I knew he wouldn't dare go back to Australia. We have a rough-and-ready justice there. We don't tolerate thieves and we don't tolerate murderers. I thought if I could make people believe he had the Green Flash, then no one would seek to rob *me* of it. I left soon afterwards, taking the Green Flash with me."

"Does Joss know this?"

"He does now. Believe me, Jessie, I'd have acted different if I'd known you were on the way."

"All those years you have allowed my father to be suspected, and my poor mother . . ."

"She should never have done what she did."

"She was driven to it."

"No, Jess, we're none of us driven. We act of our own free will, and if we find life too much to be borne, then there's no one to blame but ourselves."

I turned my face away. I was going over it all, my father caught at the safe, Ben forcing him to get out. His belongings already packed, so he had meant to go with the Green Flash . . . and leaving my mother to bear me and then destroy herself.

Ben was caressing my hand. "Don't think badly of me, Jessie," he said. "I couldn't bear there to be bitterness at the end. I've had to fight throughout my life and it's made me hard and ruthless. Perhaps I don't set so much store on morals as I should. In the outback there were men who were ready to kill me for the Green Flash. Do you understand?"

"Yes, I understand, Ben."

"And we've loved each other, haven't we? Didn't your life change for the better when we met?"

"It did, and I love you, Ben. I could never do anything but love you. I can't bear to think of your not being here. . . ."

"Never mind. I'm not leaving your life empty. There's better coming into it than was ever there before, if you'll just listen to me."

"Ben," I said, "if the Green Flash is still in your possession, it will belong to Joss when—"

"When I die. Oh, I've plans, and that's something the three of us are going to talk about tomorrow."

"Tell me now, Ben."

"Oh no. You've had enough for one day. Go home now. And don't worry, my dearest girl."

I left him then and went back to the Dower House. My grandmother was in the hall arranging a bowl of flowers.

"Oh dear," she said. "How I miss the flower room at Oakland! By the way, I see your friend has a visitor staying there. He looked slightly superior to the mining type . . . almost a gentleman. He sits his horse like one."

I did not answer. I was too full of emotion.

I SPENT a sleepless night and fancied I looked a little haggard next day. Why this unaccustomed attention to my appearance? I asked myself; but I knew it was due to that man. Ben had said he was fond of women. I thought I knew the type—wondering whether every woman he met would find him irresistible.

When I arrived that afternoon, Ben and Joss Madden were waiting for me impatiently. "Come and sit down," Ben commanded, and as we sat there I saw those peacock-blue eyes on me, and again I felt uncomfortable under Joss Madden's scrutiny.

Ben said, "I'm going to die very soon and I don't want to. There's so much I wanted to see. One of my dearest dreams was to watch my grandchildren playing on the lawns here and at Peacocks. Joss, you've never married and I used to fret about it until I met Miss Jessica Clavering. I've always had a feeling for the Claverings. I can't tell you how much I've wished I was one when I looked at that family tree in the hall. So what I want more than anything is to bring the families together. I want our blood mingled . . . that of the boy who sold gingerbread fancies and that of those who served kings in battle. I reckon there couldn't be a better combination for future generations."

I lifted my eyes and met that dark blue stare. I thought, Oh no, Ben, even you could not be so audacious as that.

"The plain fact is that I want to see you two marry. Don't fly into a rage, Jess. I know it's a shock. But Joss will be a good husband if you go along with his ways. And Jessica will be a good wife, Joss, if you're careful how you handle her."

I said hotly, "I could never go along with Mr. Madden's ways, nor would I agree to place myself in his careful handling."

"You see, Joss, our Jessie can fly into a temper," said Ben. "But you wouldn't want a meek little dove, would you?"

59

Joss did not reply.

"I should have given you more time," Ben went on, "but time is running out for me. I'd like the wedding to take place soon. Then I'll rest happy."

"You don't know what you're suggesting, Ben," I cried.

"Oh yes, I do, my dear. I've been thinking of it for a very long time. As soon as I got to know you, I said to myself, That's the girl for Joss. I've thought of nothing else for weeks."

"Now Ben," said Joss, "you see from Miss Clavering's horror that your little scheme will have to be abandoned."

For the first time I gave him a look of approval.

"Marriage is a bit of a gamble," said Ben. "Well, you've both got gambler's blood in you. When you've considered everything involved, Jessie, you'll fall in with my schemes. Joss is already half-way there."

"Not," he replied, "now that I have seen Miss Clavering's repugnance."

"Oh, proud . . . proud as a peacock! Now why are you both being so stubborn? You could search through England and Australia and not find better mates. Be sensible, both of you. I tell you this is my dying request. You can't refuse me that, can you?"

"We can," said Joss. "Ben, you're outrageous."

"Now listen to me," Ben went on. "I'm leaving everything to you, except a few minor legacies, *if* you marry."

"And if we don't?" said Joss.

"You get nothing. Do you want to see the company pass out of your hands, Joss?"

"You couldn't do that."

"You'll see. Jessica, do you want to spend your days in the Dower House with that virago of a grandmother, or do you want a life of adventure? I can't force you, of course, but I can make it very uncomfortable for you both if you don't do what I want."

We looked at each other across the bed.

"This is absurd," I began, but Joss Madden did not answer. I was aware that he was contemplating the loss of the company. Ben had conjured up a picture for me too. I saw myself ten . . . twenty years hence, growing old, growing sour because life had passed me by.

Ben lay back on his pillows and closed his eyes for a moment. I stood up and said I thought he was tired.

He nodded. "I've given you something to think about, haven't I?" He seemed full of secret amusement.

Joss Madden came with me to the door. "I'm afraid this has been a shock to you," he said.

"How could it be otherwise?" I answered.

"I should have thought young ladies in your position often had husbands chosen for them."

"That does not make the position any more acceptable."

"I suppose we are both the sort of people who would want to choose for themselves. You can always refuse."

"You surely don't mean that *you* would agree?"

I looked at him searchingly. His lips twisted into a wry smile. "There's a great deal at stake for me," he said.

I said shortly, "I'll leave you here. Goodbye."

"*Au revoir*," he called as I sped across the grass.

I WAS in a kind of daze, and I had to talk to someone. There was one to whom I could go, though once the idea of doing so would have been out of the question. Miriam!

I ran over to Church Cottage—the tiny house on the vicarage grounds. Miriam was at home. She looked several years younger and very domestic in a starched print gown.

There was no doubt that she was pleased to see me. "I'll make some tea," she said. "Ernest is out. The vicar works him too hard."

I put my head on one side and studied her. "You're a joy to behold," I said. "A walking advertisement for marriage." It was true. How she had changed! She was in love with her curate and with life; and the fact that she had turned her back on this blissful state for so long only made her appreciate it more now.

"I've had a proposal," I blurted out.

"Not . . . someone at Oakland?"

"Yes."

"Oh, Jessica! Are you sure . . . ?"

"No," I said. "I'm not."

She looked relieved. "I should be very, very careful."

"I intend to be. Miriam, suppose you hadn't married Ernest?"

"I couldn't bear to think of that," she said firmly. "And even if things hadn't turned out so well, to tell the truth, Jessica, I should have been glad to get away from the Dower House."

"Who wouldn't?" I thought of living there for years and years without the compensation of going to Oakland to see Ben, and I knew I couldn't face it. Rather marriage with Joss Madden. Perhaps we could come to terms.

"Have you known this man long?" asked Miriam.

"One does not have to know people all one's life . . . just because you and Ernest did."

"But then you can be so much more sure."

"Perhaps it's more exciting not to be."

Miriam was thoughtful for a while; then she took out a bottle of homemade wine. "We'll drink to your future," she said.

I SCARCELY slept that night, and my chores the next morning seemed endless. Immediately after luncheon I went to the stream. The world seemed to have turned upside down. Ben, whom I so dearly loved, had lied about my father. How could I reconcile myself to that . . . and yet how could I stop loving Ben? And now he had come along with a proposition which he knew was repugnant to me and to Joss. I just could not understand it. The alarming fact was that I did not understand myself, because, somewhere at the back of my mind, I was actually considering this marriage.

As I sat there, Joss Madden emerged from the trees and came towards me. "I saw you from the turret," he said. "I think we should have a talk."

I crossed over to the Oakland side of the stream, and as we walked towards the trees, Joss said, "I'm ready to go ahead."

"You mean . . . you would marry me?"

"That was the proposition. Oh come, don't look so mournful. You won't be going to your execution, you know."

"It feels rather like that."

He gave an explosive laugh. Then he was serious. "I'm afraid Ben won't live much longer. He is very weak today."

We came to a tree trunk, and he took my hand and pulled me down to sit beside him. "I gather," he said, "that you weren't contemplating marriage with someone else?"

"No."

"Then it's fairly straightforward. I could get a special licence, and we could be married very shortly."

I replied, "You seem to take all this in your stride."

"How else could I take it? I see what Ben feels. He was fascinated by your mother and all that she represented—the stately mansion, the distinguished family. Now he has the house, but he hasn't got the blood. If you and I married, our offspring would have a modicum of the blue-blooded variety through you."

That was just too much. I said sharply, "I'm afraid I never could."

He looked straight at me, and it was as though he were probing my innermost thoughts. I knew that he understood what had alarmed me. "There's a great deal at stake," he said. "Ben means what he says. He knows that the only way he could get us married at such short notice is to threaten us with what will happen to us if we don't. He can be ruthless, our Ben."

"I know that."

"He's told me a great deal about you. He's sentencing you for life to the Dower House unless you marry me. The devil or the deep blue sea. That's your choice. And for me, the loss of command of the company which I have helped to build up. I have some shares in it, but Ben has the major holding, and he's threatening to pass it to someone else. It would mean if I stayed with the company I'd be there in a minor capacity. So he has netted me. He knows I'd accept anything rather—"

"Even me?"

"Even marriage. Which for thirty-three years I have successfully eluded."

"So there have been those who have angled for you?"

"Countless numbers."

"Perhaps they came in time to regard their lack of success as good fortune. But that's beside the point."

"You're quite right. We don't want to be sidetracked into frivolous discussion when there is something so much more important to occupy us. I've made up my mind. I'll marry you immediately. All you have to do is say you'll marry me."

He put an arm about my shoulders, and I drew back in dismay. Again he gave that brief laugh.

"All right," he said. "I'll make it easy for you. We'll marry and it'll be, as they say, a marriage in name only. That's until both parties want it otherwise. What about that?"

"Ben may not agree to those terms. He wants grandchildren."

"He can't have it all his own way."

I stood up suddenly. He did the same, towering above me. There was an amused twitch to his lips as he laid his hands on my shoulders. "Negotiations seem to be progressing favourably," he said. "Shall we go and tell Ben?"

"Not yet. I'm undecided."

"All right. But don't delay too long."

I WENT to see Ben. I was glad that he was alone. He looked a little better and I commented on this.

"Yes, I'm determined to live until I see you two married. Tell me, Jess, have you thought any more about it?"

"I have. And there's one thing I have to tell you. If I did marry Joss, I couldn't live with him as his wife, and that means that your dream of grandchildren would simply not come true. I'm sure that in these circumstances the whole thing falls through."

I had expected dismay, but there was nothing of the sort. Ben laughed so much that I feared he would exhaust himself. "You know, Jessie," he said when he had recovered, "you're enlivening my last days, you are. You never fail to please me. So you've made up your mind to marry him, have you?"

"I didn't say that. I've told you why it's impossible."

"Listen. I want you two married. You were meant for each other. As to the other little matter, well, I'm ready to leave that to Joss. So it's settled. I accept your terms and you'll accept mine. I want a nice wedding in the church."

"That will take a little time."

"I reckon I've got that time left. I just won't go until I've seen you and my boy Joss joined together in holy matrimony. In years to come, you'll be grateful to old Ben, I promise you."

I DON'T KNOW what Joss said to my grandmother. He was in the drawing room with her, my grandfather, and Xavier for an hour. From my bedroom window I saw him stride back across the lawn to the bridge. Then Maddy knocked at my door. They wanted to see me in the drawing room, she said.

As I entered, I was aware of the change in their attitude towards me. I had become important, but my grandmother was not going to show me her gratification too readily.

"So," she began, "you have clandestinely been meeting this man from the wilds."

"If you mean Mr. Madden, it is true I have been meeting him."

"And have become engaged to him! He did not ask our consent

64

before asking you, which would have been the proper thing to do. But I suppose we cannot expect good manners from people brought up as he must have been."

"He has been educated in England."

She grudgingly admitted that she realized this saving grace. "I only hope this offer is genuine. If it is, all may not turn out too badly. If this man is telling the truth, he will in due course inherit Oakland Hall, in which case you as his wife will live there."

My grandfather's eyes looked watery. "It's almost like Oakland coming back to us through you, Jessica," he said.

I couldn't help being thrilled. I knew then that if a way out were offered me, I wouldn't want to take it. I wanted the excitement of marrying Joss Madden—provided, of course, that we kept to that all-important clause.

"I hope your children will be born at Oakland Hall," my grandmother said. "Perhaps we could get Mr. Madden to change his name to Clavering. That has been done before in the family."

"I know that would be quite impossible."

"It must be a wedding worthy of the old days," my grandmother went on. "We shall sell the silver candlesticks so that we can do everything as it should be done." I had never seen her look so pleased, and the knowledge that it was due to me seemed ironic.

The next Sunday, Ernest, officiating for the Reverend Jasper Crey, read out the banns.

I WAS to have a white satin wedding gown—the best possible satin from Liberty. My grandmother made a journey up to London to buy materials on the proceeds from the silver candlesticks.

I stood for hours while the seamstress, her mouth full of pins, fitted my wedding dress and my trousseau. "We don't want people in Australia to think we're savages," said my grandmother.

After the banns had been called twice, my excitement turned to apprehension. Joss Madden seemed determined to spend a good deal of time with me. "Doing his courting," as Ben described it.

Joss said, "We'd better get to know each other. Are you any good on a horse? You'll have to ride a great deal in Australia."

I said that I had been taught to ride but had little opportunity of doing so.

"There's a small stable at Oakland," he said. "I'll take you riding. I want to see what you can do."

He chose my mount, a brown horse with a frisky look that made me somewhat fearful, and then he picked out the finest horse in the stable for himself. As we walked our horses side by side, I could feel his eyes on me, appraising my posture, my hands, my heels, everything . . . and the smile I hated played about his lips.

Suddenly he broke into a canter, and my horse refused to follow him. Instead the beast lowered his head and nibbled a bush by the roadside.

Joss Madden turned and laughed. "Come on, Joker," he said, and the response was immediate. The sly Joker immediately relinquished the bush and moved on with an injured air, as though to say, What can you expect me to do with this amateur on my back?

"You have to *control* your horse, you know," said Joss.

"I'm very well aware of that," I retorted.

I hated that morning because I sensed that he was trying to show me how inferior I was. Once he galloped across a meadow and called Joker to follow. It was maddening to have him commanding my horse, and when Joker sped after him, I was helpless.

He was beside me suddenly. He seized my bridle and for a few moments we galloped side by side. When we stopped he was laughing. "I'll have to teach you to ride before we leave," he said. "You can't go out to Australia like this."

"Don't you think it would be a good idea if we abandoned the whole thing?" I asked.

"What! With the dress being made, the banns being called . . ." He was serious suddenly. "Besides, what of Ben?"

"I hate it all," I said vehemently.

"You mean you hate me?"

"You can look at it that way if you like."

"A firm basis on which to build a marriage," he mocked. "Feelings often change, they say, after the ceremony, and at least yours can't change for the worse, since they are as bad as they can possibly be now. We'd better make the best of it. Who knows, I might succeed in making a tolerable horsewoman of you and you might succeed in keeping me at a distance." His eyes glittered suddenly, and I saw the pride there. He was put out because I was not attracted to him. "Let me say," he said with a hint of anger in his voice, "I think the latter will be easier to achieve."

I certainly hated him, and he appeared to despise me. Well, at least I should not have to worry about his forcing his attentions on me; and then I began, perversely, to hope that he might—so that I could have the pleasure of rebuffing him.

AT LAST my wedding day arrived. It was like a dream, standing there at the altar while the Reverend Jasper Crey married us. As Joss slipped the ring on my finger, I felt a shiver of emotion that I couldn't quite define.

Ben came to the church in a wheelchair. I could imagine his contentment. His will had been done. Miriam played the wedding march, and as I came down the aisle on the arm of Joss Madden, Xavier, my grandfather, and my grandmother watched happily.

After the reception at the Dower House, Joss and I walked across the bridge to Oakland Hall. Ben had said that he wanted to see us. He was sitting up in bed and his eyes were shining.

"You two have made Ben Henniker a very happy man today," he said. "Come and sit on either side of me. There, that's good. Give me your hands. I want to say something to you, and I've been saving it up till now."

"You're exhausted, Ben," I said. "You should rest."

"Not till I've told you this. When I took the Green Flash to Australia with me, I had to have a hiding place for it. You're the only two who'll know where that hiding place is. I made it myself. You know *The Pride of the Peacock* in the drawing room, Joss. It's a picture, Jessie, of a magnificent peacock on our lawn. The picture is set in a thick frame of carved wood and gilt. At the right-hand corner of the frame there's a spring catch. You touch the spring and the back opens like a door to reveal a cavity. There, wrapped in cottonwool, is the Green Flash. The stone is yours jointly when I die. You can do what you like with it."

He was getting too excited. I felt alarmed and said soothingly, "Thank you, Ben. Now you must rest."

He nodded. Joss pressed his hand, and for a moment or two they looked steadily at each other. Then I bent over and kissed him. "Bless you both," he said.

The bridal suite had been prepared for us. I was apprehensive when I entered it. Joss shut the door behind him. He stood leaning against it, looking at me mockingly.

"They tell me that the mistresses of Oakland Hall spend their first night of marriage in this room," he said.

I glanced quickly at the four-poster bed. "This is a rather different case," I said.

"One's own case always is," he replied. He walked across the room. "Here's the dressing room. Shall I occupy it or will you?"

"Since you say Oakland brides traditionally occupy this bed I will do so. The dressing room can be yours. It will be quite comfortable, I daresay."

"A nice wifely concern for her husband's comfort is always to be admired," he said. He took my hand and kissed it.

"I trust you are a man of your word," I said.

He shook his head slightly. "It would be unwise to trust me too far." I snatched my hand away. "But," he went on, "have no fear. I would never force myself where I am so clearly not wanted."

"Then I will say good night."

"Good night," he said. He walked to the dressing-room door.

When it shut behind him, I ran to it and, to my dismay, saw that there was no key. As I stood there the door opened. Joss was there with the key in his hand. He gave it to me with a bow. "You will want to feel safe," he said. I took the key and locked the door.

SIX WEEKS after the wedding Ben took a decided turn for the worse. Joss and I were with him constantly.

"Remember me, Jessie," he said, "and particularly remember that everything I wanted was for your happiness. One day you and Joss are going to see what's staring you in the face, and that is that you were meant for each other. God bless you both."

After long days of waiting, Ben died in his sleep. We buried him in the churchyard not far from the Clavering section. It was what he would have wanted. Joss and I stood side by side at the grave, and as I listened to the clods of earth falling on the coffin, I knew it was the end of a phase. My new life was about to begin.

THERE WERE solicitors to be seen. Joss and I were joint owners of Oakland, the house in Australia known as Peacocks, and the Green Flash at Sunset. We were given matching shares of Ben's holding in the Opal Mining Company. There were legacies to other people, including Mrs. Laud, his housekeeper, and her children. If our marriage had not taken place before Ben's death or within a year afterwards, the shares, the houses, and the Green Flash opal would have been held in trust for the Lauds.

During the next weeks we made preparations for our departure. Miriam was delighted that it had all gone so smoothly. Xavier wished me happiness. "Weddings are infectious," he said, and I wondered if he and Lady Clara had come to an understanding.

My grandmother now and then shot an occasional barb about life in the wilds. When people had perfectly good homes in civilized surroundings, she could not understand why they must go dashing off to the other side of the globe. I could laugh more than ever. I was free of her.

Joss and I rode together each day. I both dreaded and enjoyed the lessons. I knew I had improved, and Joker would not now refuse my orders. Not that Joss would admit that I was an apt pupil. He seemed to enjoy humiliating me.

In October, Joss and I sailed for Sydney.

ON A GOLDEN autumn day we embarked on the *Hermes*. Joss was known, as Ben had been, to the captain and the crew. This meant that innumerable little concessions were granted to us.

"One of these," said Joss, "is being provided with single cabins, which they think is rather unorthodox in a newly-married pair, but I am sure you will feel exceedingly grateful."

The weather was rough at first, but I was delighted to find that I was a good sailor. Joss was, and I should have hated to have given him an advantage over me in that respect.

On one occasion the atmosphere below was so stuffy that I decided it would be more pleasant on deck in spite of the high seas. I staggered up there to find it was almost impossible to stand. The waves were pounding the side of the ship. As the prow rose up towards the sky, it seemed as though it would never come down again. The wind tore at me and lifted me off my feet.

Suddenly, as I tried to walk the deck, I was caught and held. It was Joss, and he was laughing at me.

"What are you trying to do?" he demanded. "Commit suicide? Don't you know it's dangerous on deck in weather like this?"

He was still holding me and I made an effort to free myself. "I'll be all right now," I said.

"I beg to contradict." The ship rolled and we fell against the rail. "You see?" he taunted, his face close to mine.

"I have to admit you're right, I suppose."

"Look. There's a bench in the shelter of the lifeboats." We sat

69

down and he put an arm about me. "Safer," he said with a grimace. "The only reason, I assure you."

"Had I in my folly been washed overboard, everything you now share with me would have been yours, wouldn't it?"

"That's true."

"A consummation devoutly to be wished, surely?"

"Perhaps there are other consummations which would be more devoutly wished." I drew away from him. "Be prepared, Jessica," he went on. "One of these days you're going to grow up."

"You seem to think you should instruct me in this art?"

"A husbandly duty, perhaps."

To change the subject, I asked him to tell me about his work and the new life I was going to.

"It's something you'll have to experience for yourself. You'll be in opal country; Peacocks is only about two miles from Fancy Town. You know, the town got its name because of Desmond Dereham's hunch."

"Yes, I do know. He was my father."

Joss told me about some finds which had come to light in the Fancy. He talked about the excitement of searching for opal, and it was fascinating to listen to him. He seemed to forget the need to score over me. When I saw him as the director of the company— the man who understood opals and loved them—I saw a different side to his nature from that of the conceited male whose dignity had been affronted because the woman he had married for the sake of a fortune had insisted on a marriage in name only.

So we sat there while the storm raged around us, and my feelings towards him changed a little.

OUR FIRST PORT of call was Tenerife, and Joss took me for a tour around the island. We went to Santa Cruz in a gay little carriage drawn by two donkeys. I admired the lush shrubs and the banana plantations.

At a small restaurant, we lunched on a sort of watercress soup, and delicious fish which had been caught that morning. As we sat overlooking the sea, Joss told me that the ancient Romans had called these islands Canaria, the Islands of Dogs, after the large canine population. Even his pleasure in his superior knowledge failed to dampen my delight, and I was sorry when we had to go back to the ship.

WHEN WE reached Cape Town, Joss and I went to see Kurt van der Stel, an opal dealer. We took a horse-drawn carriage to his delightful Dutch colonial house. There were stone steps leading to a terrace, and as we came up the steps, Kurt van der Stel and his wife, Grete, welcomed us. They were very pleased to see us, and while the men talked business, Grete showed me through the house. When we went back to the terrace, where the two men were sitting, we heard the sound of hoofs on the road below. A few moments later a man mounted the steps. Joss rose and shook hands with him and then drew me forward. "Jessica, this is David Croissant."

I had heard that name from Ben. David Croissant, the merchant who knew more about the quality of opals than any other.

Joss told him about Ben.

"What bad luck," murmured David Croissant. "If he still had the Flash, you'd think it was that. I wonder what happened to Desmond Dereham? He disappeared off the face of the earth."

Joss flashed me a warning look. I resented the fact that my father was still being accused of theft when at the very most he had only attempted it. However, I remained silent.

"What have you brought to show us, David?" asked Kurt.

"Ah," replied David, "some stones that will make you dance with joy. There's one in particular."

When I saw the Harlequin Opal, I had my first real understanding of the fascination a beautiful stone could convey. It was aptly named. There seemed so many colours, which changed as one watched. The stone had a wonderful gaiety about it.

Joss held it out to me. "Take a look at that, Jessica."

I held the stone in my hand, and I felt a reluctance to let it go.

"You see the beauty of it?" said Joss eagerly. "You're beginning to understand something about opals, aren't you?"

"I'm very ignorant," I said, handing the stone back to David, "but at least I'm aware that I know nothing about them."

"You've mastered the first lesson," answered Joss. Then he looked at his watch. "We must go back to the ship. I'll see you in Australia, David. I daresay you'll be coming soon."

So we said goodbye, and the carriage took us back to the ship.

THERE WERE long days in calm waters when the ship seemed to move hardly at all. I would sit on deck with Joss, and we would talk desultorily while we sipped cool drinks. Now and then we would see porpoises or dolphins sporting in the deep blue water. Once an albatross followed the ship for three days, and we would lie back in our chairs and calculate the immense strength of that twelve-foot span of wing above us. In time, even my desire to discover the truth of my father's disappearance receded. This was peace, and I wondered whether Joss felt it too.

THERE WAS great excitement on board when we approached Sydney. I stood leaning on the rail as we went past numerous coves and sandy beaches fringed with lush foliage. Then the buildings began to appear, and it was obvious that we were coming to a considerable city.

"What a beautiful place!" I cried.

Joss looked pleased. "We'll spend a week here before we go to Peacocks," he told me.

Our hotel was situated in the heart of the town, and the reception area was crowded with people, but Joss forced his way through to the desk and emerged with two keys. I saw the ironic grin on his face as he handed one to me. "All according to contract," he said.

After a good night's sleep we met at breakfast—a hearty one for Joss consisting of lamb chops and kidneys.

"We're good trenchermen here," he said. "It's the outdoor life. I'm going to spend the day taking you round. I want you to get your bearings."

After breakfast we set off in a buggy. Joss drove down to the harbour. I had seen it from the ship, of course, but this was different. We drove in and out of the coves, and from the heights we could look down on those wonderful bays. The sea was the colour of sapphires.

"It looks beautiful," he said, "but there are sharks lurking beneath that innocent blue. If you ventured in, you might easily end up by providing a shark with his dinner."

"What a horrible thought."

"Things are not always what they seem," he said. "If sharks frighten you, how are you going to like it in Fancy Town?" He had brought the buggy to a standstill and was looking intently at me. "Some people get so homesick they can't endure it. They just pack up and go home."

"Were your ancestors homesick?"

"It wouldn't have mattered if they were. They had to stay. My mother's father came out seventy years ago on a convict ship. He was no criminal, but his opinions offended some people, and a charge was trumped up against him. My father's mother was a lady's maid accused of stealing her employer's brooch. She was innocent, says the family, but all convicts were innocent according to their families. Most have a yearning to go back to England."

"And do you?"

"Sometimes. Part of me would like to stay at Oakland and become a squire, but opals are here and opals are my life. I will try to get the best out of both worlds."

"So you will return to Oakland for visits?"

"Yes," he said. "I am sure that you would like to visit the old place now and then."

"Indeed I would."

"Now we have one matter on which we agree. I think we are progressing."

I enjoyed those days in Sydney. I met some of Joss's business associates, and I did some shopping with one of the wives. In bustling George Street I bought material to make into practical garments for my new life, and two large straw hats to protect me from the fierce Australian sun.

We were to travel to Peacocks on horseback, and Joss spent a good deal of time choosing the horses we should hire. Since most of our baggage would come by coach to Fancy Town, we took only one packhorse with a few belongings and provisions.

It was the end of November when we set out, the equivalent of May in England. The wild flowers were beautiful, but most impressive of all were the eucalyptus trees, which towered over the native beech and ash. The dryness of the land was particularly noticeable after the green fields at home. The roads were rough and full of holes, and our horses raised a cloud of dust. We climbed small hills, crossed flat country, and went over dried-up creeks. At length we came to a homestead, where Joss said we should stay the night.

He dismounted, and a woman came out to greet him. Joss talked to her, and then he came back to me. "They've only one room," he said. "Shall we take it or spend the night out of doors?"

"You're welcome here, my dear," the woman said, coming forward. "It's a nice room. I'll get the bed made up. It's a good bed, with lovely soft feathers brought out from England."

73

Joss helped me to alight. He was enjoying the situation. "Cheer up," he whispered. "The unnatural embargo is bound to put us into some awkward situations, but I'm quite resourceful."

The room was pleasant—very clean—and dominated by the big double bed. Joss regarded it ruefully. "I'll take the chair," he said. Then he placed his hands on my shoulders and looked at me earnestly. "There is one thing you must never forget," he said. "I have never yet forced my attentions on a woman who didn't want me, and I feel no temptation to do so now. I'm proud, you know. . . ."

For all Joss's protestations I found it disturbing to share a room with him. He took the chair, and I removed only my skirt and bodice. I slept fitfully, which perhaps was to be expected in the circumstances.

The next day we set off on our journey in the pure morning air, and about eleven o'clock we stopped beside a river. Joss made a fire and brewed what he called quart-pot tea. Our landlady of the previous night had supplied us with sandwiches. Strangely enough, I had never drunk tea or tasted sandwiches so good.

The sun grew hotter, and both of us were feeling drowsy. I dozed and dreamed that I was on the deck of the ship in a storm. I was being buffeted from one side to the other. Joss caught me suddenly in a vice-like grip. "Are you trying to commit suicide?" he asked, and I was stung into saying, "It would be a good way out for you, wouldn't it? Everything would be yours . . . the houses, the shares, the Green Flash at Sunset." "That's a good idea," he said. "I'd be better off without you. It could look like suicide." I cried out, "No . . . no! Don't murder me."

I awoke with a start and my heart leaped in terror. There he was, his face close to mine. "What was that about?" he asked.

"I was dreaming."

"It seemed like a nightmare. You must have something on your mind. Are you disturbed about coming to a strange land?"

"I sometimes wonder how I shall fit in," I said.

"There are lawless elements here," he said. "Have you heard of bushrangers?"

"Of course."

"They're desperadoes who live by robbery. They're determined not to be caught, which would mean hanging, so they don't hesitate to kill if the occasion arises. This is a country where life is cheap."

"I believe you'd like me to go straight home."

He laughed. "Don't fret. You've got a protector." He took out a small pistol from a belt at his hip. "A beauty," he said. "I never travel without her. Neat, insignificant in appearance, and deadly in action."

We rode side by side through the bush, and I looked at the scenery. "What are those pale-looking trees over there?" I asked.

"Ghost gums. Some people believe that when men die violently in the bush, they take up their habitation inside the trees. There are some who won't pass a clump of ghost gums after dusk."

I started violently at a sudden cackle of laughter above us.

"It's only a kookaburra," Joss said, "the laughing jackass of a kingfisher. Ah, there's his mate. They are often in pairs. You'll hear them round Peacocks."

About seven in the evening Joss pulled up on a slight hillock. "We should be able to see the Trant Homestead from here," he said. "I want to get there before sundown. The bush can be treacherous. People who get lost often end up walking round in circles. They can't make a landmark, because the scenery repeats itself again and again. So don't wander out alone."

We rode on. The sun had sunk below the horizon. The first stars had appeared, and there was a thin crescent of moon. Suddenly, Joss pulled up short. "Good God!" he cried. "Just look at that!"

It was an eerie sight in the pale moonlight—a shell of a house. We rode on over the scorched grass. Fire had ravaged one side of the building; the rest had been severely licked by the flames.

We dismounted, and Joss tethered the horses to an iron fence. "Careful how you go," he said. Then he took my hand and together we stepped over the blackened threshold.

"The Trants must have lost everything," he said. "I wonder where they went. There's nothing else for miles." He looked at me. "We'll have to stay here tonight. There's a river where the horses could drink, and there might be some grass. . . ."

The blackened walls filled me with horror. "There's something haunted about this place," I said. "Couldn't we go on?"

"It's thirty miles to Peacocks. The horses need rest. We'll stay here till dawn, and then we'll get going. Let's see if there's anything we can use. We'll explore. But be careful."

As we moved across the floor, my foot struck something. I stooped and picked up a half-burned candle. Joss lighted it and held it high. His face looked different in the candlelight. His enigmatic expression gave me a twinge of uneasiness.

"I wonder who left the candle?" he said. "Some bushranger, perhaps." He kept his eyes on my face, and I had an idea that he was trying to frighten me.

I said, "There's a big tin box over there. There might be something in that."

He went over to it and opened it. "Why, look, a blanket. The tin box protected it from the fire. What a find! We can spread it on the floor."

As I lifted the blanket out, I saw a book. It was a ledger. Inside was written: "This book is the property of James and Ethel Trant who left England in the year 1873 and settled here in this house which they called the Trant Homestead."

The book had been used as a kind of register. There was one column for the date, a centre one for names, and another for comments. There were remarks like "Thanks, James and Ethel", and "Just like home". The last guests had left three months ago.

I held the candle while Joss spread the blanket on the charred floor. Then he took the candle from me and, tilting it, let some grease drip onto the floor, and in this he stuck the candle.

I sat down on the blanket and glanced idly through the register. Then a name leaped out at me. "Desmond Dereham, June 1879", and his comment: "I shall surely come again".

"What's the matter?" asked Joss.

"My father stayed here. His name's in the book. I think people ought to know that he did not succeed in stealing the Green Flash and that Ben had it all the time."

"We'll see. It's not a thing I want to decide quickly."

I glanced down at the book and saw David Croissant's name. "There's someone else we know," I said.

"I daresay I could find many people I know in that book. Everyone used this place." Joss stretched out full length on the blanket. "Aren't you sleepy?" he asked. He put out a hand and pulled me down beside him.

"Such a small blanket," he said quietly.

I shrank to the edge of it.

"You disappoint me, Jessica," he said. "I didn't think you'd be so easily frightened. This marriage suited us both. Now that it's done, why don't we try to make something of it?"

"I intend to learn all I can about the company. I want to play a part in that."

"That's not what I meant. Here you are alone with your husband. Don't be such a child, Jessica."

"You promised," I cried. "You said you were too proud—"

"You are the most maddening woman I know. I wish to God—"

"That you had refused Ben. But you wanted Oakland, Peacocks, and the Green Flash. Unfortunately you had to take me too."

Joss had risen. "I'm going to see that the horses are safe," he said, and he strode out, leaving me alone.

As I looked about that burned-out inn, a feeling of foreboding came to me. He didn't want me. His voice echoed through my mind: "This is a country where life is cheap." How easy it would be for him to kill me. I could hear his explanations: I went down to the horses. When I came back she was dead . . . shot. There were bushrangers in the neighbourhood. Her jewels are missing. . . .

"O God, help me," I whispered. Had Joss really gone to see the horses, or would he come creeping up behind me . . . ?

Nonsense, I told myself, this man is your husband.

I started. Footsteps, slow, stealthy, creeping up to the inn—and not from the direction of the river.

I was on my feet. I crouched at the door. A man pushed it open and stepped into the inn. I heard his breathing.

I cried out, and he spun around. It was David Croissant.

He stared at me. "Why, it's Mrs. Madden. Where's Joss?"

"He's looking after the horses."

Joss came in then, and there were explanations. David Croissant had caught a ship about a week after he had seen us. He was on his way to the Fancy and had planned to stay at the Trants'.

Joss made a fire and boiled a billycan of tea. David produced cold chicken and johnnycakes and we all ate ravenously. I felt immense relief because I was no longer alone with my husband.

Chapter IV

It was late the next day when we arrived at Peacocks. We turned into a gate, and before us lay a drive of about a quarter of a mile to the gracious white colonial house. The porch and terrace were supported by ornate Grecian pillars, and the lawns were immaculately kept. A peacock, followed by his meek little peahen, strutted beside the terrace as though asking for our admiration.

"Take the horses, Tom," said Joss to a man who came up to us. "Who's at home?"

"Mrs. Laud, sir, Mr. Jimson, and Miss Lilias."

We dismounted. Joss took my arm, and with David Croissant following, we stepped into the hall. It was cool inside the house, for thin wooden venetian blinds shut out the fierce sunlight. The hall was large and lofty. The floor was paved in a mosaic design, in the centre of which was depicted a magnificent peacock.

Joss said, "Ben was determined that everyone who set foot in the house would know it was Peacocks. There are reminders everywhere."

A carpeted staircase climbed from the hall, and I saw a woman standing on the landing, watching us. She was tall and slender, with fine greying hair in a knot at the nape of her neck. She wore a simple grey gown with a white collar and cuffs.

"Mrs. Laud!" cried Joss. "I've got a surprise for you. This is my wife."

She turned pale and clutched at the newel-post. "It's one of your jokes, Mr. Madden," she said.

Joss drew me forward. "No joke at all, is it, Jessica? We were married in England. Ben came to our wedding."

Mrs. Laud came down the stairs and took my hand. "What will you think of me? I had no idea. . . . We have all been so sad because of Mr. Henniker's death."

"I share your sadness," I said. "He was a very good friend of mine."

"Mrs. Laud will be able to tell you all about the house, Jessica," said Joss. "She'll take you on a tour of inspection tomorrow."

Mrs. Laud smiled at me ingratiatingly. "I'll get the servants to make some tea," she said. She opened a door and we entered a drawing room with windows which reached from floor to ceiling.

My eyes immediately went to the picture of a peacock that hung on the wall. Joss's did the same; our eyes met, and a tremendous wave of excitement passed between us. The Green Flash at Sunset was hidden there, and we were going to see it very soon.

Then we were joined by Jimson and Lilias Laud.

"This is my wife," Joss told them.

They were startled, as well they might be, I thought. Joss

grinned at me. "We seem to have delivered a bombshell," he said. "Jessica and I were married before we left England."

"Con . . . congratulations," Jimson said, recovering a little from his surprise. I reckoned him to be about Joss's age.

"Jimson works for the company," Joss explained to me. "And Lilias helps Mrs. Laud around the house."

How alike the family were! Lilias was a younger edition of her mother—meek, unassuming. I caught her expression as her eyes rested on Joss, and I was not quite sure what it meant. It was scarcely there before it was gone, and she was the meek girl of a moment before.

"You'll be staying for a while, Mr. Croissant, I daresay?" said Mrs. Laud.

"For a couple of nights. Then I have to go to Melbourne."

The tea arrived. "Shall I pour?" asked Mrs. Laud.

"I believe my wife would like to do that," said Joss, dismissing her. After the Lauds left, we were alone with David Croissant. I could feel that Joss was a little impatient by the manner in which he kept looking at that picture. I was as impatient as he.

After we finished our tea, Joss said he would take me to my room. As we mounted the stairs, he said, "At the first opportunity we'll look for the Green Flash. I hardly want to do it while David Croissant's in the house. He's got a nose for opals. I felt he was going to sense it in that room. Well, I hope you are going to like your home."

"I like very much what I have seen."

"The Lauds are a sort of institution," he went on. "Mrs. Laud was a widow with two children when she came to work here. She's been more than a housekeeper. She and Ben were *very* friendly at one time."

"You mean . . . ?"

He looked at me maliciously. "You wouldn't understand."

"I think I understand . . . perfectly," I contradicted.

"It gives them a certain standing in the household. Jimson was taken into the company. He's good at figures. And Lilias is a pleasant girl . . . more talented than you'd think."

"How do you know what I think?"

"My dear wife, I read you like a book. Ah, they have prepared the bridal suite for us."

He swept me off my feet and carried me into the room. I did not

79

protest because I realized he was hoping I would. I remained passive until he set me down.

"Oh dear," he said, clucking his tongue. "They've made the same mistake." He regarded the big four-poster bed with feigned dismay, then went to a bell rope and pulled it.

Lilias came, and I suspected that she had not been far off.

"Lilias," said Joss, "will you have my old room made ready for me?" I saw the speculative gleam in her eyes, and I wondered what the relationship had been between her and Joss.

"I will see to it immediately," she said.

She went out, and a maid came in with hot water.

"I'll leave you," said Joss. "I'll see you at dinnertime."

I looked around the room. The curtains were a light shade of yellow, the carpet a darker one, and there was a primrose-coloured counterpane on the bed. It was indeed pleasant.

I washed and changed into a green silk dress. Then I went to the window. Looking out, I could just see Fancy Town. I imagined Ben here, looking out on the town which had begun with my father's dream. "Ben, are you satisfied now?" I whispered.

I longed for Ben then. I wanted to explain to him that when he had arranged our lives he had not been aware of what danger he was putting me in. Oh Ben, I thought, you were a ruthless man, and your son is the same. You brushed aside those who stood in your way. Did you ever think, Ben, that I might be in Joss's way?

When Joss took me down to dinner, I saw that the dining room was panelled like the one at Oakland and had tall windows with blue drapes. A candelabrum stood in the centre of the table and at either end was a decoration of variegated leaves. Mrs. Laud had arranged everything very tastefully.

The Lauds dined with us, and I was aware of a certain tension at the table. I felt I had much to learn about my new home. When I looked at Lilias, I would find her eyes on me. She would smile or look hastily away, and I asked myself whether I had been right in assuming that our marriage was a great blow to her.

I was mostly a listener that night, for the conversation was all about the company, and of this, of course, I had much to learn.

Mrs. Laud said, "Mr. Paling was badly hurt. He'd been up here to see Jimson, and on the way back to town the wheel came off his buggy and he was nearly killed."

"Paling!" cried Joss. "Good Lord! He's all right now, I hope."

"He'll never walk again. Jimson took over his work, and I've heard the department is running better than it ever did before."

"That's just Mother's talk," said Jimson modestly. "But we've looked after Paling's family. And you'll see tomorrow that nothing has suffered in the department."

"What else has happened?" said Joss.

"The Trant Homestead was burned to the ground," said Lilias.

"We know that," replied David Croissant. "We called there on the way here."

"What happened to the Trants?" asked Joss. "They escaped the fire, I hope."

"By great good fortune, yes," replied Lilias. "They've set up a cookhouse in town. It's useful for people working in the offices."

"I thought," said Mrs. Laud, "that you would like me to ask the Bannocks for dinner tomorrow."

"Yes, I think it's a good idea," Joss said. "There'll be a lot of detail to discuss." He turned to me. "Ezra Bannock is our manager in chief. He lives about five miles from here. They have a homestead . . . he and his wife, Isabel—Isa."

"Oh," cried Lilias, "we haven't told Mr. Madden about Desmond Dereham."

Everyone leaned forward in their seats.

Jimson said, "Someone who stayed at the Trants' just before the place burned down said that Desmond Dereham had died in America. Before he died, Desmond told this man an extraordinary story about the Green Flash."

"What story?" demanded Joss.

"He swore he'd never stolen it. He said he had been caught in the act of trying to take it by Ben himself. Ben had forced him to leave immediately. If he didn't, Ben had said, he'd have him arrested for theft. So Desmond went to America."

"And, of course, this story is all over town," said Joss.

"People are talking of nothing else," agreed Jimson. "Apparently, Desmond Dereham said he'd had bad luck ever since he'd tried to steal the opal. But, according to him, it never left Ben's possession. In which case it's either in England or here. . . ." He was looking at Joss.

"I haven't seen the Green Flash since the night it was supposedly stolen," said Joss. "I hope people are not making much of this story about opals being unlucky. It's bad for business."

"The Flash has had rather a history," said David Croissant.

"Well, don't let's dwell on it," retorted Joss. He began to talk about our journey out from England. It was clear that he was dismissing the subject of the Green Flash.

THE BEDROOM looked very different by candlelight. Joss had called it the bridal chamber, but of course it never had been. The house had been built by Ben, and he had never married.

I sat down at the dressing table and took the pins out of my hair. Images passed in and out of my mind. The Lauds, so unassuming, interested me. Was Lilias emotionally involved with Joss? Jimson was meek enough, but when they had talked about how he was conducting the department since Mr. Paling's accident, I had detected something . . . I wasn't sure what.

I took off my dress and put on a velvet dressing gown. Then suddenly I heard a stealthy footstep in the corridor. Someone paused outside my door. There was a quiet knock.

"Who's there?" I cried.

The door opened and Joss stood there holding a candle.

He said, "I was going to look for the Flash after Croissant had gone, but I've changed my mind. I can't wait to see it. Can you?"

"No," I answered. I wrapped my dressing gown more closely around me, and he led the way to the drawing room. He locked the door and lighted more candles. Then he took down *The Pride of the Peacock* and laid it face down on a table.

"The spring Ben talked of would be somewhere here," he said. "Not easy to find, of course. Hold the candle higher."

I obeyed. Some minutes passed before he cried, "I have it. The back opens." And there in the right-hand corner of the frame was a large cavity. Eagerly he explored it.

"Jessica," he whispered with a note of excitement in his voice, "you're going to see the most magnificent—" He stopped and stared at me. "It can't be. There's nothing here. Look. Feel it."

I put my fingers into the cavity. It was empty.

"Someone has been here before us," he said briefly. As we stood looking at each other, I was sure I saw a shadow pass the window. I turned sharply, but no one was there.

"What's wrong?" asked Joss quickly.

"I thought there was someone at the window."

He took the candle from me and said, "Wait a minute." He

unlocked the door and hurried through the hall and out of the house. I saw him pass the window. In a short time he was back.

"There's no one about. You must have imagined it."

"That's possible," I admitted. "But I was almost sure . . ."

"Who could have known . . . ?" he murmured. Then he became brisk. "What are we going to do? It looks as if someone discovered the hiding place before we did."

"It must have been someone who knows the house. . . ."

"Well, there's nothing we can do about it tonight." He replaced the back of the frame and hung the picture on the wall. The proud peacock faced the room as before.

I followed Joss up the stairs, and he left me at my door. Understandably, I passed a restless night.

WHEN I AROSE next morning, Joss had already gone into Fancy Town with Jimson Laud and David Croissant. But Mrs. Laud was waiting for me when I went down.

"Mr. Henniker liked things done as they are in England," she said, "so we serve an English breakfast. There are bacon, eggs, and kidneys. Would you like to help yourself from the sideboard?"

I did so.

"Mr. Madden was anxious that I should show you everything," she went on. "If you want anything at all changed, please say so. It's a large place to run, and so many people come here. Merchants and managers from the company. The Bannocks are here a great deal."

"I believe I am meeting them tonight."

"Oh yes." Her lips tightened almost imperceptibly.

"I understand Mr. Bannock is the manager in chief."

"Yes. He's very knowledgeable about opals. His wife is quite a collector."

"How old are they?"

"He would be about forty-five. She's much younger . . . ten years, I'd say." Again that slight tightening of the lips.

When I had eaten, we started on a tour of the house. She took me through a great many rooms, and finally we came to the gallery, which was a replica of the one at Oakland.

"Mr. Henniker was very fond of this," Mrs. Laud told me. "He furnished it exactly like the one in his English home. Someone he was fond of used to play that spinet. After she died, he brought it

83

out here from England." I realized that it was the very spinet my mother used to play.

Mrs. Laud took me to the garden, which was walled in the Tudor manner. "Mr. Henniker used to say this was like a bit of England. It was difficult with the droughts here, but he wanted it to look like home. You must see the orchard."

There grew oranges, lemons, figs, and guavas, with vine bananas. "Mr. Henniker was a wonderful man," Mrs. Laud went on. "It was a pity he ever saw the Green Flash."

I looked at her sharply and she lowered her eyes. "It brings bad luck," she said passionately. "If Desmond Dereham never stole it, then Mr. Henniker had it all the time. That would account for his accident and his death. And where is it now?"

She looked at me steadily. "It could be in the house," she said. "Oh, I don't like that. It will bring bad luck."

I was surprised at her agitation.

"You can't believe all these stories about bad luck, Mrs. Laud," I said. "There's no real foundation for them."

She laid a hand on my arm. "I'm afraid of that stone, Mrs. Madden. I hope to God it's never found."

THAT AFTERNOON Lilias came to my room to ask if she could help me unpack. I thanked her and said that I could manage very well, but she sat down and watched me. She thought my clothes were very elegant and said that they would surely make Isa Bannock jealous.

"She thinks she is a *femme fatale*," Lilias added.

"It will be interesting to meet her."

"I hope you'll find it so. My mother has shown you the house, hasn't she? We're anxious that you should put us right about anything you don't like. You see, when my mother came here I was only one, so it's always been my home."

"And must continue to be . . . until you marry."

She cast down her eyes. It was a habit she shared with her mother. "We had no idea Mr. Madden would marry over there. But it's not for us to say what should be done."

"Well, I know it was a shock, but I am sure we shall all get along well together."

"We're a very close family. Jimson and I never forget what we owe to our mother. But I'm boring you, Mrs. Madden. Have you

84

room for your things? Mr. Madden's seem to be in the other room." Again her eyes lowered. Was it triumph she was hiding?

"I have plenty of room," I said coolly.

"Dinner will be at half past seven," she said.

After she left, I dressed with care in a gown of peacock-blue silk. "This," my grandmother had said, "will serve for a *dignified* occasion." And so I went down to meet the Bannocks.

They were in the parlour drinking aperitifs. Joss came forward and took my arm. "Come along and meet Isa and Ezra," he said.

Ezra, a powerfully built man, took my hand and nearly crushed it in a sincere handshake. "Congratulations, Joss," he cried in a booming voice. "You've got yourself a beaut."

I smiled and said how pleasant it was to meet him.

"And here's Isa," said Joss.

She was obviously several years younger than her husband. As she scrutinized me with topaz-coloured eyes, she reminded me of a tigress; there were tawny lights in her hair to match her eyes, and she moved like a cat with immense grace.

"So you're Joss's wife," she said. "How sly of him to spring you on us like this. I hope you'll like it here. There's a shortage of women. It makes us all so much more precious than we should otherwise be. Don't you agree, David?" She was smiling at David Croissant, who seemed overwhelmed by her charms.

"It would depend on the woman," said David, grinning at her.

"What have you brought in your peddler's pack?" Isa asked him. "I'm longing to see your opals. And I'm sure Mrs. Madden is too."

"Yes, I am," I said. "I saw some in Cape Town, and I remember one especially. The Harlequin Opal. I don't think I ever saw anything so beautiful."

"The Harlequin!" cried Isa. "What a marvellous name. I long to see it. Have you got it with you, David?"

"You shall see it later," he promised her.

Mrs. Laud said, "I think we should go in to dinner now."

Joss sat at one end of the table and I at the other. Isa was on his right hand, Ezra on mine. It was soon clear to me that the men's attention was focused on Isa, and that she revelled in it.

I scarcely noticed what I ate. My attention—like that of the men—was on Isa, and in particular on Isa and Joss. Once or twice she placed her hand over his and he smiled at her. I tried to tell myself that she was an empty-headed, frivolous woman, but there was more to her than that. She was secret, subtle, and cunning.

She brought up the subject of the Green Flash and repeated the story of Desmond Dereham's confession. "If Ben had the opal all the time," she said, "what on earth happened to it?"

There was a brief silence, and then Joss lifted his eyes and, looking straight at me, said, "Before Ben died he told my wife and me where he had hidden the Green Flash. He left it to us jointly."

Isa clapped her hands. "I want to see it."

"I can't show it to you," said Joss. "Someone has stolen it."

Mrs. Laud had turned very pale. "It's no longer in this house then," she said. "Thank God for that."

"Oh, Mother, you take the rumours too seriously," said Jimson.

"I don't want a lot of talk about unlucky stones," said Joss. "People could stop buying opals because of it." He addressed Ezra, and I noticed afresh how when Joss wanted a subject changed, he made it clear. "Have you added any good horses to your stables lately?"

"One or two. I've got a little beauty . . . a grey mare. She's called Wattle. I've never known a horse with such feeling. If you need a good horse for Mrs. Madden," he said to Joss, "I'd like to give her my Wattle. She has a will of her own, but if I drop a word in her ear, she'll be just the mount for the lady."

"I've never known anyone talk to horses as Ezra does," Jimson told me. "He has a way with them."

"It's very kind of you," I said. "Thank you."

"Well, that's settled," said Isa. "David, I can't wait to see your treasures."

After coffee we went into the drawing room, and before the eyes of the haughty peacock on the wall, David unrolled the cases.

The gems glowed in the candlelight. "Mostly from South Australia, this lot," said David. "They were hard come by. Conditions are rough in the gibber country."

Joss turned to me. "Gibber country is flat plains strewn with stones." I was irrationally pleased because he had remembered me.

"David," said Isa imperiously, "*I* want to see the Harlequin."

So he opened a case, and there it was in all its glory—even more beautiful than it had seemed on the previous occasion. Isa cupped it in her hands. "I love it," she crooned. "Look at those fantastic

86

colours." Her face glowed. "It's one of the loveliest stones I ever saw. I'd give a good deal to add it to my collection."

"I can see I'll have to start saving up," commented Ezra.

"Isa has a fine collection of opals," Joss said.

"I do have some really fine stones. I should so much enjoy showing them to you," Isa said to me.

"I should very much like to see them."

The Bannocks left soon afterwards, and I went up to my room and brooded on the evening. Dominating my thoughts was the memory of Isa's attitude towards Joss and his towards her.

"A *femme fatale*," Lilias had said.

I felt angry. How dared Isa behave flirtatiously towards my husband in my presence!

It was the first time that I had referred to him in my thoughts as "my husband"

I was ready for bed when a sound in the corridor startled me. I went to the door and listened. The footsteps were slow and stealthy. At my door they paused. I found myself trembling. Cautiously I reached for the key and turned it in the lock.

There was silence, then the footsteps retreated.

WHEN I WENT down to breakfast next morning, I was surprised to see Ezra Bannock at the table with Joss.

"I thought you and Wattle ought to get together right away," Ezra said. "As soon as you've had a bite to eat, we'll go to the stables and I'll make a formal hand-over."

Wattle and I took to each other immediately. I was rather amused by the way Ezra talked to her.

"Now, old girl, I want you to look after this young lady. It's a bit rough going out here for her."

When I mounted, Wattle seemed docile enough, but I sensed the fire in her. I leaned forward and chatted to her. Then we rode out, Ezra on one side of me, Joss on the other. I felt grateful to the big, rather clumsy man, and I wondered why Isa had married him and what he thought of her behaviour.

Very soon Fancy Town came into sight. It was not beautiful by any stretch of imagination. It had sprung up on the banks of a creek which Nature, by great good fortune, had set near the opal field. Some of the workers lived in calico tents, which bordered the town. There were also a few dwellings in the centre of town—huts made of logs or mud bricks. The shops were sheds open on one side to display their goods. Some children came running out to stare at us—rather unkempt, most of them. I noticed how respectful everyone was to Joss and how curious they were about me.

We passed a blacksmith shoeing a chestnut horse. Joss called out, "Good morning, Joe. This is my wife. You'll see a good deal of her in the future."

The blacksmith came forward, rubbing his hands together. "Welcome, ma'am," he said. "'Tis good to see the master wed at last."

Joss gave his sudden burst of laughter. "So that's your opinion, is it? Tether the horses for us, Joe."

After we alighted, Ezra went on to the offices. Joss took my arm, and we sauntered along what he called The Street. It was hot and the flies were beginning to pester. Joss grinned as I tried to brush them aside. "It's nothing to what it will be later on in the day," he said. "The sand flies are partial to fresh English blood—especially the blue variety."

"I think you're trying to make me dislike the place."

"I just want you to see it in its true colours."

We came to a wooden dwelling, where Joss introduced me to the innkeepers, James and Ethel Trant.

"I was sorry to hear what happened," said Joss.

James Trant nodded. "There's not much hope of saving a wooden house when you're in the bush," he said. "The funny thing was that only a few days before the fire, this man came along who'd known Desmond Dereham. He said Desmond had never stolen the Green Flash, that it was here in Australia. I wonder if that brought us bad luck."

"What utter nonsense," snapped Joss. "All this gossip about ill luck has got to be stopped."

James and Ethel looked crestfallen. I smiled apologetically at them, and Joss said, "We must be going."

When we were out of earshot, I said, "Those poor people suffered a dreadful tragedy. Can't you even be civil to them?"

"I'm being kind to them. Talk like that could make the price of opals slump and cookshops with them."

"I see. Being cruel to be kind."

"Exactly, and you object to it?"

"It's a mode of self-righteousness I particularly dislike."

"There's a lot about me that you particularly dislike."

I was silent and he went on. "You've accepted the conditions of Ben's will. All this and me too. You've made your bed, and now you must lie on it. . . ." Again that mocking laugh. "Though I have to admit that that's a rather unfortunate analogy."

I said angrily, "It's you who are spoiling things. I think we should at least try to behave graciously, whatever resentments we feel."

"You set me an example. Pretend that all is well. Who knows? In time you may enjoy being here among the shafts and the gougers. One day this is going to be a real town, with a town hall, proper houses, and a church. It'll be more to your taste then."

"Perhaps," I said.

"Here are the company offices," he told me as we came to a quite impressive building. "Let's go in. I want to introduce you."

Ezra had gathered the department heads in the boardroom. There were six men present, including Ezra and Jimson Laud. Of the others I felt particularly drawn to a young man called Jeremy Dickson, who was not long out from England.

As we sat around the table, Joss told them the terms of Ben's will. Then he turned to me. "You will no doubt want to acquaint yourself with all that goes on here . . . that's if you decide to take an active part. You can, of course, always allow me to take care of everything for you."

"I want to take my place here with the rest of you," I said.

So I sat there while they talked for about an hour, and I was very little wiser at the end of it. Then Joss left us, asking Jeremy Dickson to take me around the departments. As I watched men sorting the opals, Jeremy pointed out how to recognize quality. I learned to distinguish pieces likely to contain first-, second-, or third-class opal from what was merely potch.

I was fascinated by the snippers, who removed worthless layers of stone and, by means of facing wheels, revealed the beautiful colours beneath. One false move, Jeremy explained, and a precious opal could be lost.

It was most interesting, but I could not absorb it all at once. Soon I was ready to go back to Peacocks, and Jeremy offered to ride with me.

On the way he told me that he had come to Australia to make a fortune out of gold, but he had not done very well. Then he had discovered opal, and the stones had fascinated him. Ben Henniker had taken a liking to him and offered him a place in the company. Now he was in charge of the sorting department.

At Peacocks I said, "You'll come in, won't you?"

"For half an hour. Then I must get back to work. But I would like to say hello to Mrs. and Miss Laud."

I sent one of the servants to tell Lilias and her mother that we had a visitor. Lilias came in, and I was amazed at the change in her. She smiled and held out her hands to Jeremy.

"You must be hot and tired," said Lilias. "I'll send for some lemonade. I made it early this morning."

We sipped and talked, and I thought how pleasant it was. Jeremy Dickson was so English that I felt completely at home with him. As for Lilias, she seemed like a different person.

Then Mrs. Laud came in. She stood at the door, looking enigmatically at Lilias. "So Mr. Dickson has called," she said. "How nice."

Again I had the impression that everything was not as it outwardly seemed. There was something strange about my new home.

EACH MORNING I rode into town with Joss. The first event on arrival was a meeting with the department heads, with Joss presiding. If the gougers had brought in any finds of special interest on the previous day, we examined them. I was genuinely fascinated and determined to learn quickly.

I was most interested in the sorting and snipping. As this was Jeremy Dickson's concern, I saw a great deal of him. One morning he made tea on a spirit lamp in his tiny office. As we sat drinking it, he told me marvellous stories about opals.

"The ancient Turks," he said, "had a theory that a great fire stone was thrown out of Paradise in a flash of lightning. It shattered and fell in a great shower on certain areas of the world. That is now opal country." His eyes glowed. "Opal used to be called the fire stone. I've often thought these stones have some odd power because of the hold they get on people."

Just then the door opened, and Joss looked in. "Am I interrupting a tea party?" he asked.

"It's a working tea party," I replied. "Mr. Dickson is teaching me a great deal."

"I hope you are finding my wife an apt pupil." He stressed the words "my wife" as though he were reminding Jeremy Dickson who I was. Quite unnecessary, I thought.

The next day at breakfast, Joss said, "I thought we'd take a ride this morning. You'll get some idea of the layout of the land."

As we walked our horses away from Peacocks, I said, "Are you doing nothing about the theft of the Green Flash?"

"Can you suggest what should be done? This is rather an unusual theft. In the first place, no one knows when it took place."

"It must have been after Ben left for England."

A thought entered my head then that Joss had been in Peacocks after Ben had left. Surely he would not have stolen the opal from Ben. Yet that stone had a strange effect. My own father had been so bewitched by it that he had contemplated leaving my mother for it. Who could say . . . ? And it would explain why Joss was doing nothing about finding it.

He turned from me and galloped towards a gap in the hills. His horse kicked up a cloud of dust, and I lost sight of him for a few moments. How I should have liked to turn back to Peacocks, but I knew I should not be able to find my way without his guidance.

When I came through the gap, he was waiting for me. "This is Grover's Gully," he told me. "There was a flourishing opal mine here at one time, but now it's duffered out, as we say. It's full of underground chambers. There's a rumour that it's haunted by a miner who made his fortune here."

"There's certainly something desolate about the place."

We walked our horses over to the mine shaft. I saw an old iron ladder, which had been used for the descent, still in position. Although Joss was watching me, I could not repress a shudder.

"Come on," he said. "That's enough of Grover's Gully." He moved off and I followed. He was a little way ahead of me when he pulled up once more and pointed to the horizon.

"Can you see a building there?"

"I can just make it out. Is it a house?"

"It's the Bannock Homestead," said Joss, and my spirits fell. The last person I wished to see was Isa Bannock.

As we approached, the dogs started to bark and Ezra Bannock came out. He called in his hearty way, "Well, look who's here." He opened the gate and took us into a grass enclosure. Wattle gave a whinny of delight as he patted her.

"Come along in," he said. "Isa will be pleased." We went into a tiled hall and Ezra shouted, "Visitors!"

Then I saw Isa. She was wearing a soft voile morning gown with flowing sleeves. She looked fresh and, I had to admit, beautiful.

Joss kissed her hand. I was surprised at that, for it seemed out of character.

"My *dear* Joss," she murmured tenderly, "it *is* good of you to come to our little homestead."

"I hope we haven't come at an inconvenient time," I said.

"My dear Mrs. Madden . . . but don't you think we should call each other by our Christian names? Jessica, then . . . it suits you. . . ." The manner in which she said my name suggested a rather prim woman, inclined to take life very seriously. "You will stay for luncheon," she went on eagerly.

"That's an excellent idea," said Joss warmly.

"First, cool drinks in the parlour," said Isa. "Ezra, darling, please summon Emily."

The parlour was essentially hers—a frilly, feminine room. As we sat down on the chintz-covered chairs, she threw a coquettish glance at Joss. He was smiling at her in a way which was beginning to madden me. At least, I thought, he might not show his besotted admiration so blatantly in front of his wife.

They chatted about people of whom I had never heard. Isa seemed determined to shut me out. Then she mentioned a treasure hunt at Peacocks. "Haven't you heard about it, Jessica? The treasure hunt is one of the events of the year. Ben thought of it to keep his workers from being bored."

"It sounds interesting," I said, looking at Joss coldly.

"There's been such a lot to show you," he said. "I forgot to explain about it. It's a little childish, perhaps. . . ."

Isa changed the subject abruptly. "I did promise to show you my collection, Jessica, didn't I?"

She and Joss exchanged a glance. Then he said, "By all means, show her, Isa. Jessica's getting really interested in opals."

"After lunch," promised Isa. With that, we went into the dining room for cold chicken, salad, and fruit. Afterwards we settled down in the parlour to see her collection. She had some magnificent stones and she was clearly knowledgeable about them. "I only want the very best," she told me.

"That's what you have," replied Joss.

"Coming from such a connoisseur, that's gratifying," she said, smiling at him. "Now . . ." She opened a small case and laid it on the table. There on the black velvet was the Harlequin Opal.

I stared at it. It couldn't be. Isa chuckled. "Pick it up," she commanded. "I know you love it. I saw by the way you looked at it before."

"You are very fortunate to have such a stone," I said.

"I have to thank my very good friend. . . ." She was smiling at Joss, and I was astonished at the cold anger I felt. "Dear Joss gave it to me, didn't he, Ezra?"

"It was a generous gift," said Ezra complacently.

I put it back on the black velvet and hoped my fingers were not trembling with the rage which consumed me.

The collection was put away and I thought, The object of the visit is over. We sat a while, and as I listened to their talk, I kept seeing Isa's tiger eyes and the smouldering response I fancied I detected in those of Joss.

It was a great relief to go down to the stables. Ezra took a fond farewell of Wattle, and then Joss and I rode back to Peacocks. I tried to keep aloof, but he insisted on riding beside me.

"You're silent," he said.

"You should have warned me that we were going there."

"I thought it would be a pleasant surprise. Isa made us very welcome, didn't she?" he said.

"Especially you. She must be grateful to you. You give her such wonderful presents."

"Something has occurred to me. Is that rather pleasant little nose out of joint?"

"What do you mean?"

"You did rather fancy the Harlequin, I know. You should have asked me for it. Who knows, I might have given it to *you*."

"Unlike that woman, I have no wish to take expensive gifts from you."

"Yet you seem rather angry because I gave it to her."

"And what of that so-called husband of hers?"

"He doesn't really mind any more than my so-called wife does."

"Are you that woman's lover?" I demanded.

"You don't want me. Can you take me to task if I look for affection elsewhere?"

I turned to look at him. His eyes were lowered in an expression

93

of resignation. He was mocking me. When had he ever ceased to mock me? I could endure no more. I started to gallop.

"Steady," he called. "You'll be lost in the bush if you go that way. Just follow me."

So I followed him back to Peacocks.

There I went straight to my room, feeling wretched and angry at the same time. He's in love with Isa Bannock, I thought. Of course he would be; she's everything that I am not.

I lay on my bed and stared up at the ceiling.

I dislike him, I told myself. He's arrogant and conceited, heartless and ruthless. He's everything that I hate. "Peacock," I muttered. "Nothing but a peacock, flaunting your glory."

But the flashing light of the Harlequin Opal had revealed something to me. Why should I care so much? Because . . . I must face the fact. . . . I was either in love with him or fast getting into that terrifying state. It had taken his devotion to another woman to make me see the truth. I was in love with Joss Madden.

I HAD BEEN in my room for more than an hour considering this extraordinary situation when there was a knock on my door. I called, "Come in," and Mrs. Laud entered.

"I came to speak to you about the treasure hunt," she said.

"Do tell me about it. I heard of it for the first time today."

"Well, we make believe that the house is a desert island. The treasure is two opals which have been found during the year. The servants make up the clues and place them. I help them, of course, because I don't take an active part in the hunt, though Mr. Henniker used to insist that I did sometimes." She smiled reminiscently. "So we'll take care of that part of it, but I wanted to discuss other arrangements with you. We always have a buffet supper, and we like to send out formal invitations in advance."

"I daresay you could arrange all this without any help from me, Mrs. Laud."

"Oh, I thought it only right and proper that you should know how we had conducted it in the past, in case you wished to make new arrangements."

"I think it would be better to leave this treasure hunt in your capable hands," I replied. "You're so efficient. I'm really more interested in learning the affairs of the company than in running a house, Mrs. Laud."

"You're a very unusual lady. I realize that. I think you are the kind who will master what you set out to do."

Then she went, and left me with my thoughts.

I DOZED fitfully that night. I kept thinking of the Harlequin Opal. Joss had given Isa permission to show it to me, and he had even taken me there for that purpose. It was tantamount to an act of defiance. It meant: I don't care for you any more than you care for me. And yet I fancied he did not like my growing friendship with Jeremy Dickson. How dared he resent something so innocent when his relations with Isa were far from innocent?

And what did Ezra think? Was he prepared to stand aside for Joss because of the power Joss had in the company? Ezra seemed ready to grant Isa's every wish. What hold did she have over them?

At one point I dreamed we were all sitting around the table while Isa showed us the Harlequin Opal.

"Look at it," she said, and when I looked into it I could see pictures. I saw myself and Joss, and Joss was saying, "I don't want you. I want Isa. You are in the way. If you weren't here, the Green Flash would be mine. You're in the way . . . in the way. . . ." I felt his hands about my throat and I awoke trembling.

It was only a dream, I assured myself. But as I lay in the darkness the thought came to me that the dream was a warning. There was something strange about Peacocks. The Lauds, with their meek unobtrusiveness, seemed to be living two lives—the real one, which I didn't see, and the shadow one, which I did. Jimson and Lilias seemed afraid of their mother . . . not exactly afraid . . . protective, perhaps. I suppose that was natural, and yet. . . .

And then I heard footsteps outside my locked door. I sat up in bed, and in the faint moonlight I saw the door handle slowly turning. There was a brief silence and then the sound of retreating footsteps. I lay down, trembling again, wondering what would have happened if the door had not been locked.

FOR SEVERAL DAYS the bustle of preparation went on at Peacocks. The servants were absentminded, giggling together.

"It's always like this when the treasure hunt approaches," Lilias told me. She asked how I was getting on with the company, and I told her that I was growing more fascinated every day.

95

"I daresay you see a great deal of Jeremy Dickson," she said, and she looked a little mournful.

As for me, I was trying not to think of Joss, but I couldn't help it. Every time I heard his voice I felt excited. When he rode out, I wondered whether he was going to Isa. I wondered if Ben had known of Joss's infatuation with her. I did not think Ben would have liked Isa very much. Perhaps he had wanted to break that connection by giving Joss a younger wife.

I longed to be loved as Isa was loved; and I knew then how happy I should have been if my marriage had turned out differently, if Joss had fallen in love with me as I had with him.

ON THE NIGHT of the treasure hunt Lilias came to my room while I was dressing. "Why, your dress is beautiful," she cried.

It was another of the peacock-blue shade which, strangely enough, I had always loved. I had not adhered closely to fashion, because the mode of the day was not, I considered, very becoming. I had gone back to an earlier and more charming age. My dress had a billowing skirt, and a close-fitting bodice which fell off the shoulders in elegant austerity.

Lilias herself looked pretty in a modest gown of pale grey silk embroidered with pink moss roses. "You know," she said, "the ladies choose their partners for the treasure hunt. It's a tradition."

I would choose Joss, I promised myself. I had to admit that the unsatisfactory state of our relationship was to a large extent due to me, so perhaps it was up to me to set the pace.

Lilias was saying timidly, "I thought I'd ask Mr. Dickson unless, of course, you wanted to ask him."

"I hadn't thought of it," I replied, and she seemed relieved.

The door opened and Joss came in. He looked magnificent. He wore a velvet dinner jacket in a shade of peacock blue almost identical with mine. Lilias said, "Excuse me," and scuttled out.

Joss regarded himself in the mirror, approvingly, I thought. His eyes met mine and he smiled. "I know what you're thinking," he said. "Peacock!"

"I've never heard anyone but Ben call you by that name."

"They do it behind my back. They wouldn't think of using it before my loving wife."

He caught me by the shoulders and turned me around so that we stood side by side, looking in the mirror. "We're a handsome pair, you must agree. You're not exactly displeased with your appearance, are you? Is there a bit of the peacock in you?"

A great impulse came to me then to tell him that I wanted to change everything. I wanted to say, Let us give ourselves a chance to make something of our lives. One little sign from him and I should have done so.

I said instead, "I understand the ladies choose partners for the treasure hunt. I suppose I should choose you."

It sounded ungracious, as though I regarded it as a duty, when what I meant was, I want to be with you. I want us to walk through this house hand in hand, searching for the treasure which will be symbolic in a way . . . searching for that happiness which we can only find together. For a few seconds those dark blue eyes rested on my bare shoulders almost caressingly, and my heart beat fast. Then Joss said, "My dear, there is no need to choose me. In fact, it would hardly be right. Suppose we found the treasure. They would think it was collusion." I felt deflated. I knew, of course, that Isa had already chosen him.

We stood side by side in the hall and received the guests as they arrived. People shook my hand warmly and welcomed me to Fancy Town. They were noisy, friendly people out for an evening's enjoyment—the high spot of the year.

One fair-haired young woman told me that she was glad her baby had arrived in time to let her come to the treasure hunt. "I want to win the opals," she confided. "They are always lucky."

After our guests had eaten their fill of the buffet, the hunt began. "All ladies must take their partners," announced Joss.

I felt sick with misery when I saw Isa with Joss. She looked beautiful, of course, in a tawny brown and yellow gown. A topaz tiara brought out the strange colour of her eyes.

"I've taken your husband," she cried, with a hint of malice in her voice. "I hope you won't mind."

Joss was watching me closely, an unfathomable expression in his eyes. Ezra stood by sheepishly. "Then I'd better retaliate by taking yours," I answered, and Ezra beamed.

Mrs. Laud handed out the first clue. The game was the old English one in which players started with one clue which led them to the next. The first to collect the entire set was the winner.

The first clue was made easy in order to give everyone an interest in the game. It was something like:

You have come to pay a call
Take a drink beside the wall.

This led us to the hall where callers come on their arrival. The second clue was in a punch bowl on a table close to the wall. We found the third in the library, and the next led us upstairs. It occurred to me that on an occasion like this, with so many people in the house, somebody might have come upon the Green Flash. How ironic if it had been lost through a treasure hunt.

"How are you getting on with Wattle?" asked Ezra.

"Very well. But she still remembers you."

"She'll remember me till the day she dies. Faithful creatures, horses. That's more than you can say for some human beings, eh?"

I looked at him sharply, and wondered whether he was referring to Isa.

We opened the door to the gallery. There was no one there. Six candles flickered eerily in their sconces. My eyes went to the spinet at one end, and I thought of my mother.

"It looks as if it ought to be haunted," said Ezra. "Why are those drapes placed at intervals round the room?"

"That's how they are at Oakland. There the walls are partially panelled, and the drapes hang where there is no panelling."

"Can you play the spinet, Jessica?"

"A little. I had lessons when I was a child." I sat down and played a Chopin waltz as well as I could remember it.

"Hello! This place *is* haunted then." It was Joss's voice. I swung around sharply as he and Isa came into the gallery. "Why," he went on, "the ghost is Jessica."

"Why did you think I was a ghost?" I demanded.

"I didn't. But in sentimental moments Ben used to fancy he could hear the spinet being played, and said he'd like someone who played at Oakland to play for him here. He furnished this gallery just like the one at Oakland, so the ghost might come to Peacocks."

"I want to find those opals," Isa said. "Come along, Joss." They disappeared.

Ezra and I went out too. Shortly afterwards we found ourselves at the top of the house in a section which was unfamiliar to me. The rooms here were smaller, and one was furnished as a sitting room. An open workbox stood on the table. A piece of needlework lay nearby. A door led out onto a narrow terrace.

"I believe these are the Lauds' quarters," I said. "I don't think Mrs. Laud would have allowed any clues to be placed here."

"Nevertheless, I'll look round," replied Ezra.

I stepped out on the little terrace and looked up at the sky where the Southern Cross shone. It reminded me that I was far from home, where no one would be missing me very much—and, I thought with a trace of bitterness, no one here cared either. I looked over the side of the terrace wall to the sheer drop below.

Then I heard voices and stepped back into the room. Ezra was standing at the table and Mrs. Laud was at the door.

She was saying, "I wouldn't have dreamed of letting them put clues here. Oh, there's Mrs. Madden."

"I'm sorry we intruded," I said.

"Oh no, it's not that." Mrs. Laud laughed. "I was just startled when I saw a man in the room."

Ezra apologized in his hearty way and we went downstairs. "You've got a treasure in that woman," he said.

"I don't know what we'd do without her."

"And Jimson's good. The way he can juggle figures really takes your breath away. It's rare to find people out here who can do that."

"I can hear sounds from below," I put in. "I believe they've got a winner."

It was the fair-haired young woman and her partner. Joss made me stand with him to present the prize.

While everyone was examining the opals, Joss said to me, "Tactful of you not to win."

"You, too," I answered. "And your acquisitive friend?"

"My acquisitive friend had to accept the inevitable."

"Will she demand another Harlequin as compensation?"

His eyes met mine—a little stormy, a little mocking. "I wonder," he murmured.

THE NEXT DAY in the office a disturbing incident took place. I overheard raised voices in Joss's room, and as I passed, Joss and Ezra came out. Ezra's large face had completely lost its benignity. Joss looked fierce and stern. They acknowledged me rather curtly.

Later I said to Joss, "You and Ezra seemed at cross-purposes this morning."

"It happens now and then," said Joss lightly. "There's always trouble when a house in town falls vacant. Ezra promised one to a man he liked, but I gave it to a much better worker."

"So that was it."

Joss looked at me quickly, but he said nothing. I was thinking, Were they really arguing about the house, or had Ezra told Joss that he was getting tired of seeing him with his wife?

The next time I saw Ezra he was his beaming hearty self, so I thought no more of the matter until later.

Saturday at dusk Joss and I rode into town. "Saturday night is a tradition here," said Joss. "The week's work is over and there has to be revelry. The workers are far away from the bright lights of a big city, so we have to make their entertainment."

Outside the town a bonfire was burning. "We'd rather have it in the centre of town," Joss explained, "but it's dangerous with so many wooden buildings. A wind in the wrong direction and the whole place would be ablaze." We left the horses at the blacksmith's and then wandered back out to the bonfire.

"Supper will be in that large tent over there," Joss told me. "The company provides the food. Ben believed that incentives make people work harder and so do I."

"Why do you always present yourself as the hardheaded businessman?"

His face glowed in the firelight. "Because that's what I am."

"You look like a demon in this light."

"I've often thought demons might be more exciting to know than angels. I'm sure you'll agree, because you're not exactly angelic yourself."

"Indeed?"

"Most certainly. There's a flash of fire in you. They named you Opal rightly. And no one knows more about opals than I do."

"Do you see Isa Bannock as an opal?"

"That's an interesting idea."

"Of course, I couldn't hope to compare with her brilliance."

He pressed my arm against his. "You mustn't underestimate yourself . . . or pretend to, must you?"

We sat down on a hillock, where we could watch the scene. From the tent came the smell of food and the sound of excited voices. People came out with slices of roast meat on bread, and mugs of home-brewed ale. They ate and drank with great enjoyment.

"Have some," said Joss. "Just to show you're not too proud to join in." He grinned at me. We were given some meat, which we ate with our fingers.

We had just finished when I heard a horse's hoofs, and a man came riding up. He cried, "Is Mr. Madden here?"

Joss went over to the rider. "Oh, Mr. Madden, sir," I heard him say, "Mrs. Bannock sent me to find you. She says to tell you that Mr. Bannock did not return home last night and now his horse has come back without him."

Joss replied, "Tell her I'm coming right away."

He walked off. I felt sick with rage. She only had to send for him and he forgot my existence. Then I thought of Ezra and was ashamed. What could have happened?

JIMSON brought me home and I waited for Joss in my room.

It was midnight when he returned. He came straight to my room. "I can't think what's happened," he said. "Ezra must have had an accident. I'll send out search parties tomorrow."

"I hope Ezra's all right," I said. "I do like him so much."

Joss smiled, hesitated, and I thought he was going to say something, but he seemed to change his mind.

"Good night," he said, and left me.

Chapter V

The search parties found no sign of Ezra. Three days after his disappearance I rode out on my own late in the afternoon. As usual, Wattle turned towards the gap in the hills leading to Grover's Gully and the Bannock Homestead.

It was a hot day and the wind was blowing from the north. I rode through the gap and looked about me uneasily. The place was desolate. Little eddies of dust swirled just above the ground, and I thought, The wind is rising. I'd better get back soon.

"Let's go home, Wattle," I said.

Then Wattle behaved in a most extraordinary manner. I urged her to turn back through the gap, but she started to move towards the mine. "No, Wattle, not that way." I pulled on her reins, but she continued to move forward.

"Wattle!" I cried in dismay. She ignored me, and at that moment I heard a kookaburra laughing. My spine tingled.

Very resolutely, Wattle was making her way forward. I was at her mercy, and I knew that she was aware of something of which I was ignorant.

Suddenly she stopped and began to whinny. Then she turned from the mine and made her way to a ragged mulga bush. She gave a snort of distress and pawed at the sand.

"What's wrong, Wattle?" I asked. Then I saw that she had uncovered something. I leaned forward.

"Oh, God!" I whispered in horror, for she had uncovered what was left of Ezra Bannock.

HE HAD been shot through the head and someone had buried him under the bush. He might never have been discovered.

Joss held a meeting in the company's offices to discuss the crime. Everyone who had seen Ezra on the day he disappeared was questioned. It was disclosed that Ezra had ridden over to Peacocks that morning and had been with Joss for an hour. Then Ezra had ridden off, presumably to go home. Joss had gone to town some time later.

A terrible suspicion came into my mind. I asked myself again whether their disagreement some days before in the office was indeed about housing a gouger. Or was it really about Isa?

At the funeral, Isa was swathed in black, which became her well. Indeed, her widowhood seemed to have added an extra dimension to her charms. She was mysterious and, I thought, not entirely desolate. Her eyes gleamed like topaz through a fine veil, and her tawny hair seemed brighter than ever.

Several of us rode back to the Bannock Homestead afterwards for ham sandwiches and ale. I found her beside me.

"Poor Ezra," she said. "Who *could* have done it? He didn't have any enemies. Everyone liked him."

"You don't think he quarrelled with someone?"

I saw the speculative light in her eyes. "It . . . could have been," she admitted.

"The most likely theory is that a bushranger shot him."

"His purse was missing," said Isa. "And it was full of sovereigns. It was red leather with a gold ring over the top. So poor Ezra probably died for a few pounds. But perhaps someone did want him out of the way."

I could not fathom her expression. "Perhaps," she went on, "you'll come to call soon. I'll show you my collection."

"You have shown me, remember?"

"I didn't show you everything."

Joss came up and she immediately turned to him. I heard him tell her that if she needed any help she was to call on him. No, Isa had not become less attractive because she was a widow.

Joss and I rode back to Peacocks together. That evening we sat on the terrace to take advantage of the cooler air.

"What is your theory?" I asked tentatively.

"Robbery," he said. "I think Ezra was trying to stop someone from taking his purse."

"Or his wife?"

"It was his purse that was missing."

I cried out passionately, "Shall we stop talking around this? I want to know the truth. Did you kill Ezra Bannock?"

"I? Why ever should I?"

"There's a perfectly good motive. You're his wife's lover."

"Then what good would his death be to me? I have a wife. I'm not free to marry Isa even if she's free to marry."

I was deeply shocked. He had not denied being her lover. I stood up.

"I find this conversation distasteful," I said.

He was beside me. "And," he said coldly, "so do I."

I went to my room and sat at the dressing table, looking at my reflection without seeing it. He would marry Isa if he were free, I thought. But he is not free, because he is married to me.

Then it was as though the room were full of warning shadows.

I could see very clearly that I stood in the way.

SEVERAL WEEKS passed. My nights were uneasy. But I tried to forget my apprehension by concentrating more and more on the business.

One morning in the sorting room I had what I can only call a hunch about one piece. Some work was set aside so that the merits of this particular piece might be explored. To my great joy, I had picked a winner. There, revealed by the facing wheel, was as fine an opal as had been seen for many months.

"She's got it!" cried Jeremy Dickson excitedly. "Mrs. Madden, you're a real opal woman."

I went regularly to the Trants' cookshop for a midmorning cup of coffee with Ethel. One day, as I sat stirring my coffee, she brought up the recent murder. "I reckon Ezra stole the Green Flash for his wife," she said.

"Surely you don't think she has it now?"

"It wouldn't surprise me. He did well at the company, but he never got as far as she wanted him to."

"I can't believe that Ezra was a thief."

"It's not the same, stealing the Green Flash. People can't help themselves. Some evil spirit takes over. Anyway, I reckon the Green Flash brought Ezra bad luck. That's why the bushranger got him in Grover's Gully. People are saying that the Green Flash ought to be found." She was eyeing me speculatively, and I felt there was more in her mind than she would tell me.

DURING THE NEXT weeks the house seemed to oppress me. I had a feeling that there was something there from which I must escape. I thought a great deal about Ben; I fancied that his spirit was in the house, warning me of danger. Nothing had turned out as he had planned. He had bound Joss and me together, but such interference in the lives of other people could be dangerous. Had he really known just how far Joss would go to get what he wanted?

Who crept up to my room at night? Was it Joss? I believed it was. Had he come to plead with me to let us begin a new life together? No, he was too proud for that. Then why?

I often fled to the peace of the orchard. There, among the lemon and orange trees, I would admonish myself for my foolish fancies, and feel a return to commonsense.

I had several books on opal lore. I liked to take one to the orchard, find a shady spot, and read, memorizing facts with which to startle people, Joss in particular. I could see that he was impressed. He never said so, but there would be a twinkle in his eyes that I found gratifying.

There in the orchard I made an alarming discovery. The grass was coarse and the earth was brown and cracked. I suppose that was why I noticed a spot which had been dug up recently.

I put aside my book and studied the spot for a few seconds without moving. Then the sun caught something and it glittered like gold. I went over. It *was* gold. As I pulled it out, I went limp with horror. What I had found was a red leather purse with a gold ring, and I knew at once that it had belonged to Ezra Bannock.

I went to my room in a haze of horror and indecision. The theory

105

that a bushranger had shot Ezra was false. What bushranger would bury the purse in our orchard?

There seemed to be one answer to the mystery. Someone at Peacocks had killed Ezra Bannock and taken his purse to make it look like robbery. I knew only one person who had a motive.

I wanted to protect Joss, whatever he had done. I wanted to go to him and say, I have found Ezra's purse, where you hid it. We must get rid of it.

But why had he buried the purse in the orchard? That seemed like a panic-stricken action. Strangely enough, I could believe he might commit murder, but not that he would ever panic.

I did not know what to do, so I put the purse into a drawer. Then I was afraid that it might be discovered. I spent a sleepless night and twice rose to check that it was still there.

The next day I rode into town, and when I returned to Peacocks, I went straight up to my room. I went immediately to the drawer in which I had put the red purse. It was not there. Whoever had killed Ezra now knew that I had discovered the purse, and that person had taken it from its hiding place.

I went to the window and looked across the grounds to the arid bush. As I stood there, I saw Mrs. Laud returning from town with provisions. She looked up and waved in acknowledgment.

I hurried down to the hall. "You look worn out," I said to her. "You should have taken Lilias with you."

"I think she sees a little too much of Jeremy Dickson." She pressed her lips together. Then she said, "I thought I'd have a cup of tea. Would you care to join me, Mrs. Madden?"

We climbed to her room and she put the kettle on the spirit lamp. It was a very cozy little room, with a bunch of dried leaves in a pot in the fireplace and a red plush runner on the polished table. Mrs. Laud seemed upset about something, and I determined to find out what. It took my mind off that other terrifying matter.

"Has Mr. Dickson done anything to upset you?" I asked.

"Oh no . . . not he."

"Then someone else . . . ?"

She looked over her shoulder as though she were seeking some way of escape. "It's a lot of lies. . . . Mrs. Bannock's not liked in town. But you're the last one I should be saying this to."

"Now, Mrs. Laud, you have said too much to stop. I want to know what people are saying."

"If I tell you, will you promise to say nothing?"

"To my husband, you mean?"

"Yes, he'd be so angry. They say they'd always known how it was between them. Ezra put up with it for a long time because of his position in the company. Then he wouldn't have it . . . and that's why he died."

"No!" I cried fiercely, forgetting that it was exactly what I had thought myself. "It's impossible."

"They say she has the Green Flash, that he took it from its hiding place and gave it to her."

"I never heard such nonsense," I cried firmly.

She hesitated. "I don't believe it, of course, but . . . well, I think you ought to be on your guard. . . ." I stared at her and she stammered, "On your guard . . . against gossip."

WHEN I WENT into town, I imagined people watched me furtively, wondering how much I knew. In a place like this everyone knew everyone else's business. The notices asking for information about Ezra's murder looked out at me from every post.

At the office, Jeremy Dickson showed me the finished product of the opal I had had such a feeling about. "You can be proud of your hunch," he told me. "That's what we all wait for."

He was one of the few people I could talk to, and as he made tea, I brought up the subject of the Green Flash. "I only wish I knew where to start looking for it. You see, it's very awkward, because Joss doesn't want to start a fuss."

Jeremy wrinkled his brows. "That's strange," he said. "But I'll keep my eyes and ears open and do everything I can."

The door opened and Joss looked in. "Oh," he said. "A cozy chat, I see!" He turned and left.

Soon after that I went back to Peacocks. I had lain down to rest when I was startled by a gentle tap on my door. I called, "Come in," but there was no answer. I went to the door, opened it, and looked into the corridor. "Is anyone there?" I called.

There was still no answer. Then I heard the sound of the spinet playing a Chopin waltz. I started towards the gallery. When I was nearly there, the music stopped abruptly. I went into the gallery. No one was there.

I looked around in dismay. If someone had been in here playing, I would surely have seen whoever it was coming out of the room.

THE NEXT AFTERNOON Jeremy Dickson rode back to Peacocks with me. "I shall be going away for a short time," he said. "Mr. Madden wants me to go to the Sydney office."

"Are you pleased?" I asked Jeremy.

"I've become too enthusiastic about our plan to track down the Green Flash. Wouldn't it be strange if the answer was in Sydney? I'll drop hints about it." I missed him when two days later he left.

One morning as we rode into town, I asked Joss, "What's happening about Ezra? Are you nearer to discovering his murderer?"

"Quite clearly it was a bushranger. I expect Ezra put up a fight and that was that."

"His purse was taken. I thought it might have been found."

He stared at me in amazement. "His purse! The thief would have thrown it away . . . and quickly."

I wanted to tell him my suspicion, but I couldn't. It would be like accusing him of murder.

At the office I could think only of Isa and Joss . . . together. Finally I decided to go to the homestead to see her.

A servant took me into the drawing room, and a few moments later Isa came in. She looked beautiful in flowing black chiffon.

"Jessica, how nice of you to take pity on me."

"It must be lonely for you now," I said.

"Oh, people are *so* good. They call often."

A faint smile at the lips. Joss, I thought.

She rang for tea and asked how I was getting on with the company. "I've heard you're something of a genius. Processes and all that. All I can do is enjoy the finished product."

"You said that you would show me the rest of your collection. Now that I know a little more, I should really enjoy it."

"Oh yes, you were a novice when you first saw my opals. But not so much so that you couldn't recognize the qualities of the Harlequin. Now there's a gem. It *was* good of Joss."

"I'm sure he enjoyed giving it to you."

"He knew it would be in good hands."

"It's not the best in your collection though, is it?"

"No," she answered. Then she laughed. "Oh, I know what you're thinking. The elusive Green Flash. In town they're saying that Ezra stole it and gave it to me. Do you think I'd want bad luck?"

"You wouldn't believe in the bad luck, would you?"

"I'm very superstitious. And I can't show you my collection because it's packed away. I'm leaving for England in a few weeks."

"Leaving for England! You are going . . . alone?"

The tiger eyes gleamed. "I need to get away," she said.

At dinner that night I was shattered when Joss said, "I think a trip to England will be necessary soon."

I stared at him in amazement. "Why must you go?" I asked.

"There's a growing demand in London for black Australian opals. Naturally we want to exploit that."

I felt deflated and wretched. Isa was going to England, so he would go, too.

I no longer had any appetite, and as soon as we left the table I made an excuse to go to my room. I had noticed the way Joss had looked at me when he had made the announcement about England. He seemed to be waiting for me to protest.

I won't give him that satisfaction, I thought.

I CAME HOME one afternoon to a quiet house. As I went to my room, I heard again the ghostly sound of the spinet. I ran to the gallery, but the music had stopped. No one was there.

Someone was playing tricks on me. And as I looked around the gallery, I noticed that one of the curtains was disarranged. I drew it back and disclosed a partially-open door which I hadn't known was there. The trickster had left by way of that door.

I pushed it open and peered into darkness. I felt with my foot and touched a stair. Cautiously I stepped down two steps. There was a clatter, my feet slid out from under me, and I went sailing into the air. I clutched the banister and sat down abruptly.

So shocked was I that I was unable to move for some moments. I was aware of heavy objects bumping down the stairs. I called for help and tried to stand up. My eyes were growing accustomed to the darkness, and I could see the staircase going down into gloom.

Then I heard Mrs. Laud shouting from below. "What's wrong?"

I called out, "I'm here, Mrs. Laud. I've fallen."

"I'll come up. . . ."

I sat there waiting, grateful for my narrow escape. I should have had a very bad fall if I had not found the banister in time.

Mrs. Laud appeared. "Let me help you, Mrs. Madden."

I stood up gingerly, and she half dragged me back into the gallery. "I saw the open door," I said. "I'd no idea it was there."

109

"There's a stairway between this floor and the one below. It hasn't been used for years. How do you feel?"

"Stiff and sore and rather shaken."

"Perhaps I should help you to your room."

"I just want to stay here for a moment and think. Mrs. Laud, you say no one has used that staircase for years. But someone has been using it lately—someone who has been playing the spinet. I think that today, whoever it was left the door open to lure me down there."

"Oh no, Mrs. Madden, he wouldn't go as far as that."

"He? Who?"

"Whoever is playing these tricks with the—"

"I have got to get to the bottom of this, Mrs. Laud. I'm going to see what is actually on that staircase."

I lit a candle, went to the door, and peered down. I could see a huddle of boxes on the lower stairs.

"We'd better clear it out and open it," I said. "I don't like the idea of secret places."

And as I was speaking, I knew that someone had put boxes on that staircase to trip me, someone who had hoped that I would have an accident. Someone who wished me out of the way.

I SUFFERED little physical effect from the adventure, and I rode into town next morning.

I said to Joss, "Did you know there was a staircase connecting the gallery with the lower floor?"

His expression did not change as he said, "Oh yes, I remember. I used to play hide-and-seek there a lot as a boy."

"I discovered it yesterday."

"We ought to open it and use it."

"That's what I thought," I said. "Did you ever play the spinet?"

"As a matter of fact, I did. But I haven't touched it for years. I expect it's out of tune. We ought to get someone to come and have a look at it."

How could he be so calm? There were people in town who suspected him of murdering Ezra—Mrs. Laud had hinted at it—and now the other encumbrance had to be removed.

My death must appear to be natural. Joss was a great power in Fancy Town, but even he would have to be careful how he committed murder.

THE NEXT MORNING one of the maids brought a letter for me. I was astonished, because we collected our mail in Fancy Town, and for a letter to be delivered at the house was unheard-of.

"How did it come?" I asked, turning it over in my hand.

"One of the servants found it lying in the hall, Mrs. Madden."

The writing on the envelope was vaguely familiar. I opened it and read:

My dear Mrs. Madden,

I am riding in late tonight to drop this letter at Peacocks. I must see you alone and in secret. My inquiries have revealed so much that it would be very unwise for us to meet openly at this stage. You are in danger. So am I. Can you meet me tomorrow— that will be the day you get this letter—at three o'clock? The best meeting place would be Grover's Gully. I suggest that we meet in the underground chambers of the mine.

Please don't show this letter to anyone. That's very important. You will understand the reason when we meet.

Sincerely,
Jeremy Dickson

The words danced before my eyes. It sounded wildly dramatic, but then so was everything connected with the Green Flash. Of course I would do it. I was not afraid, although the mine was said to be haunted. I had always liked and trusted Jeremy Dickson.

Early that afternoon I took a candle and matches from my room. I would need the candle to find my way through the passages. Then I set out, confident that no one had seen me leave.

The sun was high in the sky—a white blazing light—and as I rode I left a cloud of dust behind me. The song of cicadas filled the air, and overhead the inevitable kookaburras laughed together.

I went through the pass to the mine. There was no sign of anyone. I looked at my watch. It was five minutes to three. Jeremy must be in the underground chambers already, although I wondered where he had hidden his mount. I slipped off Wattle, tethered her to a bush, and went to the mine.

I descended the rusty iron ladder; it had not been used for a very long time. I reached the bottom and stepped into a cavern. It led into another, and from that several passages had been hewn out of the rock. "I'm here," I called softly.

There was no answer.

111

I lighted my candle and started to explore the first chamber, but I had only taken a few steps when the flame flickered and went out. I relighted it, but it went out again.

I could not understand what was wrong. The passage turned at right angles and I was in complete darkness.

A sudden cold fear possessed me. Jeremy had not written that letter. I had only seen his handwriting once or twice. It would be easy for someone to copy it in order to deceive me.

Someone had lured me here. I would know who very soon. . . . What a fool I had been to step right into the trap.

"No, Joss," I said aloud. "Oh no, Joss . . . not you."

I had never known fear like this. It was the strangeness of everything, the darkness closing in on me . . . and most of all the silence, the terrible silence. Get out, I commanded myself. But an odd lethargy was creeping over me.

I stumbled through the passage to a faint shaft of light, but I could scarcely move, and then I slowly sank to the ground.

JOSS was holding me in his arms.

"So it *was* you," I murmured. "You've come to kill me."

Joss did not answer, but I could vaguely hear voices and I realized that I was lying on the ground outside the mine. I heard Joss say, "Don't crowd round. Give her air."

I heard him say "Jessica" in a tone he had never used before, half reproachful, half tender. Then he lifted me into a buggy and drove me home.

He put me down on my bed. I was only half conscious, but I was aware that he bent down and kissed my forehead.

When I opened my eyes he was sitting by my bed. He smiled at me.

"It's all right," he said. "I got you out in time."

I closed my eyes again, not wanting to know more just then. I wanted merely to revel in the knowledge that he had saved me and that he cared about what happened to me.

IT WAS DARK when I awoke. There were candles in the room and Joss was still sitting by my bed.

"You did a very foolish thing," he said. He was the old Joss again.

"I was going to meet Jeremy Dickson."

"I saw his letter. Lilias found it in your room. She doesn't

112

believe he wrote it. But, thank God, she had the sense to bring it to me without delay. I went straight to the mine."

"He was not there. And I began to feel so strange."

"You felt strange because you were poisoned. Jeremy Dickson sent you into that mine because he knew just what would happen. People hereabouts know that unused mines have pockets of poisonous gases. You should have noticed that your candle didn't stay alight."

"I did."

"That was a warning. It meant . . . get out quickly."

There was silence for a few moments, then he said, "When I brought you out, you said, 'So it was you, Joss. . . . You've come to kill me.' Did you really believe *that* of me?"

"Why shouldn't I believe it? You got rid of Ezra. I thought it was my turn. . . ."

He stared at me incredulously. "This farce has gone on long enough." He took me by the shoulders and kissed me.

"Joss," I began, "there's so much . . ."

But neither of us wanted explanations then. At length, he said, "Ben was right. I realized that pretty soon."

"Why didn't you say so?"

"I was too proud," he replied. "I wanted it to come from you. Many times at night I've come to your bedroom door."

"I know. I heard you. I thought you wanted to murder me."

"You're crazy," he retorted. "I have a lot to say to you. But just now you've had a shock, and you need to rest."

"Will you stay with me?"

"I will, but you must lie still. Just think of two foolish people who have said goodbye to their folly and are now going to wake up and live."

I felt light-headed, as I had in the mine—but with a difference. This was not the delirium of fear, but of joy. I must have slept, for it was midmorning when I awoke. Joss was sitting by my bed.

"Is it really true that you care about me?" I asked.

"It's the truest thing that ever happened."

"Yet you were planning to go to England with Isa Bannock."

"When I go to England you're coming with me."

"Why did you pretend . . . ?"

"Because I wanted to goad you. I wanted you to show some feeling for *me*."

"You seemed so involved with her."

"I've only been involved with one woman since I married. The rest was pretence, to try to break through her indifference."

"You gave Isa a magnificent opal."

"I gave it to her because I knew you'd hate it. I thought it might show you how foolishly you were acting and arouse some feeling in you. I thought it might be a step towards sanity. . . ."

"Rather an expensive step."

"Anything that brought about that state couldn't have been too expensive." Then he turned to me and kissed me fiercely. "Now I want you to stay quietly in the house for the rest of the day."

"Where are you going?"

"To find Jeremy Dickson. I want to know the meaning of this."

"I cannot believe Jeremy wrote that letter. Why should he want me dead? It doesn't make sense."

"That's what we have to find out. I've sent people to look for him. I'm going off now, and taking Jimson with me."

"Do you think he had anything to do with the purse?"

"What purse?"

"Ezra's. I found it buried in the orchard and later someone took it from my room."

He was puzzled. I had an idea that he thought the poisonous gases had made me a little light-headed.

He said, "We'll talk about that later. I just wanted to make sure you were all right before I went. I'm going to leave you in Mrs. Laud's care. I'll be back before sundown."

Then he took me into his arms and held me as though he would never let me go. He said, "If Ben is looking, I reckon he's laughing and saying, 'I told you so.'"

Chapter VI

I rose and dressed in a leisurely way. I was still feeling a little dazed. Mrs. Laud came to my room to offer me a cup of tea.

"Come up when you're ready," she said. "I'll put the kettle on."

Within five minutes I was knocking at her door.

"Do come in. It's all ready." I sat down in the chair she had pulled up to the table and sipped the refreshing tea. Her workbox was open and a piece of needlework lay beside it.

115

"Oh, Mrs. Madden, what bad luck you've had lately. I'd like to know what that Jeremy Dickson was up to. How's the tea?"

"It's very good, thank you."

"We're regular tea drinkers out here . . . every bit as much as they are at home. Let me give you another cup."

"Thank you, Mrs. Laud."

"Do you feel rather sleepy?"

"I feel a little . . . strange."

"I thought you did. The house is quiet, isn't it? We're the only ones here. Everybody's gone on this wild goose chase. All except two of the girls, and I said they could ride into town and get some goods for me. They're both friendly with gougers there." She chuckled. "I reckon they won't hurry back." She was watching me intently, and there was a strange gleam in her eyes.

"I'm going to show you something before you go," she said.

"Show me something . . . before I go . . . where?"

"There's a little secret drawer in my workbox. You remember the treasure hunt? Ezra knew. I could see from the look in his eyes that something had led him to my workbox."

I tried to stand up, but I couldn't. It seemed as though my legs were not part of my body.

"Don't try to go yet. You'll want to see this. I've had it since Mr. Henniker went away. He couldn't have been far out at sea when I found it. Mr. Henniker had a way of looking at that picture and laughing to himself, and it struck me that there was something special about it. So I paid particular attention to it, and I found the hidden spring."

I said, "You found the Green Flash at Sunset, Mrs. Laud. Are you telling me that you have had it all the time?"

She started to laugh. A change had come over her. She was no longer the mild housekeeper grateful to have found shelter for herself and her family all those years. Someone else looked out at me from those wild eyes. She was possessed.

She went on. "I shall never forget the moment when I found it, and it burst on me . . . all that brilliance, all that power. At first I was just going to have it in my room and look at it. I used to wake up in the night and remember I had it. I'd get out of bed and look at it. And then I saw that the Green Flash would give me anything I wanted. There's something in it, something alive . . . a living god. Do you remember Aladdin's lamp? Well, it's like that."

"Show me the stone, Mrs. Laud," I said quietly.

She fumbled in her workbox. Her mouth twitched and her eyes blazed. I thought, She really is mad. The Green Flash has driven her mad.

Her fingers shook as she unwrapped a mass of cottonwool. Then she took something in her hands and crooned over it as a mother might over a baby. She leaned across the table, and there it lay in all its fabulous glory—the stone which had shaped my destiny.

It is impossible to put into words the qualities of that magnificent stone. It was large . . . larger than I had expected it to be; and even with my sparse knowledge I knew that it was perfect in every way. It was the deep blue of a tropical sea and the lighter blue of a cloudless sky, with glints of red like sunlight breaking over the sea. But this does not convey the utter fascination, the aura, the living quality. It had a power, that stone. I was feeling more and more hazy, and I could not stop myself reaching out to take it.

"Oh, no you don't," said Mrs. Laud. "I'm only showing it to you, that's all. I thought you should see it before you died."

"Before . . . I died . . . ?"

"Feel sleepy, don't you? I put something in your tea.. It won't hurt. A nice peaceful sleep, that's all it will be. Look at my hands. They're strong. You've got a little neck, and I know just where to press. But I'll wait until you're fast asleep."

I could feel the hair rising on my scalp, and it was because she spoke in such a matter-of-fact way. I was alone in the house with a madwoman.

I wondered if I could make a dash for the door, but my limbs were already leaden. She was looking down at her hands . . . those hands which were waiting to strangle me . . . but not till I slept, so I must not sleep. I must find some way of outwitting her.

I said, "You play the spinet well, Mrs. Laud."

It was eerie—the way she slipped from the personality of the malevolent murderess to that of the homely housekeeper.

"Oh, yes. Mr. Henniker told me about this other Jessica. I guessed she was your mother. He had this fancy about her coming back. I didn't like that much, because I was fond of Mr. Henniker myself. So I played for him and he said it reminded him of her."

"And then you played for me?"

"You were prying; you were looking for the Green Flash. I saw

117

you and Mr. Madden take down *The Pride of the Peacock*. I wanted Mr. Madden for Lilias. I guessed Mr. Henniker would leave him the Green Flash, and then it would be partly hers. But then you came. It was mine and I wanted to keep it."

"You've been getting it to work for you, have you?"

She nodded. "When Mr. Paling visited the house, I went into the stables and meddled with the wheel of the buggy. Then he had his accident and Jimson had his job. You see, the Flash puts notions into your head."

"So you lured me to the gallery."

"The Flash is clever. It never does anything without reason. I wanted you to tell people that you were afraid . . . because you thought your husband wanted you out of the way. I knew how things were . . . separate bedrooms, and Isa Bannock."

"So you arranged for me to have an accident, and if I were killed you would have seen that my husband was suspected?"

"It was hardly likely that a fall down those stairs would have been the end of you. But it would have stopped your prying for a bit. Lilias spoiled it. She got hysterical about my playing the spinet, and she and Jimson tried to stop me. They were always watching me. They didn't know I had the Flash, of course; but they thought I'd changed and they got frightened."

I had to stay awake and keep her talking, so I said, "You killed Ezra Bannock?"

"Yes, I did. I waited for him at Grover's Gully, and I shot him and buried him there. He'd have stayed hidden for years if it hadn't been for that horse."

"And the letter from Jeremy Dickson?"

"I heard him tell you he was trying to track down the Green Flash. I copied his writing from his acceptance to the treasure hunt, and I think I did well. And Lilias, my own daughter, stopped it. She was prying in your room because she was jealous of you and Jeremy. Well, she found the letter and she swore it wasn't his writing. She took the letter to Mr. Madden."

Mrs. Laud looked as though she were going to burst into tears. "I could see Mr. Madden wasn't going to let it rest. Someone had threatened *you*, and he's like Mr. Henniker. He'll go on and on until he gets to the bottom of things . . . and I've got to stop him."

"You will never be able to."

118

She looked cunning. "The Flash has the answer. The Flash always has the answer. It's only when I don't let myself listen that I go wrong . . . like burying that purse. I took it because I wanted them to think it was a robbery. I should have thrown it away in the bush. So I won't act without the Flash again."

O God, I prayed, help me to keep awake.

"It won't work, Mrs. Laud," I said. "If you kill me, you'll be exposed as a murderess."

"You'll disappear," she said. She laughed, and it was a demoniacal laughter that sent cold shivers down my spine.

Oh, where are you, Joss? I wondered.

Mrs. Laud said, "Everything is ready. I shall bury you in the garden, where no one will think to look. I shall hide your travelling bag and some of your clothes. I shall tell them that you have the Green Flash, that you showed it to me, that I tried to persuade you to give it up. That you've gone away with the Flash."

"It wouldn't be possible. Unless you are going to kill Wattle and bury her too."

"Oh no. I'll say that someone came for you. He brought horses and you rode away together."

"Jeremy Dickson, I suppose."

"That could do for a start. Why don't you go to sleep? It's better if you do. Then we can get it over with."

"I'm not going to sleep."

"You must. You can't help it."

She was wildly fanatical. I saw the greed in her eyes and I thought, This stone has done this to her. This stone ruined my mother's life, and now I may well die because of it. There is evil in it and it has taken possession of this woman.

I gripped the table. Waves of weariness swept over me. I thought of Joss coming back and finding me gone. Would he really believe that I had gone off with Jeremy Dickson, taking the Green Flash with me?

The minutes were ticking by. Mrs. Laud was getting worried. "I don't understand this. You should be off by now."

"My willpower is stronger than your drug, Mrs. Laud."

"Why," she said, "anyone would think *you* had the Flash."

"It is mine by right. I share it with my husband. Perhaps it knows that." I saw the fear in her eyes, and I went on. "The Flash won't hurt me, because I'm the true owner. It's mine, Mrs. Laud."

She still held the Green Flash in her hands. "I'll never give her up . . . never," she screamed.

"Look, Mrs. Laud, it's only an opal . . . silica deposited at some time in the rock. How can you attach special powers to that?"

She stared at me blankly.

"It's done you a great deal of harm," I said. O thank you, God, I prayed. I'm fighting off my sleepiness. I'm going to live if I keep talking. "You've become obsessed by a stone . . . you've built all this up in your mind, but it doesn't really exist."

"How dare you call it just a stone! *You* haven't lived with it. You haven't held it in your hands."

I was alert suddenly. I thought I heard sounds below. Someone was coming. I looked at her, but she was staring at the opal.

The door was flung open. It was Joss. Jimson was with him. Jimson cried out in a voice of anguish, "Mother!"

She stood up, clutching the stone. "You've brought him back," she screamed. "My own son. . . ."

Joss's eyes were on me, and I stood up and tottered towards him, for now the waves of drowsiness were too much to resist.

Joss caught me in his arms. He held me against him, and I was content to stay there. I heard Jimson pleading, "Mother, I had to. I knew something was wrong."

Joss said, "Give me what you have in your hand, Mrs. Laud."

There was an agonized scream and then a silence which seemed to go on and on.

When I awoke from my drugged sleep, I remembered every intonation of her voice, every expression on her face. She had cried out that she would never give up the Green Flash, and before the men could stop her she had dashed herself onto the terrace.

When they picked her up from the stones below she was dead, but still clutching the Green Flash in her hand.

SIX MONTHS later Joss and I went back to Oakland. Lilias married Jeremy Dickson before we sailed. She told me that she and Jimson had both realized that their mother was verging on madness, though they had not been aware that she had the Green Flash. When I had been lured to the mine, they became very suspicious; and that was why Jimson, when he had heard that I had been left alone with his mother, decided to tell Joss of his anxieties for my safety.

Lilias was in great distress, but I told her I understood perfectly. They had tried hard to protect their mother, who had done everything for them when they were children. She had come to Peacocks, had worked for Ben, and had hoped to marry him. But Ben did not want marriage, and she had been a very conventional woman. The situation had worried her a great deal. If Lilias had married Joss, she might have felt everything was worthwhile.

I was sorry for Jimson and Lilias, but Jeremy would comfort Lilias, and Jimson seemed to find a certain solace in his work.

I discussed the Green Flash with Joss, and it was one of the matters over which we were in disagreement. There were, of course, many matters over which we disagreed and somehow that gave a stimulus to our life together.

Joss liked to take the stone out and look at it. "You're getting obsessed," I accused him.

"Nonsense. There's only one thing I'm obsessed with. And you know very well it's you."

"Oh, Joss," I cried. "Obsessions don't last. There was a time when you were obsessed by Isa Bannock."

He was serious suddenly. "Forget Isa. It's over. I behaved as I did because you wouldn't have me. You scorned the peacock. Peacocks don't like that. They get spiteful."

"You gave her the Harlequin."

"I'm going to make up for it. I'm giving you something a thousand times more valuable. My share in the Green Flash."

"I've been meaning to speak to you about the Green Flash. I'm frightened of it."

"You! Frightened of a stone?"

"I'm not thinking of myself, but our family. I won't run risks. Some things are too precious to be put in jeopardy."

"Me? The child?"

I nodded. He was moved, I could see, so he laughed at me tenderly.

"What do you propose to do?" he asked.

"We'll present the Green Flash to a geological museum in London. People will be able to see it, and I'll cheat the evil in it, because it won't belong to anyone."

"So you're resigning all claim of my gift to you?"

"Your gift to me, Joss, is much more than a stone."

"Do you know, you're getting sentimental as you grow up."

I WANTED my baby to be born in Oakland Hall, and Joss was ready to humour my whim. I knew Ben would have been pleased.

Oakland itself had not changed. But Miriam had a child now. "She'll live to rue the day," said my grandmother. Xavier had married Lady Clara and was managing the Donningham land.

My grandmother was quite respectful to me and even took to Joss after the first few skirmishes. I think she recognized some power in him which would be impossible for her to subdue. And he had brought Oakland back to the family.

My son was born in the vaulted chamber where my ancestors had made their first appearances. This was the culmination of my happiness. I sat up in the big four-poster bed and looked out on those lawns which had mellowed for hundreds of years, and I had a feeling that I had come home.

Joss came and marvelled at the baby as though he couldn't believe the tiny creature was real. Then he turned to me. "It's good, eh?" he said.

"What?" I asked.

"Life," he answered. "Just life."

"It's good," I agreed. "And going to be better."

Victoria Holt

I invited Victoria Holt to meet me for lunch at a fashionable London restaurant. Resplendent in a veil and an elegant dress, Miss Holt made a stately, slightly intimidating entry. However, within seconds of seating herself at my table, she had lifted her veil and was chatting away, revealing herself as a friendly, humorous person.

Miss Holt's fantastic success may, or may not, have something to do with her stars. She is a Virgo, and although she does not believe in astrology—"not seriously"—she would not deny possessing her birth sign's finest attributes: prudence, orderliness, and dependability. Her work routine allows no rule bending. She never eats heavily or touches alcohol at lunchtime if she has to work afterwards—and she always has to work afterwards. Accordingly, she ordered a well-done minute steak and a glass of lime juice and soda.

When our food had arrived, she told me more about her routine. She works at her typewriter for two hours every morning, two hours every afternoon, and another hour every evening. In this way she never gets bored, and she also manages to produce five books a year.

Her novels are published under pseudonyms, of which Victoria Holt is probably the best known. These provide the privacy necessary to such a prolific writer. Well over thirty million copies of her books have been sold worldwide.

The Pride of the Peacock was inspired during one of Miss Holt's nine around-the-world trips. When the ocean liner put into Sydney harbour, a crippled girl and her family were waiting on the quayside. The girl had come to present her favourite author with a magnificent gift: an opal. The gem immediately started Miss Holt's imagination turning.

The opal is now encircled by diamonds and beautifully decorates the third finger of Miss Holt's right hand. It is just one of the rewards of being a world-famous, well-loved novelist.   N.D.B.

The Devil's Alternative

a condensation of the book by
Frederick Forsyth

Illustrated by Mitchell Hooks

Published by Hutchinson

In the Prime Minister's private office in Downing Street there was a long silence.

"I find the idea utterly repulsive," she said at last. "Do we have such vile equipment available?"

The British secret service man studied his fingertips. "I believe the specialist department may be able to lay its hands on that sort of thing," he said quietly.

This spellbinding story of how the Western World was forced to accept "The Devil's Alternative" is master-crafted by the author of those great bestsellers: *The Day of the Jackal*, and *The Odessa File*.

One

The castaway in the skiff would have been dead before sundown but for the sharp eyes of an Italian seaman called Mario. Even when he was spotted he had lapsed into unconsciousness, the exposed parts of his near-naked body grilled to second-degree burns by the relentless sun, and those parts submerged in sea-water in the bottom of the boat soft and white between the salt-sores like the limbs of a rotting goose.

Mario Curcio was the cook-steward on the *Garibaldi*, an amiable old rust-bucket out of Brindisi, thumping her way eastward through the Black Sea towards Cape Ince and on to Trabzon in the far eastern corner of the north shore of Turkey to pick up a cargo of almonds from Anatolia.

Just why Mario decided that morning in April 1982 to empty his bucket of potato peelings over the weather rail instead of through the garbage chute at the poop he could never explain. But perhaps to take a breath of fresh Black Sea air, he stepped out on deck and hurled his garbage to an indifferent but patient ocean. He turned away but after two steps he stopped, frowned, turned and walked back to the rail, puzzled and uncertain.

He shielded his eyes against the sun and gazed abaft the beam. He was sure he had seen something out there on the blue-green rolling swell between the ship and the coast of Turkey twenty miles to the south. Unable to see it now, he mounted the outside ladders to the bridge and peered again. Then he saw it, quite clearly, for half a second between the softly moving hills of water. He turned to the open wheelhouse door behind him and shouted

127

"*Capitano!*" Captain Vittorio Ingrao's radar had revealed an echo also, so the *Garibaldi* turned back to the spot where Mario had pointed. Then Captain Ingrao saw it, too.

The skiff was a light craft barely twelve feet long. There was a single thwart across it with a hole for the stepping of a mast. But either there had never been a mast, or it had been ill-secured and had gone overboard. With the *Garibaldi* stopped and wallowing in the swell, Captain Ingrao leaned on the bridge wing rail and watched Mario and the bosun set off in the motor lifeboat to bring the skiff alongside.

The man in the skiff was lying on his back in several inches of seawater. He was emaciated, bearded and unconscious, breathing in short gasps. As the sailors lifting him aboard touched his flayed shoulders and chest, he moaned.

The castaway was taken to the sickbay and Longhi the bosun gave him a shot of morphine to spare him pain. Mario, at his own request, was given time off to tend the man, whom he soon came to regard as his personal property, as a boy will take especial care of a puppy he has rescued from death.

Being Calabrians, Mario and Longhi knew a bit about sunburn and prepared the best salve in the world. Mario brought from his galley a fifty-fifty mixture of fresh lemon juice and wine vinegar in a basin, a light cotton cloth and a bowl of ice cubes. Soaking the cloth in the mixture and wrapping it round a dozen ice cubes, he gently pressed the pad to the worst areas where the ultra-violet rays had bitten through almost to the bone. Plumes of steam rose from the unconscious man as the freezing astringent drew the heat out of the scorched flesh. The man shuddered.

The bosun then joined his skipper on the afterdeck where the skiff had been hauled. "Nothing on the man," Longhi said. "No watch, no name tag. A pair of cheap underpants with no label. And his beard looks about ten days old."

"There's nothing on the skiff either," said Captain Ingrao. "No mast, no sail, no oars. No food and no water container. No name even. But it could have peeled off."

"A tourist from a beach resort, blown out to sea?" asked Longhi.

Ingrao shrugged. "Or a survivor from a small freighter. We'll be at Trabzon in two days. The Turkish authorities can solve that one when he wakes up and talks. Meanwhile let's get underway.

Oh, and we must cable our agent there and tell him what's happened. We'll need an ambulance when we dock."

Two days later the castaway, still barely conscious and unable to speak, was tucked up between white sheets in the small municipal hospital of Trabzon.

Mario had accompanied his castaway to the hospital, along with the ship's agent. After waiting an hour by the bedside, he had bade his unconscious friend farewell and returned to the *Garibaldi*. The following day the old Italian tramp steamer sailed.

Now three men stood by the castaway's bedside: a police officer, a doctor and a short, broad man in a civilian suit—Umit Erdal, Trabzon's sub-agent for Lloyd's. The *Garibaldi's* agent had thankfully passed the matter of the castaway over to him.

"He'll pull through," said the doctor, "but he's very sick. Heatstroke, second-degree sunburns, exposure, and by the look of it he hasn't eaten for days. The sailors probably saved his life by taking the heat out of the burns. Now it's between him and Allah."

The sick man's eyelids fluttered in the nut-brown, bearded face. Mr. Erdal cleared his throat, bent over the figure and spoke slowly in his best English: "What . . . is . . . your . . . name?"

The man groaned and moved his head from side to side. The Lloyd's man bent closer to listen. *"Zradzhenyi,"* the sick man murmured, *"Zradzhenyi."*

Erdal straightened. "He's not Turkish," he said, "but he seems to be called Zradzhenyi. What kind of country would that name come from?"

Both his companions shrugged. "I'll inform Lloyd's in London," said Erdal. "Maybe they'll have news of a missing vessel somewhere in the Black Sea."

The daily bible of the world's merchant marine fraternity is Lloyd's Shipping Index which gives the movements of the world's 30,000 active merchant vessels: name of ship, owner, flag of registry, year of build, tonnage, where last reported coming from, and where bound. This organ is published in Colchester, and to this place Umit Erdal regularly telexed the shipping movements into and out of Trabzon. On that day he added a small extra for the attention of the Lloyd's Shipping Intelligence unit.

The Intelligence unit checked its records to confirm that there were no recent reports of missing, sunk or overdue vessels in the Black Sea, and passed the paragraph to the editorial desk of the

Index. Here a sub-editor gave it a mention the following morning on the front page, including the name the castaway had given.

The piece in Lloyd's Shipping Index caught the sharp eye of a man in his early thirties who worked as senior clerk in a firm of chartered shipbrokers in the City of London. His colleagues knew him as Andrew Drake.

Having absorbed the paragraph, Drake went to the company boardroom where he consulted a chart of the world which showed prevailing wind and ocean current circulation. The winds in the Black Sea during spring and summer are predominantly from the north, and the currents screw anti-clockwise round this small ocean from the southern coast of the Ukraine in the far northwest of the Sea, down past the coasts of Romania and Bulgaria, then swing eastwards again into the shipping lanes between Istanbul and Cape Ince.

Drake did some calculations on a scratch pad. Two hours later he asked for a week's holiday, and it was agreed that he could take it, starting the following Monday, 3 May. He was mildly excited as he bought a return ticket from London to Istanbul. He had decided to buy the connecting ticket from Istanbul to Trabzon for cash in Istanbul.

He was excited because there just might be a chance that, after years of waiting, he had found the man he was looking for. Unlike the three men by the castaway's bedside two days earlier, he *did* know what country the word *zradzhenyi* came from. The man in the bed had been muttering the word "betrayed" in Ukrainian. Which could mean that the man was a refugee Ukrainian partisan. And the small skiff could well have set off from the delta of the River Dniester just southwest of Odessa. Andrew Drake, despite his anglicized name, was also a Ukrainian, and a fanatic.

On arriving in Trabzon, Drake called on Mr. Erdal, whose name he had obtained from a friend at Lloyd's on the grounds that he was taking a holiday on the Turkish coast and might need some assistance. Umit Erdal, seeing the letter of introduction, was happily unquestioning as to why his visitor should want to see the castaway in the local hospital. He wrote a letter of introduction to the hospital administrator, and shortly after Drake was shown into the one-bed ward where the man lay.

Erdal had already told him that the man spent much of the time sleeping, and had so far said absolutely nothing. When Drake entered the room the invalid was lying on his back, eyes closed. Drake drew up a chair to the bedside, and stared at the man's haggard face. Then he leaned forward and said clearly in the sick man's ear: *"Shche ne vmerla Ukraina."*

The words mean "Ukraine lives on". They are the first words of the Ukrainian national anthem, banned by the Russian masters, and would be instantly recognizable to a Ukrainian nationalist.

The sick man's eyes flicked open. After several seconds he asked in Ukrainian, "Who are you?"

"A Ukrainian, like yourself," said Drake. "I am British by birth, son of a Ukrainian father and an English mother. But in my heart I'm as Ukrainian as you are."

The man in the bed stared stubbornly at the ceiling.

"I could show you my passport, issued in London, but a *Chekisti* could produce one if he wanted, to try and trick you." Drake had used the slang term for a Soviet secret policeman. "But you are not in the Ukraine any more, and there are no *Chekisti* here. You were picked up by an Italian ship and landed here at Trabzon, in Turkey. You are in the West. You made it."

The man's eyes were on his face now, wanting to believe. Drake nodded across the small room to the window, beyond which the sounds of traffic could be heard. "The KGB can dress up hospital staff to look like Turks," he said, "but they cannot change a whole city for one man. Can you make it to the window?"

A few moments later, standing at the window beside the castaway, Drake said, "The cars are Austins imported from England, Peugeots from France and Volkswagens from West Germany. The words on the billboards are in Turkish."

The man put the back of one hand against his mouth and chewed at the knuckles. He blinked rapidly. "I made it," he said.

"Yes," said Drake, "by a miracle you made it."

"My name," said the castaway, "is Miroslav Kaminsky. I come from Ternopol. I was the leader of a group of partisans."

Over the next hour the story came out. Kaminsky and six others from the Ternopol area had decided to strike back at the ruthless russification of their land that had intensified in the seventies and early eighties. In six months of operations they had ambushed and killed two low-level Party secretaries and a plainclothes KGB agent. Then had come the betrayal.

131

Whoever had talked, he too had died in the hail of fire as the KGB special troops had closed in on the country cottage where the group was meeting to plan its next operation. Only Kaminsky had escaped, running like an animal through the undergrowth, hiding by day in barns and woodland, moving by night, heading south towards the coast. Living off potatoes from the fields, he had sought refuge in the swampy country of the Dniester estuary southwest of Odessa. Finally, coming by night on a small fishing hamlet he had stolen a skiff with a stepped mast and a small sail. He had never been in a sailing boat before, and knew nothing of the sea. Holding on and praying, he had let the skiff run before the wind, southwards by the stars and the sun.

By pure luck the tiny sliver of wood which contained him had slipped past the Soviet patrol boats and the coastal radar sweeps until he was out of range. Then he was lost, somewhere between Romania and Crimea, heading south. The storm caught him unawares. He had capsized, spending the night using his last reserves of strength clinging to the upturned hull. By morning he had righted the skiff and crawled inside. His clothes, which he had taken off to let the night wind cool his skin, were gone. So also were his few raw potatoes, the bottle of fresh water, the sail and the rudder. The pain came shortly after sunrise as the heat of the day increased. Oblivion came on the third day after the storm. When he regained consciousness he was in a bed, listening to voices he thought were Bulgarian. For six days he had kept his eyes closed and his mouth shut.

Andrew Drake heard him out with a song in his heart. He had found the man he had waited years for. "I'll go and see the Swiss consul in Istanbul and try to obtain temporary travel documents for you from the Red Cross," he said. "I can probably get you to England, at least on a temporary visa. Then we can try for asylum. I'll return in a few days."

By the door he paused. "You can't go back, you know," he told Kaminsky. "But with your help, I can. It's what I've always wanted."

On 16 May, Andrew Drake flew back to Trabzon from Istanbul with travel papers for Kaminsky. He had extended his leave after a telephone call to London and a row with the broking firm he worked for, but it was worth it. For through Kaminsky he could fulfil the single burning ambition of his life.

THE SOVIET EMPIRE, despite its monolithic appearance, has two Achilles' heels. One is the feeding of its 250 millions. The other is "the nationalities question". In the fifteen republics ruled from Moscow there are several score of identifiable non-Russian nations, the biggest and perhaps the most nationally conscious being the Ukraine. By 1982 the Great Russian state numbered only 120 millions out of the USSR total of 250 millions. The next most populous and rich was the Ukraine with 70 millions; which was one reason why the Politburo had singled it out for ruthless russification. The second reason lay in its history.

The Ukraine has always traditionally been divided into two, which has been its downfall. The eastern part is more russified, having dwelt under the tsars for centuries, while during those same centuries the Western part, stretching from Kiev westwards to the Polish border, was part of the old Austro-Hungarian empire. Its spiritual orientation was and remains more western.

When Hitler swept into it, in 1941, some hoped for concessions from Moscow if they fought the Germans; others mistakenly thought Free Ukraine lay through the defeat of Moscow by Berlin, and therefore joined the Ukrainian Division, which fought in German uniform against the Red Army. They all lost; Stalin won, and pushed his empire even further westwards.

Stephen Drach, the father of Andrew Drake, had joined the German Ukrainian Division as a radio operator and was captured by the British in Austria in 1945. Sent to work as a farm labourer in Norfolk, he tumbled a Land Army girl and she became pregnant. Marriage was the answer, and on compassionate grounds he was excused the compulsory repatriation that returned two million "victims of Yalta" to the mercies of Stalin. He was allowed to stay. Freed from farm labour, he used the knowledge of radio he had gained during the war to set up a small repair shop in Bradford, a centre for Britain's 30,000 Ukrainians.

The first baby died in infancy; a second son, christened Andriy, was born in 1950, and learned Ukrainian at his father's knee. He learned too of his father's land, and he imbibed his father's loathing of Russians. But the father died in a road crash when the boy was twelve; his mother, tired of her husband's endless evenings with fellow exiles round the sitting-room fire, talking in a language she could never understand, anglicized both their names to Drake, and Andriy to Andrew.

His rebirth came at university. There were other Ukrainians there, and he became fluent again in his father's language. These were the late sixties, and the brief renaissance of literature and poetry back in the Ukraine had come and gone, most of the leading lights by then doing slave labour in the camps.

With Andrew's love for the land of his dead father came a matching loathing for those he saw as its persecutors. His hatred grew until, for him, the personification of all evil in the world was simply called KGB.

He had enough sense of reality to eschew the crude, raw nationalism of the older exiles, their divisions between West and East Ukrainians; the language nationalists for whom speaking in the tongue of their fathers was enough; the debating nationalists who talked, but did nothing. Instead, Drake, well-behaved and aloof, came to London and took a clerking job. In his spare time, he quietly put together a small group of men who felt as he did: traced them, met them, befriended them, swore a common oath with them, and bade them be patient. For Andriy Drach had a secret dream that one day he would strike one single gigantic blow against the men of Moscow that would shake them as they had never been shaken before. He would penetrate the walls of their power and meet them right inside their fortress.

His dream was one step nearer fulfilment with the finding of Kaminsky, and he was a determined and excited man as he handed Kaminsky the travel papers for England and asked for his help.

"I don't know, Andriy," Miroslav Kaminsky said. "Despite everything you have done, I just don't know if I can trust you that much. I'm sorry."

"Miroslav, everything I've told you about me is the truth. As you cannot go back, you must let me go in your place. But I must have contacts there. If you know of anybody at all . . . ."

Kaminsky finally agreed. "There are two men," he said. "They were not blown away when my group was destroyed, and no one knew of them. I had met them only a few months earlier."

"But they are Ukrainians, and partisans?" asked Drake eagerly.

"Yes, they are Ukrainians. But that is not their primary motivation. Their fathers, like mine, have been for ten years in the labour camps, but for a different reason. They are Jews."

"But do they hate Moscow as much as you or I?" asked Drake.

134

"Yes, they do," replied Kaminsky. "Their inspiration is the Jewish Defence League. Their philosophy, like ours, is to strike back; not to take any more persecution lying down."

"Then let me make contact with them," urged Drake.

The following morning Drake flew back to London with the names and addresses in Lvov of the two young Jewish partisans. Within a fortnight he had subscribed to a package tour run by Intourist for early July, visiting Kiev, Ternopol and Lvov. He also quit his job and withdrew his life savings in cash. Unnoticed by anyone, Andrew Drake, formerly Andriy Drach, was going to his private war—against the Kremlin.

Two

The main British embassy building in Moscow is a fine old pre-Revolution mansion facing north on Maurice Thorez Embankment, staring straight across the Moscow River at the south façade of the Kremlin wall. But the commercial section does not have the good fortune to dwell in this elegant cream and gold mansion. It functions in a drab complex of post-war office blocks two miles away on Kutuzovsky Prospekt. The compound also contains apartment buildings for diplomatic personnel from a score of foreign embassies.

Harold Lessing was one of the three first secretaries in the commercial section of the embassy. On one sunny morning in mid-May he sat at his desk as pale as a sheet and feeling extremely sick. His office was on the top floor of the commercial office block. When he finally fainted at around ten thirty his secretary summoned the commercial counsellor, who had two young attachés assist Lessing, by this time groggily conscious again, across the car park and up to his apartment, a hundred yards away.

Simultaneously the counsellor telephoned the main embassy, informed the head of chancery and asked for the embassy doctor to be sent over. Having examined Lessing, the doctor conferred with the commercial counsellor. To his surprise the senior man cut him short and suggested they drive over to the main embassy to consult jointly with the head of chancery, who took them to a special room in the embassy building which was secure from bugging: something the commercial section definitely was not.

"It's a bleeding ulcer," the medico told the two diplomats.

"Will it require hospitalization?" asked the head of chancery.

"Oh, yes, indeed," said the doctor. "I think I can get him admitted here within a few hours."

There was a brief silence as the two diplomats exchanged glances. Unlike the doctor, both men were aware of Lessing's real function in the embassy. "That will not be possible in Lessing's case," said the head of chancery smoothly. "He'll have to be flown to Helsinki on the afternoon shuttle. Will you ensure that he can make it?"

Then the doctor realized why they had had to drive two miles to have this conversation. Lessing must be the head of the Secret Intelligence Service operation in Moscow. "Ah, yes. Well, now. He's shocked and has lost probably a pint of blood. I've given him a tranquillizer. If he's escorted all the way, yes, he can make Helsinki. But he'll need immediate entry into hospital. I'll go with him myself to be sure."

"Splendid," said the head of chancery.

FOR YEARS it has been customary in newspapers, magazines and books to refer to the headquarters of Britain's Secret Intelligence Service, or the SIS, or MI6, as being at a certain office block in the borough of Lambeth in London. It is a custom that causes quiet amusement to the staff members of "the firm", as the SIS is more colloquially known in the community of such organizations, for the Lambeth address is a front. The real home of the world's most secret Secret Intelligence Service is a modern steel and concrete block a stone's throw from one of the capital's principal railway stations.

It was in his top-floor elegantly-furnished suite with its tinted windows looking out towards Big Ben and the Houses of Parliament across the river that Sir Nigel Irvine, director-general of the SIS, received the news of Lessing's illness. The call came from the head of personnel. Sir Nigel listened carefully.

"How long will he be off?" he asked at length.

"Several months at least."

"Pity," mused the director-general. "We shall have to replace him rather fast." His capacious memory recalled that Lessing had been running two useful Russian agents, low-level staffers in the Red Army and the Soviet foreign ministry respectively. Finally he said, "Get me a short list of possibles for his replacement by tonight, please."

It was dark by the time three files arrived on Sir Nigel's desk. He spent an hour poring over them but the selection seemed fairly obvious. Finally he telephoned the head of personnel.

"It looks like Munro, wouldn't you say?" he asked.

"I would have thought so."

"What's he like? Give me the personal touch."

"Secretive."

"Good."

"A bit of a loner."

"Blast."

"It's a question of his Russian," said the head of personnel. "The other two have good, working Russian. Munro can pass for one. He doesn't normally. Speaks to them in strongly accented moderate Russian. When he drops that he can blend right in."

Sir Nigel grunted. "Very well. Munro it is. Where is he now?"

"Instructing. At Beaconsfield."

"Have him here tomorrow afternoon. I'll have the foreign office approve the appointment as Lessing's replacement."

By mid-afternoon the following day Adam Munro was closeted in the secure library beneath the firm's HQ building, beginning to bore through a pile of buff folders. He had five days to commit to memory enough background material to enable him to take over from Harold Lessing as the firm's "legal resident" in Moscow.

On 31 May he flew to Moscow. To all but an informed few he was just a professional diplomat and the hurried replacement for Harold Lessing. To be only a first secretary in the commercial section at the relatively advanced age of forty-six was explained by his late entrance into the diplomatic corps. He met most of the staff and was taken to a round of diplomatic parties to meet other Western diplomats. He also had a conference with his opposite number at the American embassy. "Business," the CIA man confirmed to him, was "quiet."

Munro kept his use of Russian to a formal, accented version both in front of his colleagues and when talking to officials. At one party two Soviet foreign ministry personnel had had a brief exchange in rapid, colloquial Russian a few feet away. He had understood it completely, and as it was mildly interesting, he had filed it to London.

137

On his tenth day he sat alone on a park bench in the sprawling Soviet Exhibition of Economic Achievements in the extreme northern outskirts of the capital. He was waiting to make first contact with the Red Army agent he had taken over from Lessing.

Munro had been born in 1936, the son of an Edinburgh doctor, and his boyhood through the war years had been conventional, untroubled and happy. He had attended Fettes Academy, one of Scotland's best schools. It was there that his senior languages master had detected in the lad an unusually acute ear for foreign languages. In 1954, with national service then obligatory, he had chosen to go into the army as a regular and secured a posting to his father's old regiment, the First Gordon Highlanders. Transferred to Cyprus he had been on operations against the EOKA—Greek Cypriot partisans—in the Troodos Mountains during that summer.

Sitting in a park in Moscow he could still see the farmhouse on a hill, in his mind's eye. They had spent half the night crawling up through the heather to surround the place. When dawn came, Munro was posted alone at the bottom of a steep escarpment behind the hilltop house. The main body of his platoon stormed the front of the farm just as dawn broke, coming up the shallower slope with the sun behind them.

On the other side of the hill he could hear the chattering of the Stens. By the first rays of the sun he could see two partisans come tumbling out of the rear windows in headlong flight. They came straight at him, where he crouched behind his fallen olive tree, their legs flying as they sought to keep their balance on the shale. One of them had what looked like a short, black stick in his hand. Even if he had shouted, he told himself later, they could not have stopped their momentum. But he did not. Training took over; he stood up as they reached a point fifty feet from him and loosed off two short, lethal bursts.

The force of the bullets lifted them both and slammed them onto the shale at the foot of the slope. As a blue plume of cordite smoke drifted away from the muzzle of his Sten, he moved forward to look down at them. He thought he might feel sick, or faint. There was nothing; just a dead curiosity. They were boys, younger than himself, and he was eighteen.

His sergeant came crashing through the olive grove. "Well done, laddie," he shouted. "You got 'em."

Munro looked down at the bodies of the boys who would never marry or have children, never dance a *bouzouki* or feel the warmth of the sun again. One of them was still clutching the black stick; it was a sausage. A piece of it hung out of his mouth. He had been having breakfast. Munro turned on the sergeant.

"You don't own me," he shouted. "You don't bloody own me. Nobody owns me but me."

The sergeant put the outburst down to first-kill nerves and failed to report it. Perhaps that was a mistake. For authority failed to notice that Adam Munro was not completely, not one hundred per cent, obedient. Not ever again.

Six months later he was urged to consider himself as potential officer material and was posted back to England. After officer-cadet training and his commissioning as a second lieutenant, it was suggested that because of his language facility he might like to apply for the Joint Services Russian language course at a camp called Little Russia at Bodmin in Cornwall. Within six months he emerged not merely fluent but virtually able to pass for a Russian.

In 1957 he left the army for he had decided he wanted to be a foreign correspondent. He had seen a few of them in Cyprus and thought he would prefer their job to his present one. At the age of twenty-one he joined *The Scotsman* in his native Edinburgh as a cub reporter and two years later moved to London where he was taken on by Reuters, the international news agency. In the summer of 1960 he was posted to the Reuters office in West Berlin. That was the summer before the Wall went up, and within three months he had met Valentina, the woman he now realized to have been the only one he had ever really loved in his life.

A man sat down beside him and coughed. Munro jerked himself out of his reverie. Teaching his craft one week, he told himself, and forgetting the basic rules a fortnight later. Never slacken attention before a meet.

The Russian looked at him uncertainly, but Munro wore the necessary polka-dot tie. Slowly the Russian put a cigarette in his mouth, eyes on Munro. Corny, but it still worked; Munro took out his lighter and held the flame to the cigarette tip. "Ronald collapsed at his desk two weeks ago," he said softly and calmly. "Ulcers, I'm afraid. I am Michael. I've been asked to take over from him. Oh, and perhaps you can help me; is it true that the Ostankino TV tower is the highest structure in Moscow?"

139

The Russian officer in plainclothes exhaled smoke and relaxed. The words were exactly the ones established by Lessing, whom he had known only as Ronald. "Yes," he replied. "It is five hundred and forty metres high."

He had a folded newspaper in his hand, which he laid on the seat between them. Munro's folded raincoat slipped off his knees to the ground. He retrieved it, refolded it and placed it on top of the newspaper. The two men ignored each other for ten minutes, while the Russian smoked. Finally he rose and stubbed the butt into the ground, bending as he did so. "A fortnight's time," muttered Munro. "The men's toilet under 'G' block at the New State Circus. During the clown Popov's act."

The Russian moved away. Munro surveyed the scene calmly for ten minutes. No one showed interest. He scooped up the mackintosh, newspaper, and the buff envelope inside it, and returned by metro to Kutuzovsky Prospekt. The envelope contained an up-to-date list of Red Army officer postings.

Three

While Adam Munro was changing trains at Revolution Square that morning, a convoy of sleek, black Zil limousines was sweeping through the Borovitsky Gate in the Kremlin wall. The Soviet Politburo—the tiny, exclusive group of thirteen members heading the Central Committee of the Communist Party of the Soviet Union—the real government of the USSR—was about to begin a meeting that would change history.

The Kremlin is a triangular compound protected on all three sides by a fifty-foot wall studded by eighteen towers and penetrated by four gates. The southern two thirds of this triangle is the tourist area of cathedrals, halls and palaces of the long-dead tsars. At the mid-section is a cleared swathe of macadam, patrolled by guards, an invisible dividing line across which tourists may not step. The cavalcade of hand-built limousines that morning purred across this open space towards a large, rectangular building in the northern part of the Kremlin.

The southern end of the building is the old arsenal, a museum for antique weaponry. But just behind the old arsenal the interior walls are blocked off. To reach the upper floors, one must go along the side of the building and be admitted through a high wrought-iron barrier that spans the narrow space between the arsenal building and the adjacent building of the council of ministers. The limousines swept through the guarded wrought-iron gates and came to rest beside the entrance to the secret upper building.

On the third floor, overlooking an inner courtyard and screened from prying eyes, is the room where the Politburo meets every Thursday morning to hold sway over 250 million Soviet citizens and scores of millions more who like to think they dwell outside the boundaries of the Russian empire.

The three arms used to implement this rule are: the Red Army, which includes the navy and air force; the Committee of State Security, or KGB secret police; and the Party organizations section of the general secretariat of the Central Committee, controlling the Party cadres in every place from the arctic to the hills of Iran, from the fringes of Brunswick in central Germany to the shores of the Sea of Japan.

The room in which the Politburo meets is decorated in the heavy marble favoured by the Party bosses, but dominated by a long table topped in green baize. The table is T-shaped. The meeting that morning of 10 June 1982 was unusual, for Politburo members had received no agenda, just a summons. And the men grouped at the table sensed that something of dangerous importance was afoot.

Seated at the centre of the head of the T in his usual chair was the chief of them all, Maxim Rudin, president of the USSR. His real power came to him through his additional title of secretary-general of the Communist Party of the USSR. As such, he was also chairman of the Central Committee and of the Politburo.

At seventy-one, he was craggy, brooding and immensely cunning; had he not been the latter he would never have occupied the chair that had once supported Stalin, Malenkov, Khrushchev and Brezhnev. To his left and right along the head of the T he was flanked by four secretaries from his own personal secretariat, men loyal to him above all else. Behind him, at each corner of the north wall of the chamber, was a small table. At one sat two stenographers, taking down every word in shorthand. At the other, as a counter-check, two men hunched over a tape recorder. There was a spare recorder to take over during spool-changes.

The other twelve members of the Politburo ranged themselves, six a side, down the stem of the T-shaped table, facing jotting-pads, carafes of water, ashtrays. At the far end of the table—the base of the T—was one single chair. The Politburo men checked numbers to make sure no one was missing. For the empty seat was the penal chair, sat in only by a man on his last appearance in that room, a man forced to listen to his own denunciation by his former colleagues, a man facing disgrace, ruin, and once, not long ago, death at the Black Wall of the Lubyanka prison. The custom has always been to delay the condemned man until, on entering, he finds all seats taken and only the penal chair free. Then he knows. But this morning it was empty. And all were present.

Secretary-General Rudin leaned back and surveyed the twelve through half-closed eyes, the smoke from his inevitable cigarette drifting past his face. He still favoured the old-style Russian papyross, half tobacco and half thin cardboard tube, the tube nipped between finger and thumb to filter the smoke. His aides had been taught to pass them to him one after the other, and his doctors to shut up.

To his left, down the stem of the table, was his own protégé, Vassili Petrov, aged forty-nine, young for the job as head of the Party organizations section controlling the Party cadres throughout the country. Rudin could count on him in the trouble that lay ahead. Beside Petrov was the veteran foreign minister, Dmitri Rykov, who would side with Rudin because he had nowhere else to go. Next was the chairman of the KGB secret police, Yuri Ivanenko, slim and ruthless at fifty-three, standing out like a sore thumb in his elegant London-tailored suit as if flaunting his sophistication to a group of men who hated all forms of Western-ness. Picked personally by Rudin to head the KGB, Ivanenko would side with him because the opposition hated the KGB chief and wanted him destroyed.

On the other side of the table sat Yefrem Vishnayev, also young for the job. At fifty-five he was the Party theoretician, spare, ascetic, disapproving, the scourge of dissidents, guardian of Marxist purity and consumed by a pathological loathing of the capitalist West. Any opposition would come from him, Rudin knew. By his side was the defence minister and chief of the Red Army, Marshal Nikolai Kerensky, aged sixty-three. He would go where the interests of the Red Army led him.

That left seven, including Komarov, responsible for agriculture

142

and sitting white-faced because he, like Rudin and impassive KGB Chief Ivanenko, alone knew what was to come.

Rudin gestured to one of the Kremlin praetorian guards at the door at the far end of the room to admit the person waiting in fear and trembling outside. "Let me present Professor Ivan Ivanovich Yakovlev, Comrades," Rudin growled as the man advanced timorously to the end of the table and stood waiting, his sweat-damp report in his hands. "The professor is our senior agronomist and grain specialist from the ministry of agriculture. He has a report for our attention. Proceed, Professor."

The professor cleared his throat and plunged into his report. "Comrades, last December and January our long-range weather forecast satellites predicted an unusually damp winter and early spring. In accordance with habitual scientific practice it was decided at the ministry of agriculture that our seed grain for the spring planting should be given a prophylactic dressing. This has been done many times before. The dual purpose seed dressing selected was an organo-mercury compound to inhibit fungoid infection, which would be likely as the result of the dampness, and a pesticide and bird-repellant called Lindane. It was agreed, in scientific committee, that because the USSR, following the unfortunate damage through frost to the winter wheat crop, would need at least one hundred and forty million tons of crop from the spring wheat plantings, it would be necessary to sow six and a quarter million tons of seed grain."

All eyes were on him. The Politburo members could smell danger a mile off. Only Komarov, responsible for agriculture, stared at the table in misery. The professor swallowed hard and went on.

"At the rate of two ounces of organo-mercury seed dressing per ton of grain, the requirement was for three hundred and fifty tons of dressing. There were only seventy tons in stock. An order was sent to the manufacturing plant at Kuibyshev to go into immediate production to make up the required two hundred and eighty tons. Production of that amount of chemical normally takes less than forty hours. But due to a confusion in communication, the factory was undergoing annual maintenance and time was running short if the dressing was to be distributed to the one hundred and twenty-seven stations for seed-grain dressing scattered across the Union, the grain treated, and then taken back to the thousands of state and collective farms in time for planting. So an energetic young official and Party cadre was sent from Moscow to hurry things along. It appears the official ordered the workmen to stop what they were doing, restore the plant to operating order and start it functioning again."

"He failed to do it in time?" rasped Marshal Kerensky.

"No, Comrade Marshal, the factory started work again, although the maintenance engineers had not quite finished. But a hopper valve malfunctioned. Lindane is a very powerful chemical, and the dosage of the Lindane to the organo-mercury compound has to be strictly regulated. The valve on the Lindane hopper, although registering one-third open, was in fact stuck at full open. The whole two hundred and eighty tons of dressing was affected."

"What about quality control?" someone asked.

The professor swallowed again. "There was a conjunction of coincidence and error," he confessed. "The chief quality-control chemist was away on holiday at Sochi during the plant closedown. He was summoned back by cable, but his return was delayed. When he arrived, production was complete. The chemist wished to make quality-control tests on every tenth bag of dressing. The young functionary from Moscow wanted the entire production shipped at once and insisted he could only have one. That was when the third error occurred.

"The new bags had been stacked with the reserve of seventy tons left over from last year. One of the loaders selected one of the old bags for testing. Tests proved it was perfectly in order and the entire consignment was shipped."

He ended his report. There was nothing more to say. The silence in the room was murderous.

Party purist Vishnayev came in with icy clarity. "What exactly is the effect of excessive Lindane?"

"Comrade, it causes a toxic rather than protective effect against the germinating seed in the ground. The seedlings come up, if at all, stunted, sparse and mottled brown. There is virtually no grain yield from such affected stems."

"And how much of the spring planting has been affected?"

"Just about four-fifths, Comrade. The seventy tons of reserve compound were perfectly all right. The two hundred and eighty tons of new compound were all affected by the jammed valve and were mixed in with the seed grain."

144

The professor was dismissed. Vishnayev turned to Komarov from agriculture. "Comrade, it would appear you had some foreknowledge of this affair. What has happened to the functionary who produced this foul-up?"

KGB Chief Ivanenko cut in. "He is in our hands. Along with the chemist, the warehouseman, and the maintenance team."

"This functionary, has he talked?" asked Vishnayev.

Ivanenko considered a mental image of the broken man in the cellars beneath the Lubyanka. "Extensively," he said.

"Is he a saboteur, a fascist agent?"

"No," said Ivanenko with a sigh. "Just an idiot; an ambitious *apparatchik* trying to over-fulfil his orders."

"Then one last question, so that we can all be sure of the dimensions of this affair." Vishnayev swung back to the unhappy Komarov. "We already know we will only save fifty million tons of the expected hundred millions from the winter wheat. The exceptional autumn thaw saw to that, melting the snow and exposing the young shoots to later heavy frosts. How much will we now get from the spring wheat this coming October?"

"Out of the hundred-and-forty-million-ton target for the spring-sown wheat and other grains, we cannot reasonably expect more than fifty million tons," Komarov said quietly.

"That means a national shortfall of a hundred and forty million tons," breathed Petrov of Party organizations. "We could have taken a shortfall of fifty, even seventy million tons. We've done it before, endured the shortages. But this . . . ."

The members of the Politburo sat in stunned horror. They all knew it meant famine.

"We have as big a problem here as we have ever confronted," said Rudin. "I propose we adjourn and separately seek some suggestions. It goes without saying that this news does not pass outside this room. Our next meeting will be today week."

The Soviet Politburo descended to their chauffeur-driven Zil limousines still absorbing the knowledge that a weedy professor of agronomy had just placed a time bomb under one of the world's two super powers.

A WEEK LATER, as he sat in the circle at the Bolshoi Theatre, Adam Munro's thoughts were not on war, but on love; and not for the embassy secretary beside him who had prevailed upon him to

145

take her to the ballet. By the second act of "Giselle", his thoughts were straying back to Berlin, and Valentina.

It had been a once-in-a-lifetime love. He was twenty-four, a Reuters man, and she nineteen, dark and lovely. Because of her job as a secretary-stenographer with the Soviet delegation to the Four-Power Conference in Berlin they had had to conduct their affair in secret, furtively meeting in darkened streets so that he could pick her up in his car and take her back to his small flat. He had asked her to marry him, and she had almost agreed. But then came the Wall. It was completed on 14 August 1961, but it was obvious for a week that it was going up.

That was when she made her decision, and they loved for the last time. She could not, she told him, abandon her parents to what would happen to them: the disgrace, the loss of her father's trusted job, her mother's beloved apartment for which she had waited so many years through the dark times. And finally she could not bear never to see her beloved homeland again. So he watched from the shadows as she slipped back into the East through the last uncompleted section in the Wall, sad and lonely and heartbroken; and very, very beautiful.

He had never seen her again. Guarding her memory with quiet Scottish secretiveness, he had never let on that he had loved, and still loved, a Russian girl called Valentina. Which turned out to be fortunate. For, in the work he was soon to take on, such a love was against the rules.

Three years later, in London, a civilian he had known in Berlin had made a point of looking him up. There had been a dinner and another man had joined them. The Berlin acquaintance had excused himself and left during coffee. By the second brandy the newcomer made his point. "Some of my associates in the firm," he said, "were wondering if you could do us a little favour."

That was the first time Munro had heard the term "the firm". Later he would learn the terminology. To those in the Anglo-American alliance of intelligence services, the British Secret Intelligence Service was always "the firm". Its employees in the counter-intelligence arm, the MI5, were "the colleagues". The CIA at Langley, Virginia, was "the company" and its staff "the cousins". On the opposite side were "the opposition" whose headquarters were at Number 2, Dzerzhinsky Square, Moscow. This building was known as "the centre".

That proposal in the London restaurant in December 1964—confirmed later in a small flat in Chelsea—was for a "little run into the bloc". Munro made it successfully in the spring of 1965 while ostensibly covering the Leipzig Fair in East Germany. A year later he left Reuters, and had no trouble entering the foreign service, usually the cover for staffers of the firm. In sixteen years he had specialized in economic intelligence and had had foreign postings in Turkey, Austria and Mexico. He had married in 1967 but it had been an increasingly loveless union, and it was quietly ended six years later. Since then there had been affairs, and they were all known to the firm, but he had stayed single.

There was one affair he had never mentioned to the firm, and had his covering-up of it leaked out he would have been fired on the spot. On joining the service he had to write a complete life story of himself, followed by an examination by a senior officer. This procedure is repeated every five years of service. Among the matters of interest are any emotional and social involvements with personnel from behind the Iron Curtain.

The first time he was asked, something inside him rebelled, as it had in the olive grove in Cyprus. He knew that he would never be suborned over the matter of Valentina, even if the opposition knew about it, which he was certain they did not. If an attempt were ever made to blackmail him, he would admit it and resign, but never accede. He just did not want the fingers of other men rummaging through the most private part inside him. *Nobody owns me but me.* So he said "no" to the question, and broke the rules. He repeated the lie three times in sixteen years. Nothing had ever happened because of it, and nothing ever would. The affair was a secret, dead and buried.

Had he been less deep in his reverie, he might have noticed that from a private box high in the left-hand wall of the theatre he was being observed. Before the lights went up for the *entr'acte*, the watcher had vanished.

THE FOLLOWING DAY the thirteen men grouped around the Politburo table in the Kremlin were subdued and watchful, sensing a faction fight such as there had not been since Khrushchev fell.

Secretary-General Rudin surveyed them all through his drifting cigarette smoke. Petrov of Party organizations was in his usual

147

seat to his left, with Ivanenko of the KGB beyond him. Rykov of foreign affairs shuffled his papers, Vishnayev the theoretician and Marshal Kerensky of the Red Army sat in stony silence. Rudin surveyed the other seven, calculating which way they would jump if it came to a fight.

There were three non-Russians: Vitautas the Balt, from Lithuania; Chavadze the Georgian, from Tbilisi; and Mukhamed the Tadjik, an oriental and born a Moslem. Their presence was a sop to the minorities. Each, Rudin knew, was completely russified. Each had been first secretary for the Party in his republic and had overlorded programmes of vigorous repression against their fellow nationals. Each could not go back without the protection of Moscow, and each would side with the faction which would ensure his survival; that is, the winning one.

That left four more, all Russians. Komarov of agriculture; Stepanov, head of the trade unions; Shushkin, responsible for liaison with foreign communist parties worldwide; and Petryanov, responsible for the industrial plan.

"Comrades," began Rudin slowly, "you have all studied Professor Yakovlev's report. Let us consider first questions first. Can the Soviet Union survive for one year on no more than one hundred million tons of grain?"

The hour-long discussion was acrimonious but unanimous. Such a shortage of grain would lead to privations that had not been seen since the Second World War. If the state bought in even a minimum to make bread for the cities, the countryside would be left with almost nothing. The slaughter of livestock, as the beasts were left without feed grain during the winter, would strip the Soviet Union of virtually every four-footed animal. It would take a generation to restore the livestock herds. To leave even the minimum of grain on the land would starve the cities.

At last Rudin cut them short. "Very well. If we insist on accepting the famine, both in grain and, as a consequence, in meat several months later, what will be the outcome in terms of national discipline?"

Petrov of Party organizations admitted that there existed a groundswell of restiveness already among the masses, evidenced by a recent rash of small outbreaks of disorder and resignations from the Party. In the face of a true famine, many Party cadres could side with the proletariat.

148

The non-Russians nodded in agreement. In their republics the grip of the centre was always likely to be less total than inside Russia itself.

"Comrade Stepanov?" asked Rudin.

"In the event of genuine famine," said the head of the state-controlled trade unions, "it would not be possible to guarantee the absence of acts of disorder, perhaps on a wide scale."

Ivanenko of the KGB, sitting quietly gazing at the Western kingsize filter between his right forefinger and thumb, had smelt fear many times; in arrests, in interrogation rooms. He smelt it now. He and the men around him were powerful, privileged, protected. But he knew them all well; he had the files. And he, who knew no fear for himself as the soul-dead know no fear, knew also that they all feared one thing more than war itself. If the Soviet proletariat, long-suffering, patient, oxlike in the face of deprivation, ever went berserk . . . .

All eyes were on him. The repression of public "acts of disorder" were his country. "I could," he said evenly, "cope with one Novocherkassk." There was a hiss of indrawn breath down the table. "I could cope with ten, or even twenty. But the combined resources of the KGB could not cope with fifty."

The mention of Novocherkassk brought the spectre right out of the wallpaper as he knew it would. On 2 June 1962, the great industrial city of Novocherkassk had erupted in worker riots over food prices and wages. They had been viciously put down, but twenty years had not dimmed the memory inside the Kremlin.

There was silence round the table. Rudin broke it. "Very well, the conclusion seems inescapable. We will have to buy in from abroad as never before. Comrade Komarov, what is the minimum we would need to avoid disaster?"

"We will need fifty-five million tons of grain from outside, Secretary-General. That would mean the entire surplus, in a year of bumper crops, from both the USA and Canada."

"They'll never sell it to us," said Kerensky.

"They are endlessly greedy for money," Ivanenko cut in quietly. "And their Condor satellites must have warned them already that something is wrong with our spring wheat. By the autumn they will have a pretty fair idea how wrong. I can increase the production levels in the gold mines of Siberia and Kolyma. So we can raise the money for such a purchase."

"Comrade Ivanenko," said Rudin, "they may have the wheat, we may have the gold, but there is a chance that this time they might require concessions in military areas . . . ."

"Never!" shouted Marshal Kerensky, red-faced.

"We have agreed," countered Rudin, "that a nationwide famine is not tolerable. It would set back the progress of the Soviet Union by a decade, maybe more. If the imperialists exact concessions in the military field, we may have to accept a drawback lasting two or three years; but only in order to advance all the better after the recovery."

There was a general murmur of assent. Rudin was on the threshold of carrying his meeting. Then Vishnayev struck. He rose slowly as the buzz subsided. "Comrades," he said with silky reasonableness, "this is too early to reach any binding conclusion on such a massive issue. I propose an adjournment until this day fortnight while we all think over what has been suggested."

He had bought his time, as Rudin feared he would. The meeting agreed, ten against three, to adjourn without a resolution.

KGB Chief Yuri Ivanenko was about to step into his waiting limousine when he felt a touch at his elbow. Standing beside him was a major of the Kremlin guard. "Comrade Secretary-General would like a word with you in his private suite, Comrade," he said quietly. As Ivanenko followed the major, in his perfectly-fitting barathea jacket, fawn whipcord trousers and gleaming boots, towards a private lift, it occurred to Ivanenko that if any one of the Politburo came to sit one day in the penal chair, the subsequent arrest would be carried out by his own KGB border guards, with their bright green cap bands and shoulder-flashes, the sword-and-shield insignia of the KGB above their peaks.

But if he, Ivanenko, were to be arrested, the KGB would not be given the job, just as they could not be trusted almost thirty years earlier to arrest Lavrenti Beria. It would be these elegant, disdainful Kremlin elite guards who would do it.

On the third floor Ivanenko was shown into the private apartment of Maxim Rudin. It was comparatively modest for this most powerful of men. Rudin, a widower, lived alone and was cared for by an elderly cleaning woman and Misha, a hulking, silent-moving ex-soldier, who was never far away. When the KGB chief entered the study at Misha's silent gesture, he found Maxim

Rudin and his protégé, Vassili Petrov, already there. Rudin waved him to a vacant chair.

"I've asked you both here because there is trouble brewing," he began without preamble. "I'm old and I smoke too much. Two weeks ago I went out to see the quacks at Kuntsevo. They took some tests. Now they want me back again."

Petrov shot Ivanenko a sharp look. The KGB chief was impassive. He knew about the visit to the super-exclusive clinic; one of the doctors there reported back to him.

"The question of the succession hangs in the air, and we all know it," Rudin continued. "We all also know that Vishnayev wants it." He turned to Ivanenko. "If he gets it, Yuri Aleksandrovich, that will be the end of you. He never approved of a professional secret service man taking over the KGB. He'll put a Party man in your place."

Ivanenko gazed back at Rudin. Three years earlier Rudin had broken the long Soviet tradition of imposing a political Party luminary as chief of the KGB when he had appointed Ivanenko. Furthermore, Ivanenko was not only young for the job of the world's most powerful policeman and spymaster, he had also served as an agent in Washington twenty years earlier: always a base for suspicion among the haters of all things foreign in the Politburo. He had a taste for Western elegance in his private life. And he was reputed to have certain reservations about Party dogma. That, for the purist Vishnayev, was unforgivable.

"If he takes over, that will also mark your cards, Vassili Alexeivich," Rudin told Petrov. In private he called both his handpicked men by their familiar patronymics.

Petrov nodded. He and Vishnayev's chief of staff, Anatoly Krivoi, had worked together in the Party organizations section. Krivoi, the senior, had expected the top job, but when it fell vacant Rudin had preferred Petrov for the post that sooner or later carried a seat on the all-powerful Politburo. Krivoi, embittered, had accepted the courtship of Vishnayev and had taken a post as the Party theoretician's right-hand man. But Krivoi still wanted Petrov's job.

Neither Ivanenko nor Petrov had forgotten that it was Vishnayev's predecessor as Party theoretician, Mikhail Suslov, who had put together the majority that toppled Khrushchev in 1964. Rudin let his words sink in.

"Yuri, you know my successor cannot be you, not with your background." Ivanenko inclined his head; he had no illusions on that score. "But," Rudin resumed, "you and Vassili together can keep this country on a steady course, if you stick together and behind me. Next year, I'm going, one way or the other. And when I go, I want you, Vassili, in this chair."

The silence between the two younger men was electric. Neither could recall any predecessor of Rudin ever having been so forthcoming. Stalin had suffered a heart attack and been finished off by his own Politburo as he prepared to liquidate them all; Beria had tried for power and been arrested and shot by his fearful colleagues; Malenkov had fallen in disgrace, likewise Khrushchev; Brezhnev had kept them all guessing till the last minute.

Rudin stood up to signal the reception was at an end. "One last thing," he said. "Vishnayev is going to try and do a Suslov on me over this wheat foul-up. If he succeeds, we're all finished, perhaps Russia too. Because he's an extremist; he's impeccable on theory but impossible on practicalities. I have to know what he's going to spring, who he's trying to enlist. Find out for me before the Politburo meets again."

Three days later, in his office in Dzerzhinsky Square, Ivanenko took the telephone call he had been awaiting ten days. It was from a KGB agent who identified himself as Arkady, but who was actually a brigadier on the Red Army staff. When the brigadier had finished his report, Ivanenko thanked him and put down the phone. He considered the news for a long time, feeling increasingly tired and dispirited. So that was what Vishnayev was up to. He would tell Maxim Rudin in the morning.

Four

A gently warming sun shone down on Washington that middle of June, 1982, bringing rich, red roses to the garden outside the open french windows of the Oval Office in the White House. But though the fresh smells of grass and flowers wafted into the private sanctum of the most powerful ruler in the world, the attention of the four men present was focused on other plants in a far and foreign country.

President William Matthews sat where American presidents have always sat; his back to the south wall of the room, facing across a wide antique desk towards the classical marble fireplace that dominates the north wall. His chair, unlike that of most of his predecessors who had favoured luxurious, made-to-measure seating, was a factory-made, high-backed swivel chair. For "Bill" Matthews, as he insisted his publicity posters call him, had always in his election campaigns stressed his ordinary, old-folks-at-home tastes. But when he was in conclave with his senior advisers he dropped the nice-guy voice and the rumpled bird-dog grin that had originally gulled the voters into putting the boy next door into the White House. He was not the boy next door, and his advisers knew it; he was the man at the top.

Seated across the desk from the president were the three men whom he had asked to see alone that morning. Closest to him in personal terms was the chairman of the National Security Council—Dr. Stanislav Poklewski—his adviser on security matters and confidant on foreign affairs.

They made a strange pair: the blond, Anglo-Saxon Protestant from the deep South, and the dark, sharp-faced Polish Roman Catholic who had come over from Cracow as a small boy. But what Bill Matthews lacked in understanding of the tortuous psychologies of Europeans in general and Slavs in particular could be made up by Dr. Poklewski.

The other two men in front of the desk were Robert Benson, director of the Central Intelligence Agency, and Dr. Myron Fletcher, chief analyst of Soviet grain affairs in the department of agriculture.

"Bob, are you sure beyond any reasonable doubt that Condor reconnaissance and your ground reports point to these figures?" President Matthews asked the CIA chief, his eye running down the columns of estimated crop yields in front of him.

"Something strange is happening to the Soviet grain crop, sir. All the spring wheat, put down as seed in March/April after the thaw, should be coming up sweet and green by now. Instead it's coming up stunted and sparse, like it was hit by some kind of blight."

He leaned forward, detached one of the six telephones from its cradle, dialled a number, and said, "Screen it."

Then he rose and crossed to one of the bank of television sets

153

placed in the curving west wall. When civilian deputations were in the room, the screens were covered by sliding teak doors. Benson turned on the extreme left-hand set and returned to the president's desk.

The screen flickered into life. Its entire square-yard surface was filled with twenty separate stalks of young wheat. Each looked frail, listless, bedraggled. Matthews had seen them like this in pictures of the dust bowls of the Middle West, fifty years before.

He also knew about the Condor satellites. Flying higher than anything ever before, using cameras of a sophistication that could show a human fingernail in close-up from two hundred miles, through rain, fog, hail, snow, cloud and night, the Condors were the best.

"How widespread is this . . . blight?" he said.

Benson came in again. "What we have indicates it must be pretty widespread. But Condor reconnaissance shows no logical pattern. All my agronomy boys can come up with is some blight of the seed or in the earth."

Matthews turned his gaze from the screen. "Stan?" he said.

Dr. Stanislav Poklewski chose his words carefully. "Mr. President, the Soviet Union had a total grain target this year of 240 million metric tons. This breaks down into goal targets of 120 million metric tons of wheat, 60 million of barley, and the remainder a mixture of other grains. The giants of the crop are wheat and barley. And the overall shortfall now looks like being in the region of 80 million tons, not allowing for reserves."

The president looked across at the man from agriculture. "Dr. Fletcher, how does this break down in layman's terms?"

"Well, Mr. President, one has to deduct the wheat tonnage the Soviets have to keep in the countryside before any state procurements can be made to feed the industrial masses. If they cut down on the human rations, the peasants will simply consume the livestock. If they cut back on the animal feedstuff the livestock slaughter will be wholesale; they'll have a meat glut next winter, then a meat famine for three to four years."

"OK, doctor, I'll buy that. What about their reserves?"

"We estimate they have a national reserve of thirty million tons, though it is unheard-of to use up the whole of it. And they *should* have twenty million tons left over from this year's crop available for the cities—a grand total of fifty million."

The president swung back to Benson. "Bob, how much do they need through state procurements to feed the urban millions?"

"Mr. President, they cannot do with less than eighty-five million tons of state buy-in for the cities."

"Then," concluded the president, "by your figures even if they use the total of their national reserve, they are going to need thirty to thirty-five million tons of foreign grain?"

"Right, Mr. President," cut in Dr. Poklewski. "Maybe even more. And we and the Canadians are the only people who are going to have it. Dr. Fletcher?"

The man from agriculture nodded. "It appears North America is going to have a bumper crop this year. Maybe fifty million tons over domestic requirements."

Minutes later Dr. Fletcher was escorted out. Poklewski pressed his point. "Mr. President, they cannot get their wheat elsewhere. Our wheat surplus is no longer a trading matter. Therefore, it is a strategic weapon. I urge you to invoke the Shannon Act."

Passed back in 1977, the Shannon Act said simply that in any year the federal government had the right to buy the option for the US grain surplus at the going-rate per ton at the time of the announcement that Washington wished to exercise its option. The Shannon Act ensured that, if made operative, the farmers would get a fair price but speculators would be out of business. The act also gave the administration a gigantic new weapon in dealing with customer countries.

"Very well," said President Matthews. "I will activate the Shannon Act and authorize the use of federal funds to buy the futures for the expected surplus of fifty million tons of grain."

Poklewski was jubilant. "You won't regret it, Mr. President. We have the Soviets over a barrel."

FROM HIS WINDOW SEAT Andrew Drake looked down eagerly at the sprawling city beneath him as the Polish Airlines twin-jet dipped a wing over the wide sweep of the Dnieper River and settled into its final approach to Borispil Airport outside Kiev, capital of the Ukraine. Drake was tense with excitement.

Along with the other hundred-plus package tourists from London, he queued nearly an hour for passport control and customs. The man in the immigration control booth was in border-guard uniform with the green band around his cap and

156

the sword-and-shield emblem of the KGB above its peak. He looked at the photo in the passport, then stared hard at Drake. He examined the visa issued in London, tore off the incoming half and clipped the exit visa to the passport. Drake was in.

On the Intourist coach from the airport he took stock again of his fellow travellers. About half were excited Ukrainians, visiting the land of their fathers, the other half were British, curious tourists. Drake with his English name was among the second group. He had given no indication that he spoke fluent Ukrainian and passable Russian.

During the coach ride they met Ludmilla, their Intourist guide for the tour. She smiled brightly and in reasonable English began to describe the tour ahead of them: first two days in Kiev, seeing St. Sophia's Cathedral, the tenth-century Golden Gate, the Academy of Sciences. No doubt, thought Drake bitterly, no mention would be made of the 1964 fire at the academy library in which priceless archives devoted to Ukrainian culture had been destroyed, the fire set by the KGB as its answer to the nationalists.

After Kiev, there would be a trip to Ternopol, where a refugee partisan called Miroslav Kaminsky would certainly not be a subject for discussion, and then at last onto Drake's final goal, Lvov. As he expected, Drake heard only Russian on the streets of the intensively russified capital city of Kiev. It was not until Ternopol that he heard Ukrainian spoken extensively. His heart sang to hear it spoken so widely. For himself, however, he must wait until he could visit the two addresses Kaminsky had given him.

On the fifth day, the party arrived in Lvov and stayed at the Intourist Hotel. So far Drake had gone on all the guided tours on the agenda, but this time he made an excuse that he had a headache and wished to stay in his room. As soon as the party left by coach he changed into the sort of clothes Kaminsky had told him would pass without attracting attention; socks and sandals, light trousers and an open-necked shirt of the cheaper variety. With a street map he set off on foot for the seedy working-class suburb of Levandivka. He had no doubt that the two men he sought would treat him with the profoundest suspicion. He recalled what Miroslav Kaminsky, in his Turkish hospital bed, had told him about them.

On 29 September 1966 near Kiev, at the gorge of Babi Yar where over 50,000 Jews were slaughtered by the SS in 1941-42, the Ukraine's foremost contemporary poet, Ivan Dzyuba, had given an address which began as a seeming plea for remembrance of the slaughtered Jews, a condemnation of Nazism. But as it developed, his theme began to encompass all despotisms, and the *Chekisti* who had infiltrated the silent crowd realized the poet was not talking about Hitler's Germany—he was talking about the Politburo's Soviet Union.

Shortly after the speech he was arrested. In the cellars of the local barracks where the poet was taken, the chief interrogator was a fast-rising young colonel of the KGB, sent in from Moscow. His name was Yuri Ivanenko.

At the Babi Yar speech there had been, in the front row, standing next to their fathers, two small Jewish boys aged ten. They did not know each other then, and would only meet and become firm friends six years later on a building site. One was called Lev Mishkin, the other David Lazareff.

The presence of the fathers of Mishkin and Lazareff at the meeting had been noted, and when years later they had applied for permission to emigrate to Israel, both had been accused of anti-Soviet activities and drawn long sentences in labour camps. The sons lost any hope of university. Though highly intelligent, they were destined for labourers' work. Now both twenty-six, these were the young men Drake sought in Levandivka.

At the first address Kaminsky had given him Drake found David Lazareff who, after the introduction, treated him with extreme suspicion. But he agreed to bring his friend Mishkin to a rendezvous that evening.

That night Drake told the pair the story of the escape and rescue of Miroslav Kaminsky, and of his own background. The only proof he could produce was the photograph of himself and Kaminsky together, taken in the hospital room at Trabzon. Held up in front of them was that day's edition of the local Turkish newspaper. Drake had brought the same newspaper as suitcase-lining and showed it to them as proof of his story.

"If Miroslav had been washed up in Soviet territory and been taken by the KGB," he said, "if he had talked and revealed your names, and if I was from the KGB, I'd hardly be asking for your help."

The two Jewish workers agreed to consider his request overnight. Both Mishkin and Lazareff had long shared an ideal close to Drake's own—that of striking one single powerful blow of revenge against the Kremlin hierarchy. But they had been weighed down by the hopelessness of trying to do anything without outside help.

Now impelled by their desire for an ally beyond the borders of the USSR, the two agreed to take the Anglo-Ukrainian into their confidence. At the second meeting the next afternoon—Drake having skipped another guided tour—for safety they strolled through wide, unpaved lanes near the outskirts of the city, talking quietly in Ukrainian. They told Drake of their desire to strike at Moscow in a single, deadly act.

"The question is—what?" said Drake.

Lazareff, who was the more silent and dominant of the pair, spoke. "The head of the KGB—Ivanenko," he said. "The most hated man in the Ukraine."

"What about him?" asked Drake.

"Kill him."

Drake stopped in his tracks and stared at the dark, intense young man. "You'd never get near him."

"Last year," said Lazareff, "I was working on a house-painting job here in Lvov. We were redecorating the apartment of a Party bigwig. There was a little old woman staying with them. From Kiev. After she'd gone, the Party man's wife mentioned who she was. Later I saw a letter postmarked Kiev in the letterbox. I took it, and it was from the old woman. It had her return address in Kiev on it."

"So who was she?" asked Drake.

"His mother."

Drake considered the information. "You'd have to watch her flat in Kiev for a long time before he might come to visit her."

Lazareff shook his head. "She's the bait," he said, and outlined his idea.

Drake considered the enormity of it. He had envisaged the great single blow against the Kremlin in many terms, but never this. To assassinate the head of the KGB would be to strike into the very centre of the Politburo, to send hairline cracks running through every corner of the power structure.

"It might work," he conceded. If it did, he thought, it would be hushed up at once. But if the news ever got out, especially in the Ukraine, the effect on popular opinion would be traumatic. "It

159

could trigger the biggest uprising there has ever been here," he said.

Lazareff nodded. He and Mishkin had evidently given the project a lot of thought.

"What equipment would you need?" asked Drake.

Lazareff told him.

"It can all be acquired in the West," Drake said. "But how to get it in?"

"Odessa," cut in Mishkin. "I was on the docks there for a while. The place is completely corrupt. Every Western ship brings seamen who do a vigorous trade with the local spivs in Turkish leather jackets, sheepskin coats and denim jeans. The black market is thriving. We could meet you there—it is inside the Ukraine and we would not need inter-state passports."

Before they parted the plan was agreed. Drake would acquire the equipment and bring it to Odessa by sea. He would alert Mishkin and Lazareff by a letter, posted inside the Soviet Union, well in advance of his arrival. The wording would be innocent. The rendezvous in Odessa was to be a café that Mishkin knew from his days as a labourer there.

"Two more things," said Drake. "When it is over, the worldwide announcement that it has been done is vital; almost as important as the act itself. You personally must tell the world. Only you will have the details to convince the world of the truth. But that means you must escape to the West."

"We have both tried to emigrate to Israel and have been refused," said Lazareff. "This time we will go, with or without permission. Israel is the only place we will be safe ever again. Then we will tell the world what we have done and leave those bastards in the Kremlin discredited in the eyes of their own people."

"The other point follows from the first," said Drake. "When it is done, you must let me know by coded letter or postcard, in case anything goes wrong with your escape. So that I can try to get the news to the world."

They agreed that an innocently worded postcard would be sent from Lvov to a *poste restante* address in London. With the details memorized, they parted, and Drake rejoined his tour group. Two days later he was back in London. The first thing he did was buy the world's most comprehensive book on small arms. The second was to send a telegram to a friend in Canada, one of that elite

160

private list of emigrés he had built up over the years who thought as he did of carrying their hatred to the enemy. The third was to begin preparations for a long-dormant plan to raise the needed funds by robbing a bank.

AT THE OUTSET of the crucial next Politburo meeting Vishnayev took the floor. "No one, Comrades, denies that the famine that faces us is not acceptable. No one denies that the surplus foods lie in the decadent capitalist West. It has been suggested that we humble ourselves, possibly accept concessions in our military might, to buy these surpluses. Comrades, I disagree and I ask you to join me in rejection of yielding to blackmail and betraying our great inspirator, Lenin. There is one other way in which we can secure acceptance by the Soviet people of rigid rationing at the minimum level, a nationwide upsurge of patriotism and self-sacrifice, and an imposition of that discipline without which we cannot get through the hunger that has to come.

"We can use what little harvest grain we shall cull this autumn, spin out the national reserve until the spring next year, use the meat from our herds and flocks in place of grain, and then, when all is used, turn to Western Europe where the beef and butter mountains are—the national reserves of ten wealthy nations."

"And buy them?" asked Foreign Minister Rykov ironically.

"No, Comrade," replied Vishnayev softly, "take them. Comrade Marshal Kerensky has a file for us to examine."

Twelve thick files were passed round. Rudin left his unopened in front of him and smoked steadily. Ivanenko also left his on the table. He and Rudin had known for four days what the files would contain. In collaboration with Vishnayev, Kerensky the Red Army chief had taken from the general staff safe the "Plan Boris" file, named after Boris Goudonov, the great Russian conqueror, and brought it up to date. It was impressive.

Marshal Kerensky began reading it aloud. During the following May the usual massive spring manoeuvres of the Red Army in East Germany would be bigger than ever, but this time the real thing. On command, all 30,000 tanks and armoured personnel carriers, mobile guns and amphibious craft would swing westwards, hammer across the Elbe and plough into West Germany, heading for France and the Channel ports.

Ahead of them, 50,000 paratroopers would take out the fifty

principal tactical nuclear airfields of the French inside France and of the Americans and British on German soil. Another hundred thousand would drop on the four countries of Scandinavia to possess the capital cities and main arteries, with massive naval back-up from offshore.

The military thrust would avoid the Italian and Iberian peninsulars, whose governments had Euro-Communists in office and would be ordered by the Soviet ambassadors to stay out of the fight. Within half a decade, they would fall like ripe plums anyway. Likewise Greece, Turkey and Yugoslavia. Switzerland would be avoided, Austria used only as a through-route. Both would later be islands in a Soviet sea, and would not last long.

The primary zone of attack and occupation would be the three Benelux countries, France and West Germany. Britain, as a prelude, would be crippled by strikes and confused by the extreme Left which, on instructions, would mount an immediate clamour for non-intervention. London would be informed that if the nuclear strike command was used east of the Elbe, Britain would be wiped off the map.

Throughout the entire operation the Soviet Union would be stridently demanding an immediate ceasefire in every capital in the world and the United Nations, claiming the hostilities were local to West Germany, caused by a West German pre-emptive strike towards Berlin, a claim that most of the non-German European Left would believe.

"And the United States, all this time?" Rudin's protégé, Petrov, interrupted.

Marshal Kerensky looked irritated at being stopped in full flow. "The use of tactical nuclear weapons right across Germany cannot be excluded," said the Red Army chief, "but the overwhelming majority of them will destroy West Germany, East Germany and Poland, no loss for the Soviet Union. Thanks to the weakness of Washington there is no deployment of either Cruise missiles or neutron bombs. Soviet military casualties are estimated at between one hundred and two hundred thousand, at the maximum. But as two million men in all three of our services will be involved, such percentages will be acceptable."

"Duration?" asked Ivanenko.

"Units of the forward mechanized armies will enter the French Channel ports one hundred hours after crossing the Elbe. At that point the called-for ceasefire may be allowed to operate and the mopping up take place."

"Is that time-scale feasible?" asked Economics Chief Petryanov.

This time Rudin cut in. "Oh yes, it's feasible," he said mildly. Vishnayev shot him a suspicious look.

"I still have not had an answer to my question," Petrov pointed out. "What about the USA's nuclear strike forces?"

Vishnayev rose. "The American president must, at the outset, be given three solemn assurances: One, that the USSR will never be the first to use thermo-nuclear weapons. Two, that if the 300,000 American troops in Western Europe are committed to the fight, they must take their chances in conventional or tactical nuclear warfare with ours. Three, that in the event the USA resorts to ballistic missiles aimed at the Soviet Union, the top hundred cities of the USA will cease to exist. President Matthews, Comrades, will not trade New York for the decadence of Paris, nor Los Angeles for Frankfurt. There will be *no* American thermo-nuclear riposte."

The silence was heavy as the perspectives sunk in: the vast storehouse of food, including grain, of consumer goods, and technology in Western Europe; the fall of Italy, Spain, Portugal, Austria, Greece and Yugoslavia within a few years; the treasure trove of gold beneath the streets of Switzerland; the utter isolation of Britain and Ireland off the new Soviet coast; the domination without a shot fired of the entire Arab and Third World. It was a heady mixture.

"It's a fine scenario," said Rudin at last. "But it all seems to be based on one assumption. That the USA will not rain her nuclear warheads on the Soviet Union if we promise not to let ours loose on her. Had we ever believed this before we would surely already have completed the process of liberating the captive masses of Western Europe. Personally, I perceive no new element to justify the calculation of Comrade Vishnayev. Neither he nor the Comrade Marshal have ever had dealings with the Americans, or been in the West. I have, and I disagree. Let us hear from Comrade Rykov."

The elderly and veteran foreign minister was white-faced. "I have spent thirty years in foreign affairs. Ambassadors around the world report to me, and none of them, nor one single analyst in my department, nor I, have a single doubt that the US president

163

would use the thermo-nuclear response on the Soviet Union. He too can see that the outcome of such a war would be domination by the Soviet Union of almost the whole world. It would be the end of America as a super power. They will devastate the Soviet Union before they yield Western Europe and hence the world."

"I would point out that if they do respond," said Rudin, "we cannot as yet stop them. Our high-energy-particle laser beams from space satellites are not fully functional yet. The latest assessments of our experts suggest a full-blown Anglo-American thermo-nuclear strike would take out one hundred million of our citizens and devastate sixty per cent of the Union. Comrade Ivanenko, you have experience of the West. What do you say?"

"Unlike Comrades Vishnayev and Kerensky," observed Ivanenko, "I control hundreds of agents throughout the capitalist West. I too have no doubt the Americans would respond."

"Then let me put it in a nutshell," said Rudin brusquely. The time for sparring was over. "If we negotiate with the Americans for wheat, we may have to accede to demands that could set us back by five years. If we tolerate the famine, we would probably be set back by ten years. If we launch a European war, we could be wiped out, certainly set back by twenty to forty years.

"I seem to recall the very firm teachings of Marx and Lenin on one point: that while the pursuit of the world rule of Marxism must be pursued by every means, the progress should not be endangered by incurring foolish risks. I estimate this plan as being based on a foolish risk. Therefore I propose that we . . ."

"I propose a vote," said Vishnayev softly.

So that was it. The faction fight was out in the open now. Rudin had not had the feeling so clearly in years that, as now, he was fighting for his life. If he lost there would be no graceful retirement. It would be ruin, exile, perhaps the bullet in the nape of the neck. But he kept his composure. He put his own motion first. One by one the hands went up.

Rykov, Ivanenko and Petrov voted for him and the negotiation policy. There was hesitancy down the table. Then Stepanov of trade unions and Shushkin, liaison with the worldwide communist parties, raised their hands. Last, slowly, came Chavadze the Georgian.

Rudin put the counter-motion, for war in the spring. Vishnayev and Kerensky of course were for it. Komarov of agriculture joined them. Bastard, thought Rudin, it was your bloody ministry that got us into this mess. Vishnayev must have persuaded the man that he, Rudin, was going to ruin him in any case, so he had nothing to lose. You're wrong, my friend, thought Rudin, face impassive; I'm going to have your entrails for this. Petryanov the economist raised his hand. He's been promised the prime ministership, thought Rudin. Vitautas from Lithuania and Mukhamed the Tadjik also went with Vishnayev for war. The Tadjik would know that if nuclear war came, the orientals would rule over the ruins. The Lithuanian had been bought.

"Six for each proposal," Rudin said quietly. "And my own casting vote for the negotiations."

"Too close," he thought, "much too close." The faction fight would now go on until it was resolved; no one could stay neutral.

SOUTHEAST OF MOSCOW is the little village of Uspenskoye, in the heart of the weekend-villa country. In the great pine and birch forests around it stand the country mansions of the Soviet elite. Just beyond Uspenskoye bridge over the Moscow River is a beach where in summer those of the less-privileged who have their own cars come from Moscow to bathe. The Western diplomats come here too, one of the rare places where a Westerner can be cheek by jowl with ordinary Muscovite families. Even the routine KGB tailing of Western diplomats seems to let up on Sunday afteroons in high summer.

Adam Munro came here with a party of British embassy staffers on Sunday afternoon, 11 July 1982. The party left their towels and picnic baskets among the trees, ran down the low bluff towards the sandy beach and swam. When he came back, Munro picked up his rolled towel and began to dry himself. Something fell out of it. He stooped to pick up a small white pasteboard card. On it was typed in Russian: "Three kilometres north of here is an abandoned chapel in the woods. Meet me there in thirty minutes. Please. It is urgent."

He considered the angles. A dissident wanting to pass over underground literature? A religious group wanting asylum? A trap set by the KGB to identify the SIS man inside the embassy? Always possible. No ordinary commercial secretary would accept such an invitation. And yet it was too crude for the KGB. So who was the secret writer?

He dressed quickly and made up his mind. If it was a trap, then he had received no message and was simply walking in the forest. He set off alone. After a hundred yards he paused, took out his lighter and burnt the card, grinding the ash into the carpet of pine needles.

The sun and his watch gave him due north. After ten minutes he emerged on the side of a slope and saw the onion-shaped dome of a chapel two kilometres farther on across the valley. The forests around Moscow have dozens of such small chapels, once the worshipping places of the villagers, now mainly boarded up, deserted. The one he was approaching stood in its own clearing among the trees. At the edge of the clearing he stopped and surveyed the tiny church. He could see no one. Carefully he advanced into the open. He was a few yards from the sealed front door when he saw the figure standing in deep shadow under an archway. He stopped, and for long moments the two stared at each other. Then he said her name, "Valentina."

She moved out of the shadow and replied, "Adam."

"Twenty-one years," he thought in wonderment, "she must be turned forty." She looked thirty, still ravenhaired, beautiful and ineffably sad.

They sat on one of the tombstones and talked quietly of the old times. She told him she had returned to Moscow a few months after their parting, and had continued to be a stenographer for the Party machine. At twenty-three she had married a young army officer and after seven years there had been a baby. They had been happy, all three of them. Her husband's career had flourished, for he had an uncle high in the Red Army. The boy, Sascha, was now ten.

Five years ago her husband, having reached the rank of colonel, had been killed in a helicopter crash, and she had gone back to work, her husband's uncle using his influence to secure her a highly-placed job. Two years ago, after special clearance, she had been offered a post in the tiny, closed group of stenographers and typists called the Politburo secretariat.

Munro breathed deeply. That was high, very high, and very trusted. "Who," he asked, "is the uncle of your late husband?"

"Marshal Kerensky," she murmured.

Munro exhaled slowly. Marshal Kerensky, chief of the Red Army, the ultra-hawk. When he looked again at Valentina, she

166

was on the verge of tears. He put his arm round her shoulders and she leaned against him. He smelt her hair, the same sweet odour that had made him feel both tender and excited two decades ago in his youth. "What's the matter?" he asked gently.

"Oh, Adam, I'm so unhappy."

"In God's name, why? In your society you have everything."

She shook her head, slowly, and avoided his eye, gazing across the clearing into the woods. "Adam, all my life I believed in the goodness, the rightness, of socialism. Even in the times of deprivation in my country I believed in the justice of the communist ideal that we in Russia would one day bring to the world—an ideal that would give us all a world without fascism, without money-lust, without exploitation, without war. It was more important than you, than our love, than my husband and child. As much at least as this country, Russia, which is part of my soul."

Munro knew about the patriotism of the Russians, a fierce flame that would make them endure any suffering, make any sacrifice and which, when manipulated, made them obey their Kremlin overlords without demur.

"What happened?" he asked quietly.

"They are betraying it. My ideal, my people and my country."

"They?" he asked.

"The Party chiefs," she said bitterly. She spat out the Russian slang word meaning "the fat cats". "The *nachalstvo.*"

Munro had witnessed a recantation before. When a true believer loses the faith, the reversed fanaticism goes to strange extremes.

"I worshipped them, Adam. I respected them. Now, for years, I have lived close to them all, been showered with their privileges. I have seen them in private, heard them talk about the people, whom they despise. They are rotten, Adam, corrupt and cruel."

Munro took her in his arms. She was crying softly. "I can't go on, Adam," she murmured into his shoulder.

"All right, my darling, do you want me to try to get you out?"

He knew it would cost him his career, but this time he was not going to let her go. She pulled away, her face tear-streaked. "I cannot leave. I have Sascha to think about."

He held her quietly for a while longer. His mind was racing. "How did you know I was in Moscow?" he asked carefully.

"Last month I was taken to the ballet by a colleague. We were in a box. When the lights were low, I thought I must be mistaken. But when they went up in the interval, I knew it was really you. I could not stay after that. I pleaded a headache and left quickly."

She dabbed her eyes, the crying spell over. "Adam," she asked, "did you marry?"

"Yes," he said. "It didn't work. We were divorced years ago."

She managed a little smile. "I'm glad there is no one else. That is not very logical, is it?"

He grinned back at her. "No," he said. "It is not. But it is nice to hear. Can we see each other? In the future?"

Her smile faded; there was a hunted look in her eyes. She shook her dark head. "No, not very often, Adam. I am trusted, privileged, but if a foreigner came to my apartment, it would soon be noticed and reported on. The same applies to your apartment. Diplomats are watched—you know that. Hotels are watched also. It is just not possible, Adam."

"Valentina, you took the initiative for this meeting. Was it just for old times' sake? If you do not like your life here, but cannot leave because of Sascha, what is it you want?"

She composed herself and thought for a while. When she spoke it was quite calmly. "Adam, I want to try and stop what they are doing. I suppose I have for several years now, but since I saw you at the Bolshoi, and remembered all the freedoms we had in Berlin, I began thinking about it more and more. Now I am certain. Tell me if you can; is there an intelligence officer in your embassy?"

Munro was shaken. He had handled two disaffected Russians, one from the Soviet embassy in Mexico City, the other in Vienna. One had been motivated by a conversion from respect to hatred for his own regime, like Valentina; the other by bitterness at lack of promotion. The former had been trickier to handle. "I suppose there must be," he said slowly.

Valentina rummaged in the shoulder bag by her feet. She withdrew a thick padded envelope. "I want you to give this to him, Adam. Promise me you will never tell him who it came from. I cannot trust anyone but you."

"I promise," he said. "But I have to see you again. I can't just see you walk away as I did last time."

"No, I cannot do that again either. But do not try to contact me

169

at my apartment. It is in a walled compound for senior functionaries, with a single gate and a policeman on it. Do not try to telephone me. The calls are monitored. And I will never meet anyone else from your embassy, not even the intelligence chief.''

"I agree," said Munro. "But when can we meet again?"

"It is not easy for me to get away. Sascha takes up most of my spare time. But I have my own car and I am not followed. Tomorrow I must go away for two weeks, but we can meet here, four Sundays from today." She looked at her watch. "I must go, Adam. I am one of a privileged house party at a *dacha* a few miles from here."

He kissed her on the lips, and it was as sweet as it had ever been. She rose and turned to go.

"Valentina," he said, "what is in this?" He held up the package. She paused.

"My job," she said, "is to prepare the verbatim transcripts of the Politburo meetings, one for each member. From the tape recordings. That is a copy of the recording of the meeting of June tenth."

ADAM MUNRO sat in a locked room in the main building of the British embassy and listened to the last sentence of the tape recording describing what had happened to the Soviet grain. The room was safe from electronic surveillance by the Russians, which was why he had borrowed it for a few hours from head of chancery. ". . . goes without saying that this news does not pass outside those present in this room. Our next meeting will be today week."

The voice of Maxim Rudin died away and the tape hissed on the machine, then stopped. Munro switched off and let out a long, low whistle. If it was true, it was bigger than anything Oleg Penkovsky had brought over twenty years before. Penkovsky was a full brigadier-general of the GRU, with access to the highest information, who, disenchanted with the Kremlin hierarchy, had approached first the Americans and then the British with an offer to provide information.

The Americans had turned him down, suspecting a trap. The British had accepted him, and for two and a half years "run" him until he was trapped by the KGB, exposed, tried and shot. He had brought over a golden harvest of secret information at the time of the October 1962 Cuban missile crisis, but even he had never got inside the Politburo.

Munro took the spool off the machine and carefully rewrapped it. The voice of Professor Yakovlev was unknown to him, and most of the tape was of him reading his report. But in the discussion following there were at least three identifiable voices. The low growl of Rudin was well known, the high tones of Vishnayev and the bark of Marshal Kerensky.

His problem, when he took the tape back to London for voice-print analysis was how to cover his source. If he admitted the secret rendezvous in the forest the question would be: "How did she know you, Munro?" Impossible to avoid that question, and equally impossible to answer it. The only solution was to devise an alternative source, credible and uncheckable.

He had only been in Moscow six weeks, but his unexpected mastery of Russian had already paid dividends. At a diplomatic reception in the Czech embassy a fortnight earlier he had heard two Russians in muttered conversation behind him. One had said: "He's a bitter bastard. Thinks he should have had the top slot."

Munro had followed the gaze of the two and noted they were talking about a Russian across the room. He later confirmed the man was Anatoly Krivoi, personal aide to Vishnayev. So what had he got to be bitter about? Munro checked his files. Krivoi had worked in the Party organizations section of the central committee; shortly after the nomination of Petrov to the top job, Krivoi had appeared on Vishnayev's staff. Quit in disgust? Personality conflict with Petrov? Bitter at being passed over?

Krivoi, he mused. He too would have access, at least to Vishnayev's copy of the transcript. "Sorry, Anatoly, you've just changed sides," he said as he slipped the fat envelope into an inside pocket and took the stairs to see the head of chancery.

"I'm afraid I have to go back to London with the Wednesday bag," he told the diplomat. "It can't wait." Chancery asked no questions and promised to arrange it.

The diplomatic bag, actually a bag, or at least a series of canvas sacks, goes from Moscow to London every Wednesday and always on a British Airways flight. A Queen's Messenger, one of that team of men who constantly fly around the world from London picking up embassy bags and protected by the insignia of the crown and greyhound, comes out from London for it. The very secret

171

material is carried in a dispatch box chained to the man's left wrist; the more routine stuff in canvas sacks is checked into the aircraft hold. Once there, it is on British territory. In the case of Moscow the messenger is also accompanied back to London by an embassy staffer.

The following Wednesday, Adam Munro was assigned to the routine escort job. The British Airways plane lifted out of Sheremetyevo Airport and turned its nose towards London. By Munro's side the messenger, a dapper ex-army major, withdrew into his hobby, composing crossword puzzles for a major newspaper. "You have to do something to while away these endless flights," he explained.

Munro grunted and looked back over the wingtip at the receding city of Moscow. Somewhere down there the woman he loved was working among people she was going to betray. She was on her own and right out in the cold.

Five

The west coast of Norway is broken into many fragments of land and between them the sea has flowed in to form gullies, bays and gorges: winding narrow defiles where the mountains fall sheer to glittering water. These are the fjords, and it was from their headwaters fifteen hundred years ago that a race of men came out who were the best sailors ever to set keel to the water. They were the Vikings, and their descendants still live and fish along the fjords of Norway.

Such a man was Thor Larsen, ship's master, who strode on a mid-July afternoon in 1982 past the royal palace in the Swedish capital of Stockholm from his company's head office back to his hotel. People tended to step aside for him; he was six feet three inches tall, wide as the pavements of the old quarter of the city, blue-eyed and bearded. Being shorebound, he was in civilian clothes, but he was happy because he had reason to think that he might soon have a new command.

After six months attending a course, at Nordia Line's expense, in the intricacies of radar, computer navigation and supertanker technology, he was dying to get back to sea again. The summons to the head office had been to receive an invitation to dinner that

172

evening with the proprietor, chairman and managing director of the Nordia Line—Harald "Harry" Wennerstrom. The invitation included Larsen's wife, Lisa, who was flying in from Norway on a company ticket. The old man was splashing out a bit, thought Larsen. There must be something in the wind.

When Lisa Larsen arrived at the airport, he greeted her with the delicacy of an excited St. Bernard, swinging her off her feet like a girl. She was petite, with dark bright eyes, soft chestnut curls and a trim figure that belied her thirty-eight years. And he adored her. Twenty years earlier, when he had been a gangling second mate of twenty-five, he had met her one freezing winter day in Oslo. She had slipped on the ice, he had picked her up like a doll and set her back on her feet. She had been wearing a fur-trimmed hood that almost hid her tiny, red-nosed face, and when she thanked him he could only see her eyes, looking out of the mass of snow and fur like the bright eyes of a snow-mouse in the forests of winter. Ever since he had called her his snow-mouse. He drove her back into central Stockholm, asking all the way about their home in Alesund on Norway's western coast, and of their two teenage children, Kristina and Kurt. To the south a British Airways airbus passed over on its great circle route from Moscow to London. Thor Larsen neither knew nor cared.

The dinner that evening was in the famous Aurora Cellar, built in the cellar storerooms of an old palace in Stockholm's mediaeval quarter. When Thor and Lisa Larsen arrived and were shown down the narrow steps to the cellar, the proprietor was waiting for them. "Mr. Wennerstrom is already here," he said, and showed them into one of the private rooms, a small, intimate cavern, arched in 500-year-old brick. As they entered, Larsen's employer, Harald Wennerstrom, lumbered to his feet, embraced Lisa and shook hands with her husband.

Wennerstrom was something of a legend among the seafaring people of Scandinavia. He was now seventy-five, grizzled and craggy with bristling eyebrows. Just after the Second World War he had inherited from his father half a dozen small cargo ships. In thirty-five years he had built up the biggest independently-owned fleet of tankers outside the hands of the Greeks and the Hong Kong Chinese. The Nordia Line was his creation, diversifying from dry-cargo ships to tankers in the mid-fifties, building the ships for the oil boom of the sixties.

173

They sat and ate, and Wennerstrom asked after the family. His own forty-year marriage had ended with the death of his wife four years earlier; they had had no children. But if he had had a son, he would have liked him to be like the big Norwegian across the table, a sailor's sailor; and he was particularly fond of Lisa.

It was only when they sat finishing their wine that Wennerstrom came to business. "Three years ago, Thor, I made three forecasts to myself. One was that by the end of 1982 the solidarity of the Organization of Petroleum Exporting Countries, OPEC, would have broken down. The second was that the American president's policy to curb the United States' consumption of oil energy and by-products would have failed. The third was that the Soviet Union would have changed from a net oil exporter to a net oil importer. I was told I was crazy, but I was right."

Thor Larsen nodded. The formation of OPEC and its quadrupling of oil prices in the winter of 1973 had not only produced a world slump that had nearly broken the economies of the Western world, it had also sent the oil-tanker business into a seven-year decline. It was a bold spirit who could have foreseen the events between 1979 and 1982; the breakup of OPEC as the Arab world split into feuding factions; the spiralling increase in US oil consumption; and Soviet oil production so low, because of poor technology, that Russia had been forced to become once again an oil importer. The three factors had produced the tanker boom into which they were now, in the summer of 1982, beginning to move.

"As you know," Wennerstrom resumed, "last September I signed a contract with the Japanese for a new supertanker. The marketplace said I was mad; but I'm not. Next summer Clint Blake of American East Shore Oil is invading Europe. He's putting several thousand service stations across the motorways there, marketing his own brand of gasoline and oil. For that he'll need tanker tonnage. And I've got it. A seven-year contract to bring crude from the Middle East to Western Europe. He's already building his own refinery at Rotterdam, alongside Esso, Mobil and Chevron. That is what the new tanker is for. She's big and she's expensive, but she'll pay. She'll make five or six runs a year from the Arabian Gulf to Rotterdam, and in five years she'll amortize the investment. But that's not the reason I'm building her. She's going to be my flagship, my memorial. And you'll be her skipper."

174

Thor Larsen sat in silence. Lisa's hand stole across the table and squeezed his gently. Two years ago Larsen could never have skippered a Swedish-flag vessel, being himself a Norwegian. But since the Gothenburg Agreement of the previous year a Swedish shipowner could apply for honorary Swedish citizenship for exceptional officers in his employ, Scandinavian, but non-Swedish, so that they could be offered a captaincy. Wennerstrom had applied successfully on behalf of Larsen.

"I'm having her built at the Ishikawajima-Harima yard in Japan," said Wennerstrom. "It's the only yard in the world that can take her. They have the dry dock."

The days of ships being built on slipways and allowed to slide into the water were long past. The size and weight were too great. The giants were now built in enormous dry docks, so that when ready for launching the sea was let in and the ship simply floated off her blocks and rode water inside the dock.

"She's taking shape now," Wennerstrom told them. "She'll float on November first next. Then there'll be fitting-out and sea trials and you'll be on her bridge, Thor."

"Thank you," said Larsen. "What are you calling her?"

"You remember the old sagas? We'll name her to please Niorn, the god of the sea," said Wennerstrom quietly. He was staring at the flame of the candle in its cast-iron holder before him. "For Niorn controls the fire and the water, the twin enemies of a tanker captain; the explosion and the sea herself. We will call her after the daughter of Niorn, Freya, the most beautiful of all the goddesses." He raised his glass. "To the *Freya*." They drank.

"When she sails," said Wennerstrom, "the world will never have seen the like of her. And when she is past sailing, the world will never see the like of her again."

"What will be her deadweight?" asked Larsen. "How much crude will she carry?"

"She'll be carrying one million tons of crude oil."

Thor Larsen heard a hiss of indrawn breath from his wife beside him. "That's big," he said. "That's very big."

"The biggest the world has ever seen," said Wennerstrom.

IN HIS OFFICE in the firm's London headquarters, Barry Ferndale, the head of the Soviet section and Munro's controller, listened to the tape from Moscow. When it was over he began excitedly

175

polishing his glasses. Short and round, Ferndale hid his keen brain and profound knowledge of Soviet affairs behind mannerisms of great cheerfulness and seeming naivety.

"Good gracious me, my dear fellow. My dear Adam. What an extraordinary affair. This really is quite priceless."

"If it's true," said Munro carefully.

"Ah, yes, of course. Now, you simply must tell me how you got hold of it."

Munro told his story carefully. It was true in every detail, save that he claimed the source of the tape had been Anatoly Krivoi.

"Krivoi, yes, yes, know of him, of course," said Ferndale. "Well now, I shall have to get this translated into English and show it to the Master. This could be very big indeed. You won't be able to return to Moscow tomorrow, you know. Do you have a place to stay? Your club? Excellent."

Ferndale spent the night working on the translation of the tape alone in his office. His Russian was fluent and he missed nothing of the Yakovlev report, nor the stunned reaction of the Politburo.

At ten o'clock the following morning, sleepless but shaved and breakfasted, looking pink and fresh as always, Ferndale was with the director-general. Sir Nigel Irvine read the transcript in silence, put it down and regarded the tape lying before him. "Is this genuine?" he asked.

Barry Ferndale dropped his bonhomie. "Don't know," he said thoughtfully. "It's going to take a lot of checking out. Adam told me he met this Krivoi at a reception at the Czech embassy two weeks ago. If Krivoi was thinking of coming over, that would have been his chance. Penkovsky did exactly the same; met a diplomat on neutral ground and established a secret meeting later. Of course, he was regarded with intense suspicion until his information checked out. I want to do the same checking here."

Ferndale began polishing his glasses. The speed of his circular movements with the handkerchief on the lenses, so went the folklore, was in direct proportion to the pace of his thinking, and he polished furiously. "First, Munro. Just in case it is a trap and the second meeting is to spring the trap, I would like him to take some leave until we have finished with the tape."

"And inside Britain, Barry. No wandering abroad till this is sorted out. His file mentions an interest in Scotland, I see. Suggest he goes on a walking tour or something."

"Right. Then there's the tape. It breaks down into two parts: the Yakovlev report and the voices of the Politburo. No voice-print tests will be possible with Yakovlev, but what he says is highly technical. I'd like to check that out with some experts in chemical seed-dressing techniques. There's an excellent section in the ministry of agriculture which can tell us if this accident with the Lindane hopper valve is feasible."

"You recall that file the CIA lent us a month ago," said Sir Nigel. "The photos taken by the Condor satellites. Check the symptoms against the apparent explanation. What else?"

"Voice-print analysis," said Ferndale. "I'd like to chop a section up into bits, so no one need know what is being talked about. The language laboratory at Beaconsfield could check out regional dialects and so forth. But the clincher will be the comparison of voice-prints."

Sir Nigel nodded. Human voices, reduced to a series of electronically-registered blips and pulses, are as individual as fingerprints. "Very well," he said, "but I insist on two things. No one must know about this outside of you, me and Munro. If it's a phoney we don't want to raise false hopes; if it's not, it's high-explosive. None of the technical side must know the whole. Secondly, I don't want to hear the name of Anatoly Krivoi again. Devise a cover-name for this asset and use it in future."

TWO DAYS LATER a Jumbo jet arrived at London's Heathrow airport from Toronto. Among its passengers was Azamat Krim, Canadian-born son of an emigré. Andrew Drake had noted him years before as one who shared his beliefs completely, and he was waiting to meet him as he came out of the customs area. Together they drove to Drake's flat off the Bayswater Road.

Azamat Krim was a Crimean Tatar, short, dark and wiry. His father, unlike Drake's, had fought in the Second World War *with* the Red Army, and had been captured in combat. In a German forced-labour camp Chingris Krim had heard of the death of his entire family. His loyalty to Russia had availed him nothing. All the Tatar race had been accused by Stalin of collaboration with the Germans, which allowed Stalin to deport the entire nation to the wilds of the Orient. Tens of thousands had died in unheated cattle trucks, thousands more in the frozen wastes of Kazakhstan and Siberia without food or clothing.

Liberated by the Canadians in 1945, Chingris Krim had been befriended by a Canadian officer, a former rodeo rider from Calgary, who one day on an Austrian horse farm had admired the Tatar soldier's mastery of horses and brilliant riding. The Canadian had secured Krim's authorized emigration to Canada, where he had married and had a son. Azamat was the boy, now aged thirty, and like Drake bitter against the Kremlin for the sufferings of his father's family.

In his flat Andrew Drake explained his plan and the Tatar agreed to join him. Together they put the final touches to securing the needed funds by taking out a bank in Northern England.

A week later the castaway, Miroslav Kaminsky, arrived in England on his Red Cross travel papers. He had come across Europe by train, the ticket paid for by Drake who was nearing the end of his financial resources. Kaminsky and Krim were introduced and Kaminsky given his orders.

"You learn English," Drake told him. "Morning, noon and night, faster than you've ever learned anything before. Meanwhile I'm going to get you some decent papers. You can't travel on Red Cross documents for ever. Until I get them, and until you can make yourself understood in English, don't leave the flat."

THE FOLLOWING WEEK, at the end of his ten-day furlough, Adam Munro caught the breakfast flight from Aberdeen to London. The headline story in the newspaper which the air hostess handed to him concerned two unidentified men, believed to be Germans from the Red Army Faction, who had robbed a Sheffield bank of £20,000. Munro couldn't know it, but Andrew Drake, with Krim's assistance, had secured the funds he needed for the operation he was planning.

MUNRO CHECKED IN at the firm's headquarters and was shown straight into Barry Ferndale's office. Ferndale sat him down and proffered coffee. "Well now, the tape . . . . Fact is, m'dear chap, it's genuine. Everything checks. Six or seven senior functionaries of the Soviet agriculture ministry have been ousted. And the voices are genuine. Now for the big one; one of our assets working out of Leningrad managed to take a drive out of town. He swiped a stalk of the afflicted wheat. It came home in the bag three days ago. The lab report confirms there is an excess of Lindane in the

178

root of the seedling. So, you've hit what our American cousins call pay-dirt. In fact twenty-four-carat gold. By the way, the Master wants to see you. You're going back to Moscow tonight."

Munro's meeting with Sir Nigel Irvine was friendly but brief. "Well done," said the Master. "This might be a long-term operation, which makes it a good thing you are new to Moscow. There will be no raised eyebrows if you stay on for a couple of years. But just in case this Krivoi fellow changes his mind, I want you to press for everything we can squeeze out. Do you want any back-up?"

"No, thank you," said Munro. "The asset has insisted he'll talk only to me. I don't want to scare him off by bringing others in. I'll have to handle it alone."

Sir Nigel nodded. "Very well."

When Munro had gone, Sir Nigel Irvine turned over the file on his desk, which was Munro's personal record. He had his misgivings. The man was a loner, ill at ease working in a team. There was an adage in the firm: there are old agents and there are bold agents, but there are no old, bold agents. Sir Nigel was an old agent, and he appreciated caution. This new operation had come swinging in from the outfield, unexpected, unprepared-for. And it was moving fast. But then, the tape was genuine, no doubt about it. So was the summons on his desk to see the prime minister at Number Ten.

That evening Sir Nigel, accompanied by Sir Julian Flannery, the cabinet secretary, was shown straight to the prime minister's private study.

Britain's premier, Mrs. Joan Carpenter, had read the transcript of the Politburo tape, passed to her by the foreign secretary. "Have you informed the Americans of this matter?" she asked.

"Not yet, ma'am," Sir Nigel answered. "Our confirmation of its authenticity is only three days old."

"I would like you to do it personally," said the prime minister. Sir Nigel inclined his head. "The political perspectives of this pending wheat famine in the Soviet Union are immeasurable, and as the world's biggest surplus wheat producer, the USA should be involved from the outset."

"I would not wish the CIA to try to move in on this agent of ours," said Sir Nigel. "The running of this asset may be extremely delicate. I think we should go it alone."

"Of course. If pressure is brought," she said, "refer back to me and I will speak to President Matthews personally about it. In the meantime I would like you to fly to Washington tomorrow and present them with a verbatim copy of the tape. I intend to speak to President Matthews tonight."

Sir Nigel and Sir Julian rose to leave. "One last thing," said the prime minister, "I fully understand that I am not allowed to know the identity of this agent. Will you be telling Robert Benson of the CIA who it is?"

"Certainly not, ma'am." Not only would the director-general of the SIS refuse point-blank to inform his own prime minister of the identity of the Russian, but he would not tell her even of Munro who was running that agent. The Americans would know who Munro was, but never whom he was running. Nor would there be any tailing of Munro by the CIA in Moscow, he would see to that.

"Then presumably this Russian defector has a code-name. May I know it?" asked the prime minister.

"Certainly, ma'am. He's known as the Nightingale."

It just happened that Nightingale was the next songbird in the list of birds after which all Soviet agents were code-named, but the prime minister did not know this. She smiled for the first time. "How very appropriate."

Six

Just after ten in the morning of a rainy 1 August a VC-10 of the RAF Strike Command lifted out of Lyneham Base in Wiltshire and headed west. It carried one air chief marshal visiting the Pentagon in Washington and a civilian in a shabby mackintosh. The air chief marshal introduced himself to the unexpected civilian, and learned that his companion was Mr. Barrett of the foreign office who had business with the British embassy and was taking advantage of the RAF flight.

At the same time a British Airways Boeing Jumbo jet left Heathrow bound for New York. Among its passengers was Azamat Krim, heading west on a buying mission with a back pocket full of money.

Eight hours later the VC-10 landed at Andrews Air Force Base in Maryland, ten miles southeast of Washington. Two air force policemen snapped to attention as the air chief marshal came down the steps. A Pentagon limousine swept him away to Washington.

No one noticed the modest black sedan that drove to the parked VC-10 ten minutes later; no one bothered with the rumpled civilian who trotted down the steps and straight into the car. The man in the back who welcomed the guest from London was the chief of the CIA's Western European division. He had been chosen to meet the Englishman because he knew him well. "Nigel, good to see you again," he said.

"How good of you to come to meet me, Lance," responded Sir Nigel Irvine. Years before he had been the SIS liaison man with the CIA, based at the British embassy. Those had been tough days, in the wake of the Philby affair, when even the weather was classified information so far as the English were concerned. He thought of what he carried in his briefcase and permitted himself a small smile.

The car headed west into Virginia, and after thirty minutes swung off the main highway and headed into the forest. At the security gate in the great seven-feet-high, chain-link fence that surrounds Langley, it halted while Lance showed his pass, then drove to the CIA's headquarters. The car swept past the complex of five blocks and drove round the back. Here there is a short ramp, protected by a steel portcullis, running down one floor to the first basement level. At the bottom is a select car park for no more than ten cars. The black sedan came to a halt, and the man called Lance handed Sir Nigel over to his superior, Charles "Chip" Allen, deputy director of operations.

Set in the back wall of the car park is a small lift, guarded by steel doors and two armed men. Chip Allen identified his guest, signed for him and used a plastic card to open the lift doors. The lift hummed its way quietly up to the director's suite, where Bob Benson, alerted from below, welcomed the British visitor.

Benson led him past the big desk to the lounge area in front of the beige marble fireplace, and the two men sat down. Coffee was ordered, and when they were alone, Benson asked, "What brings you to Langley, Nigel?"

Sir Nigel sipped and sat back. "We have," he said, "obtained the services of a new asset." He spoke for almost ten minutes, before the director interrupted him. "Inside the Politburo?" he queried. "You mean, right inside?"

"Let us just say, with access to Politburo meeting transcripts," said Sir Nigel.

"Would you mind if I called Chip Allen of operations and Ben Kahn of intelligence in on this?"

"Not at all, Bob." Sir Nigel Irvine was not displeased that his two old contacts in the CIA should be in on the ground floor of his briefing. All pure intelligence agencies, as opposed to intelligence/secret police forces like the KGB, have two main arms. One is operations, which obtains information; the other is intelligence, which collates, interprets and analyses the mass of unprocessed material. Both have to be good. If the information is faulty the best analysis in the world will only result in nonsense; if the analysis is inept the efforts of the information gatherers is wasted. What nations are doing is nowadays often observable; what they *intend* to do is not. Which is why all the space cameras in the world will never supplant a brilliant analyst.

In five minutes Chip Allen and Intelligence Deputy Director Ben Kahn were sitting with Benson and Irvine in the lounge area, coffee forgotten.

The British spymaster talked for almost an hour. Then the three Americans read the Nightingale transcript and watched the tape recording in its polythene bag with something like hunger. When Irvine had finished there was a short silence.

"You'll want to check it all," Sir Nigel said finally. "It took us ten days, but we can't fault it. And, of course, you have your Condor photographs." From his bag he produced a small polythene bag with a sprig of young wheat inside it. "One of our chaps swiped this from a field outside Leningrad."

"I'll have our agriculture department check it out as well," said Benson.

"Can we have direct access to Nightingale?"

"Sorry, no," said Sir Nigel. "The Nightingale's too damn delicate, right out in the cold. But you'll get everything we get, as soon as we get it."

"When's your next delivery slated for?" asked Allen.

"Today week. At least, that's the meet. I hope there'll be a handover."

Sir Nigel spent the night at a CIA safe house in the Virginia countryside, and the next day "Mr. Barrett" flew back to London.

Two weeks later in the Oval Office of the White House,

President Matthews sat in conclave with his advisers: Robert Benson, Stanislav Poklewski of the National Security Council and the secretary of state, David Lawrence, a conservative Boston lawyer and pillar of the East Coast Establishment.

President Matthews flicked the file in front of him closed. He had long since devoured the translation of the first Politburo transcript; what he had just finished reading was his experts' evaluation of it. "Bob, you were remarkably close with your estimate of the grain shortfall," he said. "Now it appears they are going to be fifty to fifty-five million tons short, no matter what. And you have no doubts this transcript comes right from inside the Politburo?"

"Mr. President, the voices are real; the excessive Lindane in the root of the wheat plant is real; the hatchet job inside the Soviet agriculture ministry is real. We don't believe there is any doubt that tape recording was of the Politburo in session."

"We have to handle this right," mused the president. "There has never been an opportunity like it."

"Mr. President," said Poklewski, "this means the Soviets are facing a famine. Let them have it. Let them sort it out in their own way."

"David?" asked the president of his secretary of state.

Secretary Lawrence shook his head. The differences of opinion between him and the arch-hawk Poklewski were legendary. "I disagree," he said. "I don't think we have examined deeply enough what might happen if the Soviet Union is plunged into chaos next spring. There are massive worldwide implications."

"Bob?" President Matthews asked the director of the CIA.

"They know if they want the grain they have to come to you," Benson said. "We have the wheat, we have the Condors, we have the Nightingale and we have the time. We hold all the aces. No need to decide yet which way to play them."

Lawrence nodded and regarded Benson with new respect. Poklewski shrugged. President Matthews made up his mind.

"Stan, I want you to put together an *ad hoc* group within the National Security Council—small, absolutely secret. You, Bob and David here. Chairmen of the joint chiefs of staff, secretaries of defence, treasury and agriculture. I want to know what will happen, worldwide, if the Soviet Union starves."

One of the telephones on his desk rang. It was the direct line from the state department. Secretary Lawrence took the call, listened for several minutes, then replaced the receiver. "Mr. President, two hours ago in Moscow Foreign Minister Rykov summoned Ambassador Donaldson. On behalf of the Soviet Government he has proposed the sale by the United States to the Soviet Union by next spring of fifty-five million tons of mixed cereal grains."

Only the ormolu carriage clock above the marble fireplace could be heard for several moments in the Oval Office.

"What did Ambassador Donaldson reply?" asked the president.

"That the request would be passed on to Washington for consideration."

"Gentlemen," said the president, "I need those answers fast. I can hold up my answer by four weeks at the outside, but I shall have to reply to the Soviet Union by September fifteenth at the latest. When I do, I shall want to know what we are handling here."

"Mr. President," said Benson, "we may soon be receiving a second package of information from the Nightingale. That could give an indication of the way the Kremlin sees the problem."

President Matthews nodded. "Bob, if and when it comes, I would like it translated and on my desk immediately."

VALENTINA was waiting for him again at the chapel, standing back in the shade of the trees. His stomach was tight, knotted, for all that he was pleased to see her. She was no expert at spotting a tail and might have been followed. If she had, Adam Munro's diplomatic cover would save him from nothing worse than expulsion but it was what they would do to her that worried him. Whatever the motives, what she was doing was high treason.

He took her in his arms and kissed her. She kissed him back, trembling. "Are you frightened?" he asked her.

"A bit," she nodded. "You listened to the tape recording?"

"Yes. Before I handed it over. I shouldn't have, but I did."

"Then you know about the famine that faces us. Adam, when I was a girl I saw the famine in this country, just after the war. It was bad, but it was caused by the Germans. We could take it. Our leaders were on our side, they would make things get better."

"Perhaps they can sort things out this time," said Munro lamely.

184

Valentina shook her head angrily. "They're not even trying," she burst out. "They are just bickering, trying to save their own skins."

"And your uncle, Marshal Kerensky?" he asked gently.

"He's as bad as the rest. They all jockey for power, and to hell with the people. I can't be one of them, not any more."

Munro looked across the clearing at the pines but saw olive trees and heard a boy in uniform shouting "You don't own me!" Strange, he mused, how establishments with all their power sometimes went too far and lost control of their servants through sheer excess. "I could get you out of here, Valentina," he said. "It would mean my leaving the diplomatic corps, but it's been done before. Sascha is young enough to grow up somewhere else."

"No, Adam, it's tempting but I can't. I am part of Russia, I have to stay. Perhaps, one day . . . I don't know." They sat in silence for a while, holding hands. She broke the quiet at last.

"Did your intelligence people pass the tape recording on?"

"I think so. I handed it to the man I believe represents the Secret Service in the embassy. He asked me if there would be another one."

She nodded at her shoulder bag. "It's just the transcript. Of the following Politburo meeting. I can't get the tape recordings any more. They're kept in a safe and I don't have the key."

"How do you get them out, Valentina?" he asked.

"After the meetings, the tapes and the stenographic notes are brought under guard to the central committee building. There is a locked department where I and six others work. When the transcripts are finished the tapes are locked away."

"Then how did you get the first one?"

"The man in charge is new, since last month. The other one, before him, was more lax. There is a studio where the tapes are copied once before being locked in the safe. I was alone in there last month, long enough to steal the duplicate tape and substitute a dummy."

"A dummy?" exclaimed Munro. "They'll spot the substitution if ever they play it back."

"It's unlikely," she said. "The transcripts form the archives once they have been checked against the tapes. I was lucky with that tape; I brought it out in a shopping bag under the groceries I had bought in the commissary."

"Aren't you searched?"

"Hardly ever. We are trusted, Adam, the elite of the New Russia. The papers are easier. At work I wear an old-fashioned girdle. I copied the transcript of the last meeting on the machine, but ran off an extra copy, then switched the number-control back by one figure. The extra copy I stuck inside my girdle."

Munro's stomach turned over at the risk she was taking. "What do they talk about in this meeting?" he asked, gesturing towards the shoulder bag.

"What will happen when the famine breaks. But Adam . . . there's been a meeting since. Early in July. I couldn't copy it, I was on leave. But when I got back I met one of the girls who had transcribed it. She was white-faced, and wouldn't discuss it."

"Can you get it?" asked Munro.

"I can try. But not until early next month; I won't be on the late shift, when I can work alone in the office, until then."

"We shouldn't meet here again," Munro told her. "Patterns are dangerous." He spent an hour describing the techniques she would need to know if they were to go on meeting—and set up a number of pre-arranged places.

Five minutes later she gave him a wad of flimsy paper sheets covered with neatly typed Russian Cyrillic script and slipped away through the forest.

Munro retreated into the darkness of the church's recessed side door. He produced a roll of tape from his pocket, slipped down his trousers and taped the batch of sheets to his thigh. With the trousers up again and belted he could feel the papers snug against his thigh. Under the baggy, Russian-made trousers, they did not show. By midnight, in the silence of his flat, he had read them all. The next Wednesday they went in the messenger's wrist-chained briefcase to London.

AZAMAT KRIM had returned from New York aboard the elderly *Queen Elizabeth II*, deciding to sail rather than fly because he felt he had a better chance of his luggage escaping X-ray examination by sea.

His purchases included a standard aluminium shoulder case, such as professional photographers use to protect their cameras and lenses. It could not be X-rayed, but had to be hand-examined. Hidden under the moulded plastic sponge padding in the bottom

186

of the case were two handguns with ammunition clips. In a cabin
trunk full of clothes he had also concealed an aluminium tube
with a screw top, containing what would pass for a long-range
camera lens. Actually it was an image-intensifier, also called a
night-sight, which may be commercially bought without a permit
in the United States but not in Britain.

He had had no trouble, and the weaponry was now in Andrew
Drake's Bayswater flat. Only one more item was needed.

In late August, Somerset police were puzzled by a theft from a
sporting gunshop in the pleasant country town of Taunton. The
place had not been ransacked, and the usual haul, shotguns for
the holding-up of banks, had not been taken. What was missing
was a fine hunting rifle, a Finnish-made Sako Hornet .22, a highly
accurate precision piece. Also gone were two boxes of shells, soft-
nosed, 45-grain, hollow-point Remingtons, capable of high
velocity, great penetration and considerable distortion on impact.

In his flat, Andrew Drake sat with Miroslav Kaminsky and
Azamat Krim and gazed at their haul; it consisted of the two hand
guns, each with two magazines fully loaded; the rifle and shells,
and the image-intensifier.

There are two basic types of night-sight: the infra-red scope and
the intensifier. Men who shoot by night tend to prefer the latter,
which does not require a power source, and Krim, with his
background of three years with the Canadian Parachute Regiment,
had chosen well. The image-intensifier gathers all the tiny
elements of light that are present in a "dark" environment, and
concentrates them, as the gigantic retina of a barn-owl's eye can
concentrate what little light there is and see a moving mouse
where a human eye would detect nothing.

The rifle already had grooves along the upper side of its barrel
to take a telescopic sight. Working with a file and a vice screwed
to the edge of the kitchen table, Krim began to convert the clips
of the image-intensifier to fit into these grooves.

That same night, far away in the city of Ternopol in the
Ukraine, a plainclothes agent of the KGB left the non-commissioned
officers' club and began to walk home. He had had a convivial
evening with his colleagues, which was probably why he failed to
notice the two figures in the doorway across the street who had
been watching the club entrance.

It was after midnight and Ternopol, even on a warm August

night, has no nightlife to speak of. The secret policeman's path took him away from the main streets and into the sprawl of Shevchenko Park. Halfway across the park there was a scuttling of feet behind him; he half turned, took a blow from a cosh on the temple and went down in a heap.

It was nearly dawn before he recovered. He had been dragged into a tangle of bushes and robbed of his wallet, money, keys, ration and ID cards. Police and KGB inquiries continued for several weeks into this most unaccustomed mugging but no culprits were discovered. In fact, both had been on the dawn train out of Ternopol and were back in their homes in Lvov.

WELL BEFORE his 15 September deadline, President Matthews chaired the meeting of the *ad hoc* committee that had considered the Nightingale's second package.

"My analysts have come up with some possibilities consequent upon a famine in the Soviet Union," CIA Chief Benson told the eight men in the Oval Office, "but I don't think any of them would go as far as the Politburo themselves in predicting a pandemic breakdown of law and order. It's unheard-of in the Soviet Union."

David Lawrence of the state department agreed with him.

"So what answer do I give Maxim Rudin to his request to purchase fifty-five million tons of grain?" asked the president.

"Mr. President, tell him 'No'," urged Poklewski. "You have Maxim Rudin and the whole Politburo in the palm of your hand. For two decades, successive US administrations have bailed the Soviets out every time they have gotten into difficulties with their economy and every time they have come back more aggressive than ever. Now the world can be shown beyond a doubt that the Marxist economic system does not work and never will. I urge you to screw the lid down tight, real tight. You can demand a concession for every ton of wheat. And if he won't play, you can bring Rudin down."

"Would this . . ." President Matthews tapped the Nightingale report in front of him, "bring Rudin down?"

David Lawrence answered. "If what is described in here by the Politburo actually happened inside the Soviet Union, yes, Rudin would fall in disgrace."

"Then use the power," urged Poklewski. "Rudin has no

alternative but to agree to your terms. If he won't, topple him."

"And the successor . . ." began the president.

". . . will have seen what happened to Rudin, and will learn his lesson from that."

President Matthews sought the views of the rest of the meeting. All but Lawrence and Benson agreed with Poklewski. President Matthews made his decision. The hawks had won.

A few days later, the Cadillac of the American ambassador to Moscow hissed into the parking bay before the main doors of the Soviet foreign ministry building and Ambassador Donaldson was escorted to the office of Dmitri Rykov, the veteran Soviet foreign minister. The meeting was formal. Donaldson was attended by his head of chancery and Rykov by five senior officials. Donaldson read his message carefully in its original English. Rykov understood and spoke English well, but an aide did a rapid running translation into his right ear.

President Matthews's message expressed regret that the United States of America would not be in a position to make a sale to the Union of Soviet Socialist Republics of the requested tonnage of wheat. With hardly a pause, Ambassador Donaldson read on, into the second part of the message. This regretted the lack of success of the strategic arms limitation talks known as SALT 3, concluded in the winter of 1980, in lessening world tension, and expressed the hope that SALT 4, scheduled for preliminary discussion this coming autumn and winter, would achieve more, and enable the world to make genuine steps along the road to a just and lasting peace. That was all.

Ambassador Donaldson laid the full text of the message on Rykov's desk, received the formal thanks of the grey-haired, grey-visaged Soviet foreign minister, and left.

ON THE LAST DAY of August Andrew Drake flew from London to Athens to begin his search for a ship heading towards Odessa, his chosen entry point to the Soviet Union. The same day a small van, converted into a two-bunk mobile home such as students use for a roving continental holiday, left London for Dover and thence to France and Athens by road. Concealed beneath the floor were the guns, ammunition and image-intensifier. Fortunately most drug consignments head the other way, from the Balkans to France and Britain. Custom checks were perfuctory at Dover and Calais.

At the wheel of the van was Azamat Krim with his Canadian passport and international driving licence. Beside him, with new—albeit not quite regular British papers—was Miroslav Kaminsky.

Seven

Close by the bridge across the Moscow River at Uspenskoye is a restaurant called the Russian Izba, built in the style of the timber cottages in which Russian peasants dwell, both interior and exterior made of split pine trunks, the gaps filled with river clay. The Izba restaurant is snug and warm inside, divided into a dozen small private dining rooms. Unlike the restaurants of central Moscow it is permitted a profit incentive, and as a result, and in stark contrast to the usual run of Russian eateries, it has tasty food and willing service.

It was here that Adam Munro had set up his third meeting with Valentina on Saturday, 4 September. She had persuaded a male friend to take her to this particular restaurant. Munro had invited one of the embassy secretaries to dinner, and had booked the table in her name. The reservations record would not therefore show that either Munro or Valentina were present.

On the dot of nine o'clock each made the excuse of going to the toilet and left the table. They met in the car park and Munro followed Valentina to her own private Zhiguli saloon. She was subdued, and puffed nervously at a cigarette. Munro knew the incessant strain that begins to wear at the nerves of defectors-in-place after a few weeks of subterfuge.

"I got my chance," she said. "Three days ago. The meeting of early July. I was nearly caught."

Munro was tense. She was walking a high-wire; they both were. "What happened?" he asked.

"A guard came in. I had just switched off the copying machine and was back at my typewriter. He was perfectly friendly. But he leant against the machine. It was still warm. I don't think he noticed anything. But it frightened me. That's not all that frightened me. I couldn't read the transcript until I got home. I was too busy feeding it into the copier. Adam, it's awful."

She unlocked the glove compartment and extracted a fat envelope which she handed to Munro. The moment of handover is usually the moment when the watchers pounce, if they are there. Feet pound on the gravel, the doors are torn open, the occupants dragged out. Nothing happened.

Munro glanced at his watch. Nearly ten minutes. Too long. He put the envelope in his inside breast pocket. "I'm going to try for permission to bring you out," he said. "You can't go on like this much longer. Nor can you settle back to the old life, knowing what you know. Nor can I carry on, knowing you are out in the city, knowing that we love each other. I have a leave break next month. I'm going to ask them in London then."

This time she made no demur. "All right," she said. Seconds later she was gone into the darkness of the car park. He watched her enter the pool of light by the open restaurant door and disappear inside. He gave her two minutes then returned to his own impatient companion.

It was three in the morning before Munro had finished reading the "Plan Boris", Marshal Nikolai Kerensky's scenario for the conquest of Western Europe. He spent two hours staring at a map and by sunrise was as certain as Marshal Kerensky himself that in terms of conventional warfare the plan would work. Secondly, he was sure that Rykov too was right; thermo-nuclear war would ensue. And thirdly he was certain there was no way of convincing the dissident members of the Politburo of this, short of the holocaust actually happening.

He rose and went to the window. Daylight was breaking, an ordinary Sunday was beginning for the citizens of Moscow, as it would in two hours for Londoners.

All his adult life the guarantee that summer Sundays would remain plain, ordinary, had been dependent on the belief in a fine balance between the might and willpower of the opponent super powers, a balance of fear, but a balance for all that. He shivered, partly from the chill of morning, more from the realization that at last the old nightmare was coming out of the shadows; the balance was breaking down.

THE MEETING in the Oval Office a few days later was tense. All seven members of the *ad hoc* committee were present, with President Matthews in the chair. All had spent half the night reading the transcript of the meeting in which Marshal Kerensky had laid out his plan for war and Vishnayev had made his bid for power. All eight men were shaken. The focus was on the chairman of the joint chiefs of staff, General Martin Craig. "The question is, General," President Matthews asked, "is it feasible?"

"In terms of a conventional war across the face of Western Europe from the Iron Curtain to the Channel ports, yes, it's feasible, Mr. President."

"Could the West, before next spring, increase her defences to the point of making it completely unworkable?"

"That's a harder one, Mr. President. We could ship more men, more hardware, over to Europe. But our European allies don't have our reserves. The imbalance between the Nato forces and the Warsaw Pact forces cannot be recouped in a mere nine months."

"So they're back to 1939 again," said the secretary of treasury gloomily.

"What about the nuclear option?" asked President Matthews quietly.

General Craig shrugged. "If the Soviets attack in full force, it's inescapable. Forewarned as we are, we could slow up a Soviet advance westwards. But whether we could stop Marshal Kerensky dead—the whole damn Soviet army, navy and air force —that's another matter. By the time we knew the answer, it would be too late. Which makes our use of the nuclear option inescapable. Unless of course, sir, we abandon Europe and our three hundred thousand men there."

"David?" asked the president.

Secretary of State David Lawrence tapped the file in front of him. "For the first time in my life I agree with Dmitri Rykov. It's not just a question of Western Europe. If Europe goes, the Balkans, the eastern Mediterranean, Turkey, Iran and the Arabian states cannot hold. Our oil imports are running at sixty-two per cent, and rising. Without Arabian oil we are as finished as Europe, without a shot fired."

"Suggestions, gentlemen?" asked the president.

"The Nightingale is valuable, but not indispensable now," said Stanislav Poklewski. "Why not meet with Rudin and lay it on the table? We now know the intent of 'Plan Boris'. And we will take steps to make that intent unworkable. When he informs his Politburo of that, they'll realize the element of surprise is lost, that the war option won't work any more."

Bob Benson of the CIA shook his head vigorously. "It's not a question of convincing Rudin or Rykov. There's a vicious faction fight going on inside the Politburo. At stake is the succession to Rudin. And the famine is hanging over them. Reveal what we know to Rudin and it might cause him to fall. Vishnayev and his group would take over; they are completely ignorant of the way we Americans react to being attacked. With the grain famine pending they could still try the war option."

"Then Maxim Rudin must not fall," said President Matthews. "Last month I authorized a refusal by the United States to supply the Soviet Union with the grain it needs. I can no longer pursue that policy of rejection, because we now know what it entails. Gentlemen, I am drafting tonight a personal letter to President Rudin proposing that Secretary of State Lawrence and Foreign Minister Rykov meet on neutral territory to confer on the new arms limitation treaty, SALT Four, and *any other matters of interest.*"

After the meeting, the US secretary of state met with the Irish ambassador to Washington. "If my meeting with Foreign Minister Rykov is to succeed," said David Lawrence, "we must have privacy and discretion. The meeting has to be on neutral territory. Geneva is full of watching eyes; ditto Stockholm and Vienna. Ireland is halfway between Moscow and Washington and you still foster the cult of privacy there."

The government in Dublin agreed to host the meeting. Within hours President Matthews's personal and private letter to President Maxim Rudin was on its way to Ambassador Donaldson in Moscow.

On 20 September, President Matthews received Rudin's personal reply, agreeing to the secret meeting between Lawrence and Rykov in Ireland, scheduled for the twenty-fourth.

AT PIRAEUS, the port of Athens, Andrew Drake had found his ship: the MV *Sanadria*, a rusty old Greek cargo vessel due to sail at the end of September for stops at Istanbul and Odessa.

Drake had checked into the Cavo d'Oro hotel at Piraeus, and learned from seamen hanging out at the bar that the man to see was Captain Nikos Thanos, master of the *Sanadria*, who usually could be found at a café on the waterfront.

When Drake returned to the Cavo d'Oro one afternoon, after an unsuccessful attempt to find Captain Thanos, a message was waiting for him from Azamat Krim, saying he and Kaminsky had checked into their agreed hotel in Piraeus. An hour later Drake was with them. The van had come through unscathed. During the night Drake had the guns and ammunition transferred piece by piece to his room at the Cavo d'Oro. The following morning Krim flew back to London to live in Drake's apartment and await the next stage in the plan. Kaminsky stayed on.

Several days later, Drake made contact with Captain Thanos and arranged to be taken aboard the *Sanadria* as a temporary deckhand. For five thousand dollars, the captain asked no questions.

"We sail on the thirtieth," he said, "and should be in Odessa on the ninth or tenth. Be here at the quay where the *Sanadria* is berthed by six p.m. on the thirtieth. Wait until the agent's waterclerk has left, then come aboard just before the immigration people."

Four hours later in Drake's flat in London, Azamat Krim took Drake's call from Piraeus giving him the arrival date in Odessa that Mishkin and Lazareff needed to know.

Krim's problem was to post a card to Mishkin from inside the Soviet Union, complete with Russian stamps and written in Russian, without waiting for a visa to be granted by the Soviet consulate in London, which could take up to four weeks. With Drake's help he had solved it.

Prior to 1980 Moscow's main airport, Sheremetyevo, had been a small, shabby affair. But for the Olympic Games the Soviet government had commissioned a new terminal, and its facilities were now excellent. In the departure lounges were letterboxes for the mail of anyone who might have forgotten to post his picture postcards before leaving Moscow. The KGB vets every letter, postcard, cable or phone call coming into or leaving the Soviet Union. But the new departure lounges at Sheremetyevo were also used for long-distance flights within the Soviet Union.

Krim's postcard, which showed a picture of the Tupolev 144 supersonic passenger jet, had been acquired at the Aeroflot offices in London. Soviet stamps sufficient for a postcard were bought openly from the London stamp emporium, Stanley Gibbons. On it, in Russian, was the message: "Just leaving with our factory's Party group for the expedition to Khabarovsk. Great excitement.

Almost forgot to write you. Many happy returns for your birthday on the tenth. Your cousin, Ivan."

Khabarovsk being in the extreme orient of Siberia, a group leaving by Aeroflot from Moscow for that city would leave from the same terminal building as a flight leaving for Japan. The card was addressed to Lev Mishkin in Lvov.

Azamat Krim booked an Aeroflot flight from London to Tokyo via Moscow. In Moscow he changed planes for the Aeroflot flight to Tokyo. In the Moscow transit lounge he dropped the card in the letterbox and went on to Tokyo. From there he flew back to London.

The card was examined by the KGB at Moscow's airport, assumed to be from a Russian to a Ukrainian, both living inside the USSR, and sent on. It arrived in Lvov three days later.

ON 27 SEPTEMBER, Secretary of State Lawrence reported to the *ad hoc* committee of the National Security Council in the Oval Office. Four days earlier he had held a secret meeting in Ireland with Soviet Foreign Minister Rykov.

"Mr. President, gentlemen, I think we have it, providing Maxim Rudin can keep his hold on the Politburo and secure their agreement. The proposal is that we and the Soviets each send teams of negotiators to a resumed strategic arms limitation conference in Ireland. The Irish government has agreed to provide a suitable conference hall and living accommodation if we and the Soviets signal our assent.

"Now this is the big one; I secured a concession from Dmitri Rykov that the discussion need not exclude thermo-nuclear weapons, strategic weapons, inner space, international inspection, tactical nuclear weapons, conventional weapons and manning levels, or disengagement of forces along the Iron Curtain line."

There was a murmur of approval and surprise from the other seven men present. No previous American-Soviet arms conference had ever had such widely-drawn terms of reference. If all areas showed a move towards genuine détente, it would add up to a peace treaty.

"These talks will be what the conference is supposedly about, so far as the world is concerned," resumed Secretary Lawrence. "Now, in back of the main conference, a secondary conference of technical experts will negotiate the sale by the US to the Soviets

196

at costs probably lower than world prices, of up to fifty-five million tons of grain, consumer-product technology, computers and oil-extraction technology. At every stage there will be liaison between the up-front and the in-back teams of negotiators. They make a concession on arms, we make a concession on low-cost goodies. It seems they are in a hurry. They want to start in a fortnight."

MAXIM RUDIN did not put it to his Politburo quite like that the following day. "They have risen to the bait," he said from his chair at the head of the table. "When they make a concession on wheat or technology in one of the conference rooms, we make the absolute minimum concession in the other conference room. We will get our grain, Comrades; and at the minimum price. Americans, after all, have never been able to out-negotiate the Russians.

"There are two points we should be clear on before we decide whether to talk. One is that the Politburo will be kept fully informed at every stage, so if the moment comes when the price is too high, this council will have the right to abort the conference and I will defer to Comrade Vishnayev's plan for war in the spring. The second is that no concession we may make to secure the wheat need necessarily obtain for very long after the deliveries have taken place."

There were several grins round the table. This was the sort of *realpolitik* the Politburo was accustomed to. "Very well," said Vishnayev, "but we should lay down the exact parameters of our negotiating teams' authority to concede points."

"I have no objection to that," said Rudin. He got his vote to proceed.

THERE IS ONLY ONE direct flight a week between Athens and Istanbul, the Tuesday Sabena connection. On Tuesday 28 September, Miroslav Kaminsky was on it, instructed to secure for Andrew Drake a consignment of sheepskin coats for the trading in Odessa that was to be his care there.

On 30 September, Drake stood in the shade of a crane and watched the *Sanadria* battening down her hatches. Conspicuous on deck were Vacuvators for Odessa, powerful machines for sucking wheat out of the hold of a ship and straight into a grain silo. The Soviet Union must be trying to improve her grain

197

unloading capacity, he mused, though he did not know why.

He watched the agent's waterclerk leave the ship, giving Captain Thanos a last shake of the hand. Thanos scanned the pier and made out the figure of Drake loping towards him with a suitcase, his kitbag over one shoulder. The handguns were in the suitcase. The kitbag, about three feet long, contained the rifle.

In the captain's day cabin Drake signed the ship's articles and became a member of the deck crew.

While he was down below storing his gear the Greek immigration officer came on board and he and the captain had their usual drink together. When he scanned the crew list Drake's British nationality stood out. He riffled through the pages of his passport. A fifty dollar bill fell onto the table. "An out of work heading for the east," Thanos said lightly. "Thought you'd be glad to be shot of him."

Daylight was fading as the *Sanadria*'s ropes were cast off and she slipped away from her berth and headed for the Dardanelles. Below decks the crew were grouping round the greasy messroom table. One of them was hoping no one would look under his mattress where the Sako Hornet rifle was now stored. In Moscow his target was sitting down to an excellent supper.

Eight

While the disarmament conference opened in a blaze of world publicity at the Palladian stately home of Castletown House, west of Dublin in County Kildare, the old *Sanadria* thumped her way through the Sea of Marmara and docked at Istanbul. Andrew Drake slipped ashore and met Miroslav Kaminsky at an agreed rendezvous in central Istanbul, where he took delivery of a bundle of sheepskin coats and returned to the ship.

Captain Thanos was not surprised. His own seamen would be bringing such luggage aboard to trade the fashionable coats for five times their buying price to the black-market spivs of Odessa. Thirty hours later Istanbul dropped astern and the *Sanadria* chugged north through the Black Sea. On the evening of 9 October she dropped anchor in the roads off Odessa.

Andrew Drake leaned on the fo'c'sle rail, watching the lights of the port and city twinkle into life. Ten miles south of the harbour the River Dniester flowed into the sea through the swampy marshes where five months before Miroslav Kaminsky had stolen his skiff and made a desperate bid for freedom. Now, thanks to him, Andrew Drake, Andriy Drach, had come home to the land of his ancestors. And he had come armed.

Just after dawn the pilot boarded. The *Sanadria* weighed anchor, took a tug in attendance and moved slowly between the breakwaters and into her berth. The shore cranes started to discharge the freighter, and Drake went ashore.

His rendezvous was in a small café in the dock area of old, cobbled streets, not far from the Russian poet Pushkin's memorial. Lev Mishkin came just after noon. He was wary and sat alone, making no sign of recognition. When he had finished his coffee he rose and left the café. Drake followed him. Only when the pair had reached the wide, sea-front highway of Primorsky Boulevard did he allow Drake to catch up. They spoke as they walked.

Drake agreed that he would make his run ashore with the arms and ammunition that evening. There would be plenty of crewmen coming through at the same time for an evening in the dockyard bars. Mishkin and David Lazareff would meet him in the darkness by the Pushkin monument and take over the hardware.

Just after eight p.m. Drake came through with his consignment of arms, carrying the rifle in a kitbag wrapped in a sheepskin coat. Earlier that day he had given the customs man at the docks a bottle of whisky and another sheepskin coat, and now the man waved him jovially through immigration.

Two figures joined him by the Pushkin monument, out of the darkness between the plane trees that crowd Odessa's open spaces.

"Any problems?" asked Lazareff.

"None," said Drake.

"Let's get it over with," said Mishkin. Both men were carrying briefcases. Mishkin took the image-intensifier and stuffed it into his briefcase; Lazareff took the rifle in the kitbag, and put the handguns and ammunition into his case.

"We're sailing tomorrow," said Drake as he left them. "Good luck. I'll see you in Israel."

SIR NIGEL IRVINE selected his club, Brooks's, for his meeting with Barry Ferndale and Adam Munro. After dinner they sat down in his favourite corner of the subscription room near the windows looking down into St. James's Street. A decanter of the club's vintage port was set on the table between them and silence reigned while the cigars were lit.

"Now my dear Adam, what seems to be the problem?" asked Sir Nigel at last.

"I want to bring the Nightingale out," said Munro.

"Ah, yes. Any particular reason?"

"Partly strain. The original tape recording had to be stolen and a blank substituted in its place. That could be discovered and it's preying on Nightingale's mind. Second, every abstraction of Politburo minutes heightens the chances of discovery. We now know Maxim Rudin is fighting for his political life, and the succession when he goes. If Nightingale gets careless, or is even unlucky, he could get caught."

"Adam, that's one of the risks of defecting," said Ferndale. "It goes with the job. Penkovsky was caught."

"Penkovsky had provided just about all he could. The Cuban missile crisis was over. There was nothing the Russians could do to undo the damage. But if Nightingale comes out, the Kremlin can never know what has been passed. If he is caught, they'll make him talk. What he can reveal will be enough to bring Rudin down, and this would seem to be precisely the moment the West would not wish Rudin to fall."

"Indeed it is," said Sir Nigel. "It's a question of a balance of chances. One: if we bring Nightingale out, the missing tape will presumably be discovered and the supposition will be that even more was passed over before he left. Two: if he remains and is caught, a complete record of what he has passed will be abstracted. Rudin could well fall as a result. Even though Vishnayev would probably be disgraced also by the defection of his chief of staff, the Castletown talks would abort. Three: if we keep Nightingale in place until the Castletown arms limitation agreement is signed, by then there will be nothing the war faction in the Politburo can do. It's a teasing choice."

"I'd like him to go on," said Ferndale, "at least until the end of Castletown."

Sir Nigel reflected on the alternatives.

"I spent most of the afternoon with the prime minister," he said at length. "She has made a very strong request, on behalf of herself and the president. The Americans regard it as vital to their chances of securing an all-embracing treaty at Castletown that Nightingale keep them abreast of the Soviet negotiating position. The last transcript, when the Politburo laid out the parameters of what Rudin could or could not concede to get the wheat, were useful—not only on how far to push, but when to stop. Push too hard and Rudin could be toppled.

"I'll tell you what I'll do. Barry, prepare a plan to bring the Nightingale out, fast, that can be activated at short notice. But for the moment the Castletown talks and the frustration of the Vishnayev clique have priority. The Soviets cannot delay some sort of wheat agreement beyond February or March. After that Nightingale can come to the West, and I'm sure the Americans will show their gratitude."

A WEEK LATER Munro left his car by the Beriozka store in Moscow where the privileged shopped. He crossed the street to the ancient monastery of Norodevichi, whose grounds contain three lakes and a cemetery. He was carrying a bunch of flowers.

"Where do you hide a tree?" his instructor used to ask the class. "In a forest. And where do you hide a pebble? On the beach. Always keep it natural."

Munro traversed the cemetery with his bunch of carnations, and found Valentina waiting for him by one of the smaller lakes. Late October had brought the first bitter winds off the steppes to the east, and the surface of the water rippled in the wind.

"Our secret service man asked them in London," he said gently. "They told him that to bring you out now would reveal the missing tape, and thus the fact of the transcripts having been passed over. They feel if that happened the Politburo would withdraw from the talks in Ireland and revert to the Vishnayev plan."

She shivered slightly, whether from the chill of the lakeside or from fear of her own masters, he could not tell. He put an arm round her and held her to him.

"They may be right," she said quietly. "At least the Politburo is negotiating for food and peace, not preparing for war."

"The pressure is on," said Munro. "The low grain yield is coming in. They know the alternatives now. I think the world will get its peace treaty."

"If it does, what I have done will have been worthwhile," said Valentina. "I don't want Sascha to grow up with a gun in his hand.

That is what the warmongers in the Kremlin would have for him."

"He won't," said Munro. "Believe me, my darling, he'll grow up in freedom, in the West. My principals have agreed to bring you out in the spring."

She looked up at him, her eyes shining. "In the spring? Oh Adam, when in the spring?"

"The Kremlin needs its grain by April at the latest. When the treaty is agreed, perhaps even before it is signed, you and Sascha will be brought out. Meanwhile, I want you to cut down on the risks—only bring out the most vital material."

"There's something in here," she said, nudging the bag over her shoulder. "Most of it is so technical I can't understand it. It refers to permissible reductions of mobile Sam Twenties."

Munro nodded grimly. "Tactical rockets with nuclear warheads, highly accurate."

Twenty-four hours later the package was on its way to London.

SHORTLY AFTER, Edwin J. Campbell, chief US negotiator at the Castletown talks, took his place in the vast Long Gallery where the main conference was taking place, and gazed impassively across the gleaming Georgian table at his counterpart, Professor Ivan I. Sokolov, head of the Soviet delegation. "All right, Professor," he thought, "I know what you can concede and what you cannot. So let's get on with it."

It took forty-eight hours for the Soviet delegate to agree to cut their tracked tactical nuclear rockets in Eastern Europe by half. Six hours later, in the dining room below it was agreed that the USA would sell the USSR two hundred million dollars' worth of oil drilling and extraction technology at bargain-basement prices.

THREE DAYS BEFORE the end of the month an old lady was heading down Sverdlov Street in central Kiev towards her apartment. She had been visiting a friend two blocks away. Though she was entitled to a car and a chauffeur, she was of strong peasant stock and preferred to walk. It was just after ten in the evening when she crossed the road in the direction of her own front door.

She didn't see the car, it came so fast. One minute she was in the middle of the road with no one about but two pedestrians a hundred yards away, the next the vehicle was on her, lights blazing, tyres squealing. She froze. The driver seemed to steer right at her, then swerved away. The wing of the vehicle crashed into her hip, bowling her over. It roared away towards Kreshchatik Boulevard. Vaguely she heard the crunch of feet running towards her as the passers-by came to her aid.

The old lady was unconscious when the ambulance brought her to the October Hospital in Kiev, and remained so until the following morning. When she was able to explain who she was, panicked officials had her wheeled into a private room, which rapidly filled with flowers. That day the finest orthopaedic surgeon in Kiev operated to set her broken femur.

In Moscow, KGB Chief Ivanenko took a call from his personal aide and listened intently.

"Inform the authorities that I shall come at once," he said. "What? Well then, when she has come out of the anaesthetic. Tomorrow night? Very well, arrange it."

IT WAS BITTERLY cold that last night of October. There was no one moving in Rosa Luxemburg Street, onto which the October Hospital backs. Two long black limousines stood unobserved on the kerbside by this back entrance which the KGB chief had chosen to use rather than the grand portico at the front.

On the opposite side of the street an annexe to the hospital was under construction, its unfinished upper levels jutting above the trees. The watchers among the frozen cement sacks rubbed their hands to keep the circulation going, and stared at the two limousines parked by the door, dimly illuminated by a single bulb above the archway.

When he came down the stairs, the man with seven seconds to live was wearing a long, fur-collared overcoat and thick gloves, even for the short walk across the pavement to the warmth of the waiting car. He had spent two hours with his mother, comforting her and assuring her the culprits would be found, just as the abandoned car had been found.

An aide ran ahead of him and flicked off the doorway light. Only then did Ivanenko advance to the door, held open by one of his six bodyguards, and pass through it. The knot of four others outside parted as his fur-coated figure emerged, merely a shadow among other shadows.

He advanced quickly to the Zil across the pavement. He paused for a second as the passenger door was swung open, and died, the bullet from the hunting rifle skewering through his forehead and exiting through the rear of the cranium.

The crack of the rifle, the whack of the impacting bullet and the first cry from Colonel Yevgeni Kukushkin, his senior bodyguard, took less than a second. Before the slumping man had hit the pavement, the plainclothes colonel had him under the armpits, dragging him into the rear seat of the Zil. Before the door was closed the colonel was screaming "Drive, drive," to the shocked driver.

Colonel Kukushkin pillowed the bleeding head in his lap as the Zil screeched away from the kerbside. When it cleared the end of Rosa Luxemburg Street, the colonel flicked on the interior light. What he saw was enough to tell him his master was beyond help. His reaction was programmed into his mind. The unthinkable had happened and no one must know, save only those entitled to know. Watching the bodyguards' limousine swing out of Rosa Luxemburg Street behind them, he ordered his driver to choose a quiet and darkened street at least two miles away, and park.

Leaving the curtained Zil by the kerbside, with the bodyguards scattered in a screen around it, he removed his blood-soaked coat and set off on foot. He finally made his phone call from a militia barracks, where his ID card and rank secured him instant access to the commandant's private office and phone. It also secured him a direct line to the Kremlin.

"I must speak to Comrade Secretary-General Rudin urgently," he told the Kremlin switchboard operator.

The woman put the call through to an aide, who held it and spoke to Maxim Rudin on the internal phone. Rudin authorized the pass-through. "Yes," he grunted down the line, "Rudin here."

Colonel Kukushkin had never spoken to him before. He swallowed hard, took a deep breath and spoke. At the other end Rudin listened, asked two brief questions, rapped out a string of orders, and put the phone down. He turned to Vassili Petrov who was with him, leaning forward alert and worried.

"He's dead," said Rudin in disbelief. "Shot. Yuri Ivanenko. Someone has just assassinated the chairman of the KGB."

Beyond the windows the clock in the tower above Saviour's Gate chimed midnight, and a sleeping world began to move slowly towards war.

Nine

In the wake of the assassination of Yuri Ivanenko, Vassili Petrov took command of the cover-up. Over the telephone Rudin had instructed Colonel Kukushkin to bring the two-car cavalcade straight back to Moscow by road, stopping neither for food, drink nor sleep, refuelling the Zil bearing Ivanenko's corpse with jerry-cans, and always out of sight of passers-by.

On arrival on the outskirts of Moscow the two cars were directed straight to the Politburo's own private clinic at Kuntsevo, where the corpse with the shattered head was quietly buried in an unmarked grave. The burial party was of Ivanenko's own bodyguards, all of whom were then placed under house arrest and guarded by the Kremlin Palace guard.

Only Colonel Kukushkin was not held incommunicado. He was summoned to Petrov's private office and given one chance to save his career and his life; he was put in charge of the cover-up operation.

At the Kuntsevo clinic one entire ward was closed and guarded by KGB men. Two KGB doctors were put in charge of the patient in the closed ward—an empty bed. No one else was allowed in, but the two doctors, knowing only enough to be badly frightened, ferried in all the equipment that would be needed for the treatment of a heart attack.

Only one other man was let into the secret. Petrov summoned General Konstantin Abrassov, Ivanenko's official deputy, and informed him of what had happened. Inevitably he agreed to continue the masquerade.

In the October Hospital in Kiev, the dead man's mother continued to receive daily telegraphed messages from her son.

The three workmen on the annexe to the October Hospital who had discovered a hunting rifle and night-sight when they came to work the morning after the shooting were removed with their families to one of the labour camps in Mordovia, and two detectives, accompanied by Colonel Kukushkin, were flown in from Moscow to investigate. The story they were given was that the shot had been fired at the moving car of a local Party official; they were told to trace and identify the culprits in conditions of complete secrecy and proceeded to try.

While Colonel Kukushkin's two detectives interviewed the pedestrians who had been in Sverdlov Street on the night Ivanenko's mother had been run down, meticulously took to pieces the stolen car that had performed the hit-and-run job, and pored over the rifle, the image-intensifier and the surrounds of the hospital annexe, General Abrassov went for the nationalists in the Ukraine.

Hundreds were detained in Kiev, Ternopol and Lvov. The local KGB, supported by teams from Moscow, carried out the interrogations, ostensibly concerned with outbreaks of hooliganism.

In the seedy Lvov working-class district that November, David Lazareff and Lev Mishkin strolled through the snowy streets during one of their rare meetings. Because the fathers of both had been taken away to the camps, they knew time would eventually run out for them also. Sooner or later the spotlight of the KGB must swing away from the nationalists to the Jews.

"I posted the card to Andriy Drach yesterday, with the code message confirming the success of the first objective," said Mishkin. "How are things with you?"

"So far, so good," said Lazareff.

"We'll have to make our break soon if we are going to at all," said Mishkin. "It has to be by air. I'll see what I can discover about the airport."

Far away to the north of them an SAS jet thundered on its polar route from Stockholm to Tokyo. Among its first-class passengers was Captain Thor Larsen, on his way to his new command.

WITH ALL THE PIECES of the jigsaw puzzle of deception in place, Rudin now had the task of telling the Politburo what had really happened. In his gravelly voice, he delivered his report without frills. His audience sat stunned.

This time the room was empty of secretaries. No tape recorders turned, no aides were present. When he had finished, Rudin handed over to Petrov who described the elaborate measures taken to mask the outrage, and the secret steps then in progress to identify and eliminate the killers.

"But you have not found them yet?" snapped trade union head, Stepanov.

"Not yet," said Petrov evenly. "They will be caught, of course, and when they are, they will reveal every last one of those who helped them. General Abrassov will see to that. Then every person who knows what happened that night in Rosa Luxemburg Street will be eliminated. There will be no trace left."

"And in the meantime?" asked Komarov of agriculture.

"In the meantime," said Rudin, "it must be maintained with unbreakable solidarity that Comrade Yuri Ivanenko has sustained a massive heart attack and is under intensive care. The Soviet Union cannot and will not tolerate the public humiliation of the world being allowed to know what has happened." There was a murmur of assent.

"But it was a Western gun," insisted Shushkin, in charge of liaison with foreign communist parties. "Could the West be behind this?"

"No government," said Dmitri Rykov, "would be crazy enough to support such an outrage. Anti-Soviet fanatics, possibly. But not governments."

"Emigré groups abroad are also being investigated," said Petrov. "So far nothing has come in. The rifle and night-sight are indeed of Western make. That they were smuggled in is beyond doubt. Which means either the users brought them in, or they had outside help."

Yefrem Vishnayev watched the proceedings with keen interest but took little part. Marshal Kerensky expressed the dissatisfaction of the dissident group instead. Neither sought a further vote on the choice of the Castletown talks or war in 1983. With Ivanenko's place at the table taken by his deputy, General Abrassov, both knew the chairman's vote would again break the tie. Rudin had come one step nearer falling, but was not finished yet.

It was agreed that the announcement should be made, within the KGB and the upper echelons of the Party machine only, that Yuri Ivanenko had suffered a heart attack and was in hospital. When the killers had been identified and eliminated, Ivanenko would quietly expire.

Rudin was about to summon the secretaries to the chamber for the resumption of the usual Politburo meeting when the trade union chief, Stepanov, who had originally voted for Rudin, raised his hand.

"Comrades, I would regard it as a major defeat for our country if the killers of Yuri Ivanenko were to escape and publish their action to the world. Should that happen, I would not be able to continue my support for the policy of negotiation and further concession in the matter of our armaments levels in exchange for American grain. I would switch my support to the proposal of Party Theoretician Vishnayev."

There was dead silence.

"So would I," said Shushkin.

Eight against four, thought Rudin as he gazed impassively down the table, if these two bastards change sides.

"Your point is taken, Comrades," said Rudin without a flicker of emotion. "There will be no publication of this deed."

Ten minutes later, with the secretaries now present, the meeting re-opened with a unanimous expression of regret at the sudden illness of Comrade Ivanenko.

THE ZIL LIMOUSINE of Yefrem Vishnayev erupted from the mouth of the Borovitsky Gate at the Kremlin's southwestern corner. Inside, Marshal Kerensky sat beside Vishnayev. The partition between the spacious rear area and the driver was closed and soundproof, and curtains shut out the gaze of the pedestrians. "He's near to falling," growled Kerensky.

"No," said Vishnayev, "he's one step nearer and a lot weaker without Ivanenko, but don't underestimate Maxim Rudin. He'll fight like a cornered bear before he goes."

"Well, there's not much time," said Kerensky.

"Less than you think," said Vishnayev. "There were food riots in Lithuania last week. Our friend Vitautas was on the verge of switching sides despite the very attractive villa I have offered him next to my own at Sochi. Now he is back in the fold, and Shushkin and Stepanov may change sides in our favour."

"But only if the killers escape, or the truth is published abroad," said Kerensky.

"Precisely. And that is what must happen."

Kerensky's florid face turned brick red. "Reveal the truth? To the whole world? We can't do that," he exploded.

"No, *we* can't. So others must do it for us. With absolute proof. The guards who were present that night are in the hands of the Kremlin elite. That only leaves the killers themselves."

"But we don't have them," said Kerensky, "and the KGB will get them first."

"Probably, but we have to try," said Vishnayev. "We are not

fighting for the control of the Soviet Union any more. We are fighting for our lives. First the wheat, now Ivanenko. One more scandal, Nikolai, whoever is responsible, and Rudin will fall. We must ensure that there is one more scandal."

SIR NIGEL IRVINE read the last lines of the Nightingale transcript, closed the file and leaned back. "Well, Barry, what do you make of it?"

Barry Ferndale breathed once more on his glasses and gave them a final rub. "It's one more blow that Maxim Rudin's going to have to survive. With Ivanenko in hospital Rudin has lost one of his staunchest supporters, and one or two of the waverers might change sides."

Sir Nigel handed the folder across the desk to Ferndale. "Barry, I want you to go over to Washington with this one. Compare notes with Ben Kahn of intelligence. This exercise is becoming too damn much of a close-run thing."

Two days later, after dinner in Kahn's Georgetown house, Ferndale got down to business.

"The way we see it, Ben, is that Maxim Rudin is holding on by a thread in the face of a fifty per cent hostile Politburo, and that thread is getting very thin."

Kahn gazed at the brandy he twirled in his glass. "I can't fault you on that, Barry," he said carefully. "Our views at Langley go along pretty much with yours. Lawrence at the state department agrees. Poklewski though, still wants to ride the Soviets hard at Castletown. The president's in the middle—as usual."

"Castletown's pretty important to him?"

"Very important. Next year is his last in office. Bill Matthews would like to go out in style, leaving a comprehensive arms limitation treaty behind him."

"We were just thinking . . . Castletown would certainly abort if Rudin fell from control. He could use something from your side at Castletown to convince any waverers among his faction that he was achieving things there."

"Concessions?" asked Kahn. "We got the final analysis of the Soviet grain harvest last week. They're over a barrel. At least, that's the way Poklewski puts it."

"But the barrel's on the point of collapsing," said Ferndale.

"And waiting inside it is Vishnayev with his war plan."

"Actually my own reading of the combined Nightingale file runs along similar lines," said Kahn. "I've already got a paper in preparation on it for the president . . . ."

"THESE FIGURES," asked President Matthews the following week, "they represent the final aggregate grain crop of the Soviet Union?"

He glanced across at the four men seated in front of his desk. A log fire crackled in the marble fireplace, and beyond the bulletproof south windows the sweeping lawns held their first dusting of November morning frost.

Bob Benson and Fletcher from agriculture nodded in unison. Secretary of State Lawrence and Dr. Poklewski studied the figures.

"We could be out by five per cent either way, Mr. President, no more," said Benson.

"One hundred million tons, total," mused the president. "It will just last them till the end of March."

"They'll be slaughtering the cattle by January," said Poklewski. "They have to start making sweeping concessions at Castletown next month if they want to survive."

The president laid down the Soviet grain report and picked up the presidential briefing prepared by Ben Kahn. "They are desperate," he said. "The question is, how far do we push them?"

"If we don't push hard enough we don't get the best deal we can for America and the free world," said Lawrence. "Push too hard and we force Rudin to abort the talks to save himself from his own hawks. At this point I feel we should make them a gesture."

"Animal feedstuffs to help them keep some of their herds alive?" suggested Benson.

"What's the latest we need to give a decision on this one?" asked President Matthews.

"New Year's Day," said Benson. "If they know a respite is coming, they can hold off slaughtering the herds."

"I urge you not to ease up on them," pleaded Poklewski. "By March they'll be desperate."

"Desperate enough to concede enough disarmament to assure peace or desperate enough to go to war?" asked Matthews. "Gentlemen, you'll have my decision by Christmas Day. Unlike you, I have to take five chairmen of senate sub-committees with me on this one."

211

On 15 December Secretary of State Lawrence called President Matthews on his private line.

"Mr. President, six hours ago in Ireland, the Soviet Union conceded six major points at issue. They concern total numbers of intercontinental ballistic missiles with hydrogen-bomb warheads through conventional armour to disengagement of forces along the Elbe River."

"Thanks, David," said Matthews. "That's great news. You were right. I think we should let them have something in return."

IN HIS SUMPTUOUS MANSION, set in hundreds of acres of rigorously-guarded birch and larch forest southwest of Moscow, on the night before Christmas, a feast he had not recognized in fifty years, Maxim Rudin sat in his favourite button-back leather chair, feet towards the enormous fireplace of rough-cut granite blocks where pine logs crackled. By Rudin's chair-arm a small coffee table held an ashtray and half a tumbler of Armenian brandy, and the inevitable cigarette was clipped between his first finger and thumb. The bright yellow glare of the fire illuminated the face of Vassili Petrov who faced him.

"What news of the investigation?" asked Rudin.

"Slow," said Petrov. "That there was outside help is beyond doubt. We now know the night-sight was bought commercially in New York. The Finnish rifle was one of a consignment of sporting rifles exported from Helsinki to Britain. We don't know which shop it came from. There are two sets of footprints at the building site that cannot be traced. We are reasonably certain there were two men."

"Two dissidents?" asked Rudin.

"Almost certainly. And quite mad."

"No, Vassili. Madmen take pot-shots, or sacrifice themselves. This was planned over months by someone who has got to be silenced with his secret untold. Who are you concentrating on?" he asked.

"The Ukrainians," said Petrov. "We have all their groups in Germany, Britain and America penetrated. No one has heard a rumour of such a plan. Personally, I still think they are in the Ukraine. That Ivanenko's mother was used as a bait is undeniable. So who would have known she *was* Ivanenko's mother? Someone local, with contacts outside. We are concentrating on Kiev."

"Anything new from Ireland?" Rudin asked.

"The Americans have resumed talking, but have not responded to our initiative," said Petrov.

Rudin snorted. "Matthews is a fool. How much further does he think we can go before we have to pull back?"

"He has those Soviet-hating senators to contend with," said Petrov, "and that fascist, Poklewski. And of course he cannot know how close things are for us inside the Politburo."

Rudin grunted. "If he doesn't offer us something by the New Year, we won't carry the Politburo in the first week of January . . . ."

He reached out and took a draught of brandy, exhaling with a satisfied sigh.

"Are you sure you should be drinking?" asked Petrov. "The doctors forbade you five years ago."

"Forget the doctors," said Rudin. "That's what I really called you here for. On April thirtieth I am going to retire."

Petrov sat motionless, alert. Twice he had been close enough to feel the thunder when the most powerful tyrant in the world gave way to another. But never this close. This time he would wear the mantle, unless others could snatch it from him.

"In April I will announce to the full central committee my decision to go," said Rudin. "On May Day there will be a new leader. I want it to be you."

Petrov knew he was Rudin's choice since that meeting in the old leader's private suite in the Kremlin, when the dead Ivanenko had been with them, cynical and watchful as ever. But he had not thought it would be so sudden.

"Why so soon?" he asked.

"I got the results of the tests from the clinic yesterday. Not cigarettes and not Armenian brandy. Leukaemia. Six to twelve months. And I won't get the central committee to accept your nomination unless I can give them something they want. Grain. If Castletown fails, Vishnayev will have it all. So in the next hundred days we have to secure a grain agreement from the Americans and wipe out the Ivanenko affair once and for all."

Four days later, the United States formally offered the Soviet Union ten million tons of animal feed grains for immediate delivery and at commercial rates, to be considered as being outside any terms still being negotiated at Castletown.

ON NEW YEAR'S EVE an Aeroflot Tupolev 134 took off from Lvov airport bound for Minsk on an internal flight. Just north of the border between the Ukraine and White Russia, a nervous-looking young man rose from his seat and approached the stewardess who was several rows back from the steel door leading to the flight deck. The young man clamped his left forearm across her throat, drew a handgun and jammed it in her ribs. She screamed. There was a chorus of shouts and yells from the passengers. The hijacker began to drag the girl backwards to the locked door to the flight deck. On the bulkhead next to the door was the intercom, enabling the stewardess to speak to the flight crew, who had orders to refuse to open the door in the event of a hijack.

From midway down the fuselage one of the passengers rose, automatic in hand. He crouched in the aisle, both hands clasped round his gun, pointing it straight at the stewardess and the hijacker behind her.

"Hold it," he shouted. "KGB. Hold it right there."

"Tell them to open the door," yelled the hijacker.

"Not a chance," shouted the KGB flight guard.

"If they don't I'll kill the girl," screamed the man holding the stewardess.

The girl lunged backwards with her heel, caught the gunman in the shin, broke his grip and ran towards the KGB agent. The hijacker sprang after her, passing three rows of passengers. From an aisle seat one of them rose, turned and slammed a fist into the nape of the hijacker's neck. The man pitched face downward; before he could move, his assailant had snatched the man's gun and was pointing it at him. The hijacker sat up, looked at the gun, and began to moan softly.

From the rear the KGB agent stepped past the stewardess, gun still at the ready, and approached the rescuer. "Who are you?" he asked. The rescuer reached into an inside pocket, produced a card and flicked it open. The agent looked at the KGB card. "You're not from Lvov," he said.

"Ternopol," said the other.

The agent from Lvov nodded. "Thanks, Comrade. Keep him covered." He stepped to the speaker-phone, related what had happened to the pilot, and asked for a police reception at Minsk.

"Is it safe to have a look?" asked a voice from behind the door.

"Sure," said the Lvov KGB agent. "He's safe enough now."

The door opened to show the head of the engineer, somewhat frightened and intensely curious.

The KGB agent from Ternopol acted very strangely. He turned from the man on the floor, crashed his revolver into the base of his KGB colleague's skull, thrust his foot into the space between the flight-deck door and jamb and pushed the engineer backwards. He was through the door in a second. The man on the floor behind him rose, grabbed the flight guard's automatic, followed through the steel door and slammed it behind him. It locked automatically. Both men were to wear gloves throughout the entire operation.

Two minutes later, under the guns of David Lazareff and Lev Mishkin, the Tupolev turned due west for Berlin. At the controls Captain Rudenko sat white-faced with rage; beside him his co-pilot Vatutin slowly answered the frantic questions from Minsk control tower regarding the change of course.

By the time the airliner had crossed the border into Polish air space, Minsk tower knew the Tupolev was in the hands of hijackers and had passed on the news to Moscow. A hundred miles west of Warsaw a flight of six Soviet MiG-23 fighters swept in and formed on the Tupolev.

At his desk in the defence ministry, Marshal Nikolai Kerensky took an urgent call on the line linking him to Soviet air force headquarters. "Where?" he barked.

"Passing over Poznan," was the answer. "Fifty minutes flying time to Berlin."

The marshal considered carefully. This could be the scandal which Vishnayev had demanded. There was no doubt what should be done. The Tupolev should be shot down with all its passengers and crew. The version given out would be that the hijackers had fired within the fuselage, hitting a main fuel tank. It had happened twice in the past decade.

He gave his orders.

Five minutes later, a hundred metres off the hijacked airliner's wingtip, the commander of the MiG flight listened. "If you say so, Comrade Colonel," he told his base commander. Twenty minutes later the airliner began its letdown into Berlin. As it did so the MiGs peeled gracefully away.

"I have to tell Berlin we're coming in," Captain Rudenko appealed to Mishkin. "If there's a plane on the runway, we'll end up as a ball of fire."

215

Mishkin had never been in an aeroplane before, but what the captain said made sense. "Very well. Tell Tempelhof you are coming in. No requests, just a flat statement."

Captain Rudenko was playing his last card. He leaned forward, adjusted the channel selection dial and began to speak. "Tempelhof, West Berlin. Tempelhof, West Berlin. This is Aeroflot flight 351 . . ."

He was speaking in English, the international language of air traffic control. Mishkin and Lazareff knew almost none. Mishkin jabbed his gun into Rudenko's neck. "No tricks," he said in Ukrainian.

In the control tower at East Berlin's Schoenefeld airport the two controllers looked at each other in amazement. They were being called on their own frequency, but addressed as Tempelhof in West Berlin. No Aeroflot plane would dream of landing in West Berlin. Furthermore, Tempelhof was no longer a civil airport but a US air force base. One of the East Germans, faster than the other, snatched the microphone.

"Tempelhof to Aeroflot 351, you are clear to land," he said.

In the airliner Captain Rudenko swallowed hard. The Tupolev let down rapidly to the main airport of Communist East Germany. At five hundred feet Mishkin peered suspiciously through the streaming perspex. He had heard of West Berlin's brilliant lights, teeming streets and Tempelhof airport right in the heart of it. This airport was out in the country.

"It's a trick," he yelled at Lazareff. "It's the East." He jabbed his gun into Captain Rudenko's neck. "Pull out," he screamed. "Pull out or I'll shoot."

The Ukrainian captain gritted his teeth and held on course. Mishkin reached over his shoulder and tried to haul back on the control column. The twin impacts, when they came, were so close together that it was impossible to tell which came first. Mishkin claimed the thump of the wheels hitting the tarmac caused the gun to go off; Co-pilot Vatutin maintained Mishkin had fired first.

The bullet tore a gaping hole in the neck of Captain Rudenko and killed him instantly. Vatutin hauled back on the stick, yelling to his engineer for more power. The jet engines screamed as the Tupolev bounced twice more on the tarmac then lifted into the air, rolling, struggling for lift. Vatutin held her, nose high,

216

wallowing, praying for more engine power, as the outer suburbs of East Berlin blurred past beneath them, followed by the Berlin Wall itself. When the Tupolev came over the perimeter of Tempelhof it cleared the nearest houses by six feet. White-faced, the young co-pilot hammered the plane onto the main runway with Lazareff's gun in his back. Mishkin held the red-soaked body of Captain Rudenko from falling across the control column.

On the US air force field, Staff-Sergeant Leroy Coker was on guard duty in his police jeep. When the incoming airliner lurched over the perimeter fence, engines howling, he sat bolt upright. He knew that an attack by the Communists was always imminent, and also knew a red star when he saw one. When the airliner slithered to a stop he unslung his carbine and blew the nosewheel tyres out.

Mishkin and Lazareff surrendered three hours later. The intent had been to keep the crew, release the passengers, take on board three notables from West Berlin and be flown to Tel Aviv. But a new nosewheel for a Tupolev was out of the question; the Russians would never supply one. And when the news of the killing of Rudenko was made known to the USAF base authorities, they refused to lay on another plane. After an hour's talk with the base commander, the two men walked out with their hands in the air. That night they were formally handed over to the West Berlin authorities for imprisonment and trial.

Ten

"A disaster," snapped Andrew Drake, staring at the newspapers strewn on the floor of his London flat. "By now they should have been in Israel. Within a month they'd have been released and could have given their press conference. Why the hell did they have to shoot the captain?"

"If he refused to fly into West Berlin, they were finished anyway," observed Azamat Krim.

"Can those handguns be traced?" Drake asked Krim.

The small Tatar shook his head. "To the shop in New York that sold them perhaps. Not to me."

Drake paced the carpet, deep in thought. "I don't think they'll be extradited," he said at length. "The Soviets want them now for hijacking, shooting Rudenko, hitting the KGB man on board and of course the other KGB man they took the identity card from in Ternopol. But the killing of the captain is the serious one. Still, I don't think a West German government will send two Jews back for certain execution. They'll probably be tried and convicted for life. Miroslav, will they open their mouths about Ivanenko?"

Kaminsky shook his head. "Not if they've got any sense. The Germans might have to change their minds and send them back after all—if they believed them, which they wouldn't because Moscow would deny Ivanenko is dead, and produce a look-alike as proof. But Moscow would believe them, and have them liquidated. The Germans, not believing them, would offer no special protection. They wouldn't stand a chance. They'll keep silent."

"That's no use to us," said Krim. "The point of all this was to deal a single massive humiliation to the whole Soviet state apparatus. *We* can't give that press conference about the assassination of the head of the KGB. Only Mishkin and Lazareff have the details that will convince the world."

"Then they have to be got out of there," said Drake with finality. "We have to mount a second operation to get them to Tel Aviv. Otherwise it's all been for nothing."

"So what happens now?" asked Kaminsky.

"We think," said Drake. "And we have little time; it won't take Moscow for ever to put two and two together. They'll know who did the Kiev job on Ivanenko pretty soon. Then they'll begin to plan the revenge. We have to beat them to it."

As Drake had predicted, a few days later, despite pressure to hand the hijackers over to Soviet authorities, the Federal German government announced that they would go on trial in West Berlin as soon as possible.

THE POLITBURO meeting at the end of the week was stormy. Once again the tape recorders were off, the stenographers absent. "This is an outrage. Yet another scandal which diminishes the Soviet Union in the eyes of the world. It should never have happened," ranted Vishnayev, implying that it was due to the ever-weakening leadership of Maxim Rudin.

"It would not have happened," retorted Petrov, "if the Comrade Marshal's fighters had shot the plane down over Poland according to custom."

"There was a communications breakdown between ground

control and the fighter leader," said Marshal Kerensky. "A chance in a thousand."

"Unfortunate, though," observed Foreign Minister Rykov coldly. Through his ambassador in Bonn he knew the Mishkin and Lazareff trial would be public and would reveal exactly how the hijackers had first mugged a KGB officer in a Ternopol park for his identity papers, then masqueraded as him to penetrate to the flight deck.

"Is there any question," asked the industrial chief, Petryanov, a supporter of Vishnayev, "that these two men could be the ones that killed Ivanenko in Kiev?"

The atmosphere was electric.

"None at all," said Petrov firmly. "We know now that those two come from Lvov, not Kiev. They are Jews who have been refused permission to emigrate. We are investigating, but so far there is no connection."

"Should such a connection emerge, we will of course be informed?" asked Vishnayev.

"That goes without saying, Comrade," growled Rudin.

As the meeting dispersed the old Soviet chief drew Vassili Petrov aside. "*Is* there any connection between the two Jews and the Ivanenko killing?" he inquired.

"There may be," conceded Petrov. "We know they did the mugging in Ternopol, so they were evidently prepared to travel outside Lvov to prepare their escape. We have a finger-print taken from the car that knocked down Ivanenko's mother. We are trying to get complete finger-prints of both men from inside Berlin. If they check . . ."

"Prepare a feasibility study," said Rudin. "To have them liquidated inside their gaol in West Berlin. Just in case. If their identity is proved as the killers of Ivanenko, tell me, not the Politburo. We wipe them out first, then inform our comrades."

Petrov swallowed hard. Cheating the Politburo was playing for the highest stakes in Soviet Russia. One slip, and there would be no safety net.

A week later, West German Chancellor Dietrich Busch received his justice minister in the chancellery building in Bonn. "This Mishkin and Lazareff affair, how goes it?" he asked.

"It's strange," admitted Justice Minister Ludwig Fischer. "They are being more cooperative than one could hope for. They seem eager to achieve a quick trial. They insist on going for an admission of guilt and pleading mitigating circumstances. They claim the gun went off by accident when the plane hit the runway. Their lawyer is asking for the charge to be reduced to culpable homicide."

"I think we can grant them that," said the chancellor. "What would they get?"

"With the hijacking thrown in, fifteen to twenty years. They could be up for parole after a third of their sentence. They claim they just wanted to reach Israel the only way they knew how. There's one other thing. They want to be transferred after the trial to a gaol in West Germany. They seemed terrified of revenge by the KGB."

"Rubbish," snorted Busch, "they'll be tried and gaoled in West Berlin. The Russians wouldn't dare try to settle accounts inside a Berlin gaol. Go ahead, Ludwig. Make it quick and clean, if they wish to cooperate."

AT CHITA, Japan, in the biggest dry dock in the world, the *Freya* lay alongside her commissioning quay, her sea trials over, the silver-on-blue winged Viking helmet emblem of the Nordia Line fluttering above her.

She had cost $170,000,000 to build. She was 1,689 feet long, the length of ten city blocks. Her forward deck, alone, stretched a quarter of a mile. Her five-storey superstructure was a luxury hotel; her bridge, radio room and computer room were a low-humming complex of data banks, calculators and control systems. Each of her sixty holds was bigger than a neighbourhood cinema. Deep within her hull, four steam turbines could muster a total of 90,000 shaft horsepower to drive her twin forty-foot-diameter bronze propellers.

Chita was the only dry dock that could take a million-tonner—an Ultra-Large Crude Carrier or ULCC—and it was the first and last it would ever hold. *Freya* was the ultimate in size, power, capacity, luxury and technical refinement that the technology of man could set to float on water.

Her crew of thirty had arrived by air fourteen days earlier to familiarize themselves with every inch of her. Captained by Thor Larsen, the crew was made up of ten officers and twenty others, from cook to able seamen, deckhands and pumpmen.

The previous evening, her owner, Harry Wennerstrom, had arrived. Now high on the bridge, which towered over the vast spread of her deck, Wennerstrom drew Thor Larsen by the arm into the radio room and closed the door behind him.

"She's all yours, Thor," he said. "By the way, there's been a slight change of plan regarding your arrival in Europe. Just this once, for her maiden voyage, you're going to bring her into Europort at Rotterdam fully laden."

Larsen stared at his employer in disbelief. Fully-loaded ULCCs never entered ports; they stood well offshore and disgorged most of their cargo into smaller tankers in order to reduce their draught for the shallow seas.

"The English Channel will never take her," said Larsen.

"You're not going up the Channel," said Wennerstrom. "You're going west of Ireland, west of the Hebrides, north of the Pentland Firth, between the Orkneys and the Shetlands, then south down the North Sea, following the twenty-fathom line, to moor at the deep-water anchorage; from there the pilots will bring you down the main channel towards the Maas estuary. The tugs will bring you in from the Hook of Holland to Europort."

"The Inner Channel from KI Buoy to the Maas won't take her fully laden," protested Larsen.

"Yes, it will," said Wennerstrom calmly. "They have dredged this channel to one hundred and fifteen feet over the past four years. You'll be drawing ninety-eight feet. Thor, if I were asked to name any mariner in the world who could bring a million-tonner into Europort, it would be you. It will be tight as hell, but let me have this one last triumph. I want the world to see her, Thor. My *Freya*. I'll have them all there waiting for her. The Dutch government, the world's press. They'll be my guests and they'll be dumbfounded. Otherwise no one will ever see her because she'll spend her whole life out of sight of land."

"All right," said Larsen slowly. "Just this once. I'll be ten years older when it's over."

Wennerstrom grinned like a small boy.

"Just wait till they lay eyes on her," he said. "See you in Rotterdam, Thor Larsen."

At 3:00 p.m. on 2 February the *Freya* sailed out into the Pacific and swung her bow south towards the Philippines and Sumatra at the start of her maiden voyage.

EDWIN CAMPBELL leaned back from the Georgian table in the Long Gallery at Castletown House and looked across at Professor Sokolov. The last point on the agenda had been covered, the last concession wrung. From the dining room below a courier had reported that the secondary conference had matched the concessions of the upper floor with trade bargains from the United States to the Soviet Union.

"I think that's it, Ivan my friend," said Campbell. "I don't think we can do any more at this stage."

The Russian raised his eyes from the pages of notes in front of him. He had fought tooth and claw to secure for his country the grain tonnages that could save her from disaster and yet retain the maximum in weapon levels. He had had to make concessions that would have been unheard of four years earlier at Geneva, but it was the best he could do in the time-scale.

"I think you are right, Edwin," he replied. "Let us have the arms reduction treaty prepared in draft form."

"And the trade protocol," said Campbell. "I imagine our governments will want that also."

Sokolov permitted himself a wry smile. "I am sure they will want it very much."

ANDREW DRAKE threw down his magazine and leaned back. "I wonder," he said.

"What?" asked Krim as he entered the small Bayswater sitting room with three mugs of coffee. Drake tossed the magazine to the Tatar. "Read the first article," he said.

"You're crazy," said Krim when he had read it. Kaminsky looked from one to the other.

"No," said Drake. "Without some audacity we'll be sitting here for the next ten years. Look, Mishkin and Lazareff come up for trial in a fortnight. The outcome is a foregone conclusion. We know we're going to have to do something if they are ever to come out of that gaol. So let's start planning. Azamat, you were in the parachute regiment in Canada. Did you do an explosives course?"

"Yep. Demolition and sabotage."

"And years ago I used to have a passion for electronics and radio," said Drake. "My dad had a radio repair shop before he died. We'd need help but we could do it."

"How many more men?" asked Krim.

"We'd need one on the outside, just to recognize Mishkin and Lazareff on their release. That would have to be Miroslav here. For the job, the two of us, plus five to stand guard."

"Such a thing has never been done before," observed the Tatar doubtfully.

"All the more reason why it will be unprepared-for."

"We'd get caught at the end of it," said Krim.

"Not necessarily. And anyway, our trial would be the sensation of the decade. The whole issue of a free Ukraine would be blazoned across the world."

"Do you know five more who would come in on it?"

"For years I've been collecting names," said Drake. "Men who are sick and tired of talking. If they knew what we'd done already, yes, I could get five before the end of the month."

"All right," said Krim. "Where do you want me to go?"

"Belgium. I want a large apartment in Brussels. We'll bring the men there and make it the group's base."

ON 10 FEBRUARY the Politburo met to consider the draft treaty and trade protocol negotiated at Castletown. "What we have gained," Foreign Minister Dmitri Rykov said, "is the sale to us, at last July's prices, of fifty-five million tons of grain. Without them we faced disaster. On top we have nearly three billion dollars worth of modern technology. With these we can master the problems that have beset us.

"Against this we have to offset certain minimal concessions in arms levels and states of preparedness, which will in no way retard our capacity to dominate the Third World and its raw material resources. From the disaster that faced us last May, we have emerged triumphant thanks to the inspired leadership of Comrade Maxim Rudin."

When the meeting voted on the treaty terms, which was in fact a vote in the continuing leadership of Maxim Rudin, the six-to-six tie remained intact. The chairman's vote to accept the treaty therefore prevailed.

TWO DAYS LATER eight men grouped themselves in the apartment Azamat Krim had rented in a suburb of Brussels. The five newcomers, all of Ukrainian extraction, had been summoned by

Drake. Two of the five were German-born, one was an American, and the other two were British.

When they heard what Mishkin and Lazareff had done to the head of the KGB, there was a babble of excited comment. They agreed that the operation would not be complete until the two partisans were free and safe. They talked through the night, and by dawn had split into four teams of two.

Drake and Kaminsky would return to England and buy the necessary electronic equipment. One of the Germans, who had formerly worked in a Bavarian quarry, would partner one of the Englishmen and return to Germany to seek out the explosives. The second German, who had contacts in Paris, would take the other Englishman to buy, or steal, the weaponry. Azamat Krim took his fellow North American to seek a motor launch.

ON THE MORNING of 26 February the presiding judge in the courtroom at the top security gaol of Moabit in West Berlin began to read the judgment of himself and his two colleagues. In their walled dock, Mishkin and Lazareff listened impassively. From time to time they sipped water from glasses placed on tables in front of them. From the packed booths reserved for the international press they were under close scrutiny while the judges' findings were read out. But one magazine journalist representing a Leftist German monthly magazine seemed more interested in the glasses they drank from than the prisoners themselves. He left the courtroom and made a telephone call. Shortly after eleven Mishkin and Lazareff rose to hear themselves sentenced to fifteen years.

They were led away to begin their sentences at Tegel gaol in the northern part of the city, and within minutes the courthouse had emptied. The cleaners took over. Unobserved by her colleagues, one of them quietly picked up the prisoners' drinking glasses, wrapped them in dusters and placed them in her shopping bag. No one noticed, no one cared . . . .

On the last day of the month Vassili Petrov sought a private audience with Maxim Rudin in his Kremlin suite. "Mishkin and Lazareff," he said. "One of our people in West Berlin abstracted the water glasses they used during the trial. The finger-print on one of them matches that from the car used in the hit-and-run affair in Kiev."

"So it was them," said Rudin grimly. "Vassili, liquidate them, as fast as you can. Give it to 'wet affairs'."

The KGB department of "wet affairs" is so called because its operations not infrequently involve someone getting wet with blood. It was to this department that Maxim Rudin ordered Petrov to hand the elimination of Mishkin and Lazareff.

"I thought of giving it to Colonel Kukushkin, Ivanenko's head of security," said Petrov. "He has a personal reason to wish to succeed—saving his own skin. He would report only to General Abrassov or to me."

Rudin nodded grimly. "All right, let him have the job. The apparent reason will be to avenge the death of Flight Captain Rudenko. And, Vassili, he had better succeed first time. If he tries and fails, Mishkin and Lazareff could open their mouths. After a failed attempt to kill them, someone might believe them. And you know what that would mean to us."

"I know," said Petrov quietly. "Kukushkin will not fail. He'll do it himself."

Eleven

"It's the best we'll get, Mr. President," said Secretary of State David Lawrence. "Personally I believe Edwin Campbell has done us well at Castletown."

Grouped before the president's desk in the Oval Office were the secretaries of state for defence and treasury, with Stan Poklewski and Robert Benson of the CIA. Beyond the french windows the rose garden was whipped by a bitter March wind.

President Matthews laid his hand on the bulky draft agreement wrung out of the Castletown talks. "How about the concessions we have made?" he asked.

"The secret trade protocol," said the secretary to the treasury, "requires us to deliver fifty-five million tons of mixed grain plus oil and technology at a total cost to the United States of almost three billion dollars. On the other hand, the sweeping arms reductions should enable us to claw back that much and more by reduced defence expenditure."

"If the Soviets abide by their undertakings," said the secretary for defence.

"We have to believe they will," countered Lawrence, "and in that case by your own experts' calculations they could not launch a successful war across the face of Europe for at least five years."

President Matthews knew the presidential elections of the coming November would not see his candidacy. If he could retire leaving behind him peace for even half a decade, the burdensome arms race of the last ten years halted in its tracks, he would take his place among the great US presidents. He wanted that more than anything else this spring of 1983.

"Gentlemen," he said, "we have to approve this treaty. David, inform Moscow we join them in agreeing to the terms and propose that our negotiators reconvene at Castletown to draw up the formal treaty ready for signing. I've kept several key senators in the picture and in the circumstances I don't see senate ratification giving us much trouble. While that is going on we will permit the loading of the grain ships, ready to sail."

The following day Maxim Rudin replied formally to the proposal of the United States president, welcoming his agreement to the terms of the draft treaty. He proposed a formal signature by foreign ministers in Dublin on 10 April.

Upon receiving this message, President Matthews remarked to Secretary of State Lawrence, "Since this is more than an arms-limitation agreement, I suppose we must call it a treaty. No doubt history will record it as the Treaty of Dublin."

Lawrence consulted with the government of the Republic of Ireland, who agreed with barely hidden delight that they would be pleased to host the formal signing ceremony between David Lawrence for the United States and Dmitri Rykov for the USSR in Saint Patrick's Hall, Dublin Castle, on 10 April.

President Matthews then replied to Maxim Rudin agreeing to his place and date.

BY THE EVENING of 20 March, the mighty *Freya*, now heavy-laden with one million tons of Mubarraq crude oil from Abu Dhabi, Saudi Arabia's oil port on the Persian Gulf, moved steadily at her full-load service speed of fifteen knots past Africa's Cape of Good Hope on the last leg of her maiden voyage towards Rotterdam and her welcome.

She had sixty giant tanks or holds, three abreast in lines of twenty fore and aft. Far away in the fore part of the ship, the first row of three tanks contained a full crude tank port and starboard, with a single slop tank in the centre. This was to be used for nothing but gathering the slops or overflow from her fifty crude-carrying cargo tanks—each holding 20,000 tons of oil. One row back were the first three empty ballast tanks, used for seawater to give her stability when she was empty of cargo. The second row of three was amidships, and the third row was at the foot of the superstructure, in the fifth floor of which Captain Thor Larsen was just handing the *Freya* over to the senior officer of the watch before going down to his handsome cabin on "D" deck for supper.

The *Freya* had made good time from the Cape with the aid of southeast trade winds, and was now past Senegal, doing what she had been designed and built for—carrying a million tons of crude oil to the thirsty refineries of Europe. Her draught was at her designed ninety-eight feet and her hazard alarm devices had ingested the knowledge and knew what to do if the seabed approached too close.

FAR AWAY in Moscow, Adam Munro entered the cipher room of the British embassy and read the decoded message from London and smiled. He memorized it within seconds and passed it into a shredder which reduced the thin paper to fragments. Barry Ferndale had informed him that with the Russian/American treaty on the threshold of signature, the Nightingale could be brought out—to a discreet but generous welcome—from the coast of Romania near Constantza on the Black Sea, in the week of 16 to 23 April. There was to be a central committee fraternal delegation to the Romanian Party Congress during the first half of April and he could reasonably ask to accompany it. There were further details for the exact pick-up.

At a pre-arranged meeting in the Botanical Gardens of the USSR Academy of Sciences he told Valentina with controlled excitement of the news. She seemed overjoyed.

"I'm sure I can get permission," she said. "Sascha breaks up from school on March twenty-ninth, and we could leave for Bucharest on the fifth. After ten days at the Congress, it will be perfectly normal for me to take a bored little boy to the resort beaches for a week."

"Then I'll fix it for the night of Monday, April the eighteenth. That will give you several days in Constantza to find your way around. You must hire a car and acquire a powerful torch. Now, Valentina my love, these are the details. Memorize them, for there can be no mistakes:

"North of Constantza lies the resort of Mamaia, where the Western package tourists go. Drive there on the evening of the eighteenth. Exactly six miles north of Mamaia a track leads right from the coast highway to the beach. On the headland at the junction you will see a short stone tower, a coast-marker for fishermen. Leave the car well off the road and go down to the beach. At two a.m. you will see a light from the sea; three long dashes and three short ones. Take your own torch with its beam cut down by a tube of cardboard and point it straight at where the light came from. Flash back the reverse signal, three shorts and three longs. A speedboat will come out of the sea for you and Sascha. Identify yourself with the phrase, 'The Nightingale sings in Berkeley Square'. Have you got that?"

"Yes. Adam, where is Berkeley Square?"

"In London. It is very beautiful, like you. It has many trees."

"And do nightingales sing there?"

"According to the words of the song, one used to. Darling, it seems so short. Four weeks today. When we get to London I'll show you Berkeley Square."

"Adam, tell me—have I betrayed my own people?"

"No," he said with finality, "you have not. The leaders nearly did. If you had not done what you did, Vishnayev and your uncle might have got their war. In it, Russia would have been destroyed, most of America, my country and Western Europe. You have not betrayed the people of your country."

"But they will call me a traitor," she said, a hint of tears in her dark eyes. "I shall be an exile."

"One day, perhaps, this madness will end and you could come back. Listen, my love, we cannot stay longer. It's too risky. There is one last thing. I need your private phone number. If there should, by any remote chance, be a change of plan, or date, I may have to contact you. If I do, I will pretend to be a friend called Gregor, explaining that I cannot attend your dinner party. If that happens, leave at once and meet me in the car park of the Mojarsky Hotel at the top of Kutuzovsky Prospekt."

She nodded meekly and gave him her number. He kissed her on the cheek. "I'll see you in London, my darling," he told her, and was gone through the trees. Privately he knew he would have to resign and take the icy anger of Sir Nigel Irvine when it became plain the Nightingale was not Anatoly Krivoi but a woman, and his wife-to-be. But by then it would be too late for even the service to do anything about it.

BY 23 MARCH over two hundred and fifty grain ships were docked in thirty ports from the St. Lawrence Seaway down the eastern seaboard of the United States. Within ten days, if the Senate ratified the Treaty of Dublin, they would begin moving east across the Atlantic, bound for Archangel and Murmansk in the Soviet Arctic, Leningrad at the end of the Baltic, and the warm-water ports of the Black Sea. From a hundred North American silos from Winnipeg to Charleston the pumps spewed a golden tide of wheat, barley, oats, rye and maize into the ships' bellies, all destined within a month for the hungry millions of Russia.

ON 26 MARCH Andrew Drake rose from his work at the kitchen table of the Brussels apartment and pronounced that he was ready.

The explosives, stolen from a rock quarry in Bavaria, had been packed into ten fibre suitcases, the submachine guns, bought from an arms dealer in Paris, rolled in towels and stuffed into haversacks. Azamat Krim kept the detonators bedded in cotton-wool in a cigar box which never left him. When darkness fell the cargo was carried in relays down to the group's secondhand, Belgian-registered van and they set off for Blankenberge.

The little seaside resort facing the North Sea was quiet, the harbour virtually deserted, when they transferred their equipment under cover of darkness to the bilges of the fishing launch which Azamat Krim and his American collaborator had obtained from near Ostend. She was the kind of craft much favoured by experienced sea-anglers, steel-hulled, forty feet long with a powerful engine well capable of taking her through the wild North Sea to the fishing grounds.

On Sunday the twenty-seventh Miroslav Kaminsky bade them goodbye, took the van and drove back to Brussels. His job was to clean the Brussels flat from top to bottom, abandon it and drive the van to a pre-arranged rendezvous in the lowlands behind the dykes of Holland. There he would leave it, with its ignition key in an agreed place, then take the ferry from the Hook back to Harwich and London.

The remaining seven men left port and cruised sedately up the coast to lose themselves among the islands of Walcheren and North Beveland, just across the border into Holland. There, with fishing rods much in evidence, they hove to and waited. At a powerful radio down in the cabin, Andrew Drake sat hunched, listening to Maas estuary control and the endless calls of the ships heading into or out of Europort and Rotterdam.

"COLONEL KUKUSHKIN is going into Tegel gaol to do the job on the night of the third to the fourth of April," Vassili Petrov told Maxim Rudin in the Kremlin that same Sunday morning. "There is a senior warder, Ludwig Jahn, who will be on the night shift then, and who will let him in, bring him to the cells of Mishkin and Lazareff, and let him out of the gaol by the staff doorway when it is over."

"The warder is reliable, one of our people?" asked Rudin.

"No, but Jahn has family in East Germany. He has been persuaded to do as he is told. Kukushkin reports that he is too frightened to contact the police. Kukushkin will silence him also, just as he steps out of the doorway. There will be no trace."

"Eight days," grunted Rudin. "He had better get it right."

"He will," said Petrov. "By a week tomorrow Mishkin and Lazareff will be dead and their secret with them. Those who helped them will keep silent to save their own lives. Even if they talk, no one will believe them."

WHEN THE SUN rose on the morning of the twenty-ninth, its first rays picked up the mass of the *Freya* twenty miles west of Ireland. Meanwhile, Rotterdam was preparing for her welcome. Harry Wennerstrom had installed himself in the best suite at the Hilton Hotel. A select party of notables and press would be his guests on the flat roof of the modern Maas control building, on the north shore of the Maas estuary at the very tip of the Hook of Holland. They would watch as six tugs pulled and pushed the *Freya* those last few miles from the estuary into the Caland Kanal, from there to the Beer Kanal and finally to rest by Texan Clint Blake's new oil refinery in the heart of Europort. Already, newspapers and television had leased helicopters to give the last few miles of the

Freya's maiden voyage and her berthing complete camera coverage. Harry Wennerstrom was a contented old man.

By the early hours of 30 March the *Freya* was well through the channel between the Orkneys and the Shetlands and had turned south, heading down the North Sea. As soon as she entered the crowded sea lanes, she had contacted the first of the shore-based area traffic control officers at Wick on the coast of Caithness in the far north of Scotland.

Because of her size and draught she had reduced speed to ten knots and was following the instructions fed to her from Wick by VHF radio-telephone. All around her, unseen, the various control centres had her marked on their high-definition radars.

Ahead of the *Freya* as she crawled down the southbound traffic lane, smaller ships were informed to get out of her way. At midnight she moved away from the Yorkshire coast towards Holland. Throughout her passage she had followed the deep-water channel, a minimum of twenty fathoms. On her bridge, despite the constant instructions from ashore, her officers watched the echo-sounder readings, observing the banks and sandbars on the floor of the North Sea slide past on either side of her.

Just before sundown on 31 March, now down to her bare steerage speed of five knots, the giant swung gently eastwards and moved to her overnight position, the deep-draught anchorage twenty-seven sea miles due west of the Maas estuary, twenty-seven miles from home and glory.

She had steamed 7,085 miles from Chita to Abu Dhabi and a further 12,015 miles from there to where she now lay motionless along the line of the tide. From her stem a single anchor chain streamed down to the seabed with five shackles on deck. Each link of the chain was nearly a yard long, and the steel thicker than a man's thigh.

At the overnight anchorage Captain Larsen left his first officer Stig Lundquist, his third mate Tom Keller, a Danish-American, and an able seaman on the bridge. The officers would maintain constant anchor-watch, the seaman would carry out periodic deck-inspection.

Though the *Freya*'s engines were closed down, her turbines and generators hummed rhythmically, churning out the power to keep her systems functioning. Among these were the constant feed-in of tide and weather, of which the latest reports were heartening. Larsen could have had March gales; instead, an area of high pressure, almost stationary over the North Sea and the English Channel, had brought a mild early spring, and the sea was almost a flat calm. The sky had been a cloudless blue all day and, despite a touch of frost that night, bade fair to be so again on the morrow.

Bidding his officers goodnight, Captain Larsen left the bridge and descended one floor to "D" deck and his suite on the extreme starboard side. The spacious and well-appointed day cabin carried four windows looking forward down the length of the vessel, and two looking out to starboard. Aft of the day cabin was his bedroom, with bath. The sleeping cabin also had two windows, both to starboard. All the windows were sealed, save one in the day cabin which was closed with screw bolts which could be opened manually.

Outside the forward windows the façade of the superstructure fell sheer to the deck; to starboard the windows gave onto ten feet of steel landing, beyond which was the starboard rail and beyond that the sea. Flights of steel ladders ran from the lowest "A" deck up five floors to the bridge-wing above his head. These sets of ladders were open, exposed to the elements. They were seldom used, for the interior stairwells were heated and warm.

After dinner, Larsen decided to work the night away on a final run-through of the channel charts for the morning's berthing. It was going to be tight, and he wanted to know that channel as well as the two Dutch pilots who would arrive by helicopter at 0730 to take her over. Prior to that, a gang of ten men from ashore, the extra hands needed for the berthing operation, would arrive by launch at 0700. As midnight struck he settled at the broad table in his day cabin, spread his charts and began to study.

At ten minutes before three in the morning, inside the bridge, First Officer Lundquist and Third Mate Tom Keller shared a companionable coffee. The able seaman prowled the screens along the bridge console. "Sir," he called, "there's a launch approaching."

Tom Keller crossed to where the seaman pointed at the radar screen. There were a score of blips, some stationary, some moving, but all well away from the *Freya*. One tiny blip seemed to be approaching from the southeast. "Probably a fishing boat," said Keller. Lundquist was looking over his shoulder. He flicked to a lower range. "She's coming very close," he said.

The launch had to be aware of the mass of the *Freya*. Her deck was floodlit and her superstructure was lit like a Christmas tree. The launch, instead of veering away, began to curve in towards *Freya*'s stern.

"She looks as if she's going to come alongside," said Keller.

"She can't be the berthing crew," said Lundquist. "They're not due till seven. Go down to the head of the ladder," he told the seaman, "and tell me what you see. Put on the headset when you get there, and stay in touch."

The accommodation—or courtesy—ladder on the ship was amidships, so heavy that steel cables powered by an electric motor either lowered it from the ship's rail to sea level, or raised it to lie parallel to the rail. On the *Freya*, even full-laden, the rail was thirty feet above the sea.

Seconds later the two officers saw the seamen reach the ladder-head. He mounted a small platform that jutted over the sea, and looked down. As he did so he fitted on the earphones of a headset. From the bridge Lundquist pressed a switch and a powerful light came on, illuminating the seaman as he peered down at the black sea. The launch had vanished from the radar screen: she was too close to be observed.

"What do you see?" asked Lundquist speaking into a stick microphone.

The seaman's voice came back to the bridge. "Nothing, sir."

Meanwhile, the launch had passed round the rear of the *Freya*, under the overhang of her stern. For seconds it was out of sight. Either side of the stern, the guard rail of "A" deck was at its nearest point to the sea, just nineteen and a half feet above the water. The two men standing on the cabin roof of the launch had reduced this to ten feet. Before the launch emerged from the transom shadow both men slung upwards the three-point grapnels they held, the hooks sheathed in black rubber hose. Each grapnel, trailing rope, dropped over the guard rail and caught fast. As the launch moved on, both men were swept off the cabin roof hanging onto the ropes. They began to climb rapidly, hand over hand, unheeding of the submachine carbines strapped to their backs. In two seconds the launch emerged into the light and began to run down the side of the *Freya* towards the ladder.

"I can see it now," said the seaman high above. "It looks like a fishing launch."

233

"Keep the ladder up until they identify themselves," ordered Lundquist from the bridge.

Far behind and below him the two boarders were over the rail. Each unhooked his grapnel and heaved it into the sea, where it sank. The two men set off fast, round to the starboard side and straight for the outside steel ladders.

The launch came to rest beneath the courtesy ladder. Inside the cramped cabin four men crouched. At the wheel, the helmsman stared silently up at the seaman above him.

"Who are you?" called the seaman. "Identify yourself."

In the glare of the spotlight, the man in the black woollen helmet stared back. "He won't answer," said the seaman into his mouthpiece.

"Keep the spotlight on them," ordered Lundquist. "I'm coming to have a look."

Throughout the interchange the attention of Lundquist and Keller had been to the port side, forward of the bridge. On the starboard side of the bridge the door suddenly opened, bringing a gust of icy air. Both officers spun round. The door closed. Facing them were two men masked in black balaclavas, and wearing black roll-neck sweaters, black tracksuit trousers and rubber deck-shoes. Each pointed a submachine carbine at the officers.

"Order your seaman to lower the ladder," said one in English. The two officers stared at them unbelievingly. The gunman raised his weapon and squinted down the sight at Keller. "I'll give you three seconds," he said to Lundquist. "Then I'm blowing the head off your colleague."

Brick-red with anger, Lundquist leaned to the stick mike. "Lower the ladder," he told the seaman.

The seaman pressed a button on the small console at the ladder-head. There was a hum of motors and the ladder slowly lowered to the sea. Two minutes later five other men, all in black, were herding the seaman back along the deck to the superstructure. The six of them entered the bridge from the port side, the seaman's eyes wide with fright.

"Take it easy," Lundquist ordered him. To the masked gunman who had spoken, he said in English, "What do you want?"

"We want to speak to your captain. Where is he?"

The door of the inner stairwell opened and Thor Larsen stepped onto the bridge.

234

His gaze took in his three crewmen with their hands behind their heads, and seven black-clad terrorists. His eyes, when he turned to the man who had asked the question, were blue as a cracking glacier.

"I am Captain Thor Larsen, master of the *Freya*," he said slowly, "and who the hell are you?"

"Never mind who we are," said the terrorist leader. "We have just taken over your ship. Unless your men do as they are told, we shall start by making an example of your seaman."

Three of the submachine guns were pointing straight at the eighteen-year-old deckhand. He was white as chalk. "Mr. Lundquist," said Larsen formally, "do as these men say." Turning back to the leader he asked, "What exactly is it you want with the *Freya*?"

"We wish you no harm personally," said the terrorist, "but unless our requirements are carried out to the letter we shall do what we have to in order to secure compliance. Within thirty hours the West German government is going to release two of our friends from a West Berlin gaol and fly them to safety. If they do not, I am going to blast you, your crew, your ship and one million tons of crude oil all over the North Sea."

Twelve

The leader of the seven masked terrorists set his men to work with methodical precision, issuing a rapid stream of orders in a language neither Captain Larsen nor his officers and the young seaman could understand.

Five of the masked men herded the two officers and seaman to the rear of the bridge and surrounded them. The leader jerked his handgun at Captain Larsen and said in English: "Your cabin, if you please, Captain."

In single file, Larsen first, the leader of the terrorists next, his henchman with a submachine carbine bringing up the rear, the three men descended the stairs from the bridge to "D" deck one flight below. Larsen led his captors to his day cabin. The terrorist leader quickly went through the bedroom and bathroom. There was no one else present.

"Sit down, Captain," he said; the voice slightly muffled by the mask. "You will remain here until I return. Place your hands on the table and keep them there, palms downward."

There was another stream of orders in a foreign language, and the machine-gunner took up position with his back to the far bulkhead of the cabin, facing Thor Larsen but twelve feet away, the barrel of his gun pointing straight at Larsen's white roll-neck sweater. The leader checked to see that all the curtains were well drawn, then left.

Within minutes he was back on the bridge. "You," he pointed his gun at the boyish seaman, "come with me."

The lad looked imploringly at First Officer Stig Lundquist.

"You harm that boy and I'll personally hang you out to dry," said Third Mate Keller in his American accent.

"No one gets hurt unless they try anything stupid," said the voice behind the leader's mask. "Then there'll be a bloodbath."

Lundquist nodded to the seaman. "Go with him," he said. "Do what he wants."

The seaman was escorted back down the stairs. At the "D" deck level the terrorist stopped him.

"Apart from the captain, who lives on this deck?" he asked, in passable Swedish.

"The chief engineer, over there," said the seaman. "The chief officer over there, but he's on the bridge now. And the chief steward, there."

There was no sign of life behind any of the doors.

"The paint store, where is it?" asked the terrorist. The seaman turned and headed down the stairs to "A" deck. At the base of the superstructure the seaman opened a door and stepped out on the poop. The terrorist followed him. The cold night air made them both shiver.

The seaman led the way to a small steel structure with a steel door, closed by two great screw bolts with butterfly nuts on the outside. "Down there," said the seaman.

"Go on down," said the terrorist. The boy spun the butterfly nuts, unscrewing the cleats, and pulled them back. Seizing the door handle he swung it open. A light inside showed a tiny platform and a steel stairway running down to the depths of the *Freya*. Over seventy feet the stairs led down. When they reached the bottom they were well below the waterline, in an enclosure with four steel doors. The terrorist nodded to the one facing aft.

"What's that lead to?" he asked.

"Steering-gear housing."

Port and starboard of the steering-gear chamber were a chemical store and a paint store. The chemical store the terrorist ignored; he was not going to make men prisoners where there was acid to play with. The paint store was better—large, well-ventilated and its outer wall was the hull of the ship.

"What's the fourth door?" asked the terrorist.

"It leads to the rear of the engine room," said the seaman. "It is bolted on the other side."

The terrorist pushed against the steel door. It was rock-solid. He seemed satisfied.

"How many men on this ship?" he asked.

The boy ran his tongue over dry lips. "There are thirty men, including Captain Larsen."

The terrorist pushed the frightened young man into the paint store, swung the door closed and threw one of the twin bolts into its socket. Then he returned to the bridge. He nodded to his five companions who still held the two officers at gunpoint, and issued a stream of further orders. Minutes later the two bridge officers, joined by the chief steward and chief engineer, roused from their beds, were marched down to the paint store. There were protests, bitter language, as the rest of the crew too were herded down. But the leader of the terrorists informed them in English that their captain was held in his cabin and would die in the event of any resistance. The officers and men obeyed the terrorist's orders.

Down in the paint store the crew was finally counted: twenty-nine. The first cook and two stewards were allowed to return to the galley on "A" deck and ferry down to the paint store trays of buns and rolls, along with crates of bottled lemonade and canned beer. Two buckets were provided for toilets.

"Make yourselves comfortable," the terrorist leader told the twenty-nine angry men who stared back at him. "You won't be here long. Thirty hours at most. One last thing: your captain wants the pumpman. Who is he?"

A Swede called Bengt Martinsson stepped forward. "I'm the pumpman."

"Come with me." The time was four thirty in the morning.

It was the cargo-control room that interested the terrorist, and he ordered the pumpman to take him to it. It was on "A" deck.

238

There were no windows; it was centrally-heated, air-conditioned, silent and well-lit. Behind his mask the eyes of the terrorist chief flickered over the banks of switches and settled on the rear bulkhead. Here, behind a control console a visual display board showed in map-form the crude oil tank layout of the *Freya*.

"If you try to trick me," he told the pumpman, "I shall not shoot you, my friend. I shall shoot your Captain Larsen. Now, point out to me the ballast holds and the cargo holds."

Martinsson had sailed with Larsen twice before, and like all the crew had enormous respect and liking for the towering Norwegian. He wasn't going to argue when his captain's life was at stake.

He pointed at the diagram in front of him. The sixty holds were laid out in sets of three across the beam of the *Freya*; twenty such sets.

"Up here in the forepart," said Martinsson, "the port and starboard tanks are full of crude. The centre is the slop tank, empty now like a buoyancy tank, because we are on our maiden voyage and have not discharged cargo yet. So there has been no need to scour the cargo tanks and pump the slops in here. One row back, all three are the bow ballast tanks, now full of air."

"Open the valves between all three ballast tanks." Martinsson hesitated. "Go on, do it."

Martinsson pressed two square plastic controls on the console in front of him. There was a low humming. A quarter of a mile in front of them, down below the steel deck, great valves the size of garage doors swung open, forming a single linked unit of the three ballast tanks, each capable of holding 20,000 tons of liquid. Any liquid now entering one of the tanks would flow to the other two.

"Where are the next ballast tanks?" asked the terrorist. Martinsson pointed halfway down the ship. "Here, amidships, there are three in a row."

"Leave them alone," said the terrorist. "Where are the others?"

"The last three are here in the stern, right up close to the superstructure."

"Open the valves so they communicate with each other." Martinsson did as he was bid, knowing that if the forward and stern ballast tanks were allowed to flood with water while the centre section was buoyant with air, the ship would arch like an acrobat doing a backspring. Tankers are not designed for such strains; the *Freya*'s massive spine would break at the mid-section.

239

"Good," said the terrorist. "Now, can the ballast tanks be linked straight through to the cargo tanks?"

"No," said Martinsson. "The ballast tanks are permanent for ballast, that is seawater or air, but never oil. The two systems do not interconnect."

"Fine," said the masked man. "We can change all that. One last thing before we send you down to join your comrades in the paint store—open all the valves between all the cargo tanks, laterally and longitudinally, so that all fifty communicate with each other."

It took fifteen seconds for the necessary control buttons to be pushed. Far down in the treacly blackness of the crude oil scores of gigantic valves swung open, forming one enormous single tank containing a million tons of crude. Martinsson stared at his handiwork in horror. "If she sinks with one tank ruptured," he whispered, "the whole million tons will flow out."

"Then the authorities had better make sure she doesn't sink," said the terrorist. "Where is the master power source from this control panel to the hydraulic pumps that control the valves?"

Martinsson gestured to an electrical junction box on the wall near the ceiling. The terrorist reached up and pulled the contact breaker downwards. He removed the ten fuses and pocketed them. The pumpman looked on with fear in his eyes. The valve-opening process had become irreversible. There were spare fuses, and he knew where they were stored. But he would be in the paint store. No stranger entering his sanctum could find them in time to close those vital valves.

Bengt Martinsson knew that a tanker cannot be loaded or unloaded haphazardly. If all the starboard or port cargo tanks are filled, with the others left empty, the ship will roll over and sink. If the forward tanks are filled, but not balanced at the stern, she will dive by the nose; and the reverse, if the stern half is full of liquid and the for'ard empty.

"One last thing," said the terrorist. "What would happen if we opened all the fifty inspection hatches to the cargo tanks?"

Martinsson was sorely tempted to let them try it. He thought of Captain Larsen sitting high above him facing a submachine carbine. He swallowed. "You'd die," he said, "unless you had breathing apparatus."

He explained that when a tanker's holds are full, the liquid crude is never quite up to the ceilings of the holds. In the gap between the oil and the ceiling volatile, highly-explosive gases form, given off by the crude oil. If not bled off, they would turn the ship into a bomb. To bleed them off, inert gases—chiefly carbon monoxide—from the main engine exhaust flue are fed into the holds to expel oxygen. The danger of fire, which requires oxygen, is banished. But every tank has a one-yard circular inspection hatch let into the main deck; if these were opened by an incautious person, he would immediately be enveloped in a cloud of inert gas, and would die of asphyxiation.

"Thank you," said the terrorist. "Who handles the breathing apparatus?"

"The chief officer is in charge of it," said Martinsson. "But we are all trained to use it."

Two minutes later he was back in the paint store with the rest of the crew. It was five o'clock.

Meanwhile, the remaining five terrorists had unloaded their launch and ten suitcases of explosive stood on the deck. The leader gave orders with crisp precision. Far away on the foredeck the hatches of the port and starboard ballast holds were removed, revealing the single steel ladder descending eighty feet into the black depths of musty air.

Azamat Krim took his torch and descended into the first. Two suitcases were lowered after him on long cords. Working in the base of the hold, he placed one entire suitcase of explosive against the outer hull of the *Freya* and lashed it to one of the vertical ribs. Half of the other case went against the forward bulkhead, beyond which lay 20,000 tons of oil; the other half went against the aft bulkhead, behind which was another 20,000 tons of crude. Sandbags were packed around the charges to concentrate the blast. With the detonators in place and linked to the triggering device, he returned to the deck.

The same process was repeated on the other side of the *Freya*, and then twice again in the port and starboard ballast holds close up to the superstructure. He had used eight of his suitcases in four ballast holds. The ninth he placed in the centre ballast hold amidships to help crack the ship's spine.

The tenth was laid and primed against the bulkhead to the paint store. If it went off, the men in the store a half-inch of steel away who survived the blast, would drown when the sea came

241

pounding through. It was six fifteen and dawn was breaking over the *Freya's* silent decks when Krim reported to Andrew Drake. "The charges are laid and primed, Andriy. I pray to God we never set them off."

"We won't have to," said Drake. "But I have to convince Captain Larsen. Only when he has seen and believed will he convince the authorities. Then they'll have to do as we want."

Two of the crew were brought from the paint store, made to don protective clothing, face-masks and oxygen bottles, and proceed down the deck, opening every one of the fifty inspection hatches to the oil cargo tanks so that if the ship were sunk, the oil would bubble out all the more readily. The men were then returned to the paint store and the steel door bolted shut, not to be opened again until two prisoners were safe in Israel.

At six thirty Andrew Drake, still masked, returned to the captain's day cabin. He sat down and told Thor Larsen what had been done. The Norwegian stared back at him impassively, held in check by the submachine gun pointing at him from the corner of the room.

When he had finished, Drake held up a black plastic instrument no larger than two kingsize cigarette packets bound together; there was a single red button on the face of it, and a four-inch steel aerial sticking from the top. Larsen knew enough about radio to recognize a small transistorized transmitter.

"This is an oscillator," said Drake. "If that red button is pressed, it will emit a single VHF note, rising steadily in tone and pitch to a scream that our ears cannot hear. But attached to every single charge on this ship is a receiver that can and will hear. As the tonal pitch rises, a dial on the receivers will show the pitch, the needles moving round the dials until they can go no farther. When that happens the devices will blow their fuses and a current will be cut. The cutting of that current in each receiver will convey its message to the detonators, which will then operate. You know what that would mean?"

Thor Larsen stared back at the masked face across the table from him. His ship, his beloved *Freya*, was being raped and there was nothing he could do about it. His crew was crowded into a steel coffin inches from a charge that would crush them all, and cover them in seconds in freezing seawater.

His mind's eye conjured a picture of hell. If the charges blew,

242

great holes would be torn in the port and starboard sides of four of his ballast tanks. Roaring mountains of sea would rush in, filling both the outer and the centre ballast tanks. Being heavier than the crude oil, the seawater would push through the other gaping holes inside the tanks to the neighbouring cargo holds, spewing the crude oil upwards through the inspection hatches, so that six more holds would fill with water. This would happen right up in the forepeak, and right aft beneath his feet. In minutes the engine room would be flooded with tens of thousands of tons of green water. The stern and the bow would drop at least ten feet, but the buoyant mid-section would ride high, its ballast tanks untouched. The *Freya*, most beautiful of all the Norse goddesses, would arch her back once, in pain, and split in two. Both sections would drop straight, twenty-five feet to the seabed beneath, to sit there with fifty inspection hatches open and facing upwards. A million tons of crude would gurgle out to the surface of the North Sea.

It might take three days for the last of *Freya*'s cargo to reach the surface, but no diver could work to close the hatches among fifty columns of vertically rising crude oil. The escape of the oil, like the destruction of his ship, would be irreversible.

He stared back at the masked face but made no reply. There was a deep, seething anger inside him but he gave no sign of it.

"What do you want?" he growled. The terrorist glanced at the digital display clock on the wall. It read a quarter to seven.

"We're going to the radio room," he said. "You will talk to Rotterdam."

Twenty-six miles to the east the rising sun had dimmed the great yellow flames that spout day and night from the oil refineries of Europort. The greatest oil terminal in the world, it lies on the south shore of the Maas estuary. On the north shore is the Maas control building.

Here at six forty-five on the morning of 1 April Duty Officer Bernhard Dijkstra heard the radio-telephone speaker in front of him come to life. "Pilot Maas, Pilot Maas, here is the *Freya*."

Dijkstra leaned forward and flicked a switch. "*Freya*, this is Pilot Maas. Go ahead."

"Pilot Maas, this is the *Freya*. Captain Thor Larsen speaking. Where is the launch with my berthing crew?"

"*Freya*, this is Pilot Maas. They should be with you in twenty

243

minutes." What followed caused Duty Officer Dijkstra to shoot bolt upright in his chair.

"*Freya* to Pilot Maas. Contact the launch immediately and tell them to return to port. Inform the Maas pilots not to take off, repeat not to take off. We have an emergency, I repeat, we have an emergency."

Dijkstra covered the speaker with his hand and yelled to his fellow duty officer to throw the switch on the tape recorder. When it was recording, Dijkstra removed his hand and said carefully, "*Freya*, this is Pilot Maas. Understand you do not wish the berthing crew to come alongside. Understand you do not wish the pilots to take off. Please confirm."

"Pilot Maas, this is *Freya*. Confirm. Confirm."

"*Freya*, please give details of your emergency."

There was silence for ten seconds, as if a consultation were taking place on the *Freya*'s bridge. Then Larsen's voice boomed out again in the control room. "Pilot Maas, *Freya*. I cannot give the nature of the emergency. But if any attempt is made to approach the *Freya*, people will get killed. Do not make any further attempt to contact the *Freya*. Finally, the *Freya* will contact you again at oh-nine-hundred hours exactly. Have the chairman of the Rotterdam port authority present in the control room. That is all."

The voice ended and there was a loud click. Dijkstra looked across at his colleague. "What the hell did that mean? He spoke of men getting killed. What's he got, a mutiny? Has someone run amok?"

"We'd better do what he says until this is sorted out," said Officer Schipper.

"Right. You get on to the chairman. I'll contact the launch and the two pilots and tell them not to go near the ship."

Dirk Van Gelder, chairman of the port authority, was at the breakfast table when the phone rang. Dropping his newspaper on the chair, he shuffled in carpet slippers out to the hallway.

"Van Gelder," he said down the telephone. As he listened, he stiffened, his brow furrowed. "What did he mean, killed?" he asked. There was another stream of words into his ear. "I'll be with you in fifteen minutes," said Van Gelder.

He slammed the phone down, kicked off the slippers and put on his shoes and jacket. Two minutes later, as he climbed into his

Mercedes and backed out to the gravel driveway, he was fighting back thoughts of his abiding nightmare. "Dear God, not a hijack. Please, not a hijack."

AFTER REPLACING the VHF radio-telephone on *Freya*, Captain Thor Larsen had been taken at gunpoint on a tour of his ship, peering with torches into the forward ballast holds to note the big packages strapped far down below the waterline. He had seen the single charge in the centre ballast tank amidships, and the further charges in the after ballast tanks close by the superstructure. As he was being escorted back to his day cabin, he had noted one of the terrorists perched right up in the fo'c'sle apron of the *Freya*, the wind having blown away the poisonous inert gases from the open inspection hatches. He was watching the arc of sea out in front of the vessel. Another was a hundred feet up on the top of the funnel casing with a commanding view of the sea around him. A third was on the bridge, patrolling the radar screens, able thanks to the *Freya*'s technology to see a forty-eight-mile-radius circle of ocean around her, and most of the sea beneath her. Of the remaining four terrorists, two, the leader and another, were with him; the other two must be below decks somewhere.

The terrorist leader forced him to sit again at the table in his cabin. "Captain, please read this," the masked man said, handing Larsen three sheets of foolscap paper covered with typed writing in English. Larsen went rapidly through it.

"At nine o'clock you are going to read that message over the ship-shore radio to the chairman of the port authority of Rotterdam. No more, and no less. Just the message. Understand?"

Larsen nodded grimly. The door opened and another terrorist came in with a tray of fried eggs, rolls and coffee, which he placed on the table between them. "Breakfast," said the terrorist leader. "You might as well eat."

Larsen shook his head, but drank the coffee. He had been awake all night, and had risen from his bed the previous morning at seven. Twenty-six hours awake, and many more to go. He needed to stay alert and black coffee would help.

The terrorist signalled the remaining gunman to leave. As the door closed they were alone, but the seven-foot expanse of table put the terrorist well out of Larsen's reach. The gun lay within inches of the man's right hand, the oscillator was at his waist.

"We shouldn't have to abuse your hospitality for more than thirty hours, maybe forty," said the masked man. "But if I wear this mask during that time I shall suffocate. You have never seen me before and after tomorrow you will never see me again."

The man pulled the black balaclava helmet from his head. Larsen found himself staring at a man in his early thirties, with brown eyes and medium brown hair. He puzzled Larsen. The man spoke like an Englishman, behaved like one. But Englishmen do not hijack tankers, surely. Irish perhaps? IRA? But he had referred to friends in prison in Germany. Arab, perhaps? He spoke a strange language to his companions.

"What do I call you?" he asked the man. The terrorist thought for a moment, as he ate.

"You can call me 'Svoboda'," he said at length. "It is a common name in my language. But it also means 'freedom'."

"That's not Arabic," said Larsen.

The man smiled for the first time. "We are not Arabs. We are Ukrainian freedom fighters."

"And you think the authorities will free your friends in prison?" asked Larsen.

"They will have to," said Drake confidently. "They have no alternative. Come, it is almost nine o'clock."

Thirteen

"Pilot Maas, Pilot Maas, this is the *Freya*." Captain Thor Larsen's baritone voice echoed into the Maas control room. In the room with its sweeping picture windows gazing out over the North Sea, five men waited.

Dijkstra and Schipper were still on duty. Port Authority Chairman Van Gelder stood behind Dijkstra, ready to take over when the call came through. At another console a day-shift man was bringing ships in and out of the busy estuary but keeping them away from the *Freya*, whose blip on the radar screen was at the limit of vision. The senior maritime safety officer of Maas control was also present.

When the call came, Van Gelder sat down before the speaker, cleared his throat and threw the microphone transmit switch.

"*Freya*, this is Pilot Maas. Go ahead, please."

"*Freya* to Pilot Maas, I wish to speak personally to the chairman of the port authority."

"This is Dirk Van Gelder speaking. I am chairman of the port authority."

"This is Captain Thor Larsen, master of the *Freya*."

"Yes, Captain Larsen, your voice is recognized. What is your problem?"

On the bridge of the *Freya*, Drake gestured with his gun to the written statement in Larsen's hand. Larsen flicked his transmit switch.

"I am reading a prepared statement. Please do not interrupt and do not pose questions. At three o'clock this morning the *Freya* was taken over by armed men. I have been given ample reason to believe they are in deadly earnest and prepared to carry out all their threats unless their demands are met."

Van Gelder closed his eyes wearily. For years he had been urging that security measures be taken to protect these floating bombs from hijack. He had been ignored. The voice from the speaker went on, the tape recorder reels revolved impassively.

"My entire crew is at present locked in the lowest portion of the ship behind steel doors. So far no harm has come to them. I, myself, am held at gunpoint on my own bridge. Explosive charges have been placed at strategic positions inside the *Freya*'s hull. I have examined these myself, and can corroborate that if exploded they would blast the *Freya* apart, kill her crew instantly, and vent one million tons of crude oil into the North Sea."

"Oh, my God," said a voice behind Van Gelder. He waved an impatient hand for the speaker to shut up.

"These are the immediate demands of the men who hold the *Freya*," Larsen's voice continued. "One, all sea traffic is to be cleared at once from the area inside a ninety-degree arc between the *Freya* and the Dutch coast. Two, no vessel, surface or submarine, is to attempt to approach the *Freya* within five miles. Three, no aircraft is to pass overhead within a five-mile radius and below a height of 10,000 feet. Is that clear?"

Van Gelder gripped the microphone. "*Freya*, this is Pilot Maas. Dirk Van Gelder speaking. Yes, that is clear. I will do as instructed. Over."

There was a pause, and Larsen's voice came back. "I am

informed that if there is any attempt to breach these orders, either the *Freya* will vent 20,000 tons of crude oil, or one of my seamen will be . . . executed. Is that understood?"

Dirk Van Gelder turned to his traffic officers. "Get the shipping out of that area, fast! Get onto the airport and tell them—no commercial flights, no private aircraft, no choppers taking pictures—nothing!" To the microphone he said, "Understood, Captain Larsen. Is there anything else?"

"Yes," said the disembodied voice. "There will be no further radio contact until twelve hundred hours. At that time the *Freya* will call you again. I will wish to speak to both the prime minister of the Netherlands and the West German ambassador. That is all."

On the bridge of the *Freya*, Drake took the handset from Larsen and gestured for the Norwegian to return to the day cabin.

When they were seated with the broad table between them, Drake laid down his gun and leaned back.

"What do we do now?" asked Larsen.

"We wait," said Drake. "While Europe goes quietly mad."

"They'll kill you," said Larsen. "They may have to do what you say, but when they have done it they'll be waiting for you."

"I know," said Drake. "But you see, I don't mind if I die. I'll fight to live of course, but I'll die, and I'll kill, before I'll see them destroy my project."

"You want these two men in Germany free, that much?"

"Yes, that much. You wouldn't understand why. But for years my land, my people, have been occupied, persecuted, imprisoned. And no one cared. Now I threaten to kill one seaman or hit Western Europe in the pocket, and you'll see what they do. Suddenly it is a disaster. But for me the slavery of my land, that is the disaster."

"This dream of yours, what is it?"

"A free Ukraine," said Drake simply. "Which cannot be achieved short of a popular uprising by millions of people."

"In the Soviet Union?" said Larsen. "That will never happen."

"It could," countered Drake. "But first, the conviction by those millions that their oppressors are invincible must be broken. If it once were, the floodgates could open wide."

"No one will ever believe that," said Larsen.

"Not in the West, no. Here people would say I cannot be right in that calculation. But in the Kremlin they know I am."

"And for this . . . popular uprising, you are prepared to die?" asked Larsen.

"If I must—for the land, the people I love more than life itself. That's my advantage; within a hundred-mile radius of us here there is no one else who loves something more than his life."

A day earlier Thor Larsen might have agreed with the fanatic. But something was happening inside the big, slow-moving Norwegian. For the first time in his life he hated a man enough to kill him. Inside his head a private voice said, "I don't care about your Ukrainian dream, Mr. Svoboda. You are not going to kill my crew and my ship."

MANY OTHER EARS had heard the conversation between the *Freya* and Maas control, and at Felixstowe on the coast of Suffolk, an English coastguard officer walked quickly away from his radio set and picked up the telephone. "Get me the department of the environment in London," he told the operator.

"By God, those Dutchies have got themselves a problem this time," said his deputy.

"It's not just the Dutch," said the senior coastguard. "Look at the map."

On the wall a map showed the coast of Suffolk across to the Maas estuary. In chinagraph pencil the coastguard had marked the *Freya* at her overnight position. It was exactly halfway between the two coasts. "If she blows, lad," he said, "our coasts will also be under a foot of oil."

Minutes later he was talking to one of the men in the environment department concerned with oil-slick hazards. An hour or so afterwards the permanent under-secretary to the department was on the phone to the cabinet secretary, Sir Julian Flannery.

"It's early days yet," he said. "We don't know who they are, how many, or whether there are really any bombs on board. But if that amount of crude oil did get spilled, it would be rather messy."

Sir Julian gazed out through his first-floor windows onto Whitehall. "Good of you to call so promptly," he said. "I think I'd better inform the PM. In the meantime, could you put together a memo on the consequences if the ship does blow up? Spillage, tide flow, speed, area of our coastline likely to be affected. I suspect she'll want to know. She always does."

He had worked under three prime ministers, and the latest, Mrs. Joan Carpenter, was far and away the toughest and most decisive. The cabinet secretary had his appointment within minutes and walked briskly across the lawn to Number 10.

When he entered the prime minister's private office she was at her desk, where she had been since eight o'clock. Three red dispatch boxes were open on the floor beside her; the woman went through documentation like a paper shredder, the documents either agreed to, rejected, or bearing crisp requests for further information.

"Good morning, Prime Minister."

"Good morning, Sir Julian, a beautiful day."

"Indeed, ma'am. Unfortunately it has brought a piece of unpleasantness with it."

He took a seat at her gesture, and sketched in the details of the affair in the North Sea. She was alert.

"If it is true, then the *Freya* could cause an environmental disaster," she said flatly. "We should form a crisis management committee to consider the implications."

For thirty minutes the prime minister and her cabinet secretary listed the areas in which they would need professional expertise if they were to be informed of the options in a major tanker hijack in the North Sea.

The supertanker was insured by Lloyd's, who would be in possession of a complete plan of her layout. The British Petroleum marine division would have a tanker construction expert who could give a judgment on feasibility. Regarding spillage control, they agreed to call on the senior research analyst at the Warren Springs laboratory, run jointly by the department of trade and industry and the ministry of agriculture, fisheries and food. The ministry of defence would provide a Royal Engineers expert on explosives, and the department of the environment would calculate the ecological scope of the catastrophe. By eleven thirty the list seemed complete.

"One last thing, Sir Julian," said the PM. "If the demands cannot be met, the contingency may have to be considered of storming the vessel to liberate the crew and defuse the charges."

"Ah, yes, Prime Minister. That would of course be a last resort."

"The Israelis stormed the airliner at Entebbe," mused the PM. "The Germans stormed the one at Mogadishu. The Dutch stormed the train at Assen—when they were left with no alternative. Supposing it were to happen again, could our marines carry out such a mission?"

"To storm a vessel at sea," Sir Julian said, "a helicopter landing would not be feasible. It would be spotted by the deck-watch, and of course the ship has a radar scanner. An approach by surface vessel would also be observed. This is not an airliner on a runway, nor a stationary train, ma'am. This is a ship over twenty-five miles from land."

"What about an approach by armed divers or frogmen?" The blue eyes across the desk did not leave him. "I understand that our capacity in this regard is among the most advanced in Europe. Who are these underwater experts?"

"The special boat service, Prime Minister."

It was going to be bad, he could see it coming. They had used the land-based counterpart of the special boat service, the special air service, to help the Germans at Mogadishu. Now they were going to start another James Bond-style fantasy.

"Ask the special boat service liaison officer to attend the crisis management committee. And prepare the UNICORNE. I shall expect you to take the chair at noon, when the terrorists' demands are known." UNICORNE was the official name for this committee—the united cabinet office review group (national emergency).

The activity in Holland was already, by mid-morning, becoming frenetic. From his office in The Hague, the Dutch premier, Jan Grayling, and his staff were putting together the same sort of crisis management committee that Mrs. Carpenter in London had in mind. Dirk Van Gelder, having delivered the tape recording of the nine o'clock message from the *Freya* to Premier Grayling, drove back to Maas control. At ten thirty he placed a call to Harry Wennerstrom. Van Gelder carefully explained what had happened. There was silence from the Hilton end of the line. Wennerstrom's first reaction could have been to mention that there was 310 million dollars' worth of ship and oil being held prisoner out beyond the western horizon. It was a reflection of the man that he said at length: "There are thirty of my seamen out there, Mr. Van Gelder. I must tell you that if anything happens to any one of them because the terrorists' demands are not met, I shall hold the Dutch authorities personally responsible."

He replaced the handset and stared through the picture windows of his hotel sitting room towards the west, where twenty-five miles away his dream ship was lying at anchor. "Cancel the convoy of guests to Maas control," he said to one of his secretaries. "Cancel the reception. Cancel the press conference. I'm going to Maas control. Have my car waiting by the time I reach the garage. Also call the police chief in Alesund, Norway, and tell him to await a call from me."

Around the *Freya* the sea was emptying. Working closely with their British colleagues, the Dutch marine traffic control officers diverted shipping into fresh sea lanes west of the *Freya*. Eastwards of the anchored ship coastal traffic was ordered to stop or turn back, and movements into and out of Europort and Rotterdam were halted. Angry sea captains were simply told that an emergency had arisen. The large press corps assembled in Rotterdam reported to their editors that something serious was afoot with the *Freya*. The editor of *De Telegraaf* received a tip from a radio ham that there were terrorists on board and that they would issue their demands on Channel Twenty at noon. He at once ordered a radio monitor to be placed in readiness with a tape recorder to catch the message.

Premier Jan Grayling telephoned the West German ambassador, Konrad Voss, and told him in confidence what had happened. Voss called Bonn at once, and within thirty minutes replied to the Dutch premier that he would accompany him to the Hook for the twelve o'clock call. The Federal German government would do everything it could to help.

Lloyd's Intelligence unit had already been informed shortly after ten o'clock. The radio officer on a British vessel preparing to enter the Maas estuary had heard the nine o'clock conversation, noted it and shown it to his captain. Shortly afterwards the news was passed on to Lloyd's. A consortium of twenty-five separate firms of underwriters had put together the 170 million-dollar hull insurance on the *Freya*. Another large group of firms covered the 140 million-dollar cargo for Clint Blake in Texas. But the biggest single policy was the protection and indemnity insurance for the persons of the crew and pollution compensation. It would cost the biggest money if the *Freya* were blown apart.

Shortly before noon the chairman of Lloyd's in London stared at a few calculations on his jotting pad. "We're talking about a thousand million dollars' loss if the worst comes to the worst," he remarked to his personal aide. "Who the hell *are* these people?"

On the *Freya*'s bridge, Larsen, who now knew the nature of the demands, did not see how the authorities could refuse. The alternative was too terrible for all of them. If the man who called himself Svoboda had simply kidnapped a politician, he might have been refused his friends' release. But he had elected to endanger the coasts of five countries, one sea, thirty lives and millions of dollars.

Nothing had changed on the bridge, except that there was an extra terrorist there, curled up asleep in the corner, his gun still clutched in his hand. He was masked, like the one who patrolled the radar and sonar screens. At a word from Svoboda in Ukrainian, the man at the screens turned his gun on Larsen.

Svoboda walked over to the scanners and read them. There was a ring of clear water round the *Freya* stretching five miles on the western, southern and northern sides. To the east the sea was clear to the Dutch coast. He strode to the bridge-wing, and called upwards. From high above, Larsen heard the man atop the funnel assembly shout back.

Svoboda returned to the bridge. The time was twelve noon. "Come," he said to the captain, "your audience is waiting. One attempt at a trick, and I shoot one of your seamen."

Larsen took the handset and pressed for transmit. "Maas control, Maas control, this is the *Freya*."

Over fifty different offices heard the call. All the major intelligence services were listening, as well as ships' radio officers, radio hams and journalists. A voice came back from the Hook of Holland. "*Freya*, this is Maas control. Go ahead, please."

Thor Larsen read from his sheet of paper. "This is Captain Thor Larsen. I wish to speak personally to the prime minister of the Netherlands."

A new voice, speaking English, came on the radio from the Hook. "Captain Larsen, this is Jan Grayling. I am the prime minister."

"Is the West German ambassador with you?"

In Maas control the microphone was passed to Konrad Voss. "This is the ambassador of the Federal Republic of Germany," he said. "My name is Konrad Voss."

On the *Freya* Svoboda nodded at Larsen. "Go ahead."

The men grouped around the console in Maas control listened in silence. The two tape recorders whirled softly. Volume was switched high; Thor Larsen's voice echoed in the room.

"I repeat what I told you at nine this morning. The *Freya* is in the hands of partisans. Explosive devices have been placed which would, if detonated at the touch of a button, blow her apart. The men concerned have convinced me that they are prepared to die rather than give in. Here are their demands:

"The two prisoners of conscience, David Lazareff and Lev Mishkin, presently in gaol at Tegel in West Berlin, are to be liberated. They are to be flown by a West German civilian jet to Israel. Prior to this, the premier of the State of Israel is to give a public guarantee that they will be neither repatriated to the Soviet Union, nor extradited back to West Germany, nor re-imprisoned in Israel. Their liberation must take place at dawn tomorrow. The Israeli guarantee of safe conduct and freedom must be given by midnight tonight. Failure to comply will place the responsibility for the outcome on the shoulders of West Germany and Israel. There will be no more contact until the demands have been met."

The radio-telephone went dead with a click. Jan Grayling looked at Konrad Voss.

"I must contact Bonn urgently," the West German envoy said.

"What has just been said cannot fail to be made public within the hour," said Grayling. "I suggest we return to our offices. I shall prepare a statement for the one o'clock news. Mr. Ambassador, I fear the pressure will now begin to swing towards Bonn."

Fourteen

The reaction to the noon broadcast was frantic. Radio and television programmes were interrupted throughout Europe's Friday lunch-hour to beam the news.

In London, on the dot of five past twelve, a messenger in a motorcyclist's helmet, with goggles and scarf drawn round the lower part of his face, had walked calmly into the Fleet Street office of the Press Association and left an envelope addressed to the editor-in-chief. By twelve fifteen the editor was opening the envelope. It contained the transcript of the statement read by

Captain Larsen fifteen minutes earlier, though it must have been prepared well before that. The editor-in-chief told the metropolitan police, and the text went straight onto the wires of the PA and their cousins upstairs, Reuters.

Leaving Fleet Street, Miroslav Kaminsky dumped his helmet, goggles and scarf in a dustbin, took a taxi to Heathrow airport and boarded the 2:15 plane for Tel Aviv.

By two o'clock both the Israeli and West German governments began to receive a flood of phone calls urging them to release Mishkin and Lazareff rather than face the promised disaster.

At one forty-five Chancellor Dietrich Busch of West Germany put out a statement that an emergency cabinet meeting had been called for three o'clock to consider the situation.

Fifteen minutes later, the governor of Tegel gaol in West Berlin received a telephone call from the federal justice minister in Bonn.

The governor then summoned one of his senior prison officers. He was Ludwig Jahn, who had quietly crossed from East Berlin to the West in 1961 leaving his mother, two younger brothers and their families behind. It was Jahn who had been visited a few weeks ago by a Russian, someone the terrified warder would never know was Colonel Kukushkin of the KGB. Jahn had been shown photographs of his widowed mother, nearly eighty, and his two brothers in East German prison cells. It was then that Jahn had agreed to admit the Russian on Monday, 4 April, when he would be on night duty, and take him to the hijackers' cells. The hijackers had escaped from the East. Jahn knew that the visit would not be to bring them birthday gifts.

The prison officer's jaw dropped as the governor now told him of the demand of the terrorists on board the *Freya*.

"We'll be in the news within minutes," said the governor. "So batten down the hatches. I've given orders to the main gate; no admissions by anyone other than staff. Now, as regards Mishkin and Lazareff. I want the guard on that floor and particularly in that corridor trebled. Transfer all other prisoners in that corridor to other levels. A group of intelligence people are flying in from Bonn to ask them who their friends in the North Sea are. Any questions?"

The prison officer swallowed and shook his head.

"Now," resumed the governor, "we don't know how long this emergency will last. When were you due to go off duty?"

"Six o'clock tonight, sir. I'm to return Sunday night at midnight."

"I'll have to ask you to work right on through," said the governor. He came around the desk and clapped the man on the shoulder, "You're a good fellow, Jahn. I don't know what we'd do without you."

AT THE SAME TIME in Scotland, a Nimrod Mark Two climbed away from RAF station Kinloss and turned southeast. Squadron-Leader Mark Latham of Coastal Command was flying about the best aircraft for submarine and shipping surveillance in the world. The Nimrod could skim the waves at low level, listening on electronic ears to the sounds of underwater movement, or cruise at altitude, hour after hour, two engines shut down for fuel economy, observing by radar an enormous area of ocean beneath it. Its cameras could photograph day and night; it was unaffected by weather conditions. Its datalink computers could process the received information, identify what it saw, and transmit the picture back to base. Latham's orders were to take up station 15,000 feet above the *Freya*, well above the 10,000 feet limit specified by the terrorists, and keep circling until relieved.

"She's coming on screen, skipper," Latham's radar operator called down the intercom. Back in the hull of the Nimrod the operator was gazing at his scanner screen, watching the large blip of the *Freya* move towards the centre of the screen.

"Cameras on," said Latham calmly. In the belly of the Nimrod the F.126 daytime camera swivelled like a gun, spotted the *Freya* and locked on. Automatically it adjusted range and focus for maximum definition. From now on, the aircraft could fly all over the sky, while the cameras stayed locked on the *Freya*, swivelling in their housings to compensate for the circling of the Nimrod.

"And transmit," said Latham.

The datalink began to send the pictures back to Britain, and thence to London. When the Nimrod was over the *Freya* she banked to port, and from his left-hand seat Latham looked down on her. Behind him a camera zoomed closer, beating the human eye. It picked out the lone figure of the terrorist in the forepeak, masked face staring upwards at the silver swallow three miles above him, and another man on top of the funnel. He cradled a submachine carbine in his arms.

"There they are, the bastards," called the camera operator. The Nimrod established a gentle, Rate One turn above the *Freya*, went over to automatic pilot, closed down two engines, and began to circle and watch.

IN RESPONSE to Harry Wennerstrom's phone call, the gleaming Volvo of Trygve Dahl, the Alesund police chief, halted by the porch of the Larsens' house. Dahl had known Lisa Larsen since her marriage to his friend, and his own children played with Kurt and Kristina at school.

He climbed out of the Volvo and rang the bell. When it did not answer, he walked round to the back. He found Lisa feeding carrot tops to Kristina's pet rabbit. She looked up and smiled when she saw him. "She doesn't know," he thought.

She pushed the remainder of the carrots through the wire of the cage and came over to him. "Trygve, how nice to see you. What brings you out of town?"

"Lisa, have you listened to the news this morning on the radio?"

"No. I've been out here since breakfast." Her smile faded. "Why?"

"Look, Lisa, be calm. Something has happened. To Thor."

She went pale beneath her tan. Carefully, Trygve Dahl told her what had occurred. "So far as we know, he's perfectly all right. The Germans are bound to release these two men, and all will be well."

She did not cry. She said, quite calmly, "I want to go to him."

"Harald Wennerstrom's private jet is due at the airport in twenty minutes," the police chief said. "I'll run you there. He thought you might want to go to Rotterdam. Now don't worry about the children. They can stay with us."

Twenty minutes later Thor Larsen's "snow-mouse" was in the car with Dahl, heading back towards Alesund. Just after one thirty the Nordia Line Jetstream howled down the runway, swept out over the waters of the bay and climbed towards the south.

SINCE THE GROWING outbreaks of terrorism in the sixties and seventies the British government has maintained the basic crisis management committee known as UNICORNE.

The main meeting room two floors below the cabinet office in

Whitehall is surrounded by smaller offices; a separate telephone switchboard, linking UNICORNE with every department of state through direct lines; a teleprinter room with the printers of the main news agencies; a telex room and radio room; and a room for secretaries with typewriters and copiers.

The men who grouped under the chairmanship of Cabinet Secretary Sir Julian Flannery just after noon that Friday represented all the government departments involved. Assisting them now was a bevy of specialist and experts, including three in explosives, ships and pollution, the vice-chief of defence staff (a vice-admiral), someone from defence intelligence, from MI5, from the SIS, a Royal Air Force group captain, and Colonel Tim Holmes of the Royal Marines, the special boat service liaison officer.

"Well now, gentlemen," Sir Julian began, "we have all read the transcript of the noon broadcast from Captain Larsen. May we begin with the *Freya*. What do we know about her?"

"I have secured the plan of the *Freya* here," said the shipping expert from trade and industry. "It's detailed down to the last nut and bolt."

He went on, the plan spread on the table, to describe the size, cargo capacity and construction of the *Freya*. He pointed out where the captain's cabin would be and the exact locations of the cargo and ballast holds.

No one listened with more attention than Colonel Holmes. He was the one whose fellow marines might have to storm the vessel. He knew those men would want to know every nook and cranny of the real *Freya* before they went on board.

"There is one last thing," said the scientist from energy, "she's full of Mubarraq."

"Good God!" said Dr. Henderson, a scientist from Warren Springs laboratory. "Mubarraq is about the lightest crude oil there is."

He went on to explain that when crude oil is spilled on the sea, it contains both the "lighter fractions" which evaporate into the air, and the "heavier fractions" which are what are washed onto the beaches as thick black gunge.

"It'll spread from coast to coast before the lighter fractions evaporate," he concluded. "It'll poison the whole North Sea for weeks, denying the marine life the oxygen it needs to live."

"I see," said Sir Julian gravely. "Thank you, Doctor."

There followed information from other experts. The explosives man from the Royal Engineers explained that industrial dynamite could indeed destroy a ship this size.

"If the holes are made in the right places," he said, "the unbalanced mass of her would pull her apart. There's one other thing; the message read by Captain Larsen mentioned the phrase 'at the touch of a button'. That seems to indicate triggering by radio impulse."

The chief of the department in MI5 which dealt exclusively with terrorism as it affected Britain, underlined the strange nature of the demands of the captors of the *Freya*.

"These men, Lev Mishkin and David Lazareff," he pointed out, "are Jewish. Hijackers who tried to escape from the USSR and ended up shooting a flight captain. One has to assume that those seeking to free them are their friends or admirers. That tends to indicate fellow Jews. But in our files we haven't had Jews threatening to blow people to pieces to free their friends since the Irgun and the Stern gang. Nor do we have any trace from what Captain Larsen has broadcast to indicate their origins. It's a blank wall."

At three thirty Sir Julian recessed the meeting. It was agreed to keep a Nimrod circling above the *Freya* until further notice. The vice-chief of defence staff also proposed that a naval warship take up station just over five miles west of the *Freya* in case the terrorists attempted to leave under cover of darkness. The Nimrod would spot them if they did, and pass their position to the navy. Also the foreign office asked to be informed of any decision by West Germany and Israel on the terrorists' demands.

"There does not appear much that Her Majesty's government can do at the present moment," Sir Julian pointed out. "The decision is up to the Israeli prime minister and the West German chancellor. Personally I cannot see what they can do except to let these wretched young men go to Israel."

When the men left the room only Colonel Holmes of the marines stayed behind. He sat down again and stared at the model of the tanker in front of him. "Supposing they don't," he said to himself.

Carefully he made a note of the distance in feet from the sea to the stern taffrail.

WHEN A privately-owned Cessna began to approach the *Freya*, the plane was spotted by air traffic control zones at Heathrow, Brussels and Amsterdam. The radars put her at five thousand feet. The ether began to crackle furiously. "Unidentified light aircraft . . . identify yourself and turn back. You are entering a prohibited area . . . ." French and English were used, later Dutch. None had any effect.

On board the Cessna the pilot turned to his passenger in despair. "They'll have my licence," he yelled. "They're going mad down there."

"Switch off your radio," the journalist shouted back. "Don't worry, nothing will happen. You never heard them, OK?"

The passenger gripped his camera and adjusted the telephoto lens. He began to sight up on the approaching supertanker.

The masked lookout in the forepeak stiffened and looked up. He took a walkie-talkie from his anorak and spoke sharply into it. On the bridge one of his colleagues heard the message and snapped orders to his colleagues who ran downstairs to the day cabin.

Inside the cabin, Thor Larsen and Drake, both looking much more haggard and unshaven now, were still at the table, the gun by the Ukrainian's right hand. The masked man entered on his command and spoke in Ukrainian. His leader scowled and ordered the man to take over in the cabin.

Drake raced up to the bridge, pulling on his black mask as he did so. From the wing of the bridge he gazed up as the Cessna performed one orbit of the *Freya* at 1,000 feet and flew back to the south, climbing steadily. While it turned he had seen the great zoom lens poking down at him.

Inside the aircraft, the journalist was exultant.

"Fantastic," he shouted at the pilot. "Completely exclusive. The magazines will pay their right arms for this."

Drake returned to the bridge and sent the lookout below to summon two of his men who were catching some sleep. When the three returned he gave them instructions then returned to the day cabin.

"I think it's time I told those stupid bastards over there in Europe that I am not joking," he told Thor Larsen.

Five minutes later the camera operator on the Nimrod called his captain. "There's something happening down there, skipper."

Squadron-Leader Latham left the flight deck and walked back to where the visual image of what the cameras were photographing was on display. Two men were walking down the long lonely deck of the *Freya*. The man at the rear was in black from head to foot, with a submachine gun. The one ahead wore sneakers, casual slacks and a nylon-type anorak with three horizontal black stripes across its back. The hood was up against the chill afternoon breeze.

"Looks like a terrorist at the back, but a seaman in front," said the camera operator.

Latham nodded. "Give me a closer look," he said, "and transmit." The camera zoomed down until the frame occupied forty feet of foredeck, both men walking in the centre of the picture.

Captain Thor Larsen gazed through the wide forward windows of his cabin beneath the bridge in disbelief. Behind him the guard with the machine gun stood well back, muzzle trained in the middle of Larsen's back.

Halfway down the foredeck, the man in the black stopped, raised his machine gun, aimed at the back in front of him, and fired a short burst. The figure in the striped anorak arched as if kicked in the spine, pitched forward, and came to rest beneath the inspection catwalk.

Thor Larsen slowly closed his eyes. When the ship had been taken over, his third mate, Tom Keller, had been wearing fawn slacks and a light nylon windbreaker with three black stripes across the back. Larsen leaned his forehead against the back of his hand on the glass. Then he straightened, turned to the man he knew as Svoboda, and stared at him.

Drake stared back. "I warned them," he said angrily. "They thought they could play games. Now they know they can't."

Twenty minutes later the still pictures showing the sequence of what had happened on the deck of the *Freya* were coming out of a machine in the heart of London. Twenty minutes after that, the details in written terms were rattling off a teleprinter in the federal chancellery in Bonn where the cabinet was meeting. An aide whispered urgently in the chancellor's ear. "*Du lieber Gott,*" breathed Chancellor Busch.

He looked at his cabinet. "I regret to inform you," he said, "that one hour ago a private plane apparently sought to take pictures of the *Freya* from about a thousand feet. Ten minutes later, and under the cameras of the British Nimrod above them, the terrorists executed one of the crew."

There was dead silence in the room.

"Can he be identified?" asked one of the ministers in a low voice.

"No, his face was mainly covered by the hood of his anorak."

"Bastards," said the defence minister. "Now thirty families all over Scandinavia will be in anguish instead of one. They're really turning the knife."

"In the wake of this I really don't think we have any alternative," said Foreign Minister Hagowitz. "We should no longer delay on accepting the terrorists' demands."

It was agreed that Hagowitz should instruct the German ambassador to Israel to seek an urgent interview with the Israeli premier and ask from him the guarantee the terrorists had demanded. Following which, if it was given, the Federal government would announce that with regret it had no alternative but to release Mishkin and Lazareff to Israel.

"The terrorists have given the Israeli premier until midnight to offer that guarantee," said Chancellor Busch. "And ourselves until dawn to put these hijackers on a plane. We'll hold our announcement until Jerusalem agrees. Without that there's nothing we can do."

NATO SURFACE SHIPS had joined the RAF Nimrod in the watch. Each coastal nation wanted an on-site observer from its own navy. During the late afternoon French, Dutch, West German and British ships took up station around the *Freya*.

Meanwhile, across Western Europe the last editions of the afternoon newspapers whirled onto the streets to be snapped up by a public of three hundred millions. The latest headlines gave details of the murder of the unidentified seaman and the arrest of a freelance French photographer and a pilot at Le Touquet.

A mild and balmy dusk was ending a glorious spring day when Sir Julian Flannery completed his report to the prime minister in her office at 10 Downing Street.

"We have to assume then, Sir Julian," she said, "that the hijackers could well be in a position to blow the *Freya* apart and sink her, that they would not stop at doing so, and that the consequences would be a catastrophe of appalling dimensions."

"That, ma'am, is the most pessimistic interpretation, but the crisis management committee feels it would be rash to be more hopeful," the secretary to the cabinet replied. "From the *Nimrod*'s observations we must assume a minimum of seven terrorists. They might be too few to stop an armed boarding party, but we cannot assume that. They might not be prepared to blow the *Freya* apart and die with her, but we cannot assume that either."

The telephone tinkled and the prime minister answered it. When she replaced the receiver, she gave Sir Julian a fleeting smile.

"It looks as if we may not face the catastrophe after all," she said. "The West German government has just announced that Israel has conceded to the German request. Bonn, in its turn, agrees to the release of the two men from Tegel prison at eight tomorrow morning."

It was twenty to seven.

The same news came over the transistor radio in the day cabin of Captain Thor Larsen. Keeping him covered, Drake had switched on the cabin lights and drawn the curtains. The percolator of coffee had been exhausted and replenished five times and was bubbling again. Both the mariner and the fanatic were more unshaven and tired than ever. But one was filled with anger and grief for the death of a friend; the other triumphant.

"They've agreed," said Drake. "I knew they would."

Thor Larsen might have been relieved at the news of the pending reprieve of his ship. But the controlled anger was burning too hot. "It's not over yet," he growled.

"It will be. Soon. If my friends are released at eight in the morning, they will be in Tel Aviv by two o'clock at the latest. With an hour for identification and the publication on the news by radio, we should know by three or four o'clock tomorrow afternoon. After dark, we will leave you, safe and sound."

"Except Tom Keller out there," snapped the Norwegian.

"I'm sorry about that. They left me no alternative."

ACROSS THE Atlantic in Washington, Soviet Ambassador Konstantin Kirov telephoned US Secretary of State David Lawrence with an urgent request. He had a message for President Matthews concerning matters which Chairman Maxim Rudin personally wished to bring to the president's attention.

It was a quarter to seven in Europe, but only a quarter to two in Washington when the Soviet limousine swept into the White House grounds. The envoy was shown straight to the Oval Office to face President Matthews and Secretary of State Lawrence.

"Mr. President," said Kirov, "I am instructed personally by Chairman Maxim Rudin to relay to you this message, without variation. It is: In the event that the hijackers and murderers Lev Mishkin and David Lazareff are released, the USSR will not be able to sign the Treaty of Dublin at any time at all. The Soviet Union will reject the treaty permanently."

President Matthews stared at the Soviet envoy in amazement. "You mean Maxim Rudin will just tear it up?"

Kirov was ramrod stiff. "Mr. President, that is the first part of the message I have been instructed to deliver to you. It goes on to say that if the contents of this message are revealed, the same reaction from the USSR will apply."

When he was gone President Matthews turned helplessly to Lawrence. "David, what the hell is going on? We can't just bully the German government into reversing its decision without explaining why."

"Mr. President, I think you are going to have to. With respect, Maxim Rudin has just left you no alternative."

Fifteen

President William Matthews sat stunned by the suddenness and the brutality of the Soviet reaction. He waited while Robert Benson and Stanislav Poklewski were sent for.

None of his three principal advisers could come up with an answer. Without the treaty, the Soviet Union would receive no grain, and they were at their last few truckloads. Benson of the CIA summed up the feelings of everyone present. "It just doesn't make sense. Maxim Rudin would not react like a madman unless he had a reason."

"That still doesn't get us out from between two appalling alternatives," said President Matthews. "We let the release of Mishkin and Lazareff go through, lose the most important disarmament treaty of our generation, and witness war within a year, or we use our clout to block that release, and subject western

Europe to the biggest ecological disaster of this generation."

"We have to find a third choice," said David Lawrence.

"The answer lies inside Moscow," said Poklewski. "We must know why Maxim Rudin has reacted in this way."

President Matthews made up his mind. "I am calling Maxim Rudin," he said. "But if he declines to give me an explanation, we will have to assume he is himself under intolerable pressures of some kind. Meanwhile I am going to entrust the British prime minister with the secret of what has just happened here, and ask for her help, through Sir Nigel Irvine and the Nightingale. In the last resort I will call Chancellor Busch in Bonn and ask him to give me more time."

In careful, succinct terms, President Matthews explained to the British prime minister the message he had received from the Soviet ambassador. Joan Carpenter too was stunned. "In Heaven's name, why?" she asked.

"That's the problem, ma'am," came the Southern drawl from across the Atlantic. "There is no explanation. Incidentally, Ambassador Kirov advised me that if the content of Rudin's message became public, the same consequences to the Treaty of Dublin would apply. I take it I may count on your discretion?"

"Implicitly," she replied. "What are you going to do?"

"I've tried to call Maxim Rudin on the hot line. He is unavailable. From that I have to assume he has his own problems right in the heart of the Kremlin, and he can't talk about them. That has put me in an impossible position. But of one thing I am absolutely determined. That treaty is of the utmost importance to the whole western world. I cannot let a bunch of terrorists on a tanker in the North Sea destroy it."

"I entirely agree with you, Mr. President," said the premier from her London desk. "What do you want from me?"

"Two things, ma'am. I need to know every possible consequence and option, in the event the terrorists aboard do their worst."

"During today," said Mrs. Carpenter, "our people here have put together an in-depth study of the ship, her cargo, the chances of containing the spillage. So far we haven't examined the idea of storming her. Now we may have to. I will have all our information on its way to you within the hour. What else?"

"This is the hard one," said William Matthews. "We believe there has to be an explanation of Rudin's behaviour. If I am to handle this crisis, I have to have that explanation. I would like you to ask your people to activate the Nightingale one last time and get that answer for me."

Joan Carpenter hesitated. She had always made it her policy never to interfere with the way Sir Nigel ran his service, and had been rewarded by his unswerving loyalty. She trusted him, and he her.

"I will do what I can," she said at length. "But we are talking about something in the very heart of the Kremlin, and a matter of hours. If it is possible, it will be done. You have my word."

When the telephone was back in its cradle the prime minister ordered a pot of coffee. Then she called Sir Julian Flannery at his home and asked him to return at once to the cabinet office. Her last call, to the head office of the firm, asked for Sir Nigel Irvine to be contacted and requested to come immediately to Number 10. It was nine o'clock, and the long night had begun.

WHEN THE CALLER asked for Ludwig Jahn personally, the switchboard operator at Tegel gaol was prepared to cut him off. She had her orders—no calls. But when the caller explained he was Jahn's cousin and that Jahn was to have attended his daughter's wedding the following day, the operator softened. She put the call through to Jahn.

"I think you remember me," the voice told Jahn.

Jahn remembered the caller well. "You shouldn't call me here," he whispered hoarsely. "I can't help you. The guards have been trebled, the shifts changed. I am on shift permanently now, sleeping here in the office. They are unapproachable, those two men."

"You had better make an excuse to get out for an hour," said the voice of Colonel Kukushkin. "There's a bar four hundred metres from the staff gate." He gave its address. "In one hour," said the voice, "or else . . . ." There was a click.

When Jahn slipped into the booth at the bar he was sweating. From across the table he was regarded coldly. The warder could not know that the Russian was fighting for his own life. He listened impassively as Jahn explained the new procedures. "So you see," concluded Jahn, "I could not possibly get you into that corridor. There are three on duty night and day. Passes have to be shown every time one enters the corridor, even by me, and we

266

have all worked together for years. No new face would be admitted without a check call to the governor."

Kukushkin nodded slowly. Jahn felt relief rising in his chest. They would not hurt his family. It was over.

"You may enter the cells, of course," said the Russian.

"Well, yes, I am the *Ober Wachtmeister*. At periodic intervals I have to check that the prisoners are all right."

"At night they sleep?"

"Maybe. They have heard about the matter in the North Sea. They lost their radios just after the noon broadcasts, but one of the other prisoners shouted the news across to them before the corridor was cleared of all other prisoners."

The Russian nodded sombrely. "Then," he said, "you will do the job yourself."

Jahn's jaw dropped. "No, no," he babbled. "I couldn't use a gun. I couldn't kill anyone."

For answer the Russian laid two slim tubes like fountain pens on the table between them. "Not guns," he said. "These. Place the open end, here, a few centimetres from the mouth and nose of the sleeping man. Press the button on the side, here. Inhalation of potassium cyanide gas causes death within three seconds. Within an hour the effects are identical to those of cardiac arrest. Very simple. And it leaves you in the clear."

What Kukushkin had laid before the horrified gaze of the senior prison officer were poison-gas pistols. Inside the tubes glass globules of prussic acid rested. The trigger impelled a hammer which crushed the glass. Simultaneously the acid was vaporized and shot out of the tube into the breathing passages. An hour later the tell-tale almond smell of prussic acid was gone, the muscles of the corpse relaxed; the symptoms were of heart attack. No one would believe two simultaneous heart attacks in two young men; questions would be asked.

"I . . . . I can't do that," whispered Jahn.

"But I can, and will, see that your entire family is sent from East Berlin to an Arctic labour camp for the rest of their lives," murmured the Russian. "A simple choice, Herr Jahn." Kukushkin took Jahn's hand, turned it over and placed the tubes in the palm. "Think about it," he said, "not for too long. Then walk into those cells and do it."

He slid out of the booth and left. Minutes later Jahn slipped the gas-guns into his coat pocket, and went back to Tegel gaol. At 1:00 a.m., in four hours, he would enter the cells and do it. He had no alternative.

IN THE NIGHT, high above the *Freya*, the relief Nimrod had switched to her night-vision camera, which, peering downwards with its infra-red sights, could pick out most of what was happening fifteen thousand feet beneath. But it failed to notice the figure in the anorak, lying prostrate since the mid-afternoon, slowly begin to move, inching its way back towards the superstructure. When the figure finally crawled over the sill of the half-open doorway and stood up in the interior, no one noticed. At dawn it was supposed the body had been thrown into the sea.

The man in the anorak went below to the galley, rubbing his hands and shivering. He helped himself to coffee. When he had finished he returned to the bridge and sought out his own clothes, the black tracksuit and sweater he had come aboard with. "Jeez," he told the man on the bridge in his American accent, "you sure didn't miss. I could feel the wadding from those blanks slapping into the back of the windbreaker."

The bridge-watch grinned. "Drake said to make it good. It worked. Mishkin and Lazareff are coming out at eight tomorrow morning. By afternoon they'll be in Tel Aviv."

"Great," said the Ukrainian-American. "Let's just hope his plan to get us off this ship works as well."

"It will," said the other. "You better get your mask on and give those clothes back to that Yankee in the paint store."

MEANWHILE, SIR JULIAN FLANNERY had re-convened the crisis management committee. The prime minister had told him why the situation had changed, but he and Sir Nigel Irvine would be the only ones to know. The members of the committee were told that for reasons of state, the dawn release of Mishkin and Lazareff might be delayed or cancelled, and that the whole affair had passed into major crisis category.

After discussion the committee agreed to order the procurement during the night of every available ton of oil emulsifier—enough to break down at least the terrorists' threatened first 20,000-ton oil slick; to commandeer lorry tankers from the petroleum companies through the energy ministry; to bring the whole consignment to

Lowestoft on the east coast; and to get under way and divert to Lowestoft every single marine tug with spray equipment. By late morning it was hoped to have the entire flotilla in Lowestoft, tanking up with emulsifier.

"If the sea remains calm," said Dr. Henderson, "the slick will drift towards Holland at about two knots. That gives us time. But when the tide changes, and if the wind rises, it might move faster in any direction. We should be able to cope with a 20,000-ton slick."

"We can watch the slick from the Nimrod," said an RAF group captain. "If it moves out of range of the *Freya*, your navy chaps can start squirting."

"So far, so good, for the first 20,000-ton spillage," said the foreign office man. "What happens after that?"

"Nothing," said Dr. Henderson. "After that we're finished."

"There is one other option," said Colonel Holmes of the Royal Marines. "The hard option. These terrorists have killed one sailor in cold blood. They may well kill another twenty-nine. The ship cost 170 million dollars, the cargo 140 million dollars, the clean-up operation will treble that. If, for whatever reason, Chancellor Busch does not release the men in West Berlin, we may be left with no alternative but to try to storm the ship and knock off the man with the detonator before he can use it. I propose that we activate the special boat service."

During the UNICORNE meeting, the prime minister had received Sir Nigel Irvine in the cabinet office. "That, then, is the position, Sir Nigel," she concluded. "If we cannot come up with a third alternative, either the men go free and Maxim Rudin tears up the Treaty of Dublin; or they stay in gaol and their friends tear up the *Freya*. We have to know from the Nightingale why Maxim Rudin is taking this course."

"It is the middle of the night in Moscow," said Sir Nigel. "The Nightingale is virtually unapproachable, except at meetings planned well ahead. To attempt an instant rendezvous might well blow that agent sky-high."

"I know, Sir Nigel, that the safety of the agent out in the cold is paramount. But the destruction of the Treaty, or the destruction of the *Freya*, are matters of state. The first could jeopardize peace for years, perhaps put Yefrem Vishnayev in power, with all its consequences. The financial losses alone sustained by Lloyd's, and through Lloyd's the British economy, if the *Freya* destroyed

270

herself and the North Sea, would be disastrous, not to mention the loss of thirty seamen. I ask you to put the certain alternatives against the putative hazard to one single Russian agent."

"Ma'am, I will do what I can," said Sir Nigel.

AS SOON as the UNICORNE meeting recessed, Colonel Holmes was on the telephone to Poole, Dorset, headquarters of the special boat service. Major Simon Fallon was brought to the telephone. The two marines knew each other well.

"You've been following the *Freya* affair?" asked Holmes from London. There was a chuckle from the other end.

"I thought you'd come shopping here eventually," said Fallon.

"I have the plan of the ship here," said Holmes. "Get the boys together. Get all the underwater gear out of stores. I'm asking the navy to pick up the gear and the team. When you've left a good man in charge, jump into the car and get up to London. Report to my office as soon as you can."

Within minutes Major Fallon's men were rousing the NCOs and marines from their barracks. Before midnight they were on the stone jetty waiting for the arrival of navy patrol boats. There was a bright moon rising as the three fast patrol boats *Sabre*, *Cutlass* and *Scimitar* headed east from Portland for Poole.

THOUGH NIGHT had long settled on Europe, it was five in the afternoon in Washington. "Chancellor Busch's call will be through in a minute. What the hell do I tell him?" asked President Matthews.

"Tell him you have information that cannot be divulged on even a secure line," suggested Poklewski. "Tell him the release of Mishkin and Lazareff would provoke a greater disaster than even frustrating the terrorists on the *Freya* for a few more hours. Ask him to give you a little time."

The call to Chancellor Busch came through. President Matthews spoke for ten minutes while the German government chief listened with growing amazement.

"But why?" he asked at length. "Surely the matter hardly affects the United States?"

"Dietrich, please. Believe me. I'm asking you to trust me. On any line across the Atlantic, I can't be as frank as I'd like to be. Something of enormous dimension has cropped up. I'll be as plain

271

as I can. Over here we have discovered that for the next few hours the release of these two men would be disastrous. I'm only asking for a delay, Dietrich, my friend."

To say that the German chancellor was suspicious was putting it mildly. The trans-Atlantic line, established years before to link the NATO government heads and checked regularly, was perfectly safe. On the other hand, the president of the United States was not given to making late-night calls or crazy appeals. But what he was asking was not something Busch could decide without consultation.

"It is just past ten p.m. over here," he told Matthews. "We have until dawn to decide. I shall reconvene my cabinet during the night and consult with them. I cannot promise you more."

When the phone was replaced, Dietrich Busch stayed for long minutes in thought. There was something going on, and it concerned Mishkin and Lazareff, sitting in their separate cells in Tegel gaol. If anything happened to them, the Federal government could not escape a howl of censure within Germany from the combined media and the Opposition.

His first call was to Ludwig Fischer, his minister of justice. His suggestion to transfer the prisoners from the old-fashioned prison of Tegel to the much newer and super-secure gaol of Moabit met with immediate agreement. Fischer telephoned the instruction to West Berlin immediately.

In Moscow, an urgent summons from the senior cipher clerk at the British embassy had brought Adam Munro from his bed at midnight Moscow time—ten p.m. London time—across town to the embassy.

Thirty minutes later the telex chattered in the Moscow cipher room. The clerk turned to Munro standing by his side. "It's the Master," he said, reading the code-tag on the incoming message.

Sir Nigel had to tell Munro of the Russian ambassador's message to President Matthews. Without that knowledge, Munro could not ask the Nightingale for the answer to Matthews's question: why?

The telex rattled for several minutes. As the message spewed out Munro read it with horror. "I can't do that," he told the impassive clerk. When the message from London was ended, he told the clerk: "Reply as follows: 'Not repeat not possible obtain this sort of answer in timescale.' Send it."

The interchange between Sir Nigel Irvine and Adam Munro went on for fifteen minutes. There is a method of contacting N at short notice, suggested London. Yes, but only in case of dire emergency, replied Munro. This qualifies one hundred times as emergency, chattered the machine from London. But N could not begin to inquire until the next regular Politburo meeting, not due until Thursday following. What about records of last Thursday's meeting? asked London. *Freya* was not hijacked last Thursday, retorted Munro. Finally Sir Nigel did what he hoped he would not have to do.

"Regret," tapped the machine, "prime ministerial order not refusable. Unless attempt made avert this disaster, operation to bring out N to West cannot proceed."

For the first time Munro was caught in the net of his own attempts to keep his love for the agent he ran from his superiors in London. Sir Nigel Irvine thought the Nightingale was a dispensable embittered Russian turncoat called Anatoly Krivoi, right-hand man to the warmonger Vishnayev.

"Make to London," he told the clerk dully, "the following: 'Will try this night, stop, decline to accept responsibility if N refuses or is unmasked during attempt, stop.'"

The reply from the Master was brief. Agree. Proceed.

THERE WERE FEW cars in the park of the Mojarsky Hotel, just off the roundabout at the far end of Kutuzovsky Prospekt. Those that were there were dark, unoccupied, save two. Munro watched the lights of the other car, then got out from his own vehicle, walked across and climbed into Valentina's. She was alarmed and trembling.

"What is it, Adam? Why did you call me at the apartment? The call must have been listed."

He put his arm round her. "It only concerned Gregor's inability to attend your dinner party. No one will suspect anything."

"Nobody makes calls like that at two in the morning. I was seen to leave the apartment compound by the nightwatchman. He will report it."

"Darling, I'm sorry. Listen." He told her of the intelligence department's demand to find out why the Kremlin was taking such an attitude over Mishkin and Lazareff.

"I haven't the faintest idea," she said. "Perhaps because those animals murdered Flight-Captain Rudenko."

273

"Valentina, the Treaty of Dublin is vital to your people. Why would Rudin put it in jeopardy over these two men? There has to be another and more serious reason."

"It has not been mentioned in Politburo meetings. Your intelligence people know that."

Munro stared miserably through the windscreen. He had hoped against hope she might have an answer for Washington, something she had heard inside the central committee building. Finally he decided he had to tell her how it would affect her. She stared into the darkness and he caught a hint of tears in her eyes.

"They promised," she whispered, "they promised they would bring me and Sascha out, in a fortnight, from Romania."

"They've gone back on their word," he confessed.

She placed her head on her hands, supported by the steering wheel. "They will catch me," she mumbled. "I am so frightened."

"They won't catch you," he tried to reassure her. "The KGB acts much more slowly than people think. If you can get this information for President Matthews, I think I can persuade them to get you and Sascha out in a few days, instead of two weeks. Please try, my love. It's our only chance left of ever being together."

Valentina stared through the glass. "There was a special Politburo meeting out of sequence this evening," she said finally. "I was not there. Transcription begins this morning at ten. The staff have to give up their weekend to get it ready for Monday."

"Could you get in to see the notes, listen to the tapes?"

"In the middle of the night? There would be questions asked."

"Make an excuse, darling. Any excuse."

"I will try for you, Adam," she said eventually. "Not for those men in London."

"I know those men in London," said Adam Munro. "They will bring you and Sascha out if you help them now."

She seemed not to have heard him, and to have overcome, for a while, her fear of the KGB, exposure as a spy, the awful consequences of capture unless she could escape in time. When she spoke, her voice was quite level.

"You know the toyshop, Dyetsky Mir? The soft-toys counter? At ten o'clock."

He watched her drive away. They had demanded that he do it, and it was done. He had diplomatic protection to keep him out of

Lubyanka. But Valentina was walking right into the secret archives, without even the disguise of normal, justified behaviour to protect her. He looked at his watch. Seven hours to go, seven hours of knotted stomach muscles and ragged nerve ends.

Unlike Munro, for Ludwig Jahn the waiting was over. At Tegel gaol he watched the armoured van bearing Mishkin and Lazareff disappear down the street. For a few moments he stood by the open window of his first-floor office, then hurled one of the two cyanide pistols far into the night. He was overweight, unfit. A heart attack would be accepted, provided no evidence was found.

Leaning out of the window he thought of his mother in a cell, terrified. He thought of his gaoled brothers. He closed his eyes, held the other tube beneath his nostrils and pressed the trigger-button.

The pain slammed across his chest like a giant hammer. The loosened fingers dropped the tube, which fell with a tinkle to the street below. Jahn slumped, hit the window sill and caved backwards into his office, already dead. When they found him, they would assume he had opened the window for air when the first pain came. The chimes of midnight were drowned by the roar of a lorry which crushed the tube in the gutter to fragments. The hijacking of the *Freya* had claimed its first victim.

Sixteen

At a quarter to three in the morning the West German cabinet, after bitter argument, finally agreed to grant President Matthews an indefinite delay on the release of Mishkin and Lazareff while reserving the right to reverse that decision if it became regarded in Western Europe as impossible to continue to hold the pair.

At the same time the government spokesman was asked to leak the news to his most reliable media contacts that only massive pressure from Washington had caused the about-face in Bonn.

When the official statement from Bonn reached President Matthews, he sent back his heartfelt thanks to Chancellor Busch.

THREE IN THE MORNING is said to be the lowest ebb of the human spirit. It also marked one complete cycle of the day and night for the two men who faced each other in the captain's cabin of the

Freya. Neither had slept that night, nor the previous one; each had been forty hours without rest, each was drawn and red-eyed.

Thor Larsen was playing his own game. He was pitting his capacity to stay awake against the will of the fanatic who faced him, knowing that at stake were his crew and his ship.

Larsen knew that the man who called himself Svoboda could have ordered the Norwegian captain tied up while he himself sought rest. So the bearded mariner sat facing the barrel of a gun and played on his captor's pride, hoping that the man would take his challenge, refuse to concede defeat in the game of beating sleep.

It was Larsen who proposed the endless cups of strong black coffee. It was he who talked, through the day and the night, provoking the Ukrainian with suggestions of eventual failure, then backing off when the man became too irritable for safety. Long nights of experience as a sea captain had taught him to stay awake and alert through the night watches.

So he played his solitary game. All the superb technology built into his new command was as much use as rusty nails to him now. if he pushed the man across the table too far, Svoboda might lose his temper and shoot to kill. If he was too much frustrated he could order the execution of another crewman.

Larsen still believed that Mishkin and Lazareff would be released at eight o'clock. After their safe arrival in Tel Aviv, the terrorists would prepare to quit the *Freya*. Or could they? Would the surrounding warships let them go so easily? Even away from the *Freya*, Svoboda could press his button and blow the supertanker apart. But that was not all of it. This man had killed one of the crew. Thor Larsen wanted him dead for that. So he talked the night away, denying both of them sleep.

England was not sleeping either. In the south, bulk-tanker lorries were filling up with emulsifier concentrate. Bleary-eyed drivers rumbled through the night, moving hundreds of tons of the concentrate to Lowestoft; tugs capable of spraying liquid onto the sea were moving to the rendezvous point on the Suffolk coast.

At the same time, off the towering cliffs of Beachy Head on the south coast, the *Cutlass*, *Scimitar* and *Sabre*, carrying the complex and lethal hardware of the world's toughest team of assault frogmen, were pointing their noses north of east to bring them to the cruiser *Argyll* at anchor in the North Sea.

Twelve marines of the special boat service clung to the rails of the bucking craft, watching over their precious kayaks and the crates of diving gear, weapons and unusual explosives that made up the props of their trade. It was all being carried as deck cargo.

Meanwhile, in a room adjoining the UNICORNE conference centre, Major Fallon, their commanding officer, was poring over the plans and the Nimrod photographs of the *Freya*.

"Gentlemen," said Colonel Holmes to the assembled men next door, "I think it's time we considered one of the less palatable choices we may have to face."

"Ah, yes," said Sir Julian regretfully, "the hard option."

"The moment may come when the terrorists realize that their blackmail is not going to work," said Holmes. "They may refuse to have their bluff called, and blow the *Freya* to pieces. It seems to me this will not happen before nightfall, which gives us about sixteen hours."

"Why nightfall, Colonel?" asked Sir Julian.

"Because, sir, one must assume that they will seek their own escape. They may therefore leave the ship under cover of darkness and operate their remote-control detonator from a certain distance from the ship's side."

"And your proposal, Colonel?"

"First, their launch. It is still moored beside the courtesy ladder. As soon as darkness falls, a diver could approach the launch and attach an explosive device to it. As the launch moves away from the ship's side, the forward thrust of the launch will cause the water beneath the keel to operate a delayed action trigger. The launch will blow up before the terrorists have reached a point half a mile from the *Freya*, and therefore before they can operate their own detonator without harm to themselves."

"Wouldn't the exploding of their launch detonate the charges on the *Freya*?" asked someone.

"No. If they have a remote-control detonator, it must be electronically operated by hand. The charge would blow the launch carrying the terrorists to smithereens. No one would survive."

"But if the detonator sank, would not the water pressure depress the button?" asked one of the scientists.

"No. Once under the water the remote-control detonator could not beam its radio message."

277

"Can this plan not operate before darkness falls?"

"No," answered Holmes. "Remember there would be a ten-mile-round trip under water involved. And besides, a frogman diver leaves a trail of bubbles which could be spotted by one of the *Freya*'s lookouts."

"After dark it is then," said Sir Julian.

"Furthermore," Holmes said, "sabotaging their escape launch should not be the only ploy. If the leader of the terrorists is prepared to die with the *Freya*, he may not leave the ship with the rest of his team. We may also have to storm the ship during a night attack and get to him before he can use his device. I would like you to meet Major Simon Fallon, commanding the special boat service, who will explain the plan."

The marine major was barely five feet eight inches tall, but he seemed about the same across the shoulders. The SBS had originally been formed for conventional war, to act as specialists in seaborne attacks on coastal installations. That was why they were drawn from the marine commandos. As basic requirements they were physically fit, experts in swimming, canoeing, diving, climbing, marching and fighting. They were also proficient in parachuting, explosives, demolition and unarmed combat. In this, and their capacity for living off the countryside and leaving no trace of their presence, they shared the skills of their cousins in the special air service.

After Major Fallon had explained his plan in detail to UNICORNE, a weary Sir Julian Flannery left the smoke-charged room to ascend to the chill pre-dawn of another spring day and report to his prime minister.

On the *Freya*, the announcement from Bonn that the release of Mishkin and Lazareff was being reconsidered came over the BBC World Service at six thirty.

Drake, who was listening, burst out: "What the hell do they think they're up to?"

"Something has gone wrong," said Thor Larsen flatly. "They've changed their minds. It's not going to work."

Drake leaned far across the table and pointed his handgun straight at the Norwegian's face. "Don't you gloat," he shouted, "it's not just my friends in Berlin they're playing silly games with."

After several minutes' thought he brusquely beckoned the *Freya*'s skipper to accompany him to the bridge. Just a minute before seven Larsen, his voice sounding tired, read a new statement to Maas control:

"Following the stupid decision of the government in Bonn not to release Lev Mishkin and David Lazareff at oh-eight-hundred hours this morning, those who hold the *Freya* announce the following: in the event that Mishkin and Lazareff are not released and airborne on their way to Tel Aviv by noon today, the *Freya* will, on the stroke of noon, vent twenty thousand tons of crude oil into the North Sea. Any attempt to prevent this will result in the immediate destruction of the ship, her crew and cargo."

Almost a hundred listening-posts heard the message. It was 2:15 a.m. in Washington when the news of Drake's ultimatum was brought to the Oval Office and handed to President Matthews.

"I suppose we should have expected it," he said wearily.

"If the terrorists on the *Freya* do vent twenty thousand tons of crude," said Poklewski, "the pressures on Busch could become so overwhelming that he might decide to release the hijackers unilaterally. He doesn't know that the price would be the destruction of the Treaty of Dublin."

"There's nothing I can do to stop him," said President Matthews quietly.

"There is, actually," said Benson. When he described what it was, the faces of Matthews, Lawrence and Poklewski showed disgust. "I couldn't give that order," said the president.

"It's the only way to pre-empt Chancellor Busch," said Benson. "And we will know if he tries to make secret plans to release the pair prematurely. Never mind how; we *will* know."

"Is our new policy to spy even on our allies?" snapped Lawrence.

"We've always done it," replied Benson.

At that moment a personal message arrived for the president from Prime Minister Carpenter in London. "That's some woman," he said when he had read it. "The British reckon they can cope with the first oil slick of 20,000 tons, but no more. They're preparing a plan to storm the *Freya* with specialist frogmen after sundown. They give themselves a better than even chance."

"So we only have to hold the German chancellor in line for another twelve hours," said Benson. "Mr. President, I urge you to order what I have just proposed. The chances are it will never have to be activated."

William Matthews rubbed tired eyes with his fingertips. "Dear

279

God, no man should be asked to give orders like that," he said. "But if I must . . . . Bob, will you give the order to Captain Manning."

At seven fifty there was a knock at the door of the cabin of Captain Mike Manning, commanding the guided missile ship the USS *Moran*, which had been ordered earlier to take station five miles from the *Freya*. Manning took the message from the telegraphist.

"It's still in code," he said.

"Yes, sir. It's tagged for your eyes only, sir."

Manning dismissed the man, went to his wall safe and took out his personal decoder. When he had finished decoding, he sat at his table and stared at the message. It was a presidential order, personal to him from the commander-in-chief.

"No man can ask a sailor to do that," he breathed.

But the message was unequivocal: "In the event the West German government seeks to release the hijackers of Berlin unilaterally, the USS *Moran* is to sink the supertanker *Freya* by shellfire, using all possible measures to ignite cargo and minimize environmental damage. This action will be taken on receipt by USS *Moran* of the signal 'THUNDERBOLT' repeat 'THUNDERBOLT'. Destroy message."

Mike Manning walked to the porthole and looked across the five miles of ocean to the low outline between him and the climbing sun. He thought of his magnesium-based starshells slamming into her unprotected skin, penetrating to the volatile crude oil beneath. Normally crude oil is difficult to burn, but if heated enough it will reach its flashpoint, take fire, and explode. To plunge shells of blazing magnesium, burning at more than 1,000 degrees centigrade, into *Freya*'s holds would do the trick with margin to spare. Up to ninety per cent of her cargo would never reach the ocean; it would flame, making a fireball over 10,000 feet high. What would be left would be scum drifting on the sea's surface. Of the ship herself, there would be nothing left, but the environmental problem would have been reduced to manageable proportions.

Manning thought of the twenty-nine men, crouched deep beneath the waves in a steel coffin, waiting for rescue. He crumpled the paper in his hand.

"Mr. President," he whispered, "I don't know if I can do that."

Seventeen

Dyetsky Mir means "Children's World" and is Moscow's premier toyshop. Adam Munro was at the soft-toys counter just before ten a.m. Moscow time. He began to examine a nylon bear as if debating whether to buy it for his non-existent offspring.

Two minutes after ten Valentina moved to the counter beside him. He saw that she was pale, her lips the colour of ash. She nodded. Her voice was pitched low, conversational.

"It's charming. Yes, I did. It's serious."

She picked up a hand-puppet shaped like a small monkey and told him quietly what she had discovered.

"That's impossible," he muttered. "He's still convalescing from a heart attack."

"No. He was shot dead last October thirty-first in the middle of the night on a street in Kiev."

"And those two in Berlin were the ones?" asked Munro.

"It seems so," she said dully. "The fear is that if they escape to Israel they will hold a press conference and inflict an intolerable humiliation on the Soviet Union."

"Causing Maxim Rudin to fall," breathed Munro. "No wonder he will not countenance their release. He cannot. And you? Are you safe, darling?"

"I don't think so. There were suspicions. Unspoken, but they were there. Soon the man on the apartment telephone switchboard will report about your call; the gateman will report about my drive in the small hours. It will come together."

"Listen, Valentina, I will get you out of here. Quickly, in the next few days."

For the first time, she turned and faced him. He saw that her eyes were brimming. "It's over, Adam. I've done what you asked of me, and now it's too late." She reached up and kissed him briefly. "Goodbye, Adam, my love. I'm sorry."

She turned and walked away through the glass doors to the street, back through the gap in the Wall into the East. From where he stood with a plastic-faced milkmaid doll in his hand, he saw her reach the pavement and turn out of sight. A man in a grey trenchcoat, who had been wiping the windscreen of a car, strolled after her.

Adam Munro felt the grief and the anger rising in his throat. His hand closed round the head of the doll, crushing, cracking, splintering the smiling pink face beneath the lace cap. A salesgirl appeared rapidly at his side. "You've broken it," she said. "That will be four roubles."

IT WAS NOT until mid-morning that Chancellor Dietrich Busch received from the British ambassador the news of the intended underwater attack. He was slightly mollified. "So that's what the delay's all about," he said. "Why could I not have been told of this before?"

"We were not sure whether it was possible," said the ambassador smoothly. Those were his instructions. "We were working on it through yesterday afternoon and last night. By dawn we were certain it was feasible. We estimate the chances at three to one in our favour. The sun sets at seven thirty. Darkness is complete by nine. The men are going in at ten tonight."

The chancellor looked at his watch. Twelve hours to go. If the British tried and succeeded, much of the credit would go to their frogmen-killers, but much also to him for keeping his nerve. If they failed, theirs would be the responsibility. "So it all depends now on this Major Fallon. Very well, Ambassador, I will continue to play my part until ten tonight."

Meanwhile, on the *Moran*, Captain Manning summoned his gunnery officer, Lieutenant-Commander Chuck Olsen, to join him by the rail. "I want you to load and lay the forward gun," he said flatly. As he went on Olsen made notes of his commands.

When he had finished speaking Manning stared over the rail. Five miles away the bows of the *Freya* were pointing straight at the *Moran*. The fall pattern he had dictated would cause the shells to drop in a line from the peak of the *Freya* to the base of her superstructure, then back to the bow, then back again with the explosive towards the superstructure. First, semi-armour-piercing shells would cut open her tanks through the deck-metal as a scalpel opens skin; then starshells would drop in a line of five down the cuts; the explosive would push the blazing crude oil outwards into all the port and starboard holds.

"Fall point for first shell?" Olsen asked.

"Ten metres over the bow of the *Freya*."

Olsen's pen halted above the paper of his clipboard. He raised

his eyes to the *Freya*. "Captain," he said slowly, "if you do that, she won't just sink; she won't just burn. She'll vaporize."

"Those are my orders, Mr. Olsen," said Manning stonily.

The young Swedish-American by his side was pale. "For God's sake, there are thirty Scandinavian seamen on that ship."

"Mr. Olsen, I am aware of the facts. You will either lay that gun, or announce to me that you refuse."

The gunnery officer stiffened to attention. "I'll load and lay your gun for you, Captain Manning, but I will not fire it. You must press the fire button yourself." He snapped a perfect salute and marched away.

"You won't have to," thought Manning. "If the president himself orders me, I will fire it. Then I will resign my commission."

An hour later a Westland Wessex helicopter from the British cruiser *Argyll* came overhead and winched a Royal Navy officer to the deck of the *Moran*. He asked to speak to Captain Manning and handed him a letter. When he had finished reading it, Manning sat back like a man reprieved from the gallows. It told him that the British were sending in a team of armed frogmen from the *Argyll* at ten that night, and all governments had agreed to undertake no independent action in the meantime.

AT A QUARTER to the twelve o'clock deadline Drake sent one of his men to bring the *Freya*'s pumpman to the cargo control room on "A" deck. Leaving Thor Larsen under the guard of another terrorist, Drake descended to cargo control, took the fuses from his pocket and replaced them. Power was restored to the cargo pumps, and those that controlled the valves between the tanks.

"When you discharge cargo, what do you do?" he asked the crewman. "I've still got a submachine gun pointing at your captain, and I'll order it used if you play any tricks."

"The ship's pipeline system terminates at a single point, a cluster of pipes which we call the manifold," said the pumpman. "Hoses from the shore installation are coupled up, the main gate valves are opened at the manifold, and the ship begins to pump."

"What's your rate of discharge?"

"Twenty thousand tons per hour. During discharge the ship's balance is maintained by venting several tanks at different points on the ship simultaneously."

Drake had noted that there was a slight, one-knot tide flowing

284

past the *Freya*, northeast towards the Dutch Friesian islands. First he ordered the pumpman to shut the gigantic valves between all fifty tanks of crude oil, then pointed to a tank amidships on the *Freya*'s port side. "Open the master valve on that one," he said. The man obeyed.

"When I give the word," said Drake, "switch on the cargo pumps and vent the entire tank into the sea."

As the minutes ticked away to midday on Saturday, 2 April, Europe held its breath. In London, men of rank and influence grouped round a screen in the cabinet office briefing room on which was presented what the circling Nimrod was seeing. Her pictures were passing to the *Argyll* beneath her, and from there to Whitehall by datalink.

Down below the Nimrod, sailors of five nations passed binoculars from hand to hand. Their officers stood high aloft with telescopes to eye.

On the BBC World Service the bell called Big Ben struck noon. In the cabinet office someone shouted, "My God, she's venting!"

From the side of the *Freya* a vivid column of ochre-red crude oil erupted. It was thick as a man's torso. Impelled by the power of the *Freya*'s mighty pumps, the oil leaped the port rail, dropped twenty-five feet and thundered into the sea. Within seconds the blue-green water was discoloured. A stain began to spread, moving out and away from the ship's hull on the tide.

For sixty minutes the venting went on, until the single tank was dry. The great stain formed the shape of an egg, broadened nearest the Dutch coast and tapering near the ship. Finally the mass of oil parted company with the *Freya* and began to drift. The sea being calm, the oil slick stayed in one piece, but it began to expand as the light crude ran across the surface of the water. At two p.m., an hour after the venting ended, the slick was ten miles long and seven miles wide at its broadest.

In Washington, where the Condor satellite had been relaying pictures to the Oval Office, the slick moved off screen. Stanislav Poklewski switched off the set. "That's just one fiftieth of what she carries," he said. "Those Europeans will go mad."

CIA Chief Robert Benson took a telephone call and turned to President Matthews. "London just contacted Langley. Their man from Moscow claims that he knows why Maxim Rudin is threatening to tear up the Treaty of Dublin if Mishkin and

Lazareff go free. He's flying personally with the answer to London, and should land in one hour. He'll report to Sir Nigel Irvine, who will tell Mrs. Carpenter."

On the *Freya*, Andrew Drake had been pensive and withdrawn while the oil was being vented. At one twenty p.m., Captain Larsen was speaking to Maas control again. He asked to be patched through to the Dutch premier, Mr. Jan Grayling.

"Prime Minister, you have seen the venting of twenty thousand tons of crude oil from my ship?" asked Larsen, the gun barrel an inch from his ear.

"With great regret, yes," said Grayling.

"The leader of the partisans proposes a face-to-face conference with the captains of the NATO warships and other interested parties," Larsen read out.

Jan Grayling clapped his hand over the mouthpiece. "The bastard wants to talk," he said excitedly to two senior aides who were with him. "On behalf of the Dutch government, I accept to host such a conference," he said down the telephone.

"Not on land," replied Larsen. "Here at sea. What is the name of that British cruiser standing off us?"

"The *Argyll*," said Grayling.

"She has a helicopter," said Larsen at Drake's instruction. "The conference will be aboard the *Argyll*. At three p.m. Those present should include yourself, the German ambassador, and the captains of the five NATO warships. No one else."

"Will the leader of the partisans attend in person? I would need to consult the British about a guarantee of safe-conduct."

There was a short silence then Captain Larsen's voice came back. "No. The leader will not attend. He will send a representative. At five minutes before three the helicopter from the *Argyll* will be permitted to hover over the helipad of the *Freya*. There will be only the pilot and the winchman on board, both unarmed. There will be no cameras. The helicopter will not descend lower than twenty feet. The winchman will lower a harness and the emissary will be lifted off the main deck and across to the *Argyll*. Is that understood?"

"Perfectly," said Grayling. "Who will be the representative?"

"One moment," said Larsen and the line went dead.

On the *Freya*, Larsen turned to Drake: "Well, Mr. Svoboda, who are you sending?"

Drake smiled briefly. "You will represent me. You are the best person to convince them I am not joking."

The phone in Premier Grayling's hand crackled to life. "I am informed it will be me," said Larsen, and the line was cut.

Jan Grayling glanced at his watch. "One forty-five," he said. "Seventy-five minutes to go. Get Konrad Voss over here; prepare a helicopter to take off from the nearest point to this office. I want a direct line to Mrs. Carpenter in London."

He had hardly finished speaking before his private secretary told him Harry Wennerstrom was on the line. He had been listening on Channel Twenty. "You'll be going out to the *Argyll* by helicopter," he told the Dutch premier. "I'd be grateful if you would take Mrs. Lisa Larsen with you. The terrorists will never know. And it may be the last time she ever sees him."

"Get her here in forty minutes," said Grayling.

As Grayling put down the telephone, the jet airliner carrying Adam Munro from Moscow touched down at London's Heathrow airport. Barry Ferndale's car waited at the foot of the aircraft steps and he ushered his bleak-faced colleague into the back seat. The car had a screen between driver and passengers, and a telephone linked to head office.

As they swept down the tunnel from the airport to the M4 Ferndale broke the silence. "Rough trip, old boy." He was not referring to the aeroplane journey.

"Disastrous," snapped Munro. "I think the Nightingale is blown. May have been picked up by now."

"Bloody bad luck," Ferndale said. "Damned upsetting. Lost a couple of agents myself, you know. But that's the game we're in, Adam."

"Except this is no game," said Munro.

"Absolutely not. Sorry." Ferndale paused expectantly as their car joined the M4 traffic stream. "But you did get the answer to our question? Why Rudin is so pathologically opposed to the release of Mishkin and Lazareff?"

"Yes, I got the answer," said Munro grimly.

"And it is?"

"Mrs. Carpenter asked it. *She'll* get the answer. I hope she'll like it when I give it to her. It cost a life to get it."

"You can't just walk in on the PM, old son," said Ferndale. "Even the Master has to make an appointment."

"Then ask him to make one," said Munro, gesturing to the telephone.

"That might not be wise," said Ferndale quietly. "But I suppose I'll have to." It was a pity to see a talented man blow his career to bits, but Munro had evidently reached the end of his tether.

Ten minutes later Mrs. Joan Carpenter listened carefully to the voice of Sir Nigel Irvine on the scrambler telephone.

"To give the answer to me personally, Sir Nigel?" she asked. "Isn't that rather unusual?"

"Extremely so, ma'am. In fact unheard of. I fear it has to mean Mr. Munro and the Service parting company. But I can hardly force him to tell me. You see, he's lost an agent who seems to have become a personal friend, and he's no longer thinking straight."

Joan Carpenter paused for several moments. "I am deeply sorry to have been the cause of so much distress," she said. "I would like to apologize to your Mr. Munro. Please have his driver bring him to Number Ten. And join me yourself immediately."

The line went dead. Sir Nigel Irvine stared at the receiver. That woman never ceases to surprise me, he thought. All right, Adam, you want your moment of glory, but it'll be your last. Can't have prima donnas in the Service.

As he descended to his car Sir Nigel reflected that however interesting the explanation of Rudin's actions might be, it would soon be academic. In seven hours Major Simon Fallon would steal aboard the *Freya* with three companions and wipe out the terrorists. After that Mishkin and Lazareff would stay where they were for fifteen years.

AT TWO O'CLOCK, back in the day cabin, Drake leaned towards Thor Larsen and told him: "I know that while you are on the *Argyll* you will tell them all you know. Now listen carefully, because this is what you must also tell them, if you want to save your crew and the ship."

Thor Larsen listened impassively. When Drake had finished the Norwegian captain said: "I'll tell them. Not to save your skin, Mr. Svoboda, but to save my crew and my ship."

There was a trill from the intercom. Drake answered it and looked out through the windows to the distant fo'c'sle. Approaching carefully from the seaward side was the helicopter from the *Argyll*. Five minutes later, under the eyes of cameras that beamed their images across the world, Captain Thor Larsen, master of the biggest ship ever built, stepped out of her superstructure into the open air. He had insisted on donning his black trousers and his merchant navy jacket with the four gold rings of a sea captain. On his head was the braided cap with the Viking-helmet emblem of the Nordia Line. Squaring his wide shoulders, he began the long walk down the vast expanse of his ship to where the harness and cable dangled from the helicopter.

Eighteen

When Barry Ferndale and Adam Munro were shown into the anteroom leading to the prime minister's study, Sir Nigel was already there. He greeted Munro coolly. "I hope this insistence on delivering your report to the PM personally will be worth the effort, Munro."

"I think it will, Sir Nigel," replied Munro.

The director-general of the SIS regarded his staffer quizzically. The man had had a rough deal over the Nightingale affair. Still, that was no excuse for breaking discipline.

The door to the private study opened and Sir Julian Flannery appeared. "Do come in, gentlemen," he said. He introduced them to the prime minister, then left.

Despite not having slept for two days, Mrs. Carpenter appeared fresh and collected. She shook hands with Ferndale and Munro.

"Mr. Munro," she said, "let me state at the outset my deep regret that I had to cause you personal hazard and the possible exposure of your agent in Moscow. The answer to President Matthews's question was of truly international importance, and I do not use that phrase lightly."

"Thank you for saying so, ma'am," replied Munro.

She went on to explain that even as they talked the captain of the *Freya* was landing on the cruiser *Argyll* for a conference; and that, scheduled for ten that evening, a team of SBS frogmen was going to attack the *Freya* in an attempt to wipe out the terrorists and the detonator.

Munro's face set like granite. "If, ma'am," he said clearly, "these commandos are successful, then the hijack will be over, the two prisoners in Berlin will stay where they are, and the probable exposure of my agent will have been in vain. Merely an academic exercise."

She had the grace to look thoroughly uncomfortable. "I can only repeat my apology, Mr. Munro. The plan to storm the *Freya* was only devised in the small hours of this morning, eight hours after Maxim Rudin delivered his ultimatum to President Matthews. By then you were already consulting the Nightingale."

Sir Julian entered the room and told the premier: "They're coming on patch-through now, ma'am."

In the corner of her office a box speaker had been positioned. The prime minister asked her three guests to be seated. "Gentlemen, the conference on the *Argyll* is beginning. Let us listen to it, and then we will learn from Mr. Munro the reason for Maxim Rudin's extraordinary ultimatum."

AS THOR LARSEN stepped from the harness at the end of his dizzying five-mile ride through the sky onto the afterdeck of the British cruiser, the roar of the helicopter engines above his head was penetrated by the shrill welcome of the bosun's pipes.

The *Argyll's* captain stepped forward, saluted and held out his hand. "Richard Preston," said the navy captain. Larsen returned the salute and shook hands. "Welcome aboard, Captain," said Preston. "Would you care to step down to the wardroom?"

In the wardroom Captain Preston made the formal introductions. "The Right Honourable Jan Grayling, prime minister of the Netherlands . . . His Excellency Konrad Voss, ambassador of the German Federal Republic . . . . Captains Desmoulins of the French navy, de Jong of the Dutch navy, Hasselmann of the German navy, and Manning of the US navy."

Mike Manning put out his hand and stared into the eyes of the bearded Norwegian he had come so near to destroying. "Good to meet you, Captain." The words stuck in his throat. Thor Larsen looked curiously into his eyes, and then passed on.

"Finally," said Captain Preston, "may I present Major Simon Fallon of the Royal Marine commandos." Larsen looked down at the short, burly marine and felt the man's hard fist in his own. So, he thought, Svoboda was right.

They seated themselves at the wardroom dining table. "Captain

Larsen," said Preston, "I should make plain that our conversation has to be recorded, and will be transmitted in uninterceptable form directly from this cabin to Whitehall where the British prime minister will be listening."

Larsen nodded. His gaze kept wandering to the American; everyone else was looking at him with interest; the US navy man was studying the mahogany table.

"It has been agreed that I shall ask the questions that concern all our governments," said Preston. "First, Captain Larsen, what happened in the small hours of yesterday morning?"

Was it only yesterday? Larsen thought. Yes, just thirty-six hours ago. It seemed like a week. Briefly he described the takeover of the *Freya*.

"So there are seven of them?" asked the marine major. "You are quite certain there are no more?"

"Quite certain," said Larsen. "Just seven."

"And do you know who they are?" asked Captain Preston.

Larsen stared at the ring of faces in surprise. He had forgotten that outside the *Freya* no one knew who the hijackers were. "They're Ukrainian nationalists," he said. "The leader calls himself Svoboda."

"Then why the hell are they seeking the liberation of two Russian Jews?" asked Jan Grayling in exasperation. "Why should that help their cause?"

"Svoboda won't say. He only says that the liberation of those two men would cause such a blow to the Kremlin it could start a widespread popular uprising."

There was blank incomprehension on the faces around him. The questions about the layout of the ship, where Svoboda and Larsen stayed, the deployment of the terrorists, took a further ten minutes. Finally, Preston leaned forward. "Now, Captain Larsen, it is time to tell you. Tonight Major Fallon and a group of his colleagues are going to approach the *Freya* underwater, scale her sides and wipe out Svoboda and his men."

"No," said Thor Larsen slowly, "they are not. There will be no underwater attack unless you wish to have the *Freya* blown up and sunk. That is what Svoboda sent me here to tell you."

Captain Larsen spelled out Svoboda's message to the West. Before sundown every floodlight on the *Freya* would be switched on. The man in the fo'c's'le would be withdrawn; the entire foredeck from the bow to the base of the superstructure would be bathed in light. Every exterior door would be locked and bolted on the inside. Svoboda himself, with his detonator, would remain inside the superstructure, but would select one of the more than fifty cabins to occupy. Every cabin light would be switched on, and every curtain drawn.

One terrorist would remain on the bridge, in walkie-talkie contact with the man atop the funnel. The other four men would ceaselessly patrol the taffrail round the entire stern area of the *Freya* with powerful torches, scanning the surface of the sea. At the first trace of a stream of bubbles, or someone climbing the vessel's side, the terrorist would fire a shot. The man atop the funnel would alert the bridge-watch, who would shout a warning down the telephone to the cabin where Svoboda hid. On hearing the word of alarm, Svoboda would press his red button.

When Larsen had finished, there was silence round the table. Mike Manning watched him with anguish. The destruction of Major Fallon's attack plan now brought back to terrible possibility the order he had been given from Washington.

"Bastard," said Captain Preston with feeling. The group's eyes swivelled to Major Fallon, who stared unblinkingly at Larsen.

"We could come aboard at the bow instead," said Fallon.

Larsen shook his head. "The bridge-watch would see you in the floodlights. You wouldn't get halfway down the foredeck."

"We'll have to booby-trap their escape launch anyway."

"Svoboda thought of that, too. They are going to pull it round to the stern where it is in the glare of the decklights."

"That just leaves a frontal assault," Fallon said. "Come out of the water firing, use more men, come aboard against the opposition, beat in the doors and move through the cabins one by one."

"Not a chance," said Larsen firmly. "You won't be over the rail before Svoboda has heard you and blown us all to kingdom come."

Fallon tried one last move. "You are alone with this man much of the time, Captain Larsen. Would you kill him?"

"Willingly," said Larsen, "but if you are thinking of giving me a weapon, don't bother. On my return I am to be skin-searched. Any weapon found, and another of my seamen is executed."

"I'm afraid it won't work, Major Fallon," said Captain Preston gently. He rose from the table. "Gentlemen, I believe there is little more we can do. Captain Larsen, in my personal cabin there is someone who would like to speak with you."

A steward showed the Norwegian captain through the door of Preston's quarters. Lisa Larsen rose from the edge of the bed where she had been sitting, staring out of the porthole at the dim outline of the *Freya*. "Thor," she said. Larsen opened his arms and caught the running woman in a hug.

"Hello, little snow-mouse."

IN THE PRIME MINISTER'S Downing Street office, the transmission from the *Argyll* was switched off.

"Blast," said Sir Nigel, expressing the views of them all.

The prime minister turned to Munro. "Mr. Munro, it seems that your information is not so academic after all. If it can in any way assist us to solve this impasse, your risks will not have been run in vain. Why is Maxim Rudin behaving in this way?"

"Because, ma'am, his supremacy in the Politburo hangs by a thread. Yefrem Vishnayev has made his play for supreme power and cannot go back. He will bring Rudin down any way he can, for if he does not, then following the signature of the Treaty of Dublin, Rudin will destroy him. These two men in Berlin can deliver to Vishnayev the instrument he needs to swing one or two more members of the Politburo to join his faction of hawks."

"How?" asked Sir Nigel.

"By reaching Israel alive and giving an international press conference. By inflicting on the Soviet Union a massive public and international humiliation. You see, ma'am, during the night of thirty-first October last, in a street in Kiev, Mishkin and Lazareff assassinated Yuri Ivanenko, the head of the KGB."

Sir Nigel Irvine and Barry Ferndale sat bolt upright. "So that's what happened to him," breathed Ferndale, the expert in Soviet affairs. "I thought he must be in disgrace."

"Not in disgrace," said Munro. "In a grave. The Politburo knows this of course, and at least one, maybe two, of Rudin's faction have threatened to change sides if the assassins escape and give their achievement the worldwide publicity it needs."

"Does that make sense, in Russian psychology, Mr. Ferndale?" the prime minister asked.

Ferndale's handkerchief whirled in circles across the lenses of

293

his glasses as he polished furiously. "Perfect sense, ma'am," he said excitedly. "In times of crisis, such as food shortages, it is imperative that the KGB inspire sufficient awe in the people to hold them in check. If the terrible KGB were to become a laughing-stock, the repercussions to the Kremlin could be appalling. Those two men are a time bomb for Maxim Rudin. The fuse is lit by the *Freya* affair, and the time is running out."

"Well, gentlemen, this is all very interesting," said Mrs. Carpenter. "But it does not help solve the problem. President Matthews faces two alternatives: permit Chancellor Busch to release Mishkin and Lazareff, and lose the treaty; or require these two men to remain in gaol, and lose the *Freya* while gaining the condemnation of the world. Our own third alternative, to storm the *Freya* and liberate her, has become impossible. I fear there are no more alternatives, short of doing what we suspect the Americans have in mind."

"And what is that?" asked Munro.

"Blowing her apart by shellfire," said Sir Nigel Irvine. "We have no proof, but the guns of the USS *Moran* are trained on her."

"Actually, there *is* yet another alternative. It might satisfy Maxim Rudin, and it should work."

"Then please explain it," commanded the prime minister.

Munro did so.

There was silence. "I find it utterly repulsive," said Mrs. Carpenter.

"Ma'am, with all respect, so did I, forcing the probable exposure of my agent to the KGB," Munro replied stonily.

"Do we have such devilish equipment available?" Mrs. Carpenter asked Sir Nigel.

He studied his fingertips. "I believe the specialist department may be able to lay its hands on that sort of thing," he said quietly.

Joan Carpenter inhaled deeply. "It is not, thank God, a decision I need make. It is a decision for President Matthews. But it should be explained person-to-person. Mr. Munro, would you be prepared to carry out this plan?"

Munro thought of Valentina walking out into the street, to the waiting man in the grey trenchcoat. "Yes," he said, "without a qualm."

"Time is short," she said briskly. "If you are to reach Washington tonight."

"There is the five o'clock Concorde to Boston," said Sir Nigel. "It could be diverted to Washington."

Mrs. Carpenter glanced at her watch. It read four p.m. "On your way, Mr. Munro. I will inform President Matthews of the news you have brought from Moscow, and ask him to receive you. You may explain to him personally your somewhat macabre proposal."

FAR AWAY in the North Sea, Lisa Larsen clung to her husband in the *Argyll's* cabin. He asked her about home, and the children. They were fine, she said. Then the small talk died away.

"Thor, what is going to happen?"

"I don't know. I don't understand why the Germans will not release those two men. I don't understand why the Americans will not allow it."

"If they don't release the men, will that terrorist . . . do it?"

"I believe he will try," said Larsen thoughtfully. "And if he does, I shall try to stop him."

"Those fine captains out there, why won't they help you?"

"They can't, snow-mouse. I have to do it myself, or no one will."

"I don't trust that American captain," she whispered. "He would not look me in the face."

"He cannot. Nor me. You see, he has orders to blow the *Freya* out of the water. I don't know it for certain, but I suspect so. The guns of his ship are trained on us. If the Americans think they have to do that, they will. Burning up the cargo would lessen the ecological damage, destroy the blackmail weapon."

She shivered and began to cry. "I hate him," she said.

Thor Larsen stroked her hair, his great hand almost covering her small head. "Don't hate him," he rumbled. "He has his orders. He will do what the men far away in the chancelleries of Europe and America tell him to do." He stroked her, gently reassuring. "Do something for me, snow-mouse. Go back home to Alesund and the children. When this is over, I am going to come home. You can believe that."

"Don't go back to the ship," she begged him. "They'll kill you there."

"It's my ship," he said gently. "You know I have to go."

Five minutes later Thor Larsen was buckled by two Royal Navy

295

seamen, their hair awash from the rotors of the Wessex above them, into the harness. Captain Preston and the four NATO captains stood in a line a few yards away. As the Wessex began to lift, five hands rose to five braided caps in simultaneous salute.

Back on the *Freya*, Larsen walked into the day cabin with a submachine carbine at his back. Drake was in his usual chair. Larsen was directed into the one at the far end of the table.

"Did they believe you?" asked the Ukrainian.

"Yes," said Larsen. "And you were right. They were preparing an attack by frogmen after dark. It's been called off."

Drake snorted. "Just as well," he said. "If they had tried it, I'd have pressed this button. They'd have left me no alternative."

In Washington, President Matthews laid down the telephone that had joined him to the British premier in London, and looked at his three advisers. They had heard the conversation on the amplivox.

"So that's it," he said. "The night attack option has gone. That leaves us with the alternative of blowing the *Freya* to pieces. Is the warship on station?"

"In position, gun laid and loaded," confirmed Poklewski.

"Unless this man Munro has some idea that would work," suggested Robert Benson. "Will you see him, Mr. President?"

"Bob, I'll see the devil himself if he can propose some way of getting me off this hook."

"At least we know now that Maxim Rudin was not over-reacting," said David Lawrence. "In his fight with Vishnayev, he too has no aces left. How the hell did those two in Moabit gaol ever get to shoot Yuri Ivanenko?"

"We have to assume the leader on the *Freya* helped them," said Benson. "I'd dearly love to get my hands on that 'Svoboda'."

"No doubt you'd kill him," said Lawrence with distaste.

"Wrong," said the CIA chief. "I'd enlist him. He's tough, ingenious and ruthless. He's taken six major world governments and made them dance like puppets."

At five p.m. in London the Concorde lifted its drooping spear of a nose towards the western sky and climbed through the sound barrier. The normal rules about avoiding the sonic boom until well out over the sea had been overruled by orders from Downing Street. Halfway across the Atlantic the captain told his Boston-bound passengers that the Concorde would make an unscheduled stopover of a few moments at Dulles international airport, Washington, due to "operational reasons".

Two hours later, at nine p.m. Moscow time, Yefrem Vishnayev got the highly unusual Saturday evening meeting with Maxim Rudin for which he had been clamouring all day. They met in the Politburo room in the arsenal building. When he arrived, Vishnayev was backed by Marshal Nikolai Kerensky, but he found Rudin supported by his allies, Dmitri Rykov and Vassili Petrov.

"What brings you to the Kremlin at this hour?" asked Rudin.

"Treason, Comrade Secretary-General," snapped Vishnayev. He leaned across the table and spoke two feet from Rudin's face. "The treason of two filthy Jews from Lvov—Mishkin and Lazareff —now in gaol in Berlin. Two men whose freedom is being sought by a gang of murderers on a tanker in the North Sea. Is it not true that they killed Yuri Ivanenko?"

Maxim Rudin would dearly have liked to glance sideways at Vassili Petrov. Something had gone wrong. There had been a leak.

Petrov's lips set in a hard, straight line. Now controlling the KGB through General Abrassov, he knew that the circle of men aware of the truth was very small. The man who had spoken, he was sure, was Colonel Kukushkin, who had first failed to protect his master, and then failed to liquidate his master's killers. He was trying to buy his life, by changing camps.

"It is certainly suspected," said Rudin carefully.

"I understand it is proven," snapped Vishnayev. "It appears they may be released by West Germany and sent to Israel. The West is weak, it cannot hold out for long against the terrorists on the *Freya*. If those two reach Israel alive, they will talk."

"What are you asking for?" said Rudin.

Vishnayev rose. "I am demanding an extraordinary plenary meeting of the full Politburo here tomorrow night at nine o'clock. On a matter of exceptional national urgency. That is my right, Comrade Secretary-General?"

Rudin's shock of grey hair nodded slowly. He looked up at Vishnayev from under his eyebrows.

"Yes," Rudin growled.

"Then until this hour tomorrow," snapped the theoretician. He and Kerensky stalked from the chamber.

Rudin turned to Petrov. "Colonel Kukushkin?" he asked.

"It looks like it."

"Any possibility of eliminating Mishkin and Lazareff inside Moabit?"

Petrov shook his head. "No chance by tomorrow. Is there any way of pressuring the West not to release them?"

"No," said Rudin shortly, "I have brought every pressure on Matthews that I know."

"Tomorrow," said Rykov soberly, "Vishnayev and his people will produce Kukushkin and demand that we hear him out. And if by then Mishkin and Lazareff are in Israel . . . ."

AN HOUR LATER, on the *Freya*, Drake issued his final ultimatum.

At nine the following morning, in thirteen hours, unless Mishkin and Lazareff were airborne and on their way to Tel Aviv, the *Freya* would vent a further 100,000 tons of crude oil into the North Sea. At eight that night, unless they were in Israel and identified as genuine, the *Freya* would blow herself apart.

"That's bloody well the last straw!" shouted German Chancellor Dietrich Busch when he heard the ultimatum. "This charade is over!"

At twenty past eight the Federal German government announced that it was unilaterally releasing Mishkin and Lazareff the following morning at eight.

A personal coded message arrived on the USS *Moran* for Captain Mike Manning. It read: "Prepare for 'THUNDERBOLT' seven a.m. tomorrow."

He screwed it into a ball in his fist and looked out through the porthole towards the *Freya*. Floodlights bathed her towering superstructure in a white glare. She sat on the ocean five miles away, doomed, helpless, waiting for her executioner.

While Thor Larsen was reading the ultimatum over the *Freya*'s radio-telephone, the Concorde bearing Adam Munro touched down in Washington, at Dulles airport. The bewildered passengers noted only that she did not taxi towards the terminal building, but hove-to, engines running, in a parking bay beside the taxi track. A gangway was waiting, along with a black limousine.

A single passenger rose from near the front, stepped out of the open door and ran down the steps. Seconds later the gangway was withdrawn, the door closed and the apologetic captain announced that they would take off at once for Boston.

Adam Munro stepped into the limousine and the car swept

across the tarmac to where a small helicopter stood in the lee of a hangar, rotors whirling.

Before he boarded the helicopter Munro was exhaustively frisked for hidden weapons by two burly Secret Service agents. When they were satisfied, they escorted him aboard and the whirlybird lifted off, heading for the spreading lawns of the White House. It was three thirty on a warm Washington spring afternoon, when they landed barely a hundred yards from the Oval Office windows.

Inside the White House west wing, the two agents identified themselves and their visitor to a uniformed policeman sitting at a desk. The policeman checked with someone by house-phone, and a female secretary came and led the three up a narrow staircase to a thickly-carpeted hallway. A male aide in a charcoal grey suit glanced with raised eyebrows at the unshaven, dishevelled Englishman.

"You're to come straight through, Mr. Munro," he said.

The four men in the Oval Office were evidently waiting for him. He recognized President William Matthews, but this was a president no voter had ever seen: tired, haggard, ten years older than the smiling, confident image on the posters.

CIA Chief Robert Benson rose and approached him. "I'm Bob Benson," he said. He drew Munro towards the desk. William Matthews leaned across and shook hands. Munro was introduced to David Lawrence and Stanislav Poklewski.

"So," said President Matthews, looking with curiosity at the English agent, "you're the man who runs the Nightingale."

"Ran the Nightingale, Mr. President," said Munro. "As of twelve hours ago, I believe that asset is blown to the KGB."

"I'm sorry," said Matthews. "You know what a hell of an ultimatum Maxim Rudin put to me over this tanker affair? I had to know why he was doing it."

"You've read those reports of the Politburo discussions that the Nightingale delivered to you, Mr. Munro?" asked David Lawrence.

"Yes, Mr. Secretary," said Munro. "I know what is at stake, on both sides."

"Then how the hell do we get out of it?" asked President Matthews. "Your prime minister asked me to receive you because you had some proposal she was not prepared to discuss."

At that point the phone rang. Benson listened, then put it down. "We're moving towards the crunch," he said. "Svoboda on the *Freya* has just announced he is venting 100,000 tons of oil tomorrow morning at nine European time, just over twelve hours from now, if the two men are not released."

"So what's your suggestion, Mr. Munro?" asked the president.

"Mr. President, there are two apparent choices. Either Mishkin and Lazareff are released to fly to Israel, in which case they talk when they arrive and destroy Maxim Rudin and the Treaty of Dublin; or they stay where they are, in which case the *Freya* will either destroy herself or will have to be destroyed with all her crew on board her."

He did not mention the British suspicion concerning the *Moran*, but Poklewski shot Benson a sharp glance.

"Maxim Rudin's real fear, however, is whether Mishkin and Lazareff have the opportunity to address the world."

President Matthews sighed. "We thought of that. We have asked Israeli Prime Minister Golen to accept Mishkin and Lazareff, hold them incommunicado until the *Freya* is released, then return them to Moabit gaol, or even hold them in an Israeli gaol for another ten years. He refused. He said if he made the public pledge the terrorists demanded, he would not go back on it. And he won't."

"That was not what I had in mind," said Munro. "During the flight I wrote the suggestion in memorandum form." He withdrew a sheaf of papers from his inner pocket and laid it on the president's desk.

The United States president read the memorandum with an expression of increasing horror. "This is appalling," he said when he had finished. "Whichever option I choose, men will die."

Adam Munro looked across at him with no sympathy. In his time he had learned that, in principle, politicians have little enough objection to loss of life provided that they personally cannot be seen to have had anything to do with it.

"It has happened before, Mr. President," he said coldly, "and no doubt it will happen again. In the firm we call it The Devil's Alternative."

Wordlessly President Matthews passed the memorandum to Robert Benson who read it quickly. "Ingenious," he said. "It might work. Can it be done in time?"

"We have the equipment," said Munro. "The time is short, but not too short. I would have to be back in Berlin by seven a.m. Berlin time, ten hours from now."

"But will Maxim Rudin go along with it?" asked the president. "Without his concurrence the Treaty of Dublin would be forfeit."

"The only way is to ask him," said Poklewski who had finished reading the memorandum and passed it to David Lawrence.

The phone rang again. When Benson replaced it he turned to the president. "We may have no alternative but to seek Maxim Rudin's agreement. Chancellor Busch has just announced Mishkin and Lazareff are being freed at oh-eight-hundred hours, European time. And this time he will not back down."

"Then we have to try it," said Matthews. "But Rudin must agree to permit the plan to go ahead. I shall call him personally."

"Mr. President," said Munro. "Maxim Rudin did not use the hot line to deliver his ultimatum to you. He is not sure of the loyalties of some of his inner staff. This proposal should be for his ears alone, or he will feel bound to refuse it."

"Surely there is not time for you to fly to Moscow through the night and be back in Berlin by dawn?" objected Poklewski.

"There is one way," said Benson. "There is a Blackbird Lockheed SR-71 at Andrews which could take the polar route to Moscow and cover the distance in the time."

"Bob," said President Matthews, "take Mr. Munro to Andrews Base. Alert the crew of the Blackbird to prepare for take-off in one hour. I will personally call Maxim Rudin and ask him to permit the aeroplane to enter Soviet airspace and to receive Adam Munro as my personal envoy. Anything else, Mr. Munro?"

Munro took a single sheet from his pocket. "I would like the company to get this message urgently to Sir Nigel Irvine so that he can gain us some time in Berlin."

"It will be done," said the president. "Be on your way, Mr. Munro. And good luck to you."

Nineteen

At Andrews Base, Adam Munro was issued with a G-suit, boots, and goldfish-bowl oxygen helmet for a flight on the Blackbird, the world's fastest reconnaissance jet. Robert Benson found the pilot,

Colonel George T. O'Sullivan, in the navigation room, cigar clamped in his teeth, poring over maps of the Arctic and eastern Baltic. The angry Arizonan was in no mood to be polite. "Are you seriously ordering me to fly this bird clean across Greenland and Scandinavia, and into the heart of Rooshia?" he demanded. "And without any navigator/systems operator? With some goddam limey sitting in his seat?"

"No, Colonel," said Benson, "the President of the United States is ordering you to do it. The limey happens to bear a personal message from President Matthews to President Rudin of the USSR which has to reach him tonight."

The air force colonel stared at him for a moment. "Well," he conceded, "it better be goddam important."

The Lockheed SR-71, nicknamed the Blackbird due to its colour, stood in its hangar, swarming with ground technicians preparing it to fly. On a single, thin nosewheel-assembly, the bullet-like nose-cone thrust upwards at a shallow angle. Far down the fuselage wafer-thin delta wings sprouted. Situated almost at each wing-tip, the engines were sleek pods, so that body and engines resembled three hypodermic syringes, linked only by the wing.

Ground assistants helped Munro into the deep, narrow confines of the rear seat, the side walls of the cockpit rising above his ears. In front of him, Colonel O'Sullivan lowered himself into the front seat and began attaching his own life-support systems. When the radio was connected the Arizonan's voice boomed in his ears.

"You Scotch, Mr. Munro?"

"Scottish, yes," said Munro into his helmet.

"I'm Irish," said the voice in his ears. "You a Catholic?"

"No. Church of Scotland."

There was evident disgust up front. "Twenty years in the United States air force and I get to chauffeur a Scotch Protestant!"

The triple-perspex canopy was closed on them. A hiss indicated the cabin was now fully pressurized. From inside, the engines once started made only a low whistle. At the entry to the main runway the Blackbird paused, rocked on its wheels as the colonel lined her up, then Munro heard his voice: "Whatever God you pray to, start now and hold tight."

Something like a runaway train hit Munro squarely across the width of his back; it was the moulded seat in which he was strapped. He could see no buildings to judge his speed, just the pale blue sky above. When the jet reached 150 knots, the nose left the tarmac; half a second later the main wheels lifted from the runway. The SR-71 climbed almost vertically, powering its way to the sky like a rocket. Munro was on his back, feet towards the sky, conscious only of the steady pressure of the seat on his spine as the Blackbird streaked towards a sky that was soon turning to dark blue, to violet and finally to black.

Far below them, Philadelphia and New York went by like toy-towns; over northern New York State they went through the sound barrier, still climbing and still accelerating. At 80,000 feet, five miles higher than Concorde, Colonel O'Sullivan cut out the afterburners and levelled his flight attitude. Before the Canadian frontier passed beneath them, they had adopted a fast-cruise speed of almost three times the speed of sound. Before Munro's amazed eyes, the black skin of the SR-71, made of pure titanium, began to glow cherry red in the heat.

Within the cockpit, the aircraft's own refrigeration system kept its occupants at a comfortable body temperature. "Can I talk?" asked Munro.

"Sure," said the laconic voice of the pilot.

"How long for the flight to Moscow?"

"Three hours and fifty minutes."

Munro calculated. They would touch down at around five a.m. Moscow time on Sunday, 3 April. If Rudin agreed to his plan, and the Blackbird brought him back to Berlin, they would gain two hours by flying the other way. There was just time to make Berlin by dawn Sunday morning.

Meanwhile, in the Oval Office, President Matthews had spoken to Maxim Rudin on the hot line. Rudin had agreed to receive Adam Munro personally, and to allow the Blackbird to enter Soviet airspace.

At five a.m. Moscow time, Colonel O'Sullivan put the Blackbird down at Vnukovno II, a Moscow airport reserved for the Party elite. Forty-five minutes later a Zil limousine with Munro and two Kremlin bodyguards shot through the Borovitsky Gate into the Kremlin and headed for the side door to the arsenal building. At two minutes to six a.m. Adam Munro was shown into the private apartment of the leader of the USSR, to find an old man in a dressing gown, nursing a cup of warm milk. He was waved to an upright chair. The door closed behind him.

"So you are Adam Munro," said Maxim Rudin. "Now what is this proposal from President Matthews?"

Munro looked at Maxim Rudin. The old man appeared wearied and strained. "The proposal, Mr. Secretary-General," Munro began in fluent Russian, "is a way whereby the terrorists on the supertanker *Freya* can be persuaded to leave the ship without having secured what they came for."

"Mr. Munro, there is to be no more talk of the liberation of Mishkin and Lazareff."

"Not for the moment, sir. In fact I had hoped we might talk of Yuri Ivanenko."

Rudin, face impassive, took a sip of milk.

"You see, sir, one of those two *has* let something slip already," said Munro. He had to let Rudin know that he was aware of what had happened to Ivanenko, but he would not indicate he had learned from someone inside the Kremlin hierarchy, in case Valentina was still free.

"Fortunately," he went on, "it was to one of our people, and the matter has been taken care of."

"Your people?" mused Rudin. "Ah yes, I think I know who your people are. How many others know?"

"The director-general of my organization, the British prime minister, President Matthews and three of his senior advisers. No one who knows has the slightest intention of revealing this for public consumption."

Rudin seemed to ruminate for a while. "Can the same be said for Mishkin and Lazareff?"

"That has been the problem since the terrorists, who are Ukrainian emigrés, stepped onto the *Freya*."

"President Matthews tells me the best way out of this is to destroy the *Freya*."

"I put it to you, sir, that destroying the *Freya* would not solve the problem. Three days ago Mishkin and Lazareff were two insignificant hijackers, serving fifteen years in gaol. Now they are celebrities. People assume their freedom is being sought for its own sake. We know different. If the *Freya* were destroyed, the entire world would wonder why it had been so vital to keep them in gaol. So far no one realizes that it is their silence that is vital.

With the *Freya* destroyed, the world would believe them when they spoke about what they had done."

Rudin nodded slowly. "You are right, young man. The Germans would give them their press conference."

"Precisely," said Munro. "This then is my suggestion." He outlined the same plan that he had described to Mrs. Carpenter and President Matthews.

The Russian showed neither surprise nor horror. "Would it work?" he asked with interest.

"It has to work," said Munro. "It is the last alternative. They have to be allowed to go to Israel."

Rudin looked at the clock on the wall. It was past 6:45 a.m. In fourteen hours he would have to face Vishnayev and the rest of the Politburo. This time Vishnayev would put down a formal motion of no confidence. And, with the two assassins still unsilenced, it would be carried.

His grizzled head nodded. "Do it, Mr. Munro," he said, "and make it work. For if it doesn't, there will be no more Treaty of Dublin, and no more *Freya* either."

He pressed a bell-push and the door opened immediately. An immaculate major of the Kremlin praetorian guard stood there.

"I shall need to deliver two signals, one to the Americans, one to my own people," said Munro. "A representative of each embassy is waiting outside the Kremlin walls."

Rudin issued his orders to the guard major, who escorted Munro out. As they were at the door, Maxim Rudin called, "Mr. Munro." Munro turned. "Should you ever need another job, Mr. Munro," the old man said grimly, "come and see me. There is always a place here for men of talent."

As the Zil limousine left the Kremlin the morning sun was just tipping the spire of St. Basil's cathedral. Two long black cars waited by the kerb. Munro descended from the Zil. He passed one message to the American diplomat and one to the British. Before he was airborne for Berlin, the instructions would be in London and Washington.

At eight o'clock the bullet-nose of the Blackbird turned due west for Berlin, a thousand miles away. It would be there with Munro at seven a.m. local time.

On the *Freya*, despite his promise to choose a different cabin, Drake was so confident there would be no night attack that he elected to stay in the day cabin with Larsen. Both men were near exhaustion, but Larsen could still observe the younger man clinically, looking for signs of a weakening in concentration.

It was half-past five when the intercom from the bridge rang. The terrorist leader listened and replied in Ukrainian. The call seemed to perplex him. He sat with a frown, staring at the table, until one of his men came to relieve him in guarding the Norwegian skipper. Then he went up to the bridge. When he returned ten minutes later he seemed angry.

"What's the matter?" asked Larsen. "Something gone wrong again?"

"The German ambassador on the line from The Hague. The British have offered to assist Chancellor Busch by putting an RAF communications jet at his disposal to fly Mishkin and Lazareff to Tel Aviv."

"Does it matter?" said Larsen. "Why not accept the offer?"

Drake dismissed his colleague and resumed his seat, his gun on the table beside him. Bleary-eyed from weariness, slow from lack of sleep, he regarded the Norwegian. "You're right," he conceded. "In fact, I have accepted."

His belt, carrying the oscillator which, if the red button were pressed, would end it all, hung over the back of a nearby chair.

"Then it's over bar the shouting," said Larsen, forcing a smile. "Let's celebrate."

He had two cups of coffee in front of him, poured while he was waiting for Drake to return. He pushed one halfway down the long table; the Ukrainian reached for it. It was the first mistake he had made . . . .

Thor Larsen came at him down the length of the table with all the pent-up rage of the past fifty hours. The partisan recoiled and grabbed his gun. A fist like a log of cut spruce caught him on the left temple, flung him out of his chair and backwards across the cabin floor. As he fell, the gun skittered across the floor. He came up empty-handed, fighting, to meet the charge of the Norwegian, and the pair went down again in a tangle of arms and legs. Evading the grip of the big man's hands, Drake wriggled free and scrambled for the door. His hand was reaching for the knob when Larsen launched himself across the carpet and brought both his ankles out from under him.

No other terrorist was within earshot. Drake fought in silence, wrestling, biting, gouging, kicking, and the pair rolled over the carpet among the broken furniture and crockery. Somewhere beneath them was the gun.

In two minutes it was all over; Thor Larsen pulled one hand free, grasped the head of the struggling Ukrainian and slammed it into the leg of the table. Drake slumped. From under his hairline a thin trickle of blood seeped down his forehead.

Panting with weariness, Thor Larsen raised himself from the floor and looked at the unconscious man. Carefully, he took the oscillator from the chair-back, held it in his left hand and crossed to the one cabin window which was closed with butterfly-headed bolts. One-handed, he began to unwind them. The first one flicked open; he started on the second. A few more seconds, a long throw, and the oscillator would sail out of the porthole and into the North Sea.

On the floor behind him the young terrorist's hand inched to where his gun lay. Larsen had the second bolt undone and was swinging the brass-framed window inwards when Drake lifted himself painfully onto one shoulder, reached round the table and fired.

The crash of the gun in the enclosed cabin was ear-splitting. Thor Larsen reeled back against the wall by the open window and looked at his left hand. The Ukrainian stared in disbelief.

The single shot had hit the Norwegian captain in the palm of the hand that held the oscillator, driving shards of plastic and glass into the flesh. For ten seconds both men stared at each other, waiting for the rumbling explosions that would mark the end of the *Freya*.

They never came. The soft-nosed slug had shattered the detonator device into small pieces, and it had not had time to reach the tonal pitch needed to trigger the detonators. Slowly the Ukrainian climbed to his feet, holding on to the table for support. Thor Larsen looked at the stream of blood running from his broken hand, then across at the panting terrorist.

"I have won, Mr. Svoboda. I have won. You cannot destroy my ship and my crew."

"You may know that, Captain Larsen," said the man with the gun, "and I may know that. But they...." He gestured to the open porthole and the lights on the NATO warships; "... they don't know that. The game goes on. Mishkin and Lazareff *will* reach Israel."

Twenty

On the upper floor of Moabit gaol David Lazareff and Lev Mishkin were awakened in their separate cells by the prison governor at six on the morning of Sunday, 3 April 1983.

"You are being flown to Israel this morning," he told them brusquely. "We leave for the airfield at seven thirty."

Ten minutes later the military commandant of the British sector was on the telephone to the governing mayor of West Berlin. "I'm terribly sorry, Herr Burgermeister," he said, "but a take-off from the civil airport at Tegel is out of the question. Refuelling and maintenance facilities for RAF aircraft are far better at our own airfield at Gatow. There we can also easily prevent an invasion by the press. London has suggested that these blighters be put in an armoured wagon inside Moabit, and driven straight into Gatow. Your chaps can hand them over to us inside the wire."

Privately the governing mayor was relieved. If the British took over the whole operation, any possible disasters would be their responsibility.

Inside Gatow Base there had been controlled activity for hours. At four o'clock a Dominie executive jet, fitted with long-range fuel tanks, had flown in from Britain. Its 500 mph cruising speed would enable it to complete the 2,200 mile journey to Tel Aviv in just over four hours.

So keen were the press on observing the gaol of Moabit and the airport at Tegel that no one noticed a sleek black SR-71 reconnaissance jet sweep over the East Germany–West Berlin border and drop onto the main runway at Gatow just three minutes after seven o'clock. The Blackbird had done its job.

Colonel O'Sullivan's passenger left the hangar and was greeted by a youthful squadron leader with a Land-Rover. "Mr. Munro, there are two gentlemen waiting for you in the mess."

The two gentlemen, who posed as low-grade civil servants, were actually concerned with experimental work in a top secret laboratory. Both men were neatly dressed and carried attaché cases. One had medical qualifications and the other was a former male nurse.

"You have the equipment I asked for?" said Munro.

The senior man opened his attaché case and extracted a flat box no larger than a cigar case. He opened it and showed Munro what nestled on a bed of cottonwool inside. "Ten hours," he said, "No less."

"That's tight," said Munro. "Very tight."

It was seven thirty on a bright sunny morning.

ON THE *FREYA*, as the minutes to eight o'clock and the release of Lazareff and Mishkin ticked away, nerves became even more strained and taut. Andrew Drake, supported by two men with sub-machine guns to prevent another attack from the Norwegian skipper, had allowed Captain Larsen to use his first-aid box on his hand. Grey-faced with pain, the captain had plucked from the pulped meat of his palm such pieces of glass and plastic as he could, then bandaged the hand and placed it in a rough sling round his neck. Drake watched him from across the cabin.

"You're a brave man, Thor Larsen, I'll say that for you," he said. "But nothing has changed. If the Germans break their promise, I'll vent every ton of oil on this ship at nine o'clock."

At precisely seven forty the double gates of Moabit prison opened and the nose of an armoured van appeared. Simultaneously, outside-broadcast units rolled their cameras and radio reporters chattered excitedly into their microphones. The voice of the BBC man echoed into the day cabin of the *Freya*.

"They're on their way," Drake said with satisfaction. "Time now to broadcast the final details of their reception in Tel Aviv. I shall do it myself." He left for the bridge, the two men remaining to cover the injured captain, slumped in his chair at the table.

In West Berlin, the armoured van, preceded by motorcycle outriders with howling sirens, swept through the twelve-foot-high steel-mesh double gates of the British base at Gatów and the gates swung to, shutting out the following cars bulging with reporters and photographers.

Inside the base, Adam Munro walked into the hangar where the Dominie stood, accompanied by the wing commander in charge of aircraft maintenance. "How is she?" Munro asked.

"Hundred per cent, sir," said the warrant officer in charge of the fitters and riggers.

"No, she's not," said Munro, thinking of the experts' ten hours. "I think if you look under one of the engine cowlings, you'll find an electrical malfunction that needs quite a bit of attention."

The warrant officer looked at the stranger in amazement, then across to his superior officer. "Do as he says, Mr. Barker," said the wing commander. "The Dominie must not be ready for take-off for a while. But the German authorities must believe it's a genuine technical delay. Open her up and get to work."

The "electrical malfunction" was reported to the German authorities, and in a special flash cut into the BBC eight a.m. news. It was heard on the *Freya*.

"They'd better hurry up," said Drake.

Just after eight o'clock, Adam Munro and the two civilians entered the military police cells where the prisoners were being kept until the plane was ready. The junior civilian let Munro and his colleague enter the corridor leading to the row of four cells, then closed the door and stood with his back to it. "Last minute interrogation," he told the outraged MP sergeant in charge. "Intelligence people."

Munro entered the first cell with the other civilian. Lev Mishkin was sitting on the edge of the bunk bed smoking a cigarette. He had been told he was going to Israel at last, but he was still nervous and uninformed about most of what had been going on the past three days.

Munro stared at him. But for this man and his crazy scheme to assassinate Yuri Ivanenko in pursuit of some far-off dream, his beloved Valentina would now be preparing to leave for the boat that would take her to freedom. He saw again the back of the woman he loved going through the plate glass doors to the Moscow street, the man in the trenchcoat straighten up and follow her.

"I am a doctor," he said in Russian. "Your friends the Ukrainians who have demanded your release have also insisted you be medically fit to travel."

Mishkin stood up and shrugged. He was unprepared for the four rigid fingertips that jabbed him in the solar plexus, and the small cannister held under his nose as he gasped for air, unable to prevent himself from inhaling the aerosol vapour. When the gas hit his lungs his legs buckled and Munro caught him before he reached the floor. Carefully, he was laid on the bed.

"It'll act for five minutes, no more," said the civilian. "Then he'll wake with a fuzzy head but no ill effects. You'd better move fast."

Munro opened the attaché case and took out a hypodermic syringe. The injection ensured that Lev Mishkin would remain under its effects for almost two hours.

310

The two men closed the cell door and went down to where David Lazareff, who had heard nothing, was pacing up and down. Two minutes later he, too, had had his injection. The civilian accompanying Munro reached into his breast pocket and took out a flat tin. He held it out. "I'll leave you now," he said coldly. "This isn't what I am paid for."

A mixture of two narcotics had been injected into each hijacker. In combination they cause the patient to remain awake, albeit slightly sleepy; able to obey instructions. They also have the effect of telescoping time, so that coming out from their effects after almost two hours, the patient has the impression of having suffered a dizzy spell for several seconds. When the effects wear off the patient has not the slightest recall of anything that happened during the intervening period. Only reference to a clock will tell him that time has passed at all.

Munro re-entered Mishkin's cell. He helped the young man into a sitting position on his bed. "Hello," he said.

"Hello," said Mishkin and smiled. They were speaking in Russian, but Mishkin would never remember it.

Munro opened his flat tin box, extracted two halves of a long torpedo-shaped capsule called a spansule, such as is often used for cold remedies, and screwed the two ends together.

"I want you to take this pill," he said, and held it out with a glass of water.

"Sure," said Mishkin, and swallowed it without demur.

From his attaché case Munro took a battery-operated wall clock and adjusted it. Then he hung it on the wall. The hands read eight o'clock but were not in motion. He left Mishkin sitting on his bed and returned to the cell of the other man. Five minutes later the job was finished. Drowsy from the narcotics, neither men noticed what he was doing. He repacked his bag and left the cell corridor.

"They're to remain in isolation until the aircraft is ready," he told the MP sergeant at the orderly-room desk as he passed through. "No one to see them at all. Base commander's orders."

FOR THE FIRST TIME Andrew Drake was himself speaking to the Dutch premier, Jan Grayling. Later English linguistics experts would identify the tape-recorded voice as having originated within a twenty-mile radius of the city of Bradford, England.

"These are the terms for the arrival of Mishkin and Lazareff in

311

Israel," said Drake. "I shall expect no later than one hour after the take-off from Berlin an assurance from Premier Golen in Israel that they will be abided by. If they are not, the release of my friends will be regarded as null and void.

"One: the two are to be led from the aircraft on foot and at a slow pace past the observation terrace on top of the main terminal building at Ben Gurion airport.

"Two: access to that terrace is to be open to the public. No controls of identity are to be carried out by the Israeli security force.

"Three: if there has been any switch of the prisoners, if any look-alike actors are playing their part, I shall know within hours.

"Four: three hours before the aeroplane lands at Ben Gurion, the Israeli radio is to publish the time of its arrival and inform everyone that any person who wishes to come and witness their arrival is welcome to do so. The broadcast is to be in Hebrew and English, French and German. That is all."

"Mr. Svoboda," Jan Grayling cut in urgently, "all these demands will be passed immediately to the Israeli government. I am sure they will agree. Please do not cut contact. I have urgent information from the British in West Berlin."

"Go ahead," said Drake shortly.

"The RAF technicians working on the executive jet at Gatow airfield have reported a serious electrical fault developed this morning in one of the engines. I implore you to believe this is no trick. They are working frantically to put the fault right. But there will be a delay of an hour or two."

"If this is a trick, it's going to cost your beaches a deposit of one hundred thousand tons of crude oil," snapped Drake.

"It is not a trick," said Grayling urgently. "It is disastrous that this should happen to the RAF plane right now."

There was silence as Drake thought.

"I want take-off witnessed by four different national radio reporters. I want live reports, in English, by each one of them of that take-off."

Jan Grayling sounded relieved. "I will ensure the RAF personnel at Gatow permit four such reporters to witness the take-off," he said.

"I am delaying the venting by three hours," said Drake. "At noon we start pumping."

In Jerusalem, Premier Benyamin Golen was at his desk in his

office when his personal adviser on security matters brought him the transcript of the *Freya* broadcast. Golen read it quickly. "What are they after?" he inquired.

"They are taking precautions against a switch," said the adviser. "It would have been an obvious ploy to make up two men to pass for Mishkin and Lazareff at first glance."

"Then who is going to recognize the real Mishkin and Lazareff here in Israel?"

"Someone on that observation terrace," the security adviser said. "Probably someone whom Mishkin and Lazareff also can recognize. Some message or signal will presumably be passed to the media for broadcasting, to confirm to the men on the *Freya* that their friends have reached Israel safely. Without that message, they will go ahead with their threat."

"Another of them? Here in Israel? I'm not having that," said Benyamin Golen. "I want that observation terrace put under clandestine scrutiny. If any watcher on that terrace receives a signal from these two when they arrive, I want him followed. He must be allowed to pass his message, then arrest him."

On the *Freya*, the morning ticked by with agonizing slowness. Meanwhile on the *Cutlass*, one of the three fast patrol boats moored in the lee of the cruiser *Argyll*, Major Fallon had assembled his group of twelve commandos.

"Some time in the next couple of hours, those two men will take off from West Berlin for Israel," he told them. "They should arrive about four and a half hours later. So during this evening or tonight, if they keep their word, those terrorists are going to quit the *Freya*. They'll probably head towards Holland. The sea is empty of ships on that side. When they are three miles from the *Freya*, and out of possible range to detonate the explosives, Royal Navy experts are going to board the *Freya* and dismantle the charges. But that's not our job. We're going to take those bastards, and I want that man Svoboda. He's mine, got it?"

There was a series of nods and several grins. They had been cheated of action so far and their hunting instinct was high.

"Their launch is much slower than ours," Fallon resumed. "They'll have an eight-mile start, but we can take them three to four miles before they reach the coast. We have a Nimrod overhead, patched-in to the *Argyll*. The *Argyll* will give us the direction. When we get close to them we'll spot them with our searchlights.

Then we take them out. London says no one is interested in prisoners."

A few miles away Captain Mike Manning on the USS *Moran* was watching the minutes tick away. The news he had received in the small hours of the morning, while he sat sleepless in his cabin awaiting the dreaded order to fire and destroy the *Freya* and her crew, had surprised him. Out of the blue, the United States government had reversed its attitude. Washington now held no objection to the release of the men from Moabit. But not until the two Ukrainian Jews had touched down in Israel would Manning be completely convinced that he would not have to shell the *Freya*.

Meanwhile, at a quarter to ten, Mishkin and Lazareff began to come out of the effects of the narcotic they had ingested at eight o'clock. Almost simultaneously the clocks Adam Munro had hung on the walls of each cell came to life. The sweep hands began to move round the dials.

Mishkin shook his head and rubbed his eyes. He felt sleepy, slightly muzzy in the head. He put it down to the sleepless night, the excitement. He glanced at the clock on the wall, which he did not remember noticing before. It read two minutes past eight. He knew that when he and David Lazareff had been led through the orderly room towards the cells, the clock in that room had said eight exactly. He stretched, swung himself off the bunk and began to pace the cell. Five minutes later at the other end of the corridor Lazareff did much the same.

At ten thirty, Adam Munro strolled into the hangar where Warrant Officer Barker was still fiddling with the starboard engine of the Dominie. "How is it going, Mr. Barker?" asked Munro.

The technician withdrew himself from the guts of the engine and looked down at the civilian with exasperation. "May I ask, sir, how long I am supposed to keep this up? The engine's perfect."

"In one hour exactly," Munro said, "I'd like you to telephone the base commander and report that she's fit and ready to fly."

In the cells, David Lazareff glanced again at the wall clock. He thought he had been pacing for thirty minutes, but the clock said nine. An hour had gone by, but it had seemed a very short one. It never occurred to him or Mishkin that their clocks were moving at double-speed to catch up on the missing hundred minutes in their lives, or that they were designed to synchronize with the clocks outside the cells at eleven thirty.

314

At eleven thirty precisely, Warrant Officer Barker closed the cowling of the engine, climbed down and called the base commander at the officers' mess. "She's ready, sir," said the technician.

The RAF officer turned to the men grouped around him, including the governor of Moabit gaol and four radio reporters holding telephones linked to their offices. "The fault has been put right," he said, "she'll be taking off in fifteen minutes." From the windows of the mess they watched the sleek little executive jet being towed out into the sunshine.

At 11:35 the two prisoners were driven across the tarmac to the waiting jet. Followed by the air quartermaster sergeant who would be the only other occupant of the Dominie on its flight to Ben Gurion, they went up the steps.

At 11:45 the Dominie climbed away from the runway of Gatow airfield, and disappeared into the blue sky.

Within two minutes all four radio reporters were informing their listeners across the world that Mishkin and Lazareff were airborne and on their way to Israel and freedom.

Thirty-five minutes later Israel agreed to abide by the demands made from the *Freya* for the reception of Mishkin and Lazareff at Ben Gurion airport.

In his sixth-floor hotel room in Tel Aviv, three miles from Ben Gurion airport, Miroslav Kaminsky heard the news on the radio. He leaned back with a sigh of relief. Now for him, too, the hours were ticking away until the touchdown of the Dominie.

On the *Freya*, Andrew Drake heard the news of the take-off and Israel's agreement to his demands. "Four hours to Tel Aviv and safety," he told Larsen. "Another four hours after that, we'll be gone. The navy will come on board and release you. You'll have proper medical help for that hand, and you'll have your crew and your ship back. . . . You should be happy."

The Norwegian skipper was leaning back in his chair, deep black smudges under his eyes. For him it was not over until the explosive charges had been removed from his holds, until the last terrorist had left his ship. He knew he was close to collapse. The searing pain from his hand had settled down to a dull throb that thumped up the arm to the shoulder, and the waves of exhaustion swept over him until he was dizzy. But he would not close his eyes. He raised them to the Ukrainian with contempt. "And Tom Keller?" he asked. "My third officer. The man you shot out on the deck?"

Drake laughed. "Tom Keller is down below with the others. The shooting was a charade. One of my own men in Keller's clothes. The bullets were blank."

The Norwegian grunted. Drake looked across at him with interest. "I can afford to be generous," he said, "because I have won. I brought against the whole of Western Europe a threat they could not face, and an exchange they could not wriggle out of. In short I left them no alternative. But you came within an inch of beating me. You're a brave man, Thor Larsen. Is there anything you want?"

"Just get off my ship," said Larsen.

Twenty-one

At Ben Gurion airport the little Dominie touched down at 6:15, local time. The upper terrace of the passenger building was crowded with curious sightseers. Despite the demands of the terrorists, the Israeli Special Branch was also there, but discreetly —some of them in the uniform of El Al staff, others selling soft drinks, sweeping the forecourt, or at the wheels of taxis. Detective Inspector Avram Hirsch was in a newspaper van.

After touchdown the RAF plane was towed to the apron of tarmac in front of the passenger terminal. Here officials waited to take charge of the two passengers from Berlin.

Not far away an El Al jet was also parked, and from its curtained portholes two Israeli Special Branch men with binoculars peered at the crowd atop the passenger building. Each man had a walkie-talkie set.

Somewhere on the observation terrace Miroslav Kaminsky stood, indistinguishable from the other sightseers.

An Israeli official went inside the Dominie and after two minutes emerged, followed by David Lazareff and Lev Mishkin. They stared up at the crowd on the terrace as they were led along the front of the terminal building, preceded by the officials and with two uniformed policemen behind them.

Lev Mishkin saw Kaminsky first and muttered something quickly in Ukrainian out of the side of his mouth. It was picked up at once by a directional microphone aimed at the pair from a catering van a hundred yards away. The man in the cramped van, with earphones over his head—picked for his knowledge of Ukrainian—muttered into a walkie-talkie, "Mishkin just said to Lazareff quote there he is, near the end with the blue tie unquote."

Inside the parked El Al jet the two watchers swung their binoculars towards the end of the terrace. Meanwhile, Lazareff, his eyes along the line of faces above him, spotted Miroslav Kaminsky and winked. That recognition was all Kaminsky needed; there had been no switch of prisoners.

One of the men in the airliner began to talk into his hand-held radio. "Medium height, early thirties, brown hair, dressed in grey trousers, tweed sports jacket and blue tie. Standing eighth from the far end of the observation terrace."

Mishkin and Lazareff disappeared into the building. The crowd on the roof began to disperse, pouring down the stairwell to the main concourse. At the bottom of the stairs, a sweeper spotted a man striding away in a tweed jacket and blue tie. The sweeper reached into his barrow, took out a small black box and muttered, "Suspect moving towards exit gate five."

Outside the building Avram Hirsch hefted a bundle of evening newspapers from the back of the van onto a trolley held by one of his colleagues. The man in the blue tie passed within a few feet of him, made for a parked hire-car, and climbed in. Hirsch slammed the rear doors of his van, walked to the passenger door and swung himself into the seat. "The Volkswagen Golf over there in the car park," he said to the van driver.

When the rented car left the car park, the newspaper van was two hundred yards behind it. Ten minutes later Avram Hirsch alerted the other police cars coming up behind him. "Suspect entering Avia Hotel car park."

Miroslav Kaminsky passed quickly through the hotel foyer and took the lift to his sixth-floor room. He picked up the telephone and asked for an outside line. When he got it he began to dial.

"He's just asked for an outside line," the switchboard operator told Inspector Hirsch who was at her side.

"Can you trace the number he's dialling?"

"No, it's automatic for local calls."

"Blast," said Hirsch, "come on." He and his constable ran for the lift.

The telephone in the BBC Jerusalem office answered at the third ring. "Do you speak English?" asked Kaminsky.

"Yes, of course," said the Israeli secretary.

"Then listen," said Kaminsky, "I'll only say this once. If the supertanker *Freya* is to be released unharmed, the first item in the six o'clock news on the BBC World Service, European time, must include the phrase 'no alternative'. If that phrase is not included in the first news item of the broadcast, the ship will be destroyed. Have you got that?"

The young secretary scribbled rapidly on a pad. "Yes, I think so. Who is that?" she asked.

Outside the hotel bedroom door, Avram Hirsch was joined by two other men. One had a short-barrelled shotgun. Hirsch listened at the door till he heard the tinkle of the telephone being replaced, then he drew his revolver and nodded to the man with the shotgun.

The gunner aimed at the door lock and blew the assembly out of the woodwork. Avram Hirsch went past him at a run, dropped to a crouch, gun held forward in both hands, pointed straight at the target, and called in Russian to the room's occupant to freeze.

Miroslav Kaminsky was standing by the bed, the telephone directory in his hand. He dropped the book. When the cry to freeze came, he did not see a hotel bedroom outside Tel Aviv; he saw a small farmhouse in the foothills of the Carpathians, and uniformed Russians closing in on the hideaway of his group. He began to run backwards, through the open glass door to the tiny balcony. The balcony rail caught him in the small of the back and flipped him over. When he hit the car park sixty feet below it broke his back, pelvis and skull.

THE AIRCRAFT that had brought the two specialists to Gatow from Britain returned westwards soon after the take-off of the Dominie. Adam Munro hitched a lift on it as far as Amsterdam, where the Wessex helicopter from the *Argyll* met him and took him to the missile cruiser. All Captain Preston knew was that his visitor was from the foreign office and had been in Berlin supervising the departure of the hijackers.

"Any news of the Dominie?" asked Munro.

"Landed fifteen minutes ago at Ben Gurion," said Captain Preston. He took in Munro's dishevelled appearance. "Care for a wash and brush-up?" he asked.

"Love one," said Munro. "And a thick sweater. It's turned damn cold out there."

318

"There's a belt of cold air moving down from Norway. We could could get a spot of sea mist this evening."

The sea mist when it came, just after five o'clock, was a rolling bank of fog. When Adam Munro, washed, shaved and dressed in a borrowed thick white navy sweater, joined Captain Preston on the bridge, the fog was thickening.

"Damn and blast," said Preston. "These terrorists seem to be having everything their own way."

By half past five the fog had blotted out the *Freya*, and swirled around the stationary warships, none of whom could see each other, except on radar.

The circling Nimrod above could see them all on its radar, and was still flying in clear air at fifteen thousand feet. But the sea itself had vanished in a blanket of grey cottonwool. Just after five the tide turned and began to move towards the Dutch shore, bearing the drifting oil slick with it.

THE BBC CORRESPONDENT in Jerusalem, as soon as he learned of the telephone call his secretary had taken, contacted a friend in one of the Israeli security services. "That's the message," he said, "and I'm going to send it to London right now. But I haven't a clue who telephoned it."

There was a chuckle at the other end. "Send the message," said the security man. "As to the man on the telephone, we know."

It was just after four thirty European time when the first news flash was received on the *Freya* that Mishkin and Lazareff had landed at Ben Gurion. Andrew Drake threw himself back in his chair with a shout. "We've done it," he yelled at Thor Larsen.

"Congratulations," Larsen said sardonically. "Now perhaps you can leave my ship and go to hell."

The telephone from the bridge rang. There was a rapid exchange in Ukrainian, and Larsen heard a whoop of joy from the other end.

"Sooner than you think," said Drake. "The lookout on the funnel reports a thick bank of fog moving towards the whole area from the north. With luck we won't even have to wait until dark. But when we do leave, I'm afraid I'll have to handcuff you to the table leg. The navy will rescue you in a couple of hours."

At five o'clock the main newscast brought a dispatch from Tel Aviv that the Israeli government would keep the two from Berlin in custody until the *Freya* was released safe and unharmed. If she was

319

not, the government would regard its pledges to the terrorists as null and void, and return Mishkin and Lazareff to gaol.

On the *Freya*, Drake laughed. "They won't need to," he told Larsen. "I don't care what happens to me now. Within twenty-four hours those two men are going to hold an international press conference. And when they do, Captain Larsen, they are going to blow the biggest hole ever made in the walls of the Kremlin."

Larsen looked out the windows at the thickening fog. "The commandos might still use this fog to storm the *Freya*," he said. "In a few minutes you won't be able to see any bubbles from frogmen underwater."

"It doesn't matter any more," said Drake, "nothing matters any more. Only that Mishkin and Lazareff get their chance to speak. That was what it was all about."

Meanwhile, in Tel Aviv, the two Jewish-Ukrainians had been taken to the central police station and locked in separate cells. Prime Minister Golen was not prepared to have the unknown Svoboda play him a trick. For Mishkin and Lazareff it was the third cell in a day, but both knew it would be the last. As they parted in the corridor, Mishkin winked at his friend and called in Ukrainian, "Not next year in Jerusalem—tomorrow."

From his office the police station superintendent made a routine call to the police doctor to give the pair a medical examination, and the doctor promised to come at once.

The last thirty minutes before six o'clock dragged by on the *Freya*. In the day cabin Drake had tuned his radio to the BBC World Service and listened impatiently for the six o'clock newscast. At the *Freya*'s stern, Azamat Krim and three of his colleagues shinned down a rope to the sturdy fishing launch that bobbed beside the hull, and began preparations for departure.

At six o'clock the chimes of Big Ben rang out from London and the evening news broadcast began. Andrew Drake sat motionless, watching the radio unblinkingly.

"In Jerusalem today, Prime Minister Benyamin Golen said that following the arrival earlier from West Berlin of the two prisoners David Lazareff and Lev Mishkin, he would have no alternative but to abide by his pledge to free the two men, provided the super-tanker *Freya* was freed with her crew unharmed. . . ."

"No alternative," shouted Drake. "That's the phrase. Miroslav has recognized them. No switching has taken place." He slumped back in his chair and exhaled a deep sigh. "It's over, Captain Larsen. We're leaving."

The captain's personal locker contained one set of handcuffs, with keys, in case of the need to restrain someone on board. Drake slipped one of the cuffs round Larsen's right wrist and snapped it shut. The other went round the table leg. The table was bolted to the floor. Drake paused in the doorway, and laid the handcuff keys on top of a shelf.

"Goodbye, Captain Larsen. I'm sorry about the oil slick. It need never have happened if the fools out there had not tried to trick me. I'm sorry about your hand, but that too need not have happened. We'll not see each other again, so goodbye."

He locked the cabin door and ran down the three flights to "A" deck and outside to where his men were grouped on the after deck. He had taken his transistor radio with him. He looked at his watch. It was twenty past six. "Right. At six forty-five Azamat hits the ship's siren, and the launch and the first group leave simultaneously. Azamat and I leave ten minutes later. You've all got papers and clothes. After you reach the Dutch coast, scatter."

He looked over the side. By the fishing launch two inflatable Zodiac speedboats bobbed in the foggy water. Each had been dragged out from the fishing launch and inflated in the previous hour. One was a fourteen-foot model, big enough for five men. The smaller ten-foot model would take two. With the forty-horsepower outboards behind them, they would make thirty-five knots.

Major Simon Fallon was standing at the forward rail of the *Cutlass*. "They won't be long now," he said.

The three fast patrol boats now lay tethered beneath the *Argyll's* stern, noses pointed to where the *Freya* lay, five miles away through the fog.

There were four marines to each boat, armed with submachine carbines, grenades and knives. One boat, the *Sabre*, also carried four Royal Navy explosives experts, and this boat would make straight for the *Freya* to board and liberate her as soon as their radar had spotted the terrorist launch leaving the side of the supertanker and achieving a distance of three miles from her. The *Cutlass* and *Scimitar* would hunt down the terrorists before they could lose themselves in the maze of creeks and islands that make up the Dutch coast south of the Maas. Major Fallon would head the pursuit group in the *Cutlass*. Standing beside him, to his considerable disgust, was the man from the foreign office, Mr. Munro.

"Just stay well out of the way when we close with them," Fallon said. "They have submachine carbines and handguns. Personally, I don't see why you insist on coming."

"Let's just say I have a personal interest in these bastards," said Munro, "especially Mr. Svoboda."

"So have I," growled Fallon. "And Svoboda's mine."

As on the four other warships, the USS *Moran*'s radar scanners swept the ocean for signs of the launch moving away from the *Freya*'s side. Six fifteen came and went and there was no sign. Mike Manning had heard the news of the safe arrival of Mishkin and Lazareff in Israel with as much relief as Drake. In its turret the forward gun of the *Moran*, still loaded, moved away from the *Freya* and pointed at the empty sea.

AT TEN PAST EIGHT, Tel Aviv time, Lev Mishkin was standing in his cell when he felt a pain in his chest. A rock seemed to be growing fast inside him. He opened his mouth to scream, but the air was cut off. He pitched forward, face down, and died on the floor of the cell.

An Israeli policeman on guard outside the door with orders to peer inside every three minutes, pressed his eye to the judas-hole. He let out a yell of alarm and opened the locked door. Farther up the corridor, a colleague from in front of Lazareff's door ran to his assistance. Together they burst into Mishkin's cell and bent over the prostrate figure.

"He's dead," breathed one of the men. The other rushed into the corridor and hit the alarm button. Then they ran to Lazareff's cell. The second prisoner was doubled up on the bed, arms wrapped round himself as the paroxysms struck him.

"What's the matter," shouted one of the guards, but he spoke in Hebrew, which Lazareff did not understand. The dying man forced out four words in Russian. Both guards heard him clearly and later repeated the phrase to senior officers, who were able to translate it.

"Head . . . of . . . KGB . . . dead."

That was all he said. His mouth stopped moving; he lay on his side on the cot, sightless eyes staring at the blue uniforms in front of him.

The ringing bell brought the chief superintendent, a dozen other officers and the doctor who had been taking a coffee in the police chief's office. The doctor examined each prisoner rapidly. When he was done, he stalked out into the corridor.

"What the hell's happened?" the superintendent asked, following him out, a badly worried man.

"I can do a full autopsy later," said the doctor, "or maybe it will be taken out of my hands. But they've been poisoned."

"But they haven't eaten anything. They haven't drunk anything. Perhaps at the airport . . . on the plane. . . . ?"

"No," said the doctor, "a slow-acting poison would not work with such speed, and simultaneously. Each either administered himself, or was administered, a massive dose of instantaneous poison, which I suspect to be potassium cyanide, within the five to ten seconds before they died."

"That's not possible," shouted the police chief. "My men were outside the cells all the time. Both prisoners were searched before the entered the cells. There were no hidden poison capsules. Why would they commit suicide?"

"I don't know," said the doctor. "But they both died within seconds of the poison hitting them."

"I'm phoning the prime minister at once," said the chief superintendent grimly, and strode off to his office.

The prime minister's personal security adviser, an ex-soldier called Barak, took the police superintendent's call from Tel Aviv and informed Benyamin Golen of what had happened.

"Inside the cell itself?" echoed a stunned premier. "Then they must have taken the poison themselves."

"I don't think so," said Barak. "They had just arrived in freedom. They had every reason to want to live."

"Then who would want them dead?"

"The KGB, of course. One of them muttered something about the KGB, in Russian. It seems he was saying the head of the KGB wanted them dead."

"But they haven't been in the hands of the KGB. Twelve hours ago they were in Moabit gaol. Then for eight hours in the hands of the British. Then two hours with us. In our hands they ingested nothing. So how did they take in an instant-acting poison?"

Barak scratched his chin, a dawning gleam in his eye. "There is a way, Prime Minister. A delayed-action capsule."

He took a sheet of paper and drew a diagram. "It is possible to make a capsule like this. It has two halves; one is threaded so that it screws into the other half just before it is swallowed. One half of the capsule is ceramic, immune both to the acidic effects of the gastric juices of the human stomach, and to the much stronger acid inside it. The other half is plastic, tough enough to withstand the digestive juices, but not enough to resist the acid. In this portion lies the cyanide. Between the two is a copper wafer. The two halves are screwed together, breaking the seal in the ceramic half. The acid begins to burn away at the copper. Several hours later, depending on the thickness of the copper, the acid burns through it. It quickly cuts through the plastic of the second chamber, and the cyanide floods out into the body system. I believe the minimum delay is ten hours, by which time the indigestible capsule has reached the lower bowel. Once the poison is out, the blood absorbs it quickly and carries it to the heart."

Barak had seen his premier angry before, but he had never seen him white and trembling with rage. "They send me two men with poison pellets deep inside them," he whispered, "two walking time bombs, triggered to die when they are in our hands? Israel shall not be blamed for this outrage. Publish the news of the deaths at once. Do you understand? Immediately?"

"If the terrorists have not yet left the *Freya*," suggested Barak, "that news could reverse their plans to leave."

"The men responsible for poisoning Mishkin and Lazareff should have thought of that," snapped Premier Golen. "Any delay in the announcement, and Israel will be blamed for murdering them. And that I will not tolerate."

THE FOG rolled on, thickened, deepened, swirling around the *Cutlass*, *Sabre* and *Scimitar* as they lay under the stern of the *Argyll*. It shrouded the biggest tanker in the world at her mooring between the warships and the Dutch shore. The time was six thirty-five—ten minutes after Premier Golen's order.

At six forty-five all the terrorists but two climbed down into the larger of the inflatable speedboats. One of the five jumped into the old fishing launch that had brought them to the middle of the North Sea, and glanced upwards. From the rail above him, Andrew Drake nodded. The man pushed the starter button and the sturdy engine coughed into life. The prow of the launch was pointed due west, away from the Dutch coast, her wheel lashed with cord to hold her steady. The terrorist steadily increased the power of the engine, holding her in neutral gear.

Across the water, keen ears, human and electronic, had caught the sound of the motor; urgent commands and questions flashed from the *Argyll* to the circling Nimrod overhead.

Drake spoke quickly into his hand-held radio, and far up on the bridge Azamat Krim jammed down the *Freya*'s siren button. The air filled with the booming roar as the siren blew away the silence of the surrounding fog and the lapping water.

On the *Argyll* Captain Preston snorted with impatience. "They're trying to drown the sound of the launch engine. No matter. We'll have it on radar as soon as it leaves the *Freya*'s side."

Seconds later the terrorist in the launch slammed the gear into forward and the fishing boat, its engine revving high, pulled violently away from the *Freya*'s stern. The terrorist leaped for the swinging rope above him and let the empty boat churn out from under him. In two seconds it was lost in the fog, ploughing its way strongly towards the warships to the west.

The terrorist lowered himself into the speedboat where his four companions waited. The outboard coughed and roared. The inflatable dug its motor into the water, cleared the stern of the *Freya*, lifted its blunt nose high and tore away across the calm water towards Holland.

The radar operator in the Nimrod high above spotted the steel hull of the fishing launch instantly; the rubber-compound speedboat gave no reflector signal. "The launch is moving," he told the *Argyll* below him. "Hell, they're coming straight at you."

Captain Preston glanced at the radar display on his own bridge. "Get 'em," he said, and watched the blip separating itself from the great white blob that represented the *Freya*. "What the hell are they trying to do?"

"Shall we send the *Cutlass* to intercept?" asked the first officer.

"I'm not risking good men," said Preston. "Orders from Admiralty are quite specific. Wait till they're three miles out from the tanker then use the guns."

The other four Nato warships were asked not to open fire, but to leave the job to the *Argyll*. Her fore and aft five-inch guns swung smoothly onto target, waited, then opened fire. Somehow the launch survived the first salvo. Whatever was happening out there in the fog was invisible; only the radar could see the target boat.

And the radar could not tell its masters that no figure stood at the helm, no men crouched in her stern.

Andrew Drake and Azamat Krim sat quietly in their two-man speedboat close by the *Freya*. When they heard the first muffled boom of the *Argyll*'s guns, Drake nodded at Krim, who started the outboard engine. Drake released the rope from the *Freya* and the inflatable sped away eastwards, skimming the sea as the speed built up, its engine noise drowned by the roar of the *Freya*'s siren.

The *Argyll*'s sixth shell stopped the fishing launch with a direct hit. The explosive tore the launch apart, the fuel tank blew up and the steel-hulled boat sank like a stone.

"Let the *Sabre* go," said Captain Preston quietly. "They can board and liberate the *Freya* now."

The radar operator in the Nimrod peered closely at his screen. He could see all the warships, and the *Freya* to the east of them. But somewhere beyond the *Freya*, two tiny specks seemed to be moving away to the southeast; each was no bigger than the blip made by a medium-sized tin can; in fact they were the metallic covers to the outboard engine of two speeding inflatables. Tin cans do not move across the face of the ocean at thirty knots.

"Nimrod to *Argyll*, Nimrod to *Argyll*. . . ." The officers on the bridge listened to the news from the circling aircraft with shock. Two seconds later the *Cutlass* and the *Scimitar* were away, the booming roar of their twin diesel marine engines filling the fog around them. "Damn and blast them," shouted Major Fallon to the navy commander who stood with him in the tiny wheelhouse of the *Cutlass*, "how fast can we go?"

"Over forty knots," the commander shouted back.

Not enough, thought Adam Munro, both hands locked to a stanchion as the vessel shuddered and bucked like a runaway horse. The *Freya* was five miles away, the terrorists' speedboat another five beyond that. It would take them an hour to come level with the inflatable carrying Svoboda to safety in the creeks of Holland where he could lose himself. But he would be there in forty minutes.

The inflatable in which Andrew Drake and Azamat Krim were making for safety followed the traces of the wake made by their companions ten minutes ahead of them. It was odd, Drake thought, for the traces to remain on the sea's surface for so long.

On the bridge of the USS *Moran*, lying south of the *Freya*, Captain Mike Manning also studied his radar scanner. Away to the east he could spot the tiny blip of the racing speedboat. He looked at the gap between the refugee and the hunters charging after it. "They'll never catch it," he said, and gave an order to his executive officer. The five-inch forward gun of the *Moran* began to traverse slowly to the right, seeking a target through the fog.

A seaman appeared at the elbow of Captain Preston on the *Argyll*. "Just come over the news, sir. Those two men who were flown to Israel today, sir. They're dead. Died in their cells."

"Dead?" queried Captain Preston incredulously. "Then the whole bloody thing was for nothing. Wonder who could have done that. Better tell that foreign office chappie when he gets back. He'll be interested."

The sea was still flat calm for Andrew Drake, a slick, oily flatness unnatural in the North Sea. He and Krim were almost halfway to the Dutch coast when their engine coughed and coughed again.

"It's overheating," Azamat Krim shouted. He leaned out and dipped his hand in the water. It came out streaked with sticky brown crude oil. "It's blocking the cooling ducts," he said.

"They seem to be slowing down," the operator in the Nimrod informed the *Argyll*, who passed the information to the *Cutlass*.

"We can still get the bastards!" shouted Major Fallon.

The distance began to close rapidly. The inflatable was down to ten knots. What Fallon had forgotten was that the *Cutlass* was speeding towards the edge of a great lake of oil lying on the surface of the ocean. And their prey was in the centre of it.

Ten seconds later Azamat Krim's engine cut out. The silence was eerie. Far away they could hear the boom of the engines of *Cutlass* and *Scimitar* coming towards them through the fog. Krim scooped a double handful from the surface of the sea and held it out to Drake. "It's the oil we vented, Andrew."

"The *Argyll* says they've stopped," said the *Cutlass* commander to Fallon. "Perhaps they've hit that oil slick."

On the USS *Moran* gunnery officer Chuck Olsen reported to Manning, "We have range and direction."

"Open fire," said Manning calmly. "The nearest one first. Armour-piercing and star."

The commander of the *Cutlass* could not hear the shells, but the *Argyll* could, and told him to slow down. "What the hell are you doing?" shouted Major Fallon. "They can't be more than a mile or so ahead."

The answer came from the sky. Somewhere above them there was a sound like a rushing train as the first shells from the *Moran* homed in on their target. Three semi-armour-piercing shells missed the bobbing inflatable by a hundred yards. The starshells had proximity fuses. They exploded in blinding sheets of white light a few feet above the ocean surface, showering gobbets of burning magnesium over a wide area.

The men on the *Cutlass* were silent, seeing the fog ahead of them illuminated. Four cables to starboard the *Scimitar* was also hove-to, on the edge of the oil slick.

The magnesium dropped onto the oil, raising its temperature beyond its flashpoint. The sea caught fire; a gigantic plain, miles long and miles wide, began to glow; a ruddy red at first, then brighter and hotter.

It only lasted for fifteen seconds. In that time the oil on the sea blazed. For several seconds it reached five thousand degrees centigrade, burning off the fog for miles around, the white flames reaching five feet high off the surface of the water. In utter silence the sailors and marines gazed at the blistering inferno starting a hundred yards ahead of them. From the midst of the fire a single candle spurted, as if a petrol tank had exploded. From the heart of the flames, carrying across the water, a single human scream reached the ears of the sailors.

"*Shche ne vmerla Ukraina. . . .*"

Then it was gone. The flames died down, fluttered and waned. The fog closed in.

"What did that mean?" whispered the commander of the *Cutlass*. Major Fallon shrugged.

"Don't ask me. Some foreign lingo."

From beside them Adam Munro gazed at the last flickering glow of the dying flames. "Roughly translated," he said, "it means 'Ukraine will live again'."

Twenty-two

It was eight p.m. in Western Europe but ten in Moscow, and the Politburo meeting had been in session for an hour. Yefrem Vishnayev knew he was strong enough; there was no point in further discussion. He rose portentously to his feet.

"Comrades, we have heard the arguments for and against the so-called Treaty of Dublin. We have heard of the escape to Israel of the murderers Mishkin and Lazareff, men who it has been proved to you beyond doubt were responsible for assassinating our dear Comrade Yuri Ivanenko. My motion is as follows: that the Praesidium of the Supreme Soviet can no longer have confidence in the continued direction of our great nation by Comrade Rudin. Mr. Secretary-General, I demand a vote on the motion."

He sat down. There was silence. Even for those participating, the fall of a giant from Kremlin power is a terrifying moment.

"Those in favour of the motion. . . ." said Maxim Rudin.

Yefrem Vishnayev raised his hand. Kerensky followed suit. Vitautas the Lithuanian did likewise. There was a pause of several seconds. Mukhamed the Tadjik raised his hand. The telephone rang. Rudin answered it, listened and replaced the receiver.

"I should not, of course," he said impassively, "interrupt a vote, but the news just received is of some passing interest. Two hours ago Mishkin and Lazareff both died instantaneously in the central police station of Tel Aviv. A colleague fell to his death from a hotel balcony window outside that city. One hour ago two boatloads of the terrorists who had hijacked the *Freya* died in a sea of blazing oil. None of them ever opened their mouths. And now none of them ever will . . . . We were, I believe, in the midst of voting for Comrade Vishnayev's resolution. Those for the motion?"

No one moved. "Those against the motion?"

Vassili Petrov and Dmitri Rykov raised their hands. They were followed by Abrassov, Chavadze the Georgian, Shushkin and Stepanov. Petryanov, who had once voted for the Vishnayev faction, glanced at the raised hands, caught the drift and raised his own.

"May I," said Komarov of agriculture, "express my personal pleasure at being able to vote with complete confidence in favour of our secretary-general."

He raised his hand. Rudin smiled at him. Slug, he thought, I am personally going to stamp you into the garden path.

"Then with my own vote the issue is denied by nine votes to four," said Rudin. "I don't think there is any other business?"

Twelve hours later, Captain Thor Larsen stood once again on the bridge of the *Freya* and scanned the sea around him.

British marines had found and freed him. Navy demolition

experts had carefully plucked the detonators from the dynamite, bringing the charges gently up from the bowels of the ship to the deck. Strong hands had turned the steel cleats to the door behind which his crew had been imprisoned for sixty-four hours.

Gentle hands of a navy doctor had laid Thor Larsen on his bunk and tended his wounds. "You'll need surgery, of course," the doctor told the Norwegian. "And it'll be set up for the moment you arrive by helicopter in Rotterdam. OK?"

"Wrong," said Larsen. "I will go to Rotterdam, but I will go on the *Freya*."

During the dark hours the tugs and fireships had sprayed their emulsifier-concentrate onto the scum of oil which still clung to the water. Most had burned off in the single, brief holocaust caused by the magnesium shells of Captain Manning.

Just before dawn Thor Larsen awakened from a deep sleep. The chief steward helped him gently into his clothes, the full uniform of a senior captain of the Nordia Line. He slipped his bandaged hand carefully down the sleeve with the four gold rings, then hung the hand back in the sling round his neck.

At eight a.m. he stood beside his first and second officers on the bridge. The two pilots from Maas control were also there. With the inner channel barely fifty feet wider than the *Freya*, he really would need them this morning.

To Thor Larsen's surprise the sea to the north, south and west of him was crowded. Merchant vessels flying a dozen flags mingled with the warships of five NATO navies, all hove-to within a radius of three miles and outwards from that.

At two minutes past eight the gigantic propellers of the *Freya* began to turn, the massive anchor cable rumbled up from the ocean floor. From beneath her stern a maelstrom of white water appeared.

Little sirens like tin whistles, booming roars and shrill whoops echoed across the water as over a hundred sea captains gave the *Freya* the traditional sailor's greeting.

Thor Larsen looked at the crowded sea about him and the empty lane leading to Euro Buoy Number One. He turned to the pilot.

"Mister Pilot, pray set course for Rotterdam."

ON SUNDAY, 10 APRIL, in Saint Patrick's Hall, Dublin Castle, two men approached a great oak refectory table and took their seats. In the Minstrel Gallery the television cameras peered through the arcs of white light that bathed the table and beamed their images across the world.

Dmitri Rykov carefully scrawled his name for the Soviet Union on both copies of the Treaty of Dublin and passed the copies, bound in red Morocco leather, to David Lawrence, who signed for the United States. Within hours the first grain ships, waiting off Murmansk and Leningrad, Sebastopol and Odessa, moved forward to their berths. A week later the first combat units along the Iron Curtain began to pull back from the barbed wire line.

ON THURSDAY, 14 April the Politburo held its routine meeting. The last man to enter the room, having been delayed outside by a major of the Kremlin guard, was Yefrem Vishnayev.

When he came through the doorway, he observed that the faces of the other twelve members were all turned towards him. Maxim Rudin brooded at the centre place at the top of the T-shaped table. Down each side of the stem the chairs were all occupied. There was only one chair left vacant—the one at the far end of the table, facing up the length of it.

Impassively, Yefrem Vishnayev walked slowly forward to take his seat in the penal chair for his last Politburo meeting.

ON 18 April a small freighter rolled in the Black Sea swell, ten miles off the shore of Romania. Just before two a.m. a fast speedboat left the freighter and raced towards the shore. At three miles it halted and a marine took a powerful torch, pointed it towards the invisible sands and flashed a signal; three long dashes and three short. There was no answering light from the beach. The man repeated his signal four times. Still there was no answer.

The speedboat returned to the freighter. An hour later a message was transmitted to London. From London another message went in code to the British embassy in Moscow.

"Regret. Nightingale has not made the rendezvous."

ON 25 APRIL there was a plenary meeting of the full central committee of the Communist Party inside the Kremlin. The delegates had come from all over the Union.

Standing on the podium beneath the outsized head of Lenin, Maxim Rudin made them his farewell address. He spoke of world peace, and reminded one and all of the constant danger posed by the territorial and imperial ambitions of the capitalist West, occasionally aided by enemies of peace within the Soviet Union.

But, he went on with an admonishing finger, these secret co-plotters with the imperialists—the anti-peace faction—had been uncovered and rooted out, thanks to the eternal vigilance of the tireless Yuri Ivanenko, who had died a week earlier in a sanatorium after a long and gallant struggle against a heart ailment.

There were cries of condolence for the departed comrade, who had saved them all. Rudin raised a regretful hand for silence.

But, he told them, Ivanenko had been replaced since his infirmity began by his ever loyal comrade-in-arms, General Abrassov, who had completed the task of safeguarding the Soviet Union as the world's first champion of peace.

Maxim Rudin waited till the ovation for Abrassov was almost over before he raised his hands, and dropped his speaking tone.

As for himself, he had done what he could, but the time had come for him to depart.

The stunned silence was tangible.

He had toiled too long perhaps, and it had sapped his strength and his health. On the podium, his shoulders slumped with weariness. There were cries of "No . . . no. . . ."

He was an old man, Rudin said. And the time had come for him to admit openly that the doctors had informed him he had only a few more months to live. With his audience's permission he would lay down the burden of office and spend what little time remained to him in the countryside he loved so much.

One last question remained, said Rudin. He wished to retire in five days, on the last day of the month. The following morning was May Day, and a new man would stand atop Lenin's mausoleum to take the salute of the great parade. Who would that man be?

It should be a man of youth and vigour, of wisdom and unbounded patriotism; a man who had proved himself in the highest councils of the land. Such a man, Rudin proclaimed, the peoples of the fifteen socialist republics were lucky to have, in the person of Vassili Petrov. The election of Petrov to succeed Rudin was carried by acclamation.

Adam Munro was not present in the diplomatic gallery for the address. Since his meeting with Maxim Rudin his cover was blown and he could not function as an agent in Moscow. The ambassador and head of chancery regarded him with misgiving, and his name was carefully excluded from any diplomatic invitations. Sir Nigel Irvine had wished him to remain in London, or at least not to return to Moscow. But Munro had appealed personally to the prime minister to be allowed one last chance to ensure that the Nightingale was safe at least. His wish had been granted.

Now he hung about the city like a forlorn and unwanted party guest, hoping against hope that Valentina would contact him to indicate she was safe.

Once he tried her private telephone number. There was no answer. She could have been out, but he dared not risk it again. Following the fall of the Vishnayev faction, he was told he would be recalled to London at the end of the month and his resignation from the service would be gratefully accepted.

It was therefore surprising when a reception in St. George's Hall in the Kremlin Great Palace on the evening of 30 April was announced, and invitations arrived at the British embassy for the ambassador, the head of chancery, and Adam Munro. It was hinted to the embassy that Munro was expected to attend.

Over a hundred of the elite of the Soviet Union mingled with four times that number of foreign diplomats. Maxim Rudin moved among them like an old lion, accepting the plaudits of well-wishers as no more than his due.

Munro spotted him from afar, but he was not included in the list of those presented personally. Before midnight, pleading a natural tiredness, Rudin excused himself.

Twenty minutes later Adam Munro felt a touch at his arm. Standing behind him was an immaculate major in the uniform of the Kremlin's own praetorian guard. The major spoke to him in Russian. "Mr. Munro, please come with me."

Munro was not surprised; evidently his inclusion in the guest list had been a mistake; he was being asked to leave. But instead the major passed through into the high, octagonal Hall of St. Vladimir, up a wooden staircase guarded by a bronze grill and out into the warm starlight of Upper Saviour Square.

Munro followed him across the square and into the Terem Palace. Silent guards were at every door; each opened as the major approached and closed as they passed through. At a door at the far end of the Cross Chamber, the major paused and knocked. There was a gruff command from inside. The major opened the door, stood aside and indicated that Munro should enter.

The third chamber in the Terem Palace is the Throne Room, the holy of holies of the old tsars, most inaccessible of all the rooms. In red, gilt and mosaic tiles, with parquet floor and deep burgundy carpet, it is smaller and warmer than most of the other rooms, the place where the tsars worked or received emissaries in complete privacy. Standing staring out through the Petition Window was Maxim Rudin. He turned as Munro entered.

"So, Mr. Munro, you will be leaving us, I hear."

It had been twenty-seven days since Munro had seen him, in dressing gown, nursing a glass of milk, in his personal apartments in the arsenal. Now he was in a beautifully-cut Savile Row charcoal-grey suit, bearing the two Orders of Lenin and Hero of the Soviet Union on the left lapel. The Throne Room suited him better this way. "Yes, Mr. President," said Munro.

Maxim Rudin glanced at his watch. "In ten minutes, Mr. ex-President," he remarked. "Midnight I officially retire. You also I presume, will be retiring?"

The old fox knew perfectly well that his cover was blown the night he met him, thought Munro, and that he had to retire. "Yes, Mr. President, I shall be returning to London tomorrow."

Rudin did not approach him or hold out his hand. He stood across the room representing the one-time pinnacle of the tsarist empire, and nodded. "Then I shall wish you farewell, Mr. Munro."

He pressed a small onyx bell on a table, and behind Munro the door opened. "Goodbye, sir," said Munro.

He had half turned to go when Rudin spoke again. "Tell me, Mr. Munro, what do you think of our Red Square?"

Munro stopped, puzzled. It was a strange question for a man saying farewell. Munro answered carefully. "It is very impressive."

"Impressive, yes," said Rudin. "Not perhaps as elegant as your Berkeley Square, but sometimes, even here, you can hear a nightingale sing."

Munro stood as motionless as the painted saints on the ceiling above him. His stomach turned over. They had got her, and, unable to resist, she had told them all, even the reference to the old song.

"Will you shoot her?" he asked dully.

Rudin seemed genuinely amazed. "Shoot her? Why should we shoot her?"

"Then what will you do to her?"

The old Russian raised his eyebrows in mock surprise. "Do?

Nothing. She is a loyal woman, a patriot. She is also very fond of you, young man. Not in love, you understand, but genuinely fond. . . ."

"I don't understand," said Munro. "How can you know that?"

"She asked me to tell you," said Rudin. "She cannot see you again—ever. But she does not want you to fear for her. She is well, privileged, honoured among her own people. She asked me to tell you not to worry."

The dawning comprehension was almost as dizzying as the fear. Munro stared at Rudin as his disbelief faded.

"She was yours," he said dully, "she was yours all along. From the first contact in the woods, just after Vishnayev made his bid for war in Europe. She was working for you. . . ."

The grizzled Kremlin fox shrugged. "Mr. Munro," he growled, "how else could I get my messages to President Matthews with the absolute certainty that they would be believed?"

The impassive major returned and drew at his elbow; he was outside the Throne Room and the door closed behind him. Five minutes later he was shown out, on foot, through a small door in Red Square. The clock above his head struck midnight.

He turned left towards the National Hotel to find a taxi. A hundred yards further on, as he passed Lenin's mausoleum, to the surprise and outrage of a militiaman, he began to laugh.

Frederick Forsyth

This year Frederick Forsyth has two special reasons for celebration: the publication of *The Devil's Alternative*, which bids fair to be as hugely successful as his previous novels, and the birth this summer in Dublin of his second son, Shane.

Nowadays Forsyth and his Belfast-born wife Carrie live quietly in a spacious Victorian mansion in the Wicklow hills (with Shane and his two-year-old brother Stuart), but Forsyth's life has by no means been so quiet in the past. Born in Kent in 1938, his thirst for adventure was evident even when he was a schoolboy at Tonbridge. At the age of sixteen he used to disappear from organized sports to ride a forbidden motor-cycle to Rochester Flying Club for lessons. He qualified for his pilot's licence a few days after his seventeenth birthday. Three months later he was in southern Spain, frequenting the bullrings and practising in the arena at Malaga with other aspiring matadors. After a short spell as a pilot in the RAF he decided to become a journalist, because "it was the only job I could think of that might enable me to write, travel and keep more or less my own hours."

As a correspondent for Reuters, he travelled all over Europe, covering the OAS campaign against de Gaulle in Paris and spending a whole year as the sole Western reporter based behind the Iron Curtain in East Germany and Czechoslovakia. In 1965 he joined the BBC as a diplomatic correspondent, and this job took him all through Europe and the Middle East before he ended up covering the Biafran war which was then raging in West Africa.

These experiences gave him the vital background knowledge which has made his four major novels so chillingly convincing. *The Day of the Jackal* was based on an attempted assassination of de Gaulle which occurred while Forsyth was working in France; *The Odessa File* drew on his detailed knowledge of post-war Germany; *The Dogs of War* sprang from his experiences in Biafra. All were previous Condensed Books selections.

With his usual incredible speed, Frederick Forsyth wrote *The Devil's Alternative* in only forty-four days. He was lured out of self-chosen retirement to write this book after a five-year interval. Let us hope that in future he can be persuaded to give his readers yet another Forsyth "spectacular".

Friends and Friendly Beasts

by Gerald Durrell

ILLUSTRATED BY DAVID KNIGHT

A SELECTION FROM *MY FAMILY AND OTHER ANIMALS*,
PUBLISHED BY GRANADA PUBLISHING, *FILLETS OF PLAICE
THE GARDEN OF THE GODS* AND *THE PICNIC AND
SUCHLIKE PANDEMONIUM*, PUBLISHED BY COLLINS

The three episodes in *Friends and Friendly Beasts*, spanning twenty years of Gerald Durrell's life, have been specially selected by the editors of Condensed Books from his enchanting books about his family and his many friends, both human and animal.

In *The Rose-beetle Man*, set in the Corfu of Gerry's idyllic childhood, we meet the Durrell family in all its glorious eccentricity and charm, the friends the ten-year-old boy makes on the island, and some of the animals he owned. Five years later on the outbreak of war, the family reluctantly returned to England. In *A Transport of Terrapins* teenage Gerry makes the best of London life and finds himself a job in a pet shop, which leads to a number of amusing encounters.

Our final selection, *Maiden Voyage*, taken from Gerald Durrell's new book *The Picnic and Suchlike Pandemonium*, is a wickedly funny account of a nostalgic post-war journey to Greece. Carefully planned by Mrs. Durrell as a treat for the family, everything goes hilariously wrong.

Warm, affectionate and extremely funny, these stories will delight Durrell's admirers and make him many new friends.

The Rose-beetle Man

Corfu lies off the Albanian and Greek coastlines like a long, rust-eroded scimitar. The hilt of the scimitar is the mountain region of the island, for the most part barren with towering rock cliffs haunted by blue-rock thrushes and peregrine falcons. In the valleys of this region, however, where water gushes plentifully from the red and gold rocks, you get forests of almond and walnut trees, casting shade as cool as a well, thick battalions of spear-like cypress and silver-trunked fig trees with leaves as large as a salver. The blade of the scimitar is made up of rolling greeny-silver eiderdowns of giant olives, some reputedly over five hundred years old and each one unique in its hunched, arthritic shape, its trunk pitted with a hundred holes like a pumice stone.

When my family first came to live on the island in 1935, we settled into a bright crushed-strawberry-pink villa with green shutters that crouched in a cathedral-like grove of olives that sloped down the hillside to the sea. We were all quite young at that time: Larry, the eldest of the family, was twenty-three; Leslie was nineteen; Margo eighteen; while I was only ten. We were never quite certain of my widowed mother's age, as she could never remember her date of birth.

Each morning, when I woke, the bedroom shutters would be barred with gold from the rising sun. The air would be full of the scent of charcoal, of eager cockcrows and the melancholy tune of the goat-bells as the flocks were driven out to pasture.

We ate breakfast out in the garden, under tangerine trees. The sky was fresh and shining, a clear milky opal. Breakfast was, on the whole, a leisurely and silent meal, but by the end of it the influence of the coffee, toast and eggs made itself felt, and we started to revive, to tell each other what we intended to do and why we intended to do it. I seldom joined in these discussions, for I knew perfectly well what I intended to do, and would concentrate on finishing my food as rapidly as possible.

"Must you gulp and slush your food like that?" Larry would inquire in a pained voice, delicately picking his teeth with a matchstick.

"Eat it slowly, dear," Mother would murmur, "there's no hurry."

No hurry? With Roger, my dog, waiting at the garden gate, an alert mountain of black curls, watching for me with eager brown eyes? No hurry, with the first sleepy cicadas starting to fiddle experimentally among the olives? No hurry, with the island waiting, morning-cool, to be explored?

Finishing at last, I would slip from the table and saunter towards the garden gate, where Roger sat gazing at me with a questioning air. Together we would peer through the wrought-iron gates into the olive groves beyond. Roger would place a large black paw on the gate, and then look at me, lifting one side of his upper lip, displaying his white teeth in a lopsided, ingratiating grin, his stumpy tail wagging in a blur of excitement. Then I would fetch my matchboxes and my butterfly net, the garden gate would creak open and clang shut, and Roger would be off through the olive groves as swiftly as a cloud-shadow.

In those early days of exploration Roger was my constant companion. Together we ventured farther and farther afield, discovering quiet, remote olive groves and narrow valleys where the cypress trees cast a cloak of mysterious, inky shadow. He was the perfect companion for an adventure, affectionate without exuberance, brave without being belligerent, intelligent and full of good-humoured tolerance for my eccentricities. If I found something that interested me—an ant's nest, a spider wrapping up a fly in swaddling clothes of silk—Roger sat down and waited until I had finished examining it. If he thought I was taking too long, he gave a gentle yawn, sighed deeply and started to wag his tail.

During these trips Roger and I came to know and be known by

a great number of people in various parts of the surrounding countryside. One was the immensely fat and cheerful Agathi, who lived in a tiny tumbledown cottage. She was always sitting outside with a spindle of sheep's wool, twining and pulling it into coarse thread. She must have been well over seventy, but her hair was still black and lustrous, plaited carefully and wound round a pair of polished cow's horns, an ornament that some of the older peasant women adopted. As she sat in the sun, like a great black toad with a scarlet head-dress draped over the cow's horns, the bobbin of wool would rise and fall, twisting like a top, her fingers busy unravelling and plucking, as she sang.

Sitting on an old tin in the sun, eating grapes or pomegranates from her garden, I would sing the peasant songs with her, and she would break off now and then to correct my pronunciation. We sang the gay, rousing song of the river, "Vangeliò", and of how it dropped from the mountains, making the gardens rich, the fields fertile and the trees heavy with fruit. Then we would strike a mournful note and sing, perhaps, the slow, lilting song called "Why are you leaving me?" We were almost overcome by this one, and would wail out the long, soulful lyrics, our voices quavering. When we came to the most heartrending bit, Agathi would clasp her hands to her great breasts, her black eyes would become misty and sad, and her chins would tremble with emotion.

Then she would turn to me and say, "What fools we are, sitting here in the sun, singing. And of love too! I am too old for it and you are too young, and yet we waste our time singing about it. Ah, well, let's have a glass of wine, eh?"

Apart from Agathi, the person I liked best was the old shepherd Yani, a tall, slouching man with a great hooked nose like an eagle, and incredible moustaches. I first met him one hot afternoon when Roger and I had spent an exhausting hour trying to dig a large green lizard out of its hole in a stone wall. At length, unsuccessful, sweaty and tired, we had flung ourselves down beneath five little cypress trees that cast a neat square of shadow on the sunbleached grass.

Lying there, I heard the gentle, drowsy tinkling of a goat-bell, and presently the herds wandered past us, pausing to stare with vacant yellow eyes, bleat sneeringly and then move on. The soft sound of the bells had a soothing effect on me, and by the time they had drifted slowly past and the shepherd appeared I was nearly asleep. He stopped and looked at me, his little black eyes fierce under his shaggy brows.

"Good afternoon," he greeted me gruffly; "you are the foreigner . . . the little English lord?"

By then I was used to the curious peasant idea that all English people were lords, and I admitted that that's who I was.

"I will tell you something, little lord," he said; "it is dangerous for you to lie here, beneath these trees."

I asked why he thought they were dangerous.

"Ah, you may sit under them, yes. They cast a good shadow, cold as well-water; but that's the trouble, they tempt you to sleep. And you must never, for any reason, sleep beneath a cypress."

He paused, stroked his moustache, waited for me to ask why, and then went on: "*Why?* Because cypresses are dangerous. While you sleep, their roots grow into your brains and steal them, and when you wake up you are mad, head as empty as a whistle. So be warned, little lord, and don't sleep here."

He gave a fierce glance at the dark blades of the cypress and then picked his way carefully through the myrtle bushes to where his goats grazed, scattered about the hill, their great udders swinging.

One of the most weird and fascinating characters I used to meet during my travels was the Rose-beetle Man. I first saw him on a high, lonely road leading to one of the remote mountain villages. I could hear him long before I could see him, for he was playing a rippling tune on a shepherd's pipe, breaking off now and then to sing a few words in a curious, nasal voice. As he rounded the corner I stopped and stared at him in amazement.

He had a sharp, foxlike face with large, slanting, vacant-looking eyes of such a dark brown that they appeared black. He was short and slight, with a thinness about his wrists and neck that argued a lack of food. On his head was a shapeless hat with a very wide, floppy brim, speckled and smeared with dust. In the band were stuck a fluttering forest of feathers: cock feathers, hoopoe feathers, owl feathers, the wing of a kingfisher, the claw of a hawk, and a large dirty white feather that may have come from a swan. His shirt was frayed and grey with sweat, and round the neck dangled an enormous cravat of the most startling blue satin. His shapeless coat had patches of different hues here and there; on the sleeve a bit of white cloth with a design of rosebuds; on the shoulder a triangular patch of wine-red and white spots. The pockets of this garment bulged with combs, balloons, little coloured pictures of the saints, olivewood carvings of animals, cheap mirrors, a riot of handkerchiefs, and long twisted rolls of bread decorated with seeds. His patched trousers drooped over a pair of scarlet leather shoes with upturned toes decorated with large black-and-white pompons. This extraordinary character carried on his back bamboo cages full of pigeons and young chickens, several mysterious sacks and a large bunch of fresh green leeks. With one hand he held his pipe to his mouth, and in the other a number of lengths of cotton, to each of which was tied an almond-size rose-beetle, glittering golden-green in the sun, all of them flying round his hat with desperate, deep buzzings, trying to escape from the thread tied firmly round their waists.

When he saw us the Rose-beetle Man stopped, gave a very exaggerated start, doffed his ridiculous hat and swept me a low bow. Then he smiled, put on his hat again, raised his hands and waggled his long, bony fingers at me. Amused and rather startled by this apparition, I politely bade him good day and asked him if he had been to some fiesta. He nodded his head vigorously, raised his pipe to his lips and played a lilting little tune on it, pranced a few steps in the dust of the road, and then stopped and jerked his thumb over his shoulder, pointing back the way he had come. He smiled, patted his pockets and rubbed his forefinger and thumb in the Greek way of expressing money. I suddenly realized that he must be dumb. So, standing in the middle of the road, I carried on a conversation with him and he replied with a very clever pantomime. I asked what the rose-beetles were for, and why he had them tied with pieces of cotton. Pointing up at the sky, he stretched his arms out and gave a deep nasal buzzing, while he banked and swooped across the road. Aeroplane, any fool could see that. Then he pointed to the beetles, held out his hand to denote children and whirled his stock of beetles around his head.

Exhausted by his explanation, he sat down by the edge of the road and played a short tune on his flute, breaking off to sing in a series of strange gruntings and tenor squeaks. He produced these sounds with such verve and such wonderful facial expressions that you were convinced they really meant something. Presently he stuffed his flute into his bulging pocket and then swung a small sack off his shoulder, undid it and, to my delight and astonishment, half a dozen tortoises tumbled into the dusty road. Their shells had been polished with oil until they shone, and he had decorated their front legs with little red bows. Slowly and ponderously they unpacked their heads and legs from their gleaming shells and doggedly set off down the road. I watched them, fascinated; the one that particularly took my fancy was quite a small one with a shell about the size of a teacup. Its shell was chestnut, caramel and amber, its eyes were bright and its walk alert. I sat contemplating it for a long time. I convinced myself that the family would greet its arrival at the villa with tremendous enthusiasm. The fact that I had no money on me did not worry me in the slightest, for I would simply tell the man to call at the villa for payment the next day. It never occurred to me that he might not trust me. The fact that I was English was sufficient, for the islanders had a love and respect for the Englishman out of proportion to his worth. I asked the Rose-beetle Man the price of the little tortoise. He held up both hands, fingers spread out. However, I hadn't watched the peasants transacting business for nothing. I shook my head firmly and held up two fingers. He closed his eyes in horror at the thought, and held up nine fingers; I held up three; he shook his head, and after some thought held up six fingers; I, in return, held up five. The Rose-beetle Man shook his head, and sighed deeply and sorrowfully, so we sat in silence and stared at the tortoises crawling heavily and uncertainly about the road. Presently the Rose-beetle Man indicated the little tortoise and held up six fingers again. I shook my head and held up five. Roger yawned loudly; he was thoroughly bored by this silent bargaining. The Rose-beetle Man picked up the reptile and showed me in pantomime how smooth and lovely its shell was, how erect its head, how pointed its nails. I remained implacable. He shrugged, handed me the tortoise and held up five fingers.

Then I told him I had no money, and that he would have to come the next day to the villa, and he nodded as if it were the most natural thing in the world. Excited by owning this new pet, I wanted to get back home as quickly as possible to show it to everyone, so I thanked him and hurried off along the road.

The new arrival was christened Achilles, and he turned out to be a most intelligent and lovable beast, possessed of a peculiar sense of humour. At first he was tethered by a leg in the garden, but as he grew tamer we let him go where he pleased. He learned his name in a very short time, and we had only to call out once or twice and then wait patiently for a while until he appeared, lumbering along on tiptoe, his head and neck outstretched eagerly. He loved being fed, and would squat regally in the sun while we held out bits of lettuce, dandelions or grapes for him. He loved grapes as much as Roger did, so there was always great rivalry. Achilles would sit mumbling the grapes in his mouth, the juice running down his chin and Roger would lie nearby, his mouth drooling. When the feeding was over, if I didn't keep an eye on him, Roger would creep up to Achilles and lick his front vigorously in an attempt to get the dribbling grape juice. Achilles, affronted at such a liberty, would snap at Roger's nose, and retreat into his shell with an indignant wheeze.

But the fruit that Achilles liked best were wild strawberries. He would become positively hysterical at the mere sight of them, lumbering to and fro, gazing at you pleadingly with his tiny boot-button eyes. As well as developing a passion for strawberries, Achilles also developed a passion for human company. Let anyone come to sit in the garden, before long there would be a rustling among the sweet williams, and Achilles's wrinkled and earnest face would be poked through. If you were sitting in a chair, he would sink into a deep and peaceful sleep at your feet, his head drooping out of his shell, his nose resting on the ground. If, however, you were lying on a rug, sunbathing, Achilles would surge onto the rug with an expression of bemused good humour on his face. He would survey you thoughtfully and then choose a portion of your anatomy on which to practise mountaineering. Suddenly to have the sharp claws of a determined tortoise embedded in your thigh is not conducive to relaxation. If you shook him off and moved the rug it would only give temporary respite, for Achilles would circle the garden grimly until he found you again. This habit became so tiresome that, after many complaints from the family, I had to lock him up whenever we lay in the garden. Then one day the garden gate was left open and Achilles was nowhere to be found. Search parties were immediately organized, and the family, who up till then spent most of their time openly making threats against the reptile's life, wandered about the olive groves, shouting, "Achilles . . . strawberries, Achilles . . . strawberries . . . ." At length we found him. He had fallen into a disused well, the mouth of which was almost covered by ferns. He was, to our regret, quite dead. Even Leslie's attempts at artificial respiration, and Margo's suggestion of forcing strawberries down his throat (to give him, as she explained, something to live for), failed to get any response. So, mournfully and solemnly, his corpse was buried in the garden under a small strawberry plant (Mother's suggestion). A short funeral address, written and read in a trembling voice by Larry, made the occasion a memorable one.

For some time after this the Rose-beetle Man would turn up at the villa fairly regularly with some new addition to my growing menagerie: a frog, perhaps, or a sparrow with a broken wing.

One spring, when I was up on the hillside picking wine-coloured anemones for Mother, I became aware that he was down on the road below piping an urgent call on his flute. I hurried down the hill, and said "good morning". He smiled and, doffing his floppy hat with an exaggerated bow. The beetles, tied to its shapeless brim, buzzed sleepily on the end of their strings like a flock of captive emeralds. Presently, after inquiring after my health by leaning forward and peering anxiously into my face, he told me that he was well by playing a gay, rippling tune on his flute and then drawing in great lungfuls of warm spring air, his eyes closed in ecstasy. Thus having disposed of the courtesies, we got down to serious business.

What, I inquired, did he want of me? He raised his flute to his lips, gave a plaintive, quavering hoot, and then, taking the flute from his lips, opened his eyes wide and hissed, swaying from side to side and occasionally snapping his teeth together. As an imitation of an angry owl it was so perfect that I almost expected the Rose-beetle Man to fly away. My heart beat with excitement, for I had long wanted a mate for my scops owl, Ulysses. But when I asked him the Rose-beetle Man laughed to scorn my idea of anything so common as a scops owl and carefully tipped the contents of a large cloth bag at my feet.

To say that I was struck speechless was putting it mildly, for there in the white dust tumbled three huge owlets, hissing and swaying and beak-cracking in what seemed to be a parody of the Rose-beetle Man, their tangerine-golden eyes enormous with rage and fear. They were baby eagle owls and, as such, so rare as to be a prize almost beyond the dreams of avarice. I knew I must have them. The fact that the acquisition of the three voracious owls would send the meat bill up was neither here nor there.

I squatted down by the owlets, and as I stroked them into a state of semi-somnolence I bargained silently with the Rose-beetle Man. But it was a buyer's market and he knew it; who else in the length and breadth of the island would be mad enough to buy not one but three baby eagle owls? Eventually the bargain was struck.

As I was temporarily embarrassed financially, I explained to the Rose-beetle Man that he would have to wait for payment until the beginning of next month when my pocket money was due. I would, I explained, leave the money with our mutual friend Yani at the café on the crossroads where the Rose-beetle Man could pick it up during one of his peregrinations across the countryside. Thus having dealt with the sordid, commercial side of the transaction, we shared a stone bottle of ginger beer from the Rose-beetle Man's capacious pack. Then I placed my precious owls carefully in their bag and continued on my way home.

It was the lusty cries that the owlets gave that suddenly brought home to me the culinary implications of my new acquisitions. It was obvious that the Rose-beetle Man had not fed his charges and judging from the noise they were making they were extremely hungry. I could see I would have to rely on my mother's unfailing kindness of heart.

I found her ensconced in the kitchen, stirring frantically at a huge, aromatically bubbling cauldron, frowning at a cookbook in one hand, her spectacles misty, her lips moving silently as she read. I produced my owls with the air of one who is conferring a gift of inestimable value. My mother glanced at the three hissing, swaying balls of down.

"Very nice, dear," she said in an absent-minded tone of voice. "Put them somewhere safe, won't you?"

I said they would be incarcerated in my room and that nobody would know that I had got them.

"That's right," said Mother, glancing nervously at the owls. "You know how Larry feels about more pets."

I did indeed, and I intended to keep their arrival a secret from him at all costs. There was just one minor problem, I explained, and that was that the owls were hungry—were, in fact, starving.

"Poor little things," said Mother, her sympathies immediately aroused. "Give them some bread and milk."

I explained that owls ate meat. Had Mother perhaps a fragment of meat she could lend me so that the owls did not die?

"Well, I'm a bit short of meat," said Mother. "We're having chops for lunch. Go and see what's in the icebox."

I went and peered into the icy, misty interior of our massive icebox. All I could unearth were the ten chops for lunch and even these were hardly enough for three famished eagle owls. I went back with this news to the kitchen.

At that moment, one of the babies swayed so violently he fell over and I was quick to point this out to Mother as an example of how weak they were getting.

"Well, I suppose you'd better take the chops then," said Mother, harassed. "We'll just have to have vegetable curry for lunch."

Triumphantly, I carried the owls and the chops to my bedroom and stuffed the hungry babies full of meat.

As a consequence of the owls' arrival we sat down to lunch rather late. "I'm sorry we're not earlier," said Mother, uncovering a tureen and letting loose a cloud of curry-scented steam, "but the potatoes simply wouldn't cook for some reason."

"I thought we were going to have chops," complained Larry aggrievedly. "I spent all morning getting my taste buds on tiptoe with the thought of chops. What happened to them?"

"I'm afraid it's the owls, dear," said Mother apologetically. "They have such huge appetites."

Larry paused, a spoonful of curry halfway to his mouth. "Owls?" he said, staring at Mother. "What owls?"

"Oh!" said Mother, flustered, having realized that she had made a tactical error. "Just owls . . . birds, you know . . . nothing to worry about."

"Are we having a plague of owls?" Larry inquired. "Are they attacking the larder and zooming out with bunches of chops in their talons?"

"No, no, dear, they're only babies. They have the most beautiful eyes, and they were simply starving."

"Bet they're some new creature of Gerry's," said Leslie sourly. "I heard him crooning to something before lunch."

"Then he's got to release them," barked Larry.

"Nonsense, dear. After all, it's only some baby owls."

"Only!" said Larry bitingly. "He's already got one owl and we know that to our cost."

"Ulysses is a very sweet bird," put in Margo defensively.

351

"Well, he might be sweet to you," said Larry, "but he hasn't come and vomited up all the bits of food he has no further use for all over your bed."

"I think we've talked quite enough about the owls," said Mother firmly. "Who's going to be in for tea?"

It transpired that we were all going to be in for tea.

"I'm making some scones," said Mother, and sighs of satisfaction ran round the table, for Mother's scones, wearing cloaks of home-made strawberry jam, butter and cream, were a delicacy all of us adored. "Mrs. Vadrudakis is coming to tea so I want you to behave," Mother went on.

Larry groaned. "Who the hell is Mrs. Vadrudakis?" he asked. "Some old bore, I suppose?"

"Now don't start," said Mother severely. "She sounds a very nice woman from her letter; she wants my advice. She's very distressed by the way the peasants keep their animals. You know how thin the dogs and cats are, and those poor donkeys with sores. Well, she wants to start a society for the elimination of cruelty to animals here in Corfu, rather like the RSPCA, you know. And she wants us to help her."

"She doesn't get my help," said Larry firmly. "I'm not helping any society to prevent cruelty to animals. I'd help them to promote cruelty. If this Vadrudakis woman spent a week in this house she'd feel the same. She'd go round strangling owls with her bare hands."

"Well, I want you all to be polite," said Mother firmly, adding, "and you're not to mention owls, Larry. She might think we're peculiar."

"We are," concluded Larry with feeling.

After lunch I discovered that Larry had alienated the two people who might have been his allies in his anti-owl campaign, Margo and Leslie.

Margo, on seeing the owlets, went into raptures. She had just acquired the art of knitting and, with lavish generosity, offered to knit anything I wanted for the owls. I toyed with the idea of having them all dressed in identical, striped pullovers but discarded this as impractical.

Leslie offered to shoot a supply of sparrows for me. Laboriously, for mathematics was not my strong point, I worked out how many sparrows (supplemented with meat) I would need a week and took the result to Leslie in his room, where he was cleaning a magnificent old Turkish muzzle-loader.

"Yes . . . OK," he said, looking at my figures. "I'll get 'em for you. I'd better use the air rifle."

So, armed with the air rifle and a large paper bag, we went round the back of the villa. Leslie loaded the gun, leaned back against the trunk of an olive tree and started shooting. That year we had a plague of sparrows and the roof of the villa was thick with them. As they were picked off by Leslie's excellent marksmanship they rolled down the roof and fell to the ground, where I collected them.

After the first few shots, the sparrows retreated to the apex of the roof. Here Leslie could still shoot them but they rolled down to fall on the veranda on the other side of the house.

He continued shooting for some time, rarely missing, and each faint "thunk" of the rifle coincided with the disappearance of a sparrow from the rooftop.

Holding my paper bag, I went around to the front of the house, and saw, to my consternation, that Mrs. Vadrudakis, whom we had forgotten, had arrived for tea. She and Mother were sitting somewhat stiffly on the veranda clasping cups of tea, surrounded by the bloodstained corpses of sparrows.

"Yes," Mother was saying, obviously hoping that her visitor had not noticed the rain of dead birds, "yes, we're all great animal lovers."

"I hear this," said Mrs. Vadrudakis, smiling benevolently. "I hear you lof animals like me."

"Oh, yes," said Mother. "We keep so many pets."

She smiled nervously at Mrs. Vadrudakis, and, at that moment, a dead sparrow fell into the strawberry jam.

Mother stared at it as though hypnotized; at last, she moistened her lips and smiled at Mrs. Vadrudakis, who was sitting with her cup poised, a look of horror on her face.

"A sparrow," Mother pointed out weakly. "They . . . er . . . seem to be dying a lot this year."

At that moment, Leslie, carrying the air rifle, strode out of the house. "Have I killed enough?" he inquired.

The next ten minutes were fraught with emotion. Mother kept saying that she was sure the sparrows had not suffered. Mrs. Vadrudakis said that we were all fiends in human shape. Leslie, loudly and belligerently, went on repeating that it was a lot of bloody fuss about nothing and, anyway, owls ate sparrows and did Mrs. Vadrudakis want the owls to starve? But Mrs. Vadrudakis refused to be comforted. She wrapped herself, a tragic and outraged figure, in her cloak, shudderingly picked her way through the sparrows' corpses, got into her cab and was driven away through the olive groves at a brisk trot.

"I do wish you children wouldn't do things like that," said Mother, shakily pouring herself a cup of tea while I picked up the sparrows.

"Well, how was I to know the old fool was out here?" said Leslie indignantly. "I can't be expected to see through the house, can I?"

Two pots of tea and several aspirins later, Mother was beginning to feel better. I was sitting on the veranda giving her a lecture on owls, to which she was only half listening, saying, "Yes, dear, how interesting," at intervals, when she was suddenly galvanized by a roar of rage from inside the villa.

"Oh dear," she moaned. "What is it now?"

Larry strode out onto the veranda. "Mother!" he shouted. "This has got to stop!"

"Now, now, dear, don't shout. What's the matter?" Mother inquired.

"It's like living in a bloody natural history museum! Life here is intolerable."

"But what's the matter, dear?" Mother asked, bewildered.

"I go to get myself a drink from the icebox and what do I find?"

"What do you find, dear?" asked Mother with interest.

"Sparrows!" bellowed Larry. "Bloody great bags of suppurating unhygienic sparrows!"

It was not my day.

A Transport of Terrapins

Towards the end of 1939, when it looked as though war was inevitable, my family uprooted itself from Corfu and came back to England. We settled for a time in a flat in London while my mother made repeated forays into the English countryside in search of a house. And while she was doing this I was free to explore London, which I found fascinating. After all, the biggest metropolis I was used to was the town of Corfu, about the size of a small English market town, and so the great sprawling mass of London had hundreds of exciting secrets for me to discover.

Quite close to our flat was a shop that always had my undivided attention. It was called "The Aquarium", and its window was full of great tanks full of brightly coloured fish and rows of glass-fronted boxes that contained grass snakes, pine snakes, great green lizards and bulbous-eyed toads. I had a great desire to possess these beautiful creatures, but as I already had a whole host of birds and a marmoset in the flat, I felt that the introduction of any other livestock would bring down the wrath of the family upon me, and so I could only gaze longingly at these lovely reptiles.

Then, one morning, when I happened to pass the shop, my attention was riveted by a notice leaning against an aquarium. It said, "Wanted: Young, reliable assistant".

"They've got a job going in that pet shop down the road," I said to my mother when I got back to the flat.

"Have they, dear?" she said, not really taking any notice.

"Yes. They said they want a young, reliable assistant. I . . . I thought of applying for it," I said carelessly.

"What a good idea," said Larry. "Then perhaps you could take all your animals there."

"How much do you think they'd pay?" I asked.

"Not very much, I shouldn't think," said Larry. "I doubt that you are what they mean by reliable. And are you old enough?"

"I'm almost sixteen," I said.

"Well, go and have a shot at it," he suggested.

So the following morning I went down to the pet shop. A short, dark man with very large horn-rimmed spectacles danced across the floor towards me. "Good morning! Good morning, sir!" he said. "What can I do for you?"

"You, um . . . you want an assistant . . ." I said.

He cocked his head on one side and his eyes grew behind his spectacles. "Do you mean to say you want the job?"

"Er . . . yes," I said.

"Have you any experience?" he inquired doubtfully.

"Oh, I've had plenty of experience," I said. "I've always kept reptiles and fish and things like that."

The little man looked at me. "How old are you?" he asked.

"Sixteen . . . nearly seventeen," I lied.

"Well," he said, "we can't afford to pay very much, you know. I could start you off at one pound ten."

"That's all right," I said. "When do I start?"

"You'd better start on Monday," he said. "Then I can get all your cards stamped up and straight. Otherwise we get in such a muddle, don't we? Now, my name's Mr. Romilly."

I told him my name and we shook hands rather formally, and then we stood looking at each other. It was obvious that he had never employed anybody before and did not know quite what the form was. I thought perhaps I ought to help him out.

"Perhaps you could just show me round," I suggested, "and tell me a few things that you will want me to do."

"Oh, what an excellent idea," said Mr. Romilly. "Excellent!"

He danced round the shop waving his hands like butterfly wings and showed me how to clean out a fish tank, how to feed the frogs and toads, and where the brush and broom were. Under the shop was a large cellar where stores were kept, and it included a constantly running tap that dripped into a large bowl containing what at first glance appeared to be a raw sheep's heart. This, on close inspection, turned out to be a closely knitted ball of threadlike tubifex worms. These bright red worms were the favourite food of all the fish and some of the amphibians and reptiles as well. I discovered that as well as the delightful things in the window there were hosts of other creatures in the shop—cases full of tortoises and treacle-shiny snakes, tanks full of moist, gulping frogs, and newts with frilled tails like pennants. The shop was, as far as I was concerned, a Garden of Eden.

"Now," said Mr. Romilly, when he had shown me everything, "you start at nine o'clock sharp on Monday, hm? Don't be late, will you?"

Nothing short of death would have prevented me from being there at nine o'clock on Monday, so at ten to nine I paced the pavement outside the shop until eventually Mr. Romilly appeared, waving his bunch of keys musically.

"Good morning," he trilled. "I'm glad to see you're on time. What a good start."

In the shop I started on the first chores of the day, sweeping the comparatively spotless floor and then feeding little knots of wriggling tubifex to the fishes.

I very soon discovered that Mr. Romilly, though kindly, had little or no knowledge of the creatures in his care. Most of the cages and fish tanks were unsuitably decorated for the occupants' comfort. Also, Mr. Romilly worked on the theory that if you got an animal to eat one thing, you then went on feeding it with that thing indefinitely. I decided to take a hand in brightening up the lives of our charges, but I would have to move cautiously.

"Don't you think the lizards and toads would like a change from mealworms, Mr. Romilly?" I said one day.

"A change?" said Mr. Romilly, his eyes widening behind his spectacles. "What sort of change?"

"Well," I said, "how about wood lice? I always used to feed my reptiles on wood lice."

"It won't do them any harm, will it?" he asked anxiously.

"No," I said, "they love wood lice. It gives them variety."

I spent one afternoon in the park collecting a very large tin full of wood lice, which I kept in decaying leaves down in the cellar. When I thought that the frogs and the toads and the lizards had

357

got a bit bored with the mealworms, I would give them some wood lice. At first, Mr. Romilly used to peer into the cages with a fearful look on his face, as though he expected to see all the reptiles and amphibians dead. But when he found that they not only thrived on this new mixture but even started to croak in their cages, his enthusiasm knew no bounds.

My next little effort concerned two very large and benign leopard toads from North Africa. Now, Mr. Romilly's idea of Africa was an endless desert where the sun shone day and night and where the temperature was never anything less than about a hundred and ninety in the shade, if indeed any shade was to be found. So in consequence he had incarcerated these two poor toads in a small glass-fronted cage with a couple of brilliant electric lights above them. They sat on a pile of plain white sand, they had no rocks to hide under, and the only time the temperature dropped at all was at night when we switched off the light in the shop. In consequence, their eyes had become milky, their skins dry and flaky, and the soles of their feet were raw.

I knew that suggesting to Mr. Romilly anything so drastic as putting them into a new cage with some damp moss would horrify him, so I started surreptitiously. I pinched some olive oil from my mother's kitchen for a start, and when Mr. Romilly went out to have his lunch, I massaged the oil into the skin of both toads. This improved the flakiness. I then got some ointment from the chemist and anointed their feet with it. I also got some Golden Eye Ointment, and applied it to their eyes with miraculous results. Then, every time Mr. Romilly had his lunch hour I would give them a warm spray and this they loved. They would sit there, gulping benignly, blinking their eyes and, if I moved the spray a little, they would shuffle across the floor of their cage to get under it again. One day I put a small section of moss in the cage and both toads immediately burrowed under it.

"Oh, look, Mr. Romilly," I said with well-simulated surprise, "I put a bit of moss in the toads' cage by mistake, and they seem to like it."

"Moss?" said Mr. Romilly. "Moss? But they live in the desert."

"Well, I think some parts of the desert have got a bit of vegetation," I said. "Cactuses and things. Anyway, they seem to like it, don't they?"

"They certainly do," said Mr. Romilly. "Do you think we ought

358

to leave it in? They can't eat it and strangle themselves with it, can they?"

"I don't think they will," I said reassuringly.

So from then onwards my two lovely toads had a bit of moss to hide under and, what was more important, a bed of moss to sit on, and their feet soon healed up.

The next thing that I wanted to do was to decorate the cages and tanks to try and make them look more attractive. Now, this was a task that Mr. Romilly always undertook himself, and he did it with a dogged persistence. I don't think that he really enjoyed it, but felt that, as the senior member of the firm, as it were, it was his duty.

"Mr. Romilly," I said one day. "I've got nothing to do at the moment. You wouldn't let me decorate a fish tank, would you? I'd love to learn how to do them as well as you do."

"Well, now," said Mr. Romilly, blushing. "Well, now, I wouldn't say I was all that good . . . ."

"Oh, I think you do it beautifully," I said.

"Well, perhaps you can do a small one," said Mr. Romilly. "Now, let's see . . . . Yes, now, that mollies' tank over there. They need clearing out."

And so, with the aid of a little net, I moved all the black mollies, as dark and glistening as little olives, out of their tank and into a spare one. Then I emptied their tank and scrubbed it out and called Mr. Romilly.

"Now," he said. "You put some sand at the bottom and . . . um . . . a couple of stones, and then perhaps some . . . Vallisneria, I would say, probably in that corner there, wouldn't you?"

"Could I just try it on my own?" I asked. "I . . . er . . . I think I'd learn better that way—if I could do it on my own. And then, when I'm finished you could tell me where I've gone wrong."

"Very good idea," said Mr. Romilly.

It was only a small tank but I worked hard on it. I piled up the silver sand in great dunes. I built little cliffs. I planted forests of Vallisneria through which the mollies could drift in shoals. Then I filled it carefully with water, and when it was the right temperature I put the mollies back in it and called Mr. Romilly to see my handiwork.

"By Jove!" he said, looking at it. "By Jove!"

He glanced at me and it was almost as though he was

disappointed that I had done so well. I could see that I was on dangerous ground.

"Do . . . do you like it?" I inquired.

"It . . . it's remarkable! I can't think how you managed it."

"Well, I only managed it by watching you, Mr. Romilly," I said. "If it hadn't been for you teaching me how to do it I could never have done it."

"Well, now. Well, now," said Mr. Romilly, going pink. "But I see you've added one or two little touches of your own. Most commendable."

The next day he asked me whether I would like to decorate another fish tank and I knew I had won the battle without hurting his feelings.

The tank that I really desperately wanted to do was the enormous one that we had in the window. It was some four and a half feet long and about two feet six deep, and in it we had a great colourful mixed collection of fish. But I knew that I must not overstep the bounds of propriety at this stage. Only when Mr. Romilly had got thoroughly used to the idea of my doing the smaller fish tanks, did I broach the subject of our big show tank.

"Could I try my hand at that, Mr. Romilly?" I asked.

"What? Our show piece?" he said. "It's most important, you know. It's the piece that attracts all the customers."

He was quite right, but the customers were attracted by the flickering shoals of multi-coloured fish. They certainly were not attracted by Mr. Romilly's attempts at decoration, which made it look rather like a blasted heath.

"Well, could I just try?" I said.

It took me the better part of a day to do, because in between times I had to attend to various customers. I worked on that giant tank with all the dedication of a marine Capability Brown. I built rolling sand dunes and great towering cliffs of granite. And then, in the valleys, I planted forests of Vallisneria and other, more delicate, weedy ferns. On the surface of the water I floated the tiny little white flowers that look so like miniature waterlilies. When I had finally finished it and replaced the brilliant scarlet swordtails, the shiny black mollies, the silver hatchet fish, and the brilliant neon-tetras, and stepped back to observe my handiwork, I found myself deeply impressed by my own genius. Mr. Romilly, to my delight, was ecstatic about the whole thing.

"Simply exquisite!" he exclaimed.

After that, I was allowed to decorate all the tanks and all the cages. I think, secretly, Mr. Romilly was rather relieved not to have to urge his non-existent artistic sense into this irksome task.

I always took my lunch hour at a little café not very far away from the shop. Here I had discovered a kindly waitress who, in exchange for a little flattery, would give me more than my regulation number of sausages with my sausages and mash, and warn me against the deadly perils of the Irish stew on that particular day. It was one day when I was going to have my lunch that I discovered a short cut through a narrow little alleyway. It was cobblestoned and as soon as I got into it, it was as though I had been transported back to Dickensian London. Part of it was tree-lined, and farther along there was a series of tiny shops. It was then that I discovered that we were not the only pet shop in the vicinity, for I came across the abode of Henry Bellow.

The dirty window of his shop measured, perhaps, six feet square by two deep. It was crammed from top to bottom with small square cages, each containing chaffinches, green finches, linnets, canaries, or budgerigars. The floor of the window was inches deep in seed husks and bird excrement, but the cages themselves were spotlessly clean and each sported a bright green sprig of lettuce or groundsel and a white label on which had been written in shaky block letters "SOLD". The glass door of the shop was covered with a lace curtain which was yellow with age, and between it and the glass hung a cardboard notice which said "Please Enter" in gothic script. Never, in all the days that I hurried past for my sausages and mash, did I ever see a customer entering or leaving the shop. I wondered, as the weeks passed, why all the birds in the window were not claimed by the people who had bought them. Surely the various owners of some thirty assorted birds could not have decided simultaneously that they did not want them? It was a mystery that in my limited lunch hour I had little time to investigate. But my chance came one day when Mr. Romilly, who had been dancing round the shop singing "I'm a busy little bee", suddenly went down into the basement and uttered a falsetto screech of horror.

"What's the matter, Mr. Romilly?" I asked cautiously, peering down the stairs. Mr. Romilly appeared clasping his brow, distraught.

"Stupid, stupid, me!" he intoned. "Tubifex and daphnia!" He removed his spectacles and started to polish them feverishly.

"Have we run out?"

"Yes," intoned Mr. Romilly sepulchrally. "What negligence! I deserve to be sacked. The farm always sends it up every weekend. And I, crass idiot that I am, never ordered any."

"Can't we get some from somewhere else?" I asked, interrupting Mr. Romilly's verbal flagellation.

He climbed laboriously up the wooden stairs, mopping his brow, and emerged like the sole survivor of some pit disaster. He gazed round him with vacant, tragic eyes.

"But where?" he said at last, despairingly. "But where?"

"Well," I said, taking the matter in hand. "What about Bellow?"

"Bellow?" he said. "Most unbusinesslike chap. He deals in birds. Shouldn't think he'd have any."

"But surely it's worth a try?" I said.

Mr. Romilly thought about it. "All right," he said at last, averting his face from the serried ranks of accusing-looking fish, "take ten shillings out of petty cash, and don't be too long."

I extracted a ten shilling note from the tin petty-cash box and a moment later I was out on the broad pavement, weaving through the vacant-eyed throng of shoppers, making my way towards Bellow's shop, while the mountainous red buses thundered past. I came to the tiny alleyway and turned down it, and immediately peace reigned. The thunder of buses became muted. On one side of the alley was a blank soot-blackened wall; on the other iron railings which guarded a piece of ground that led to the local church. Here had been planted a rank of plane trees. They leaned over the iron railings, roofing the alley with green, and where they ended the shops began. There were no more than six of them, each Lilliputian in dimension.

There was Clemystra, Modes for Ladies, with a rather extraordinary fur in their window as the *pièce de résistance*; a fur which, with its glass eyes and its tail in its mouth, would have curdled the heart of any anti-vivisectionist. There was the Pixies' Parlour, Light Luncheons, Teas and Snacks, and next door to it A. Wallet, Tobacconist, whose window consisted entirely of cigarette and pipe advertisements. I hurried past all these and past William Drover, Estate Agent, with its fascinating pale brown pictures of desirable residences, past the shrouded portal, decorated rather severely by one rose-pink lavatory pan, of Messrs. M. & R. Drumlin, Plumbers, to the end of the row of shops where the faded notice above the door stated simply and unequivocally: Henry Bellow, Aviculturist. At last, I thought, I had the chance of getting inside the shop and solving, if nothing else, the mystery of the birds with the "SOLD" notices on their cages. But as I approached the shop something unprecedented happened. A woman in tweeds, wearing a ridiculous Tyrolean hat with a feather, strode purposefully down the alley and, a brief second before me, grasped the handle of the door marked "Please Enter" and swept inside, while the bell jangled melodiously. I was astonished. It was the first time I had ever seen a customer enter any of the shops in the alley. Anxious to see what happened I rushed after her.

In an almost lightless shop the woman and I were caught like moths in some dingy spider's web. The melodious chimes of the door, one felt assured, would have someone running to attend shop. Instead of which there was silence, except for the faint cheeping of the birds in the window and the sudden shuffling of feathers from a cockatoo in the corner. It put its head on one side and said, "Hello, hello," softly and with complete lack of interest.

We waited what seemed a long time. My eyes gradually grew accustomed to the gloom. I saw that there was a small counter and behind it shelves of cuttlefish and other accoutrements of the aviculturist's trade, and in front of it a number of large sacks containing seed. Suddenly a very large and very ancient retriever padded its way solemnly through the door at the back of the shop and came forward, wagging its tail. It was followed by a man I took to be Henry Bellow. He was tall and stout with a great mop of curly grey hair and a huge bristling moustache, like an untamed gorse bush, that looked as though it were a suitable nesting site for any number of birds. From under his shaggy eyebrows his periwinkle-blue eyes stared out through gold-rimmed spectacles. He moved with a sort of ponderous slowness rather like a lazy seal. He came forward and gave a little bow.

"Madam," he said, and his voice had the rich accents of Somerset. "Madam, your servant."

The Tyrolean hat looked rather alarmed at being addressed in this fashion. "Oh, er . . . good day," she said.

363

"What may I get you?" inquired Mr. Bellow.

"Well, actually, I came to get your advice," she said. "My young nephew's going to be fourteen soon and I want to buy him a bird for his birthday . . . ."

"A bird," said Mr. Bellow. "And what kind of bird have you got in mind, madam?"

"Well, er, I . . . I don't really know," said the lady in the Tyrolean hat. "What about a canary?"

"I wouldn't touch canaries at this time of year," said Mr. Bellow, shaking his head sorrowfully. "I would be a dishonest man if I sold you a canary, madam."

"Why at this time of year?" asked the lady. She was obviously impressed.

"It's a very bad time of the year for canaries," said Mr. Bellow. "Bronchial trouble, you know."

"Oh," said the lady. "Well, what about a budgerigar?"

"Now, I wouldn't advise those either, madam. There's a lot of psittacosis around," said Mr. Bellow. "The parrot's disease. Most of the budgerigars have got it at this time of the year. It's fatal to human beings, you know."

"Well, what bird would you suggest, then?" said the woman, getting rather desperate.

"Actually, madam, it's a very, very bad time of the year to sell birds," said Mr. Bellow. "They're all in moult, you see."

"Then you wouldn't advise me to get a bird?" she said. "How about something else, like a . . . like a white mouse?"

"Ah, well, I'm afraid you'd have to go somewhere else, madam. I'm afraid I don't deal in them," said Mr. Bellow.

"Ah," she said. "Oh. Well, I can always go to Harrods."

"A very fine emporium, madam," said Mr. Bellow. "I am sure they will be able to satisfy your wants."

"Well, thank you so much," she said. "Most kind of you." And she left the shop.

When the door closed Mr. Bellow turned and looked at me. "Good afternoon, sir," he said. "And what can I have the pleasure of doing for you?"

"Well, actually, I came to see whether you had any tubifex," I said. "I work at the Aquarium and we've run out."

"Well, well," said Mr. Bellow. "And what makes you think that I would have tubifex? I deal in birds."

"That's what Mr. Romilly said, but I thought there was just a chance you might have some."

"Well, it so happens that you're right," said Mr. Bellow. "Come with me."

He led me through the door at the back of the shop and into the small and untidy but comfortable sitting room. It was quite obvious, from the look of the chair and sofa covers, that the dog enjoyed them as much as Mr. Bellow did. He led me through the back into a little paved yard where the plane trees from the churchyard hung over, and there was a small pond with a tap dribbling into it, and in the middle of it a plaster cupid standing on a mound of rocks. The pond was full of goldfish; at one end of it was a big jam jar in which was a large lump of tubifex. Mr. Bellow fetched another jam jar and ladled some of the tubifex into it. Then he handed it to me.

"That's very kind of you," I said. "How much do I owe you?"

"Oh, you don't pay me for it," said Mr. Bellow. "Take it as a gift."

"But . . . but it's awfully expensive," I said, taken aback.

"Take it as a gift, boy," he said.

He led me back into the shop.

"Tell me, Mr. Bellow," I asked, "why are all the birds in your window labelled 'SOLD'?"

His sharp little blue eyes fastened on me. "Because they *are* sold," he said.

"But they've been sold for ages. Ever since I've been coming down this alley. And that's a good two months. Doesn't anybody ever come and claim them?"

"No, I just . . . keep them until they're able to have them. Some of them are building aviaries, constructing cages, and so forth," said Mr. Bellow.

"Did you sell them when it was the right time of the year?" I asked.

A faint flicker of a smile passed over Mr. Bellow's face. "Yes, indeed, I did," he said.

"Have you got other birds?" I asked.

"Yes, upstairs," he said.

"If I come back another day when I've got more time, can I see them?"

Mr. Bellow gazed at me thoughtfully and stroked the side of his chin. "I think that might be arranged," he said. "When would you like to come?"

"Well, Saturday's my half day," I said. "Could I come then?"

"I'm normally closed on a Saturday," said Mr. Bellow. "However, if you'll ring the bell three times, I'll let you in."

For the next couple of days I thought very deeply on the subject of Mr. Bellow. I did not believe for one moment that the birds in his window were sold, but I could not see the point of having them labelled as such. Also, I was more than a little puzzled by his obvious reluctance to sell a bird to the woman in the Tyrolean hat. I determined that on Saturday I would do my best to prize the answer to these secrets from Mr. Bellow himself.

I arrived at Mr. Bellow's shop sharp at two o'clock on Saturday. The notice on the door said, "We regret that we are closed". Nevertheless, I pressed the bell three times and waited hopefully. Presently Mr. Bellow opened the door.

"Ah," he said. "Good afternoon to you. Do come in."

I went in and he locked the shop door carefully after me. Then he took me through his living room and up a very tiny rickety staircase. He ushered me into a room which was lined from floor to ceiling with cages full of birds of all shapes, sizes, colours and descriptions. There were groups of tiny vivid seed-eaters from Africa and Asia. There were parakeets, green as leaves, and Red Cardinals that were as crimson as royal robes. I was fascinated. Mr. Bellow proved to be much abler at his job than Mr. Romilly, for he knew the name of every bird and its scientific name as well, where it came from, what its food preferences were, and how many eggs it laid.

"Are all these birds for sale?" I asked, fixing my eyes greedily on a Red Cardinal.

"Of course," said Mr. Bellow, and then added, "But only at the right time of year."

"Surely if you're selling birds you can sell them at any time of year?" I asked, puzzled.

"Well, some people do," said Mr. Bellow. "But I have always made it a rule never to sell at the wrong time of the year."

I looked at him and I saw that his eyes were twinkling.

"Then when is the right time of the year?" I asked.

"There is never a right time of year as far as I am concerned," said Mr. Bellow.

"You mean you don't sell them at all?" I asked.

"Very rarely," said Mr. Bellow.

"And all those birds in the window marked 'SOLD', they aren't really sold, are they?"

Mr. Bellow gazed at me, judging whether or not I could keep a secret. "Actually, between you and me, they are not," he admitted.

"Well, then how do you make a profit?" I asked.

"Ah," said Mr. Bellow, "that's the point. I don't."

I must have looked utterly bewildered for Mr. Bellow gave a throaty chuckle and said, "Let's have some tea, shall we, and I'll explain it to you. But you must promise that it will go no further."

"Oh, I promise!" I said.

We went down to the little living room where Mr. Bellow's retriever, Aldrich, lay stretched, sublimely comfortable, across the sofa. Mr. Bellow lit a little gas ring and toasted crumpets over it and then buttered them quickly, and when he had made a tottering, oozing pile of them, he placed them on a little table between us. He made the tea and set out thin and delicate china cups for us to drink it out of.

He handed me a crumpet, took one himself and sank his teeth into it with a sigh of satisfaction.

"What . . . what were you going to tell me about not making a profit?" I asked.

"It's rather a long and complicated story," he said. "The whole of Potts Lane once belonged to an eccentric millionaire called Potts. When he built this line of shops he laid down special regulations governing them. The people who wanted the shops could have them on an indefinite lease and every four years their rent would come up for revision. If they were doing well, their rent was raised accordingly; if they were not doing so well, their rent was adjusted the opposite way. Now, I moved into this shop in 1921. Since then I have been paying five shillings a week rent."

I stared at Mr. Bellow disbelievingly. "Five shillings a week? But that's ridiculous for a shop like this. Why, you're only a stone's throw away from Kensington High Street."

"Exactly," said Mr. Bellow.

"But why is the rent so ridiculously small?" I asked.

"Because," he said, "I make no profit. As soon as I discovered this section in the lease I immediately saw that it would provide me with a convenient loop-hole. I had a little money put by,

367

enough to get along on. And what I really wanted was a place to live where I could keep my birds. Well, this provided me with the ideal opportunity. I went round to see all the other people in Potts Lane and explained about this clause to them, and I found most of them were in a similar predicament; that they had small amounts of money to live on, but what they really wanted was a cheap abode. So we formed the Potts Lane Association and we got ourselves a very good accountant. We meet once every six months or so and he examines our books and tells us how to run at a loss. Then when our rents come up for revision they either remain static or are slightly lowered."

"But can't the present owner change the leases?" I asked.

"No," said Mr. Bellow, "that's the beauty of it. I found out that by the terms of Mr. Potts's will these conditions have to stand."

"But they must have been furious when they found out that you were only paying them a pound a month?"

"They were indeed," said Mr. Bellow. "They did their very best to evict me, but it was impossible. They met with an equally united front from all the other shops in the lane, so there was really nothing they could do."

I did not like to say anything because I did not want to hurt Mr. Bellow's feelings, but I felt sure that this story was a complete make-up.

We sat and ate crumpets and chatted. Mr. Bellow I found a fascinating companion. In his youth he had travelled widely round the world and knew intimately a lot of places that I longed to visit. After that I used to go and have tea with him about once a fortnight.

I still didn't believe this story of Potts Lane, so I thought I would conduct an experiment. I visited in turn each shop in the lane. At Clemystra's, for example, I went to buy a hat for my mother's birthday. They were terribly sorry, said the two dear old ladies who ran it, I couldn't have come at a worse time. They had just run out of hats. Well, had they got anything else, I inquired? Well, no, as a matter of fact, they said, all the stuff they had in the shop was bespoken at the moment. They were waiting for a new consignment to come in.

Mr. Wallet, the tobacconist, told me that he did not stock the brand of cigarettes I wanted. He also did not stock cigars, or pipes. Reluctantly, he let me buy a box of matches.

I next went to the plumbers. I had called, I said, on behalf of my mother because there was something wrong with our cistern and could they send a man round to look at it?

"Well, now," said Mr. Drumlin, "we've only got one man here and he's out on a job . . . quite a big job. Don't know how long it will take him . . . . Maybe a day or two."

"Couldn't he come round and do a bit of overtime?" I asked.

"Oh, I don't think he'd like to do that," said Mr. Drumlin. "There's a very good plumber in the High Street, though. You could go to them."

Thanking him, I left. I next went to William Drover, the estate agent. He was a seedy little man with glasses and wispy hair like thistledown. I explained that my aunt was thinking of moving to this part of London and had asked me if I would go to an estate agent and find out about flats for her.

"Flats?" said Mr. Drover, pursing his lips. "It's an awkward time. Lots of people moving into the district, you know. Most of them are snapped up before you have a chance."

"So you've nothing on your books?" I asked. "How about a small house, then?"

"Ah, they're just as bad," he said.

I next went to the Pixies' Parlour. They had quite an extensive menu but all they could offer me was a cup of tea. Most unfortunately their van, carrying all their supplies for the day, had broken down somewhere in North London and they were bereft of food of any description.

After this I believed Mr. Bellow's story about Potts Lane.

It was at about this time that another rather strange character appeared in my life. Periodically Mr. Romilly would send me down to the East End of London to collect fresh supplies of reptiles, amphibians and tropical fish. These we got from the wholesalers, whereas the farm sent us all the freshwater fish that we needed. I enjoyed these jaunts where, in gloomy, cavernous stores in back streets, I would find great crates of lizards, basketfuls of tortoises and dripping tanks green with algae, full of newts and frogs and salamanders. It was on one of these forays into the East End that I met Colonel Anstruther.

I had been sent down to Van den Goths, a big wholesaler who specialized in importing North American reptiles and amphibians, and I had been given instructions by Mr. Romilly to bring back

150 baby painted terrapins—those enchanting little freshwater tortoises with green shells and yellow and red markings on their skins. They were each about the size of a half crown. We did quite a brisk trade in these for they were a good and simple pet to give a child in a flat.

Mr. Van den Goth himself placed my terrapins in a cardboard box with moss, but what I did not notice was that both the terrapins and the moss in their box were excessively moist. The not unnatural result was that as I was just about to take my seat on the top of the bus, the entire bottom of the box gave way and a cascade of baby terrapins fell on the floor.

It was fortunate for me that there was only one other person on the top of the bus and he was a slender, military-looking man, with a grey moustache and a monocle. He had a carnation in his buttonhole and a malacca cane with a silver knob. I scrabbled madly on the floor collecting the terrapins, but baby terrapins can move with extraordinary speed and I was heavily outnumbered. Suddenly, one of them rushed up the central alley of the bus and turned in by the military-looking man's foot. Feeling it clawing at his well-polished shoe, he glanced down. Now I'm for it, I thought. He screwed his monocle more firmly into his eye and surveyed the baby terrapin.

"By George!" he said. "A painted terrapin! *Chrysemys picta!* Haven't seen one for years!"

He looked round to see the source from which this little reptile had emanated and saw me crouched, red-faced, on the floor with baby terrapins running madly in all directions.

"Hah!" he said. "Is this little chap yours?"

"Yes, sir," I said. "I'm sorry, but the bottom has fallen out of the box."

"By George, you're in a bit of a stew, what?" he shouted. He picked up the baby terrapin that had managed to get on the toe of his shoe and came down the bus towards me.

"Here," he said, "let me help. I'll head the bounders off."

"It's very kind of you," I said.

He got down on his hands and knees and we crawled together up and down the bus collecting baby terrapins.

"Tally-ho!" he would shout at intervals. "There's one going under that seat there."

Once, when a small terrapin approached him at a run, he

pointed his malacca cane at it and said, "Bang! Bang! Back, sir, or I'll have you on a charge."

Eventually, after about quarter of an hour of this, we managed to get all the baby terrapins back into the box and I did a rough splinting job on it with my handkerchief.

"It was very kind of you, sir," I said. "I'm afraid you've got your knees all dusty."

"Well worth it," he said. "Haven't had sport like that for a long time. Tell me. What are you doing with a box full of terrapins?"

"I . . . I work in a pet shop and I've just been down to the wholesalers to get them."

"Oh, I see," he said. "Do you mind if I come and sit near you and have a chin-wag?"

"No, sir," I said.

He came and planted himself firmly on the seat opposite mine, put his malacca cane between his knees, and gazed at me thoughtfully.

"Pet shop, eh?" he said. "Hmmm. Do you like animals?"

"Yes, very much. They're about the only thing I really do like," I said.

"Hmmm," he said. "What else have you got in this shop?"

He seemed genuinely interested and so I told him. When we reached my stop I got to my feet.

"I'm sorry, sir," I said. "I've got to get off here."

"Hah," he said. "Hah. So have I."

It was perfectly obvious that this was not his stop and that he wanted to continue talking to me. We got down onto the pavement. My rather liberal and eccentric upbringing had left me in no doubt that even military-looking gentlemen with monocles could be inclined towards boys, and the fact that he had got off at a stop that was not his argued an interest in me which I felt might possibly turn out to be unsavoury. I was cautious.

"Where's your shop, then?" he said, swinging his cane between his finger and thumb.

"Just over there, sir," I said.

"Ah, then I'll walk there with you."

He strolled down the pavement gazing intently at the shops as we passed.

"Tell me," he said, "what do you do with yourself in your spare time?"

"Oh, I go to the zoo and the cinema and to museums," I said.

"Do you ever go to the Science Museum?" he inquired. "All those models?"

"I like that very much," I said.

"Do you? Do you?" he said, screwing his monocle in and glaring at me. "You like to play, do you?"

"Well, I suppose you could call it that," I said.

We paused outside the shop.

"Well, if you'll excuse me, sir," I said. "I'm . . . I'm rather late as it is."

"Ah," he said. "The Aquarium. Wondered." He pulled out a wallet and extracted from it a card. "There's my name and address if you'd like to come round one evening, we could play a game."

"That's, er . . . very kind of you, sir," I said.

"Don't mention it," he said. "Hope to see you, then. Don't bother to ring up . . . just call. Any time after six."

He strolled off down the street, very much the military man. There was no trace of effeminacy about him, but I knew that was not an essential manifestation of homosexuality in a person's character. I stuffed his card into my pocket and went into the shop.

"Where have you been, you naughty boy?" asked Mr. Romilly.

"I'm sorry I'm late," I said. "But I had a little accident on the bus. The bottom fell out of the box and all the terrapins got out, and a colonel chappy helped me to pick them all up but it delayed us a bit. I'm very sorry, Mr. Romilly."

"That's all right," he said. "It's been a very quiet afternoon."

I put the baby terrapins in the tank and watched them swimming about, and then I took out the colonel's card and looked at it. "Colonel Anstruther," it said, "47 Bell Mews, South Kensington," and it had a telephone number. I mused a bit.

"Mr. Romilly," I said. "Do you know a Colonel Anstruther?"

"Anstruther?" said Mr. Romilly, delighted. "Yes, yes . . . yes. A fine soldier. And a very fine man, too. Was he the person who helped you pick up the terrapins?"

"Yes," I said.

"Ah, just like him. Always a man to help a friend in need," said Mr. Romilly. "They don't breed them like that nowadays, you know."

I pondered on this information for some time, and then I

thought that perhaps I would take the colonel up on his invitation. After all, I thought, if the worst came to the worst I could always scream for help. A few days later I phoned him up.

"Colonel Anstruther?" I asked.

"Yes. Yes," he said. "Who's that?"

"It's . . . um . . . my name is . . . Durrell," I said. "I met you on the bus the other evening. You were kind enough to help me catch my terrapins."

"Oh, yes," he said. "Yes. How are the little chaps?"

"They're doing fine," I said. "I wondered if, perhaps, I could take you up on your kind offer of coming round to see you?"

"But of course, my dear chap!" he said. "Delighted! Come round about six thirty," he said. "Come to dinner."

"Thank you very much," I said. "I'll be there."

Bell Mews, I discovered, was a short, cobbled cul-de-sac with four small houses on each side. What confused me to start with was that I did not realize that the colonel owned all four houses on one side which he had knocked into one, and he had, with a brilliant display of the military mind, labelled each door "47". So after some moments of confusion I finally knocked on the nearest door marked "47" and waited to see what would happen.

At that moment, the door that I had knocked on was flung open and there stood the colonel. He was dressed in a bottle-green velvet smoking jacket with watered silk lapels, and he brandished in one hand a carving knife of prodigious dimensions. I began to wonder whether I had been wise to come after all.

"Durrell?" he said inquiringly, screwing his monocle into his eye. "By Jove, you're punctual!"

"Well, I had a little difficulty," I began.

"Ah!" he said. "The forty-seven foxed you, did it? It foxes them all. Gives me a bit of privacy, you know. Come in!"

I edged my way into the hall and he closed the door, then led the way, at a brisk trot, through the hall, holding the carving knife in front of him as though leading a cavalry charge. Then we were in a large, spacious living room, simply but comfortably furnished, with piles and piles of books everywhere and colour reproductions on the walls of various military uniforms. He led me through this and into the large kitchen.

"Sorry to rush you," he panted. "But I've got a pie in the oven and I don't want it to get burnt."

He rushed over to the oven, opened it and peered inside.

"Ah, no, that's all right," he said. "Good . . . good."

He straightened up and looked at me.

"Do you like steak and kidney pie?" he inquired.

"Oh, yes," I said, "I'm very fond of it."

"Good," he said. "It'll be ready in a moment or two. Now, come and sit down and have a drink."

He led me back into the living room and poured me a glass full of ruby red wine which was crisp and dry. We sat chatting, mainly about terrapins, for ten minutes or so and then the colonel glanced at his watch.

"Should be ready now," he said. We went into the kitchen and the colonel laid the table; then he mashed some potatoes and heaped a great mound of steak and kidney pie onto them and put the plate in front of me.

The steak and kidney was excellent. I inquired whether the colonel had made it himself.

"Yes," he said. "Had to learn to cook when my wife died. Quite simple, really, if you put your mind to it. It's a wonder what you can do with a pinch of herbs here and there."

After we had finished off the steak and kidney pie he got some ice cream out of the fridge and we ate that.

"Ah," said the colonel, leaning back in his chair and patting his stomach, "that's better. I only have one meal a day and I like to make it a solid one. Now, how about a glass of port?"

We had a couple of glasses of port and the colonel lit up a fine thin cheroot. When he had finished the port he screwed his monocle more firmly in his eye and looked at me.

"What about going upstairs for a little game?" he asked.

"Um . . . what sort of game?" I inquired cautiously, feeling that this was the moment when, if he was going to, he would start making advances.

"Power game," said the colonel. "Battle of wits. Models. You like that sort of thing, don't you?"

"Um . . . yes," I said.

"Come on, then," he said.

He led me up a staircase and through a small room which was obviously a sort of workshop; there was a bench along one side with shelves on which there were pots of paint, soldering irons, and various other mysterious things. Then he threw open a door and a most amazing sight met my gaze. The room I looked into ran the whole length of the house and was some seventy to eighty feet long. It was, in fact, all the top rooms of the four mews houses knocked into one. But it was not so much the size of the room that astonished me as what it contained. At each end of the room was a large fort made out of papiermâché. They must have been some three or four feet high and some four or five feet across. Ranged round them were hundreds of tin soldiers, glittering and gleaming in their bright uniforms, and amongst them there were tanks, armoured trucks and guns.

"Ah," said the colonel, rubbing his hands in glee, "surprised you!"

"Good Lord, yes!" I said. "I don't think I've ever seen so many toy soldiers."

"It's taken me years to amass them," he said. "I get 'em from a factory, you know. I paint 'em myself. Much better that way, get a smoother, cleaner job . . . . More realistic, too."

I bent down and picked up one of the tiny soldiers. Normally a tin soldier is a fairly botchy job of painting, but these were meticulously done. Even the faces appeared to have expression on them.

"Now," said the colonel. "Now. We'll have a quick game—just a sort of run-through. Once you get the hang of it we can make it more complicated, of course. Now, I'll explain the rules to you."

The rules of the game were fairly straightforward. You each had an army. You threw two dice and the one who got the highest score was the aggressor and it was his turn to start first. He threw his dice and from the number that came up he could move a battalion of his men in any direction that he pleased, and he was allowed to fire off a barrage from his field guns or anti-aircraft guns. These worked on a spring mechanism and you loaded them with matchsticks. The springs in these guns were surprisingly strong and projected the matchsticks with incredible velocity down the room. Where every matchstick landed, in a radius of some four inches around it, was taken to be destroyed. So if you could gain a direct hit on a column of troops you could do savage damage to the enemy.

I was enchanted by the whole idea, but principally because it reminded me very much of a game that we had invented when we were in Greece. My brother Leslie had collected a whole navy of toy battleships and cruisers and submarines. We used to range them out on the floor and play a game very similar to the colonel's, only we used marbles in order to score direct hits on the ships. Rolling a marble accurately over a bumpy floor in order to hit a destroyer an inch and a half long took a keen eye. It turned out, after we had thrown the first dice, that I was to be the aggressor.

"Hah!" said the colonel. "Filthy Hun!"

I could see that he was working himself into a warlike mood.

"Is the object of the exercise to try and capture your fort?" I inquired.

"Well, you can do that," he said. "Or you can knock it out, if you can."

I soon discovered that the way to play the colonel's game was to distract his attention from one flank so that you could do some quick manoeuvring while he was not aware of it, so I kept up a constant barrage on his troops, the matches whistling down the room, and while doing this I moved a couple of battalions up close to his lines.

"Swine!" the colonel would roar every time a matchstick fell. "Dirty swine! Bloody Hun!" His face grew quite pink. "You're too bloody accurate."

"Well, it's your fault," I shouted back. "You're keeping all your troops bunched together. They make an ideal target."

"It's part of me strategy. Don't question me strategy. I'm older than you, and superior in rank."

"How can you be superior in rank, when I'm in command of an army?"

"No lip out of you, you whippersnapper," he roared.

So the game went on for about two hours, by which time I had successfully knocked out most of the colonel's troops and got a foothold at the bottom of his fort.

"Do you surrender?" I shouted.

"Never!" said the colonel. "I'll fight you every inch of the way, you Hun!"

He crawled rapidly across the floor on his hands and knees, moving his troops frantically. But all his efforts were of no avail; I had him pinned in a corner and I shot him to pieces.

"By George!" said the colonel when it was all over, mopping his brow, "How did you manage to get so damned accurate when you haven't played it before?"

"Well, I've played a similar game, only we used marbles," I said. "But I think once you've got your eye in . . . it helps."

"Gad!" said the colonel, looking at the destruction of his army. "Still, it was a good fight."

After that I would spend two or three evenings a week with the colonel, fighting battles up and down the long room, and it gave him tremendous pleasure—almost as much pleasure as it gave me.

Not long after that, my mother announced that she had finally found a house and that we could move out of London. I was bitterly disappointed. It meant that I would have to give up my job and lose contact with my friends, Mr. Bellow and Colonel Anstruther. Mr. Romilly was heartbroken.

When the day finally came for me to leave, with tears in his eyes he presented me with a leather wallet. On the inside it had embossed in gold "To Gerald Durrell from his fellow workers". I was a bit puzzled since there had been only Mr. Romilly and myself, but I thanked him very much and then I made my way for the last time down Potts Lane to Mr. Bellow's establishment.

"Sorry to see you go, boy," he said. "Very sorry indeed. Here, I've got you a little parting present."

He put a small square cage in my hands and sitting inside it was the bird that I most coveted in his collection, the Red Cardinal.

"But, is it the right time of year for a present?" I inquired.

Mr. Bellow guffawed. "Yes, it is," he said. "Of course it is."

That evening I went round to play a last game with the colonel. When it was over—I had let him win—he led me downstairs.

"Shall miss you, you know, my boy. However, keep in touch, won't you? I've got a little, um . . . a little souvenir here for you."

He handed me a slim silver cigarette case. On it had been written "With love from Margery". I was a bit puzzled by this.

"Oh, take no notice of the inscription," he said. "Present from a woman I knew once. Thought you'd like it. Memento, hmmm?"

"It's very, very kind of you, sir," I said.

"Not at all, not at all," he said, and blew his nose and polished his monocle and held out his hand. "Well, good luck, my boy And I hope I'll see you again one day."

I never did see him again. He died shortly afterwards.

Maiden Voyage

Under a full daffodil-yellow summer moon, Venice was ravishing. It was spoiled only by my belligerent family, clustered around two tables in the Piazza San Marco.

It was several years after the war had ended and it was my mother's idea that we should be there, on our way to revisit the scenes of our youth in Corfu. Unfortunately, as had often happened throughout her life, what she had produced as a treat had already, even at this early stage, started turning into a fiasco.

"I wouldn't mind if you had had the decency to tell me in advance. I could, at least, have risked death travelling by air," said Larry, looking despondently at one of the many glasses that an irritatingly happy waiter had put in front of him. "But what in Heaven's name possessed you to go and book us all on a *Greek* ship for three days? It's as stupid as deliberately booking on the *Titanic*."

"I thought it would be more cheerful, and the Greeks are such good sailors," replied my mother, defensively. "Anyway, it's her maiden voyage."

"You always cry wolf before you're hurt, Larry," put in Margo. "I think it was a brilliant idea of Mother's. After all, we will be among the Greeks."

"I think that's what Larry's worried about," commented Leslie gloomily.

We paid our bill, straggled down to the canal and climbed on board one of the motor launches which the Italians call

379

vaporettos. Venice was a splendid sight as we chugged our way down the canal, past the great houses, past the rippling reflections of the lights in the water. We were landed eventually at the docks which, like docks everywhere, looked as though they had been designed (in an off moment) by Dante while planning his Inferno. We huddled in puddles of phosphorescent light which made us look like something out of an early Hollywood horror film and completely destroyed the moonlight, which was by now silver as a spider's web.

A ship slid into our view which, even by the most landlubberish standards, could never have been mistaken for seaworthy. At some time in her career, she had probably been used as an in-shore steamer, but even virginal and freshly painted she could not have been beautiful. Now there were large patches of rust, like unpleasant sores and scabs, all along her sides, and as she turned to come alongside the docks, we saw an enormous tattered hole in her bows that would have admitted a pair of Rolls-Royces side by side. No first aid, even of the most primitive kind, had been attempted. The plates on her hull curved inwards, like a giant chrysanthemum. Struck dumb, we saw her name above the huge hole in her bows: the *Poseidon*.

"But it's our boat," squeaked Margo.

"Nonsense, dear, it can't be," said Mother, peering hopefully up as the boat loomed above us.

"Three days on this," said Larry. "It will be worse than the Ancient Mariner's experience, mark my words."

"I do hope they are going to do something about that hole," said Mother worriedly, "before we put out to sea."

"What do you expect them to do? Stuff a blanket into it?" asked Larry.

"But surely the captain's noticed it," said Mother, bewildered.

"I shouldn't think that even a Greek captain could have been oblivious of the fact that they have, quite recently, given something a fairly sharp tap," said Larry. "Our snorkels and flippers will come in handy. What a novelty to have to swim down to dinner. How I shall enjoy it all."

We made our way up the gangway and at the head of it were met by a romantic-looking Greek steward, with eyes as soft and melting as black pansies, wearing a crumpled and off-white suit, with most of the buttons missing. He appeared to be the purser, and his smiling demand for passports and tickets was so redolent of garlic that Mother reeled back against the rails.

"Do you speak English?" asked Margo.

"Small," he replied, bowing.

"Well, I don't want waves in my cabin," said Margo firmly. "It will ruin my clothes."

"Everything you want we give," he answered. "If you want wife, I give you my wife. She . . ."

"No, no," exclaimed Margo, "the waves. You know . . . water."

"Every cabeen has having hot and cold running showers," he said with dignity. "Also there is bath or nightcloob having dancing and wine and water."

"I do wish you'd stop laughing and help us, Larry," said Mother, covering her nose with her handkerchief to repel the odour of garlic, which was so strong that one got the impression it was a shimmering cloud round the purser's head.

Larry pulled himself together and in fluent Greek (which delighted the purser) elicited the information that the ship was not sinking and that there were no waves in the cabins. While Mother and Margo were taken in a friendly and aromatic manner down to the cabins by the purser, the rest of us followed his instructions as to how to get to the "nightcloob", which apparently contained the only bar.

This, when we located it, made us all speechless. It looked like the lounge of one of the drearier London clubs. Great chocolate-coloured leather chairs and couches cluttered the place, and dotted about were Benares brass bowls in which sprouted dusty palm trees. There was, in the midst of this funereal splendour, a minute parquet floor for dancing, flanked on one side by a small bar containing a virulent assortment of drinks, and on the other by a small raised dais, surrounded by a veritable forest of potted palms. In the midst of this, enshrined like flies in amber, were three lugubrious musicians in frock coats, celluloid dickies, and cummerbunds that would have seemed dated in about 1890. One played on an ancient upright piano and tuba, one played a violin with much professional posturing, and the third doubled up on the drums and trombone. As we entered, this incredible trio was playing "The Roses of Picardy" to an entirely empty room.

"I can't bear it," said Larry. "It'll drive us all mad."

At Larry's words, the band stopped playing and the leader's

face lit up in a gold-toothed smile of welcome. He gestured at his two colleagues with his bow and they also bowed and smiled. We three could do no less, and so we swept them a courtly bow before proceeding to the bar. The band launched itself with ever greater frenzy into "The Roses of Picardy" now that it had an audience.

"Please give me," Larry asked the barman, "in one of the largest glasses you possess, an ouzo that will, I hope, paralyse me."

The barman's face lit up at the sound of a foreigner who could not only speak Greek but was rich enough to drink so large an ouzo.

"*Amessos, kyrie*," he said. "Will you have it with water or ice?"

"One lump of ice," Larry stipulated. "Just enough to blanch its cheeks."

"I'm sorry, *kyrie*, we have no ice," said the barman apologetically.

Larry sighed. "It is only in Greece," he said to us in English, "that one has this sort of conversation. It gives one the feeling that one is in such close touch with Lewis Carroll that the barman might be the Cheshire Cat in disguise." He turned to the barman. "Water, then, a tiny amount."

The barman went to the massive bottle of ouzo, as clear as gin, poured out a desperate measure, and then went to the little sink and squirted water in from the tap. Instantly, the ouzo turned the colour of watered milk.

"God, that's a strong one," said Leslie. "Let's have the same." I agreed. The glasses were set before us. We raised them in a toast: "Well, here's to the *Marie Celeste* and all the fools who sail in her," said Larry, and took a great mouthful of ouzo. The next minute he spat it out in a flurry that would have done credit to a dying whale, and reeled back against the bar, clasping his throat.

"Ahhh!" he roared. "The bloody fool's put hot water in it!"

"Why did you put hot water in the ouzo?" asked Leslie belligerently.

"Because we have no cold," said the barman, surprised that Leslie should not have worked out this simple problem in logic for himself. "That is why we have no ice. This is the maiden voyage, *kyrie*, and that is why we have nothing but hot water in the bar."

"I don't believe it," said Larry brokenly. "A maiden voyage and the ship's got a bloody great hole in her bows, a Palm Court

Orchestra of septuagenarians, and nothing but hot water in the bar."

At that moment Mother appeared, looking distinctly flustered. "Larry, I want to speak to you," she panted. "It's Margo. She went to the you-know-where and she's got the slot jammed."

"I don't know what you expect me to do," said Larry. "I'm not a plumber. Can't she climb out?"

"No," said Mother. "She's tried, but the hole at the top is much too small, and so is the hole at the bottom."

"But at least there are holes," Larry pointed out. "We can feed her through them during the voyage."

"Try putting another coin in the slot thing," suggested Leslie. "That sometimes does it."

"I did," said Mother. "I put a lira in but it still wouldn't work."

"That's because it's a Greek lavatory and will only accept drachmas," Larry pointed out. "Why didn't you try a pound note. At least the rate of exchange is in its favour."

"Well, she can't stay in there all night," said Mother. "Supposing she banged her elbow and fainted? You know she's always doing that." Mother tended to look on the black side of things.

"In my experience of Greek lavatories," said Larry judiciously, "you generally faint immediately upon entering without the need to bang your elbow."

"Well, for Heaven's sake do something!" cried Mother. "Don't just stand there drinking."

Led by her, we eventually found the lavatory in question. Leslie, striding in masterfully, rattled the door.

"Me stuck. Me English," shouted Margo from behind the door. "You find stewardess."

"I know that, you fool. It's me, Leslie," he growled.

He fiddled ineffectually with the door, swearing under his breath.

"I do wish you wouldn't use bad language, dear," protested Mother. "Remember, you are in the Ladies."

"There should be a little knob thing on the inside which you pull," said Leslie.

"I've pulled everything," rejoined Margo indignantly. "What do you think I've been doing in here for the last hour?"

"Well, pull it again," suggested Leslie, "while I push."

He humped his powerful shoulders and threw himself at the door.

"It's like a Pearl White serial," said Larry, sipping the ouzo that he had thoughtfully brought with him and which had by now cooled down. "If you're not careful we'll have another hole in the hull."

"It's no good," said Leslie panting. "It's too tough. We'll have to get a steward or something." He went off in search of someone with mechanical knowledge.

"I do wish you'd hurry," said Margo, plaintively. "It's terribly oppressive in here."

"Shall I go and get her a hot ouzo? We can slide it under the door," Larry suggested helpfully.

He was saved from Mother's ire by the arrival of Leslie, bringing in tow a small and irritated man with a lugubrious face. "Always the ladies doing this," he said to Mother, shrugging expressive shoulders. "Always they are getting catched. I show you. It is easy. Why woman not learn?"

He went to the door, fiddled with it for a moment, and it flew open.

"Thank God," said Mother, as Margo appeared in the doorway. But before she could emerge into the bosom of her family, the little man held up a peremptory hand. "Back!" he commanded, masterfully. "I teaches you." He pushed Margo back into the lavatory and slammed the door shut.

"What's he doing?" squeaked Mother in alarm. "Larry, do something."

"It's all right, Mother," shouted Margo, "he's showing me how to do it."

"How to do what?" asked Mother, alarmed.

There was a long and ominous silence, eventually broken by a flood of Greek oaths.

"Now he's locked us both in," wailed Margo.

"Disgusting man," cried Mother, taking command. "Hit him, dear, hit him. Larry, you go for the captain."

"Please to find purser," wailed the little man. "Please finding purser for opening door."

Anyone who does not know the Greek temperament and their strange ability to change a perfectly normal situation into something so complicated that it leaves the Anglo-Saxon's mind unhinged, may find the ensuing scene incredible. Leslie returned with the purser, who not only added to the redolence of the Ladies with his garlic, but in quick succession complimented Larry on drinking ouzo and Leslie on his Greek accent, soothed Mother with a large carnation plucked from behind his ear, and then turned such a blast of invective on the poor little man locked up with my sister that one expected the solid steel door to melt. He rushed at it and pounded with his fists and kicked it several times.

Larry repaired to the bar to get drinks. At that moment three fellow passengers arrived, all large, big-bosomed, thick-legged peasant ladies, with heavy moustaches and black bombazine dresses three times too small. All of them smelt of garlic, scent and perspiration in equal quantities. Seeing the purser dancing with rage and pounding on the door, they paused like massive war-horses that have scented battle. Any other nationality would have complained about the purser's presence in this shrine to woman-hood, but this is where the Greeks so delightfully differ from other races. They knew it was a SITUATION with capital letters, and this above all is what Greeks love. The presence of three men (if you include the invisible one closeted with Margo) in their lavatory was as nothing compared with the SITUATION. Their eyes glittered, their moustaches whiffled and, a solid wall of eager flesh, they enveloped the purser and demanded to know what was afoot. As usual in a SITUATION, everyone spoke at once. The volume of sound made one's head spin, like playing the noisier bits of the Ride of the Valkyries in an iron barrel.

Having grasped the elements of the SITUATION from the harassed purser, the three powerful ladies, each built on the lines of a professional wrestler, swept him out of the way with scarlet-tipped spade-shaped hands and proceeded to lift up their skirts. With deafening cries of "Oopah, oopah," they charged the lavatory door. Their combined weights must have amounted to some sixty stones of flesh and bone, but the door was stalwart and the three ladies fell in a tangle of limbs. They got to their feet with some difficulty and then argued among themselves as to the best way to break down a lavatory door. One of them, the least heavy of the three, demonstrated her idea against one of the other doors. This, unfortunately, was not on the latch and so she crashed through, full tilt, into the lavatory pan.

At that moment Larry arrived accompanied by the barman

carrying a tray of drinks. For a time we all sipped ouzo companionably. Fresh interest in the SITUATION was aroused by the arrival of what appeared to be the ship's carpenter. He, like a magician, rolled up his sleeves and approached the door. Silence fell. He produced a minute screwdriver from his pocket and inserted it into a minute hole. There was a click and a gasp of admiration, and the door flew open. He stood back and spread his hands like a conjurer.

The first little man and Margo emerged like survivors from the Black Hole of Calcutta. The poor little man was seized by the purser and pummelled and shaken and abused. The carpenter, at this stage, took over. We listened to him with respect as he expounded the cunning mechanism of locks in general and this one in particular. He drained an ouzo and waxed poetic on locks. With his little screwdriver or a hairpin or a bent nail he could open any lock. He took the first little man and the purser by the wrist and led them into the lavatory like lambs to the slaughter. Before we could stop them, he had slammed the door shut. My family and the three fat ladies waited with bated breath. There were strange scrapings and clickings, then a long pause. This was followed by a torrent of vituperation from the purser and the steward, mixed with confused excuses and explanations from the lock expert. As we furtively crept away, the three ladies were preparing to charge the door again . . . .

THE FOLLOWING MORNING, we went down to the dining room for breakfast. The years had mercifully obliterated our memories of the average Greek's approach to cuisine. Greece provides most of the ingredients for good cooking but the inhabitants are generally so busy arguing that they have no time left to pursue the effete paths of *haute cuisine*.

In the dining saloon the tables were covered with off-white tablecloths covered with the ghosts of stains that some remote laundry in Piraeus had not succeeded in quite exorcising. Mother surreptitiously but determinedly polished all the cutlery on her handkerchief. The four young waiters, since we were the only people there for breakfast, saw no reason to disturb their noisy bickering until Larry, tried beyond endurance, bellowed, "*Se parakalo!*" in such vibrant tones that Mother dropped three pieces of Margo's cutlery on the floor, and the waiters surrounded our table with the most healthy obsequiousness. Mother, to her delight, found that one of them had spent some time in Australia and had a rudimentary knowledge of English.

"Now," she said, beaming at her protégé, "what I would like is a nice, large pot of hot tea. Make sure the pot is warmed and the water is boiling, and none of those teabag things that make one shudder when one refills the pot. Then I shall have some grilled tomatoes on toast."

We sat back expectantly. Mother had never given up a pathetic hope that she would one day find a Greek who would understand her requirements. As was to be expected, the waiter had let Mother's instructions regarding the tea pass unnoticed. Tea grew in teabags as far as he was concerned, and to tamper with nature would, he felt, involve dire consequences for all concerned. However, she had now introduced into his life a complication, a species of food unknown to him. "Gill-ed tomatoes?" he queried uncomfortably. "What is?"

"Gill-ed tomatoes," echoed Mother, "I mean tomatoes grilled on toast."

The waiter clung to the one sane thing in the world, toast. "Madam want toast," he said firmly, trying to keep Mother on the right track, "tea and toast."

"*And* tomatoes," said Mother, enunciating clearly, "grilled tomatoes."

A faint bead of perspiration made itself apparent upon the waiter's brow. "What is 'gill-ed tomatoes', madam?" he asked.

We had all relaxed around the table having ordered our breakfast, *sotto voce*, and now we watched Mother launch herself into battle. "Well," she explained, "You know, um, tomatoes . . . those, those red things, like plums."

"Madam want plums?" asked the boy, puzzled.

"No, no, *tomatoes*," said Mother. "Surely you know tomatoes?"

The gloom on the young Greek's face lightened. She wanted tomatoes.

"Yes, madam," he answered smiling.

"There," said Mother, triumphantly, "well then, tomatoes grilled on toast."

"Yes, madam," he said dutifully.

After a long interval, the waiter came back with the things we had ordered and plonked a pot of tea in front of Mother and a

plate upon which there was a piece of bread and two raw tomatoes cut in half.

"But this is not what I ordered," she complained. "They're raw, and it's bread."

"Madam say tomatoes," said the boy stubbornly.

"Look," said Mother, as one explaining to an idiot child, "you make toast first, you understand?"

"Yes," replied the boy dismally.

"All right, then," said Mother. "Then you put the tomatoes on the toast and you grill them. Understand?"

The boy wandered off carrying the plate. We watched, fascinated, as he put the plate of tomatoes and bread on a table and then spread out a paper napkin with the air of a conjurer about to perform a very complicated trick. He then placed the bread and the tomatoes carefully in the middle of the napkin.

"What on earth is he doing?" asked Mother.

"Performing some ancient Greek rite," explained Larry.

The waiter now folded up the napkin with the bread and

tomatoes inside and solemnly made his way across the saloon to lay his burden upon the big oil stove in the centre of it. Although it was spring, the weather was chilly, and so the stove was almost red hot and giving out a comforting heat. Before our fascinated eyes he placed napkin, bread and tomatoes carefully on the glowing lid of the stove and then stepped back to watch. There was a moment's pause and the napkin burst into flames to be followed, almost immediately, by the bread. The waiter, alarmed that his novel form of cookery was not being effective, seized another napkin from a nearby table and tried to extinguish the blaze by throwing it over the top of the stove. The napkin, not unnaturally, caught fire too.

"I don't know what Greek delicacy that is," said Larry, "but it looks delicious, and cooked *almost* by the table, too. Think what fun you'll have picking the bits of charred napkin out of your teeth."

"Don't be so disgusting, Larry," protested Mother. "I'm certainly not eating that."

Two other waiters had joined the first and all three were trying to beat out the flames with napkins. Bits of tomatoes and toast flew in all directions. An old gentleman, who had just sat down, had his tie pinned to him with a piece of flaming toast like a red-hot Indian arrow. The purser, emerging from the kitchen, seized a large jug of water and running forward, threw it over the stove. It certainly had the effect of extinguishing the flames, but all the closer tables were immediately enveloped in steam.

"It smells just like minestrone," said Larry. "I do think after all the boy's efforts you ought to try just a little, Mother."

"Don't be ridiculous, Larry," cried Mother. "They've all gone mad."

"No," said Leslie, "they've all gone Greek."

One waiter had now hit another for some inexplicable reason, the purser was shaking the original waiter by his lapels and shouting in his face. The threatening gestures, the pushing, the rich invective, were fascinating to watch but, like all good things, they eventually ended with the purser slapping the original waiter over the back of his head and the waiter ripping off his dingy white coat and hurling it at the purser, who threw it back at him and ordered him out of the saloon. The purser then made his way over to our table, drew himself up to his full height beside us, plucked a fresh carnation from his buttonhole and put it in Mother's left hand, while seizing her right hand and kissing it gracefully.

"Madam," he said, "I am apologetic. We cannot give you grilled tomatoes. Anything else you want, we do, but grilled tomatoes no."

"Why not?" asked Larry, in a spirit of curiosity.

"Because the grill in the kitchen it is broken. You see," he added by way of explanation, "it is the maiden voyage."

"It seems the most unmaidenly voyage to me," commented Leslie.

"Tell me," inquired Larry, "why was the waiter trying to grill on that stove?"

"The boy very stupid," said the purser. "We have only experienced personnel on this ship. He will be dismantled in Piraeus."

"How do you dismantle a waiter?" asked Larry, fascinated.

"Larry, dear, the purser is a very busy man, so don't let's keep him," said Mother hastily. "I'll just have a boiled egg."

"Thank you," replied the purser with dignity and he bowed and disappeared into the kitchen.

When the eggs arrived (two of them, which were put before her ten minutes later), not only were they hard but they had been carefully deprived of their shells by loving but unwashed fingers.

"There!" exclaimed Larry. "What a treat! Cooked to a turn and covered with fingerprints that Sherlock Holmes would have found irresistible."

Mother had to conceal these strange avian relics in her bag and then throw them overboard after breakfast when she was sure no one was looking, for, as she observed, we didn't want to hurt anyone's feelings.

"There's one thing to be said for it," said Larry, watching Mother casting the eggs upon the waters. "Three days on a diet of nothing but red-hot ouzo will render us slim as minnows and we'll all be as convivial as Bacchus by the time we land."

But he was wrong.

The evening meal was, by Greek standards, almost epicurean. There were three courses, the first of which was cold by intention, being an hors d'oeuvre, and the other two cold because they were served on cold plates accompanied by the usual altercation between the waiters. However, everything was edible.

As we had lingered over our meal, we found that the "night-cloob" was in full swing. Our three fat ladies, and an assortment of other passengers, were, to the strains of a Viennese waltz, jostling for position on the minute square of parquet. An eager steward materialized at our elbows and showed us to the most illuminated and conspicuous table in a place of honour. It was, we were told to our alarm and despondency, specially reserved for us by the captain. We were just about to protest that we wanted a dim and obscure table when, unfortunately, the captain himself appeared. He was one of those very dark, romantically melting Greeks, slightly on the fleshy side but giving the impression that this made him more attractive, in that curious way Levantines have.

"Madam," he said, making it seem like a compliment, "I am enchanted to have you and your most beautiful sister on board our ship on her maiden voyage."

It was a remark that, had the captain known it, was calculated to offend everyone. It made Mother think he was what she always used to call darkly "one of those sort of men", while Margo felt that there was some difference between Mother's seventy odd summers and Margo's well-preserved thirties. For a moment, the captain's fate hung in the balance; then Mother decided to forgive him as he was, after all, a foreigner, and Margo decided to forgive him because he was really rather handsome. With the suavity of a professional head waiter, the captain arranged us round the table, seating himself between Mother and Margo, and beamed at us, his gold fillings twinkling like fireflies in his dark face. He ordered a round of drinks and then, to Mother's horror, asked her for the first dance.

"Oh, no!" she said. "I'm afraid my dancing days are quite over. I leave that sort of thing to my daughter."

"But, madam," implored the captain, "you're my guest. You must dance." So masterful was he that, to our astonishment, Mother—like a rabbit hypnotized by a stoat—rose and allowed him to escort her out onto the dance floor.

"She's gone mad," said Leslie gloomily. "She'll have a heart attack and we'll have to bury her at sea."

Being buried at sea had been her last choice anyway. Mother spent much of her time choosing places in which to be buried.

"She's more likely to be trampled to death, with those three enormous women about," observed Larry. "Fatal to attempt to get onto that floor. It's like entering an arena full of rogue elephants."

Indeed, the floor was so packed that the couples were gyrating at an almost glacial slowness. The captain, using Mother as a battering ram and aided by his broad shoulders, had managed to fight his way into the solid wall of flesh and he and Mother were now embedded in its depth. Mother, owing to her diminutive size, was impossible to see but we caught an occasional glimpse of the captain's twinkling teeth. Finally, the last liquid notes of "Tales from the Vienna Woods" crashed out and the dancers left the floor. Mother, crumpled and purple in the face, was half-carried back to our table by the beaming captain. She sank into her chair, too breathless to speak, and fanned herself with her handkerchief.

"The waltz is a very good dance," said the captain, gulping his ouzo. "And it is not only a good dance but it is good exercise also for all the muscles."

It was Margo's turn next but being lighter on her feet and more agile than Mother, she survived rather better. Then, using all her undoubted charms, she persuaded the captain that, although Viennese waltzes were all right as a toning-up exercise, no Greek ship worthy of its name could ignore the cultural inheritance of Greece as embodied in her national dances. The captain was much struck by both Margo and the scheme and before we had orientated ourselves to the idea, had taken control of Greece's national heritage. He strode over to the septuagenarian band and demanded of them in loud tones what fine old cultural Greek tunes they knew. Tunes of the peasantry, of the people. Tunes that brought out both the wonders of Greece and the valour of her people, the poignancy of her history and the beauty of her architecture, the subtlety of her mythology, the sparkling brilliance that had led the world.

The violinist said they only knew one such tune and that was "Never on Sunday".

The captain came as near to having an apoplectic fit as anyone I've ever seen. With veins throbbing in his temple he turned, threw out his arms, and addressed the assembled company. Had anyone, he asked, rhetorically, ever heard of a Greek band that did not know a Greek tune? "Send for the chief officer!" he roared. "Where is Yanni Papadopoulos?"

The chief officer presently arrived looking faintly alarmed, presumably fearing that another hole in the bows had appeared.

"Papadopoulos," snarled the captain, "are not the songs of Greece one of the best things about our cultural heritage?"

"Of course," said Papadopoulos, relaxing slightly, since it did not seem from the conversation that his job was in jeopardy. It was obvious, he thought, that he was on safe ground. Even an unreasonable captain could not blame him for the brilliance or otherwise of the musical heritage of Greece.

"Why you never tell me, then," said the captain, glowering fiendishly, "that this band don't know any Greek tunes, eh?"

"They do," said the chief officer. "They play 'Never on Sunday'."

"My spittle on 'Never on Sunday'!" shouted the captain. "I ask you for the cultural heritage of Greece and you give me a song about a '*poutana*'. Is that culture? Is there no one on this ship who can play any real Greek songs?"

"The electrician, Taki, has a bouzouki, and I think one of the engineers has a guitar."

"Bring them!" roared the captain. "Bring everyone who can play Greek songs."

Having shown his authority, the captain beamed twinklingly and returned to the table. Presently, from the bowels of the ship, struggled a motley gang, most of them half-dressed, carrying between them three bouzoukis, a flute and two guitars. The captain was delighted.

The rest of the evening went splendidly, with only minor accidents to mar the general air of cultural jollification. Leslie ricked his back while trying to leap in the air and slap his heels in the approved style during a strenuous *Hosapiko* and Larry sprained his ankle by slipping on some melon pips that somebody had thoughtfully deposited on the dance floor. The dance went on until dawn when, like a candle, it flickered and went out. We crept tiredly to our beds as the sky was turning from opal to blue and the sea was striped with scarves of mist.

All was bustle and activity when we dragged ourselves out of bed and assembled in the main saloon. Presently, the purser materialized, and bowed to Mother and Margo. The captain's compliments, he said, and would we all like to go onto the bridge and see the ship dock? Mother consented to attend this great moment with such graciousness that you would have thought that they had asked her to launch the ship.

The captain, with no loss of charm after his hard night, greeted us with great joy, presented Mother and Margo with carnations, showed us round the wheelhouse with pride, and then took us out on what Larry insisted on calling the quarterdeck. From here, we had a perfect view over both the bows and the stern of the vessel. The chief officer stood by the winch round which the anchor chain was coiled like a strange rusty necklace, and near him stood at least three of the sailors who had made up last night's band. They all waved and blew kisses to Margo.

"Margo, dear, I do wish you wouldn't be so familiar with those sailors," complained Mother.

"Oh, Mother, don't be so old-fashioned," said Margo, blowing lavish kisses back. "After all, I've got an ex-husband and two children."

"It's by blowing kisses at strange sailors that you get ex-husbands and children," remarked Mother, grimly.

"Now," said the captain, his teeth glittering in the sun, "you

394

come, Miss Margo, and I show you our radar. Radar so we can avoid rocks, collisions, catastrophes at sea. If Ulysses had had this, he would have travelled farther, eh? Then we Greeks would have discovered America. . . . Come." He led Margo into the wheelhouse and busily showed her the radar.

The ship was now pointing straight at the docks, travelling at the speed of an elderly man on a bicycle. The chief officer, his eyes fixed on the bridge like a retriever poised to fetch in the first grouse of the season, waited anxiously for instructions. In the wheelhouse, the captain was explaining to Margo how, with radar, the Greeks could have discovered Australia, as well as America.

Leslie began to get worried, for we were now quite close to the docks. "I say, Captain," he called. "Shouldn't we drop anchor?"

The captain turned from beaming into Margo's face and fixed Leslie with a frigid stare.

"Please not to worry, Mr. Durrell," he said. "Everything is under control."

Then he turned and saw the dock looming ahead like an implacable cement iceberg. "Mother of God help me!" he roared in Greek, and bounded out of the wheelhouse. "Papadopoulos! Let go the anchor!"

This was the signal the chief officer had been waiting for. There was a burst of activity, and a clatter as the anchor chain ran out. The ship, however, went inexorably on its way. More and more chain rattled out, and still the ship slid on. It was obvious that the anchor had been released too late to act as a brake. The captain, ready for any emergency, leaped into the wheelhouse, signalled full astern, and brought the wheel hard over, pushing the helmsman out of the way with great violence. Alas, his brilliant summation of the situation, his rapid thinking, his magnificent manoeuvre, could not save us.

With her bow still swinging round, the *Poseidon* hit the dock with a tremendous crash. Everyone, including the captain, fell down. Larry received a nasty cut on the forehead, Mother bruised her ribs, Margo only laddered her stockings. The three fat ladies, who had been descending the companionway, were flung down it like an avalanche of bolsters.

The captain, with great agility, regained his feet, did various technical things at the wheel, signalled the engine room, and then— his face black with rage—strode out onto the bridge.

"Papadopoulos!" he roared at the poor chief officer, who was getting shakily to his feet and mopping blood from his nose, "you imbecile, you donkey! You illegitimate son of a ditch-delivered Turkish cretin! Why didn't you lower the anchor?"

"But Captain," began the chief officer, his voice muffled behind a bloodstained handkerchief, "you never told me to."

"Am I expected to do everything around here?" bellowed the captain. "Steer the ship, run the engines, produce the band which can play the Greek songs? Mother of God!" He clapped his face in his hands.

All around arose the cacophony of Greeks in a SITUATION. With this noise, and the captain's tragic figure, it seemed rather like a scene from the Battle of Trafalgar.

Eventually, the walking wounded were allowed ashore and we straggled down the gangway. We could now see that the *Poseidon* had another, almost identical, hole in her bows, on the opposite side to the previous one.

"Well, at least now she matches," said Leslie gloomily.

"Oh, look!" said Margo, as we stood on the docks, "there's that poor old band."

She waved, and the three old gentlemen bowed. We saw that the violinist had a nasty cut on his forehead and the tuba player a piece of sticking-plaster across the bridge of his nose. They returned our bows and, obviously interpreting the appearance of the family as a sign of support that would do something to restore their sense of dignity which had been so sorely undermined by their ignominious dismissal the night before, they turned in unison, and glancing up at the bridge with looks of great defiance, raised tuba, trombone and violin, and started to play.

The strains of "Never on Sunday" floated down to us.

Gerald Durrell

Gerald Durrell was born in Jamshed-pur, India in 1925. After his father died, his mother eventually settled in Corfu with her four remarkable children, of whom Gerry was much the youngest. According to her son, Mrs. Durrell "steered her vessel of strange progeny through the stormy seas of life with great skill, like a gentle, enthusiastic and understanding Noah", and the family's five-year stay there was idyllic.

"I had a truly happy, sunlit childhood," Gerry recalls, "a thing which a number of children nowadays seem to lack."

At a very early age he had made up his mind that the only thing he wanted to do was to study animals, and in Corfu he kept a large number of local wild animals as pets and made a special study of zoology. By his teens he knew without a shadow of doubt that he wanted to be a zoo-owner, and in 1945, as a first step in this direction, he joined the staff of Whipsnade Zoo as a student keeper.

Later he organized animal-collecting expeditions all over the world. He wrote his first book, *The Overloaded Ark*, about an expedition to the Cameroons, and has since written more than twenty equally popular books about animals.

In 1958 Gerald Durrell achieved his greatest ambition, a zoo of his own. The Jersey Wildlife Preservation Trust which he founded there has a particular purpose: the building up of breeding colonies of various species threatened with extinction in their wild state. At his zoo at Les Augres Manor in Jersey there are breeding groups of many rare creatures such as the Mauritious Pink Pigeon (reduced now to only thirty-five birds in the wild), the Pigmy Hog and the Golden Lion Marmoset.

Durrell is excited about future developments at the zoo. He has just bought more property in Jersey and hopes to be given permission to build a small college where students of conservation can be trained in animal care. Chances are that once more Gerald Durrell will achieve his aims.

EARTH
EARTH
EARTH
EARTH
EARTH

SOUND
SOUND
SOUND

A CONDENSATION OF THE BOOK BY
Arthur Herzog

Illustrated by Barbara Fox

PUBLISHED BY HEINEMANN

SOUND
SOUND

For Harry Vail, formerly a seismologist—
a specialist in the phenomena of earthquakes—
the remote farmhouse in New England, with
its sturdy red stones and quaint charm, was a
welcome haven from the tensions of city life
and the anguished memories of his past.

Then slowly, insidiously, the foundations
of his world began to crumble. The relentless
summer rain seemed to breed hostility—
within the village, within his marriage, and
finally, within the earth itself. As Harry
struggled to cope with the sinister forces
around him, he found himself utterly alone
before an awesome opponent. Here is the
gripping story of his battle for survival.

TREMOR

SATURDAY, June 15. Vail was up on a high stepladder, pruning a dead branch from a tree with a saw. He said, "Good to get outside for a change. This is the first Saturday morning it hasn't rained in . . . how long would you say?"

"More'n a month."

"Easy. Maybe two."

The blade bit into the tough wood of the elm. Vail put his shoulder into it, then stopped. "Can you hold the ladder tighter, Dun?" He began sawing again, and again the ladder shook. "Dun!"

He looked down. The old handyman had vanished. From the barn Vail could hear hammerblows. The legs of the ladder seemed firmly planted in the moist ground. "What the—"

It was as though the earth had shrugged gently, like an animal twitching its hide. The ladder swayed, and Vail dropped the saw and scrambled down as fast as he could.

Not far from the ground, the toe of his boot must have slipped on a muddy rung. Flailing out with his foot, he lurched drunkenly and fell with a cry.

Stunned, he lay with his eyes shut, his big frame outstretched, head pressed against the naked soil. Through his earth-fused ear he thought he heard a sound, like a grunt—a small grunt, far away, and yet he sensed incredible power.

"MR. VAIL?" the voice implored.

He did not want to be interrupted. He needed to remember, record the experience indelibly. He squeezed his eyelids and flattened his ear to the ground.

"Son?" The handyman's voice lost its indecision. "Better get the missus."

Shuffling feet. Piano music that stopped, then a child's cry, a dog's bark, more footsteps. Damn! He wanted to hear the earth-sound again.

"Harry! Are you all right?"

Magic Fingers, he thought. You put a quarter into a slot in a motel room and the bed vibrates. That's what the shaking was like. What was the grunt?

"Are you all right?" Kay demanded once more.

A tongue, wet, warm, furtive, touched his lips. Dog breath. Opening his eyes, he muttered, "Yes."

"Daddy's okay!" Mark shouted.

Dun stepped forward, hand outstretched, but Kay stopped him. "No. He might be hurt. I'll call Dr. Bjerling."

Harry wiggled his fingers and toes and questioned the rest of his body. "I'm all right," he said, standing up to prove it.

"What happened?" his wife asked anxiously.

"I slipped coming down the ladder." He glanced at Dun.

The handyman mumbled, "Should have held the ladder for you. Shouldn't have gone off." Watchful gray eyes blinked.

Harry reached out and shook the ladder, which seemed stable enough. "Not your fault," he said to Dun. He started for the house and stopped. "About the time I fell, did either of you feel or hear anything strange?"

Dun and Kay exchanged glances. Kay said, "No."

"You, Mark?" he asked the boy.

"No, Daddy."

"Why?" Kay said.

"No reason." But he had been positioned up on a stepladder while Dun had been hammering and Kay playing the piano. And Mark was only six.

In the kitchen, Kay cleaned dirt from his head and ear while Mark watched. "You have a bump." She fussed as she touched his skull gently. "I hope you haven't really hurt yourself. Have you a headache?"

"No," he lied. "Funny what happened up there before I fell. The ladder shook exactly as though there were"—he paused in surprise at his own words—"an earthquake."

"In Rhode Island?" Kay said with a smile.

"I didn't say there *was* an earthquake. It just felt like one. The saw must have stuck on a knot, and the ladder shook when I pushed." Harry gazed solemnly at his son. "Come to think of it, sawing is something like an earthquake." He went on to explain. "In an earthquake, instead of a saw scraping on wood you have two big pieces of stone trying to push past each other. The stone slabs stick. When the pressure gets too great they finally slip and the ground shakes. Buildings can fall down."

"With people in them, Daddy?"

"Sometimes." His big hand ruffled the child's red hair. "I'd better get moving." He started to rise, felt wobbly, and had to sit again.

"You ought to check with Dr. Bjerling," Kay said, eyeing him. "People can fracture their skulls and not know it for days."

Harry smiled. "I'm okay." This time he gained his feet.

The boy and the Shetland sheepdog went outside, while Kay returned to the grand piano in the living room. She played nicely, but a bit too heavily for the state of his head. Also, the piano sounded out of tune. Vail went to his study and closed the door.

The small room contained an old couch, a desk with a swivel chair, a filing cabinet. A bookshelf ran along one wall. Below it, Vail found books scattered on the floor. Mark? He was into everything. Or the cat—Judy sometimes jumped onto the shelves. Or the books might just have been unbalanced. Still . . .

Vail replaced the books and sat down at the desk, nerves twitching. His eyes scanned the shelves above his desk which contained books on geology and seismology. He reached for a volume but pulled back his hand. No, he warned himself, don't. That episode is over. Forget about it—you fell from the ladder. End of story.

But the room suddenly seemed constricting as a cell, and he fled. Outside, he stood indecisively, unable to put the earthsound from his mind. It was a damp morning, cool for the season. Bunches of clouds scudded in under a gray sky. Shoulders hunched, he started toward the sea.

The stone house where the Vails lived stood on six acres of land. The trail to the beach led through an overgrown field where farmers, and Indians before them, had planted corn; occasionally Vail found arrowheads. He hopped on stepping-stones over a stream known as Torturous Creek, swollen by recent rains, and skirted a

long, brackish pond lined by sedges. Swans paddled aimlessly. After the pond came a marsh, then a copse of trees and a small field, and finally a ten-foot bluff that overlooked their rocky beach.

When he reached a spot curtained from the house by a grove of trees, he dropped abruptly to the ground and placed one ear to it; the earth was mute. He got up and continued to the bluff, where he stood at the base of a shallow coastal indentation. To his left down the coast, close to the sea, loomed the Demming mansion, three stories high; on the right lay Shonkawa Point, the tip of Old Brompton peninsula, where the village of Old Brompton was, on the far side of the cliffs. When the wind drove in from the east the sea became rough here, but otherwise, partly protected, the water was calm. Today a big surf ran.

On the edge of the bluff was a chairlike rock, with arms and a back, in which he sometimes sat hypnotized by the unending motion of the waves. He stared intently at the surf splattering the exposed rocks, then pressed his ear against the stone slab and listened once again.

All right, all right, think about it if you have to, just don't think about it too much. The shaking on the ladder was easy to explain; it was the earthsound that bothered him. He must have imagined it as he lay in a daze, and yet he was not normally given to flights of fancy. What could the noise have been? The earth for Vail was familiar terrain, and he ticked off conceivable causes: blasting, excavation, underground water, deposits of natural gas struggling to reach the surface. . . . None of these answers was plausible.

Had he then experienced a tiny tremor? Vail had been a professor of seismology at the California Institute of Technology in Pasadena before he had quit academic life a decade ago and moved east, where he became a working geologist. He knew that noise sometimes accompanies quakes and that even stable Rhode Island was not entirely free of seismic activity. He took a deep breath and slowly the Modified Mercalli scale of earthquake intensities as they affect human observers came back to him:

I. Not felt except by a few under especially favorable circumstances.
II. Felt only by a few persons at rest, especially on upper floors of buildings. Delicately suspended objects may swing.

And so on up to the maximum intensity:

XII. Damage total. Waves seen on ground surfaces. Lines of sight and level are distorted. Objects thrown upward into air.

Little earthquakes—premonitory tremors, earthquake swarms— could be precursors of big ones, deadly ones—Stop! His mind balked, refused to continue the self-torture. He forced back the memory and the image of himself as shaken and helpless.

When Vail returned from the ocean, he found his son in the back-yard poking a patch of new yellow mud which lay along a narrow strip Dun had dug for a pipe to the studio.

"Mark! You're getting yourself filthy."

Kay appeared from the house. "Where did that mud come from? It hasn't rained yet today."

"I guess the new pipe is leaking. Where's Dun?"

"He left in a hurry right after you did."

"I'd better get him back. I don't know a thing about pipes." He surveyed the yellow patch. "It's funny—Dun doesn't usually make mistakes."

They expected company that evening, and Kay said, "If you're going to the village, I'll give you a small list." She added anxiously, "Head all right?"

He sensed that the ache was there dormantly. "Do until I get a new one."

Under a canopy of trees Vail maneuvered his twenty-year-old Rolls-Royce. The car, which he kept in perfect condition, was rather an affectation—it gave him a country-squire look he didn't deserve —but he had so few airs that one more wouldn't matter. The long driveway was filled with holes, exposing sharp rocks. He would have the drive graded and graveled when the rain stopped.

The Rolls-Royce turned onto Point Road, the only thoroughfare down the narrow four-mile-long peninsula. Between the stone house and the village lay a half-mile section of empty land belong-ing to Fred Demming. The stretch was a buffer zone between the rich summer people up the peninsula and the villagers whom none of the others wanted to know socially. The Vails were neither rich nor summer people, since they lived on the peninsula year-round, but socially they allied themselves with the rich because the villagers were, well, impossible.

Nobody seemed to know how many people lived in Old Brompton

Village—or Shonkawa Village, as its inhabitants called it, using the Indian name. A hundred or so, Vail guessed, the descendants of the early settlers. The more enterprising local people had broken with the past and moved away. Those who remained took a bare livelihood from the sea, and from occasional work for the summer people, who came in June and left after Labor Day. Except for a small general store and a grubby bar, the village had no stores, nor even the inevitable shore restaurant. The few tourists who came turned around and departed.

Bleak against the slate sky, the village appeared after a bend, almost as though whoever laid out the road had wished to keep the place out of sight. The buildings consisted of shacks and old trailers set on cinder blocks, and everything needed paint. Vail could imagine how the town green, which testified to the village's self-image, had once looked, with grass and trees and a proud cannon from the War of 1812. Now filled with abandoned vehicles, torn fishing nets, staved-in boats, old lumber and weeds, the square was nothing more than a dump in the middle of town.

On the square appeared a faded white church, the village's only vaguely presentable building. Too large for the present population, it had no minister, and so Dun, as archdeacon, performed the services. The church, the old man said, housed a valuable old Aeolian-Skinner pipe organ, and Vail took his word for it, never having been inside. The place was always locked except on Sunday mornings.

The town looked deserted except for Sam Wilbore, a tall, long-haired, athletic-looking youth, who stood on the ramshackle pier, a pile of flat white stones beside him. He reached down, took a stone and launched it across the bay, where it skipped half a dozen times on the water. When Vail parked the car and got out, Wilbore turned to reveal a face in which hardness mixed with craft and stupidity.

Uncomfortable with most of the villagers, and especially with the Wilbore clan, Vail made himself say, "Where is everybody?"

Wilbore hesitated before responding. "Church."

"Saturday?"

"Memorial service," Wilbore mumbled. He turned his back and launched another stone.

Vail's eyes, following the trajectory, saw a distant column of smoke against the overcast horizon. "What's that?"

Wilbore said over his shoulder without turning around, "Tank farm blew up near Newport."

"Anyone hurt?" The kid shrugged. An idea jabbed at Vail's brain. "What time did it blow?"

" 'Bout an hour ago."

"An hour!" That was when he had fallen from the ladder. He calculated: the storage tanks were about five miles across the water, too far for shock waves to have traveled through the ledge rock below. He said, "Thanks."

The Wilbore General Store was locked. Mrs. Wilbore, Sam's mother, must be in church, toward which, Vail noticed, the boy now sauntered. Try as he might, he could not rid his mind of the earthsound; if there had been a tremor, mightn't it have left clues? He began to prowl the street, looking for cracks in the pavement, broken windowpanes, fallen objects; but he found nothing unusual. As he neared the church he heard the bleat of the pipe organ; suddenly the music stopped, and the villagers poured out.

In their plain-colored clothes, they regarded him with blank eyes, as if he were a curiosity. Such strange folk, he reflected, from another culture almost, in some other time. How little he had learned about them in the three years he had lived in Old Brompton; but after all, they kept to themselves.

"Looking for something, Mr. Vail?" Dun inquired, appearing from the throng. Vail explained about the mud and the leaking pipe. Creases deepened in Dun's weathered face. "Wonder what went wrong. Go right over."

Vail thanked him and returned to the store. Mrs. Wilbore was a tall, strongly built woman with short hair and a lined, stony face. Invariably he wondered what went on behind the red-rimmed eyes. She might be piqued because the Vails did their major shopping elsewhere. His vocal objections to the driving habits of her teenage sons, Sam and Cy, might have annoyed her. The boys tooled down Point Road day and night, honking, tailgating, driving fast. Perhaps she lumped him with the rich summer people whom the villagers appeared to resent and envy. But Vail believed that what really bothered Mrs. Wilbore was his purchase of the stone house from her spinster sister-in-law, for Mrs. Wilbore had been cold from the start. Vail had questioned Dun about her, but the old man failed to enlighten him.

In the back of the store Vail almost tripped on a can, then saw that several had fallen from a stack against the wall. When he put his purchases on the counter, he said to Mrs. Wilbore, "Some things have fallen down in back. Just thought I'd tell you."

She stared at him bleakly over the register. "Oh?"

"Mrs. Wilbore, this might sound silly to you, but do you remember hearing the cans fall?"

"Pardon?"

"I'm trying to find out when they fell."

"No idea, Mr. Vail. Somebody must have knocked them down." Her glance included him among the suspects. "That'll be six twenty-seven."

Vail produced six dollars, and fished in his pockets for change, coming up with a quarter, which he placed on the counter.

"Six twenty-*seven*," she repeated, not touching the money.

He blinked in annoyance, found a ten-dollar bill in his wallet, and handed it over silently. Mrs. Wilbore made change without speaking. He swung the box of groceries under his arm and left the store hurriedly.

Two cents! And the way she overcharges! He'd see to it they shopped there even less. Feeling demeaned, he slipped too easily into what happened next.

Cy and Sam Wilbore leaned against the fender of the carefully polished Rolls. Cy was about eighteen and Sam about two years younger; both were almost as tall as Vail but lean, without his heft. They had dark hair and pointed faces like their mother's, with the same narrow red-rimmed eyes. Vail said, "Get off the car."

Neither boy moved. " 'Fraid we'll scratch your fancy buggy, Mr. Vail?" Cy Wilbore said. He asked his brother, "Sam, you got a burr on your pants?"

"Why, have a look," Sam clowned. He bent and turned the seat of his Levi's toward Vail.

Cy Wilbore leaned over and looked. "No burr." He laughed and settled back on the fender. "Lose something?" he said to Vail. "Saw you poking around."

"Well, it's a free country."

"Yeah? Never know it from all you rich folks' signs that say 'Private Property—Keep Out.' "

"I didn't put them up," said Vail. He was losing his temper, and he surveyed the peeling shacks on the town square deliberately. "Though, considering the looks of this place, I can see why people do."

Cy's face twisted. He extended his finger and made an X on the hood of the Rolls. "That," he said distinctly, "for you."

The ache in Vail's head jerked like a muscle spasm. *"Get off the car!"* he roared. Neither boy budged. He lunged, grabbed their necks, and with all his two hundred pounds lifted them from the Rolls and threw them to the ground. Sam Wilbore lay gasping for breath while Cy got to his feet and backed away, white-faced.

Vail jumped into the car and drove off. He hit his driveway too fast and the Rolls shuddered in the holes. The dog barked as he sat in the car trying to calm himself. After a decade in New England, Vail still thought of himself as a Californian—easygoing, essentially unflappable—as opposed to Easterners, who were tense and erratic. As he considered the scene in the village he wondered if he had become an hysterical Easterner, too. Surely there must have been a better way to handle the Wilbore kids.

THE barking persisted and Vail, himself again, left the car. "Shut up, Punch. Don't you ever know me?" Playfully he picked up the dog by its long bushy tail, an act to which Punch never seemed to object. He put the groceries in the kitchen and went to the backyard where Dun was digging an oblong trench. "I'll give you a hand, Dun," he said.

Kay appeared in the doorway of the studio. "Oh no you don't. No physical exercise until we're absolutely sure there's nothing wrong with that head of yours."

"No problem, son. Ground's soft. Almost finished already."

"Well, all right."

Vail joined his wife in the studio. Over the winter, the renovation of the stone house finished at last, Dun had converted a storage room in the barn into a studio for Kay. Now neat and cozy, with a picture window that overlooked the massive gray rock in the backyard, it would replace the cramped bedroom she had painted in before. It was Vail's hope that the studio would help keep Kay busy during the long winters, which were hard on her, especially the last one, with Mark in first grade and himself away frequently on business. She sometimes complained of being lonely, depressed, and waited eagerly for June, when the summer people arrived like a rescue mission. Unlike Harry, Kay was gregarious.

During the morning Kay had been hanging her pictures, and for the first time the studio looked like one. Harry said, "Terrific."

She kissed him. "It's a wonderful present. Like the arrangement?"

He inspected the pictures in their clear plastic frames. Perhaps because of his geological training, he often displayed a better spatial sense than she did. He said, "They're all at a slight angle."

"Angle?" She stepped back.

"Look at the frames in relation to the floor."

"You're right. How spooky. I'd have sworn I had them straight. Well, what about the layout?" she repeated.

He pointed to a picture. "That's too high. It ought to go there— to the left of the one of the boulder."

He put in a new hook and took down the picture, staring at it. As time passed, Kay's work had become more literal—this painting was almost photographic. It showed part of a wall of the stone house. "Have I seen this before?"

"It's new. I just painted it. Like it?"

"Yes, I do. It's just that . . ." Something seemed wrong—some minor detail he could not quite extract from the pattern of stones and mortar. Dun entered the studio.

"Found the problem, Mr. Vail. Care to come outside?"

Vail followed the short, spare figure. It had started to drizzle. Dun pointed at the trench he had dug. "Leak in the coupling. Guess I messed up." He smiled, revealing small brown teeth. "Fix it now, before the rain gets too bad."

"What about the hole?"

"Put a piece of plywood over her so nobody falls in, and finish up tomorrow."

Vail looked away from the open trench. "Okay," he said with a frown.

LATER, in their bedroom, Kay said, "You'd better hurry."

"They never come on time." Vail combed his hair, slipped on clothes, and said, "Your turn to step on it."

"I'm ready," she said from her dressing table. She stood up, gave a final look in the mirror at her long blue skirt and white blouse, and turned to appraise her husband.

Vail was a muscular man a little over six feet tall, with a round, friendly face, green eyes, and a complexion ruddied from the outdoors. He wore an old tweed jacket over a sport shirt, cavalry-twill trousers, suede shoes. Kay was thirty-four, three years younger than Vail. Like him, she had reddish hair and ruddy skin. But she was eight inches shorter and not much more than half his weight.

They were still as they examined each other's faces. "You're a good strong man, Harry Vail," she said. "I'm lucky to have you. We have a fine life."

"Yes," he said. "We have just about all anybody could want. We're awfully lucky."

She became subdued. "I just wish the rain would stop. It's like summer hasn't started yet, and the winter was so long."

"We'll go on a trip next winter, I promise."

"That's what you said last winter and the winter before. It always costs too much. I wish we had as much money as our friends."

"The Demmings and the Pollidors? Well, I guess they'd be even unhappier without it. I'm going to say good night to Mark." His gaze slid past her to the window. "Look, it's stopped raining. See how lucky we are?"

THE Pollidors and the Demmings were the Vails' closest neighbors. As Harry had predicted, all were late. Waiting for them, Kay fluttered around the living room, patting couch cushions and rearranging flowers. Harry put wood in the fireplace and lit it. Smoke billowed. Using tongs, he pushed the logs deeper into the fireplace; smoke continued to pour into the room. "The flue is shut," he said. "I don't remember closing it."

"I didn't," she said, "so you must have."

"I could say exactly the same thing," he retorted.

"Better open the windows," she said. He did, with effort, and the smoke cleared.

When the shelty's high-pitched barks telegraphed guests, "Big Ben," the grandfather clock, said 9:30. "Ssssh, Punch," Kay scolded as she opened the door.

Polly Pollidor, an heiress from a manufacturing family, entered first. A short, pretty woman in her late thirties or early forties, with shoulder-length brown hair, Polly contrived to look simple and expensive at the same time. There was a sharp frown line on her forehead, which she tried to hide with makeup. She and her husband, Bill, had married young and recently celebrated their twentieth anniversary. They had no children.

"My dear," Polly said to Kay, "don't you look glamorous! How do you keep your hair so nice? Mine looks like a mop and not a hairdresser in the village. Not that it would do any good, with all this rain. Pretty soon Old Brompton will be under water and we'll have to move—or grow gills. Why, the peninsula's half submerged already...."

Bill Pollidor stood behind her. A balding man in his middle forties, he was a New York tax lawyer who spent summers in Old Brompton, conducting his business by phone. Not gently, he tapped his wife's shoulder and said, "You're forgetting our guest."

"This is Jeffrey Carmichael," Polly said. "We've been in love for years, even though he is my first cousin."

Carmichael stepped forward, hand outstretched. He was a handsome man about Vail's age, and was wearing a tartan blazer. A television reporter, whose wife had recently left him, he needed, Polly had told the Vails, warmth and reassurance.

"We've seen you on the tube, of course!" Kay told him.

"Always glad to hear that," Carmichael said with a bright smile under his mustache. As they entered the living room from the foyer he exclaimed, "What a lovely place!"

Kay looked pleased. "When we fixed it up we tried to keep it pretty much as it was."

"You were right." He glanced quickly at the Pollidors, who the year before had converted their old farmhouse into a modern dwelling, with glass walls and high ceilings. "Not that starting over isn't all right, too!" He examined the beams nestling in white plaster, the marble fireplace, the old peanut vendor's cart on sturdy wheels which Kay had converted into a bar. He pointed at the brass birdcage. "That's a pretty bird. What kind is it?"

"It's called a singing greenfinch," Kay said. "It's supposed to have a nice voice, except this one doesn't seem to know how to sing. It never has, anyway."

"Maybe it needs another finch to sing to." Jeff then nodded toward a row of squat jugs with painted faces and three-cornered hats on a lighted glass shelf. "What are those?"

"I picked them up at an antique auction. They're called toby

413

jugs. The faces are all different, but they're modeled after an eighteenth-century Englishman who's supposed to have drunk two thousand gallons of beer without eating."

"Bill Pollidor could do that," Polly said quickly. "You won't believe what he's done. He's bought a bar with a computer! It was supposed to come today from New York, but it didn't—which will ruin Bill's weekend."

Pollidor broke in. "It can be programmed to make a hundred kinds of drinks, if you provide the liquor."

Harry laughed and took their orders while Carmichael asked Kay, "Are there many stone houses around here?"

"No. We have the only one on the peninsula."

"You must be very special. How old is the house?"

"That's a bit of a mystery," Kay said. "The woman we bought it from three years ago wanted all the money in cash. Then as soon as the deal was made she vanished. We know her family, the Wilbores, but they're not very . . . well, communicative. Anyway, the builder must have been a Wilbore because most of the property on the peninsula generally has stayed in the same family. The house is definitely a post-Civil War farmhouse, and Harry believes it must be built on the foundation of another house, because it's a good location."

"Why did this particular farmer use stone?" Carmichael inquired.

"Who knows?" Kay said. "But my bet is that the stone gave him a feeling of stability, of security." Under Jeff's stare she blushed beneath her freckles. "You *do* ask a lot of questions."

Carmichael replied gaily, "Of course! It's my business. Where did the stone come from? Or is that a mystery, too?"

"Yes," Kay confessed with a sigh. "The stone looks local because it's the same color as the sea cliffs, but it couldn't have come from there, because the cliffs are crumbly. And yet Harry can't find a quarry on the peninsula. He's a geologist, you know."

"I was told. Are you also interested in geology?"

"Me?" Kay cried. "What do I know about science? People are more interesting to me than rocks, though not to Harry. He's fascinated by the earth, aren't you, honey? He believes it's alive."

Just then Punch exploded like a string of firecrackers, and the door opened to Fred and Wende Demming. With extensive real estate in Boston and on the peninsula, as well as inherited wealth,

Fred Demming was surely the richest man in affluent Old Brompton, but he seemed to have paid a price. His hands shook as though from a mild palsy, and his gruff face looked older than his fifty years. He wore thick glasses and walked with a cane.

Wende was a former beauty queen and still reigned as one in Old Brompton. Twenty years younger than her husband, tall, small-boned, she had a narrow waist and long, supple legs. Her face—white-skinned, blue-eyed—looked fragile, deceptively. Wende was immensely competitive and delighted in being a general at games. She was not entirely happy, however, she once confessed to Kay, who had a way of bringing people out. There was some deep need in her that Fred failed to satisfy, and sometimes, impetuously, she would depart in her cream-colored Mercedes convertible for days at a time.

Vail brought the newcomers into the circle and introduced them to Carmichael. Kay was suddenly silent, Harry saw, and understood. She was eager to unveil her studio. "Come and see the new studio," he said.

Chattering, they trooped across the lawn toward the square of light from the picture window. Harry had to push hard on the door to open it. "I thought you were going to straighten the pictures, Kay," he said as they filed in.

"I thought I did," she said vaguely. "I guess I didn't."

To all but Jeff Carmichael the scenes on the walls were familiar, yet in a sense they were new to the summer people, since they depicted winter in Old Brompton: the brackish pond with a lone swan huddled in the sedges; the jutting block of granite behind the house, that looked like a giant gravestone; the soaring black elm in the backyard, with the clay bell hanging from a branch.

"Kay, you've changed your style!" Polly exclaimed.

Kay smiled gratefully as she straightened another picture. "I'm trying to be more realistic, that's all."

"Do you exhibit in New York?" Jeff asked.

"Oh no, I'm just an amateur. Painting's therapy for me. It keeps me from going crazy when Harry's away on business and our son's in school."

"Pretty good for an amateur," Jeff said. He pointed to a picture of a deer by a little house. "Where's that?"

Wende answered, "It's in the woods, right where the Pollidors', the Vails', and our property all meet. It's a playhouse Fred built for his children." She added lightly, "His kids by his first wife."

"You didn't need to tell me," Jeff said. His gaze rested on Wende's clear face a little longer than necessary. "What's that big rock? I haven't seen anything like it around here."

"It's granite," Harry explained. "You're right—there's nothing like it within thirty miles. It was carried here when the last glacier receded about 10,000 B.C. Can you imagine the power involved? It weighs tons."

"I guess Mother Nature hasn't got the stuff she used to have," Jeff observed. "Not here in the East anyway."

"Oh, I don't know. The trouble is, tucked away in our cities, we're losing the feel of the earth. If Mother Nature gets in a bad mood, we don't know what to do. And things can happen. Hurricanes, floods . . . earthquakes."

"Earthquakes? When has there been an earthquake anywhere but out West?" Jeff demanded.

"You can get tremors everywhere."

"Sure, sure. But I mean a *real* earthquake."

"Even a tiny tremor *is* an earthquake. As for severity, one in early Salem was strong enough to knock down chimneys, and there was a good-sized earthquake in Boston last century."

"That's a long while back," Jeff argued.

"By our standards, maybe, but by the earth's it was just a second ago. You never know what Mother Nature is up to."

"Oh yes. You think the earth is alive, your wife said."

"The earth isn't exactly alive, but in many ways it's comparable to a living organism. The crust would be its skin, rocks its bones, veins of metal its nerves, water its blood. And it has a heart—its core. There's movement under the earth; it changes, too, just as living things move and change."

They turned to the watercolor that Kay had finished that morning, depicting a stone wall of the house. Vail had been aware before of a peculiar detail in the painting. Now, inspecting it closely, he saw that Kay had painted a tiny crack, like a series of diagonal Ws, in the stones near the roof. "Kay," he said, "there's no crack like that in our house."

She glanced at him. "Of course there is."

"Since when?"

416

"Since always."

"I'm sure it wasn't there when we bought the house. Where is it?"

"On the wall outside Mark's room. You've just forgotten." Kay turned to the others and said, "Harry fell today and whacked his head. It's affected his memory, which is usually sharp."

"Nothing's wrong with my memory," he insisted.

"Well, darling, you can see the crack for yourself tomorrow. And ask Dun if it hasn't always been there."

She turned to leave the studio, but Harry insisted, "Kay, didn't we take pictures when we bought the place?"

"I think we did—for a before-and-after album. Why do you ask?"

He said, trying to keep his voice even, "Where are the photos, do you remember?"

"How should I know?"

"Try to remember."

Kay said to the others, "Shall we go?"

Vail remained in the studio to turn off the lights after the group had found its way to the house. He stood by the picture window, thinking about the crack. Why couldn't he quite bring himself to believe Kay? And if by some dreadful chance he was right, a new crack could mean that the house was shifting in subsoil turned to treacle by the unprecedented rains. He told himself to stop imagining things.

About to leave the studio, he heard Kay's mare, Brioche, champ in her stall on the other side of the barn and, almost simultaneously, Punch's staccato bark. He turned again to the picture window. Usually he put the Rolls in the barn, but today, preoccupied by the scene with the Wilbore boys, he had left it out. It stood in front of the Demmings' and Pollidors' cars, on the edge of the pool of light. His eyes probed the darkness. Did he detect movement behind the Rolls, the white of a hand, a retreating figure? He went outside. Clouds curtained the sky and the dark was almost total.

Heads raised a little too quickly when he entered the living room. Kay said sharply, "Why did Punch bark?"

"Wild animal—deer, fox, owl."

"Sure it wasn't a prowler?" Kay asked.

"Didn't see anybody. Why?"

"Polly says there have been robberies on the peninsula recently.

417

And Bill's had a burglar alarm installed. He thinks he's seen people in the woods. Who would they be?"

"The village idiots, who else?" Bill Pollidor said.

Jeff broke in. "Who are these villagers?"

Fred Demming leaned forward to explain. "The so-called summer people like myself own much of the land on the peninsula but by no means all. The locals come from farming families, and though they no longer farm, they still own quite a bit of land. They made a collective decision some time ago not to sell until the price went higher. And it was a good idea so far as it went. The price of land *is* rising."

"Then why don't they sell?"

"The fact that the price rises confirms their expectations that it will rise still more. If the price of land dropped, they would sell at once, but it won't drop, and so we have the status quo. They will always hope for a still higher price, and we do our best to preserve the expectation."

Demming waved his cane. "Some of us—I don't mean the Vails here; they're a little naïve about such things—have influence on the town council."

"Run it, you mean," Bill Pollidor said.

Demming ignored him. "We see to it that there are strict zoning laws, and that real estate taxes don't strain the locals' pocketbooks. The summer people pretty much finance the town through charitable donations. And from time to time blind offers to purchase the villagers' lands are made through us. The price is always high enough to be interesting and low enough to be turned down."

Jeff said, "So! But surely there comes a time when someone wants to sell. How do they keep each other in line?"

"Oh, it's a matter of a handful of families, really. Any one of them who thinks of selling faces ostracism, like the Wilbore woman who sold to the Vails here. Afterward she just vanished. Forced to move away, I suppose. That was the last land sold in these parts—three years ago. They haven't forgiven Vail yet, just for buying the property."

Polly said, "They're practically like an Indian tribe, clinging to their old ways!"

"She's right," Kay remarked. "The village is almost a reservation,

418

and in it the villagers are dying off just like the Indians. I hope they don't come back to haunt us, too."

"Haunt us?" Harry asked.

Kay said wanly, "Mrs. Wilbore told me that people hereabouts used to believe that Indian ghosts haunt the peninsula, seeking revenge on the early settlers who squeezed them off their lands. Eventually the whole tribe died of starvation."

"It's just like the villagers to believe in ghosts," Polly said.

"A surprising number of people do," Jeff remarked, "though they won't admit it. Anyway, it's *how* you die that counts, not what comes after. Don't we all pick our own form of death in a way? Say, I know a game . . ." He stopped, as if he had thought better of what he was about to say.

"I hate all this talk about ghosts," Kay said. "Who's hungry? I have sandwiches in the dining room."

AFTER the guests had gone they cleaned up in silence. Kay said finally, "Have a good time?"

"So-so. Carmichael's kind of a know-it-all."

"Wende liked him. I hope nothing's starting, for Fred's sake." She stood up from the dishwasher and looked at him. "You weren't yourself tonight, the way you carried on about that crack. It was embarrassing, Harry."

"Was it? Would you be embarrassed if the house fell down?"

"I just don't understand why one silly crack bothers you so."

"I don't remember seeing it, that's all. I'd still like to look at those photos."

"All right!" she snapped, setting down a pot with a bang. "I'll look for them in the morning. In the meantime try to remember the crack is in your head! I'm going to bed."

He took a flashlight from the hall closet and went outdoors. Below Mark's window he shone the light, seeing nothing except tangled patterns of shadow and stone. He put both cars in the barn and started back to the house, when the light picked up the whitish shape of plywood over Dun's trench.

He stopped, wrestling with his emotions. Something inside him demanded that he look beneath, into the open hole, into the earth. No, no, he argued, but the compulsion was too strong. He knelt, put the light on the grass, and lifted the plywood with both hands.

His skin cringed at the outline of the cadaverously thin body at the bottom of the trench. *Dammit, it's only a pipe!*

He replaced the plywood and entered the house, alarmed by his own reactions. Inside, he became aware of Kay's half-fearful cry from the bedroom, as though she had called before. "Harry? You were gone forever. Where were you?"

"Checking the house," he muttered.

"Poor Harry, I'm sorry I snapped at you," she said as he got into bed.

AFTER Kay fell asleep he lay coiled like a watch spring, recalling the day's events. Once as he started to doze something seemed to fall on him, and he woke with a start.

The room was still except for the soft sounds entering the open door, sounds of which he was usually unaware—the whine of the refrigerator, the crack of a beam, the faint clanging of the clay bell in the tree. Every house has its own sounds, like its own personality, he thought. His house was old, slightly complaining. Vail shifted uncomfortably, senses alert.

Ever since he had hurt his back playing football he had sat on hard chairs and slept with a board beneath his mattress, and he was uncertain whether the rumble reached him from outside, far away, or from the bed, transmitted by the board. He ran to the window. Just for an instant he thought he saw two dots of red that danced in the night and vanished. *Must be a truck.* But why a truck at that hour?

He returned to bed. Sweat rose on his forehead. Careful not to wake Kay and let her see him in this state, he stayed as motionless as he could.

Dawn found him exhausted. The wind had ceased; the room was utterly still. He sighed and started to sleep, and then he felt it: quick, light, evasive, almost gentle, a shudder in the bed. Kay rolled over without waking.

VAIL woke at nine thirty feeling terrible. Kay entered the bedroom and put her palm on his forehead. "The sheet's wet, as if you've been sweating, but you don't have a fever."

"I'm all right," he grumbled. "Dun here?"

"Yes. He's finishing up before he goes to church."

Vail dressed and had breakfast, though he lacked appetite. He went outside, eyes on the inevitable clouds.

"Watch out!" Dun cried.

Vail walked gingerly around the open trench. Dun set down the wheelbarrow and said, "Don't want no more accidents, do we? Feeling all right, Mr. Vail?"

"I've been better," he said. "Tell me, Dun, did a truck come to the village late last night?"

"Yes, as a matter of fact. Something to deliver to the Pollidors from New York. Supposed to get here yesterday afternoon, but the truck broke down on the highway. Come here, did they?"

"No. I heard the truck on the road." It showed how capable he was of misreading evidence. "Come with me, Dun."

"Oh, Mr. Vail." Dun, walking by his side, seemed eager to speak. "Your car has a flat front tire. Looks like a gash in it."

"Maybe one of those sharp rocks in the driveway. Hit it too hard," Harry surmised. "I'll look at it later."

"I'll change it for you, Mr. Vail."

They turned the corner of the house and stood below Mark's window. Looking up, Harry saw a thin, steplike crack near the roof, exactly where Kay had painted it. "How long has that crack been there?"

Dun had been working around the place since the Vails had bought it. He scratched his cheek with yellowed nails and squinted, as though having difficulty locating the break. "Just a surface crack in the mortar. Don't mean a thing."

"I know. But how long has it been there?" Vail said impatiently.

The handyman shifted his weight from one foot to the other and opened his lips to speak.

"Dun!" Standing behind them, Kay spoke sharply. She intimidated the old man a little, Harry was aware. "It's always been there. You know that."

The handyman gave Kay a hesitant sideways glance. "Reckon that's right," he said.

"You don't have to put words in his mouth," Harry snapped.

Kay's face filled with surprise. She held a manila envelope. "I found the photos." She removed one from the envelope and handed it to him. Dated three years earlier in his own writing, it showed a thin crack on the outer wall. "Now are you satisfied?"

"I'm sorry, Kay," he said humbly.

That afternoon Vail found still another crack in the stone house. He had gone to the basement on an errand and discovered water on the floor. Considering the amount of rainfall, this was not unusual, though he wondered how the water had gotten in. Mopping up, he realized that it seemed to come from under a pile of cartons, containing tax records and outgrown toys and clothes, that stood against one wall. He decided to move the boxes to the other side of the cellar, where it was dry.

As Vail picked up the last carton he saw what appeared to be a defect in the concrete.

He approached slowly, praying his eyes were deceived in the dim light, and placed his fingers on the wall. Up from the floor ran a thin crack about a foot long.

The crack had not been there a few months before, when he had moved the boxes from the storeroom to make way for Kay's studio, of that he was sure. What would have caused it? But maybe he was wrong about this crack, too, just as he had been wrong about the one on the outside wall. Suddenly his mind began to whirl. What was real and what wasn't?

Vail told Kay he was headed for the beach, and soon he sat in his rock chair overlooking the sea. The water was flat, almost motionless, and the fading sun lurked behind thin clouds.

He would try to come to terms with himself, to penetrate the layers of his own experience which held pain and terror.

How many of his actions during the past decade had been taken to escape anxiety? Abandoning a seismological career and moving from California were clearly two of them; locating his Fall River office on a low floor of the building might be included, and so, for that matter, might be the choice of an imposing old car that he associated with stability. His love for Old Brompton? Subtly, yes; protected from outsiders, operating according to strict standards, it was as unchanging a place as might be found.

But more to the point was his recent obsession with tremors. What had happened, he believed, was that the fall from the ladder and the hearing of an earthsound had triggered a neurosis he thought to have buried for good, a neurosis that tricked him into finding earthquake clues, made him feel shakings when there were none. The clinical name of this difficulty he did not know.

Seismophobia, the fear of shaking, would be close, he imagined. Harry Vail was terrified of earthquakes.

Vail recalled himself as a nature-loving youngster who liked to backpack, climb mountains, fish. He delighted in the contour of a hill, the strata in canyon walls. When first he cracked open a rock with a hammer, he had been amazed at the complexity hidden beneath the drab exterior. In sparkling layers the rock explained the enormous scope of its life.

Without articulating it, Vail had formed an idea of the earth as awesomely ancient and, if not quite friendly, at least a reliable platform. Vail had lived with his parents not far from Bakersfield, California. In 1952, when he was fourteen, the area was hit by an earthquake strong enough to earn a name—the Tehachapi earthquake, after the nearest town. Like any Californian living near the San Andreas Fault, Vail was accustomed to earthquakes—but not one of this awful power. The world tilted, becoming a heaving place in which nothing stable existed.

As the ground rippled beneath him it seemed to say "I'm alive, I'm alive," and he responded with joy at the earth's almost playful vitality. Then a few days later the aftershock was worse than the main one. Buildings collapsed; a boy Vail knew was crushed beneath a falling water tower.

For nights afterward he woke up shaking in anticipation of a new blow. Later, when he studied geology at Stanford and went on for his Ph.D. in seismology, he would sometimes wonder whether scientific interest was the goad, or whether in some complicated way he was trying to put himself against the earth in order to prove that it held no terror. But he liked the work and displayed an instinctive feel for it.

Besides, seismology took its adepts away from the lab and out into the field. Such a chance came to Vail in 1964 when . . . On his rock seat by the ocean his memory again balked, would not proceed without instructions on how to handle the pain. If he could avoid thinking her name . . . if he could depersonalize her . . .

She was an undergraduate and he, a professor, married her. She had looked something like Wende Demming, he remembered, tall, blonde, but rounder of face, sweeter. He had taken a leave of absence from Cal Tech, and she a semester off, for him to work with an oil company in Anchorage, Alaska. By analyzing seismic waves

423

sent off by underwater explosions in Cook Inlet, he might be able to predict the location of oil. In summer, when his work was complete, they would travel north to the Denali Fault, carrying a mercury tiltmeter that would record minute changes in ground level.

They arrived in Anchorage the middle of March. On Good Friday, March 27, the library where Vail pored over seismic records closed early, and he came home to their house in Turnagain-Bluff-by-the-Sea. They strolled to the edge of the bluff in light flurries of snow. Sea and sky blended into smooth nothingness, a gray void. The face she turned to him lacked expression. "It's like a hole to nowhere," she said, or had she said that? His memory was unreliable, because at that instant the ground shuddered.

"Earthquake!" He seized her arm and they scrambled away from the swaying bluff. Trees rocked, their car creaked on its springs, the picket fence danced like a chorus line. The churning subsided.

"You're safe here," he told her. "Wait. I'm going inside for the tiltmeter. I'll be right back."

She clutched his hand so tightly he had to wrench it free. He took the flagstones at a run, leaving the front door open behind him. The instrument, which he had been testing, lay on the living-room floor. He started toward it. The front door shut with a bang. The house shook as though in the grip of a monstrous animal. Walls weaved. Books and dishes flew across the room.

"Hurry, Harry, hurry!" He heard her thin cry through the broken windows. He wanted to go to her, but the tremendous shaking made him weak, dizzy. The house groaned, and the roar grew until it resembled a jet aircraft overhead. "*Harry . . . Harry, hurry!*"

Above him was a wood chandelier made from a ship's wheel. He watched, hypnotized, as it spun on its chain, shooting pieces of wood in every direction. Struck on the head, Vail fell.

It was too late to retrieve the instrument. The floorboards opened. Fountains of sand spewed into the room. He lurched like a steel pellet in a pinball machine. Furniture lunged at him. He did not know whether he escaped by door or window. Dazed and terrified, he squatted on the ground.

In thunderous jerking jolts the land shattered. The flat stones heaved. Trees fell in crazy patterns and the earth cracked into a jigsaw puzzle. In the uproar he heard her monotonous cry of terror, "*Hurry-Harry-HUUAAARY!*"

"Hang on!" he screeched as the picket fence behind her disappeared. The futile words mocked him. Hang on to what? The ground leaped, split into smaller pieces, until she knelt alone on a rocking island in a sea of earth.

Paralyzed, he watched as a tree fell on her silently, deadly as a guillotine. The ground began to slide toward the edge of the bluff, taking the house with it. The earth opened brutal brown lips, swallowed her body, and moved on.

Whimpering, he crawled away. He woke in a hospital. Diagnosis: shock.

The Alaska earthquake of Good Friday, 1964, lasting from three to four minutes, was the largest ever recorded in North America: between 8.3 and 8.6 on the Richter scale, on which the greatest known earthquake is 8.9. In the Turnagain section alone, seventy-five homes were lost. Somewhere down the bluff lay her body, a permanent part of the earth's displacement.

Vail had returned to California, where he found that the slightest vibration made him jump, caused nausea, trembling, fear. He was constantly anticipating earthquakes in a region prone to them. To remain in California or even to continue in seismology was out of the question, and he moved to an area where the prospect of serious earthquakes was considered remote.

After his old balance returned, the mere thought of an earthquake no longer upset him. He told Kay about the experience before they were married but had not mentioned it again. And he withheld completely the shame of his failure. The memory of it deep within himself stirred only fitfully. Now it demanded that he remember the tortured earth, the startled face, the cry, the terror, the desolation.

FRACTURE

JUNE 17. The grayness on Monday looked reversible, as though the sun might actually come out. At the end of the driveway Vail stopped and scooped the morning mail from the box without leaving the car. Among the usual bills and alumni bulletins was a letter to himself, addressed by hand, from P. Kelly of Lamont-Doherty Geological Observatory, Palisades, New York. Vail put the rest of the mail back in the box and slipped the envelope into his jacket to read at the office.

A rough spot appeared just past his driveway and he drove over it slowly, then briskly up Point Road. The dashboard clock said just past 9:00, and Vail flicked on the radio for the last part of the news. ". . . crippled a gasoline storage facility near Newport. The seventh victim died last night, and two others remain on the critical list. The cause of the blast is still being investigated. Donald Brown, chief engineer at the refinery, told WROK that sabotage has not been ruled out. Police are trying to locate a former employee of the company. That's the news, folks. Now stay tuned for, 'Morning Rock'—spelled W-R-O-K—with Kip Smith."

Vail switched off the radio, and his mind picked up the bearded visage of Kip Smith, the young entrepreneur who owned WROK. Smith had employed Vail, who had gone into business as a geologist in Boston, to do a profile of the ground where the broadcast tower for the radio station would be built. One day Vail had driven to nearby Old Brompton just to have a look, and had been struck by the sense of isolation of the finger of land. In the village's general store, where he had stopped for a soft drink, he had inquired of the small, narrow-faced woman behind the counter whether there were houses for sale here. Mrs. Wilbore's sister-in-law had studied him a moment, asked about his occupation, and said warily, "Mebbe. A stone house." But would he have roused himself to look if she hadn't mentioned stone? As a geologist he dealt in stone. When he saw the roomy, rundown place with its thick walls, beamed ceilings and jutting cupola, he wanted it.

Old Brompton was too far from Boston to commute. To move there had meant shifting the small geological concern to Fall River, where Vail's partner already lived. Kay, too, adored the old stone house. She had always wanted a saddle horse and on the peninsula she could have one. But she worried about being marooned in the winter when the summer people left. "It'll work out fine, you'll see," he had told her, and it had, except that now he had worries.

Just outside Old Brompton, Vail pulled into the filling station, pointed to the flat tire in the trunk, and asked, "Could that have been done with a knife?"

Yesterday Dun had showed him an X in chalk near the hole in the tire of the Rolls. It was like the ones made at filling stations to mark a leak. Dun wanted to know if he'd had another flat fixed recently, for maybe it was the same one.

Harry said that he had had a flat, but on a rear tire. He had examined the mark, and suddenly remembered Cy Wilbore's X on the hood of the car, the tussle, the moving figure seen through the picture window. He swore. "The village kids!"

Dun's weathered hand rested briefly on Vail's arm. "Possible. But think of it this way, son. Only a tire. Forget about it."

"Can you fix it?" Vail now asked the attendant.

"Do for a spare. Stop by on your way home, Dr. Vail."

After his handling of the Wilbore boys Vail felt some complicity. In any case, he could see no advantage in making the quarrel worse, even if a teenager's knife had been responsible for the gash. He decided to heed Dun and forget it.

He continued on to Fall River, entered the downtown section, and stopped before the old Academy Building. The elevator took him to the third floor, where dark wood doors carried the inscription VAIL AND LECHINE, INC. GEOLOGICAL SYSTEMS.

The firm performed typical geological functions: developing water supplies, finding sand and gravel deposits, testing soils for the foundations of buildings and bridges. The job was honest and useful, if to Vail a bit routine.

The secretary, Mrs. Conner, was already at her desk. Vail said good morning and went to his office with the morning mail. Then he remembered the letter from Paul Kelly and opened it.

Kelly had been Vail's professor at Cal Tech and now, at forty-five, was a leading seismologist. His infrequent missives, written in a wiggly script that resembled a seismograph after a tremor, were really scientific reports, and Vail translated as best he could. ". . . understanding earthquakes better . . . time not far off when . . . have capability to predict . . . exciting period for all of us. . . ."

Kelly, though sympathizing with his friend's reasons, had strongly opposed Vail's decision to abandon seismology. "The trouble with escape," Kelly had warned his younger colleague, "is that you can never escape far enough."

Over the years the two men had kept in touch by letter, and they had been able to see each other occasionally after Kelly joined the staff at Lamont.

Vail missed his former vocation and colleagues, of whom there were probably not more than a few hundred over the country. Lugging their equipment about, pure seismologists searched out earthquakes with the enthusiasm others displayed in prospecting for gold. But Vail was a plain geologist now, he thought with mild regret.

Vail looked up at the sound of a cough to see Jim Lechine standing in the doorway. "You sure can concentrate, Harry," Lechine said with admiration. "We have to talk." Vail invited his partner to sit down.

The two men had contrasting strengths and temperaments, and handled different sides of the business. Lechine, thirty-nine, had been an engineer. Finding himself too much at a desk, he had returned to college and gotten a degree in geology. But his real talent was public relations. Open and friendly, Lechine dealt easily with clients, soliciting business, arguing fees with tightfisted town councils. Vail liked him, with minor reservations. Lechine could be opinionated at times. Also, Jim, of French-Canadian extraction, had a large family to support, which made him a little greedy as far as Vail was concerned. He was always soliciting new business—more than the firm could really handle.

Wearing a bow tie and red suspenders, Lechine put his feet on the desk and said, "Hey, Harry, you look a little pale. Too many parties down there on the peninsula?"

Vail smiled wryly. "It's not that. Like a damned fool, I slipped from a ladder and hit my head. I'm still not quite myself."

"Ouch. You didn't break anything, did you?"

"No, luckily. That's one thing to thank the rain for—the ground's soft." Vail looked moodily out the window at sky damp as soggy tissue. "What's this—the third year of record rain?"

"I forget. Anyway, these clouds have silver linings. The rain's bringing us plenty of work. Friday, when you were out, I got a call from a contractor in Eastport, Mass. There's an old people's home called Summerset Villa which has developed cracks in the walls. It's a relatively new building situated on a hillside, and the contractor thinks the foundation might be settling because the hill is saturated. He asked me to take over the job, but I have quite a day today. So I just wondered if you could do it. It's not far from your place."

Vail had plenty to do himself. But buried in Lechine's voice lay an urgency Vail had learned to understand. Lechine wouldn't say so, but he worried whether his geology was up to the problem. Vail said, "Any immediate danger?"

Lechine frowned. "The contractor doesn't seem to think so. Still, there are people living in the building."

"Did the builder ever do a soil study?" Vail asked, knowing the answer.

"No."

Vail said fretfully, "People just build things without understanding the ground. We've lived in New England three hundred years, and half the time we don't even know what's underneath it. Nothing would surprise me. Not even an earthquake," he blurted out.

"Earthquake? Why did you say that?"

"I don't know." Vail looked at his partner. "Tell me, Jim, have there been many earthquakes in this area?"

"Doubt it. Seems to me the U.S. Geological Survey did a seismic study of the Northeast Corridor six or seven years ago, when the government was considering a new high-speed railway between Boston and Washington. I may have it."

Lechine went to his office and returned with a manila envelope. It was labeled:

ENGINEERING GEOLOGY OF THE NORTHEAST CORRIDOR
WASHINGTON, D.C., TO BOSTON, MASSACHUSETTS
Earthquake epicenters recorded in or near
the Northeast Corridor from 1534 to 1965

Vail opened it and stared at a map covered with circles. "Those government geologists are certainly thorough," he said. "Yes, there have been earthquakes in this area."

"Not for a long time, probably. Why do you care?"

Vail said something about writing a paper. "May I keep this?"

"Too much in my files already."

Embarrassed by the turn the talk had taken, Vail looked out the window. Water dripped on the panes. "I'll take on the old people's home," he said. He added casually, "Speaking of cracks, I found one about a foot long in the concrete wall of my basement. I keep wondering why it's there."

Lechine shrugged. "The building's settling, that's all."

"No, the stone house is old and would have settled long ago."

"Water pressure then. The crack's small—nothing to worry about."

"I hope not," Vail said, fighting a vision of falling stone.

SUMMERSET Villa was a large brick building with white, pseudo-colonial trim. From its hillside facing the water Vail might have been able to see, with field glasses, his own house across the bay.

He parked and entered the lobby, where old people lolled in chairs, doing nothing. Summerset seemed to be a place in which you dumped ancient relatives and forgot them.

Vail was wondering how to find the manager when an old lady looked up from her knitting and smiled. "May I be of assistance?"

"I'm looking for Mr. Robinson, the manager. Would you know where he is?"

"No need to shout, young man," she said. "My hearing's quite as good as yours. Of course I know where he is—in his room. Mr. Robinson is always in his room."

"What does he do in his room?" Vail asked.

"He looks at his photograph book. And dreams, I suspect. Certainly he pays very little attention to his work."

"What are the photographs of?"

"Of Mr. Robinson, of course. Our manager is a former actor. Didn't you ever wonder what happened to actors when the last show closed? Now you know. They manage old people's homes."

"There must be worse fates."

"Not for Mr. Robinson. He hates old people. We remind him of what he'll become. He avoids us as much as he can. I'll get him for you. What is your name, young man?"

"Vail." He noted the gold band on her finger. "But Mrs. . . ."

"Alma Benjamin. I need the exercise. Besides, I enjoy disturbing Mr. Robinson's foolish reveries."

Mrs. Benjamin, he saw when she rose, was a tiny woman, no more than five feet tall and a hundred pounds; her hair was in a bun, and she walked youthfully.

A few minutes later Robinson emerged, a nattily dressed man in his fifties. "Ah, Vail. I was told to expect you."

Vail said, "Are you the owner as well as the manager here, Mr. Robinson?"

"I wish I were. It's plenty profitable. The owner, Mr. Summerset,

lives in Florida and has a chain of homes just like this one."
Robinson showed a neat row of false teeth.

"You make all the decisions, then?"

"The buck stops here," Robinson said. "Of course, when it comes
to spending money, I have to get authorization—when I can find
Mr. Summerset. Let's get going. I have a great deal to do."

Outside, the sun was struggling to take off its mask, but no one
sat on the benches or walked on the paths. "Your old people like
it indoors, it seems," Vail observed. "Dampness bother them?"

"They'd love to go outside," Robinson snapped. "But I won't
permit it in this weather. I don't want them tracking mud all over."

They reached the back of the building. Part of the hillside had
been cleared for a lawn which had never been planted. The
glistening mud looked like the icing on a chocolate cake. Robinson
examined his polished shoes with obvious distaste—they bore
splotches of mud. He pointed. "What you want to see is there. I'll
wait here, if you don't mind."

In the car Vail had put on boots. The mud sucked them as he
moved toward the wall of the building. Then he saw the cracks—
four squiggles that ran up the cement base into the brick.

He returned to Robinson. "When were the cracks discovered?"

"Middle of last week. The maintenance man noticed them on the
inside of the cellar wall."

"How old is the building?"

"Eight or ten years. It was built before I came."

"How deep are the footings—the foundation? I'm trying to find
out how good the construction is."

"I don't know anything about construction."

Vail turned toward the hillside. "See those ridges?"

Robinson squinted. "Sure. So what?"

"Those are hummocks, where the earth has slipped. Behind the
ridges is a depression called a slump. It's a miniature landslide,
meaning that the soil is saturated with water. In the West, when
you get a condition like that, whole hillsides can begin to creep.
The mud carries buildings with it."

"This isn't the West," Robinson insisted.

Vail replied, "Just the same, something of the sort could happen.
The hill could be unstable, the foundation could shift, and the
building could collapse without much warning. We'd better drill

some holes and get a reading on the soil." He stared toward the cracks again. "It ought to be done right away."

"How much will it cost?"

"Not much to bore the holes. After that, we'll see."

Robinson's face turned angry. "You contractors are all alike—always gouging. It better not be expensive. Mr. Summerset would blame me for it."

"I'm not a contractor, I'm a geologist," Vail answered. "In any case, I wouldn't suggest work that doesn't have to be done."

"Well, all right," Robinson conceded. He departed, and Vail climbed the slope, inspecting the slump and the nearby trees. The hill, on one side, had a steep drop that ended in the bay, and he stood staring at the water. He retraced his steps to the front of the building. About to get in his car, he saw a small figure standing just inside the entranceway. He went over and poked his head inside. "Good-by, Mrs. Benjamin," he said, "You'd better watch out for Robinson. He's on the warpath."

"I know. Don't worry about me, Mr. . . . or is it *Dr.* Vail? Robinson said you're a geologist."

"Dr. Vail," he agreed. "Tell me, Mrs. Benjamin. Is the construction of the building shoddy?"

"Shoddy! The walls are *that* thick." The old woman made a narrow gap between her thumb and forefinger. "You can hear everything. And the plumbing is unmentionable."

"Why do you stay?" he asked her.

She shrugged. "The obvious reason. Where else to go?"

ARRIVING home, Vail hoisted the dog by its bushy tail and said, "Shut up, Punch. It's only me."

Kay, running from the studio, gasped, "Harry! There's a rumble in the basement. The house is shaking."

He could feel the vibration through the floor. The dining-room chandelier tinkled. He had to force the basement door, swollen because of humidity. The sound reverberated off the cement walls, and his ears focused on a machine protruding from a square well in the floor. He kicked the pump angrily; the noise stopped.

"What was it?" she asked anxiously when he came upstairs.

"Sump pump's on the blink. Didn't you notice when you looked in the cellar?"

432

Her thin nose pointed away. "I didn't go down."

Harry shook his head. "I'll get Dun to come in the morning."

That evening Kay was scheduled to play bridge at the Demmings'; she asked if he wanted to come. Harry, whose bridge was not of the best, shook his head. Conversation was desultory at supper. She told of her day: "Went for a ride on Brioche. Took Mark to the beach. Shopped. Piano's out of whack, just like the grandfather clock. The repair people said they'd come tomorrow. They won't, of course. Oh, did you call me today?"

"Too busy. Why?"

"Phone rang a couple of times when I was in the backyard, but by the time I got there nobody was on the line."

Kay put Mark in his pajamas while Harry cleaned up. She kissed the boy good-night, and her station wagon disappeared down the drive. He liked evenings alone with his child. They wrestled on the floor, fending off affectionate lunges from the dog and cat. "Read to me, Daddy!" Mark cried finally.

Harry lay on his back on the floor, holding a book called *At Paddy the Beaver's Pond* over his head, with Mark and the animals curled up beside him. He read: "Down from the mountainside on the still air came the sound of deep grunts. They came from places some distance apart. They were angry grunts. What is more, each grunt sounded more threatening than the previous grunts." Harry cleared his throat and continued, "'They are coming this way,' declared Uncle Paddy."

"Go on, Daddy!" Mark cried.

Harry sat up. "Did you hear anything, Mark?"

Mark's eyes, blue like his mother's, had opened wide. "Yes. The grunts. I heard the grunts. Go on, read!"

He read on for a few moments and, after the usual protests, carried Mark upstairs to bed. Mark's room lay at the opposite end of the carpeted hall from his parents' room. On the wall was a circus poster with lions, tigers and clowns. A mobile of blue plastic fish hung from the ceiling. Mark favored the top of the double-decker bunk, and Harry threw him into it, firmly resisting the boy's demand that he get into bed, too. Harry went downstairs and pulled his hard chair to the light. He was rereading Kelly's letter when he felt a vibration crawl up the chair legs. The shaking was slight; reading to Mark, he had experienced it as sound, he realized.

He returned to the basement. The pump grumbled. When he kicked it the machine fell silent. His eyes turned to the crack. Vail froze—he was convinced it had grown longer.

The steps creaked as he clambered up, returning with a tape measure, pad and pencil. He measured up the wall from the floor and was about to record the result when, upstairs, the phone rang. He ascended hurriedly, but the caller had hung up. In the basement again, he searched for the pencil. He had left it by the phone.

To hell with it! He went to the far end of the basement and opened a door to an exercise room, installed at the time of the renovation. He kept a robe, slippers and shorts there, and now he worked himself to the limit on the bicycle and rowing machine. Then he sat in the burning sauna.

FEW of the villagers had phones, and Dun was no exception. The next morning Vail drove past the village and took a rutted road along the shore. About halfway to the red cliffs at Shonkawa Point stood a row of one-room shacks with stovepipes protruding from the roofs. Dun's old truck was gone, and Vail left a note in the mailbox marked D. SOWLES.

As he headed for the office Vail considered the anomaly of shanties occupying the best beachfront in Old Brompton. He wondered why Dun went along with the villagers' pact not to sell, when he probably could get enough to retire to a warmer climate. The old man *was* different from the others.

Dun had traveled. While the other villagers rarely left the peninsula, he had lived all over the Northeast, even been a logger, farmer, carpenter. Unlike the others, too, Dun was hardworking, reliable. He was in demand throughout the peninsula, though he seemed choosy about whom he worked for. Like the rest of the villagers, however, Dun looked poor, and Vail wondered why. He had no family to support, and surely he had Social Security. Perhaps he salted his money away; then, too, the season was short and the rich summer people were notoriously ungenerous.

Toward Harry Vail, Dun always displayed a special partiality, coming as quickly as asked and often calling him son. Spending most of his life on the move, he had never married.

"I bet he wanted a son like you," Kay said to Harry. "Big, smart, educated. Nice but tough down deep, like he is."

Vail respected the old man and would have been flattered if that were true, yet Kay's notion seemed too simple. Between Vail and himself Dun maintained a wall of habitual reserve, never offering personal information. Vail sometimes had the sensation that behind the wall Dun was on guard.

When Vail returned home that evening, the old man came out of the barn to announce, "Your missus is horseback riding. Asked me to keep an eye on the boy." He hitched up his dungarees with his thumbs, shuffled his feet, and said suddenly, "You were right about the tire. Not a rock but a knife."

"I knew it! How did you find out?"

"Everything here is known sooner or later. Reckon the boys felt they had a score to settle. If you let be, that'll be the end of it."

"Okay. But don't tell Mrs. Vail about it, all right? It'll just make her nervous." The old man nodded.

Vail took a piece of paper from his pocket. "So many things to be done I had to write them down. Doors stick." He told Dun which ones. "The leaf in the dining-room table is fouled up. The sump pump and the upstairs toilet don't work."

Dun said, "There's also a leaking pipe in the boy's bathroom. Missus showed it to me. I'll have to replaster the wall after I've fixed it."

Vail said, "What caused that?"

"Things happen in an old house."

Vail reminded himself that everything had functioned perfectly until Saturday, the day he fell from the ladder.

The two men descended to the basement. Again water stood on the cement floor, and Vail told of the noise the now silent pump had made. Dun said, "Too much groundwater, I reckon, for that old pump to handle."

"That account for the puddle?" Dun nodded, and Vail went on, "Unless water leaks through the wall. Look." He pointed to the crack. "That I'm sure is new."

Dun moved closer to the wall. He had put in the concrete lining himself. His silence affirmed that the crack was new. His keen eyes searched the surface. "Hard to say if the crack leaks. Anyhow, crack don't mean nothing—cement most likely just dried out on the inside, even with the rain. Get a new pump and see what happens."

A folding rule stuck from Dun's back pocket. Vail said, "Measure it, will you?"

Dun bent and measured. "Fourteen and five-eighths."

"Are you sure?"

"Measure it again?"

"No. I'll take your word for it." He remembered $14\frac{1}{8}$ inches the evening before, but perhaps he was wrong.

"Harry?" he heard Kay call. "The Pollidors are expecting us."

MARK was no problem. They'd taken him along and put him in a bedroom. It was almost dark as they drove home, with Mark silent in the back seat. "What an awful evening," Harry exclaimed.

"I can see how *you'd* think so," Kay said. "You really got Pollidor angry telling him cement was falling from between the fireplace bricks and nails were working out of the wood. You made it sound as though his house was falling down."

"I didn't say that. I just said there were signs of stress."

"And the business about how the ball veered when you were playing croquet. Nobody felt the ground shake but you. That fall from the ladder did something to your balance. You *must* see Dr. Bjerling."

"You were all so busy at the computer bar you couldn't have felt anything," he said defensively. "Still, maybe I ought to pay Bjerling a visit if this keeps up." He turned onto Point Road. "I was sore when Pollidor scared Mark with the burglar alarm."

"It wasn't nice of him," Kay agreed. "I wish they wouldn't talk so much about crime. You'd think we're having a crime wave in Old Brompton. Maybe they're right. I keep wondering if we shouldn't have a burglar alarm, too. There's the china, silver, my toby jugs. The collection's worth two thousand easily."

"A thief wouldn't know what a toby jug is," he reassured her.

"I'm just nervous, I guess." She shifted in her seat. "And Jeff with his game about predicting how we'll all die. He really wants to play it."

"I can't believe Fred Demming will do it."

"He does anything Wende wants. And she loves games. Including the one she's playing with Jeff. Fred must be blind."

"I'm tired of talking about those people," he said as he turned into their driveway. "What else is new?"

"Did I tell you that both the piano tuner and the clock man came today? A minor miracle."

"What was wrong with Big Ben?"

"Something rubbing against something."

Punch barked from inside the house as they drove up. Already fed at the Pollidors', Mark went reluctantly to bed. They had a pickup supper from the refrigerator. "Will you clean up?" she asked as she started for the living room. When she turned on the light she screamed softly, "Harry!"

A toby jug lay broken on the floor. Her gaze was shocked. "One of my best jugs. How could that have happened, Harry?"

Kay seemed greatly agitated and he wanted a reasonable explanation to calm her down. Punch and Judy stood near the bar cart, staring up at them solemnly. "Did you do that, Judy?" he asked.

"Judy doesn't walk on furniture."

"But she does sometimes. I've caught her at it."

Kay's face was disbelieving. "She wouldn't go up on a glass shelf."

"She wouldn't have to," he insisted. "She jumped on the cart and nudged the jug with her tail. It fell, hit the corner of the bar, and broke." He showed her a mark on the cart.

Kay seemed satisfied with the explanation, but he wasn't—not quite. He began to prowl. On the mantel stood some arrowheads he had found in the cornfield; ordinarily they leaned against the chimney, but a few were down. He picked them up. The cart on its sturdy wheels was an inch away from the wall and he pushed it back. She watched him closely. "Stop pacing," she said suddenly.

"Kay, why did you leave the record cabinet open?"

"Haven't been near it. Must have been Mark. He can play the machine by himself now." She sucked in her cheeks. "Any cigarettes in the house?"

"No! You're *not* going to start smoking again."

"All right, all right." She pulled on her index finger until it popped. "We're both in a funny mood, aren't we? Maybe it's because the sun never shines. I read somewhere about a valley in the Northwest which has a fantastic rate of suicides. There's always rain or fog and people get depressed." Kay sat down abruptly at the piano, played a few bars, and frowned. "The piano is out of tune again. The man must have done a lousy job." She went to the birdcage, drumming the brass with her nails. "Bird, bird, why

438

won't you sing?" She whirled to face him. "It's too much! Nothing works. Look! The clock is still slow, too. I want a cigarette."

"There aren't any."

"Then I'll drive to the village and buy some."

"You win," he said coldly. "Cigarettes somebody left are in my desk."

She returned at once. "Harry, did you throw books on the floor of the study?"

"Me?" They raced to the study. Books were strewn over the desk and the floor. She found the cigarettes and lit one quickly. "Somebody's been in the house!" she shouted.

"Nobody's been in the house. Calm yourself." He pointed to the empty shelf supports over the desk. "I had books on one end of the shelf and a light on the other. The whole thing came down. It must have been unbalanced." He returned the shelf to the wall, then switched on the clip light. "The bulb isn't even broken." He took the books from the floor and glanced at the last one—Charles F. Richter's famous *Elementary Seismology*.

"It's enough to make you believe in a poltergeist," she muttered.

"A what?" he asked sharply.

"Poltergeist—a spirit that moves things, throws them, sets fires. Poltergeists haunt people."

He looked at her carefully. "You sound like you believe in them."

"Of course I don't," Kay said defensively. "It's just that so much is happening at once. I'm going to bed."

"I'm going to check the basement," he announced.

The floor was dry—today it had only drizzled. He found the tape in the pocket of the old robe he kept by the sauna. He knelt in front of the crack. It measured exactly $14\frac{3}{4}$ inches. What had been its length the first time he measured it? Had Dun's measurement been wrong? Or had the wound in the wall grown since the day before yesterday? That, he understood suddenly, was how he regarded the crack—as a wound in the body of his house.

He studied the crack. What, exactly, was happening? You really only have two ways to go, he told himself. You either decide that a lot of small things are happening at the same time by chance—or you conclude an earthquake is under way. But suppose that conclusion is right, what then? Don't say anything until you have more. Try to be a scientist for a change. Watch and wait, and keep your emotions out of it. If there really is a big quake coming, it'll surface and you'll know, you'll *know*.

The stairs squeaked, and whirling, he saw Mark in pajamas.

"I woke up, Daddy. I'm hungry."

"Okay." In the kitchen he poured the boy a glass of milk and sent him back to bed. His eye fell on the blackboard where Kay listed errands, doctors' appointments. Seizing the chalk, he returned to the basement. At the tip of the crack he placed a white dot.

THE next morning when he entered the office Mrs. Conner asked, "Can I get you some coffee, Dr. Vail? You don't look quite yourself."

"I'm not," he admitted. "I'd love some coffee. Lechine in?"

"I'll get him."

Vail's desk calendar said Wednesday, June 19. Vail hadn't talked to Lechine yet about Summerset Villa. He motioned his partner to a chair and said, "I'm worried about the old people's home. There's been some creep on the hillside it stands on, and it looks like some of the trees are angled."

Born in the region, Lechine knew it like his own skin. "The hill must be made of Mother Nature's Irish stew—a till of old glacial debris consisting of hard clay, sand, gravel and boulders. It ought to be stable."

"But it's saturated. Till doesn't absorb water easily. And the hill edges on a bluff. I got Charley to take his rig over there yesterday and drill some holes. If the ground is as wet as I think, we could try digging a well and pumping out the water."

Lechine said uneasily, "Do we have a contract with the owner?"

"No. The manager's trying to find him."

"Suppose he won't pay for it?" Lechine demanded. "Aren't you a little premature?"

Vail's mind saw the wrinkled face of Alma Benjamin. "The construction of that building is cruddy," he snapped. "You want it to go down? It's too risky to wait, contract or no contract."

BY FRIDAY there had been no change in the crack in the basement, with the white dot on top of it like the head of a long insect. Kay now made biting remarks whenever Vail went to check it.

In the office, he asked Mrs. Conner whether the test results on Summerset Villa had come.

440

"I'm afraid not, Dr. Vail."

"I marked the job rush," he complained. "I'll call Charley."

He dialed the number on Mrs. Conner's phone. "Charley, it's Vail. I want those test-drilling results today. This is top priority."

Lechine wandered out of his office and said, "By the way, apropos of nothing, looks like they've located the guy who blew up the gasoline storage tanks. Man named Williams. He's in Florida. Only a matter of time before they extradite him."

"What's supposed to be his motive?" Vail asked.

"Something about being in an industrial accident and not getting compensated. I hope they throw the book at him. I hate kooks."

"Maybe he didn't do it," Vail said.

"Sure he did. How else could it have happened?"

That afternoon Mrs. Conner handed Vail the test report on Summerset Villa. He read it, made two telephone calls, and walked quickly to his partner's office. "I've got the Summerset drilling results, and I don't like them at all," Vail said.

"Water saturation?"

"That's part of it. The hillside is like molasses. The water table has risen twenty feet."

"That's enormous!"

"But not unheard of. Don't forget, we've had a huge amount of rain. The bedrock won't let the water seep out. I put in a call to Robinson, the so-called manager, to get authorization to dig a well and try to drain the water, but he's away for the weekend, nobody knows where. I've gone out on a limb and ordered Charley to start digging the well on Monday."

"I still think you should talk to the owner first."

"I haven't given you the whole story. Something in the report surprised me. There are limy layers."

Lechine's gaze faltered. Sometimes the deficiencies of his geological training showed like an outcropping of rock.

"Limestone might be significant," Vail said. "Water passing through vegetation becomes acidic. Limestone contains calcium carbonate and magnesium carbonate. They're soluble in acid. When water reaches limestone, openings occur in the stone. You could get a cave."

"That would take centuries," Lechine scoffed.

"True. But an existing cave could have grown larger because

441

of the excessive rainfall during the last several years. Especially if there's a fault line there. Water would collect along the fault."

"What makes you think there's a fault?"

"I just say it's possible."

Back in his office, he went to his desk and removed the envelope with the survey reports. In addition to the chart depicting earthquakes in the region, he found one on its bedrock geology. No fault was shown near Summerset Villa, but one did exist at the mouth of the Sakonnet River, not far away. He drew a black square around the area. Then the phone rang.

"Anything new?" Kay asked.

"The supply store called. The sump pump came. I'll pick it up on my way home."

"Have you forgotten there's a picnic at the club beach? Also we're invited to the Demmings' on Sunday."

"I think I'll pass up the club party." He looked outside. "Anyway, it's raining."

"Weatherman says it's due to stop."

"Oh sure," he retorted.

But the rain had stopped when Vail drove down the beach road. Seeing Dun's old pickup outside the shack, Vail climbed the steps and knocked. He heard the scuffle of slippers. Dun squinted from behind the screen door. "Oh, Mr. Vail." He seemed surprised.

"I've got the new pump, Dun. Could you come tomorrow?"

The old man nodded. "Care to come inside?"

Perhaps Dun was merely being polite. Yet Vail wanted to understand him better; besides, he had something to ask.

"I didn't know you were eating," Vail apologized, seeing a sturdy table upon which were a glass of milk and a plate of food.

Dun took his plate into the alcove kitchen. "Wasn't hungry anyway. How about a drink, Mr. Vail?"

The back windows faced the sea. The horizon was touched with pink for a change. Kay and Mark would be at the picnic. Vail nodded, and Dun returned with two shots of rum.

On the table, open and face down, lay a soft-cover book which, Vail observed, Dun carefully closed and placed under his hand. Vail glanced around. Stones of various colors and shapes lined the windowsills, and on a table and chest stood glass jars filled with stones. "Nice rocks," he said.

"Red ones from the cliff, white ones from the beach." There was a silence and then Dun said, "Don't get much company."

"It must get lonely, especially in winter," Vail answered.

"Oh, don't mind. Work. Fish. Read. Every Sunday, church."

"The whole village attends your church, doesn't it? Yet your people don't strike me as especially religious."

Dun laughed. "You religious, Mr. Vail?"

Vail shifted in his chair. This was the closest thing to a personal question Dun had ever asked, and he wanted to answer truthfully. "I'm a scientist, Dun. Ultimate questions aren't my affair."

"You mean answers," Dun said. "All of us got the same questions. It's our answers that ain't the same. Maybe there ain't answers for some things."

"There are answers. We just don't know them yet."

Dun scratched his cheek. "How can you *know* there are when you ain't got them?"

"Faith, I guess."

"Well, Mr. Vail, that's religion."

"You'll make a convert of me yet," Vail said with a laugh. "What denomination are you?"

The old man hesitated. "Ain't exactly connected with any church. Got our own ways. Sort of . . . earthy in our views."

He picked up the book and went to the alcove, returning with a bottle. He refilled their shot glasses and said jocularly, "Trouble at the church. Pipe organ's ailin'. Gives some bad notes. Know anything about pipe organs, Mr. Vail?"

"I'm afraid not." It occurred to Vail that he did know a pertinent fact, but he could not recall it. His mind switched to the book Dun had removed from the table. In the second it lay open Vail had glanced at the title. "I noticed the book you were reading, by Edgar Cayce. I've heard that name, but I can't place it."

Dun's face gave nothing away. "*Kay-see*, not *Case*, Mr. Vail. He was a clairvoyant."

"Of course! I remember hearing about him in California. Claimed he could predict disasters—stock market crash of '29, World War Two." He paused. "Earthquakes."

"That's him." The gray eyes opened wide. "Something to wonder at, if he could do the things they say."

Vail grunted. "Where did he predict earthquakes for?"

"California, Japan."

"Hard to miss there. Tremendous amount of seismic disturbance in both areas. Do you know how many earthquakes there are every year over the world?" Dun shook his head. "A hundred thousand, at least," Vail said.

"Your missus told me you studied earthquakes once."

"Yes, I was a seismologist. Where else did Cayce claim earthquakes would happen?"

"Alabama."

Vail smiled. "That was last century."

"Major earthquake in Alaska."

Vail scowled. "When?"

"Between 1959 and 1998," Dun said.

Vail said, "That's a forty-year period, and that area is earthquake prone, too. There's been a big one already. Anywhere else?"

Dun said slowly, "Here. In New England. He believes that everything will fall apart."

"Cataclysm," Vail said after a moment. "Is that what you teach in church?"

Dun hesitated. "No. But respect nature."

As he rose to go Vail shot the question which had been on his mind. Waving toward the darkening sea through the windows, he said, "Dun, this stretch of beach must be worth a fortune. Why don't you sell and retire to a warm climate?"

"Can't. Now you could sell and go. Someone might make you a good offer. Why don't you take it?"

"Me? Sell? Of course I won't. Who told you to ask?"

"Didn't say anybody did. Just that they might." Vail had reached the front door. Dun added, "Been thinking about the crack in your basement. Nothing to worry about. Simple break in the masonry caused by water pressure. We'll reinforce her when the rain stops."

Out on the stoop Vail heard a deep, guttural moan, seeming to emanate from beneath the shack. "What is that?"

"Wind's coming up, that's all," Dun said impassively. "Come back again. Pleasure to have you."

Vail drove carefully in the semidarkness, still worried by the sound. But Dun was right about the breeze. When he reached home he brought the new pump into the kitchen, then, hearing the rumble of the old one, went downstairs to kick it into silence.

444

The dot had vanished from the crack. He raced up to his study. The tape measure was not in the drawer where he had put it. He searched frantically, returning at last to the basement with Mark's one-foot ruler. The crack measured 15 inches on the nose.

There had been another tremor.

Wait a minute, he cautioned. There was a slight bulge in the concrete where the crack was, which would throw the reading off, since the wooden rule could not lie flat on the wall.

He visualized Kay's lipstick on her dressing table and ran upstairs for it, sweating and panting. Down the length of the crack he drew a thick red line and, dropping the lipstick on the floor, stood up to look. Now the crack resembled a real wound, and he left the cellar hastily.

The next morning Dun came before Vail was up. He found the old man in the cellar installing the new pump. Kay and Mark stood facing the wall with the crack, and Kay held a rag in her hand. The crack had been wiped clean. She said, "I've told you a hundred times *not* to come to the basement alone, Mark."

Harry stepped forward. "What did he do?"

"He smeared the wall with one of my lipsticks."

"But I didn't," Mark protested. "I just put Daddy's tape there like Daddy does." The boy showed her the tape in his hand.

"I found the lipstick on the floor," Kay said angrily. "How did it get there?"

"I did it," Harry said.

She looked at him with a kind of horror. "But why?"

"There's a crack there. I marked it."

She peered at the wall and then at her husband. "I didn't even notice it. What's the big deal?"

After Kay and Mark had gone upstairs Dun took the folding rule from his pocket and placed it on the crack. "Fifteen inches," he announced. "Guess I wasn't careful when I measured before."

Harry said bitterly, "Oh, come on, Dun. The crack *has* grown."

"Doubt it," Dun insisted.

SUNDAY morning Vail discovered that the stone house had sprung another leak. Mark entered the bedroom in his pajamas and said, "Daddy, my circus poster is wet."

Harry sat up with a start and went to the boy's bedroom. The

445

poster was damp to the touch, and behind it brown watermarks ran from ceiling to floor.

"Why?" Kay asked as he started to dress.

"It poured last night. A shingle's loose or an old crack has opened up. I'll try some waterproofing compound on it."

On summer Sundays, Kay went riding with others from the club, with Mark sitting sidesaddle in front of her. After breakfast she saddled Brioche and rode the patient old sorrel to the house, where Harry hoisted Mark to its back.

"Harry, look!" Kay pointed to narrow ridges on the lawn.

"Mole traces, I guess," he muttered.

"What'll we do? They'll ruin the yard."

"Poison," he decided. "The stuff we used on the mice."

"But won't Punch get into it?"

"I'll put it where he can't. But the dead moles may stink."

Kay sniffed the air. "Talk about the power of suggestion!"

He sniffed. "The septic tank is backing up, I'm afraid."

"Let's go, Mark, before anything else happens," she said.

When they had gone he located some mole holes and inserted the pellets of poison in them with his bare hand, reaching in until the earth seemed to grab at his arm.

In the barn, he put the poison away and found a can of water-proofing compound and a long brush. He returned to the house and went through a trapdoor in the attic onto the roof. From there something he had not seen on the ground was clearly discernible. The ridges below were not irregularly placed, as he had assumed, but crossed the lawn in a definite north-south pattern. Earthquake activity could leave such traces.

Vail's examination showed no loose shingle or open places through which water might seep. On his hands and knees he went down the gently sloping roof until his head hung over the cornice and he could see the crack directly below. A piece of mortar had fallen out. Lying on his stomach at the edge of the roof, he began smear-ing the crack with compound. He had just completed the job when he felt the shaking.

Careful! You'll fall!

Warily, he crawled back to the trapdoor and entered the house. He took the tape to the basement, to find the crack, his primitive seismometer, unchanged.

ON THEIR way to the Demmings' the three Vails walked under sky that was pasty but bright. Kay said, "You're not very talkative this evening."

The shelty barked and they turned. Punch was on top of the giant gray boulder and Mark was trying to scale the side.

"Mark!" Kay shouted. "You come right down. You'll be filthy."

They crossed Torturous Creek by the stepping-stones, with Punch wading beside them. Halfway over, Mark bent and dipped his finger in the stream. "Warm water!" he cried.

Harry put his finger in, too. "It does feel warm," he agreed.

"Maybe summer's coming at last," Kay said.

Mark ran ahead on the leaf-slick path. Suddenly he vanished. Kay glanced around. "Mark?" The boy was not to be seen.

"The playhouse," Harry said.

The side trail was obscured by a branch that he pulled aside, revealing a small clearing and the playhouse with a shingled roof. Harry knocked on the door. "Anyone home?"

A giggle. "Come in."

He poked his head through the narrow doorway. The room contained child-size furniture, and was large enough for a grownup to lie outstretched but not to stand up straight. He noticed an air mattress rolled in the corner. Mark, on his knees beside it, held something in his hand.

"Come on out, honey," Harry said.

The boy emerged, holding out a glittering object. "See what I found?"

It was a gold cigarette lighter with WBD engraved on the side. Harry took it, and Mark ran on ahead. "WBD—Wende Baldwin Demming." His eyes met Kay's.

"Playing around in the playhouse," she said.

"Well, it's her business. What'll I do with the lighter?"

Kay said, "Keep it out of sight so Mark won't remember. Put it under a chair cushion where Wende will find it."

The path opened on an expanse of emerald lawn the size of a football field, passed manicured bushes and a formal garden. Farther on was the three-story house with its carved wood exterior, turrets, and numerous bedrooms, mostly unoccupied. By the forty-foot pool the usual faces cried, "Hello, hello," to kisses and handshakes, while Mark went off to be given early supper.

Wende said, "It's just us folks again. I was afraid to ask anybody else. Jeff's game could be . . . well, revealing."

"It *has* to be revealing or it's no fun," Jeff exclaimed. "You find out exactly what other people think of you."

Harry surreptitiously slid the lighter beneath the cushion of his chair as Demming snapped, "What is this fool game of yours?"

"It's called Inquest," Jeff said. "We're the coroners, and we have to determine the cause of death of each of us."

Fred said loudly, "I don't get the point."

"Doesn't the manner of a person's death often explain how he lived? What kind of person he was? That's our job: to figure out how each of us died by how we lived. But we must be frank."

"One doesn't go to an inquest for amusement," Bill warned.

Wende said, as if to stop discussion before too many negative ballots were cast, "It's getting chilly. Shall we go inside?"

The house, in Fred's family for generations, had remained intact: yellow plaster, dark paneling, bulky mahogany furniture, harsh ancestral faces in wood frames. Nobody mentioned the game at supper, but afterward Wende said to Jeff, "I like to try new things. Explain the rules."

"We each die in turn," he replied. "As we file around the bier we give our verdict on how the person died from what we understand about his life. The fun of it is saying what you've always wanted to tell someone."

"It's only a game, I suppose," Fred said.

"Okay?" Wende, victorious, glanced at each. "You'll have to give me a moment to set the stage." She rang for the servants and pushed the company out of the dining room.

While they waited, Harry, with Mark on his shoulders, climbed the stairway to an unoccupied bedroom, and Kay followed behind.

After putting the boy to bed Kay said listlessly in the hall, "How quiet it is! Even the sea is still."

"You don't really want to play. Why don't we just forget it?"

"We'll ruin the game, and Wende's determined to do it."

They returned to the living room. Soon a servant entered quietly and put on a record of sorrowful music. At the same instant the dining-room doors opened. The heavy chairs had been pushed back to the walls and the thick draperies shut. A sheet lay on the long oak table, on both ends of which candles burned.

"Come in, come in," Wende called gleefully.

They entered slowly, as if unwilling to cross the threshold. "It's so realistic," Kay muttered. "Seven candles and seven of us."

"How observant you are, Kay. Each of our candles has to go out. Who's first?" Wende asked.

Polly pointed at her husband. "Him. He deserves it."

Pollidor was pulled protesting to the table and commanded to lie down. Wende folded his hands across his chest, closed his eyes with the tips of her fingers, and wrapped him in the sheet.

Giggling, Polly began to walk around the table, the others in train. "What am I supposed to say?" she asked.

"Tell what you thought of him." Jeff laughed.

"Well, a fine, upstanding man, a leading New York lawyer, a credit to his profession . . ."

"Come on, needle him a little," Wende said gaily.

"Well . . ." Polly stared at her husband's still face. "He looks sort of small and pathetic."

Bill opened baleful eyes, but Wende shut them with her fingers. "You're dead," she warned.

Jeff said, "Tell us more, Polly. Did he have any bad qualities?"

For once Polly groped for words. "I wouldn't know where to start. I mean, he is . . . was my husband, after all, but, oh well, he's dead now, isn't he?" A smirk played briefly on her features. "Take his pride. He wouldn't listen when Harry said the contractor was gypping us, and now we've a house that trembles in the wind. And extravagant—when it came to himself.

"I guess money was his real passion—how he envied Fred Demming his wealth. For money Bill would do just about anything. He saw himself as a man of action, but what he did mostly was bend his arm. I could have put up with his drinking except for his violent rages, when he was capable of slugging his own wife." Tears came to her eyes, but then her face brightened. "They did an autopsy on him and guess what they found! No heart, stomach, nothing. He was all liver. That's what he died of—cirrhosis."

Kay extended her hand and ran it gently across the ridges of Pollidor's skull gleaming in the candlelight. "No. He was shot," she announced with authority. "Shot in the head."

Pollidor rose, and as Wende blew out one candle, pointed at his wife. "You're next."

He circled the table on which Polly lay wrapped in the sheet. "Poor Pol. She worried terribly about growing old. I wouldn't want to accuse a woman cold on her bier of lying about her age, but I wouldn't be completely surprised if her birth certificate showed that she was older than she admitted. A certain plastic surgeon knows about it."

Polly struggled to disentangle herself from the sheet. "Bill Pollidor, you know that isn't true."

"No squabbling!" Wende shouted. "Polly, don't you want to know how you died?"

"All right." Polly sank back on the table.

"Of premature old age," Pollidor said mercilessly.

"Maybe she died of boredom from having to listen to you." Kay chuckled, and then her face grew serious. "I believe she died a natural death."

Polly rose, looking relieved. "Your turn, Jeff," she said as Wende blew out a second candle. Jeff wound the sheet about him and lay down, arms crossed, the light flickering on his profile.

"The dear boy," Polly babbled. "He had almost no faults. He was charming, handsome, intelligent."

"The girls will certainly miss him," Wende joshed. "I wonder how he died?"

Demming said softly, "Perhaps a jealous husband murdered him."

Polly said quickly, "I'm sure he died doing something heroic, like covering a war for television."

Harry, unable to resist, put in, "He was something of a thrill seeker, wasn't he? I bet he died doing something foolhardy."

Kay mumbled, "He drowned." Her voice was almost mechanical.

"You really sound like you know what you're talking about, Kay," Wende told her, but Kay said nothing.

Wende blew out Jeff's candle and swung her long legs up on the table as Jeff, smiling, came down. She closed her eyes and murmured, "Be nice to me when I'm gone."

Jeff's words were careful and cool. "She was a lovely woman in all respects. Everyone will miss her very much."

Kay walked behind him. "She's beautiful even in death. She must have died young. How?" she asked no one in particular.

Fred paced slowly, gazing at his wife's smooth oval face. "I loved her," he said somberly, "and I hope she hears that, wherever she

is. But she was not perfect except in appearance. She was a willful woman who indulged her every impulse. She was a child, essentially, whose whole universe was herself."

"But how did she die?" Polly called.

Fred seemed surprised by the query. "I haven't the vaguest idea."

"It was shock," Kay said. Her lips were slack, her eyes dull. "A shock. I know."

"Know?" Harry studied her. "This is a game, remember?"

"Game? Oh yes."

Wende blinked but lay quite still for a moment, eyes clear and depthless, hands folded across the waist. Sitting up, she said in an even voice, "Your turn, Fred."

Demming mounted the table with effort and evident reluctance. "No sheet for me," he said bossily, pushing it away. His hands shook a little as he closed his eyes behind the thick glasses.

"Now that's a man who didn't die from worrying about money," Pollidor said.

"Grief?" Polly suggested to Wende. "Over you?"

Wende asked Kay, "Well?"

Kay studied Demming's face, gray in the ever darker room. "Yes, that's part of it, but not all. Fred fell into a hole."

"This dame's got some imagination," Bill roared. "Why a hole?"

"I'm just guessing, like everyone else," Kay said.

Wende bent and kissed Fred's brow. "So I'm the widow Demming. I wish I'd had the courage to tell him alive what I'm able to now that he's dead. That he lived too much for power. He wanted to control everything around him, including me. He was too unfeeling, too ungiving, and if he'd been different, I might not have done some things I did."

Fred snorted slightly and his body shook. Pollidor roared, "He's fallen asleep!"

"Come on, Fred, get up," Wende said with deep impatience. Demming rose sheepishly, and his wife blew out a candle and said coldly, "Only two left. Kay?"

Kay took a step back. "Well . . ."

"What's the matter, Kay?" "Come on, Kay . . ." "Don't do it, darling, if you don't want to." Kay's head twisted helplessly toward each speaker in turn before she went to the table, wrapped herself in the sheet, and lay down, fists crossed on her breast.

452

Pollidor said, "What happened to her, do you think?"

"Nice-looking woman," said Jeff, "but a nervous type."

"Something in her face says she didn't die peacefully," Wende offered.

"Maybe we ought to perform an autopsy," Bill said.

"Not necessary," Jeff objected. "She died of fright."

Kay's thin frame shuddered slightly, and Harry glared at them. "She died peacefully in bed, of old age. Didn't you, Kay? Come on, darling," he coaxed, "join the living."

A single candle burned. It was Harry's turn. He reclined on the table, hands outstretched, palms flat. Words floated down to him: "A nice fellow but he had this *thing* about the ground . . . thought the earth was alive . . . something in his past . . . wonder how he died. . . ."

Then the table shook; he could sense a faint vibration through his hands, his back. In his mind a crevasse opened and he glimpsed the shape of his anxiety, which was insupportable. He opened his eyes. Their faces hovered above, and he blew out the candle as though to extinguish the sight.

LATER, the Pollidors dropped them off at home. Harry carried the sleeping boy up to his room while Kay made coffee in the kitchen.

When he returned he found Kay walking agitatedly back and forth. "That's a game I can live without," she said.

"Me, too. But what scared you so?"

"I don't know. It was, well . . ." Her eyes would not look at him. "Like there was someone else in the room."

"Is that where you got your predictions about how people would die? You believe somebody talked to you?"

"I hardly remember what I said." She popped a knuckle.

"That's a brand-new habit, Kay. Where did you get it?"

"What?"

"The noise you made with your finger."

"Oh. You've got a funny habit, too—telling people things shake when nobody else feels it. Tomorrow you'll see a doctor. You promised, remember?"

They went to bed, turning away from each other as they searched uselessly for sleep.

SLIP

MONDAY, June 24.⁕ At the office, Vail made a number of calls that morning: to Dr. Bjerling, asking to be squeezed in during the next few hours; to Robinson at Summerset Villa, learning that the manager was not expected back until later; to the outfit that drained septic tanks; to the phone company about the false rings.

Through his doorway he called, "Mrs. Conner, send Walter in."

Walter Johnson was the company draftsman. When the partners worked up a report he turned their data into drawings, diagrams, or graphs.

Johnson entered the office. Vail handed him the Summerset Villa data from the drilling outfit. "I'd like drawings today of the hill—a cross section and a topographical sketch."

With the visit to the doctor impending, Vail prowled the office impatiently. He was oddly unconcerned about his own health. What mattered more was to establish the reason for his shakiness. For if nothing was wrong with him—as he suspected—then he was that much nearer to proving the existence of an earthquake.

Bjerling's office was only a few blocks away, and Vail walked there rapidly. The receptionist waved him in at once, and Vail seated himself before a crisp, white-coated man his own age.

Bjerling gazed at his patient thoughtfully. "You look a little pale, Harry. What's the trouble?"

Vail explained his fall from the ladder, the continuing dizziness and sense of imbalance. "It's like being on a rolling sea. Or in an earthquake."

Bjerling checked off a list of questions, examined Vail's eyes, and took his blood pressure. "Normal. All right, stand up. Put your feet together and close your eyes. If you fall, I'll catch you." Vail smiled and closed his eyes. He outweighed the doctor by fifty pounds. He did not fall.

A test for hearing followed. Here, too, Vail was normal.

At last Bjerling returned to his desk. "I can't find anything the matter with you. My bet is a mild case of labyrinthitis—disturbance of the inner ear. We don't know what causes it—virus, most likely. Probably what made you fall off the ladder in the first place. I'll give you some Dramamine, which will help your dizziness, and

the nurse will take skull X-rays just to be sure there's no fracture."
He extended his hand. "Take it easy, Harry. You're fine."

Vail frowned. He had wanted a clean bill of health or a clear
diagnosis. Labyrinthitis sounded like neither one, and the ambiguity
of the shaking, maddeningly, remained.

Later, at Summerset Villa, Charley, the foreman of the drilling
rig, told Vail, "That Robinson character won't let us work. He
came in about an hour ago and started to scream."

"I'll talk to him."

Vail climbed the hill. The sun was out, and a few old people sat
on the benches and strolled the paths. Among them he saw a
familiar face.

"Ah, Dr. Vail. You're here about the cracks, aren't you? Well,
they've gotten bigger. The janitor says you can see daylight through
one of them. The building is safe, isn't it?"

"There's nothing to worry about, Mrs. Benjamin," Vail said,
feigning confidence.

"Well, if you say so. You seem like such a nice, dependable
young man. Intelligent, too." She made a wrinkled smile. "You'd
better go talk to Mr. Robinson. He's waiting for you."

This time their discussion took place in the manager's office, and
he was angry. "I gave you permission to drill some holes, and now
you're back on my lawn with ugly machinery and a heavy truck.
What is it this time?"

"This hill is too wet. I want to dig a well and dewater it. It won't
take more than a couple of days."

"It'll cost a fortune. I'll need Mr. Summerset's permission."

"There's no time. The cracks must be sealed. You can see daylight through one. Also, I want to dig a hole on top of the hill."

"All right, dig your fool holes. But that is absolutely *all* I
authorize. I wish I could reach Mr. Summerset." Robinson wrung
his hands. "Vail, I hope you don't cause any more trouble."

Vail laughed bitterly. "Me? It's the rain, Mr. Robinson, the way
this place is built, the ground."

PUNCH's bark sounded hollow and far away. Vail walked to the
back of the house, where the shelty, scratching vainly at a mole
hole, greeted him with another bark and resumed scratching.

Kay appeared in a flowered apron. "Hello, you're early."

"I decided to quit at five like normal people." He kissed her.

"Oh, Dr. Bjerling called. He said you don't have a concussion. All you suffer from is a little virus. We haven't had a nice evening alone for a while. I'll feed Mark early and put him to bed."

She reappeared later in a blouse and long skirt. She looked nice, he told her, without mentioning that she seemed wan. He made a fire. Kay sat in the rocker, he in his straight-backed chair. Outside, the wind had started to gust. "Storm's coming," she remarked. "I hope we have good weather for the holidays. When is the Fourth?"

"A week from Thursday." He listened to the windows rattling.

"I hate the Fourth of July," Kay said suddenly. "Firecrackers make me jumpy. Did you call about the septic tank?"

"Yes. They'll come as soon as they can."

"Polly called. She had trouble getting through; you did call the phone company?" He grunted. "She said that Jeff is returning to New York on Wednesday, though he hopes to be back for the Fourth. Did I tell you that I saw him and Wende in the Wilbore store this afternoon? They said they were off to play tennis, but there was a blanket in Wende's convertible, and it looked like they were heading for the beach. Those two are together constantly. It's the talk of the club, but Wende doesn't seem to care."

"You don't think she'd leave Fred for Jeff?" he asked.

"I don't think so. She's too practical to abandon her nest for a TV reporter in the middle of a divorce." Kay pondered a moment. "Still, she did say she was going away for a few days. . . ."

"Anybody mention the game last night?"

"Not a word. It's like they all want to forget it, too."

There was a loud rap on the door and Kay whirled in her chair. "What's that?"

Harry opened the door to find Fred Demming leaning on a cane. His Cadillac loomed behind him in the dark. "Come in," said Harry. "What brings you out on a night like this?"

Demming entered hesitantly, his heavy face slack. "Wende went out hours ago. I thought she might be here and tried to call, but your phone is on the blink."

"Yes, we've reported it. Maybe she's at the Pollidors'."

"No. I called."

"How about a drink, Fred? Maybe she'll show up here."

"Please," he said aimlessly.

456

The phone rang and Kay, with a startled expression, picked it up and put it down again. "Nobody there."

"My phone's been acting funny, too," Demming said. "Kind of spooky, with the wind whistling and Wende not home and a dead phone in your hand. I wonder if it's a prank."

"Prank?" Kay asked sharply.

"The village kids, dialing and hanging up."

"They don't have phones," Harry reminded him.

"There's one in the bar they could use."

"Fred," Harry said in a slightly embarrassed voice, "strangest thing. Dun Sowles said somebody was interested in buying *my* house. Have any idea who?"

Demming seemed surprised. "No idea at all. Somebody up the peninsula, I imagine. Interested in selling?"

"*Me?* Definitely not."

"You didn't tell me about it," Kay said.

"I forgot."

Another rattle sounded, which Harry took to be the wind, but after it happened twice he went to the door, to find the Pollidors. "Hello, hello," he greeted them.

"What took you so long?" Polly asked. "I was practically blown off the porch."

Harry, considering why he had not gone to the door at once, realized that he would have expected Punch to bark had there been people outside. "Where's the dog?" he asked Kay.

She shrugged. "Up in Mark's room, I guess."

Bill said, "We only popped over to look for Jeff."

Polly said rapidly, "He must still be at the club. Gracious, what a terrible night! It's absolutely scary. The wind's making our whole house shake. I feel so much safer here in the stone house."

The phone rang and Kay went to it hastily. "Jeff," she said. "Yes . . . I'll ask them." She said to the Pollidors, "Jeff's back from the club. He wants to know if he should come over."

"Tell him we'll be right home," Polly said.

When they had left Fred picked up the phone and dialed. "Maybe Wende's shown up. . . . Nobody," he said, hanging up. "I guess she's walking on the beach. Walks a lot lately."

Several sharp raps sounded, and Harry ran to open the door. There was no one outside. "Punch?" he called.

457

"Punch is in Mark's room, I told you," Kay said.

He closed the door and switched on the porch light.

"What's going on?" Fred asked.

"That's what I'd like to know," Kay said.

The rapping sounded again. Harry ran to the door and jerked it open.

"What's the matter, Harry?" Wende Demming said.

He felt foolish. "I didn't mean to frighten you, Wende. Come in. Fred's here."

Wende came into the room—hair tousled, cheeks flushed—wearing a sweater and tennis shorts. "Fred, darling," she breathed, "after tennis I took a walk on the beach. The big surf is marvelous. I went farther than I meant to. I figured Fred might be here," she said to the Vails, "but your line was out of order so I came over. Poor Fred, you haven't had dinner." Kay started to speak, and Wende said rapidly, "Don't even suggest it, dear. We'll eat at home."

"Wasn't she in a hurry to get out of here," Harry remarked when the front door closed.

"She was afraid I'd blab about seeing her at the store, which I wouldn't have, of course. Well, I guess we should eat."

As Kay was removing the soufflé from the oven he felt a shake. "I don't know what happened," she said, arriving in the dining room. "The soufflé fell."

"It'll taste fine anyway."

After dinner he stoked the fire in the living room, adding logs. Kay entered with coffee and said, when they were seated, "Polly was afraid to stay in her house. Could it really fall?"

"If a storm were big enough, yes. And in California the Pollidors' house wouldn't have a chance of surviving. It's too fragile."

"Survive what? Oh, I get it, an earthquake."

"Neither would ours, probably. Stone houses don't fare well in earthquakes."

She sighed. "Everybody has one irrational fear, I guess." The wind spluttered. "Mine comes out on nights like this."

He chuckled. "Don't say it. Ghosts again. Next you'll tell me you really believe in them."

"Maybe I did once," she said softly.

"You mean it's true? You never told me."

"Because you're a scientist. You would have laughed at me."

"With you," he corrected her. "When did you stop being a believer?"

"Years ago, when I got to college."

"When you got to college!" His big hand rested on her knee. "You mean you believed in ghosts as late as that?"

"In a way. It was strongest when I was a teenager. At that age almost anything's believable." She smiled faintly into the fire. "Shouldn't we use the screen, Harry?"

"The fire's small. Go on."

"Well, my ghosts were nasty spirits who could read your mind and know just what frightened you."

"What—" he started to say when he heard the pounding.

"What's that?" Kay shrieked.

"A loose shutter," he said. "In the laundry room, I think. That must have been the noise we heard before." He marched down the hall, latched the shutter from the inside, and came back. "There's a big draft in here," he observed. "Is anything open?"

"Not that I know of."

"Well, go on. When you were a girl, what frightened you that ghosts would know about?"

Kay said absently, "Unexpected things. I never thought I saw a ghost. It was more like sensing an evil presence."

Upstairs a door slammed. "Oh, Harry," she moaned.

He took the stairs two at a time. Mark's door was shut. He opened it and saw that the boy lay on his back in a deep sleep. Harry propped the door open and went downstairs.

"Mark's door. Draft, I guess. What did the ghosts do?"

"They didn't actually *do* anything," she said. "It was just the sensation that they *could*, if they chose."

"And what was your reaction?"

"You honestly want to know?" He nodded vigorously. "I tried never to be alone. I slept in my sister's room whenever I could, hung around with my parents or friends as much as possible. I figured that when I got old enough the ghosts would understand I wasn't vulnerable and go away for good. And they did."

There was an interval of silence as they examined the fire, and then Harry said, "Kay, I thought you said that Punch was in Mark's room. He isn't there now."

"How could he have gotten out?" she said in a worried voice.

459

"Maybe the screen fell off the study window again."

"Go look." The study door was shut. It resisted when he opened it, and the chandelier in the dining room tinkled like tiny bells as a wind whipped through the house. He switched on the light. "Kay," he called. "The window is broken."

She entered the room hesitantly. The floor was strewn with papers and glass. "How . . ."

He inspected the shattered pane and raised the sash. "Broken branch down there. It knocked off the screen and broke the window. Punch must have been trapped in here and jumped outside."

Examining the floor, her eyes fastened on something. She knelt and rose, holding out a flat white stone. "What's this doing here?"

"Mark bring it in?"

"I don't think so."

He secured the papers on his desk, closed the door behind them, and they returned to the living room.

He listened to the groaning trees. "What a wind! The surf must be over the bluffs. I hope the studio's all right. Dun hasn't quite finished caulking the picture window. I'd better go look."

"Not on your life. Stay with me. Where do you suppose that dog is? I hope he hasn't gotten hurt."

"I bet he's out checking the mole holes, wind and all. I'll call him." The wind roared as he stepped outside and called into the darkness, "Punch! Punch!" There was no response. He closed the door and returned to the living room.

Kay sat stiffly in the rocker, clutching the arms of the chair, staring in the direction of the birdcage. "Kay! What's the matter? Why are you sitting there like that? Say something!"

She did, in a very small voice: "Bird."

"I can barely hear you. Come on, honey, what gives?"

She opened her mouth. "Harry, something horrible just happened. I had this funny feeling, like somebody was shaking me, and the rocker began to rock without me rocking it. And then those fireplace tools began to rattle and then—you won't believe it—the bird sang. The singing greenfinch actually sang. Only it wasn't a pretty song, but this awful croak. I tried to call, but I choked up. Harry, that bird was scared to death." She began to sob.

Suddenly the lights went out. "Damn," he muttered. The fire seemed to burn brighter in the darkness, flickering in a burst of wind down the chimney. "Storm's knocked out the power. Or is it just our house? I'll go upstairs and see."

He took the flashlight from the closet, brought candles from the dining room, and lighted them. Then he went upstairs. When he returned Kay sat in her chair, rocking slowly, eyes closed. "I thought maybe we'd blown a fuse," he said, "but the Pollidors' house is dark, too."

"Harry," she said dreamily, "I smell something burning."

"Nonsense, honey, you— The rug's on fire!" He stamped the burning ember with his foot. "You were right. We should have used the screen. Well, there's only a small hole."

"*They* start fires."

He took her into his arms, telling her that a downdraft caused the fire and that the birdsong and all the rest were in her imagination. Once they were in bed everything would be all right. She allowed herself to be led upstairs as he held a candle. Then, deep and guttural, a creak like that of a huge hinge filled the house.

"Harry, what was that?" she said, her voice pathetically controlled.

He tried to think. "That was the elm swaying in the wind."

He watched her undress, then went to check on Mark, who still slept soundly. In their bedroom again, he saw her shake two pills from a bottle into her palm. "What's that?" he demanded.

"Seconal."

"Don't. That stuff's rotten for you," he pleaded. But she had already swallowed the pills. Dramamine, Seconal, a fine pair we are, he thought. He returned to the living room for the flashlight, went to the basement and measured the crack, which was unchanged. Then he went outside. The wind had abated. The flashlight revealed the trunk of the elm to be sound, and he could detect no big broken branches.

After checking the studio, his keen eyes detected movement by the barn, and he shone the torch. Dun emerged from the darkness, shielding his eyes. "Dun! You scared me."

" 'Fraid I'd do that. Parked the truck on the road and walked in so I wouldn't disturb you people. Wanted to be sure the picture window was okay. Looks to be. Everything else all right?"

"Seems to be. Hear that noise a while back?"

Dun nodded. "Elm tree creaked."

"I thought so. Oh, Dun, there's a broken window in the study.

Falling branch did it, I think. If you could fix it tomorrow . . . ."

After saying good night Vail turned toward the house. There was one more task, he thought. With the flashlight he slowly began examining the stone stoop. He was about to give up when he found what he was looking for: two flat white stones, identical with the one Kay had found.

THE NEXT MORNING Kay and Mark overslept as if exhausted. The electricity was on again, and Vail set the electric clock in the kitchen. He made himself breakfast and dressed and shaved silently. He backed the Rolls from the barn and drove away.

Near Point Road he remembered Punch. Where could the rascal be? Once before he had run off, and it had been days before he returned, muddy and covered with sores and ticks. If the dog wasn't back by evening, he would search for him.

A broken place on Point Road seemed to resist the repair crew's every effort. Vail wondered if perhaps an underground stream, a swollen tributary of Torturous Creek, weakened the road.

As he headed toward Summerset Villa he switched on WROK. "Williams contends that he was in Florida at the time of the Newport gasoline explosion and so could not have perpetrated the crime, but in the absence of a witness to corroborate the suspect's story, Rhode Island authorities are moving for his extradition. . . ."

Vail turned off the radio, maneuvered the Rolls around a bad spot in the road near Summerset Villa, and drove up the hill. On the crest behind the building the rig was in place, its pyramidal scaffolding outlined against the sky. He got out of the car. Charley and his helper stood in front of the home, holding coffee mugs.

"Good morning, Charley," Vail said. He looked toward the entranceway, crowded with old people. The drilling operation was probably the most exciting thing to happen at Summerset Villa all year. "Give me a report."

Charley said, "The well is in. Got hoses down there. The hill's dewatering, but not as much as I'd like."

"Let's give it some time. What about the top of the hill?"

"All set. We'll take a sample."

The front door opened and a frail figure appeared, bearing a cup. "Good morning, Dr. Vail," Mrs. Benjamin said. "I brought you some coffee."

462

"Good morning, Mrs. Benjamin!" Vail took the cup with a smile. "Did you have a good night?"

"It was ghastly, Dr. Vail. The building shook as though a terrier had hold of it. I hate to think what might have happened had the storm been worse. Well, most of us here have lived long enough."

"Don't talk like that, Mrs. Benjamin. You've a lot of years left."

Vail made his way up the muddy hill. The rig was twelve feet high. Within its confines, a 350-pound steel weight hammered the drill head into the ground with a steady *pum, pum, pum.*

"What are you getting?" Vail asked Charley.

"About fifty, I guess." Vail understood what this meant. If it took the hammer three hundred blows to drive the drill into the ground, the drill bit was encountering solid rock. The fewer blows it took, the softer the ground. Fifty blows for the same distance meant soft ground, but not quite as soft as Vail had expected.

Charley kept an eye on the drill shaft. He said suddenly, "It's going down faster. Twenty, I'd say now." Twenty meant silty, clayey soil, very wet. It was like driving a pin through gauze. "Slower now," Charley said. "Looks like we're hitting rock."

Vail felt relieved. If it was bedrock, this close to the surface, the ground was more stable than he had supposed. His optimism abated as Charley shouted, "Faster, much faster!"

Vail's gaze shot to the top of the rig, which began to move back and forth. "Watch out!" he bellowed. He lunged, and seizing Charley's helper, dragged him away. At the same moment there was a pop. The ground buckled and the rig crashed into the hole.

The rig man dusted himself off. "Thanks, Dr. Vail."

"You may have saved his life," Charley gasped, examining the opening. Water sloshed below. "There's a cave down there. The drill went through the roof."

"We've got to find out how big it is," Vail said. "Drill some more, Charley, farther down the slope."

"Do our best," Charley said glumly. "This ground is dangerous."

SILENCE greeted him at the stone house. When he entered the kitchen Mark ran up to him. "I miss Punch."

"Daddy will look for him." Vail circled the house, whistling and calling Punch's name at the trees, in the field, until he found himself at the house again.

"I'm going to the village and see if he's there," he told Kay.

On the end of the pier Sam Wilbore was throwing stones over the water. Vail called, "Sam?" The boy turned. "Did you see my dog? Shetland sheepdog. Missing since last night."

Wilbore's head responded negatively while he bent and picked another flat white stone from the pile beside him. He launched it over the bay.

Vail went home. "Nothing much we can do. . . . He'll turn up," he said in a comforting voice. "Well, what happened today? Septic-tank people come? The yard stinks."

"No. Nobody came," Kay replied mournfully.

A hand pulled at Vail's sleeve, and he stared down at the small pale face. "What is it, Mark?"

"Daddy, I want to show you something. Come." Mark tugged at his hand. He followed his child. "I found a funny plant. Over there." He pointed to the far side of the giant boulder. Vail walked faster, with the boy hanging behind. Vail stopped abruptly. A brown growth of some kind stuck up from the ground—or was it a stick? He put his hand on his stomach and said tensely, "Go back to the house, Mark. Tell your mother to stay where she is." Mark ran.

He approached reluctantly, forcing his legs to move. He reached down, pulled, and looked away from the dead shelty hanging from his hand by its stiffened tail.

"Harry!" said her broken voice behind him. "I told you not to use poison!"

"I don't see how he got to it. I don't remember putting poison on this side of the boulder." He examined the dog more carefully. "Punch's head looks crushed."

"Crushed? By what? By *whom?*" Kay fainted.

She was not very heavy, he reflected as he carried her to the house. She must have lost weight. As he thought of it, he could not recall Kay eating a decent meal in days.

He placed her on the couch and rubbed her temples with cold water. Her eyes opened. "What are you going to do?"

"Bury him."

"Mark, stay here with me," she said.

Vail took a shovel, and carrying the dog, looked for a suitable burial place. Up the small hill, at the foot of the giant boulder, seemed right: the slab resembled a gravestone, as Kay's painting recorded. The ground here was soft. There were gentle ridges he hadn't noticed before. He dug a pit quickly and laid the shelty under the sod. He marked the grave with a rock.

Inside, Kay rested in bed while Mark paged through a book in the living room, now and then stifling a sob. Harry decided to give the boy his dinner. He was in the kitchen when Dun appeared at the back door. Harry went outside. The old man was agitated. "Came by to repair the broken window," he began apologetically, then blurted out, "Mr. Vail, somebody been digging on the hill?"

Vail said slowly, "The dog's dead. I buried him."

"Oh." His face could not control relief. "That's too bad. Nice little doggie." He shuffled from one foot to the other as if searching for something to say. "Well, one thing about dogs, if one dies, you can get another. Not like people. Look at it that way, Mr. Vail."

"I guess so." Vail studied him suspiciously.

Dun faltered. "How did the little dog die?"

"Well, either he got into some poison or he was killed somehow and put in the mole hole where I found him."

"Ain't nobody around here who'd do that."

"The head was crushed." Vail glanced up at the elm, black against the twilight. It seemed to him that the tree looked different in some way. He heard something. "Hear anything, Dun?"

"Nope. What'd it sound like?"

"A crash. Like a small tree came down."

"Could be. Lots of trees weakened by the windstorm," Dun explained. "Sorry about the dog."

POISON, acting instantly, was bad enough; that Punch might have suffered a violent death affected Kay even more, and several times after Mark went to bed she referred to it.

"But I've told you already," he said, "on thinking it through I'm sure that the condition of the head was due to rigor mortis."

"I wish I could believe you," she said. "Crazy ideas are running through my head. I'll go to the studio and try to work."

When she had left he went to his study and took down Richter's *Elementary Seismology* from above his desk. He skimmed a table showing the effects of big quakes that caused tremendous convulsions over a large area and would measure in the upper magnitudes. The Richter scale, which the seismologist had devised to measure magnitudes, was divided into ten segments, with each segment representing a magnitude ten times greater than the one preceding. Thus an earthquake with a magnitude of 8.4—like the Alaska quake—would be twenty million times more powerful than a quake with a magnitude of 3.5, itself large enough to be perceptible to humans. Vail wondered if a quake of a magnitude of 5, enough to cause considerable damage, could occur in a small geographical area, as an earthquake of low magnitude would.

He was studying the page when he heard the knocks. There were three this time, one sounding as though it had struck the front door, the others the wall of the house. Racing to the front door, he flung it open. A flat white stone lay in the doorway. "You!" he shouted angrily into the darkness. "That's enough."

Kay stood beside him. "Who are you yelling at?"

"The village kids. They're throwing stones at the house."

"They couldn't throw that far."

"Sam Wilbore could. The kid has an arm like Hank Aaron. Listen. Hear their car starting up?"

"No." Kay turned and he closed the door. "Why would they do it?" she asked.

"Revenge because I dressed them down."

"Maybe. If it was them. Did they kill the dog, too?"

He hesitated. "I don't think so."

"What did, then?" Her eyes showed white around the irises.

He said slowly, "The ground did it. The earth crushed him."

"Harry, is that what you believe? Isn't it clear that—"

He put his hands on her shoulders and shook them. "Kay, snap out of it. Punch's death has driven you over the line. Come back to normal."

"What's normal?" she said bitterly.

He would consider later how differently they experienced the same event. For him the floor leaped upward slightly, accompanied by sounds of pots rattling in the kitchen, mugs jiggling on the glass shelf, arrowheads falling from the mantel. The phone rang once and stopped. "They're all over the house!" Kay cried.

"Kay, it's not—"

From above came a thump and a scream. Vail ran up the stairs and found the boy on the floor, whimpering. The fishes in the mobile swung slowly, like live aquatic creatures.

466

"He's all right. He fell out of bed," he said to Kay, whose white face flashed in the doorway and vanished. "Come on, Mark, it's all right. Get in the lower bunk this time."

He covered the boy with a blanket and squeezed in next to him, cradling the small body with his own until Mark stopped trembling and fell asleep.

The door to his own bedroom was closed. He entered to find Kay in bed, completely covered by blankets and pillows. "Better leave me alone," she said in a muffled voice.

He went to the basement and measured the crack. It was now 18 inches long.

Old Brompton, Vail knew, was experiencing a certain kind of earthquake—spasmodic, slow, but it might be building up. It had killed his dog. Perhaps there would be further victims.

FAULT

WEDNESDAY, June 26. Rising early, Vail trotted to the beach and sat in his rock chair, watching the waves and the gulls. Clouds spotted the horizon like warning flags.

Having identified the adversary, Vail felt a certain relief; at least he faced an actual thing and not his fantasies. Still, though convinced that an earthquake was under way, what should he do? The slow quake might remain at its present magnitude and intensity, causing no real harm; but it could also grow from a baby into a monster, and that worried him, because people ought to be warned. How? The newspapers, if he went to them, would take him for a freak. Kip Smith at WROK would make a joke of it. Paul Kelly at Lamont was the natural recipient of his information, but he would want proof. If only reliable, corroborating witnesses existed or if only proof existed . . .

Perhaps there was such evidence. Vail remembered the elm tree in the backyard. What he had perceived in the twilight, he now believed, was a slight list to the tree. Such a thing could happen if the earth had crept during the tremors. Prove it, he thought.

He jogged back to the studio and removed Kay's painting of the black elm from the wall. Out in the yard, he changed positions, trying to find the exact point from which she had painted it. At last he found the spot on the bank of Torturous Creek.

Her voice startled him. "What are you doing?"

"I was comparing the elm with your picture. Look—the tree leans now. There's been a change in the ground."

Kay looked at the picture. "You're imagining things."

"You should talk," he said coldly. "Where did you put those before-and-after photos? Maybe there's one of the backyard."

The pinched look of her face was new to him. "I don't remember. Maybe in the hall closet. Look for yourself."

But the photograph he found was too small to permit him to make a judgment. He placed it in his jacket and drove off.

He took the print to a photography shop on the street level of his office building, then rode the elevator to the third floor.

In his office, Walter Johnson handed him a geological profile of the Summerset Villa area, with surface features—the home, the road, the hill—depicted on a sheet of acetate.

"Nice job," he told the draftsman. "This morning I'd like you to cover the end of Old Brompton peninsula, too. There are three houses, one of which is mine, a road called Point Road, a fishing village, and finally some cliffs. Oh yes—" He went to the filing cabinet and returned with the map covered with circles. "These represent earthquake epicenters in this region." A confused look appeared on Johnson's face and Vail went on, "The epicenter is the point on the surface above the earthquake. What I'd like you to do is to give me the direction and distance of every recorded earthquake in a radius of, say, a hundred miles from here. Put them on the acetate, around the sides."

Lechine appeared in the doorway with a newspaper. "What's all this?" he demanded when Johnson had left.

"There's a cave in the hill at Summerset Villa which could indicate a fault," Vail replied. "If there's a fault around here, I want to find out where it runs."

"First a crack in your cellar and you think your house is in trouble. Now a cave and you detect an earthquake. In the meantime, how do we get paid?" Lechine snapped. "You neglect the paying jobs for a charity project on a building—it will surely be standing longer than you!" He paused. He looked sorry. "Didn't mean to shout. It's just that we've got to pay the bills or we'll be on the street even without that earthquake of yours. Vail's earthquake!" He laughed and socked Harry playfully on the arm. "Say, did you read the paper? They let that Williams guy loose. The one who blew up the tank farm. They believe his alibi."

WHEN Vail came home he removed a large sheet of poster board from the back seat. Facing the elm, he held the board in his hands and studied it.

Kay emerged from the studio. "What's that?"

He showed her the mounted 5 x 3-foot photograph. "It's a blowup of the photo I found this morning. Look, the tree *does* lean."

Kay covered her eyes with her thin hands. "Harry, I don't want to encourage you in any way. What you're into is nuts." She turned and ran to the kitchen.

He stood still, trying to capture the meaning of the tree's list, ignoring her disbelief. If he was right about the creep, the tree would eventually fall and crush the barn.

He went inside, where Kay was talking excitedly into the telephone. "That was Polly," she said when she hung up. "Wende has been missing since last night."

A few minutes later Polly came over. Harry took her arm and led her to the couch. "Calm down, Polly. What happened exactly?"

"Fred went to Boston on business yesterday. He called around five to say he'd be late—Wende was home. He got back at ten and she was gone. So was her Mercedes. He thought she must have gone to a party and waited up, but she never came back."

"Wouldn't the servants have known where she was?" Kay asked.

"The servants know nothing."

"Did he report her disappearance to the police?" Harry said.

Polly answered, "I learned only because I went over there. He hasn't told anyone else, much less the police, because he's afraid Wende's run off with Jeff Carmichael. It all fits," Polly insisted. "They spent the day together and Jeff came back for an early supper. Then he left for New York in his car. That must have been about the time she disappeared."

"What did she do with her Mercedes?"

"Hid it someplace so Fred would believe she'd gone off on one of her little trips. No, I'm certain she's with Jeff. I feel so guilty for letting it happen. Fred is really suffering."

"Shouldn't you call Jeff and make sure?" Kay asked.

"Me? I never want to speak to Jeffrey Carmichael again."

When she had left, Kay turned a bleak face to Harry. "I hope Wende's all right. I have a terrible feeling."

"But she told you she planned to go away for a few days."

"I wish I knew for sure that she was with Jeff. I'd call him, but I don't have any right to poke into her business."

"I'm going to the village," he told her.

In the square, he wandered about, mentally cataloguing the pieces of scrap that had accumulated there. In particular, he noted a pile of creosote-covered boards. Climbing back into the Rolls, he heard a clatter of stone on metal and saw Sam Wilbore on the pier, winding up for another throw into the square. Vail ignored him.

Dun was at home. "Good evening," Vail said, stepping into the shack. "A couple of things, sort of important, Dun. I believe the village kids—the Wilbores, Bill Pabodie, maybe—are throwing rocks at my house." He took from his pocket a white stone like those in Dun's glass jars. "I found that on the porch."

"Lots of stones around like that."

"Not ones that fly through the air and hit doors and windows. If they don't stop, I'll call the police." He sighed inwardly, thinking of Old Brompton's one ancient policeman.

Vail followed an agenda now. "Crack in my basement, sump pump that failed, leaking pipe in the bathroom, other things—they add up to the possibility of small earthquakes happening during the past few weeks. Do you know of anything that would support that idea, Dun? Anything cracked, broken, bent?"

Dun's voice turned cold. "Don't believe I do."

"In case I'm right, it might be smart to take precautions," Vail said. "I'd like to brace my cellar, Dun. Can you do it?"

" 'Fraid not this week. Too busy."

"Too busy for *me?*"

Dun said with stiff lips, "Yes. Awful lot happening to that house, Mr. Vail. Maybe you should sell and move away to get your mind off this earthquake of yours."

Vail turned angrily to the door. They're all alike, he found himself thinking, even Dun. Hand on the knob, he heard several loud pops.

"What's that noise?" he asked sharply.

"Firecrackers," Dun said. "Kids impatient for the Fourth of July."

Vail headed for home. As he was slowing down for his driveway he heard a rush from behind and pulled in sharply, twisting his neck to see Cy Wilbore's souped-up blue car receding down the road. Catcalls. It's a war of nerves, he thought. But why?

He found Kay watching the six-thirty news. On the screen bobbed a thin mustache. "This is Jeffrey Carmichael, filling in for Bill Ducksworth, who is on vacation."

"I'm going to call him after all," Kay said when the show was over. But after chatting with Carmichael she returned, her face startled. "Where can Wende be? She's not with Jeff."

"We'd better tell Fred," he said.

"Not yet. It might worry him even more."

THEY LOOK terrible, he said to himself at supper, Kay with her pallor, Mark with blue rings about his eyes.

"Harry," she informed him, "the tap water has started to run brown. And Mark has a little diarrhea. Is there a connection?"

"No. I don't think so. If there were, we'd be sick, too. It's just brackish water getting into the well from the pond because the water table's so high. Nothing to worry about."

"There are little cracks in the ceiling of Mark's room."

"Because of the leak in the pipe, probably."

She poured coffee. "Harry, let's leave the house and go stay in a motel at Fall River for a while. I don't think this atmosphere is at all good for Mark—or for me."

"Why don't you go to your mother's until the Fourth of July?"

"No. I don't like to leave you alone here."

"Think it over," he muttered.

In the cellar, he measured the crack—now almost two feet long.

AS HE parked the car in front of Summerset Villa he could hear Charley's drill pummeling the hill. He walked through mud which still hadn't dried after three days of sunshine. "Morning, Dr. Vail," Charley said. "A few more holes to drill, but looks like that's a small cave, extending to about there." He pointed to an imaginary spot some distance up from the building.

"How's the draining going?"

"Pretty good. Water is coming out."

"Call me at the office when you're finished."

471

"Yes. Dr. Vail, there's something I want to show you."

Vail followed Charley to the hilltop. From the hole through which the drill had fallen, water burbled and flowed down the hillside.

"And look." Charley pointed to a line of small cones running down the hill. They were about a foot high, each capped by a hole, like a miniature volcano. "I think those are caused by water."

"Earthspouts," Vail said. "You get them in California."

"Never seen nothing like that around here."

"Me neither."

Vail went back down the hill. As he entered the reception room Alma Benjamin sprang at him. "Just the person I want to see."

"Any trouble, Mrs. Benjamin?"

"There's always trouble these days. The clothes driers won't spin, basement's flooded, lights have gone off several times. Mr. Robinson doesn't work either."

"I must talk to him."

"I'll try to get him."

Fifteen minutes later Robinson appeared, cheeks creased by sleep lines. "Did you reach Summerset?" Vail asked.

"No. He usually returns my calls quicker than this."

"Look, Mr. Robinson, there's a decision to be made. By draining the hill we've stabilized the ground to some extent. Of course, if the rains start again, all bets are off. And if there were seismic activity . . . tremors. Little earthquakes. Or even a big one . . ."

"Nonsense. What are you getting at?"

"Well, there's a procedure for strengthening unstable ground, called pressure grouting. What it amounts to is digging holes and inserting liquefied cement."

Robinson said with an edge of contempt, "If I told Mr. Summerset he had to shell out a bundle because some local geologist said there was going to be an earthquake, he'd fire me. It'll be hard enough to get him to pay for what you've already done."

"Perhaps you'll change your mind. I'll stop by early next week—Oh, Mr. Robinson?"

The manager had already started to leave. "What now?"

"If I were you, I'd put scaffolding around the building."

Robinson's small eyes stared accusingly. "Vail, are you insane?"

Back at the office, Vail asked Mrs. Conner to place a call to Paul Kelly at the Lamont-Doherty Geological Observatory in Palisades,

New York. Lechine was nowhere to be seen. Vail poked his head into Johnson's office. "How's it coming?"

"Jim threw a rush load at me," Johnson complained. "I don't see how I can get to the drawing until tomorrow."

"I'd like it this afternoon, please. Lechine's stuff can wait."

"Your party's on the line," Mrs. Conner called.

He went to his office and picked up the phone. Kelly's brisk voice was clear. "Harry? How's the geology?"

"It has its ups and downs." He laughed briefly. "Thanks for your letter." After chatting for a few moments Vail said, "I have a question. Have your seismic stations picked up any unusual activity recently up my way?"

Kelly sounded surprised. "No, I don't think so. Why?"

"I believe there's an earthquake under way here."

Vail laid out his evidence of shakings and cracks; of the north-south direction of what he had first perceived as mole ridges; of the earthspouts at Summerset that could be a sign of a fault, along with the limestone cave. He did not mention the dog.

Kelly's tone was doubtful. "The nearest seismic activity to you at present is at Moodus, Connecticut, but that earthquake swarm is not new. The noises have been going on a long time."

"Noises?"

"Ground noises. We're getting them on tape."

Vail said quickly, "Suppose I come down and borrow a portable seismometer. Will you be in on Saturday?"

"I'm always in on Saturdays. All right, I'll dig up a machine."

Vail saw Lechine in the doorway. "Portable seismometer?" Lechine shook his head. "Nuttier and nuttier."

BY LATE afternoon Johnson's drawing was ready, and Vail took it home with him. The survey covered both sides of the body of water separating Old Brompton peninsula from Massachusetts. Arrows indicated the location of previous earthquakes in the vicinity within the ordered radius. There had been dozens of them, the map showed, none major.

Vail marked on the acetate sheet the location of the cones he had seen that morning on the hillside, and the pavement breaks below Summerset Villa and on Point Road. But the location of the fault—if there was one—remained purely speculative: the pocked roads didn't necessarily mean a thing. He needed more evidence.

Vail marched down to the basement and glared at the crack. It looked thicker as well as longer. He drove to the village.

Sam Wilbore stood on the pier, flipping stones over the water. He watched as Vail prowled the square. Vail found what he wanted in a pile of rusty machinery—a long, thin metal strip with holes around the edges. Under the weight he struggled, carrying the piece to the car.

From the side of his eye he saw Wilbore bend and throw. A stone bounced and clanked among the machinery close to where he walked. Then came another. Vail moved faster, put the plate in the trunk, and gazed accusingly at Wilbore. The boy, he thought, had been trying to frighten but not hit him. He suppressed an instinct to run to the pier and confront him. That, he realized, was just as well, for as he got into the car to drive off, Cy Wilbore and Bill Pabodie emerged from behind the store. It had been a trap: the three youths would have ganged up on him.

At home, he lugged the metal piece to the basement, held it to the wall, and made marks through the holes with a pencil. He found the electric drill, and began to drill into the hard face.

An hour was needed to bolt the plate to the wall. The metal covered the crack completely, hiding it from view. Perhaps the break could not be contained, but at least he was fighting back, and it felt good.

Upstairs, Kay murmured dejectedly, "Wende hasn't shown up. We'd better give Fred the news. I called and said we'd come over."

"WHERE can she be?" asked Fred Demming. In the last few days he seemed to have aged; the hand holding the cane head trembled. "I was certain she was with Carmichael—counted on it, I guess, in terms of her safety."

"Wende's taken little trips before," Harry pointed out.

"Yes," Demming confessed, "but she's always left a note."

"Maybe you should call the state police," Harry suggested.

Demming looked horrified. "Police? It would get in the newspapers. Better to wait."

The place seemed oddly silent. Harry asked, "Where is the staff?"

Demming's thin lips barely moved. "They quit today, the whole lot. Complained the atmosphere made them nervous. I'm all alone."

That evening Kay was subdued to the point of utter silence, and Harry asked what she was thinking.

"Of Fred. I saw something in his face that I don't want to talk about. Listen!" A hum, like a bee's, faded and rose again. Stealthily, Kay crept across the room to the piano. She seized the tuning fork and the sound stopped. "What caused that? Tell me!" She brandished the tuning fork like a weapon.

"Vibrations passing up through the floor, through the piano, to the tuning fork. Kay, I want you to listen." He gave her the information he had presented to Kelly. "There are tremors so small a human can't feel them. We're in the middle of an earthquake."

"Harry, I want to believe you, but I can't. Make me a drink, will you?"

He went to the bar.

"Watch out!"

He stepped back quickly, and a toby jug crashed where he'd stood, spreading its grin on the floor.

"They're turning dangerous, Harry. Before, they only wanted to frighten us. Now they'd like to kill. We can't stay in this house."

"Get hold of yourself," he said as he eyed the row of mocking faces. "The jugs have been shaken to the edge of the shelf by the tremors. That's the reasonable explanation."

"You and your reasonable explanations. Can't I make you see, Harry? There are spirits in our house. They followed us to the Demmings' the night we played Inquest and told me in some weird way how everyone was going to die—"

A sharp rap sounded at the front door. He ran outside and bellowed, "You rotten kids!" From the darkness a stone struck the wall near his head. Inside, locking the door, he opened and closed his big fists in fury. Kay knelt on the floor, sobbing. He pressed her to him, stroking her hair. "Those kids again. One more stone and I'm going after them."

"Not the kids," she said with a sharp intake of breath. "It's them. I started to tell you what they're saying: Wende is dead. Demming is dying. Something about the Pollidors. Now we're being warned. I'm leaving, Harry. And *I want you to come with me!*" she shrieked.

"I'm staying," he said severely. "Kay, there are no such things as spirits, you know that. What about the crack? No spirit could cause *that*, could it?" He grasped her arm.

"No," she said in a small voice, "I guess not. But—"

"No buts. There aren't any spirits. There are tremors and bad kids. Will you believe me?"

"I'll try."

SIMULTANEOUSLY with the peal of the telephone a scream sounded from far out in the night, louder and louder. As Kay switched on the bed light and reached for the phone, Vail realized that he had never heard an ambulance siren on the peninsula before. He could see lights flashing through the trees.

"Hello . . . Oh no . . . You poor dear . . . ." As she hung up she said, "Bill Pollidor shot himself in the head. He was loading his shotgun and it accidentally went off."

"Is he alive?"

"Well, he's breathing." Vail got out of bed and started to dress. "No, don't. Polly's going in the ambulance with him to the hospital in Fall River. She was barely coherent, but she did say she'd call tonight—if he dies. Otherwise we can go to the hospital in the morning. . . . In the head," Kay kept repeating. "In the head . . ."

The next morning Pollidor remained alive but unconscious. The doctors refused a prognosis, but even if he pulled through, it looked as though he would suffer brain damage.

The Vails, leaving Mark with a sitter, spent most of the day at the hospital. Afterward, at home, Kay said carefully, "I've decided to take Mark to Mother's tomorrow. I wish you'd come, but I know you won't. Many more sleepless nights and I'll get sick. I just lie there waiting for the noises. I hate to abandon Polly, but I can't help it. She's got relatives arriving tomorrow and Jeff's scheduled to return next week, so I feel less guilty about leaving."

He said slowly, "It stands to reason that the shooting—I mean the fact that poor Bill got it in the head—just confirmed what you said at the party and your worst fears, didn't it? But Bill was loading or cleaning his shotgun. A tremor came and the gun fired accidentally. Couldn't you be satisfied by that explanation?"

She shook her head mutely.

"I guess each of us has to see things in his own way," he said helplessly. "You've got this crazy notion about spirits, and I know there's an earthquake. Well, I think there's one thing we can agree on—we ought to put breakable things in a safe place."

"Where in this house is a safe place?" she cried.

"The cellar, I guess, is the safest." He found a box and together they packed the toby jugs, the glassware and the china.

CREEP

AT THE Lamont-Doherty Geological Observatory on the lofty palisades west of the Hudson River, not far from New York City, Kelly greeted Vail ebulliently. A short, broad-shouldered man with a snub nose, Kelly had come to Lamont from Cal Tech four years before, but the two men had met infrequently since, and never on either's home ground.

After the preliminaries Kelly asked warily, "You've been experiencing tremors, have you?"

Vail said cautiously, "I think so. And if I could prove there are tremors, or an earthquake swarm, it might help my wife. She's begun to interpret these events as psychic phenomena."

"You're kidding! Well, your location's about the last place you'd expect seismic stuff."

"Earthquakes have occurred in the region before, though," Vail observed. "And we've had a tremendous rainfall. There could be an old fault and water could have collected, activating it."

"Well, anything's possible when it comes to earthquakes," Kelly said dubiously. "Moodus isn't so far away, I'll grant that. Seismic activity has been going on there for centuries. You don't feel the occasional Moodus quakes—the tremors are zero magnitude—but you can hear them. The name Moodus itself is an Indian word meaning place of noises. There hadn't been many such noises in a long while, but in the past year they started up again near Mount Tom. We have a team studying the phenomenon."

"How do local people react?"

"They take the sounds for granted. But in the old days the noises turned the Indians into devil worshippers of some sort. The early settlers had some quaint ideas, too. Somewhere around here I've got a paper on them. Want it?"

Vail nodded, and Kelly looked bleakly at the morass on his desk. "I'll dig it up before you leave. Anyway . . ." and he launched into a lecture on the latest in seismology, to which Vail listened with care. "All right," Kelly said finally, "let's go to the lab."

In the hall they passed a large room where banks of seismographs silently recorded action in the Northeast from twenty stations hooked into Lamont-Doherty by telephone line. Kelly said, "Any sizable tremor in your neck of the woods would show up here."

"Where's the nearest station to me?"

Kelly checked a chart on the wall. "New London, Connecticut."

"Too far to pick up tremors as small as the ones I'm getting, I imagine," Vail said.

Kelly's lab was a maze of machinery. He showed Vail around and then pointed to an aluminium box the size of a large suitcase. "There's your seismometer. Don't lose it; it's worth four grand. If you get anything on it—though I doubt you will—call me."

Kay had left for Boston, and Vail returned at dusk to an empty house. The kitchen door stuck and he forced it with his shoulder, carrying the seismometer inside. He looked around. The refrigerator was wide open, as were the drawers Dun had built.

He began to explore the house carefully. Everywhere he found evidence of possible mischief—screens down, angled pictures, books on the floor. But the most spectacular damage was in their bedroom—a crack ran the length of the mirror on the closet door.

He carried the fifty-pound seismometer to the basement and opened the instrument. Battery-run, it consisted of a drum covered by smoked paper on which rested a delicately balanced stylus. Kelly had given him a week's supply of the paper, which had to be changed daily. He attached the cords to the two geophones—microphones for picking up vibrations—and placed one on either side of the room. As he switched on the machine the drum turned slowly. The stylus drew a straight line.

Upstairs again, he went to his study and read the paper Kelly had given him.

The Moodus noises, he learned, had occurred in the town of East Haddam since the beginning of recorded Connecticut history. Superstitions associated with them began with the Wangunk Indians, who claimed that the god of evil, Hobomoko, was angry at the white man and caused the sounds by the light of a carbuncle —a dark red precious stone—under Mount Tom, where the Indians often met to worship and offer sacrifices.

Some of the early settlers also believed that the noises were caused by the red stone and that its removal would stop the sounds. A doctor reportedly found the stone in a cave and removed it, stating that the piece he had left behind would grow and again produce noises—a prediction strikingly fulfilled with noise and vibration about fifteen years later.

Over the years there had been hundreds of earthquakes in the limited area. Most were tiny, but one in 1791 had been assigned, on the basis of a written record of its effects, an intensity of VIII on the Modified Mercalli scale. That would have been a powerful earthquake, capable of knocking down buildings.

Vail went down to check the seismometer, which had recorded nothing. He got into bed and listened in the dark. The old stone house, once so pleasantly grumbling, seemed full of menace.

The first alien noise he heard resembled a low cry, far away, as if from a prisoner in a pit. Vail jerked involuntarily, then sagged back on the mattress. Ground noises, he decided, like the ones at Moodus. How easy it was to slip into unscientific explanations, as the Indians, the early settlers, and Kay had done.

The next noise was like footsteps, like someone scuffling across the stone floor of the cupola . . . scrape, scrape . . . somewhere below, a door slammed. He could see why Kay was scared. The scraping sound must be from the stones moving slightly in a tremor, which would also twist a doorjamb and make a portal close.

He raced downstairs. A jagged line had been traced on the seismograph paper. Vail was excited—he, and he alone, had detected it: "Vail's earthquake," he recalled Lechine saying, and smiled.

Then the smile vanished. The little tremors could be harbingers of a bigger one. Vail had a vision of the crack shooting up the wall, breaking his house in two; of red stones falling down. He left the basement hurriedly, his old fear clutching at him.

By morning several tremors had been recorded. At his desk, Vail studied Johnson's drawing. He felt safe now in drawing a dotted line, representing the fault, from Summerset Villa to the stone house. Next he analyzed the question of why his immediate neighbors had not noticed the tremors. If the shakings at the Demmings' or the Pollidors' had been as hard and sustained as at the stone house, people would have noticed. Since the stone house had taken the brunt of the seismic action, the fault was extremely narrow.

Vail extended the dotted line to the broken pavement on Point Road and beyond to the village, where it arrived at the church. Dun had said something about the church that might have been a clue, but Vail could not remember what. He would have to visit the place, but the church was always locked except during Sunday services.

He decided to arrive late, to minimize his presence. No cars were parked outside. Except for the sound of singing and the pipe organ, he would not have known a service was in progress. As he approached the closed white door, he became aware of his curiosity about the villagers' creed—earthy, Dun had called it.

He entered quietly. Backs toward him, about a hundred people —the entire population of the village, he believed—stood in the nave singing.

> *"O safe to the Rock that is higher than I,*
> *My soul in its conflicts and sorrows would fly;*
> *So sinful, so weary, Thine own would I be;*
> *Thou blest 'Rock of Ages,' I'm hiding in Thee. . . ."*

Vail hung back in the doorway, partially concealed, and examined the interior of the early-eighteenth-century church. Except for the pipe organ, everything about the church was plain, from its stark lines to the straight-backed pine pews, dark and cracked with age. In front of the pews, in the center of the church under the pulpit, was a square pit filled with sand. He recalled that churches like these used to be heated by potbellied stoves that rested in sandpits. Beside the pulpit—an unadorned box—was a raised platform on which stood an altar flanked by two neat pyramids of rocks, the familiar red rock of the stone house.

Dun, the archdeacon, led the singing from the altar. He wore a surplice the color of the rock, and a large necklace of the same red stone. Scrutinizing the parishioners, Vail saw that all clothing was dark red, brown or gray, colors associated with earth.

After the singing Dun climbed the small pulpit and began to speak, his voice clearer and more resonant than Vail had ever heard it. "Friends, we are gathered here to celebrate the good Lord Who dwells among us, Who speaks to us if we will listen.

"For some time the Lord has not chosen to visit us, but has stayed in His hiding place, His dark hole in the earth, listening through the rocks, watching through His eye of the waters. And now He has returned. In recent days the Lord has been raising His voice, as before. He grumbles and He mutters, and in this way tells us of His displeasure at our iniquities. What does He wish? How are we to appease Him and make His angry voice fall silent?

"It is time to ask these questions, for the Lord's lips open and His tongue peals the bell of doom. Catastrophe approaches." Dun's words seemed to echo from every corner of the church. "We are the chosen ones and to us, in Shonkawa Village, does the Lord say, 'Live in peace with your brethren. Cease thy iniquities or ye shall be destroyed! I shall make the sea to heave up its waters, for I *am* the sea! I shall cause the earth to shake and tremble. I will crush ye with the rock for I *am* the rock!' " Suddenly Dun held a large rock high above his head and smashed it into the sandpit. The church seemed to tremble from the blow. "Let us pray. Lord of the Earth, Earth God, Noisemaker, protect us . . ."

"For we have sinned."

"Be our solid rock. Cause the earth to be silent and still."

"For Thou art the Lord, our God. Amen."

The pipe organ played and the parishioners began to jiggle and shake, holding their arms out and jabbing their fingers vigorously toward the ground. In the midst of this ritual, Vail heard the off-key notes and instantly remembered what he had forgotten about pipe organs. At that moment the congregation knelt, leaving him exposed. From the pulpit Dun stared at Vail, eyes alert and frightened.

The organ died and Dun came rapidly down the aisle. "Shouldn't have come here, Mr. Vail," he mumbled.

Vail said, "Dun, I know what's wrong with your pipe organ."

The parishioners turned and muttered. Their faces dark with anger, the Wilbore boys stepped toward him, followed by Bill Pabodie. Dun placed himself in front of Vail and raised his arms. "No, not *here!*" he shouted.

"He has no right . . ."

"Trespassing on the Lord's ground!"

"The stone! The stone!"

"Listen to me!" Vail cried. He seized Dun's arm and propelled him roughly to the organ. "Pipe organs don't have strings; they don't get out of tune. But yours is, and for a reason." He pointed. "Two of the pipes are bent at the top."

Dun squinted and said reluctantly, "It's true. Another sign from the Lord."

"No!" Vail shouted. "Don't you see? You've had an earthquake here! Nothing else could have caused that."

"A sacrilege! A sacrilege!" Mrs. Wilbore shouted.

Dun frowned as the Wilbore boys came closer. "Better go now, son." Through the growling throng he escorted Vail to safety.

Returning home, Vail remembered the hate-filled faces he had seen in church. What iniquities had Dun commanded them to cease? What had led Dun to predict a cataclysm? Was it apocalyptic mumbo jumbo? Or did he know something that Vail did not?

He checked the seismometer. There had been a tremor while he was in the village—one large enough to be apprehended by human senses. Yet in the church he had felt nothing. What was the meaning of that?

At his desk, he stared at Johnson's map. With felt pen he extended the dotted fault line to the church, then beyond to the bay, where the drawing ended. He pictured Sam Wilbore hurling stones across the water toward the column of smoke. Of course, the gas tank farm! An alignment of his map with one from a Rhode Island guidebook proved that the fault line went there unerringly.

It was not difficult to imagine what had happened. A quick jolt at exactly the same moment he had felt the shaking on the ladder. A leak in a pipe. Contact with fire or fumes. A blast.

He decided to appraise the situation from the beach. Crossing Torturous Creek, he put his hand in water, which still seemed abnormally warm. Were there thermal springs beneath the ground, which because of the shaking had begun to feed into the creek? He passed the pond and saw fish jumping straight out, as though they longed to escape the water. The swans, too, were acting strangely, darting this way and that.

Suddenly Vail became conscious of something new: the pond lay in a low hollow that paralleled what he now presumed to be the fault line. This was not a natural position for the water, according to the direction of ground drainage, and it occurred to him that the water could be a sag pond created by the fault itself. In that case, further seismic activity could destroy it. The water would simply disappear into the sea, as a result of a phenomenon known as a seiche. When the ground tilts, a body of water on it naturally tilts, too, running to one bank. Then, when the earth's equilibrium is re-established, the water rushes back in a wave, overflowing the other side.

A seiche wasn't as frightening as a tsunami, of course. Caused by a seaquake and popularly called a tidal wave, a tsunami, or seismic ocean wave, hurtled over the deep-sea surface at nearly 500 mph. A ship at sea would hardly feel the ridge of water racing beneath it. But when the wave reached shore and the water became shallow, the ridge could grow into a monster 50, 60, 70 feet high.

Vail sat down in the rock chair, and began to theorize. Outside of the explosion, nothing unusual had been reported across the bay, so it seemed reasonable to assume that the tank farm lay at the other end of the fault. This made the fault about ten miles long and under water except for the ends and the peninsula's tip.

No shaking, moreover, had been reported at the old people's home, nor did anything untoward appear to have happened at the gas storage facility after the blast. In the church he hadn't felt the tremor recorded at his house by the seismograph. From this evidence it was reasonably certain that the stone house stood precisely over the epicenter of the earthquake swarms, at the breaking point of the seismic storm.

He supposed that the fault woke up at long intervals, shook itself, then went back to sleep again. One factor could be decisive—the prodigious rainfall. Suppose the rains had triggered the tremors in the first place. It hadn't rained for several days, yet the tremors seemed to be increasing in number and intensity. Suppose there was more heavy rain—how large a quake might be set off then?

In the early evening half a dozen tremors were picked up by the machine, one large enough for Vail to feel. Simultaneously the phone rang with no one on the line. He reached Fred Demming after getting two wrong numbers. They commiserated about Pollidor and then Vail said, "Any word about Wende?"

"No," said Demming heavily, "and I'm worried sick. I'm starting to believe she's been kidnapped."

Harry was startled. "But there's absolutely no evidence of that. You'd have heard from the kidnappers."

"Not yet perhaps. I did notify the police finally. There's a four-state alarm out."

"Fred, why don't you go to Boston and wait there?"

"If she's been kidnapped," Demming muttered, "I've got to be here when they call."

Vail next phoned Polly. "Is Bill conscious?"

She said in a voice weary to the breaking point, "No, not quite."

"What does the doctor say?"

"He gives Bill every chance to get well."

"Polly," he told her, "you ought to have somebody with you. When is Jeff coming?"

"Oh. Soon, soon."

It would be next to impossible to jolt his distraught neighbors into believing anything was wrong. Wanting to get his mind off the tremors for a moment, he went down to the exercise room and took a sauna bath. The heavy wood door stuck a little when he opened it, and he made a mental note to sandpaper it. Upstairs again, he telephoned Paul Kelly.

"Paul? Listen, something is happening. I've recorded about a dozen tremors in the last twenty-four hours."

Kelly whistled. "How big?"

"Zero magnitude, mostly. But will they stay small? Suppose the swarm turns into a convulsion?"

Kelly scoffed, "Not a chance. The fault must be short—a couple of hundred yards, probably." The length of the fault, both men knew, can be a determining factor in the size of a quake.

"Well, I wonder about that. There was an unexplained explosion at a gas storage facility five miles away from here two weeks ago. Suppose a tremor caused the blast? The fault could extend to there. If so, I'm sitting right on top of a potentially large earthquake. Vail's earthquake," he said with a bitter laugh.

"Vail's earthquake. That's a hot one. Don't spook out on me, Harry. It's a tiny fault—the seismometer tells you that."

Vail said, "The earthquake's been around a long time, Paul. Ground noises exist here, too. I imagine there's a cave below the village through which the earthsounds reverberate. Over the years the villagers built a religion around the noises, just as the Moodus Indians did. The locals think that a fearsome God lives under the ground and periodically speaks to them. They invented a scary religion to fit their fear of ground noises."

"That sounds right." Kelly hesitated. "Harry, I'm sorry I misjudged you—I thought your earthquake was imaginary. I lent you the seismometer to prove it. Now that you're back at seismology, why don't you make it permanent? There's always an office for you here."

Vail grinned despite himself. "We'll see. Can you come up? I need some help here."

"I'll put a team together next week."

"Can't make it sooner?"

"Doubt it. Stop worrying, will you, Harry?" Kelly said.

"I just hope it doesn't rain."

He called Kay, then went to bed. About four, he was awakened by a loud noise which his sleepy mind finally identified as thunder. Outside the bedroom window, water was pouring down.

THE gray sky on Monday looked like a layer of shale. The seismometer informed Vail of a dozen mild tremors during the night. He was about to extinguish the basement light when he saw a shadow on the wall. Close up it became a thin line which darted two feet up from the metal strip. The crack had broken out.

Easy, now, he told himself.

Upstairs, he tried to feed the cat, but Judy wouldn't eat. He didn't feel like eating either. The horse! He had forgotten Brioche. With oats and a bucket of water he entered the stall. Instead of nuzzling him as usual, the mare shied and launched a hoof at him. He backed off, leaving the door open, and Brioche followed. Outdoors she seemed herself once more, rubbing her head against him. The tremors had frightened the mare.

He went to the kitchen where the clock said just past 9:00. He phoned the office. "I'm not coming in today, Mrs. Conner, and maybe not for several days. I have something to finish here."

He went to the studio. The easel was toppled and pictures and paint jars were strewn on the floor. He returned to the living room with Kay's charcoals. He made a drawing of the wall which showed a brace fastened to it, like a Roman numeral X, with the crosspieces avoiding the windows and front door.

Wood, he said to himself. Where? He visualized the pile of two-by-fours in the town square, and taking a tarp and rope from the barn, drove off. He found the creosote-soaked pieces, about eight feet long, which had been stacked in the square for years. He looked about—no one was in sight.

486

Filthy though it was, the wood was perfect for his purpose. He carried it to the car on his shoulders, two boards at a time, until he judged he had enough. After spreading the tarp on the roof of the Rolls, he tied the wood in bundles and secured them there.

As Vail backed up and turned he saw a blue car sidle around the square. It halted before him, and three youths got out.

"There's Mr. Vail," Sam Wilbore said in a loud voice.

"Sure it's Mr. Vail?"

"Sure I'm sure. Who else has a shiny old Rolls-Royce?"

"Howdy," Cy Wilbore said. His red-rimmed eyes flickered. "Notice your load of wood. Anyone give you permission to take it?"

"Come on! That wood's been there for years. Nobody wants it."

"We want it," Bill Pabodie shouted, "for a bonfire on the Fourth of July."

Cy Wilbore reached for the door handle of the Rolls. No, no, Vail cautioned himself. Don't fight with three adolescents, probably armed with knives. He shoved the Rolls in gear, maneuvered it around the blue car, and shot off down Point Road.

That had been an error, he realized, as he glanced in the rearview mirror. Cy Wilbore driving, the blue car caught up quickly and began to graze the Roll's bumper dexterously. The car, already hard to steer because of the load, shuddered and began to veer.

Mastering the timing of Wilbore's repeated bumps, he touched his brakes lightly in unison, hoping the sturdy old car would withstand the impacts. He heard a twang as Wilbore's bumper broke, a snap as the Rolls's bumper crushed the blue car's grille. Wilbore swung sharply, in time to avoid the wood that fell from the Rolls.

The blue car again took up pursuit but halted at the edge of Vail's driveway. It came no farther.

The Rolls looked undamaged, and though Vail had lost some lumber, enough remained for the job. The breeze shifted and the backyard foully breathed at him. The tremors must be agitating the contents of the cesspool.

He dropped the load of wood. The mole holes had become cone-shaped boils like the earthspouts at Summerset Villa. He remembered the earth's insidious embrace of his arm, Punch's flattened head. His spirits sagged. It was as though the quake were following him. Against a trio of punk kids he could fight. But what was his strength against the earth's?

He returned to his labor, bringing in the wood, gathering tools, sawhorse, nails. Kay, he thought, would be furious if she saw the living room, with the furniture pushed back, the rug rolled up, and lumber piled on the floor. He drilled, sawed and hammered until the living-room wall above the crack in the basement was girdled with boards. "That's that," he said aloud. Jerry-built as it was, perhaps it would support the wall.

He swept the sawdust and shavings from the floor, replaced the rug and the furniture. Then he decided to visit Demming. Brioche needed exercise and he bridled her in the stall. As he passed the playhouse he saw that a tree had gone down just off the trail—that must have been the sound he heard when talking with Dun in the backyard a few days before.

At the Demmings', the lawn needed to be cut. Leaves littered the swimming pool. A telephone on a long cord beside him, Fred sat in a wicker chair, pale, unshaved, surrounded by newspapers and plates of half-eaten food. "Have you moved out here?" Vail asked.

Demming shifted. "Inside, I'm reminded of Wende."

"Pool's leaking," Vail said, trying to avoid the main issue. Studying the bottom, he saw small cracks.

"They've been here twice to fix it," Demming said.

They were silent until Vail finally asked about Wende.

"Police found her car at the gas station," Demming said. "She was supposed to pick it up. That proves she's been kidnapped."

"But Fred . . ."

"I've got the kidnappers figured," Demming said in a monotone. "They've spent time in prison. Time means nothing to them; they've learned how to wait. One of these days the phone will ring and a voice will tell me they've got Wende." He began to cry.

Shocked, Vail said softly, "But you don't know for certain she's been kidnapped, Fred."

"What else could it be?"

"I don't know. Accident, maybe."

Vail went home more depressed than ever. He was eating dinner when he heard the crack of a stone against the house. He closed the front shutters. With the brace on the living-room wall the stone house was like a beleaguered citadel.

In the basement the seismometer needle had recorded a dozen tremors, small but steadily increasing in magnitude. His eyes stole to the crack. Sprouting like bamboo, it reached almost to the ceiling. He quailed. Would the scaffolding above suffice?

He went to the exercise room and worked out, trying to divert the rush of his mind. Crack, slide, shift, thrust, rift, slip, slump, fissure, spout, slipstick fault . . . Stop! He turned the sauna on high and stepped inside, still trying not to think of quakes.

Then he was too hot and decided to leave the sauna. As he touched the handleless door he felt a quick, deceptively delicate motion—a tremor! He pushed against the door. It stuck. He pushed harder, but the door refused to budge.

He retreated to the opposite wall and charged, using his whole strength, but the chamber wasn't big enough to permit momentum. He struck the door futilely and fell to his knees.

The control was outside. Heat poured in. A puddle formed on the floor as sweat flowed from his body. *Your heart will stop.*

He rose and pressed his face against the glass diamond on the door, peering into the room where the cool air was, disarmingly close. The tremor had altered the hang of the door, enough to keep him inside to die by degrees. Suppose he came at it from a different direction? He charged low, without result. Panicking, he flung himself against the unyielding cedar door again and again.

He lay on the wood slats gasping, blinded by sweat. He imagined his body melting like a piece of lard in a frying pan.

The solution came to him almost like a reflex. Lying down, he placed his feet against the opposite wall, and straightening his knees, gave a powerful shove with his shoulders, his whole arched body behind the effort. The door snapped open.

He lay on the floor outside for a few minutes, breathing in cool air. He got on his knees, then his feet, and turned off the sauna. The mirror showed his face bright red up to the hairline. He put on a robe. It might be irrational, but he was angry.

The tremor had registered on the seismometer and had sent the crack like an arrow from a bow, up the wall beyond the ceiling. He found the tip upstairs on the living-room wall, just above the baseboard. Mouth grim, face set, he went up to his room.

HE WOKE on Tuesday with an answer to the problem, not much of an answer perhaps, but the only possible one.

In Kelly's theory, he remembered, earthquakes were explained in terms of pressure too great for dry rock pores to contain as they absorb water. The increased pore pressure further weakens the rock and triggers the earthquake. If that was correct, then the heavy rains around Old Brompton, funneling into an old fault, had increased pore pressure to the point of inducing earthquakes more powerful with each passing day. It might be possible, therefore, to pacify the ground by lowering the pore pressure in the fault zone.

At 7:30 a.m. Vail picked up the phone. "Charley? Vail."

"You're up early, Doctor. What can I do for you?"

Vail glanced outside. It was drizzling and the cloud ceiling looked low enough to touch. "Bring your rig to my place this morning and dig me a hole, a deep hole."

The rig man sounded bewildered. "I don't get it. Why? Besides, Lechine's got me on a road job."

"That can wait. Remember those cones we saw on the hillside near the old people's home? They're here, too, now. Water pressure's building up and I'm worried about my house."

"You're the boss."

About 9:00 a.m. Charley arrived in his truck with a helper. "There's a blue car parked by your drive," he reported. "As soon as we showed, it took off."

Vail nodded. He showed Charley a spot near the giant boulder where he wanted the hole.

"How far down?" Charley asked.

"Drill until you hit water. It's trapped between layers of rocks. Hopefully, it'll spew out like an artesian well."

Charley sniffed the unpleasant air. "What's that stink?"

"Cesspool's backing up. I can't get anybody to drain it. Everything around here is falling apart."

Vail went inside. What he had told Charley about the house was true; one by one, the dwelling's systems were showing signs of strain. The phone was erratic, and so was the electricity. The tap water had become sulfurous. He drank bottled water now.

After several tries Vail reached Summerset Villa by telephone and persuaded the receptionist to ring Robinson's room.

"What do you want this time?" the manager said irritably.

"Robinson, remember I talked of scaffolding for the back of the building? You should put it up without delay. And you ought to have a plan for evacuating the home."

"You're crazy, Vail," Robinson said, and hung up.

"You're crazy, Vail," Lechine said angrily into the phone later. "What are you doing with Charley? Send him back at once. I need him."

"I do, too. He's got his rig operating in the backyard, trying to rid the ground of excess pressure."

"Why?"

"Because there are tremors, that's why," Vail answered. "I've got a seismometer going. It's been recording them for days."

"I bet. The tremors must be caused by Charley's rig."

"Just because there hasn't been an earthquake in this area doesn't mean there can't be a first time," Vail said, angry, too, now. "How can I convince you, you stubborn bastard?"

"You can't. You've turned into a kook right under my nose, Vail, and you know how I feel about kooks."

"You can't talk to me that way, Lechine. Get yourself a new partner," Vail said, slamming down the receiver.

He got himself under control and went outside. "How's it going?" he called to Charley above the beat of the drill.

"Pretty slow. We're hitting rock." Charley sniffed. "If we have to come back tomorrow, I'll bring a gas mask."

As Harry neared the house Dun stepped from behind the barn. "Mr. Vail?" he called.

Vail stopped. "Well, Dun?"

The old man said nervously, "Mr. Vail, beg you to stop what you're doing in the backyard. You've got no right."

"Why? It's my land," Vail snapped.

"Only the top of it."

Vail guffawed. "Who owns the rest?"

"God," Dun said stiffly.

"Everywhere under the ground, or just here?" Vail cried.

"Here," Dun admitted. "Where the Indians were. They believed God lived right under that big rock."

"You believe that, too?"

The smile Dun attempted failed. "Not under the rock, no. But we accept the principle. This is sacred ground."

Vail sighed. "It's because of those noises, isn't it? Your religious views, I mean. Listen to me. The ground noises have nothing to do with a holy spirit. They can be explained. They originate because

491

of small tremors—tiny earthquakes. Come down to the basement and I'll show you."

"Don't know what you're talking about. All I know is you're not supposed to offend this ground by digging deep holes." The old man's voice sounded stronger. "Folks in the village are upset. Want you to stop. Mean it. God don't like holes dug in Him." Dun kicked the ground angrily and walked off.

THAT afternoon the machine in the basement reported a sharp increase in seismic activity. Vail finally decided to alert the public to the imminence of a major earthquake—or try to. He determined to drive to WROK, a few miles away.

There was no receptionist. He opened a door and found himself staring at the bearded face of Kip Smith, the disc-jockey entrepreneur, who was talking into a microphone behind a glass plate. Smith looked up and waved Vail in. "If it isn't the geologist! Have a seat, Harry. Is it business or social?"

"Business, if you can call it that." Vail fidgeted. He wanted to be as convincing as possible and for this reason his explanation of the recent seismic activity was belabored.

"You mean a big earthquake, man?" Smith asked finally, smiling. "Like in San Francisco?"

"Well, no, not that powerful. Still, buildings could collapse, people could be hurt or killed. They ought to be warned to go outdoors if the earthquake happens. You could do it over the radio."

"Hey, a freaky quake like that around *here* would be a real trip," Smith chanted. "Great! The kids'll eat it up. I'll put it out right now, if you want to stick around."

"No, thanks," Vail said despairingly. He left.

That evening he closed the shutters and locked the front door. The little tremors arrived continually now. He felt them in the balls of his feet, heard them in the clanging of pots in the kitchen, the brief bursts from the telephone, the erratic booming of Big Ben. Occasionally, too, he heard earthsounds, deep belching noises like the one he heard when he fell from the ladder and lay with his ear to the ground.

In the basement, Vail found an old tape recorder which he took upstairs to record the earthsounds. He had started the machine when he heard a persistent knocking at the front door.

492

"Open up. Hurry." He unlocked the door and Kay entered carrying the sleeping boy, whom she passed to him. "I tried calling you, but no answer. I decided to come tonight and here I am." Her startled eyes saw the scaffolding. "What in the world . . ."

He pointed to the crack halfway up the wall. "I'm bracing the building." He carried Mark upstairs and put him to bed.

"Poor darling," Kay said in a controlled voice when he returned. "Dun could have plastered that silly crack in minutes. Tomorrow you'll remove the nasty wood. Oh, Harry, those boys are in a blue car down at the end of the driveway, drinking and yelling. I'm calling the police." She went resolutely to the phone and picked it up. "Harry, the phone's dead."

"Most of the time it doesn't work now."

"We're practically marooned." Her confidence seemed to falter as her eyes darted this way and that. "Harry, what's *that?*"

It was a sound like a hollow gong. "That's the ground—earth noises. It's because of the earthquake. Listen."

He reversed the tape on the recorder and played back their conversation. Then he switched it off. "The machine didn't pick up the noise."

"Of course it didn't. They don't let themselves be recorded. What do you think you're dealing with?"

"Natural phenomena." He tried vainly to reason with her.

She went upstairs, and he heard her shrill cry. He ran to the bedroom to see her face stare from the full-length mirror on the closet door. Their reflections were separated by the break that cut the mirror in two.

IN THE morning Kay dropped a milk bottle on the kitchen floor. "I'm so nervous. That's the last bottle."

"We'll have to make do," he said, mopping up. "Sit down, darling. I'll fix breakfast."

Through the window Mark saw the drilling rig at which Charley and his man had just begun to work. "What's *that?*" he cried excitedly.

"That's for making a hole in the ground."

"Now what?" Kay said drearily.

"A lot of water is trapped there. That's what causes the tremors."

"Tremors," she said impatiently.

"Come look." He almost had to force her to the basement. The

493

seismometer had recorded some thirty tremors during the night. "You can't argue with a seismometer," he said trimphantly.

"*They* could do that!" she screamed. "All they'd have to do is jiggle the needle."

Upstairs again, Kay sat over coffee. "Please eat something," Vail urged. Kay hadn't touched her cereal.

She stood up. "I'm going to the village and call the phone company. Also, I'll talk to Mrs. Wilbore about her sons."

"Don't," he begged. "Those people are trouble."

"The villagers?" she said scornfully.

He decided not to argue. Kay got along with Mrs. Wilbore—the clan's grudge was against him.

As soon as she left he went to the crack. His mouth contracted. The thin line had disappeared above the scaffolding. He climbed the stairs to Mark's room and lifted the circus poster: the crack had slithered into the room like a snake.

He stood at the window studying the blue car at the end of the drive. It was positioned on the Fall River side of the road, which suggested that the boys might oppose an attempt to leave the peninsula. Mentally, Vail ransacked the house for materials which would serve as a brace for the wall in Mark's room. If only he hadn't lost part of his wood. A piece of plaster fell from the ceiling. The house seemed to be disintegrating around him.

He waited downstairs for Kay, whose station wagon finally bounced down the drive. "It's the craziest thing," she muttered. "Remember when you said somebody wanted to buy our house? Well, it's Mrs. Wilbore. She was as sympathetic as she could be. She has always known there are evil things here. They all do. That's why the boys are there—to protect us. They won't come on the property because they don't want to be rude. It isn't they who've thrown the stones—it's the evil spirits, just like I told you. They're Indians—this used to be their burial ground—and *very* resentful against whites. Mrs. Wilbore didn't want you to buy the house in the first place, and she was angry with her sister for selling it because she knew we'd have trouble. She'll pay a fair price."

"Why does she want to buy it?"

"She believes the spirits bring bad luck to the whole community. She says she'll turn the house into a shrine to the Indians and placate the spirits. It makes perfect sense."

"Well, it accounts for what Dun said, but the rest is nonsense. They want to get me out of here before I report the earthquake and ruin their property values. That's the whole idea, I bet."

"Harry, I want to sell the house to her. Now, today!"

His mouth turned stubborn. "We're not selling, and that's that."

IT WAS possible that the boys wanted to frighten, not hurt him, that he could slip in and out of the square without injury. He gathered rope and tarp and placed them in the Rolls. He turned toward the village with no more than a glance at the waiting blue car. It started to follow him at a discreet distance.

Firecrackers popped somewhere as Vail left the car and entered the square. Tomorrow, he remembered, was the Fourth of July. There was no sign of the blue car. He carried a load of lumber and dumped it by the road. Then the first stone hit the lumber, just missing his head. He ducked behind the woodpile. The popping of firecrackers had ceased; the village was silent.

Another stone landed some distance away, but the next pinged viciously into the wood close to him. Vail scuttled on his hands and knees to a scrapped car. He glanced up in time to see Sam Wilbore bend and heave from beside the old cannon.

This was no game—they wanted to kill him. He spotted the other two boys at different points in the square, arms back, ready to throw. He was pinned.

He ran to a pile of drums, but a stone caught him painfully in the calf. He looked toward the end of the square; a knot of villagers watched, like spectators at an execution. Dun was not among them. Vail moved behind some fish netting, but a stone struck him in the stomach. He ran to the carcass of a boat. Stones flew, splintering the old wood. Vail was afraid to make a run for it—if he was struck on the head he would fall, and that would be fatal—yet he could not remain where he was.

His eyes, scouring the square, saw the battered lid of a garbage can. He ran for it in a hail of stones, scooping it off the ground, raising it as a shield into which a missile aimed for his head clanked harmlessly. He clung to the lid, which wrenched at his wrist as stones landed, and began to back from the square. Then he was in the Rolls as a stone smashed the rear window.

Vail drove off hurriedly, leaving the wood behind, the blue car in pursuit. He had just reached Point Road when the steering wheel became stiff in his hands. He hung on as the Rolls veered. Then it was over and the car steered normally. In the rearview mirror he saw the blue car twist sharply and overturn.

He stopped and sat breathing deeply, trying to grasp what had just happened. Wilbore's car had gone out of control at the same moment his own had refused to respond. Whatever gripped one car had also gripped the other—a tremor! Saved by the quake, he thought grimly, and turned the Rolls around.

He approached cautiously, torn between compassion and anger. Sam Wilbore and Bill Pabodie stood dumbly staring. Cy Wilbore's head was crushed against the bloody windshield.

Vail heard running, Mrs. Wilbore's scream, saw the menace in the faces of the arriving villagers, felt the hand grasp his arm. "Go, son," Dun said. "Quick."

"LOOK WHAT they've done!" Kay screamed. A crack ran down the picture window of her studio.

He inspected the damage solemnly. "We've had an earthquake. Didn't you feel it?"

"No," Kay shouted.

He turned to Mark. "Mark, did the ground shake?" The boy's lips moved but nothing came out. "Scared, huh?" He picked him up and squeezed him. "Kay, take him away from the house for a while. Walk over and see how Polly is. Okay, honey?"

"Yes," she said. "Come, Mark."

Vail walked to the rig standing near the giant boulder. Charley had stopped drilling. "Ground shook a little while back—we're checking the equipment. Wonder what caused it?"

"It was an earthquake—a little one," Vail answered.

"Golly. Could the drilling have caused it?"

"No, but if you hit water in time it might stop a bigger one."

"Well, we're getting there. Look!" *Pum-pum-pum* went the drill. From the drill hole water flowed slowly.

In the barn Vail found a few wood slats that he hammered to the wall in Mark's room without hope—even the heavy bracing below had failed, and it seemed inevitable that the new crack would unite with the old one on the outer wall.

Back in the studio, Vail morosely studied the broken picture window, wondering if he should remove the glass before the earthquake did it for him. Staring out the window, he noticed that the hillside below the giant boulder appeared to have changed.

Reaching the hill, Vail saw that a small landslide had occurred at the base of the rock, revealing an outcropping of freshly exposed rock—not the gray of granite, but the red stone of his own house.

With utter astonishment he saw the graveyard that lay in the depression. Five gravestones had been revealed. Four were covered with strange, grotesque whorls, but the fifth was plain and seemed new. Under the gravestones were bits of bone, but before the new one a skull grinned brightly.

Vail clambered into the pit and emerged with the skull. It had belonged, he surmised, to a small adult, probably a woman. The top of the skull looked crushed, as though by a heavy blow. Vail turned to find Dun standing beside him.

The gray eyes looked sorrowful. "Told them Wilbores trouble would come."

"You understand I had nothing to do with Wilbore's death? He is dead, isn't he?"

The old man nodded. "Instant. It was God who made the land to shake and kill young Wilbore because he was trying to kill you. God's punishment."

"Why did they want to kill me?"

Dun blurted out, "Afraid that you, messing around with the rig, would find that." He pointed to the graveyard.

"The tremor was responsible for the slippage. Why were they so frightened?"

Dun paused. "Guess you've got some answers coming. Told you there was an Indian graveyard here?" Vail nodded. "God lived under the ground and the Indians worshipped Him, and then some of the settlers did. About a hundred years ago God got mad. Used to be another stone house here, but when God made the ground shake it fell into smithereens. A Wilbore farmer built a new one and used up all the red stones left in the quarry . . . there"—Dun pointed to the outcropping of red stone.

"Folks here didn't want anybody to know about the shaking. Figured people would blame an earthquake, just like you do. It was a limited step God took—a warning. Ground shook here, and only here. So they decided to keep it a secret because He was

498

their God, and they—we—His chosen people. Nobody was supposed to sell their property to newcomers who'd find out, and especially not to sell this house where God lives underneath. People were told if they sold they'd be killed. But a few houses were sold. Result's what you see in the graveyard." Dun took a deep breath.

Vail held up the skull. "This isn't all that old."

Dun's silence seemed interminable. Finally he said, "That was Miss Wilbore, who sold you this house. She was lonely and wanted to clear out."

"What happened to her?"

Something in the old man's face told Vail that Dun had wanted to unburden himself. He said rapidly, "Wilbores dropped a stone on her. And today Cy got his punishment for trying to kill you. God forgave the Wilbores once, but not twice."

"So they put the bodies of those they executed here and covered them over?"

"That's right," Dun said. "Oldest one's been here about a century. Hadn't been a killing for years before Miss Wilbore."

"How could they be sure nobody would find the graveyard?"

"Couldn't. Kept watch on it. Came through the woods. But never actually set foot on the sacred ground. Only the archdeacon, me now, can do that."

So Pollidor had been right—the villagers had been prowling the woods. "They didn't fully trust you," Vail suggested.

"Maybe not. Especially after Mrs. Wilbore killed her sister-in-law, or her sons did. Knew I didn't like that."

"What did they do with Miss Wilbore's money after they killed her? I assume they got it."

"Yes. Hope was to buy the house back from you. From the common fund. We pool our money. Keeps me poor, the rest are so lazy."

Vail's head was ablaze with questions. "Dun, why didn't you just clear out of here?"

Dun lowered his eyes. "We're waiting a sign from the Lord that we can sell our property and go. Besides, they would have killed me, too. They'd kill me now if they knew what I'd told you, Mr. Vail. But, see, kind of look at you as a son. Don't want anything to happen to you."

"But Dun, why don't you believe that earthquakes, not God, are responsible for the action under the ground?"

Dun said quietly, "It's my faith."

In the house, analyzing Dun's revelation, he heard the scream. Fool . . . he should never have let Kay see the graveyard.

Crying, she permitted herself to be led inside, Mark whimpering behind her. "It's all right, Mark," he told the boy, embracing him. "Go watch TV."

He tried to hold Kay, but she shook free, saying, "Jeff's at Polly's."

"Could he give any information on Wende?"

"He insists she's gone off somewhere and forgot to leave a note."

Every so often a tremor shook the house. In the kitchen the dishes and pots rattled as he tried to coax a light supper down his family, without success. Judy sat in the corner and howled.

"Get that cat out of here," Kay begged. The cat clawed him painfully when he reached for it, then fled from the room, tail up.

The lights flickered. "The power might go out. We'd better let Mark sleep with us," Harry said, wiping his bleeding hand with a paper napkin. He heard a gust of wind and added, "Maybe it would be better if we all sleep in the living room."

"You won't agree to leave?" Kay asked. She looked at his face and said, "All right, the living room."

As Vail came downstairs with pajamas and blankets the lights flickered and went out with a certain finality. Kay moaned.

He moved to the dining room, took candles from the chest, and returned, placing them on the coffee table. The candlelight flickered on the scaffolding, which looked ominous. "Who'd have thought we'd end like this—refugees in our own living room," Kay said.

Locating his flashlight, he answered, "We ought to go to sleep early tonight. God knows what will happen tomorrow."

She lay on her back on a couch, staring up. "Sleep! *Look*."

The shadow of the birdcage began to sway. At the same time he felt the vibration through his legs. "Another tremor," he said.

"And what's that?"

He heard a metallic scratching and a faint cry. "An owl," he said tentatively.

The tremor was the largest yet. The house groaned and Big Ben chimed once and stopped. A hollow noise sounded. Kay sprang into his arms like a frightened child, her damp cheek pressed against his. Gradually her body relaxed and her breathing slowed. "Harry," she muttered, "it's over. They've gone. At least for tonight."

500

It was true that the tremors seemed to have ceased, and so had the mysterious noise. "Poor Kay," he murmured, stroking her hair.

He put a blanket over her and, flashlight in hand, explored the house. In his study the beam of light passed an open place over the bookcase. The grate of the heating duct had fallen. He climbed up the bookcase and called into the duct, "Judy, come here."

He listened to claws scraping metal. Terrified, Judy had sought refuge in the hole, then lost her way in the ducts. "Ghosts!" he said contemptuously as the cat's head appeared in the aperture.

Vail descended to the basement and shone the light on the slowly turning drum. The paper showed that there had been dozens of tiny earthquakes that evening, but now the needle ran straight.

At last the earthquake swarm had stopped; a stillness lay on the earth. Perhaps the tension in the fault had been eliminated by the movement of the rock; perhaps the earth was exhausted. Vail switched off the machine, placed the geophones inside the aluminium case, and closed it. He was not sure why, but the precaution seemed sensible.

QUAKE

THURSDAY, the Fourth of July. A loud noise awakened Vail. Kay stirred on the couch, and Mark breathed lightly from a mattress on the floor. Vail had slept in his clothes and, rising, went to the kitchen. The power was still off. Daylight glowed, but if the sun was up, a heavy mist obscured it. He did not know the time.

The noise seemed to have come from the sea's direction and resembled a load of gravel being dumped from a truck. He started down the mist-arched path. Crossing Torturous Creek he lost his footing and stepped into water that was almost hot.

Long before he reached the rock chair he heard the ocean, and looked out at surf higher than he remembered having seen on his shore. Dead fish littered the beach. Through the fog came the squawk of gulls headed inland.

Vail walked back to the house, still unable to account for the noise. Misty shapes were emerging from the wood—deer, pheasants, skunks, badgers—moving rapidly away from the sea. From the pond fish leaped again and again, as swans' clamorous wings announced their departure. *They* know, he thought.

When he passed the creek Vail understood that he had not missed his footing earlier, as he had supposed. Where land should have been there was water. The sound he had heard in his sleep was the clatter of pebbles as the creek abruptly shifted course. Suddenly he feared for the elderly residents in the cheaply constructed building on the unstable hillside. He ran.

He shook her awake. "Kay! Take Mark and go outside. Understand? An earthquake's starting—a big one."

"Go away, Harry." She pulled the blanket over her head.

He ripped it off. "I mean it. Go outside."

"All right, all right."

He should have stayed until he was certain that she got up, he thought, as the Rolls pounded down the driveway. The clock on the dashboard said 6:45. He hit the brakes where an ugly gash stretched across the road. The simple break in the pavement was now a fissure about six inches wide. The car bounced over it.

The fog vanished as he moved away from the sea. There was no traffic this early, and he drove rapidly under cloudy skies.

The crack in the road before Summerset Villa was fissurous, too. He had been right, then, about the line of fault. Climbing the hill, he saw that the cones running down the slope had grown, and each spouted a mighty gush of water, perhaps twenty feet high.

In the lobby he found a throng of anxious old people in bathrobes, pajamas and slippers. Alma Benjamin rushed up to him. "Dr. Vail! Something's terribly wrong. There are cracks all over the building and we feel vibrations. Look!" Over the reception desk a crack appeared in the ceiling and a piece of plaster fell, sending up a white puff as it hit the floor. A frightened murmur rose in the room. "What'll we do?"

"Get everybody outside. Stay well clear of the building, to the side of it, in case the structure slides. You'll be all right. Hurry."

He raced back to the peninsula. As he neared his house he encountered fog again. The fissure had widened, and the Rolls navigated it at the cost of what sounded like a broken spring and shock absorber. The car limped down the potholed drive. He found Kay in the kitchen trying to make Mark eat. Cracks ran over the ceiling, and a seam had opened in the terra-cotta floor.

502

"Kay!" He felt a small tremor, quick and determined. "Go outside!"

"There's no reason," she said, sounding dazed. "They don't come out this early."

Mark cried, "Daddy's right! Let's go, Mommy. Come!" The boy seized her hand.

"Where's Judy?" Harry shouted.

"Here, Daddy, under the table." The animal stood stiff-legged. He grabbed it and they went outside.

On the lawn, squat cones ejected plumes of water. Then, with a rumble, the ground above the cesspool burst open, spewing a brownish geyser that smelled sulfurous and fecal.

"It's hell. We're in hell," Kay cried. The studio's picture window suddenly shattered and fell.

"Get up on the boulder," he yelled at her.

"Wait. Brioche is trying to get out." She raced to the barn and returned with the terrified mare, which trembled and foamed at the mouth. "There, there," Kay said, trying to soothe her.

"I'm going to the Demmings'," he said. "I'll be right back. Get on the rock." He set off at a run, passing between the boulder and the black elm, whose list was obvious now. He took the creek in a leap and stumbled down the path, thrashing through thick bushes until he came upon the fallen tree he had seen a few days before. The fog opened momentarily; he looked down and gasped.

He saw the face of Wende Demming shrouded in the haze, her body pinioned by the fallen tree. She had been there a week, he knew with dreadful certainty. He went to the playhouse and leaned against it, unable to continue. On the night that Jeff left she must have wandered out to the playhouse, the scene of her tryst, and the tree, weakened by the windstorm, had crushed her. In death she reminded him once again of the pale face lying beneath another tree, long ago. Harry, he pleaded with himself, hang on.

Knees shaking, he proceeded down the path to Demming's lawn. "Fred! Fred!" he shouted. Then he saw the thick eyeglasses that lay shattered on the cement deck by the wicker chair. Through a foot-wide crack the water had emptied from the pool as though a bathtub drain had opened. On the hard bottom lay the crumpled body of Fred Demming. In the tremor Fred must have dropped his glasses, groped for them in the fog, come too close to the empty pool. Nothing could be done for him now.

Vail found himself on the path again, brain reeling. Long before he reached the Pollidors' he heard the mocking shriek of the burglar alarm and, seeing the house, felt certain that Polly was dead, too. The chimney had collapsed, taking with it the roof and the large glass window. He stepped into the debris. Polly sat on the floor, speechless, clasping her knees.

"Polly," Vail commanded, "come." She followed dumbly. Outside, he asked, "Where's Jeff?"

"On the beach with a movie camera," she was able to report.

Seeing them from the top of the boulder, Kay ran down to help. Together they pulled Polly to the flat top of the rock.

"Look!" Kay cried as the boulder shuddered. Chimney stones were falling and the TV antenna went. A sharp metallic snap rang from the Rolls-Royce, whose front end sagged. The elm tree groaned.

"I'm going to the village. Keep everybody on the rock—don't go back in the house," Harry yelled at Kay as he ran toward Brioche, tied to a pole of the clothesline. The mare shied and reared, flailing out with her front hoofs. Harry seized the reins and mounted, hoping he was too big to throw.

Horse and rider moved across open fields to the village. Vail was about to dismount by the church when he saw that the beach seemed abnormally large. A man stood on the pier with a movie camera. He rode over and shouted, "Jeff! Get away!"

Carmichael lowered the camera. "What's up, Harry?" He smiled.

The water had drawn back. "Leave the pier or you'll drown."

"Expecting a tidal wave?" Jeff asked. "That's low tide."

"It isn't low tide. It's because of a seaquake. The water will rush back, I tell you."

Jeff grinned. "Oh, come on. Say, this is my first earthquake. Think a building might fall down?"

"Listen to me, Jeff," Vail pleaded as he turned the horse.

INSIDE the church Cy Wilbore's body lay in an open coffin before the altar. Dun, in his russet surplice, chanted from the pulpit: "*God is our refuge . . . Therefore will not we fear . . . though the waters thereof roar . . . though the mountains shake with the swelling thereof. . . .*" The villagers were trying to propitiate the Earth God just as they must have been in the Saturday memorial service —was that only a few weeks ago?

504

"Dun!" he cried. "Take your people and go to the cliffs. A big wave is coming and the village may be washed away." The church trembled, as though underscoring Vail's words.

Mrs. Wilbore screamed, "The Earth God will save us!" She pointed at Vail. "Kill him. The stone! The stone!"

"This is an earthquake," Vail shouted. "Go to the cliffs!"

The congregation parted, and Sam Wilbore came toward him carrying a heavy stone from the altar, other parishioners behind him. He raised the stone over his head, glaring at Vail.

"Wait!" Vail said in a loud voice. "If your Earth God is angry with you and shakes the ground, shouldn't Cy Wilbore's death be enough of a sacrifice? If he isn't propitiated, wouldn't he be an evil God, who wants to hurt you? Either your God deserves hating, for he is the devil, or this is an earthquake and your God has nothing to do with it. Flee!"

"Mr. Vail is right!" Dun roared. "His words are sound. I sense the truth through the very wood of the pulpit. There is danger in Shonkawa Village. Brethren, let us take refuge on the cliffs." He removed his surplice and started out.

"Never!" cried Mrs. Wilbore. "We stay in church with our God."

Looking back, Vail saw Mrs. Wilbore, Sam, Bill Pabodie, and a few others by the open coffin.

He returned past the pond, whose water had left its banks on the side of the ocean. A seiche was starting. When the water came back it would overflow toward the house, and if that were accompanied by a seismic ocean wave . . . He refused to think further.

Reaching the backyard, he saw that Kay and Mark had left the rock. At the same moment the ground gave a violent lurch and Charley's rig toppled over. A jet of boiling water rose thirty feet.

"Where are they?" Vail yelled as he slid from the horse.

Polly pointed mutely to the house.

Hurriedly he entered. The crack in the terra-cotta floor cut the kitchen in two. As he ran into the dining room the chandelier tinkled in the quick, hard tremors and smashed on the table, showering glass. All over the house objects fell, windows broke, doors slammed. In the living room the noise was intense; fireplace tools jiggled, piano rumbled, Big Ben boomed incessantly. From the birdcage the finch emitted a penetrating screech.

Kay cowered behind a couch, clutching the boy. The floor rippled as he tried to cross it and he almost fell. "Look out!" Kay called. He whirled in time to see the heavy bar cart bearing down on him. It rolled across the room, then, as the floor canted again, lumbered toward him once more. He seized the cart and hurled it at the wall, where it collapsed into a pile of twisted metal.

He recrossed the room. A large piece of plaster struck him on the back, and he staggered and fell. Part of the scaffolding dropped from the wall and rapped him behind the ear. Dazed, he knelt on the floor in terrified paralysis, unable to move, he on his island of floor, they on theirs, as the house rocked in its misery. A pipe burst in the ceiling and brown water poured down. The scaffolding abruptly collapsed to reveal the full extent of the crack, through which daylight showed. *Bong, bong, bong,* sounded the clock.

And above it all he could hear Kay's thin, monotonous cry, "Harry-Harry-Help-Help-Harry-Harry-Help-Help-HARRRRY . . ."

No! He struggled to his feet, started to fall again as a convulsive tremor struck, but made himself move across the tossing room to his wife and child. "Come on!"

Kay stood. Mark cried, "The bird!"

"He ran in to get it. I followed him!" she screeched.

He carried Mark and Kay to the birdcage, put them down, snatched the cage off its hook, and handed it to Kay. "Go to the rock," he told her when they staggered outside.

Somehow he made his way back through the kitchen. The basement staircase shuddered violently as he descended, snatched the seismometer from the floor, and raced back up. Just as he reached the top the stairs collapsed, and he clawed his way out of the disintegrating house, lugging his burden.

They watched from the shivering boulder. The tremors came rapidly now, one after the other, as the earth strained to release the pressure inside. Vail, counting the shocks, realized that the main paroxysm was at hand, but even so he was unprepared for its severity and brute energy. This was the dark side of the earth that he feared and admired, the pent-up fury wracking the ground.

The earth wasn't made for living things, he thought. The shapes and forms of life had to find their place upon it and, in the last reckoning, take it as it came, survive the vicissitudes that were visited, endure. That great ball hurtling through space was not a haven built by God, but an impersonal sphere whose workings might be discovered but never changed, whose mysteries, laid bare, only revealed more mysteries, whose purpose was no purpose as humans understood the term, whose meaning was no meaning except existence itself. And that existence had to be clung to, even as they clung now to the rock, solid yet shaking.

From the cornfield a deep rustle sounded though there was no wind, and the ground seemed to ripple as the earth wave passed through, sending fence posts into the air, leaving a pile of broken machinery that had been a Rolls-Royce. The clay bell on a branch of the elm tolled incessantly, and suddenly shattered as the tree tottered and crashed on the barn, leaving the building in splinters. Now the house itself began to rumble in protest as great cracks appeared in the heavy walls. What remained of the chimney crashed through the roof, red stones fell down in a shower of shingles, the cupola collapsed, the second story became the first, red rocks rained down, until nothing remained but a pile of debris and a cloud of dust that hovered above it.

The earth was still under advancing water.

On the rock they were silent in awe, and then Kay muttered, "So that was an earthquake."

"That was an earthquake," he said.

"To think I believed all that about ghosts. It was unforgivable of me. I failed you and I'm sorry." Her eyes were clear and sharp.

"I almost failed you, too. I came close to panic in there."

"But you didn't panic," she said gratefully. She looked at the masonry that rose from the flood. "Well, what now? Rebuild?"

"I don't think so," he said slowly. "We've had it here. Kay, I want to go back into seismology. If I work at Lamont, we can live in New York."

"Civilization! Maybe I could do something useful there, like teach school. Mark's old enough for me to work, aren't you, honey?"

Mark said proudly, "Next year I'll be in second grade."

Kay sighed and glanced at Polly's sightless eyes. As if she had been avoiding the question she asked, "What about the others?"

"Some of the villagers died, I think," he said. "Wende's dead, Fred's dead, and Jeff, probably."

"Our whole world in pieces, just like that." Kay permitted herself a tiny tear. "You were right, but nobody listened. How different it would be if they had."

"I wonder," he said somberly. "The thing is . . ."

"What?"

"Well, what happened to our friends was exactly what you said would happen. I can't account for it. Can you?"

Kay picked up the cat and stroked it. "Look," she said, "there's a helicopter."

EPILOGUE

AT Lamont-Doherty a graduate student had duty on the Fourth of July. Shortly after 8:00 a.m. he unlocked the building, went upstairs to the bank of instruments, and did a double take. The seismometer pens were furiously scratching large arcs.

The student quickly determined that the tremor had been picked up first by the seismic station at New London, Connecticut, then by other seismometers farther west. He raised the phone and dialed. "Dr. Kelly? Sheel, at Lamont. Sorry for waking you, but there's just been an earthquake in New England. Magnitude four—or bigger. The pens have jumped off scale."

Kelly's voice rose. "Where in New England?"

"Well, it's east of the seismic network, which would put it at sea or possibly Cape Cod or Rhode Island."

"I'll be right over! Locate it precisely, will you? And notify Gold."

The graduate student phoned Gold, like Kelly a senior seismologist, and hurriedly triangulated reports from three seismic stations to find the quake's focus. He had just finished when Kelly walked in.

"Got it?" the seismologist asked.

"Within about ten miles. It's northeast of Newport."

"Check the Wood-Anderson," Kelly ordered.

The graduate student left at a run, heading for the vault on the bluff. There, resting on concrete pillars, under perfectly controlled heat, light and humidity conditions, the Wood-Anderson was kept. A low-sensitivity seismometer which did not go off scale as the ones in the main building did, its results were recorded on photographic paper. Working by red light, Sheel took the paper from the drum and went to the darkroom.

Meanwhile, Kelly called the airport and summoned a helicopter.

Gold entered, with several students who had also been alerted hurrying behind. "What's up?"

Kelly said, "Remember the fellow I told you about? Vail, the ex-seismologist, who worried about a quake in Rhode Island? Well, he was right. There's been a biggish one. I'm going up to have a look. Want to come?"

"Wouldn't miss it."

The phone screamed and Gold picked it up. "A reporter."

"Yes?" Kelly said impatiently, taking the receiver.

"Scott from the Associated Press. We have received a report of a high-intensity earthquake in a small area near Fall River. Can you throw some light on it?"

"You know everything I do," Kelly said tersely. "It was strong, Richter scale four or larger." He hung up.

Sheel entered with his results. "The earthquake was magnitude five or even six, according to the Wood-Anderson."

A clamor rose in the room. "Five or six!" Kelly exclaimed. "Nobody even suspected a major fault there. It's one for the books."

A buzz sounded, grew louder. Gold said, "The helicopter."

As the helicopter scurried northeast Kelly mused, "If Vail is right—and I bet he is—the fault line is about ten miles long. Imagine it producing such a magnitude." He leaned forward, tapped the pilot on the shoulder, and shouted, "See if you can find out what happened at Fall River and Newport."

The radio crackled and the pilot shouted back, "A few light tremors were felt and an abandoned factory collapsed in Fall River. But most people aren't even aware that there's been an earthquake."

"What about the quake zone?"

The radio crackled again and the pilot reported, "It's a lightly populated peninsula. Damage there is considerable. The area's flooded, and they're waiting for the water to recede."

"Flooded!" Kelly said in a startled voice. He turned to Gold. "Is there a tsunami?"

"Could be," Gold said, staring at the map. "The quake area seems mostly underwater."

"It adds up to an earthquake with a very shallow focus," Kelly said. "The impact was concentrated in one place. That kind of event could pack a wallop."

The pilot said, "We're here."

Old Brompton township lay below them. In the distance a radio tower had fallen. A narrow road was badly cracked, which accounted for the absence of vehicles, Kelly thought, but otherwise everything seemed normal at first, except for the military helicopters hovering over the end of the peninsula. Gold, who had field glasses, pointed to the mainland across the bay. "A largish building on a hill by the water has collapsed. And ahead of us there's flooding."

"A tsunami, all right," Kelly said. "It's like a big coastal earthquake in miniature."

"There are people up on the cliff," Gold said, moving the field glasses. "About a hundred of them."

"They're lucky," Kelly answered, staring at what remained of a village—a flooded square, ruined church, smashed houses, wrecked pier. "Still, it's good-by to property values. They'll have the peninsula to themselves. Nobody will want to live here. I wonder if anyone got hurt."

The helicopter veered, passing above a large three-story house which appeared to have survived the quake intact, a smaller house that had disintegrated into a ruin of glass and brick, and finally what appeared from the rubble to have been an old stone house. A tree had fallen on an outbuilding, and half immersed in water was a car which would never be driven again. A horse swished its tail on the side of a hill, on top of which was a large boulder. Three adults and a child had taken refuge there.

"The water's receding. They'll get to them pretty soon," Kelly said. He squinted. "Let me have those field glasses. See that big fellow who's waving? That's Harry Vail." He smiled. "He's even got the seismometer."

Arthur Herzog

Arthur Herzog is delighted and a bit bemused by his new career as a novelist, after an already full lifetime of magazine journalism. "I vastly prefer writing novels," he says. "Now that I've learned how to harness my imagination, once I sit down at a typewriter it's like pushing a button. The scenes start to unroll. In nonfiction, I couldn't find a way to use the ideas I was constantly having."

Herzog, born in New York City, grew up in Tucson, Arizona, and in 1950 graduated from Stanford University, where he was editor of the campus humour magazine. He took a year off to travel around Europe, then returned to a job on the *National Police Gazette*, which he edited while completing his M.A. in English literature at Columbia University. In 1962 he became the first reporter to cover the rebels in Angola, writing mostly for *The New York Times Magazine*.

He wrote five nonfiction books before his first novel, *The Swarm*, appeared in 1974. A "science gothic" about killer African honeybees assaulting mankind, it has been made into a film by Irwin Allen–Twentieth Century Fox. For Herzog the exposure to fiction proved as powerful as the sting of his famous bees, and *Earthsound* is the result.

Herzog says he has never been in an earthquake, has never heard an earthsound. But he has thoroughly researched his story with men who have, at the Lamont-Doherty Geological Observatory in Palisades, New York, as well as consulting the Anchorage, Alaska, *Times* and many other sources.

What would be Herzog's advice to those in an earthquake? "Go outside!"